MW01128911

Timewreck Titanic

Timewreck
Titanic

Rhys B. Davies

SEA LION PRESS

First published by Sea Lion Press, 2017
Copyright © 2017 Rhys B. Davies
All rights reserved.
ISBN: 1977837719
ISBN-13: 978-1977837714

PROLOGUE

FLIGHT 401

The North Atlantic
Monday, April 15th 1912, 3.30am local time

"Mayday, Mayday, Mayday. Air Station Elizabeth City, this is Coast Guard Flight 401 declaring a mid-air-emergency. We believe ourselves to have been heavily damaged during a flyby of the Titanic Memorial Fleet, are losing fuel and are down to two engines. Our position... estimated position, is 300 miles south-southwest of Halifax, now turning north and attempting to reach Nova Scotia, please respond. Hello, Hello? Elizabeth City, please respond..."

"...can anyone hear me?"

*

Marconi Wireless Telegraph Message

Captain Haddock, 'Olympic' – Please ascertain full situation and report as soon as possible – Franklin, New York.

*

"Come on boys, faster, swing those boats out!"

"I say, Officer, what's all with the hullabaloo?"

"We're going to the aid of another ship sir; please keep yourself and your wife clear. You there, keep those lines straight!"

The agitated clatter of the lifeboat gear played over the voices of passengers and crew alike, men shouting instructions to try and make themselves heard. There were groups of them spread out along the boat deck working at the lifeboat stations, cranking away at the windlasses. Above them towering funnels belched out thick clouds of black smoke that trailed for mile upon mile behind the ship like an angry welt on the face of heaven. The night was clear, but the stars were veiled behind swirling spirals of a strange blue and green light that washed across the sky in waves, sometimes coiling into arcane eddies.

Captain Herbert Haddock stood at the side of the bridge of the Royal Mail Steamship *Olympic*, his thick mutton-chop whiskers rustling in the ship's headwind and hands tightly clenching the rail as he stared up at the unnatural lights that writhed over the ocean like shimmering snakes, lending everything a sickly pallor. Entranced, he watched in silence, until the sound of footsteps on the wooden deck alerted him to the approach of the Officer of the Watch.

"Engine room reports that she's sped up from nineteen to twenty-one knots," the man said softly. "The Chief Engineer assures me she'll go to twenty-three once the auxiliary boilers are brought online."

His voice was hushed with awe and reverence at the sight, and Haddock nodded in understanding, his mouth feeling dry as he forced words out of himself.

"What do you make of it?"

"Honestly sir, I don't know what to think about any of this."

Reluctantly Haddock turned his eyes away from the illuminated heavens, a grim smile on his face.

"I've been sailing this Western Ocean for over thirty years, and have never experienced anything such as this," he said with quiet conviction, and as if thinking in unison they glanced behind themselves, at the groups of men swinging the lifeboats out high over the black water surging past far below. Through the deck Haddock could feel the engines racing ahead, churning relentlessly deep in the heart of the ship. The rail was trembling slightly beneath his resting hand as he mentally calculated their rate of travel.

"We need to go faster still…" he said at length, turning to face forward again. "At twenty-three knots it will still take us almost a full day to reach the spot where she is sinking. We would not arrive before eleven o'clock tomorrow night."

"What else can we do, sir?" the Officer replied, his words tinged not with disrespect, but with a quiet despair. "She's over five hundred miles away; we can't just slice that distance in half, no matter how much steam we put to the engines."

He swallowed.

"And sir, given that no-one seems to have heard from her in the past hour, she may have sunk already."

"Impossible…" Haddock's hands clutched at the rail as if in desperate need of strength. "We all know that modern shipbuilding has gone beyond that…"

Olympic charged on into the dark. Somewhere, far out beyond the horizon, her twin sister *Titanic* had struck an iceberg and was sinking.

Overhead the sky continued to burn with brilliant colours.

*

It was an aurora, the most incredible he had ever seen. By all accounts it should have been impossible. Not for the first time Gareth King shook his head and swallowed back a malignant dread gnawing at him. In fifteen years flying both planes and helicopters for the United States Coast Guard, he had never seen an aurora this far south on the Atlantic. It was a stunning sight.

"Mayday, Mayday, Mayday. Is anyone out there?" he messaged.

The hiss of static on the radio seemed to perfectly match the slow-boiling lightshow being played out above. But in contrast to the burning sky, the ocean beneath was as dark as an open grave. And it stretched out on all sides, an endless pane of black glass reaching right to the dim horizon.

"You don't land a Hercules HC-130J on water, you crash it!"

His training's sole piece of advice on making an emergency water landing bounced around persistently in King's head as he fought against the controls, struggling to correct how the damn plane kept trying to pull to one side. Reaching for the trim controls he glanced across the vacant co-pilot's seat to the window beyond. Two of the Hercules's four turboprop engines were off to that side, slung under the wings and roaring away, struggling to keep the plane airborne. Turning his head in the opposite direction King saw the other two engines idling, the propellers freewheeling in the airstream. A dim glow visible through holes torn in the engine cowlings suggested lingering fires.

Warily, his eyes slid back to the controls in front of him, hazard lights blinking owlishly from the avionics display. Low fuel warning, multiple hull breaches, loss of hydraulic pressure, and the possibility of fires in the two stalled engines were just the most prominent of them. Worse yet was that those glaring warnings were the only activity coming from the instrument panel, as the other displays, the computerised communications and navigation screens, were alarmingly blank, or littered with nonsensical error messages.

The plane was dying. As if voicing its pain, it buffeted through a patch of turbulence and the strained airframe took up the motion, its stringers and ribs rattling and creaking arthritically. Once again the yoke tried to snatch its way out of King's hands and he winced, glancing down. Through a glass panel at his feet the ocean's surface was alarmingly close to the plane's belly, the black waves faintly outlined with the same effervescent light that glimmered on the edges of his vision, and he spared himself a glance up through the windshield, as if to confirm he was not dreaming.

The colours in the sky were not the Northern Lights, he knew that much.

Something incredible and terrible had happened to him and his crew, he was now convinced. Slowly his gaze fell back to the darkened navigation computer as he wished he knew where they were.

"Air Station Elizabeth City, please respond," he tried again. *"This is Coast Guard Flight 401, returning from the Titanic Memorial wreath-dropping. We are lost over the North Atlantic, critically damaged and loosing fuel. Hello! Hello!"*

*

"Captain!" a new voice broke into Haddock's thoughts, as one of *Olympic*'s two wireless operators came running up, a sealed envelope in his hand. "Sable Island just relayed us another urgent message from New York, sir!"

"Thank you Bagot," Haddock replied, and bypassing protocol he plucked the envelope directly from the younger man's hands and tore the seal open.

"Herbert," he read aloud, noting with surprise the use of his Christian name, which perhaps suggested just how serious the situation was. *"Please confirm rumours that various ships have already reached Titanic – Franklin."*

That would be Phillip Franklin, Vice-President of the White Star Line shipping company, owners of both *Olympic* and *Titanic*, and head of the line's American operations. Haddock tried to imagine the crowds gathering outside the company's New York offices on Broadway, anxious for news and hounding Franklin for answers where he had none to give. He did not envy the poor man, and wondered whether the scene was being repeated outside Oceanic House, White Star's London offices.

"Well Bagot?" Haddock folded the slip of paper up and nodded towards the wireless operator. "You're better qualified to answer than me. What are ships up ahead of us saying?"

"Honestly sir," Bagot replied, pausing to swallow. "It's a mess. Some are saying that *Titanic* has sunk, others are saying she's under tow by a German oil tanker, and one ship is insisting that *Titanic*'s boilers exploded, blowing her to atoms and causing... this".

He pointed at the aurora overhead. "The only thing that they agree on is what we saw ourselves."

Haddock nodded. *Olympic* had been peacefully steaming east, following the same course travelled by all the great transatlantic liners, when just a few hours ago the horizon ahead of them had suddenly lit up for a second with brilliant light. Bagot and Moore, the wireless operators, had at the same time reported *"the loudest, rudest 'X' imaginable"*, a term in their trade for atmospheric interference. Moments later the two of them had come to the bridge in a near-state of panic, as when they had sent out messages of enquiry as to the source of the flash, they had received within seconds a faint cry for help from *Titanic*. *Olympic*'s sister, five days into her maiden voyage from New York to Southampton, had been in a collision with an iceberg it seemed, and was floundering. Haddock had immediately ordered all steam to the engines, and instructed Bagot and Moore to ascertain *Titanic*'s full situation. But not long had passed before this impossible aurora had begun to manifest itself over *Olympic*, playing havoc with the Marconi equipment and closing off direct communication.

"Very well," Haddock said at last. "Do you have a spare form on which I can write a reply?"

"Yes sir." From one of his waistcoat pockets Bagot produced a scrap of lined paper, letter-headed with the crest of the Marconi Wireless Company. Using the rail as a rest for his pen, Haddock quickly jotted down a message.

'Franklin, New York. Lost contact Titanic 0200. Endeavouring to re-establish communication by Cape Race and other ships. At last word, Titanic flooding in forward compartments, women and children being set off in boats.'

After a lengthy pause, in which he struggled to give structure and form to the conflicting theories bobbing around his mind, he scribbled in a final line: *'Reports other ships taking aboard Titanic's passengers remain unconfirmed – Haddock, Olympic'*

There. It was hardly anything Franklin did not already know, but for the moment, it was all he had to offer. As Bagot ran off towards the wireless room to put the message out, Haddock gazed along the deck, watching as the men swung out *Olympic*'s boats in readiness to receive survivors, and for a second wondered if his fellow captain, EJ Smith, was witnessing the exact same vignette aboard *Titanic*. The chattering of the ratchet windlasses, the shouts of men heaving on ropes, and the anxious expressions of the first few passengers to come out on deck, roused by the racket. Overhead the safety valves on the funnels would be roaring with deafening volume, venting the ship's full head of steam, and the deck would be slowly but noticeably trimming down as the bow began to settle into the icy Atlantic…

He shivered, wondering for a moment what he would do in Smith's place.

*

Like a dying creature trying to end its own misery, once again the plane yawed sickeningly to one side and King had to force

10

the controls over to keep it from going into a spiralling dive. Momentarily he wondered what his flight instructors would say about trying to fly upside down, and clenched his teeth to not laugh. Holding himself against the yoke, he reached out with one hand and again sought out the trim controls. Ballast pumps whirred somewhere to aft, and in fits and starts, struggling all the time against him, the ailing plane came back onto an even keel. King once again took in the dead engines, the useless telemetry screens, the sickly aurora, and struggled to make sense of events.

What's happened to us?

They had been passing over a group of ships, the Titanic Memorial Fleet, flying low and fast, putting on a show for the passengers watching on from below. Just as King was bringing them around to drop the first of several commemorative wreaths, something on one of the ships had, he suspected, exploded directly underneath them, peppering the Hercules' underside with debris. The two portside engines had immediately burst into flames, and King had been struggling to keep the plane from plunging into the Atlantic when something... *else* happened, a pulse of brilliant light that seemed to knock out every display in the cockpit. For a moment he had been struck with the terrified realisation that they were flying blind.

That was when he had seen the aurora suddenly manifest overhead, giving him enough light to make out the outlines of the ships wheeling outside the windows, off which he had taken a best-guess heading and turned back towards what he hoped was the American Eastern Seaboard.

With a sudden grunt someone climbed into the seat next to him. His co-pilot, Lieutenant Connie Ramirez, a resourceful woman whose striking features were currently screwed up with concentration and suppressed anger.

"Everything checks out behind, sir," she said bluntly as she strapped herself into the safety harness and then reached up, resetting the circuit breakers on the overhead switchboard. After a moment's attention directed at the navigation console, which still mocked them with glassy blankness, she scowled and began repeating the procedure.

"Trying setting them to AUX," King suggested, and Ramirez grunted that she already had. After another minute's silence, in which she made a final attempt to cycle the power and recover navigation, she fell back into her chair with a shout of anger.

"*Shit!* No navigation, no GPS, no radio! We don't know where we are or which way we're headed, and can't even get a positional fix from the stars!"

Her abrupt unprofessional outburst stopped when she caught the warning glance King was directing at her.

"Sorry," she held up a hand in apology. "It's just... no, it's nothing."

Pulling herself together she sat forward to check what few instruments still worked.

"Only about fifteen minutes worth of fuel left, altitude is thirteen hundred feet, and our bearing is approximately 340 degrees from magnetic north." She paused, seeing the magnetic compass in front of her swinging in sick arcs from side to side, and managed a faint grin. "Either that or we're headed for Bermuda."

The two of them laughed nervously at the joke, and as their chuckles petered out Ramirez turned to stare upwards through the glass canopy at the aurora.

"Do you think that thing up there is what's messing with the instruments?"

"Maybe," King said. "Or maybe we took something to the transceiver when that ship exploded. Try hailing Elizabeth City again, Lieutenant."

Nodding, Ramirez repeated their distress calls; that they were losing fuel and altitude, flying north in the hopes of making landfall, with only minutes left before they would be forced to ditch at sea. King sat in silence as she tried multiple channels, staring forwards towards what he hoped was the horizon. Briefly he glanced past Ramirez towards her window; if that was east, then dawn should soon be making itself felt. Should he climb higher to increase their chances of getting a sun sighting and a fix on their position?

As if in answer, the steady rhythm of the propellers was suddenly broken, the turboprops rasping like chainsaws. The cockpit bounced violently in time with the struggling engines, before they snarled back into howling life, running on dregs and fumes.

Calls for help silenced, Ramirez removed her helmet and pulled the radio headset off her head, allowing her short-cut hair to fall free. King noted, not for the first time, that the Lieutenant was an extremely attractive woman, and wondered at what had led her to becoming a United States Naval Aviator.

The Hercules continued to fly into the dark, engines howling in the void between blackened sea and fractured sky, while pilot and co-pilot stared in wonderment at the trails of light writhing like fighting snakes.

"It's beautiful," Ramirez said with reluctant awe. "Like flying in space."

*

"Yes Mr Fleming, that's what I said," Haddock spoke into the telephone that connected *Olympic's* bridge to the main engine room. "I want you to squeeze off the steam and hot-water lines to the cabins, and so conserve that power for the engines. A little discomfort for our passengers is no bother if you can draw a few extra knots from the ship."

He ended the call with the Chief Engineer and, restless, paced through the bridge and out onto the boat deck. In his pocket he carried the latest message the wireless operators had picked up from *Titanic's* vicinity.

It was something they had overheard, a bit of gossip flashing between two other ships, but Moore and Bagot's alert ears had snatched it out of the ether.

'Carpathia approaching Titanic's position – has sighted 1000 foot ship named Oceanic.'

It was amazing how much a single line of text had shaken him. *Carpathia*, a ship he also understood to be racing to *Titanic's* aid, belonged to the Cunard Line, White Star's closest rivals on the North Atlantic. Haddock knew her captain, Arthur Rostron, to be a no-nonsense fellow, and for him to declare that he had sighted a 1000-foot long ship named *Oceanic* was like being presented with proof of the existence of sea monsters, both exciting and unnerving. All the more so in that Haddock's last command before taking over *Olympic* was named *Oceanic*, and while a fine ship, she was in no way a thousand feet long, being not even half *Olympic*'s size. Indeed, there was no ship in the world a thousand feet in length. *Titanic*, at just shy of nine-hundred, was currently the largest vessel in existence.

All the facts considered, he could only conclude that something bizarre and inexplicable was taking place around where *Titanic* was sinking. It was on that strength that he had ordered steam diverted from passenger comforts to the engines, and had the lifeboats swung out even though they were still many hours from *Titanic*'s position. Out in the night there was something terrible and possibly dangerous, and he was charging headlong into that danger to render assistance. Many of *Titanic*'s crew, picked from the best White Star had to offer in its talent pool, were known to him, either by name, reputation or acquaintance. Some, like Captain Smith and Purser McElroy, fondly nicknamed the Eastern Despot, were good friends. He would not allow them to face this alone.

With his hand pushed into his pocket, the Marconigram tight in his grasp, Haddock headed aft along the boat deck, arriving at the wireless cabin. Moore was taking his turn at the headphones, and a growing stack of messages was growing around him, while Bagot was down on his knees, sorting the correspondence into small clusters on the floor.

"Well gentlemen, have there been any more 'strange' messages?" Haddock asked as he entered.

The two men shared a glance, before shaking their heads.

"No sir," Moore ventured. "No one's heard from *Titanic* in hours, and now they've lost touch with *Carpathia* as well."

"You can't say that she's sunk as well?"

"No sir. The next nearest ship to them is the *Mount Temple*, and the Old Man on her says that something is interfering with his wireless. So what we think is that something is jamming both *Titanic* and *Carpathia*'s signals."

Before Haddock could respond, Moore stood up from his wireless key, a scrap of paper in hand.

"There's this too sir. When we got that message about a ship named '*Oceanic*', well, we thought it was a bit odd, and so we put out a question asking if anyone knew where 'our' *Oceanic* is right now."

Haddock nodded. *Oceanic* was hard to misidentify. He himself had last laid eyes on her in Southampton two weeks previous, the venerable liner having been laid up for want of coal. In light of the recent miners' strike, many of White Star's ships had been temporarily withdrawn from service so that their fuel supplies could be scavenged for more prestigious vessels, like *Titanic*, and *Oceanic* was among those whose sailings had been cancelled.

"Well we just got this back," Bagot continued, offering him the message. Trying to hide how his hand trembled, Haddock took the Marconigram. It was from Benjamin Steele, White Star's Marine Superintendent at Southampton, confirming that *Oceanic* was still moored there, her coal bunkers empty.

"Very well; understand that the contents of these messages," he waved the unnerving missives, "are to remain secret to the three of us."

He realised the command was unnecessary but felt it important to say. No one ship had the range to broadcast right across entire oceans, instead relying on a relay system of passing on each others' messages. Any station listening in on Moore and Bagot's traffic would have heard that there were now apparently two *Oceanic*s, one of which was impossibly large. He had no doubt that Philip Franklin and Ben Steele would be chasing down the same questions at the same time, along with every other White Star official on both sides of the Atlantic. The only ones not privy to the 'secret' would be most of *Olympic*'s passengers and crew.

He was just stepping out onto the deck when from far ahead the bell in the crow's nest rang out several times, the code to signal that the lookouts had sighted an object. Before he could even pause to comprehend, Haddock found his feet carrying him onto the bridge with full speed. One of the junior officers was on the telephone that connected to the crow's nest, and as he ended the call his eyes were wide and his face pale, even by the ever-present corpse-light of the aurora.

"Captain, lookouts report navigation lights off to the south-east, and… *they say they're in the sky!*"

Haddock felt his mouth fall open in incredulity. In the hushed silence that followed he heard only a soft creak from the decking as the helmsman turned to look over his shoulder at them, his face now equally drained of colour. Turning, Haddock strode out onto the exposed bridge wing, where the Officer of the Watch was peering off to the south-east, a pair of binoculars pressed to his eyes.

"I see it sir," said in astonishment, his body as rigid as a figurehead. "This sounds impossible – but I think it's an aircraft, a flying machine!"

*

"You like science-fiction, right Connie?" King said abruptly.

"Pardon sir?" Ramirez answered.

"Science-fiction, *Star Trek*, that anime junk from Japan, you're into all that, correct?"

"Yes…" Ramirez replied hesitantly.

"Have you ever seen *Close Encounters of the Third Kind?*"

She nodded.

"There's this bit at the end," King continued, "where the aliens give back all the people they've abducted over the years. Some of them are Navy Airmen, from Flight 19."

"You're hoping aliens are coming to rescue us?" she smirked, eyebrow arched wryly. "Isn't Flight 19 that Bermuda Triangle story?"

"Not exactly; Flight 19 was a group of Grumman bombers that vanished off of Fort Lauderdale in 1945, during a training exercise. Their planes turn up at the beginning of *Close Encounters*, in the desert."

"Okay," she nodded in understanding. For a few seconds the cabin buffeted, and King focused on the controls, but then loosened his grip and rolled his eyes in her direction.

"Well, I was always a wild-west, cowboys and pioneers kind of boy, but I read about Flight 19 in *Argosy* magazine as a kid. Scared the shit out of me, almost made me swear off the dream of being a pilot. But I always wondered where those planes went. Did they get lost and wreck at sea, or did they…"

He trailed off, and both he and Ramirez turned to regard the aurora. It truly was like flying under a nebula, as if they had warped into a picture from the Hubble Telescope. King's voice reflected the awesome sight, sounding like that of a man in prayer.

"…well, did Flight 19 possibly go somewhere like this?"

The engines spluttered again, and the two of them reached up to adjust the fuel flow and squeeze a few more seconds of flight time out of the plane. With the impending ditch postponed, Ramirez reached behind her seat and produced a wreath.

"Sir, Jenkins gave this to me while I was checking the electronics. He never got a chance to drop it before things went to hell."

King glanced over at the wreath, one of three the plane was carrying. Red, white and blue ribbons had been twisted into the laurels, and attached to it was a small placard. It would have been his job to read the message inscribed on it, and he had committed the words to his memory.

"The reason we're here, isn't it?"

"I suppose it is…" Ramirez regarded the wreath, and respectfully laid it at her feet. Then she jumped in her seat. *"Sir!"*

"What is it?"

"We just flew over something; I saw it through the floor viewport!"

King moved to ask whether she was sure, but the look of conviction in her face brooked no argument. He nodded and hauled on the stick, guiding the limping plane into a banking turn. "Put your helmet back on, Lieutenant."

Ramirez was already pulling the grey plastic fishbowl back on, clipping it into place and reaching forward to rest her hands on the throttle levers, adjusting the power to help King make the turn. Both of them peered forward, until they spotted a small cluster of lights, almost lost in the expanse of the ocean.

"You were right, Lieutenant," King exhaled in hope. "We've found a ship."

The engines spluttered again, and this time did not recover, continuing to choke on the fumes as the plane began to shudder into its death throes.

"Shut off engine three," King said sharply. "Let engine four have whatever fuel's left."

"Sir?"

"Prepare to ditch, Lieutenant!" King ordered as he wrestled with the controls. "We're aiming for right alongside that ship!"

Ramirez hauled back on one of the throttles and gently pressed the other forward until engine four's gasps steadied up into a final burst of power. Without waiting for King's order she reached forward and lifted the safety latch on a button marked 'flares', then rested her finger over it.

"Wait, Connie. Not just yet. We're going too high and too fast. I'm going to try and bleed off some airspeed through several turns and passes. Wait until we're down at their level before igniting the flares. And when we do, wave like Hell!"

*

"Good Lord…" Haddock breathed slowly. Explosions, an aurora, and *Titanic* sinking amid mystery ships. What else did this night intend to throw at him?

Over the roar of *Olympic*'s bow-wave, they could hear a rising drone, like the swarming of hundreds of bees, the sound peaking as the immense aircraft flew right over them. As it passed overhead, he gazed up and saw its elongated black hull, from which two long horizontal wings extended. The craft was clear as daylight against the light-show above, and now was turning back towards them.

"It's immense, sir," the Officer of the Watch said softly. "Quadruple screws, and a wingspan of at least a hundred feet."

Haddock slowly scratched at his head, a nervous habit of his, and he felt his eyes widen until he supposed he resembled a confused child struggling to comprehend. Only three years ago the French aviator Louis Blèriot had become the first man to cross the English Channel by aeroplane, and he understood that an American woman, Ms Harriet Quimby, aimed to reproduce the feat in just a few days. The public were wild with adoration for these dashing adventurers, but when Haddock had seen images of Blèriot's self-designed flying machine, the EX-1, he had reacted with a private and cynical laugh at the opinion widely proclaimed, by figures who should know better, that these fragile machines of canvas and wood, so prone to the temperaments of wind and weather, would someday replace the battleship and the ocean liner as engines of war and peace.

Now he felt like a man being force-fed his own words, as crew and passengers alike began to notice the gigantic aircraft now coming back towards them with the unstoppable will of a bullet. Haddock ducked instinctively as it soared over *Olympic*, roaring angrily, cutting through the liner's smoke trail and scattering the black exhaust like an infant would his colouring paints. For a moment, as it eclipsed the aurora overhead, the ship's lights were reflected in the aircraft's silvery underbelly, and then Haddock saw red flames gushing from underneath one of the craft's wings and realised something was severely wrong.

"The binoculars!" he shouted, hand extended, and quickly they were pressed into his grasp. Raising them, he aimed the lenses towards the quick-moving aircraft, which was now listing heavily to one side and turning back towards *Olympic*. Despite its speed, it seemed to be handling sluggishly, like a ship fighting against a jammed rudder, and as it presented its side to him he confirmed his suspicions; three of the four propellers were without power, lazily spinning in the air current, and black smoke interspersed with bursts of fire were pouring back from two of the engines.

Half-hidden by the streaking exhaust, he could see the words 'US Coast Guard' painted on the side of the hull.

The aeroplane made another pass, this time well off to *Olympic*'s side, coming low down enough to throw up spray from where it skimmed over the surface. Then, in a series of hissing spurts, a cascade of white flares burst from the underside of the wings, burning with bright flames where they touched the water. Conjoined to them by trails of smoke like the wings of an angel, the plane climbed away again, heading out several miles before beginning another limping turn. Under the swirling light of the aurora it was staggeringly beautiful, but it was evident now that the craft was in trouble as it turned back towards them. And in the light of the flares, Haddock had caught a brief glimpse of one of the crew through the glass canopy of the cockpit, face obscured by a bulbous helmet, but waving frantically through an open window, palm turned to the ocean below.

"He's going to try and land on the water…" he said, before spinning on his heel towards the wheelhouse. "Hard a starboard! Turn the ship right around!"

*

"If they haven't seen us, they'll have spotted that!" King said, fighting the Hercules through their last banking turn, the plane almost right on its side. Glancing down he saw the port wingtip pointing straight down at the water like a hydrofoil. "Get back into the aft fuselage and strap in with the rest of the crew, Lieutenant!"

"But I…"

"Do it, Connie! It's not a suggestion!"

"Yes Sir!" Ramirez said, instinctively responding to an order, but then pausing to add "Good luck, Gareth."

Grabbing the wreath, she vanished into the depths of the plane. Completing the turn, King pushed the controls over and held them there, and the plane rolled back level with sluggish speed as engine four turned its last, dying with a final scream instead of asphyxiated spluttering. Now they were gliding, only a few hundred feet over the water, and the lights of the ship were just a mile straight ahead, and coming closer with every second. One hand flying to the flap controls, King glanced up and down several times, trying to keep an eye on the altimeter while steering close enough to the ship for the crew to be rescued without actually hitting the damn thing.

Well, let's see if you can land one of these at sea.

*

Olympic was turning hard, heeling over and digging her bow into the water as she made the emergency left-hand turn under full power, but it was still not fast enough.

"Full astern on the portside engine!" Haddock bellowed, eyes fixed on the approaching plane. He heard the engine-order telegraphs ringing, and after a terse few moments felt the ship lurch as the port propeller swung into reverse and began backpedalling furiously. Now *Olympic* started to shudder and shake, deck bouncing underfoot and her stern pitching as engines and rudder worked together to swing her around as quickly as possible. Glancing aft, Haddock saw the lifeboats hanging away from the side of the ship like pendulums and passengers clinging to anything upright in order to maintain their footing.

Well, this is bound to drag everyone out of bed, he thought to himself, before turning and striding 'up' the canting deck and through the bridge, several crewmen trailing behind him.

"Rudder amidships!" he ordered as they came out on the port bridge wing. The helmsman straightened up the wheel and on momentum alone *Olympic* completed the turn, now travelling parallel to the aircraft, which was rapidly overhauling them from astern. The flying machine had brought its nose up slightly, adopting what Haddock hoped was a proper attitude for a water landing, and was now coming in with eerie silence; the engines had failed.

"Full astern!" he yelled. "Emergency stop!"

The crashing sound of the main and emergency order telegraphs chattered from within the bridge, but Haddock's eyes were glued to the plane, now so close that the binoculars were unnecessary. Like an albatross on the glide it reared back, spreading the broad underside of its wings to snatch at the air, and for a moment it hung over the water, impossibly vast and heavy.

Then the underside of the tail smacked into the water and ploughed up a huge furrow of foam.

*

King felt the Hercules' flat ducktail dig into the sea, the sudden resistance throwing him into his restraints so hard it felt like they had grounded onto a beach. For a second they skidded along, nose in the air and black water flashing by beneath his feet, then the Hercules lost its grip on the sky and fell forward, burrowing its nose into the ocean as the cockpit caved in.

Lieutenant Commander Gareth King died instantly, hit in the face by a wall of water at over a hundred miles an hour. But he had managed to put his command down on a level keel, and for the first crucial seconds after splashdown the airframe remained intact.

And then the speeding Hercules listed heavily, and the portside wingtip and one of the burning engines dug hard into the water, dragging the fuselage over. The wings sheared off, propellers flying free like decapitated flower heads, tumbling across the surface of the ocean. The flooded cockpit tore away, and the shattered remains of the fuselage, shipping water, sank in less than a minute.

*

Haddock stared, along with what felt like the entirety of the ship's complement. Vast crowds had gathered on deck just in time to see the whole aircraft plunge underwater like a torpedo as it landed. With a sickening crack the two wings broke away, fluttering like giant steel butterflies and turning several cartwheels before they smashed back into the water.

And then, silence. The aircraft seemed to have vanished into the Atlantic. Haddock felt his own heart pounding as underfoot *Olympic*'s engines jumped in time with it. Finally they arrested her momentum and the liner came to rest, a backwash of water cascading down past her bows in twin arcs, like a dog panting with its tongue hanging out. Mercurial coils of light roiled in the sky, mockingly silent as they looked down on mortal suffering.

"Sound on the whistles!" he shouted. "Call out to any survivors!"

Someone jumped to the whistle cord and hauled down on it. *Olympic* bellowed, the brassy notes of her whistles proud and strident in the empty night. A pause, a lingering silence in which no answering cry or signal came from the crash site, and then they were blown again.

Haddock swallowed, looking towards where flickering pools of floating fire, fuel oil he supposed, formed a ring of flame that marked the point where the plane had finally sunk. He wondered how many crew, or even passengers, had been travelling aboard the machine, and as *Olympic* roared aloud for a third time, he feared none had survived.

And then, like a hoisted standard, a green flare shot up from the ocean, trailing a stream of sparks as it arced across the water.

His breath caught in his throat for a second, before he spun and pointed at the first of his officers.

"Launch lifeboat number two immediately!" he ordered, before turning like a top to call into the wheelhouse. "Dead slow ahead!"

Slowly, her engines turning over warily, *Olympic* edged towards the expanding circle of burning fuel, and finally pushed through, the flames lapping with futile hunger against her steel hide and achieving little except blistering the paintwork. Inside the ocean was eerily still, with little sign of wreckage. Haddock thanked the heavens that they had seen fit to swing the lifeboats out now as boat number two, loaded with eight men to man the oars and an officer at the tiller, slithered quickly down the lifeboat falls and smacked into the water, before pulling off into the dark void beyond the glow of *Olympic*'s state-of-the-art electrical lighting.

State-of-the-art, Haddock laughed snidely to himself. *An aircraft, which even when crashing travels with a speed and endurance that defy my comprehension, mystery ships over a thousand feet long, and here I am thinking of a simple electrical installation as being state-of-the art.*

*

Ramirez did not remember how she escaped from the crushed fuselage of the plane; when her senses returned to her she had found herself treading water, pinning an unconscious Ensign Jenkins to her chest with one arm. Ensign Orion was there too, waving from only a few feet away and buoyed up by his lifejacket like an orange Michelin Man.

And then a deafening roar burst across the water, and she had looked up. The nearby ship was hailing them. Pushing wet, matted hair out of her eyes she had pulled a flare gun from the belt on her flight suit and fired it into the burning sky. Then there was nothing to do except to wait for rescue, and fight against the urge to close her eyes…

Then, without warning, a heavy wooden oar splashed down in the water beside her head, the shouts of men's voices shaking her back into reality. The hull of a lifeboat bumped gently into her shoulder.

"Two men in the water here!"

"Another to this side!"

"Careful there, watch where you put your oars!"

Strong hands grabbed a hold of Jenkins and hauled him head-first out of the water. Kicking her legs, Ramirez turned and got a hand on the lifeboat's gunwale. Right in front of her was a metal plate bolted to the wooden hull, cut in the shape of a white star on a red flag. She knew it from somewhere.

Wait, go back Connie, you're running ahead of yourself. This boat is made of wood. It's being rowed by men with oars.

Something here was not right. Fumbling, she found the button on her lifejacket that triggered its built in torch, and with its beam to provide light found herself looking up at a man dressed in a ye-old-time sailor's uniform, complete with a wide collar and Donald Duck's Fauntleroy hat. The words *White Star Line* were stitched in gold on the brim.

Did I hit my head…? she thought groggily. *White Star… isn't this the scene from the movie where Jack dies?*

They stared at each other for what felt like forever, and then the man's face lit up in disbelief.

"Sir, this one's a woman!"

"Don't hang about man," was the shouted reply. "Pull her in!"

They were gentler with her than they had been with Jenkins, easing her up with soothing words like *"up you come miss"* and *"you'll be alright now"*. Ramirez would have objected to the benevolent sexism, if not for the fact that her eyes were fixed on the ship they hailed from, which was now slowly manoeuvring closer; it was large, but not massive, maybe a medium-sized cruise liner, because it definitely had too many lights on it to be a freighter. Once again it bellowed, its voice the baroque note of a steam whistle, not the rude tones of an air horn. She blinked…

…then the mystery vessel came into the light of one of the burning puddles of fuel, and she gasped with shock. Four pillar-like funnels rose from its back, and the lines of the hull were sleekly cut in a style a century out of fashion to her eyes. It was a profile instantly recognisable.

She turned to her crewmates. Jenkins was unconscious, but Orion was sitting upright, staring mouth agape at the vessel looming towards them. He was clutching at one of the memorial wreaths as if it was a lifebelt, and looked insensible.

Is that what I look like as well? she thought, forcing herself to shut her mouth and pulling herself upright, trying to act as Lieutenant King would have done in her place. Some of the men crewing the boat sat back in surprise when they saw the Naval Aviator wings carried proudly on her chest, along with her name and rank.

"Thank you for rescuing us. I'm Lieutenant Ramirez, United States Coast Guard," she began, and took a deep breath. "What the fuck is the *Titanic* doing here?"

Now it was their mouths that fell open, though she was not sure if it was due to her gender, her rank, or her strategic use of language.

On reflection, it was probably not the most diplomatic First Contact scenario.

*

Haddock could hear the subtle reverberations of hundreds of footfalls on the decks below as people climbed through *Olympic*'s hull to her promenades. It seemed as if the entire ship was already on deck, and he wondered where all these people were coming from, and where they found the energy to climb all those stairs. Speaking for himself he suddenly felt haggard, as if he had aged ten years in just a few hours.

If a few Marconigrams and some pretty lights in the sky did this to me, I can't imagine what EJ Smith is going through right now on Titanic... assuming she's still afloat.

Before he could explore that thorny path of thought further, a series of bright flashes out on the water drew everyone's eye.

"Boat Two is hailing us by Morse-Lamp, sir," an officer interpreted on everyone's behalf. "Three souls brought safely aboard."

His words were spoken loud enough for several passengers to overhear, and they repeated them at a shout to their travelling companions. Someone gave a cheer, and others took it up and leant it their voices, until it seemed the very ship itself was roaring lustily in appreciation of the mysterious aviators' salvation.

"Excellent," Haddock felt himself nod. "Instruct them to return to the ship; we'll have the doctor prepare to receive casualties."

"Wait sir, there's more..." the officer's mouth twisted as Boat 2's lamp continued to flash in the dark, and then he slowly twisted around to face Haddock. He had a look of a man falling off into an abyss from which he could not climb out. His mouth moved, but the cheers of the passengers drowned him out. Haddock nodded towards the cab on the bridge wing and the two of the crossed over into its sheltered interior.

"Now tell me, what is wrong?" Haddock said, his teeth biting into his lip like a schoolboy about to be thrashed.

"Captain..." the officer said, and then paused to pull off his cap and wipe away the sweat on his brow. His skin was pale and clammy, like a fish pulled straight from the water.

"Herbert," he said at last. "The survivors believe the year to be two-thousand-and-twelve."

*

Olympic's safety valves were blowing off loudly by the time the last of the survivors had been brought aboard. Rather than draw the fires while the ship was stationary, instructions had been sent down for as full a head of steam as possible to be built up, and from the surplus pressure erupting from the valves, the boilers in the bowels of their ship were being pressed to their limit.

"Mr Fleming, this is the Captain!" Haddock was again using the telephone to the Engine Room, shouting to be heard over the roar of venting steam. "Do you remember my last order? Well I want you to carry it out to the fullest. We're going to be making a full-speed dash for *Titanic*'s position now, and I require every knot you can coax from the engines. Shut down all but the auxiliary dynamos if necessary, get every man available working the furnaces, but I need a sustained twenty-four to twenty-five knots from her and I'm granting you power to do everything possible to make it happen short of tying down the safety valves."

The future. The year 2012. While a small part of him still clung to the hope that this was all just a mass misunderstanding, and that the crashed aircraft's crew had simply been left delusional by the impact, the rest of him was already charting a course forward through these new waters. He might not have been as dashing or famous as his colleague, EJ Smith – 'the Millionaire's Captain' – but let no-one say that Captain Herbert Haddock was not qualified to helm a ship.

"All have been brought aboard sir," came the report from aft on the Boat Deck, where Boat 2 was being secured into place. "And one wishes to speak to you."

"Very well…" Haddock moved to the centre of the bridge, straightened his cap, and folded his hands behind his back, maintaining an image of calm decorum.

The person presented to him seconds later was dressed in a baggy orange pair of overalls, and carried a bowl-shaped helmet under her arm. Stepping onto the bridge, she stopped and saluted crisply.

"Lieutenant Connie Ramirez, United States Coast Guard. It's a pleasure, Captain."

Haddock returned the salute. "Captain Herbert Haddock of the *Olympic*, it is *our* pleasure to be of assistance to you, Lieutenant."

Their mutual salutes completed, Haddock reluctantly reached forward and extended a hand in greeting. Normally when meeting a lady for the first he would take her hand gently and motion as if to kiss it, but now he and Ramirez simply shook hands. Her grip was firm, hinting at considerable physical strength hidden beneath the concealing uniform, and from her bearing he suspected that, in spite of her youth, she was of a greater maturity than some of his junior officers.

A female soldier, he noted in amazement, seeing the gold wings sewn to a patch on her breast, *and an aviator as well*.

She was also evidently Hispanic, and Haddock, against his best instincts, was impressed by both her smart presentation and evident intelligence, contrary of his expectations of anyone outside of the Anglo-Saxon race; he could see that her bright eyes were now darting around the bridge, taking in as much detail as possible.

Had any woman of his own time presented themselves in such a manner and form of dress, Haddock would have immediately requested that she return the uniform she had surely stolen to its rightful owner, but this Ramirez carried herself with an erect discipline that spoke of a genuine military training. And her confidence went beyond vulgar brazenness; it was evident that she considered it her right to be considered the equal of a man, not something she was forced to prove.

"I'm not familiar with the United States Coast Guard," he admitted. "What happened to the Americans' Revenue Cutter Service?"

"We are their successors, sir, founded in 1915," she replied, and he saw a flash of pride in her eyes, tempered by what he supposed was a growing realisation of their situation. "But we continue the traditions of the 'First Fleet'. Or we will, I suppose…"

"I see," Haddock smiled nervously, wondering at how to adjust tenses to the circumstances of time travel. But his mind was already turning over these new concepts and scrutinising them like a jeweller might a rough gem, searching for facets and where to cut.

"Lieutenant, do you know what the date is?"

"No, sir," Ramirez replied, and he indicated that she should follow him to the chart room, where he showed her a calendar.

"April 15th, 1912," she said slowly. "We've moved exactly a hundred years in time…"

Amazing… Haddock wondered to himself. *And intriguing; if they are coastguards, then what was their aircraft was doing so far out to sea? Perhaps they were on some form of patrol, or a rescue mission?*

He felt his mood darken at the sudden reminder of *Olympic*'s own circumstances, and opened his mouth to speak when he saw that Ramirez had turned her attention to the ship's log, lying open on a stand. The time-traveller slowly extended her fingers and brushed them against the most recent entry, which detailed the events of the last few hours.

"Titanic," she breathed, palm now pressed against the log as if to confirm it was real. *"Oh, my God…"*

The tone of her words was of mixed awe and dread, and struck at Haddock with frightening force. More worrying though, was that he now realised Ramirez was carrying a wreath in one hand. In the dim light of the wheelhouse he had assumed the ring-shaped object to be a lifebelt of some kind, but he could now see clearly that it was a tightly woven hoop of leaves, as one might place on a grave...

He felt a sudden chill, a grim fatalism gnawing at the fringes of his mind as his thoughts gave structure to disparate thoughts.

One hundred years from now, on this very night, this woman was flying over the Atlantic, bearing a wreath of commemoration... oh Lord above, please don't say that...

At that moment the bridge telegraphs all chimed, signalling that the Reciprocating and Turbine Engine-Rooms were standing by, and Haddock turned and strode into the wheelhouse with a sudden, electrified energy, as if fighting against the current of history.

"Helmsman, resume course! All engines, ahead full! Make for *Titanic* with all speed!"

Two of the officers stared in surprise at his sudden orders, and then they sprang forward and forced the telegraph levers over to their stops. One, clearly sensing Haddock's intent, even leapt to the emergency telegraph and shoved it to 'Full Ahead', lending further weight to the order. Seconds later the roar from the safety valves cut out as steam surged into the main reciprocating engines, which began to pound away within the hull, mightily flexing their iron sinews. The deck trembled, and far forward, Haddock heard a rising roar as *Olympic* began to push a bow wave. The ship noticeably surged forward as the turbine engine powering the central propeller came on-line, and the foaming rush grew louder, laced with the sound of cascading spray.

"Engine room reports all ahead full, sir! Making revolutions for seventeen knots, and rising!"

"Send word to the pursers and chief stewards in all three classes," he instructed, eyes fixed forward to where the first light of dawn was drawing the line of the horizon. "They are to place notices in each of the main companionways explaining that we are making full speed for *Titanic* on a mission of mercy, and that any discomfort suffered by the passengers is in the aid of saving lives. Instruct them to hand out additional blankets if necessary, and have the galleys prepare a steady supply of hot food and drinks to keep those who need them warm, but make it clear that we shall not reduce speed under any circumstances until we have reached *Titanic*."

Now *Olympic* was storming into the chase, full steam ahead and no holds barred. Exiting onto the bridge wing, Haddock was struck in the face by a blast of cold air. The roar from forward was hungry and relentless as the ship cleaved through the swells, shovelling miles under her keel and engines racing away below like forty thousand galloping horses wrestled into harness. By mid-morning, when the remaining boilers came to full pressure and the engines had limbered up, *Olympic* would be travelling flat-out, as had never been asked from her before. Hopefully they would be able to make up the time they had lost in rescuing Ramirez and her crew.

Hopefully we will be able to make any difference at all, Haddock thought to himself as he turned and beckoned to Ramirez, who loomed in the wheelhouse door like a grim spectre of doom. She was still carrying the wreath.

"Lieutenant, your flight took you out to the site of *Titanic's* sinking," he said bluntly. It was a statement of fact, not a question.

"Yes sir," she dipped her head. "Our service has dropped a wreath in commemoration of *Titanic* every year for the past century. And because this was meant to mark the centenary, we were not the only ones participating. There was an entire fleet of ships gathered over the wreck site."

"Is that so?" Haddock said grimly as he visualised what she was describing. "Might I see it?"

Hesitant, and seemingly unwilling to relinquish the wreath, she instead plucked a small card from it and placed it in Haddock's hand. With not a little dread, he read the message inscribed on it.

"Good Lord…"

Slowly, his mind reeling, he lowered the card and cleared his throat.

"Fifteen hundred lives? Is there nothing that can be done to avert this… catastrophe? There is no-one close enough to aid her immediately?"

"I'm not sure… to my knowledge, she would have sunk over an hour ago by now, and help did not arrive until dawn."

Haddock slowly removed his cap and rubbed at the thin strands of hair on top of his head, and then paused, an idea blazing bright in his mind like a flare.

"Lieutenant," he said softly. "Were you the only craft to have been moved in time?"

She opened her mouth to reply, and then paused, the light of realisation dawning on her face.

"No. I'm sure how many might have been brought along, but immediately after we… shifted… I looked out of a window, and I'm pretty sure I saw the lights of the largest ship of the Memorial Fleet."

"Was her name *Oceanic*?"

Ramirez looked at him, one eyebrow lifted in curiosity. Haddock hoped fervently for several seconds, and then she tipped her head in confirmation.

"Yes sir, it was."

Haddock trembled. "Then there is still hope."

He looked down at the card in his hands, and this time he read the inscription aloud.

"It is with great respect and reverence that we commemorate the 100th anniversary of the sinking of the RMS Titanic on April 15th 1912, remembering the 1500 souls who perished on that fateful morning. Presented on behalf of the International Ice Patrol by the United States Coast Guard, in association with Project 401 and the Titanic Centennial Expedition. April 15th, 2012."

He prayed that it was a prophecy that would not come to pass.

Smoke pouring from her stacks, powering across the darkened ocean beneath the broken sky, *Olympic* charged towards the morning.

ACT ONE

TITANIC CENTURY

CHAPTER ONE

From:	j.laroche@cml.net
To:	admin.mckinn@project401.net
Subject:	ETA *Seguin Laroche*
Sent:	18:45, April 14, 2012

Bonsoir, Mme McKinn

I'm not sure if this will reach you, but it's worth a try. Apologies for not having contacted you sooner to confirm our ETA, but we have been having some technical difficulties with our radar which has taken up my time. It also seems to be affecting our radio and satellite uplink, about the only thing still working on the ship is the compass!

Unfortunately, besides these issues, the weather has not been with us, so we are running several hours late, but we are doing our best to make up for what we've lost. We'll make about twenty knots once the seas abate, and expect to reach the Memorial Fleet just in time for tonight's ceremonies.

Thank you again for extending an invitation to Compagnie Maritime Laroche to participate in the Titanic Centennial. Although I've never been able to confirm my suspicions of a family link to the disaster, I know my father and grandfather would both be honoured by your graciousness, and we aim to not let you or their memory down.

Yours

Joanna Laroche
Captain, MV *Seguin Laroche*

*

On the evening of April 14th 2012, the wild North Atlantic was a field of writhing gold scattered with diamonds, white-capped waves sparkling as they fought each other in the light of the setting sun. A lone cargo ship valiantly fought her way east, white letters on her green hull declaring her to be the Motor Vessel *Seguin Laroche*. Turned head-on into the weather, the ship surged into cresting waves, each slamming against her bow and breaking over the containers stacked in regimented formations on her decks.

The brisk wind lifted the spray high enough to reach the bridge, and pelted it against Joanna Laroche's turned back, even as it tried to snatch the baseball cap stencilled with the rank of '*Capitaine*' away from her head.

"*Can you see any damage, Pierre?*" she struggled to make her herself heard over the wind and rolling waves, hands clenched tightly onto a railing as she called upwards towards the mast, where the ship's electrical engineer had secured himself to the radar assembly. Struggling to hear his reply she felt the deck jump under her feet, and braced herself as the ship took a wave nose on, sliding over into the following trough. For a second she felt the engines race away as the propeller was hoisted out of the water, and then with a roller-coaster surge the ship slammed back down, water exploding around Joanna as eighty thousand tons of metal plunged into the sea. From her position high up on the compass bridge, an exposed platform perched atop the wheelhouse, the ocean below looked dark and hungry, foam from the ship's wake running over the waves like saliva. She did not want to imagine what it was like for the electrician, secured by a carabiner to the spire of the mast, hundreds of feet above the waterline, where the motion of the ship would be at its worst.

But despite the thirty-foot seas and the wind, Joanna was not afraid. The North Atlantic was a capricious road to travel, and both she and the ship had weathered it together many times. It was simply part of their job.

"That's enough Pierre! Come back down!" she ordered at last. "If you can't identify the problem, then there's no point in trying to fix it!"

Her throat burned as she strained her voice to reach the masthead, and part of her noted that it would have made sense to have brought a loudhailer with her out on deck, rather than rushing straight off to find the electrical engineer when the radar screens on the bridge had dissolved into static.

His windbreaker smothering him against the ladder in the wind, Pierre finally began to descend the mast. Joanna crossed the compass bridge to him, water sloshing around her boots.

At last, he reached the foot of the mast and grabbed her outstretched arm.

"The emitter's fine," he said, confusion creasing his face. "And the transceiver checks out as well; I thought that seawater might have gotten into the junction box, but all the seals are all in place. I can't understand it."

"Never mind that now, you're a mess!" Joanna could see the young man was shivering. "Get yourself a drink, have a shower and then try and trace the fault with the help of the other engineers. We're alright for now, but if conditions deteriorate we'll just be a hazard to ourselves and other ships unless we can get the radar working."

Pierre did not need any encouragement to get out of the driving spray, but Joanna hung behind at the foot of the mast, her gaze falling on a metal-and-Plexiglas box welded to it just below eye level. Within the translucent case was the ship's good-luck totem, a silver medal, and beneath it was inscribed a quote from Baudelaire's '*L'Homme et la mer*'.

Love the sea always Man, ye both are free!
For it is thy mirror: thou canst find thy soul
In the mighty waves' surging roll...

She smiled wistfully; it had been a happy day when they fixed the box in place, while the *Seguin Laroche* was still under construction in the shipyard. The medal had been her grandfather's, and his pride in the family's new flagship was immense. She always found it a bitter pill that he had not lived long enough to see the ship's maiden voyage.

Then again, it was probably a blessing that he had been spared having to see Compagnie Maritime Laroche being sold into the hands of 'outsiders'. She often wondered if CML would have fallen so far had he lived a few more years. Glancing around the compass bridge, she noted where rust was beginning to show through peeling paint, and where water was pooling up behind blocked scuppers. With a disgusted shake of the head, she crossed to the rear of the deck and glared down, arms folded, towards the stern staff, the flagpole that stood at the very rear of the ship. Until just a few years ago the French tricolour had proudly flown from it, until CML's new owners, M&B Holdings, had re-registered the fleet in the Marshall Islands 'for purposes of competitive economy', by which they meant escaping the stringent Safety Of Life At Sea regulations enforced in developed countries.

Right now though, the pole was naked, no flag flapping in the sharp breeze.

Oui, I volunteered to hoist our colours for tonight's ceremony... she berated herself for having almost forgotten. It was the fourteenth day of April, and tonight would mark one hundred years since the sinking of the *Titanic*. That was also the reason why the *Seguin Laroche* was charging head-on into the swells at full speed, rather than altering course for an easier passage. They had a rendezvous to make.

The thought of the famed ship gave her pause, for ever since she had learned one piece of *Titanic* trivia, she had suspected a personal connection to the disaster; that she *might* have had family on board the famed liner.

Joseph Philippe Lemercier Laroche, Third Class, Ticket #2123. Born in Haiti, May 26th 1886, died April 15th 1912. Body never recovered...

As she stood in brooding contemplation, gazing down from the compass bridge, she noticed some brave person moving around on the aft container deck, exposing themselves to the lash of wind and spray. She recognised him as one of her youngest crew-members, a twenty-something Egyptian.

His full name was Nashat Abu Shakra, but everyone referred to him as 'Nash', one of several Arabs who had joined the crew only a month ago, replacing a group of men who had jumped ship in Tripoli. These newcomers had been a mixed bunch of nationalities, ranging from British to Pakistani, their only shared trait being their ethnicity, and short of crew but with little alternative, Joanna had signed them on, despite harbouring fears that she might be hiring a group of radicals.

But the new recruits had given several voyages' worth of competent, reliable work, and mostly got along well with the rest of the crew. Jabril Hab Allah, the little group's ringleader, was now training for a position as a bridge officer, and Nash's mechanical abilities had earned him the position of ship's Bosun, responsible for co-ordinating shipboard maintenance among the deck crew.

Now, however, the usually cheerful and upbeat young sailor was working his way nervously about the containers, checking around as if afraid of being caught. Her curiosity piqued, Joanna leaned over the rail to get a better view.

What's he doing, and is that a copy of the ship's manifest in his hand?

Before she could get an answer however, Nash turned out of sight, and when he did not reappear after several minutes, she gave up and headed back to the ship's wheelhouse, resolving to have a quiet word with him when the opportunity arose. Diligence in his duties was well enough, but responsibility for the cargo rested with Marc Pètain, her Chief Officer.

As she passed the base of the mast, she brushed her fingers over the box welded to its forefoot, for luck, before descending the stairs to the Bridge Deck.

The ship's actual wheelhouse was sparse and utilitarian, filled with workstations and control panels that ran the full width of the room. The tall, rugged Officer of the Watch was checking each console as he made his rounds, but aside from himself and Joanna, the only other man present was the lookout, Benjamin Khan, another Arab seaman, scanning the horizon through the long bank of windows that overlooked the containers stacked forward of the bridge. The ship itself was on autopilot, following waypoints laid into the navigational computer.

Marc Pètain, the Watch Officer, was Joanna's Chief, her second-in-command. He was also her fiancé. Hanging her rain-slicked jacket on a rack inside the bridge vestibule, Joanna came up beside him, and saw that he was regarding a pair of radar displays, the monitors clouded by green and grey static.

"Pierre couldn't find anything wrong up on the mast, Marc," she said as she joined him.

"Well, that makes no sense," he replied, offering her a mug that still contained a tepid inch of coffee. Gratefully downing the bitter dregs, she shared a smile with him and tapped the engagement ring on her left hand against the surface of the radar screen. The two of them had been sailing together for six years, and had finally announced their engagement only a month ago.

"Have we considered the possibility that it's just a glitch with the monitors?" Marc suggested, turning to her with a wryly arched eyebrow. "Certain people are, after all, looking for some failure they can point to as evidence of mismanagement."

Joanna feigned shocked insult, holding a hand to her chest. "Are you suggesting I'd send the electrical engineer climbing up the mast in gale force winds just to try and find proof that my family's ships are being allowed to fall apart?"

"Yes," he replied. "Pierre looked like a drowned rat when he passed through. For shame, Capitaine."

She smirked unrepentantly. "If you think I am going to apologise, then you are quite mistaken, Chief Officer Pètain."

In response he offered her a roguishly winning grin, one that suggested a decidedly unprofessional relationship. "I suppose we'll have to work out our differences of opinion later, then."

Shaking her head and laughing lightly, Joanna turned away.

"I will see you at eight bells," she said pointedly, returning his mug to its place on the chart table. "I'll be back to relieve you then. But first, I'm going to get some actual coffee."

"Be warned. Mr Abercrombie is probably still lurking around the officers' lounge. Are you sure you want to be in proximity to him?"

"I'll have to if I want to get anything done. Anyway, he might represent the owners, but while at sea, this is still my ship. If he steps out of line, I can confine him to quarters."

"You sound almost eager to," Marc laughed cautiously. "So, I'll see you back in our cabin after the evening festivities. Anything you'd like for a midnight snack?"

"*Un petit croissant*, perhaps," she called teasingly over her shoulder as she went below decks. Marc was incorrigible out of bed, but a stallion in it.

Neither of them noticed how Khan, the young coffee-skinned man on lookout, though keeping his eyes fixed on the spray-lashed windows, had clenched his mouth tight with disapproval.

*

You have (one) new Private Message:

Mr Abercrombie, where are you? I agreed that we'd be best served by transporting the device discretely, but the captain cannot be expected to ignore that something aboard is beginning to jam the radar. And Nashat has just come running with word that the container is hot to the touch and the external power couplings are smoking! We need to bleed it now!

Meet me beside it immediately!
Jabril Hab-Allah

*

The officer's lounge was quiet, a few off-duty members of the senior crew gathered around a TV. Some noticed Joanna's quiet entry and nodded respectfully, while still keeping their focus on the film that was playing on an old VHS player.

"...like scraping off trays in a cafeteria, or cleaning out toilets!"

With such an internationally diverse crew, English was the lingua franca for entertainment on the *Seguin Laroche*. Crossing to the coffee machine Joanna searched on the sideboard for her usual mug, and found it to be missing. Pulling another one off the shelf, she glanced curiously at the grainy image on the television screen and recognised it as an American thriller from some years back. This was the scene where the embittered older convict hectored an ignorant young buck about the value of hard work.

"...and when that man walks in at the end of the day; when he comes to see how you've done, you ain't gonna look at his eyes; you're gonna look at the floor!"

The coffee machine percolated softly and chimed once it had filled the mug. Grabbing it and a handful of sugar sachets, Joanna turned to leave. But then she paused, frowning at a man seated in the corner of the room, typing away on a laptop computer. His tailored jacket was folded neatly over the back of a chair and a pair of gold arm-binders held his silk shirt neatly in place.

Adrian Abercrombie, a middle-level executive with M&B Holdings, had been placed onboard allegedly to oversee the ship's participation in the Titanic Centennial, but had in actuality left all those details to Joanna's own discretion, choosing to keep his own company. That said, neither the crew nor the Capitaine herself had felt particularly put out to make the man feel welcome. Mostly he had hidden away in the cabin provided for his use, except for meals, as now. Her favourite mug was resting within reach of one of his hands, steaming softly. Feeling her gaze on him, he looked up and smiled unpleasantly. His mild eyes seemed small and colourless behind a pair of frameless glasses.

"Because you don't wanna see that fear in his eyes, when you jump up and grab his face, and slam him to the floor, and make him scream and cry for his life…"

Joanna slowly pressed her tongue against the inside of her clenched teeth, resisting the urge to make a comment. As if reading her mind Abercrombie rolled his attention towards the television, mouth working obscenely as he chewed on a sandwich. Onscreen the older convict was working himself up into a rage as he continued to berate the other man.

"And then he's gonna look around the room and see how you've done. And he's gonna say, "Oh, you missed a little spot over there. Jeez, you didn't get this one here. What about this little bitty spot"."

Abercrombie swallowed and looked back at Joanna, a slight smirk curling the corner of his lips, enjoying some personal joke. Isolated in the centre of the room, Joanna could only stand and watch as he raised his drink to her in mocking salute. The company logo was embossed on the ceramic surface of the mug he had 'borrowed'. Her *arrière-grand-père* had designed it when he founded the Compagnie Maritime Laroche.

"And you're gonna suck all that pain inside you; and you're gonna clean that spot, and you're gonna clean that spot, until you get that shiny clean!"

Turning on her heel, Joanna left the lounge, suddenly feeling like a king who has found himself alone in a besieged keep.

"And on Friday, you pick up your pay check."

All she had left was her pride.

*

You have (one) new Private Message:
I don't take orders from you, Cadet Officer. We agreed to the terms and conditions on how we would transport your toy, and I've no intention of stepping back on them.

As for getting access, I'm not going to pull anything while the captain is prowling around. She was in here just now, glaring at me like a beaten dog. Her watch starts at eight. Once she's on the bridge, you can get Pètain to open the container. Until then, do nothing.

And likewise, the cooperation of both Pètain and me is guaranteed only by payment, regardless of the condition the device is in upon arrival.

A. Abercrombie

*

The *Seguin Laroche's* office was a space behind the bridge wheelhouse into which two desks and several filing cabinets had been squeezed, along with a sofa and coffee machine. Joanna refilled her mug and sat down behind the more cluttered of the desks, sifting through the reams of paperwork that kept a ship running just as much as crew and machinery. Missives from the company were scattered throughout the stacks of forms, mostly rejections of her multiple requests that the *Seguin Laroche* be soon laid up for overhaul, the bureaucrats citing overt expense and difficult economic conditions as the reason that any such work be deferred for another six months.

Sighing, she spun a paperweight around, so that the green-on-white emblem stamped on the side was facing her. It was the same crest that decorated the mug Abercrombie had repurposed; a proud fleur-de-lis and anchor encircled with stars, crowning the words *Compagnie Maritime Laroche*. Slumping forward with her hands supporting her chin, she pulled her cap from her head, allowing her auburn locks to fall down the back of her neck. Holding the cap by the brim, she looked at the same logo emblazoned on the front, surrounded by a gilded garland of leaves.

From the deck outside the ship's bell rang out, a mechanical hammer striking it seven times to mark seven bells. The bell itself was a relic, having been carried on each company flagship since the Crimean War. Joanna herself had been baptised in it as a baby. Cradling the mug, she tipped back in the chair, hefted her boots up on her desk and stared at a tricolour that had been pinned to the wall opposite. It was the flag that had flown from the ship's stern staff for years.

Regarding the flag she suddenly sat upright, remembering her mental agreement to fly the ship's colours in time for tonight's show. The blue and gold Marshallese flag would be secured in the stern flag locker, and her hand automatically drifted to the thick ring of keys she wore secured to her belt, and began to rifle through the tiny metal objects for the right one. She had half an hour to get the job done before her bridge watch began at eight bells.

Still working her way through the keys she left the office and descended the stairs, coming out on the side of the superstructure. The wind was slackening off and the sea seemed to be settling, and through the deck she could feel the engine revolutions steadying as the ship worked up towards twenty knots, her full speed when travelling against moderate swells. Heading aft, she passed under the ship's single lifeboat in its launch cradle and then paused suddenly, hearing raised voices. They were speaking in English, a language with which she was familiar. One of them was Nash, recognisable by an excitable twang that coloured his language;

"...but Abercrombie wants the captain out of the way before we do anything."

"If we wait much longer it's not going to be salvageable, Nashat."

The second voice was gruffer, but softer, the speaker maintaining a careful calm. Cautiously she approached, ducking behind one of the access ladders for the lifeboat to hide herself.

Nash was walking down a narrow corridor between the stacked containers, talking with a bearded, leanly-muscled man. Jabril Hab Allah, the Pakistani Cadet Officer.

Wondering at what they were doing, Joanna followed them, her rubber-soled shoes making no noise on the deck. The two men continued on until they stopped beside a particular cargo unit. It was right in the middle of the aft deck, other containers stacked around and even on top of it. Keeping herself hidden, she watched as Hab Allah felt around the container's near end, inspecting several fat power cables connecting it to the ship's electrical systems. He then inhaled deeply and swore aloud, all the more shocking in the amount of quiet vehemence he put into the expletive. Mimicking him in sniffing the air, Joanna smelled an acrid reek, like burning plastic, and then noticed a few coils of smoke rising off the cables Hab Allah had been examining. Feeling the cold weight of dread sinking like a stone into her stomach, she saw him pace along the object, running his hands over patches of rust in the steel plating, as if searching for some defect.

"Abercrombie says to wait!" he said aloud. "When the damn thing is about to catch fire!"

As the two continued to talk, Joanna stared at the forty-foot container, trying to imagine it through their eyes. Pulling out her PDA she accessed a digital copy of the manifest and matched the container to its ISO number.

PLBU8727506

Almost immediately the worry began to eat at her like a malignant growth. The container was *wrong*. According to the manifest, container 506 had been loaded at Philadelphia, containing 'auto parts' for onward shipping after arrival in Le Havre. No final destination was given. But the container itself was a *reefer*, a refrigerated unit meant for the transportation of perishable goods, hence the power conduit that fed electricity from the ship's generators to the container's refrigeration plant. The white paint that should have marked it out, however, had been painted over with red oxide, the original colour showing where rust had nibbled away at the overcoat. She wondered if the ISO code had been falsified as well.

It was all wrong. Something suspicious, possibly dangerous, and almost certainly illegal, was being transported on her ship, and Abercrombie seemed to be personally escorting it. Her crew had even been infiltrated by people who had business with that container's contents. And they had come aboard weeks before container 506 was loaded, meaning that this had been planned in advance.

But what troubled her most was that cargo handling was the personal responsibility of the Chief Officer, her fiancé. When 506 had been taken aboard, Marc would have seen the discrepancies, and had done nothing. Worse yet, he would have had to help conceal them.

Betrayal. The hot, sickly feeling twisting in her gut was one she had come to know very well ever since the family sold CML to

M&B Holdings, only now it was directed at Marc, and carrying her along faster than she could think.

There was a soft click, and Joanna felt a cool metal object press against the side of her head. She slowly turned.

Jabril Hab Allah stood over her, calmly wielding a gun in her face, giving her a bullseye view down a black barrel that seemed the size of a canon.

"Mademoiselle Capitaine," he said politely. "You have been relieved of command."

The *Seguin Laroche* groaned darkly as she rolled over another wave.

*

Delivery Error. E-Courier (Seguin Laroche).
Cannot Find External Network.
Your message (Seguin Laroche ETA) failed to deliver.
A report has been sent to the system administrator.

*

The grey periscope cutting through the sea close at hand went unnoticed. Seen through it, the container ship was a square silhouette, an artificial island set like a rock in the heaving ocean.

"*Seguin Laroche*, Majuro."

Lieutenant Commander Scott Thresher slowly worked the zoom and contrast on the scope controls, tracking up from where the ship's name and homeport were painted at the stern, to focus on the mast above the bridge, where the radar receivers were motionless, braving the wind defiantly.

That's interesting.

Thoughtful, Scott swept the periscope along the length of the foreign ship, and then stepped back. "Sonar, any contacts?"

"No contacts to report sir," the senior technician reported.

Scott blinked, struggling to keep a straight face. "Down scope!"

With a soft whir, the periscope retracted into the floor and Thresher glanced around the control room of Her Majesty's Vanguard-class submarine *Viking*. Ratings in blue coveralls manned computerised workstations, supervised by officers in pressed white uniforms. Thresher instinctively brushed a piece of lint off of his shoulder-boards and called towards the navigation consoles.

"Helm, maintain this course, make your depth twenty metres."

He grabbed a small microphone and thumbed an internal channel. "Engineering, this is the Executive Officer. Set speed two-zero."

Twenty knots, not far short of full speed. Then, on another channel, he made a public announcement. "Captain to the Conn please, Captain Furness to the Conn."

Some of the crew murmured softly amongst themselves at the unusual orders, but none questioned Thresher's words.

"Maintain course," confirmed the helmsman. "Make depth twenty metres, aye sir."

The deck began to thrum softly as, further aft, the submarine's power plant came up to cruising speed. Moments later the skipper, Commander Robert Furness, entered. Greeting him with a silent salute, Scott waved towards the empty Officer's Wardroom, indicating a need to speak in private. With a raised eyebrow the captain stepped through, and Thresher drew the curtain behind them as Furness sat himself on the edge of a table which had just been cleaned from dinner.

"We've put on speed Scott," he said evenly. "Care to explain why we're bombing along like an underwater jet-ski, advertising ourselves to the world?"

"Sorry sir, but something occurred when we went to periscope depth and extended the antennas to pick up our weekly radio traffic."

"Would you care to elaborate on 'something'?"

"Yes sir. We couldn't pick anything up on any bandwidth, from ELF through to SHF. Radio assures me it is not a fault in the system, but something external causing interference. When I put the scope up to see if there was anything up there, I spotted a merchant vessel just a mile off."

Furness had been sitting with a hand held patiently cupping his chin, but now he silenced Thresher with a motion of his index finger. "You brought the boat to periscope depth in the presence of another ship? You do understand patrol procedure I hope, Lieutenant?"

"Yes sir; hide and keep quiet, pretend to be a hole in the water, don't show yourself to anyone. But that's it, sir; sonar reported no contacts within twenty nautical miles before we stuck our head up."

Thresher was now moving through a library cabinet as he spoke, until he located and pulled down a thick volume on merchant vessel recognition. "That ship is not showing up on any of our instruments. Sonar can't hear it and radar can't see it. I think this is her here."

He flipped open the correct page and laid it down for the skipper to see. "One of the larger container ships belonging to CML shipping."

Furness ran his finger down the ship's particulars. "*Ile* Class. Marshallese registry, single screw propulsion, top speed twenty-five knots, forty metres beam, three hundred metres in length, deadweight displacement 83,000 tons; hardly an easy thing to misplace." He pursed his lips, and Thresher could see the light of curiosity mirrored in his eyes. "Okay, maintain our current course, but keep tight to her. Banging along like the damn *Sean Connery Express*, the most we can hope is that anyone listening in confuses our noise with that of the ship."

Thresher nodded and moved to the curtain.

"Scott," Furness raised his voice gently, and his executive officer turned back towards him. "Don't make rash decisions without consulting me first, ever," the Captain said, pausing to let the words sink in before dismissing him with a nod. "You have the Conn."

As Thresher, now somewhat more subdued, returned to the control room, Furness ran a hand over the scraps of hair that still clung to his bald pate, and one of his hands pushed inside his pocket, slowly turning over the key to his personal safe. Exiting through another doorway, he descended a deck and headed aft, emerging into the room which housed his command's reason for existence.

He was in a forest of metal, vertical launch tubes marching away along the length of the compartment. Each contained an ICBM, an Intercontinental Ballistic Missile. This was 'Sherwood Forest', *Viking's* nuclear armoury.

After a moment contemplating the missiles, sheathed and sealed in their launch housings, Furness turned on his heel and returned to the officers' quarters, ducking into his own private cabin and closing off the corridor.

It was a compact space, as was every other compartment on the submarine, but comfortable compared to the enlisted crew's quarters, containing a small bunk and cupboard, and a desk about two feet square. Beside the desk was his personal safe, and opening it, Robert reached into the back, where several thin red folders were neatly racked, on a shelf stamped **FOR CAPTAIN'S EYES ONLY**.

The Roswell Files, he and the other captains in the submarine service called them. Seven red dossiers, all sealed, and all allegedly containing instructions on what action to take in the event of one of Her Majesty's submarines encountering a phenomenon or circumstance beyond explanation.

Rumour said that one of them detailed procedures for carrying out first-contact with alien visitors, and that another was prepared in the event of an undisclosed 'non-nuclear event', which some had joked might be anything from the supposed December 21st 2012 apocalypse, to the Second Coming of Christ.

They also said that one captain who broke the seals and read all the folders out of curiosity was never seen again after his command returned to port. And not only physically – any attempts to track down family members or paper evidence of his existence turned up dead ends, as if he had been completely 'disappeared' from existence, sponged away by sinister government forces.

Bob Furness, for his part, had always treated those stories with a mixture of humoured condescension and respect. Although the myths surrounded the Roswell Files were definite nonsense, they also served as a cautionary reminder of the responsibilities that came with the captaincy of a ballistics sub:

You are entrusted with secrets, you are responsible for the defence of the realm, and if necessary, you are expendable.

Or in other words: *don't take this job lightly.* One day he might be asked to actually launch *Viking*'s missiles on an enemy state, and risk destruction at the hands of that country's own armed forces.

As much as he and the other sub-drivers liked to joke about their work on the V-Boats, they were all serious men when out at sea.

Still, he had never expected one day actually being in a position to unseal one of the Roswell Files, and so when he finally selected the right one of the seven he handled it as he might an armed bomb, gently setting it down on the desk before relocking the safe and returning the key to his pocket. Integrated into one bulkhead of his cabin was the rare luxury of a personal washstand, and pouring himself a glass of water he finally turned his attention to the folder, sipping slowly.

Dossier 7000
Seal To Be Broken Only Under Prescribed Circumstances:
Radar/Sonar Anomalies, With Regard To Other Vessels
All Contents Classified Under The Official Secrets Act, 1989.

Furness sat in a staring contest with the final line of text for some time, wondering about that captain who had allegedly been erased from existence, until he realised that he had drained his glass of water. Then, with a speed that surprised him, he jammed a paper knife under the lip of the file, broke the seal, and removed from it a few meagre sheets of paper, tightly-packed with typed text and reproduced photographs. Feeling a little disappointed at first, he scanned through them quickly.

Two minutes later he stood and crossed to a cubby-hole beside the washstand, refilling his glass from a hidden bottle of Irish Whisky. His hands were trembling.

Her single propeller churning with newfound purpose, HMS *Viking* invisibly stalked the *Seguin Laroche* into the gathering dark.

*

Delivery Error. E-Courier (*Seguin Laroche*).
Cannot Find External Network.
Your message (Error Report) failed to deliver.
A report has been sent to the system administrator.

CHAPTER TWO

Project401.net

Home >> Ships and Teams >> RV Anatoly Sagalevich >>
Philippa Paik >> Pippa's Blog

Date:	*April 14 2012, 7.40pm*
Location:	*Big Russian ship in middle of Atlantic, da?*
Status:	*Erm... still single, still crushing on poor Jack*

Thayer

Mood: *Excited, Awesomely Excited! And kinda terrified.*
I know, lolwut!

Listening To: *BBC News 24, Celine Dion*

Blog It: *I can't believe it! Tonight's the night. I mean, tonight is THE night. The Night They Remembered! It's going to be exactly 100 years since the ship sank, and I get to be where it all happened! They're about to feature us on the news, and in just a few hours, I get to give a lecture on Titanic!*
...

Sorry, began panicking a little there. Being a part of Project 401 is, well it's kinda humbling, you know. Oh Gawwwwd. I've gotta give a lecture on Titanic, to how many people? Save me!

*

Kai Alinka's rebreather bubbled in his mouth as he sank beneath the surface, the weight of the oxygen tank on his back pressing him down as he descended into the depths. The water around him was bitterly cold, despite the dive suit sheathing his body, and the LEDs mounted around his mask threw only a meagre cone of illumination, an icy light that glinted on specs of plankton and debris. He glanced down, and beyond his flippered feet saw absolute dark, a void two miles deep.

Na aumakua mai ka po mai,
Nana i na pua,
Ho'okomo iloko o keia po o ka malamalama.

Scuba-diving in the North Atlantic was like taking a casual swim over some mythical underworld. Glancing upwards he saw the bright sky beyond the veil of the surface and was suddenly reminded of mythical heroes, the champions who journeyed into the afterlife to rescue loved ones from the grip of death, and the spirits that acted as their guides.

Aumakua of the night,
Watch over your offspring,
Enfold them in the belt of light.

He recited the old Hawaiian poem again in his head, uncomfortably remembering his childhood in *'the Aloha State'*, before a female voice broke into his thoughts.

"Kai, are you having a *'moment'* again?" it crackled in his ear, and he reached up to feel at a hard bump where his earpiece sat snugly underneath the neoprene cowl of the wetsuit, before his hand drifted down to the watertight keypad strapped to his forearm, on which he tapped out *'maybe'*.

"Well, while you're repeating poetry to yourself, would you kindly test the video feed?"

Rolling his eyes, Kai held up his hand in front of his face and wiggled 'hello' with his fingers for the benefit of the fibre-optics suite integrated with his mask. As happened whenever he was partnered with an obnoxious radio operator, he considered giving the camera 'the finger' instead, but professionalism advised against it; someday, maybe, *but never today.*

"Video checks out," the operator confirmed. "Sonar shows the chunk is ascending towards one hundred feet. It should be with you any second."

Feet kicking against the swells Kai inverted himself in the water, letting gravity pull him on down, the dive-meter on his wrist slowly marking his descent until he came to a halt.

'holdin @ 15 metrs' he tapped out on his keypad. Even only a short distance down the water was noticeably colder and darker, and he hung in a dim twilight between the bright surface and the inky depths. It reminded him of an occasion when he had gone

diving in a flooded quarry in the Appalachians; there had been an entire town at the bottom of the pit, sheds and workshops now a home only to fish; cranes and diggers rearing up from the bottom like the ruins of Atlantis...

...and now Atlantis was rising.

"There it is!" the operator said, her voice now tinged with quiet awe.

Kai could not fault her; the cone of light from his mask was now shining on a balloon-like lifting bag that was rising ghostlike towards him with patient slowness. As it drew nearer he could see more of the white bags emerging from the depths, each shaped like a tapering torpedo, their canvas skins stretched taut. There were twelve of them, each secured to a sturdy line.

And attached to the lines was an immense chunk of metal, almost a hundred feet in width. Kicking his feet again, Kai skirted the lines cautiously and swam over the top of the object, which was caked with thick tendrils of rust. Beneath them he could see huge steel plates riveted together in neat rows known as 'strakes'. Running across the centre of the object was the keel, a thick girder to which they were rooted, like ribs to a backbone. At either end of the chunk, however, the keel had been hideously torn, bent and deformed by immense forces. Tentatively, Kai reached out a hand; the metal was old, rotting and decayed. Touching it, he shivered; suspended from the bags, the immense object swayed softly back and fro with a motion like the breathing of an animal. It was an eerie sensation.

"Check the mounting points," the operator instructed, and tapping out '*o-k*' Kai swum over the side of the object. Underneath the thick metal skin the structure of the object was honeycombed and subdivided into metal cells, which had been pumped full of a thick grey foam to expel water and increase buoyancy. To his hands the expanded foam, riddled with bubbles of trapped gas, felt like hardened pumice, and at intervals steel rods had been anchored in it to act as securing points for the lift lines.

More lights shone in the murk, and Kai turned to see other divers joining him, laying their own hands on the object as if in reverence. Through their masks he made eye-contact with one, and she waved in excited greeting. Shaking his head, Kai checked his dive-watch and saw that they were approaching the surface; the blue glare from above was getting brighter and stronger. With a whine of electric motors a submersible joined them, keeping a cautious distance, and now he waved hello for the high-definition cameras mounted on its robotic arms.

In the glare of the tiny metal craft's halon lights, the dark metal object showed itself to be painted; patches of deep red anti-fouling paint showing through the rusticles. It reminded Kai of just where this object had come from, and shuddering in sudden revulsion he spared a final glance down into the void from which it had risen. Milu, the realm of dark, and above them Wakea, the realm of light.

And hovering in between, basking in daylight for the first time in a century, a several-hundred-ton fragment from the wreck of the *Titanic*.

*

"We now go live to Dean Simmons over the North Atlantic."

"Thank you London," someone shouted over the roar of a helicopter engine. *"I'm currently hovering over the Russian research ship Anatoly Sagalevich, and while the level of activity out here is almost impossible to describe, from the air you can see huge cranes and derricks swinging into place over the side of the deck, directly above where divers are in the final stages of one of the most ambitious and controversial operations in the history of marine salvage..."*

The television tuned to BBC News 24 continued to natter away as Philippa 'Pip' Paik stepped out from the en-suite shower attached to her cabin, one towel wrapped around her body and a second tying up her hair like a turban. Slipping her feet into a pair of fuzzy pink slippers, she hunted around for the remote control, tossing aside books and notes that were littered across the cabin's desk and bunk. From beyond her open porthole she could hear the sound of the helicopter from which the news broadcast was being filmed, and turning momentarily back to the TV she saw the futuristic shape of the ship she was on, the *Anatoly Sagalevich*, appear onscreen, the vessel's slab-sided superstructure and open work deck supported on twin catamaran hulls.

Hey, I can see my house from here! she thought with a smile, before returning to her search for the remote control.

"If you look around," the broadcast continued, *"you can see for yourself the amount of interest in this event, as more and more ships converge on this desolate stretch of ocean for what must be a once-in-a-lifetime gathering. Closest to us at this moment is the other vessel from which this salvage operation is being directed, the USNS Rescue."*

The camera panned to another ship several hundred yards away. The *Rescue*, dark and sharp-edged, looked like a pocket-sized warship that had been stripped of all its guns, but before the viewer's attention could linger, Simmons pointed down from the helicopter, and the cameraman panned with the newscaster's gesturing arm away towards where a tiny yellow craft was surfacing in the open water between the two vessels.

"...coming to the surface right now is one of the Mir submersibles which have made this project possible, capable of diving to depths of over two miles..."

Pip grabbed hold of a stack of papers and turned them over in her hunt, spilling them onto the floor. Then with a triumphant shout she found the remote buried in a discarded pile of clothes.

"...in the distance I can see the ocean liner Oceanic III approaching, delayed by rough seas but still arriving in time for tonight's ceremony. And from aboard Oceanic, I am now joined live by Adrienne McKinn; founder of Project 401, the organisation that co-ordinated this event. Mrs McKinn, can you please describe to us what is happening here?"

Whipping around with the recovered remote in hand Pip held down on the volume key, just as a willowy woman in an elegant gown appeared in a separate window onscreen.

"Well Dean, what's happening is that we're raising the Titanic," she smiled serenely. *"A hundred years to the day of the sinking of the world's most famous ship, the largest section of her ever recovered will break the surface before the eyes of the world, thanks to the partnership of the National Oceanographic and Atmospheric Administration, the United States Navy and the Russian Academy of Sciences, as well as RMS Titanic Inc., the wreck's official salvors-in-possession."*

"And what role does your organisation play in this?"

"Besides conceiving the expedition and arranging the involvement of the various participants, Project 401 aims to create a complete, living encyclopaedia of Titanic history; our web servers, graciously

hosted aboard the ships of the fleet, are home to a growing, floating database collating photographic records, testimonials, archives and ongoing research articles covering the Titanic phenomenon. And to add context, we're also showcasing video-diaries and articles prepared by all manner of people from around the world, giving their thoughts and opinions on why it is that Titanic continues to hold such a grip on the world's imagination."

Pip bit her lip and hunched forward on the edge of her bed, eyes wide as a selection of clips began to play. Faces, familiar and unknown scrolled past, some praising the centennial expedition, others condemning. And then, for a few seconds she herself appeared onscreen.

"That's where Titanic should have docked! And in a month and a half, part of her will complete that voyage! Isn't that amazing!?"

"Yes!" Pip all but punched the air as Adrienne McKinn returned onscreen.

"Project 401 has had a massive response, not just from people around the world, but from organisations and shipping companies that want to participate in commemorating the centenary. Oceanic herself, specially chartered from her owners, the revived White Star Line, is right now making full speed to join Rescue, the Anatoly Sagalevich and seventeen other ships at Titanic's final resting-place, to pay our respects and remember what transpired here a hundred years ago."

"Thank you Adrianne," the newscaster took back the screen, turning into the camera to smile. "So tonight at 11.40pm, at the precise time Titanic began to sink, a part of her will return to the surface, and we will return then for further coverage. From the Titanic Centenary Expedition, at 41 Degrees 43 Minutes North, 49 Degrees 56 Minutes West, here in the North Atlantic, this is Dean Simmons for BBC News 24."

The second the broadcast wrapped up, Pip's phone began to ring from somewhere in the clutter of her cabin, and she dived onto the bed to recover it.

"Hello, sis? Marilyn? Yes, I saw it!" she squealed happily. "It's so awesome being out here, being a part of this!"

Someone banged on the door of the cabin, interrupting her. "Hey Pip! The Big O's coming up in a few minutes, get on deck quick or you're going to miss it!"

"Thanks! No, no, Mari, don't go!" Pip said. Cradling the phone between her ear and her shoulder she began to pull on her clothes, talking away even as she fumbled to pull her jeans on. "Yes, the weather's improving, so we will be going across to the *Oceanic* this evening for the presentations…"

She pushed open the cabin's small closet and pulled a thick jersey out. "The dress?"

Her eyes turned. Hanging at the far end of the clothes rack was a royal blue fantasy of velvet and silk, protectively wrapped in plastic. "The dress is fine; I haven't taken it out of the carrier since you left it with me… yes it fits – or at least I hope it does…" nervously she felt around her waist. "I don't think I've gained anything since you took my measurements, but with the food they serve in the galley… How bad? Well, just be glad you've never had to try *borscht*."

She listened for several moments and then recoiled. "You did what with the fitting-session photos? Marilyn, I don't need a boyfriend… you are just teasing me, right? Phew…" she sighed in relief, and then laughed nervously. "Yes, OK, I'll get someone to take a few of me wearing it tonight. Just, don't go spreading them around on Facebook. Promise?"

She smiled softly and checked her watch, before grabbing hold of her digital camera and camcorder. "Right, I've got to go. I love you too Sis', and I'll talk to you soon, take care… bye."

Ending the call with a feeling of warmth and pride conflicting with embarrassment at her sister's threats, she ran out into the corridor and made her way through the mazelike interior of the ship, following signs labelled bilingually in English and Cyrillic Russian towards the laboratories.

"Hey guys!" she ducked her head into the first room. Artefacts recovered from the wreck site below sat in saltwater vats for careful documentation and restoration. "The *Oceanic's* arriving… oh!"

Her voice trailed off and her eyes widened as they fell on what the team were gathered around. "Is that what I think it is?"

"It was brought up just twenty minutes ago," one scientist said by way of answer, a grin splitting his face. "The crown-jewel itself."

Several of the technicians were hoisting between them a basket, straining with the weight. Inside was an evidently very heavy piece of electrical equipment, badly corroded after a century underwater, but still recognisable as a motor, or maybe a generator. Mounted on the shaft that extended from one end was a metal disc studded with electrical terminals. Any other parts of the device, not made from ebonite and metal, had long since rotted away.

Pip immediately brought up her camera and began taking quick shots, walking once around the device and capturing it from every angle. At most it was only two feet long from end to end, and looked like a piece of junk you might find rusting in peace in a farmyard, but she reverently documented it as thoroughly as if it were a priceless relic straight from the Valley of the Kings.

The digital camera continued to click as the men hoisted the device, cage and all, up from the floor. Only when they had deposited it in the largest saltwater bath available did she lower the viewfinder from her face, her mouth curling upwards in a faint, sad smile.

"*Titanic*'s rotary spark discharger..." she said aloud. "The heart of her Wireless installation, through which she put out her distress calls... what did they do to the wreck in order to get it out?"

Her voice was muted, and a few of the lab techs looked away uneasily, as if suddenly confronted with similar feelings of guilt, but the first shrugged casually. "They cut through the roof of the silent room and pulled it out by brute force, after one of the robots secured lift-lines to the bedplate. No different to pulling a tooth."

The analogy was blunt and a little sickening. Pip rested a hand on the side of the tank and looked at the bottom of the spark discharger. It was still resting on fragments of deck plating, the edges mangled from where they had been torn away. She tried not to visualise the gaping hole left behind from where the device had been ripped from the ship's broken corpse. "We can't leave the poor thing in peace, can we?"

Her mood suddenly sombre, she looked around the room at other relics removed from the ship for preservation. "We're tearing her to pieces. This isn't like the 'Big Piece' of 98', or the double-bottom section they're raising today; all of those are just being plucked out of the debris field. But now we're cutting into the wreck itself to remove her fittings. What's next – the rudder, or the anchors, or maybe even the propellers, like they did to the wreck of the *Lusitania*?"

After a sad pause, she added: "No wonder this expedition lost the support of Doctor Ballard and the Titanic Historical Society. It's like we're looting a dead body…"

"But respectfully…" someone else spoke up, their voice quavering a little with uncertainty. "We're not treasure-hunters; all these things are being removed out of respect to their value in history, not because they're worth money…" he gestured towards the spark distributor. "That's worth a few dollars if you melted it down for the metal, and given a few more years on the ocean floor, it would have just ended up as worse, a puddle of rusty mulch. But now, it's here with us, and priceless, and because it's going into a proper museum, not a travelling fair, it will last for as long as people remember *Titanic*… that's the best reason, the only reason, for our being here."

"I mean, why else would we be disturbing a mass grave…" Pip answered softly.

The sudden bellowing of a horn from outside drew their attention away from ethics, and in groups of two and three they trickled away to watch. Pip left last, slowly scrolling through the photographs stored on her camera's flash-drive, and wondering why she felt so passionately excited, and so ashamed, over a collection of decaying scrap.

*

"DRP, it stands for Deepwater Recovery Procedure," Kai said, arms crossed over his chest in an attempt to make himself more impressive for the newscasters. That it also drew attention to where the *Rescue*'s crest was printed on the shoulder of his dive-suit probably helped as well. "It's what helps us do the impossible, as you can see here".

He indicated towards the lift bags just breaking the ocean surface. The raised section of *Titanic*'s hull was out of sight below them, still submerged underwater as *Rescue* manoeuvred it and herself towards the *Anatoly Sagalevich*.

"Can you explain that in more detail for us?" prompted one of the interviewers, collecting footage for editing into future broadcasts. "And why the US Navy is volunteering its services for a civilian enterprise?"

"Right…" Kai paused for a moment, the words catching in his throat. Seeking escape, he glanced up towards *Rescue's* superstructure and saw a figure in a baseball cap and bomber jacket leaning on a rail, a corncob pipe elevated in a toast of challenge to him. It was the ship's captain, Jordan Jones.

Ready for your close-up, Mr Alinka?

Groaning to himself, Kai's attention snapped back to the cameras, and waved his arm around as if to take in the whole of the ship. "Well to start with, *Rescue*, a modified *Safeguard*-class salvage ship, is actually assigned to the Military Sealift Command, the US Navy's civilian department; likewise, although I'm the ship's Lead Salvor, I'm not a US Navy Diver, just a professional salvage engineer. *Rescue's* job, and ours, is to support military operations through transportation, resupply, towing and salvage, and this is where DRP comes in."

Leading them across *Rescue's* open rear deck he gestured towards a cluster of cylinders connected with a complex network of plumbing, which came together in a long lance-like gun studded with intermix chambers.

"We've been using polyurethane foam like this to refloat wrecks for years, but have never tried applying the technology in extreme depths," he said, hefting the foam gun to illustrate its full six-foot length. "But this causes a problem if we lose a ship or submarine in the open ocean and need to raise it, either whole or in part. Like the USS *Scorpion*, a nuclear sub lost southwest of the Azores in 1968. What if, all these years on, her wreck's power plant begins to leak radioactive waste into the environment; how can we recover it safely if we don't have the technology, the equipment or the experience needed to raise something as heavy as a nuclear reactor from several miles down? That is why the Navy is testing DRP in conjunction with Japan's IJN Ishiyama Shipyards and Doctor Oshiro, who developed the technology."

He pointed across the deck and several of the cameras turned away to a quiet, bespectacled figure standing by the rail, charcoal-grey hair drawn back into a lengthening ponytail. Doctor Akira Oshiro noticed the sudden attention and waved politely with the clipboard in his hand, before stepping out of sight behind tanks of DRP foam. Kai grinned with a vapid dread as the focus of the newshounds returned to him, and he held up the foam gun as if to defend himself. IJN Ishiyama's emblem, a samurai warrior riding atop a rearing pegasus, sword drawn and wings spread, was branded onto the stock.

"Well, we had the technology, but needed to prove it. And while searching for a suitable field-test, we were approached by Project 401, and so here we are, proudly assisting the Titanic Centennial Expedition in something that's never been done before, raising several hundred tons of metal from over two miles down."

"So refloating this large section of the *Titanic*'s double-bottom is actually an opportunity for the Navy to test DRP in advance of some possible disaster?"

"That's correct," Kai clarified. "The Cold War may be over, but as recent events like the sinking of the *Kursk* show, the world's navies need to be prepared for worst-case scenarios."

And it lets us bag some free publicity, he mentally added, wondering if they were thinking it in turn. Turning to return the gun to its rack he saw two helicopters flitting about overhead, the *Anatoly Sagalevich's* Sikorsky Seaking now being joined by a smaller Bell model-407 that had just arrived on site, carried on the back of the *Oceanic.* Now the two craft wheeled over the assembled vessels, camera-bubbles slung from their noses filming everything.

A metric ton of publicity.

The interview wrapped up shortly afterwards, and as the news crew continued to mill around and did their best to make a nuisance of themselves, Kai gratefully accepted a towel to wrap around his shoulders and climbed the steep staircase to *Rescue's* upper deck, fleeing their attention. Standing to one side of the bridge, one foot up on a bollard and quietly stuffing tobacco into his pipe, was Captain Jones, tall, broad-shouldered and bearded.

"Bravo Kai!" he said teasingly, bringing his hands together in joking applause. "That was a stunning film debut. Talent agencies will be all over you once we make port."

Jones' eyes were hidden behind a pair of reflective sunglasses, but Kai suspected they were crinkled up in silent laughter. Despite being about twenty years his senior and a graduate of the Maine Maritime College, *Rescue's* master regularly seemed to comport himself with all the grace and decorum of a college frat-boy.

"I'd rather they didn't, captain," he said quietly, drawing the towel a bit tighter around his shoulders and pulling down his baseball cap to shield his eyes from the glare of the evening sun.

"Fame, glory, hordes of willing girls ready to drape themselves over you," the Captain genially continued to expand on the idea. "Sounds like a good deal to me."

Kai managed a laugh and rolled his eyes at the Captain. "I've lived through that once already; Hilo High School class of 1993."

"Oh, really?" Jones smirked wryly, before trailing off into a series of puffs on the stem of the pipe, struggling to light it in the sharp ocean breeze. Finally, with one of the matches cupped in his free hand, he was rewarded with a light curl of blue smoke. Shaking the match out, he tossed it overboard, still grinning. "Can I guess that you were one of those insufferable kids who actually enjoyed reciting the Alma Mater in assembly?"

"Beneath the tropic skies of Hilo, stands dear old Hilo High School," Kai sang out in response. *"Dearer ever shall it grow, with the spirit of Blue and Gold."*

He trailed off into an embarrassed laugh.

"Pretty appropriate lyrics," Jones said by way of response, pointing upwards with his pipe. Kai's eyes followed it, and he smiled ruefully at the sight of two dashes of colour on the funnel that marked *Rescue* as a ship of the Military Sealift Command; one band of blue, and another of gold. "My school's colours were black and silver," Jones added. "North Marion High, West Virginia. And, for what it's worth, I was one of those same insufferable kids."

"I would never have guessed," Kai responded, the sarcasm rebounding off Jones' ever-present grin like a ball off a wall. Oh shit, dodgeball sessions in Phys Ed. That was another unpleasant school memory to repress.

"Captain?" he said eventually. "I do have a question."

"Fire away."

"Why did you nominate me to give the interview? The Brits were meant to be speaking with you."

"Well, first of all, I have terrible acne, so I thought it was better to spare them and their viewers the horror," Jones quipped, and Kai withheld a snort. It was widely regarded on *Rescue* that the skipper's claim to various chronic skin ailments was just an excuse to get his beard past the dress-code regulations 'on doctor's orders'.

"Secondly, I get stage fright." That was another lie. Men like Jordan Jones stood legs astride on the stage of the world, challenging its slings and arrows.

"And most importantly, I decided it was the only way to get you to do something other than studying and brooding poetically in the mess," Jones concluded bluntly, the humour still lurking in the shallows of his voice, but a quiet seriousness taking the main channel. "You need to socialise more, Kai, try and live a life beyond just your work."

Before Kai could answer, the bellowing roar of an air horn broke over the assembled fleet, and both he and Jones turned to regard the megaship now cruising slowly up towards them.

"The Big O…" Kai muttered quietly. "Even that seems like an understatement."

"The Royal Mail Ship *Oceanic III*," Jones said with reverence. "What a beast."

The *Oceanic* was a suitably massive ship, big enough to more than justify her nickname. Long and sleek with a smooth, rounded front to her superstructure she bore a close family resemblance to her sister, Cunard Line's *Queen Mary 2*, but wore a different set of colours to mark her apart. Her single huge black funnel was flanked with a pair of angular tan smoke deflectors, and a continuous gold band ringed her hull from stem to stern. Lights gleamed from thousands of cabin balconies and constellations of portholes. From atop her slender radio mast, a single pennant flapped in the breeze. Even with eyes narrowed Kai could not make it out, and mentioned it to Jones, who chuckled.

"It's a five-pointed white star on a red fishtailed burgee," he said calmly, and Kai's eyes widened in disbelief.

"You can see that from a mile out, without binoculars?"

"I eat plenty of carrots," Jones chuckled, tapping at his sunglasses, before explaining. "It's the company flag of the old White Star Line."

"And the new..." Kai added, his attention drifting down from the flag to where the letters **'WHITE STAR'** were branded on the side of the vessel's white superstructure. In contrast to the subtle but ever-present roll to *Rescue*'s deck, the approaching cruise liner seemed as steady as a rock planted in the waves, lending weight to her impressive size.

"Ocean Liner, not Cruise Liner," the captain corrected when Kai voiced his observation. "That ship is built to run to a timetable back and forth across the Atlantic, not stroll around the Med and the Caribbean like she's got nothing better to do."

It seemed like an arbitrary distinction to Kai, and the Captain continued to pontificate on how ships designed for 'the Atlantic Ferry' were built to higher standards than cruise ships in order to withstand the rough seas and rogue waves that often menaced the Western Ocean. Stronger steel, reinforced bows, provision of a greater reserve of power to fight their way through storms.

"...and of course, they carry on tradition," Jones concluded, nostalgia lacing his words. "Proper ocean travel isn't just about luxury and easy entertainment; it's about evoking the spirit of the liners that once ruled the seas. *Andrea Doria* and *Christoforo Columbo*, *Aquitania* 'the ship beautiful', the great *Normandie*..."

"And the unsinkable *Titanic*," Kai added, prompting Jones to pause and peer down at the surface below, as if he could see the colossal wreck two miles below.

"Yes, her too," he said, his voice tinged with melancholy.

From *Oceanic*'s decks the sound of laughing voices echoed across the water, along with strains of party music.

"Well, there goes the neighbourhood," Jones observed, turning away to call out to a subordinate officer. "Miller, make sure our signal flags warn *Oceanic* to keep well clear of us. Manoeuvring with that piece of seabed flotsam attached is a proper bugbear."

As if to prove his point, *Rescue* caught a swell on her starboard quarter and swung against the submerged section of *Titanic*'s hull, throwing up a blast of spray that reached high above the bridge deck. From below decks the collision between several thousand tons of ship and several hundred tons of ex-ship rang like a collapsing belfry.

"Well, she's built to do the work of an icebreaker," Kai heard Jones say to himself, even as he winced at the sound. "This is no problem."

With those words the Captain strode off to oversee transferring the chunk of wreckage to the *Anatoly Sagalevich*, but momentarily clapped his hand on Kai's shoulder as he passed behind him.

"Think a little on what I said," he said softly, before vanishing into the darkened depths of the wheelhouse, shouting orders to the helmsman. With a muffled bang *Rescue's* engines tore into reverse and she swung around, dragging the hull section with her until it was facing towards the *Anatoly Sagalevich*.

The Russian deep-sea research platform was now showing off one of her party-tricks, flooding ballast tanks that allowed her to settle deeper into the water, so that a her low-slung portion of her deck could submerge to take on the recovered hull-section.

More orders were shouted out, and, riding sideways on her bow thrusters, *Rescue* presented the segment of *Titanic* towards the other ship like a proffered chalice and slowly began to push it into place. Sparing a last glance at the towering *Oceanic*, now coming to a halt in the prized position set aside for her right in the centre of the gathered flotilla, Kai scurried below.

*

From *Oceanic's* upper decks, the other ships looked like toy boats floating on a golden sea, dark in the last light of day. Quickly, Janice Patton brought her digital camera up to her eye and pressed down on the shutter, capturing the moment forever.

"Hello there…" someone said, and Janice turned, brushing a strand of pale hair out of her eyes so that she could see who had approached her.

"Hey Adrienne," she smiled cheerily. "I saw you filming downstairs. It went okay?"

"About as well as you could expect," replied the founder of Project 401, resting her own weight on the rail beside them and peering around, looking for someone. "Where's your other half?"

"Terri's running laps on the promenade," Janice replied, holding up her camera. "I'm just getting some inspiration for my next commission."

"After the success we had with the sales of *Titanic Century*, the Project might hire you to illustrate a follow-up volume," Adrienne replied, a light grin on her face. "You know, there's still a lot of people who'd love you hear your thoughts as the artist behind the book."

"No no," Janice replied, waving her finger to make a point. "I told you before Addy, that this voyage was going to be my honeymoon, not a press junket. I pushed back my wedding by months in order to meet publishing deadlines and help promote the Project, but I'm not going to go up on a stage and bore everyone to death with an art lecture when I could be…"

"…whispering sweet nothings into your newlywed's ear?" Adrienne finished for her, a teasing grin on her face. When Janice did not reply the other woman chuckled and turned her face to the setting sun. "Ah, to be young and wild again."

"More than you know…" Janice said to herself, thinking back to her wedding night.

"So then," Adrienne persisted, jokingly nudging against her. "What are you doing tonight? It is the centennial after all. Marking the occasion with anything special?"

"We've booked a table for two in the White Swan Restaurant, on the Promenade Deck," Janice replied cautiously.

"I see… small, private, intimate, and the food is to die for…" Adrienne said, almost wistfully. "Though the Waldorf Pudding goes straight to your hips… and then?"

Well, if I can get my way tonight, that won't be the only thing aiming towards my hips… Janice thought in response, before snapping back to reality.

"What happens then," she said, trying to hide the blush rising to her cheeks. "Is none of your business, Mrs McKinn."

"Oh really…" Adrienne said softly, all but winking raunchily to drive home that she could see right through Janice's false bluster. "Well, if you feel like it after food and *ahem*, before bed, I've reserved the Cafe Parisien, just across from the White Swan.

Feel free to come along, have a few cocktails, and bask in the appreciation of others for what you made possible…"

Janice made a move to protest, but Adrienne held up her hand. "I'm serious. There's a lot of people coming aboard tonight, guest lecturers and prominent sponsors, all of whom I think would love to do a little meet and greet with you. It wouldn't hurt to talk up your accomplishments a bit, and I'm sure your young spouse would agree."

She had a point there.

"Okay, we'll consider it…"

"So it's a date?"

"I said we'd consider it," Janice laughed. "You're relentless at times."

"Had to be when I was a Congresswoman, and I find it still helps if you want to get anything done in this world," Adrienne said, before giving her a light shove. "Now stop wasting time on me and go find Terri. You've got a romantic dinner for two to get ready for, remember?"

"Oh, I'm way ahead of you…" Janice was already heading towards the stairs, but then paused and turned back. "And Adrienne – thanks, for making all of this possible."

She waved around at the whole of the ship, and then suddenly brought the camera back up and caught her in the viewfinder. The shutter clicked.

"Gotcha!"

"Get on with you…" Adrienne shooed her away, laughing. "Or else I'll have Captain Waters set the hounds on you!"

Unable to hold back her own laughter, Janice began descending through multiple decks towards the promenade, scrolling through folders of pictures on the camera. Her graduating as a Master of the Arts; her holding the first print copy of *Titanic Century*, the book she had collaborated on to promote Project 401; herself in her wedding dress, getting married, throwing the bouquet, kissing her bride…

Speaking of… she had just come out onto the promenade that wrapped around the ship's beltline, and spotted a familiar figure running with long easy strides along the jogging track marked out on the deck. Feeling a thrill at the sight of her wife clad in only a tank top and bike shorts, Janice waved.

"Hey Terri!"

Terri Patton, dark skin gleaming with sweat, broke away from the track and loped up to her, throwing her arms around Janice in a welcoming hug.

"Hi lover!"

"Ew… you stink of sweat…" even as she said it Janice realised the slew of double-entendres she had just run head first into, but in response Terri just smirked and raised an eyebrow, as if to say *'you never complained about that before…'*

"You know I didn't mean it that way!" Janice blurted in protest.

"Didn't mean what?" Terri folded her arms smugly.

"Oh, I give up. Come on; let's get somewhere where we can get a drink before dinner."

"Now you're just being whiny," Terri laughed. "Listening to you anyone would think we were married. Oh, wait…"

"Come on…" Janice lightly shoved her forward. "We can bicker like old wives in the Red Pennant Bar; at least there I can get a decent sundowner."

"You and your weird cocktails," Terri laughed as she let Janice drag her along. "I thought you weren't meant to drink those until the sun set."

"Well it's near enough for me," Janice said firmly, waving her arm at the fiery orb beginning to melt into the western horizon.

But then she paused, and shivered…

They had come to a halt by a corridor running right through the ship and out onto the opposite promenade, revealing the dark ocean reaching out to the east. As the sun set, sea and sky were blurring together into a single looming shadow, and it was like peering through the ship into a black void.

"Janice… hello, Earth to my wife…" Terri called, and Janice tore herself away from the oncoming night.

"Sorry, let's get those drinks."

"Sounds good to me."

Arm-in-arm they began to stroll further down the promenade, to where a brightly lit sign advertised the Red Pennant Bar. Inside, the atmosphere was warm and cosy, and familiar voices quickly called out in greeting as the two of them entered. It was a perfect moment.

But for some reason, Janice found it hard to shake that sudden chill, and a strange fear, as if something somewhere nearby was extremely wrong…

…and coming closer.

CHAPTER THREE

The weight of the FAMAS F1 assault rifle felt worrying familiar in Jabril Hab Allah's hands, and he reflexively brushed one of his fingers against the safety switch, ensuring the weapon was secured.

"What are you, some kind of idiot?"

The words of his former weapons trainer rang in his memory for a moment, and Jab shook his head to clear it. Faisal Massad had been a ruthless disciplinarian and a skilled expert in firearms, but he was not a woman, and the voice yelling at him in accented English was definitely female.

"We're in the middle of the North Atlantic, *in twelve thousand feet of water*! What do you hope to gain from seizing my ship when we're hundreds of miles from the nearest port? This isn't Somalia; you can't just anchor here and issue demands!"

The captain was showing remarkable courage in the face of two men armed with machineguns, even when forced to stand with her hands and face pressed against the rear bulkhead of the *Seguin Laroche's* bridge. Jab ignored her as he moved from console to console, checking the ship's vital statistics. Marc Pètain, the Chief Officer, was manning the helm, face uneasy but composed.

Benjamin Khan, however, the young English-born Arab who had been standing lookout, was not so calm.

"Shut up right now, you bitch!" he snapped from where he was sitting on the radar display, his voice full of contempt as he waved his own FAMAS menacingly between the two officers. "We're in charge now. How'd you like that, hah, tables turned haven't they? And all of your worthless crew are either under armed arrest, or dead!"

"We've not killed anyone yet," Jab interrupted firmly, not looking up from the navigation computer, "and we do not aim to. Get down from there."

Expression dark as storm clouds, Khan slipped from off his perch on the radar scope and began to stalk nervously like a jungle cat up and down the length of the bridge, carrying his FAMAS with the trained enthusiasm of someone who has never used a firearm in anger, but who would really like to. Again, Jab twitchily fingered the safety on his own weapon, identical to Khan's. Like the ship and most of the crew, the guns were French. He wondered if he was the only one to appreciate the irony.

"So, what's in the magic box?" enquired the captain again, referring to the shipping container.

"You can shut your trap!" Khan snapped back, tapping the barrel of his gun against her cheek. "Or you can give this 45mm a blowjob."

"What does it matter if I speak, *dèbile!*" she hissed, even as Khan threatened her with the gun. "It's not like I can do anything to stop you, so how does talking hurt, or is it simply that you can't handle polite conversation?"

Khan let off a furious tirade in what Jab could only assume was English street slang and strode towards her, pressing the muzzle of the gun to her head. "Fucking French slag. I could kill you right now bitch, can you handle that?"

"Khan!" Jab snapped finally, confronting the other man in Arabic. "That's enough."

The other man snapped round, boyish face clouded with anger. The two of them locked eyes for a moment, inky black staring into turbulent hazel, while Captain Laroche and Chief Pètain maintained a wary silence.

"The whole point of this mission is to show the world that we are not all violent fanatics," Jab hissed, his pride wounded by Khan's aggression. "And you scream and wave a gun as if you're taking vengeance for the Crusades!"

Khan seethed for several seconds. "She is trash, and if you grew up like I did you would know that. These 'liberated' women are fucking poison, Jabril; they raise broken homes and Godless children."

"Like yourself?" Jab challenged. "You are acting disgracefully on what should be a mission of divine peace, where she is showing courage in her duty as Master of this ship. Who is the better person, *Benny?*"

Khan gritted his teeth as if he was about to blow a blood-vessel, but then his shoulders slumped and he withdrew his gun from Laroche's head.

"Now make yourself useful, and bind her wrists and ankles," Jab said evenly, reverting to English and indicating with a nod of his head towards the ship's office. "There should be handcuffs in the security strongbox, and the keys to it are on the *capitaine*."

Mouth working in silent fury, Khan all but tore the ring of keys from Joanna's belt, stalking away down the aft corridor. Trading places with him, Jab leaned back casually against the radar scope, drawing the bolt on his own rifle to chamber a round. His thumb rested against the safety, while his index finger stayed well clear of the trigger guard. The ship purred with reassuring smoothness beneath his feet as he ensured he had a line of fire on both the Captain and her fiancé.

"I apologise for that," he said, making sure he enunciated clearly in French, more that Khan could not listen in than for the captain's benefit. "When recruiting for this mission I asked for qualified Muslim sailors more interested in peace than war, but my young colleague is quite passionate to make himself a martyr before God, and as a result he can be very... excitable, and more likely to make martyrs of others. But rest assured that we intend you no harm, and that once we have docked in a friendly port you will be free to depart from the ship. This does depend, however, on your co-operation."

The captain nodded, and then her head shifted slightly, turning towards her first mate as if examining him for flaws. Jabril was aware of their engagement, and wondered at how they managed to maintain a professional relationship.

"You have a question?" he enquired. "If so, feel free to speak it."

Cautiously she turned to face him, keeping her hands raised. "You smuggled something aboard my ship. It required electrical power, so you modified a reefer so that it could be run off of the *Seguin Laroche's* power circuit."

He nodded politely.

"That is correct, Capitaine Laroche."

She swallowed, but did not avert her eyes from the tip of the rifle aimed just to the side of her head. "And you had a deal with

Abercrombie to transport it, while posing as crewmen to ensure it made the passage safely?"

"You are a very perceptive woman," he replied. "Though we are all certified mariners, so it was hardly a charade. And I will admit that you have been a respectable captain to sail under, regardless of Khan's rhetoric about the place of women."

"Flattery will get you nowhere…" she replied with a certain Gallic élan, and even as Jab smiled he reminded himself not to relax so much as to allow the gun to drop towards the floor.

"So, is this the point where I divulge my evil scheme to you?" he chided.

"No," she replied. "I don't expect you to explain what is going on with your group, Abercrombie and that container…" she was staring at his face now, trying to challenge a reaction from him. He smiled softly. One had to admire her brazen courage.

"Mr Abercrombie and his superiors have made a long and lucrative career out of transporting questionable goods for questionable people." Jab inclined the FAMAS slightly towards the first mate and voiced what he knew her to be thinking already. "Perhaps the gentleman to whom you are affianced could elucidate on some of the more… unusual 'auto parts' he and Mr Abercrombie have smuggled in the past aboard Compagnie Maritime Laroche's vessels."

"Marc…" she said softly, turning her head towards the man standing stoic at the helm. *'J'accuse?'*

"Oui," he said softly. "Abercrombie's 'business partners' first approached me about a month after the sale of CML. The money from these jobs is paying for our future."

She wetted her lips, which shook slightly. In an admittedly sad moment, Jab felt certain he saw the light of love die in her eyes as she turned back to him. Shame.

"So, you're one of those terrorist networks that smuggle restricted technologies to various countries?" she said bluntly. "If so, why suddenly expose yourself in the middle of the ocean?"

"I am not a terrorist, *capitaine*," Jab answered curtly. "But yes, I trained as a seaman in order to help transport sensitive materials to those nations that needed them. You do not need to know anything else, save that the particular device being shipped aboard the *Seguin Laroche* poses no radiological or biological threat to the ship, yourself or the crew."

"Don't lie, it's a bomb," Marc said. "I saw inside the container, and that thing is too small to be a nuclear reactor, and too whole to be a dismantled set of parts."

"You brought a bomb on my ship, Marc!?" Laroche exclaimed, her frustration now directed at the man beside her. "What did you hope to accomplish!?"

"The money was good," he pleaded. "And I was afraid for our safety if I said no." Then he smirked. "And besides, I kept full records of every job and how the dirty money ties back to Abercrombie and M&B Holdings. I thought that after the wedding I could give you the gift of publicly shaming the men running your family firm into the ground."

"How could I marry a man who smuggles weapons for terrorists?!" she all but screamed. "After my Grandfather smuggled Jews out of Europe during the Holocaust!"

Jab's thumb pressed against the FAMAS's safety and he rose to his feet.

"That's enough!"

"Did you honestly believe I could ever condone this Marc!? If you had, you would not have hidden the truth from me!"

"I said that's enough!"Jab shouted, trying to get the situation under control.

But the first mate was now trembling in shock at the sudden rejection. "But, Joanna…"

"You shamed everything CML stood for Marc! *That's it!*"

"It is not a bomb!" Jab loudly interjected, but at that moment Khan stepped back onto the bridge, rifle pointed casually at the floor, and Marc lunged madly for him with a madden cry.

"I'm sorry!"

Safety off, weapon up, fire. Jab had paid attention years ago, and had practised his guncraft since.

The FAMAS jerked once in his hands, the shot deafening in the small space, and Marc fell to the deck atop Khan, pinning him.

"Get it off me! Oh God, get it off me!"

Laroche had flinched and covered her ears at the gunshot, but now her horrified eyes focused on an orchid burst of blood that had splattered over the wall beside her, mingled with chunks of pink and grey matter, glowing luridly in the golden evening light. Mouth open in a silent scream she brought one of her hands to her face, and found red droplets scattered like new freckles over it. Slowly she looked down, finding Marc's body lying prone atop the struggling Khan, a neat red hole in the back of his head. Her chest heaved and a strangled moan, like a dying breath, forced its way out of her.

Jab sighed to himself, the safety once again engaged on his rifle.

"Murderer!" she whispered acidly, turned to regard him with burning contempt. Calmly he directed the gun back towards her, seeing the light that had gone out in her eyes now rekindled with the coals of rage.

"A name I have been called many times before Capitaine, enough that it has long since ceased to affect me," he calmly replied, before curtly ordering Khan to pull himself together. "I am sorry that it came to this."

The young British expatriate was frantically trying to get the corpse off him, blood from the shot to the head liberally caking his face and hair. As the boy rolled the carrion off of himself, Jab spared it a glance. The bullet had exited through the temple, tearing out a cup-shaped chunk of bone and tissue, leaving the impression that someone had attacked the first mate with a sharpened ice-cream scoop. With the gun he directed Khan to cover the Captain, freeing him to kneel beside the body.

First closing its wide-open eyes, he then reached inside the man's open shirt collar and felt around, pulling out a piece of jewellery – a crucifix; perhaps Marc had been a Christian, one of the Peoples of the Book afforded respect by Islam. Removing it from around the neck he placed the totem in the body's still-warm hands and then clasped them together; he hoped God would show mercy to someone killed before their time, and overlook the man's transgressions in betraying the trust of his fiancée and captain.

"Secure the *Capitaine* to the wheel," he said quietly as he rose back to his feet. "We might need her expertise in ship-handling later."

Silenced, and acting like a man in shock, Khan laid his gun down a safe distance away and pulled Laroche forward, handcuffing her to the helm. Her eyes travelled to the discarded FAMAS, and Jab lightly inclined his own gun towards her, face still impassive. Her own expression was inscrutably blank as Khan snapped the handcuff shut with a soft *clink*.

"Stay with her," Jab instructed Khan, his own hand reaching out to disengage the ship's gyrocompass autopilot. "You have the helm, Capitaine."

Looking up he regarded the seascape before them, the waves from earlier now settling down for the night, which was growing thick and black out ahead towards the eastern horizon. The ship's long main deck, stacked high with containers, was aimed squarely at the heart of the gathering darkness. "We have good sailing conditions tonight, Capitaine; I trust there will be no further distractions?"

Laroche's hands slowly gripped hold of the wheel, and her mouth opened and shut several times before she suddenly found her voice.

"The Titanic Centennial… we were to take part in it, and we're still on course for the wreck site. Can I at least steer clear of them?"

Jab paused at the door to the bridge and turned to meet her pleading eyes. "Actually Capitaine, I would prefer if you steered directly for them. I do not want to draw unwanted attention by skipping out on a scheduled rendezvous."

He pointed at Khan. "Ensure she does nothing to change our course."

Khan's face was pale beneath the blood, but he still managed to scowl as he clutched his FAMAS to his chest. "Why not take her below with the others?"

"She deserves to be treated with respect," Jab replied calmly. "As I said, she is the master of this vessel."

With that, he headed downstairs. Though he kept his face composed, he felt a certain regret boiling within him. Regret that he had taken a life, when after the Libyan revolution he had sworn he would never again. Regret for Khan, who despite his fervour, had just witnessed his first killing, his first blood. Regret for the Capitaine, and the dead man. If events had not gone beyond his control, she would have remained ignorant of what was being shipped aboard her vessel, and he would still be alive.

He hoped there would be no more deaths in this mission. And yet he knew, as he had known ever since his first campaign in Palestine, that once blood was spilled, once the red line was drawn and crossed, there was no turning back. Already he could feel the urge rising within him, the evil thoughts suggesting that it would be simpler to just outright kill all the remaining crew and so cut off any attempt at a rebellion.

Exterminate all the brutes!

And as always, he took those thoughts and trod them underfoot like serpents. God would no less frown on someone who shed blood needlessly, than he would on someone not prepared to take a life in the pursuit of a divine objective.

Remember the great Dr. Siddiqui, he thought to himself. *He helped give both America and Pakistan the atomic bomb, and is respected in both. His daughter is an Ambassador to the United States and a campaigner for women's rights. They are the example you should aspire to, not the lunatics who scream for blood and merciless vengeance...*

The remaining deck crew had been confined to the lounge below the bridge, but Jab continued down further to the main deck, stepping out into the last, cool rays of sunset. Soon the cold of night would be setting in. Despite the bloodshed, the ship seemed as light as a feather, gliding freely over the waves as he proceeded aft to the disguised container. Nash had retrieved an angle-grinder from the Bosun's locker and was cutting swiftly through the cargo unit's steel sides, allowing the excessive heat being generated within to vent. The remaining members of their team were down below, ensuring the engineering staff did not attempt anything silly.

"Is it safe?" he asked, trying to temper his impatience as the saw continued its relentless assault.

"It's still hot in there, but not dangerously so," Nash replied, turning the cutting tool on the container's padlocks. After a few seconds work, the fastenings sheared, and the doors to the inside of the container swung open by a few feet, as if of their own violation.

Laying down his weapon, Jab reached up and undid a light chain around his neck. On the end of it was a small phial half filled with fine purple dust; like something from a child's chemistry set. He waved it towards Nash.

"You know what this is, Nashat?"

"Yes…" the word was accompanied by an eager nod, Nash's face tinged with the curiosity of a budding engineer. "It's a sample of the Apergy; a failed batch."

"And you know that if we can't stabilize the machine, then all we'll have to show for our efforts is a ton of scrap and more of this dust," Jab said, rolling the phial between his fingers. The two of them exchanged a serious glance, and Nash turned towards the ship's superstructure.

"I'll fetch the documentation on my laptop, and get back as soon as possible."

As the younger man ran forward, Jab turned to the open container. The heat inside was intense, but he stepped in with all the reverence of entering a mosque.

The Liberty Bell…

Laying his eyes on the softly humming device, the source of both the heat and the electromagnetic fields jamming the ship's radar and telecommunications, he felt the words of the Shahada coming to him unbidden, full of life, purpose and promise.

"There is no god but God, and Muhammad is his messenger."

To which he added a fervent. *"Allahu Akbar."*

God is greatest.

CHAPTER FOUR

Despite the way the dress Pip had donned for tonight pinched around her waist, putting it on had been strangely liberating. After weeks of thick coveralls and hardy work clothes wear, the feel of silk on her skin was like stepping into a cool shower. It was a pretty thing, the blue offset with an exotic dash of gold embroidery around the hem. Her sister Marilyn, who had attended the Fashion Institute of Technology before opening her own dressmaking business in New York, had assured her endlessly that the filigree was genuine *geumbak*, a perfect way to draw attention to their Korean heritage. When the two sisters had last met, just hours before the *Anatoly Sagalevich* sailed from New York, all Pip had cared about the dress was that she look nice for her presentation.

Now? Well right now, it honestly made her feel like a goddess.

Guttural voices shouted in Russian as the small launch she had climbed aboard bounced against the ship's grey hull, and a spray of saltwater made her glad she'd donned a waterproof jacket over the dress. As the engine started and the launch pushed away from the side of the *Anatoly Sagalevich*, she tightly clutched a duffel bag she carried on her lap. It contained her laptop, camera, camcorder, several bundles of wires and a pair of high-heel shoes; like with the jacket, she'd decided it made more sense to wear trainers for the boat ride.

The piercing whine of a crane winch drew her attention back to the *Sagalevich* as the launch came around the ship's stern. The Russian research vessel was lit up with a corona of light as deckhands scurried around one of its two beluga-like submarines. She smiled and waved, and several shouted back as they readied *Mir-4*, nicknamed 'Saga', for its next dive. The sound of their voices, along with several catcalls, drifted faintly over the water as the gap between the launch and the ship increased. But as Pip looked around, she could see the other ships coming into view, all riding motionless on the black surface of the ocean. Right now the launch was coming around the *Rescue's* bow, and directly ahead the *Oceanic* was revealed, sleek and majestic. Her full thousand-foot length was blazing with lights, which washed together into a dazzling glow; a city that floated on the ocean, hundreds of miles from the nearest land. Pip stuck her head through one of the launch's open windows, and smiled at the floodlit pennant flying from the mast.

Drawing alongside, the launch came to rest against a jetty that unfolded from the immense vessel's side like a medieval drawbridge, thumping against collapsible rubber bumpers. Crewmembers on lines held it tight while Pip and the other passengers stepped up and over the gap to be greeted by the ship's hotel manager, an elegant man in pressed whites.

"Good evening and welcome aboard the RMS *Oceanic III*."

*

Dinner was provided courtesy of the ship's company in the *Olympic* Restaurant, a towering three storey chamber hollowed out of the vessel's interior. As the second seating of passengers supped around them, Pip and several other guests were directed by waistcoated stewards to the Captain's Table in the centre of the room. *Oceanic's* master, Captain Waters, noting her lack of an escort, had even taken her arm and accompanied her down the restaurant's elaborate staircase to their privileged seats. With his high-peaked hat carried underarm and the creases in his uniform ironed to a razor-sharpness, he was every inch the master mariner, and Pip felt like she was being presented to a royal court. Mentally she thanked Marilyn for attiring her appropriately as the assembled diners' eyes all turned to them. Waters might have been old enough to be her father, but the attention that came with his presence was certainly helping to shore up her flagging confidence. With that in mind she kept her head high and her back straight, as Marilyn had taught her.

Just smile and don't trip up; the dress will do the rest of the work for you.

She must have still been trembling, however, because Water's arm tightened softly around her arm and he subtly whispered to her, whilst still keeping his head turned towards the crowd. "If it makes you feel any better, the Duchess of Cambridge snapped a shoe heel on the bottom step at the ship's Christening."

"Really?"

"Yes indeed, but she did not even break step. Genuine class on her part, I felt. We found the broken heel of her shoe in an air conditioning cavity a week later, during the maiden voyage."

She stifled a snigger. "What did you do with it?"

"We sent it back to her with the ship's compliments, of course. She then had it mounted on a plaque and returned to us; it's now got pride of place in the crew bar down below, which was eventually named *The Broken Sole.*"

Pip held a hand to her mouth to mask another giggle, and found that in the time they had been speaking they had passed by the interested and curious (and some disapproving) stares from the various tables to arrive at the Captain's Table. The light from a chandelier overhead sparkled like diamonds on the varnished wood. It was not so hard to imagine that this was the *Titanic* herself, or at least a worthy spiritual successor.

Eat your heart out Kate Winslet, she crowed to herself in a manner most unladylike, as a steward seated her, while another presented a selection of drinks. Not having to worry about costing, she immediately requested a glass of whatever had the most digits in its price. It turned out to be a spectacularly aged French white, which went down like a glass of liquid summer, bright and cool.

*

The night air played over Jabril Hab Allah's bare arms, bringing blessed relief from the sweatbox that was the inside of the container.

"Have you sourced the problem with the *Liberty Bell*, Nash?" he asked.

"It's not hardware…" the young Bosun replied as he stepped out, his own arms looking like wet spaghetti. "Though honestly, I know that machine inside-out and I still could not tell you 'how' it works, and I doubt the idiot geniuses who designed it did either. There's a reason why the core of it is a sealed unit."

Jab offered him a bottle of water, which the youth gratefully poured over himself. "I'm pretty sure it's a programming error. The governor subroutines keep crashing every time they try to reset the machine's power cycle. I think the internal clocks are out of sync, or something."

"Why wasn't it a problem before?"

"Because our contacts in America were discharging it manually, every day, right until we took delivery and sealed it into the container. We've not touched it since then, and the automated subroutines took over the responsibility of purging the system, except they're fighting themselves; crashing, rebooting and crashing again – it's done it five times just in the hour I've been working on it. So instead of idling or running at minimal power, the system has spent the entire voyage gathering a… frighteningly massive charge."

"Is it fixable?"

"If this was just software, fixing it would be a point-and-click thing, but the problem is in the firmware as well, the programming pre-loaded onto the drives and processors, and some of those are original parts from the nineteen nineties. The internal computer governing the *Bell* is Frankenstein's monster, and it's on a rampage. Give me an hour though, and I could fix it, but then we'd still have to discharge the system, and the computer won't let me."

"Why not?"

Nash swallowed. "Because now it's got too much power; the emitter coils are cycling beyond their specified full speed and it won't let me bleed the charge they've accumulated because the system can't calculate what will happen if I do! It's telling me that we have to kill the power and let the machine die completely."

Jab groaned softly, resting his head against the container as Nash came close and mirrored his posture.

"Jabril… every second we leave the *Liberty Bell* racing away on the Critical Mass threshold is like leaving a car in neutral with a brick on the accelerator. It's going to critically damage itself and burn out. Our only other option is to fire it right now."

For a second they stood in wordless silence, Nash's face flushed and Jab's pale. He felt as if the world had been pulled out from under him, and slowly he began to massage his temples, trying to drown out the oppressive roar of the overloading machine.

"Jabril, you wanted the power to shape history. Well that power is only seconds away from you. Either we trigger the machine now, or we allow it to go into its emergency sequence and shut itself down."

"We CAN'T!" Jab snapped in response, one hand still pressed to the sides of his head as if trying to keep his skull from exploding. "We are in the wrong place to trigger the machine, you know this!"

"If we went back right now, we could sail the ship to Egypt," Nash protested. "And then travel overland to Medina! With the *Seguin Laroche* and the *Liberty Bell* as proof of our story, we would surely be granted an audience with the Prophet!"

"And what then? It would take weeks, and by that point a return to here would be impossible. The whole point was to fix this world, not hide away in another! The timeframe we had to carry out the entire mission was miniscule to begin with, even when we planned to carry out the entire excursion from within Medina itself. We can't try and stretch it out to include a Mediterranean cruise as well!"

The two of them fell into silence. Staring failure in the face, Jab slumped to the deck, his back to the container, so that he stared out across the darkened sea.

"…and we can't let the *Bell* burn out or power itself down," he said, holding up the phial of dried crystals. "All the Apergy that we sourced would become inert if we shut off the power. Even if we spent another seven years stealing and scrounging parts, there's no way we can replace this stuff."

The *Seguin Laroche's* wake churned softly behind them. Closing his eyes Jab focused on the soothing rush, and dug deep. Think.

Nashat says the machine is on a rampage. It is certainly making enough noise…

That was it.

"Nashat…" he said slowly. "You say the machine is Frankenstein's monster. Would it be possible to… sedate it?"

"You're not listening, Jab," Nash began, only for Jab to hold up a hand and cut him off.

"No, I am. I was educated in nuclear physics, and I've studied disasters like Chernobyl. When things were already dangerous, the power plant's computer automatically tried to SCRAM the reactor, which set off the disaster. It's the same here; the Bell wants to shut itself down, which will make it useless to us. But could you trick the safety systems into thinking everything is fine, and take manual control of the machine?"

Nash ran a hand over his eyes and held it there, as if the solution was written on the inside of his palm. "The *Bell* was designed to be operated manually if need be, but the safeties are an integrated part of the computer system… we'd need to take out several of the circuit boards, maybe hotwire some other parts, but yes, it could be done…"

He lowered his hand and stared at him. "But Jab, you must understand the risks. Even with the errors, at this point the machine is not a threat. Bypassing the safeties would enable us to possibly make an even worse mistake. We don't really understand what the *Bell* does to space-time or what else may be wrong with it. You mentioned Chernobyl; I would not like to see what this machine would do were *it to melt down*."

To the older man's eyes, Nash was eclipsed by a light from behind, lending him a brilliant halo. The laptop computer in his hands looked like a book. Was this how the angel Gabriel had appeared to the Prophet, with the divine commandment to 'read'? He had hoped to find out for himself.

No, he *still* hoped to. For that hope's sake, anything was worth the risk.

"Do it Nashat," he said softly, tipping his head. "Everything depends on it."

"Alright…" Nash nodded. "I will need tools, and electronic components."

"Get Pierre, the ship's electrical engineer," Jab said wearily. "Explain the situation, and I'm sure he will co-operate with obtaining what you need from the stores."

82

Then he looked up, eyes fierce.

"But just in case he doesn't, make sure you have a gun."

*

About a mile astern of the *Seguin Laroche*, and thirty feet below the surface, a deathly silence had settled over *Viking*, broken only by the thrum of the reactor pumps, the whine of the steam turbines and the distant, distorted echo of a looping song;

London calling to the faraway towns.
Now that war is declared, and battle come down.
London calling to the underworld.
Come out of the cupboard all you boys and girls...

Scott Thresher lay in his berth, lanky legs folded up into the compressed space, listening to the music drifting through from the adjacent wardroom.

The Clash, 'London's Calling'. Doc Montgomery's playing his old LPs again... he thought to himself, leafing through a small bundle of papers in his hands and inspecting them, one-by-one. *Sounds appropriate, though...*

The papers were all familygrams, short messages to members of the crew broadcast from ashore during the mission. Family members back home were given a stock of forms with numbered spaces for up to one hundred and twenty words, with the choice of sending either one long, or two half-length messages per week. It was the only contact allowed between crew on the Royal Navy's ballistic missile submarines and their wives and girlfriends, children and parents, and was one-way only. *Viking*, just like her sisters *Vanguard, Vigilant, Vengeance, Victorious* and *Valorous*, sailed under strict orders to maintain radio silence for the whole of her three-month patrols, so as to prevent potential enemies having any knowledge as to her position. Meaning she was permitted to receive messages, but not broadcast back.

It was a brutal doctrine, but logical. On their previous patrol, one of the engineering officers had been scalded to death when a steam line burst. The worst part had been that *Viking* had continued to receive familygrams from the dead man's wife, writing with news of little joys and pains like their baby boy's first

83

words, completely unaware of the fact that she was now a widow, and that her infant son was going to spend many years of his life asking where 'daddy' was. It had almost broken Scott's heart, to the extent that he seriously considered breaking radio silence and notifying home of the casualty. In the end, however, Captain Furness had reined him in, but it had still been a sombre day when *Viking* returned to her home base at Faslane in Scotland.

Now, he had actually gone and broken the rules, by sending *Viking* off in pursuit of that strange container ship that refused to show up on radar. The other great taboo of operating a missile sub was to never give away your position by running at high-speed, which generated noise that potential enemies, other submarines, might pick up on.

The fact that the Captain had not countermanded the order, but maintained speed and vanished into his cabin for several hours now had left Scott wondering what was happening, and what else he might be able to get away with.

His own handful of familygrams made him all the more thoughtful. Until last week, all had been from Jess, his wife of some months. They had married after that last patrol, and honeymooned on Cyprus, where Jess had seemed to pick up a little stomach bug, which Scott had thought would pass in just a week. But it had lingered, and from the short messages from home, was coming back in fits and starts, mingled in with the brilliant news that she was pregnant.

But last week, his familygram had been from his father-in-law, cryptically hinting that Jess had been admitted to hospital. The bad news was conveyed in a code he had agreed on with his family as a means of informing him if a close relative had died or was ill, information normally censored by the Royal Navy if written in plain language; it was against the rules, but after the incident with the dead engineer Scott had decided that if something had gone wrong at home he wanted to know about it, rather than fret about what *could* be happening unbeknownst to him.

After that message he had worried quietly for his wife all week. Today was meant to have been the day for the next batch of messages to be broadcast from Faslane, but whatever was happening on the *Seguin Laroche* was completely blocking all radio and microwave transmissions. The mystery of the Marshallese-registered container ship had given Scott a temporary outlet for his anxiety, but now it was returning, full-strength.

The ice age is coming, the sun is zooming in.
Engines stop running and the wheat is growing thin.
A nuclear error, but I have no fear.
London is drowning, and I live by the river!

Unable to rest he finally swung himself out of his bunk and stuck his head into the corridor that bisected the officer's quarters. No-one was to be seen. Since *Viking* had put on speed the crew had retreated into quiet worry themselves, wondering at what might have happened to bring about the change of agenda.

They were on edge anyway, *Viking's* assigned mission already showing significant deviation from the norm; instead of patrolling the North Sea and Arctic Ocean, after leaving Faslane in Scotland the boat had in fact sailed to America, specifically to Naval Submarine Base Kings Bay in Georgia, the facility that held the warhead stockpile for the British and American missile defence programs. As part of a joint project to extend the life of the Trident II weapons system into the 2040s, at Kings Bay *Viking* had taken on a Lockheed-Martin test warhead containing prototypes of the next-generation of guidance and navigational arrays. Once this unarmed 'package' had been mated to one of her British-built missiles, the sub put back to sea, spending the next sixty days quietly roaming the North Atlantic at little more than walking pace, monitoring the missile in at-sea conditions. With the patrol now ended *Viking* was proceeding back towards the States, first to pick up US Navy observers from Kings Bay, and then to a designated firing-range off the coast of Florida, where the life-extension missile (or Trident LE), currently stowed in the number-one firing tube, would be fired under test conditions. The 'weapon' would then be tracked by NATO forces until it splashed down harmlessly, marking the climax of the mission.

And then *Viking* would go home.

Except now no-one seemed certain as to what might happen next, a dangerous state-of-mind to be in when sealed into a submerged metal tube with one-hundred-and-twenty-nine other men. Turning, Scott knocked lightly on the door of the cabin adjacent to his own.

"Captain… it's Lieutenant Thresher."

"Come in…" came the beleaguered reply. Scott frowned at the despondent tone in Commander Furness' voice, and stepped through.

The first thing he noticed was Bob Furness lying on his own bunk. Second was the open red dossier on the desk, next to an empty glass that smelt suspiciously of strong spirits. Struggling not to gape he turned to the captain, who was watching him, expression guarded.

"You've opened one of the Roswell files?" he said at last.

"Obviously…" Furness replied, waving a hand languidly. A small sheaf of familiar papers was clutched in it, and Scott felt a note of camaraderie with Furness; when in doubt, the Captain had turned to his own familygrams for support. "Do you want to know what we've stumbled across, Scott?"

"Excuse me sir!" Scott felt his own voice rise into an involuntary retort, almost as if he were accusing the Captain of a crime. "The files are for your eyes only!"

"Except I'm not the only one that knows about that ship, First Lieutenant…" Furness replied, a hand drawn over his eyes as if to block out the world. "One way or another, I doubt we're going to get much peace from home when we return with the news we have. It'll be debriefs all around… read the file Scott, and tell me what you think."

Scott bit down on his lip, his previous concerns now swept aside in the face of something interesting. "Alright…" Warily he sat at the desk, sorted the scattered papers into some order, and began to read aloud.

*"An Intelligence Report into **SS PROJECKT VALKYRIE (1941-1944)** and **US NAVY PROJECT LESTERPACK (1943-1994)**. Complied by Naval Intelligence for Admiral Sir Jock Slater…"*

That would backdate the document to the mid-1990s, if he recalled correctly, when Jock Slater was First Lord of the Admiralty. After holding on the cover for a long while, as if entranced, he slowly turned the page and began to read on, eyes growing wider and wider as he went deeper down the rabbit hole.

When he had finished reading, Captain Furness sat up, poured a fresh shot of whiskey, and pushed it across the desk to him.

Now get this.
London calling, yeah I was there, too.
An' you know what they said? Well, some of it was true!
London calling at the top of the dial.
After all this, won't you give me a smile?

*

Oceanic's Grafton Ballroom had been reserved especially for a series of presentations spread out over the course of the voyage. Fifteen minutes previously Doctor Oshiro from the *Rescue* had completed his own lecture on how the massive section of *Titanic*'s double-bottom was being raised, and now Pip hung nervously in the wings, watching as seats laid out in neat rows began to fill with murmuring voices. Eventually the lights dimmed and a projector whirred softly, throwing a title card onto the ten-foot screen set up onstage.

'Titanic's Heirlooms'
by Philippa Paik
Nautical Archaeology Undergraduate, Texas A&M University
Student Intern; National *Oceanic* & Atmospheric Administration

Pip wetted her lips as she stepped up beside her laptop, which had already been connected to the projector. Several hundred expectant faces were turned towards her as she nervously started the slideshow. On-screen appeared a black-and-white photograph of a steamship anchored in the English port of Southampton, bedecked with flags for Easter. Four funnels, elegantly balanced lines, a proud, sheer bow. It was an unmistakable vessel.

"The RMS *Titanic*," she began, her voice quavering, "Pride of the White Star Line. At the time of her maiden voyage, the largest moving object to ever issue forth from the hand of man."

The slides advanced through old publicity materials, illustrating the ship's great dimensions in comparison to skyscrapers and historical wonders. The *Titanic*, turned on her end like some avant-garde obelisk, dwarfing the Great Pyramid of Giza.

"Symbolic of man's dominion over nature, she was the product of an age we wrongly remember as a time of peace, prosperity and progress, but in truth an era of..." for several seconds she caught stage fright and her mouth froze. She suddenly felt like she was back at the NOAA applications panel, justifying her presence on this expedition. Why hadn't she been better prepared?

"...an era of complacency," she finished lamely, the words coming out in a whisper, struggling to hide her nerves with a faltering grin.

The slideshow cycled to an image of *Titanic*, advancing on her maiden voyage with all the expectations of an age drawn along in her wake. The ship seemed to fill the screen, her bow pointing towards a confident future.

"*Titanic* then, and today, exactly one hundred years after she sank..." she said, and clicked for the next slide.

There was a murmur as another familiar sight appeared. It was the same elegant bow, tapering to a slender tip, but submerged over twelve thousand feet below the Atlantic surface, tinted blue by artificial light, and wizened with a hundred years of deep-sea decay.

"...a monument to fifteen hundred lives lost due to that complacency, in a time of boundless confidence and wilful ignorance gone mad."

More images began to scroll as Pip blindly searched for the glass of water her hosts had provided. Finding it without spilling it all over her laptop, she sipped nervously as the audience were shown further visuals of the legendary ship's withered remains.

The bridge from where Captain Smith had overseen his last command, torn away in the long fall to the seabed. Long, airy promenades, now blocked by vine-like tendrils of rust that hung from the ceiling. Mangled metal where the hull had been torn in two, collapsed decks falling down to hide the unsightly wound. Grey boilers, like blinded eyes, peeking out from the shattered hull. Pip felt a repressed shudder ripple through her, a memory of her own dive to the wreck, took hold of that lingering fear and directed it at her audience.

"When I first saw *Titanic*, from the *Mir-3* submersible, it was a terrifying experience. I felt like I was trespassing on a grave, and worse, robbing from the dead."

Video footage now, of the inky black North Atlantic seabed, a world where the sun's light never shone, and where strange creatures eked out meagre lives in the cold, dark deep.

"Two and a half miles directly below us, it is an alien landscape. When we explore *Titanic*, we are in an environment that is lethal to the human body, with pressures great enough to kill instantaneously. It has all the dangers of outer space travel, with few of the compensations. Space is beautiful and full of twinkling life, but the ocean floor is deathly, a void without starlight or sunlight, drowning in cold."

Out of the dark, a vertical wall of metal appeared, a barrier spotted with portholes. *Go no further*, it seemed to say.

"Seeing this, I was a little child again, sharing ghost stories with friends, and afraid of what lurked beyond the torchlight… when you dive on *Titanic*, ghosts become very real. And what we are attempting to do on this centennial expedition to keep *Titanic*'s own ghost alive, long after her wreck's mortal remains have gone to their final rest."

The images began to scroll faster and faster, photographs of the shipwreck blurring together with the faces of long-lost passengers and crew.

"It is not enough to simply hold a photo in your hands, or even explore a virtual recreation of the ship. To truly understand something, we need to be able to see with our own eyes, touch it, and feel it. And so, this expedition has made the controversial choice to salvage historical artefacts from the ship before further decay takes them from us forever."

An older image of *Titanic*'s mainmast, laid flat along the forward superstructure like a fallen redwood. A twisted shroud of thin metal clung to the levelled mast, overhanging the open mouth of a gaping cargo shaft.

"The crows' nest, from where lookouts Fredrick Fleet and Reginald Lee spotted the fatal iceberg, is a perfect illustration of why we feel this step has to be made. When Doctor Robert Ballard took these first images in September of 1985, the crows' nest still clung to the mast, but at some point since, either due to the ravages of time or careless exploration of the wreck, it vanished."

She called up a modern photo of the mast, now bare and naked, sagging in the middle as it succumbed to old age.

"It's irrelevant as to whether the nest was knocked free by a submersible, stolen, or simply decayed and fell into Cargo Shaft Two of its own choice. The fact is that it is gone, and we feel *Titanic*'s other treasures must be salvaged before the same occurs again. Rather than be lost within the hull, from where they can never be recovered, they will instead be preserved for all the peoples of the world to see, and remember."

Now she took them aboard the *Sagalevich*, to the artefacts laboratory. Technicians were working on carefully cleaning a bronze pedestal that stood about waist high, set with mounting points for long decayed fittings. An inset photo showed the same device as it once appeared on the exposed bridge of the wreck, a row of dedication plaques from various expeditions laid respectfully before it. Many voices murmured in the audience, some in approval, and others in dissent. Pip was certain she heard the word "blasphemy" muttered from the front row.

"This was the stand for the bridge telemotor, on which Quartermaster Hichens spun the ship's wheel to try and steer *Titanic* clear of danger. It was the only piece of equipment left standing on the bridge, and since the wreck's discovery it has served as a marker to the lives lost in the sinking. The decision to save it for posterity was not easy, and has cost the expedition the support of many. Some rightly say that we have defaced a tomb, but at the same time we had no option but to recover the telemotor now, before it fell through the rotting deck, lost to us forever."

As the presentation continued, Pip continued to explain and describe the relevance of the major artefacts that had been recovered from the wreck. A pair of lifeboat davits, one still cranked back from where crewmen, led by First Officer Murdoch, had tried to launch an additional liferaft as the deck submerged, moments before his *alleged* suicide (and the emphasis on 'alleged' was something Pip made sure to stress). The hatch to Cargo Hold One, blasted clear of the bow when it ploughed into the seabed. A set of whistles, the non-ferrous metal brilliantly preserved, recovered from a crumpled funnel. Pip played an audio file of compressed air being blown through the whistle, waking the aged resonating chambers, and *Titanic's* voice spoke out from across the gap of a century, raising goosebumps.

Gangway doors, sections of hull. Chandeliers and deck fittings, fine china now clean enough to eat off again. Deck fittings and even the anchor crane from the very tip of the ship's prow. Pip winced as she illustrated the slight scorching where underwater cutting tools had cut through the fastening bolts on the last.

"But how far is too far?" she was beginning to wrap up the event. "These artefacts tell us nothing new about the people who lived, and died on *Titanic*. The china recovered is indistinguishable from the replicas off which we have all dined while aboard *Oceanic*. But in an age where mass media has blurred the line between reality and fiction, when green-screens and special effects can recreate history on demand, there must be something worthwhile in preserving something that is real, and genuine."

She paused on another photograph, of one artefact that had been left in peace. *Titanic's* massive starboard propeller, half-buried in muck. In the centre of one blade, cast into the metal over a hundred years ago, could be seen the numerals 401; the ship's build number.

"All this may seem like a twisted form of death worship, glorifying, even enshrining, objects whose only value to history is from association with disaster. But there is life too. The final object I wish to share with you, which was recovered only today, demonstrates this."

She clicked the pointer, and the slideshow began to cycle through the photos she had taken only a few hours ago aboard the *Sagalevich*.

"This device is a Rotary Spark Distributor, built by the Marconi Wireless Company for installation onboard ships. It represented a step away from the first crude wireless systems, and effectively doubled the transmission range of these ships' telegraph sets. In 1912, this was the bleeding edge of telecommunications, and *Titanic* was the first ship in the world to be fitted with such a system."

She paused, and tried to push additional emphasis into her words.

"It was through this object that *Titanic*'s wireless operators Jack Phillips and Harold Bride sent her calls for distress, summoning the Cunard liner *Carpathia* to the rescue of the survivors. For a hundred years this life-saving machine was buried in the twisted wreckage of the ship's wireless suite, but now recovered from the wreck, we can see it, know it and understand it with our own eyes. And in the same way, through all these items, the great ship's heirlooms, bequeathed to us for generations to come, we can know *Titanic*."

After almost an hour of continuous speaking, she paused for breath. The resulting silence was expectant, and with a flash of gratified surprise she realised the audience was hanging on her for more. Inside, she felt sorry to have to disappoint them.

"Thank you for your time," she bowed at the waist, and was greeted with applause, some polite, some more enthusiastic. Even the grudging responses however justified the theory at the core of her presentation, and the pitch she had made to the NOAA board when called upon to justify her request to join the expedition; even after a hundred years, *Titanic* could inspire passionate emotions.

But why?

CHAPTER FIVE

When he was young, Scott Thresher had heard of an urban myth which claimed the US Navy had conducted high-energy cloaking experiments on a docked warship, the USS *Eldridge*, resulting in the vessel being teleported instantaneously all the way from Philadelphia to Norfolk, Virginia, over two hundred miles away. It was an engaging enough fantasy to spark the imagination, and there had even been a film adaptation which used the alleged experiment as the jump-off point for a time-travel story. Now though, he wondered if all of that might have been a smokescreen, an elaborate cover-up.

A fiction based off a legend thrown up to mask a truth, and possibly closer to the truth than intended…

"I heard that the Americans tried to cloak a ship back in '43, and instead managed to teleport it out of the Philadelphia Naval Shipyard, but this…" Scott waved a hand at Dossier 7000, his other clutching the glass of whiskey Captain Furness had poured him. "This says that it not only happened, but that their 'cloaking device' managed to move the USS *Eldridge* through *time* as well."

He breathed deeply for a moment and rubbed a hand over his face, before striking out against the desk as if to convey his amazement. "The US Navy accidentally built a time machine, and then spent fifty years trying to weaponise it!"

"Seems hard to believe, doesn't it?" Bob Furness replied, still seated on his bunk and swirling his own glass, refilled with water. Neither of them had taken a sip of their respective drinks. "Thank God the Nazis didn't get there first…"

"Yeah, but they nearly did from the look of things," Scott replied, directing his attention back at the dossier, examining a photo of an upright metal cylinder with a thickened metal base, branded with the sinister image of an eagle clutching a swastika in its talons.

"Device GLOCKENSPIEL. At the Riese facility, Wenceslaus, December 23ʳᵈ 1943…"

The device rather looked like a giant bell, and closely examining the grainy, black-and-white image Scott felt a chill, fearing what might have happened if the Third Reich had had control of time and space. The idea of Infinity and Eternity married into the custody of Adolph Hitler and his cronies was terrifying, and yet, like marvelling at the lethal potential of a Messerschmitt fighter or a U-Boat, thrilling at the same time…

"I wonder how they did it…" Furness mused. "Right when quantum physics was in its infancy and nuclear physics was still toddling around with the safety-wheels on. 1943 was only a year after the first self-sustaining nuclear reaction… and that took all the resources of the Manhattan Project."

"I know, sir," Scott replied. As the second-in-command of an atomic submarine, the history of nuclear fission was something he had learned by rote. This, though…

"Someone in Germany must have made a breakthrough…" he said at last, turning to the second photo, of a similar device branded with the fouled-anchor and eagle of the United States Navy, dated June of the same year, 1943. "And so did the Americans, at almost the exact same time… parallel research or stolen secrets, perhaps?"

"Einstein fled to America in 1933, like many great European geniuses, to escape fascism, and this evokes his unified field theory," Furness mused. "Perhaps someone else, some forgotten grandmaster of physics, was working on the same path, but sided with the Nazis…"

He downed his glass of water. "After the war the Americans might have gotten hold of him to collaborate on their own projects, like Werner von Braun, Heisenberg, and all those other German engineers and technicians that *Operation Paperclip* snatched up to work for Uncle Sam. We'll probably never know."

He rose from his bunk. "What we do know, is that there is a ship out there that is, to all intents and purposes, cloaked, which was what these machines, these 'Apergy engines' were first intended to do. Time-travel was an unexpected side-effect, a 'happy accident'…"

"Happy for someone…" Scott mouthed back, turning to the final page, a photocopy of an internal document from the US Department of the Navy. "But for whatever reason, even though they had a time-machine, something must have prevented the US from using it to it change history…"

The duplicate was a termination order, dated June 6th 1994. Several sections had been highlighted, and he found himself speaking aloud as he read them.

"…after review of project by SecDef Perry… continued failure to produce practical results after fifty years of research… undue expenditure on scientific curiosities… all funding for Project Lesterpack to be cancelled and all personnel reassigned… all Apergy devices to be decommissioned and placed into secure storage…"

He took up a pen and circled the last part, thinking intently.

Not so secure after all… somehow one must be on that ship. Perhaps they stole it or… reverse engineered a similar device… but who are 'they' and what do they plan to do with it?

His eyes slid to the final image attached to the file, a line-drawing showing the ultimate evolution of the Americans' project. It was a refined 'Apergy engine', jacketed in ceramic plating, so that the thick, protruding flange at the bottom now flowed smoothly into the vertical part of the casing. The whole device was crowned with a rounded cap, like the sensor suite of an AEGIS chain gun, or a radar dome.

Possible LIBERTY BELL configuration, 1993, extrapolated by MI6, the notation said.

"You know me Scott, I was never one for guesswork," Furness answered, now standing at the door to the cabin. "Fascinating as it is, we don't accomplish anything by sitting here speculating. But our orders are clear…"

Nodding Scott regarded a covering letter attached to the report;

In the event of any Royal Navy vessel encountering evidence of such a device, all reasonable efforts must be made to gather ancillary data and, if possible, to secure the machine for study…

"So we've gone from being a hole in the water, to the brink of piracy…" Scott questioned. "What do we do, blow tanks, pop the hatch and ask 'hey, mind handing over your one-of-a-kind time machine'?"

"In so many words," the Captain replied. "But first, I'd like to know more about where that ship is heading."

"Alright," Scott nodded, feeling the same excitement from earlier swelling inside him. "So we keep stalking her."

"Yes, for now…" Furness stretched. "It's my watch in a few minutes… get some rest while you can Scott, I doubt we'll have much of it once we have a reasonable bead on that ship's course."

"Aye Captain," Scott replied, lightly saluting and stepping out of the cabin. Nodding by way of parting, the two of them turned in opposite directions; Furness towards the Conn, Scott back to his own cabin.

Lying back in his bunk, Scott opened a hand he had kept clenched shut since he rose from Furness' table. Crumpled up inside was a sheet of paper that he had spotted lying beneath the red dossier. The captain had evidently been writing a letter on it before the rules of the game had changed. Parts of it were heavily crossed-out and annotated, like a first draft that was meant to be tidied up later, but several lines of Bob Furness's tightly cramped handwriting could be read easily.

Lieutenant Commander Thresher has shown excellent organisational skills during his three patrols as First Lieutenant aboard HMS Viking, and strong qualities of initiative and improvisation. His positive demeanour and ease of conversation have also enabled him to build a strong rapport with both senior crew and ratings, and his genuine interest in mastering the technical aspects of submarine operation and warfare have furthermore made him an asset to the crew. However, at this time, I cannot recommend him for the soon-to-be vacant position of Captain aboard HMS Valorous, and instead would suggest he remain aboard Viking in his current position, until certain impulsive tendencies in his…

The remainder was unfinished. Mouth pursed, breathing slowly, Scott crumpled it back up into a ball, only to then spread it back out on the bulkhead, beside his pinned up familygrams.

Not for the first time, he wondered where his future lay. And now the sudden introduction of potential time-travel into the equation only made his possible options all the more numerous and confusing. For once, he could well understand Captain Furness's dislike for uncertainty…

*

"Oceanic, Oceanic, hailing Oceanic."

"*Oceanic* here. We read you, please identify."

"This is United States Coast Guard Flight 401, pilot-in-command Gareth King speaking, on-course for the wreath-dropping at your position. We're approaching you from due west, and we expect to be directly over you and the fleet on-time at approximately 23:25. Once the fleet has set off their fireworks at 23:40 we plan to make several passes for the benefit of your passengers, before dropping our wreaths."

"Copy 401, we'll let you take the lead."

"We also have some information for your consideration; our weather radar is showing a localised low-pressure front developing and moving east towards you. Wind speed is Beaufort three and rising, with visible swells on the ocean below. The estimated wave height is between two and four metres. Please notify your companions in the fleet accordingly."

"Thank you 401. We'll relay that immediately."

"See you soon then Oceanic. CG401, over and out."

"Godspeed and good flying 401, over and out."

*

"Ladies and Gentlemen!" a familiar figure in a flowing gown called out, tapping a fork against her champagne flute to draw attention. "On behalf of the Project and everyone aboard *Oceanic*, I want to say thank you for all you've contributed towards today's celebration of *Titanic*…"

Pip quietly sipped at her own flute as Adrienne McKinn continued to praise her and the other guest lecturers from the small stage at the far end of *Oceanic's* 'Cafe Parisien', an elegant space meant to emulate a sidewalk bistro. The ship's band, or one of them at any rate, were arranged around the room playing what would in 1912 have been described as 'festive airs'.

Off to one side by herself, Pip tapped away at her laptop's keyboard, having found a comfortable nook on one of several

97

couches arranged around a six-foot-long model of a ship. It was an ocean liner, the hull long and sleek, the superstructure cut in sharp modernist lines, and crowned with three squat funnels.

"The original *Oceanic III*, from 1928," someone voiced aloud, and she turned towards them. It was Captain Lloyd Waters, cap carried underarm and a flute of what was *probably* fizzy water in his hand.

"I know the story," she nodded, saluting him with her glass. "White Star Line had plans for a thousand-foot liner named *Oceanic* to rival Cunard Line's Hull 534, the *Queen Mary*. But the funds ran out due to the Great Depression and bad management, and the project was scrapped not long after they laid the keel. White Star was folded into Cunard at about the same time."

She tapped at the keyboard and stabbed the return key decisively. "And that's all she wrote."

"Until now," he replied, still admiring the model of a ship that never was. Slowly he turned to take in the opulence of the room, full of mingling guests. "Decades later, here we are aboard a sister ship to Cunard's *Queen Mary 2*, rebranded as a new White Star Line vessel. Old rivalries back from the dead."

"False rivalry," Pip amended quietly. "The 'new' White Star is now just a subsidiary of Cunard; it's all just a publicity stunt playing on people's nostalgia."

"Nostalgia translates directly into money, in a world where people want to escape from everyday life," someone said, and they turned to see Adrienne McKinn approaching, accompanied by a pair of young ladies who were walking hand-in-hand. One was dressed a ballroom gown, while the other wore a tailored tuxedo, offset with a pink bow-tie. "Might I introduce Janice and Terri Patton?"

"Good evening ladies, I hope you're enjoying your time aboard," Waters said by way of genial greeting, turning his attention back to Pip after an exchange of pleasantries. "So, tell me, Ms Paik. Did you find an answer to the question I posed you at dinner?"

Terri Patton, lithe and dark-skinned, her hair styled in a series of short spikes in sharp contrast to her tux, raised a curious eyebrow, and Adrienne explained.

"The captain asked Phillipa what it is that should distinguish the new White Star Line from its parent company."

"Not even my employers could tell me when I asked them that," Waters clarified. "I climbed the ranks in Cunard, imbibing the traditions of that company, but was suddenly asked to transfer to captain this new division's flagship, with no explanation for the tone I should set. Now, as you said Ms. Paik, it's obvious to anyone that all of this is just a publicity stunt playing off the interest in *Titanic*, but I was wondering if someone could tell me what it is that should set my ship, and my crew, apart from a disaster one hundred years old, and a parent company that cannot define what we should be."

"Back in 1912 White Star was the brasher, fashionable alternative to Cunard," Pip replied, looking up at length from her laptop. "The two companies were in rivalry for decades over who controlled the North Atlantic passenger traffic. Cunard prided itself on speed and grandiose decoration, which won them the custom of the British well-to-do, where White Star advertised stability, comfort, and tasteful luxury, which drew the patronage of America's wealthiest."

"Tasteful?" Waters smirked ironically. "Have you noticed the carpet your feet are resting on?"

Pip had. Tiny White Star pennants were woven into the pattern, as if the ship was trying to beat its faux heritage into everyone who walked over it, surely a signifier of the vessel's identity crisis.

She smiled nervously. "The comparison does break down after nearly a century though."

"Well, it's not entirely a show," suggested Terri Patton. "We've just come from the White Swan Restaurant, and the wall panelling in there was originally fitted to *Titanic*'s older sister."

Several heads nodded at that. It was well-known that a small fortune had been spent purchasing or 'leasing' vintage fittings to lend *Oceanic's* public spaces a genuine strand of 'White Star DNA'. For those who were interested, there were tours available that guided passengers from one treasure to the next, allowing people to marvel at staircase banisters and window-frames that once again were ploughing the ocean deep. The main dining room below decks even sported sideboards and panelling from 'old reliable' *Olympic's* a-la-carte restaurant, materials that at auction had been the subject of a bidding war between Carnival

Corporation, corporate owners of Cunard-slash-White Star, and Celebrity cruises, who had wanted to install the historic woodwork on a ship of their own.

"And there's the organ at the bottom of the Grand Staircase," added Adrienne, referring to a spectacular 250-pipe Welte-Philharmonie mechanical organ that had pride of place in the ship's main lobby. "That was intended for installation on the class's third sister, *Britannic*, before she sank in WW1 as a hospital ship… took us a crazy amount of effort to get the Schloss Bruchsal Museum to loan it to us for the duration of this voyage…"

"Star patterns and chandeliers," interjected Janice, shaking her head. "Wall fittings and fireplaces, paintings and pillars. Those are just trimmings. They're a nice touch with the past, but they aren't what it means to be a White Star vessel…"

"Well then, what is?" prodded Waters, and Janice shrugged as if it was the most obvious thing in the world, her blonde locks bobbing around her head as she spoke.

"White Star is *Titanic*. You can't escape from the fact that the ship, the company and the disaster are all tied together nowadays. So what you're aiming for is to capture the romance of the Edwardian era."

"Glitz and glamour," nodded Terri in agreement. "Elegant women and dashing gentlemen."

"So says the girl whose cummerbund is falling off?" Adrienne McKinn lightly laughed.

"That's rich coming from the former Congresswomen dressed up like she's ready to attend a 1912 debutante ball!" Terri responded with a sly grin.

"You have me there," Adrienne conceded. Pip snuck a glance at the older woman's gown – a waterfall of elegant fabric, tied with a floral sash – and compared it to the modern cut of her own attire. Both shared Asian influences, but differed in approach, Pip's dress going for straightforward elegance while Adrienne's was a symphony of Edwardian exuberance. Most of the women present at dinner and her presentation were dressed similarly, as if attending a themed event.

"So ladies," Waters mused, stroking his chin. "You're saying my ship should emulate the four days between *Titanic* sailing sail, and her brush with an iceberg?"

"Whether they know it or not, that's what people will be looking for when they climb on board," Adrienne said with confidence. "Pip, you said in your lecture how *Titanic* was the product of a faux Golden Age, a concept that quickly broke down once you scratched the surface, and which World War One shattered forever. But real or not, that ideal is what this ship needs to be. Comfort, stability and the promise of prosperity, everything people want in a modern world lacking almost any semblance of those things. Isn't that right?"

"Yes…" Pip managed to squeak, suddenly feeling overwhelmed.

"Think about it, Lloyd," Adrienne continued, rising back to stand with her arms folded, chin resting on a cupped fist. "People want that false romance. *Titanic* is remembered as a floating palace for the idle rich, but really she was an immigrant ship with a frosting of opulent icing slapped onto the top decks. Of the 2,200 people on board the ship that night, over seven hundred were travelling in Third Class, people who'd saved everything to purchase a one-way ticket to America with the dream of achieving the same power and privilege as those travelling for fun and profit in First or Second Class. *Oceanic* allows people from today to live that dream, even if just for the duration of a week-long holiday."

The conversation was just getting interesting to Pip's ears, when a musical tone suddenly sounded from one of the Captain's pockets, and he produced a small pager. Checking its screen, he frowned for a moment and then made a polite bow.

"Ladies. Sorry to leave you but I'm required on the bridge. I trust the three of you will not trash the place in my absence."

"Get off with you, Lloyd…" Adrienne shooed him away teasingly. "Go steer us away from any dangerous icebergs."

Returning his hat to his head, Waters saluted them smartly and vanished up into the highest reaches of the ship. Pip could not help but notice how Adrienne watched him go with an appreciative eye. Then, trying to hide her own attention, she pulled a thick hardback book out of her backpack. "Erm, Mrs Patton, would you sign my copy of *Titanic Century*?"

Janice smiled graciously. "It would be a pleasure."

"Even out in the middle of the Atlantic, you have your fangirls," Terri chuckled, rolling her eyes as Janice autographed the inside jacket. Pip, for her part, just kept quiet.

"Congratulations Janice," Adrienne said softly. "And thank you. Sales from the book made all of this possible."

"It was your ideas that made this happen, Addy," Janice ended her signature with a flourish. "I just footed part of the bill."

"You and everyone who bought a copy of *Titanic Century…*" Adrienne's eyes slid over to Pip, and graced her with a dazzling smile. "Like our wallflower there. Come over here, Pip; don't shirk from the spotlight."

Nervously, Pip closed her laptop and stood with them. She was just noting, to her chagrin, how she barely came up to Adrienne's collarbone when the taller woman suddenly bent over and gave her a light hug too, as if they were old friends. "I've been following your blog. You're almost the poster girl for the Project. The network technicians tell me that more people have bookmarked your page than the main website."

The Korean-American's response was once again, a strangled squeak. Adrienne barked in laughter, like a dog that had just found a particularly fun chew-toy. "What will it take to get you to stand up like you did in your lecture? Did you use the old trick of visualising everyone in the audience to be naked?"

Pip felt a blush blooming on her face and struggled to find her voice. "Actually, I just tried to think about facts. Facts are easy. You don't have to worry that someone's going to call you out if you just keep to the unvarnished truth of something." She paused, realising that she was launching off into a spiel, and dipped her head back towards her champagne glass so that her hair hid her face as she sipped. "As you can see."

"So I can…" their hostess smiled gracefully.

"Well, if my beau here has done enough meet and greet tonight," Terri Patton smirked again, teasing mirth in her eyes as she wrapped one arm around Janice. "I'm going to be stealing her away now…"

"Have fun girls," Adrienne embraced them. "And Terri, don't go breaking my superstar artist."

"I promise nothing!" was the joyful reply before the two women vanished into the crowds, leaving Pip and Adrienne standing beside the model of an *Oceanic* that never was.

"They're a wonderful couple," Adrienne said softly. "They were finally married in Massachusetts last month, and it was a proper marriage at that, officiated by a minister who was happy and willing to wed them."

"Lucky them…" Pip said, smiling sadly. "Back in 1912 John Jacob Astor had to pay a priest to officiate over his own remarriage. Then he and his teenage wife were run out of town by the judgemental masses, though that might have had something to do with the fact she was pregnant *before* the wedding."

"Well, everyone loves a scandal, now and then. 'JJ' at least was one of the wealthiest men in the world, and could afford to take his blushing bride away on a several month Grand Tour of Egypt…"

"…followed by a First Class passage back to the states on board *Titanic*. Madeleine Astor survived but her husband became the richest man to die in the sinking," Pip mused, drumming her fingers on the casing of her laptop, lost in thought until Adrienne suddenly nudged her on the shoulder.

"Alright Ms Serious Academic, what are you working on?"

Hesitantly, with all the fear of rejection weighing her down, Pip turned the laptop around so that the founder of Project 401 could read the monitor.

"*The New Atlantis: The Sinking of the Titanic in the Public Consciousness*," Adrienne read aloud, skimming through the first few paragraphs. "This is what you were arguing, that *Titanic* is a touchstone event in history?"

"Well, yes," Pip began to explain. "You said yourself that the Edwardian Golden Age was actually just a Gilded Age; a time of poverty and strife masked over with gloss and veneer. All at the same time you have the rise of the middle-class and the growth of democracy out of the industrial revolution, matched with the last vestiges of imperialistic ambition as countries vie for overseas colonies, while Germany strives to build an empire, to hell with the consequences. All the signs of the coming war are there to see, and yet people of the time seem blinded to it, placing their faith in the progress of man and the march of industrialisation!"

Her movements were becoming more impassioned, and with a wild sweep of the arm she sent the contents of her champagne flute flying into the crowd. Suddenly abashed, she pushed a loose hair back into place. "Sorry. But into the midst of all this *madness*, a ship sails into an iceberg, *and the entire world gasps in shock*. The greatest product of shipbuilding technology sinks in less than three hours, and over one thousand five hundred people die with her. The great and the poor, rich and impoverished, carried to their doom together. It was so unprecedented that everyone sat up and took notice."

Her hands flew over the keyboard and called up a page of text. "Here's an example. Jack Thayer, one of the survivors of the sinking, wrote an account of it during WW2. Listen to what he says: *'In my eyes the modern world awoke with a start on April 14th 1912'*. It's the perfect quote to sum up my theories."

Adrienne's eyes were bright with interest. "And this is going to be your final dissertation for university?"

"Probably; I've been working on it ever since I was accepted for the expedition. But I've been asking the same questions ever since I saw James Cameron's *Titanic* when I was a kid: why do people care so much about a ship that sank a hundred years ago?"

"Why not ask me?" the former Congresswoman chuckled, wrapping a shawl around her shoulders. "Come on, at the very least, I can give you *my* story."

Despite the late hour, the air was mild as *Oceanic* and the other ships held position over *Titanic's* wreck, but the atmosphere was electric, pressure and excitement building like a rising swell. Passing through the bustle of mingling guests, Adrienne led Pip out of the Cafe Parisien onto the promenade deck.

"First off, yours was one of the best presentations we've seen today, Pip," she began. "I have to say that openly courting controversy was unexpected, after the majority of lecturers played their hands close to their chests. You certainly got a response."

Pip's shoulders fell at the unpleasantly weighty praise as she glanced out across the sea. The stars were hidden behind gathering clouds. "I honestly don't know how I feel. I believe what I said, that parts of the wreck need to be salvaged, but at the same time I feel guilt for endorsing the robbing of a gravesite."

"A mass grave, to be precise."

"Gee, thanks."

"Pip, you want to write about how people feel about *Titanic*, right? Just consider this; the story means so much to me that I took up permanent residence on *Oceanic* just to try and recapture some of that spirit. This ship is my home year round now."

"You're a widow right, if that's not too personal?" Pip asked, with cautious interest.

"Don't worry about it. Yes, my late husband Mike was born an Ulsterman, and it was him who introduced me to the pride in *Titanic* that still lingers in Belfast. When he died, I felt that connecting with something he loved would help me hold onto the memory of him. But *Titanic* is infectious, and now that the ship's legend has really got its hooks in me I find myself not only the founder of Project 401, but living aboard *Oceanic* and becoming an unofficial crewmember who assists in organising shipboard events."

Pip suddenly felt very cold. The notion of family and the death of loved ones played uneasily in her mind. And as she wrestled with those feelings, her ears picked out the distant drone of a powerful engine rolling over the waves.

"Aha..." Adrienne peered into the night. "Well, here comes the US Coast Guard."

For a moment, lightning flashed in the distance, sheets of white fire roiling in the clouds. Against them, Pip briefly saw the dark shape of a plane soaring towards them, high in the sky. She glanced at her watch. 11.25pm. Fifteen minutes to blast-off.

"Ladies and Gentlemen, this is your Captain speaking!" Lloyd Waters' voice suddenly boomed over the ship's public address system. "Please be advised that weather conditions seem set to deteriorate. As such, we ask for guests from the other ships of the Memorial Fleet to please make their way to the ferry station so that we can return them to their lodgings before the chop becomes too rough. Thank you."

Pip had turned her head up to the nearest loudspeaker, disappointment welling up in her. Forcing a smile onto her face she turned and shrugged. "Well, that's my cue to leave."

"*Bon voyage*, Pip," Adrienne smiled. "I'll see you soon."

CHAPTER SIX

"For passengers remaining aboard *Oceanic*, the time is now 23:25…" Lloyd Waters spoke clearly into the microphone. "An aircraft from the United States Coast Guard is approaching us to carry out their annual wreath-dropping, and Captain Gorbachev of the *Anatoly Sagalevich* has sent up a flare notifying us that they are ready to surface the recovered section of *Titanic*'s hull. Thank you everyone, and we hope you enjoy the fun and fireworks. A service of commemoration will follow at 2.20am."

He pulled his finger off the button and spun around, tone and expression hardening. "Right, what's the situation?"

Oceanic's bridge, a symphonic orchestra of high-tech displays, was currently crowded with crew overseeing the complex ballet of launches that would ferry guests back to their ships. Catherine Vickers, the Safety Officer, clucked her tongue to draw Waters' attention and handed over a typewritten sheet.

"The weather report we received from the plane was just ratified; there's a low-pressure front developing out of nowhere right on top of us. Wind speed is climbing fast and the seas are rising too."

"So I see…" Waters turned to peer down from the nearest window. A ship of *Oceanic*'s size was near impervious to weather, but there was a definite motion now to what had until half an hour ago been tranquil, placid seas. "Well at least we'll have the guests back to their own ships before the worst of the weather closes in."

"Here's hoping sir, but there's something else," Vickers pointed. "Look off to the west, sir."

He squinted, and then requested a pair of binoculars. "It's a ship, motoring hard towards us…" he determined at last, lowering the glasses. "I think she's the *Seguin Laroche*, the late arrival to the party."

"Yes Captain, but that's just it…" Vickers had moved to the navigation console. "She's not showing up on radar."

"That's impossible…" he began to reply, but when he reached her side he stopped dead. The radar scope was clouded with an odd green pixilation, but the other ships of the fleet still stood out as bright blots against the background static. He glanced towards the window, and then matched the bearing on the *Seguin Laroche's* position to the scope. There was nothing there.

Wordlessly he walked down the length of the console to the backup display, which showed the same anomalies. Neither did the approaching ship show up on the GPS Display, which tracked each ship within a hundred nautical miles by their individual GPS callsign.

"Try hailing that ship…" he said at last. "Ask Captain Laroche if she's having any technical issues, and then request she adjust course. On her current heading she's going to ram straight into the *Anatoly Sagalevich.*"

"Aye Capt…" the radioman began, but then paused. "Captain, listen to this."

"What the hell now?" Waters cursed softly as he crossed over and accepted an offered pair of headphones. Wailing tones and static burst in his ears, warbling as the system tried to find a clear radio channel. "We're being jammed?"

"That's what it sounds like. And it's getting stronger every second. Just a minute ago I was talking to my counterpart on the *Rescue*, and now I can't reach him."

"Sir!" called Vickers, voice raised in urgency. "We're losing radar now, GPS too!"

Captain Waters slowly lowered the headphones and looked to the flickering computer screens on the bridge. Then he peered out into the night, to where the bright patch of lights that was the *Seguin Laroche* was growing larger and larger.

Something hit one of the bridge windows with a sharp **tap**, a fat, heavy raindrop. More followed, and within moments a full-on cloudburst broke overhead, the water pouring down and hiding the oncoming ship from view.

"What the hell is happening?"

*

"What the hell is this?" someone gasped, and Nash turned to see Adrian Abercrombie slowly approaching the open container, keeping his hands slightly upraised. Their co-conspirator was wet from the rain, his jacket lost or discarded, but his face was clouded with anger.

"You lock me up with the crew," he seethed. "And then you 'send' for me like I'm some dogsbody? That's just going to incriminate me with the rest of you bastards!"

Jab stared blankly at him, and then shrugged. "I thought you would like to see what it is that you've made possible."

Warily, Abercrombie stepped up alongside him and gazed into the depths of the steel box, now lit with portable lights. Jab saw his eyes widen.

Nash and Pierre were on their knees inside the container, comparing several reams worth of paperwork to the display of Nash's laptop computer. Circuit boards and cut wires were scattered around them.

"Any success?" Jab asked the two of them, keeping one eye on Abercrombie.

"Yes," Nash gave him a thumbs' up. "We've set up a work-around to fool the safeties and let us discharge the system with a one-second jump into the future. After that the machine will idle back into standby mode. I just need to synchronise the internal clocks and then we can start the sequence."

Both he and Pierre were wet with their own sweat, the source of their discomfort being the hulking machine secured in the centre of the container, plumbed into the banks of cooling units and power capacitors that filled the back of the confined space. The roiling heat was intense. Even standing just inside the brightly lit container, Abercrombie's silk shirt was steaming slightly as it dried, and Jab had rolled down his overalls, leaving his upper body clad only in a T-shirt.

"Well?" Abercrombie asked, eyes now full of fear. "What is it?"

"It's called the *Liberty Bell*," answered Jab, his arms folded impassively. "It is a device with which we intend to travel backwards in time and meet with the Prophet Muhammad."

108

Abercrombie gaped, even as he wiped sweat from his face. "It's a… time machine? That… that's not possible."

"It is very possible," Jab indicated towards the machine. "What you are looking at a piece of scientific apocrypha, the rumoured product of an abandoned experiment, which we have brought back into service after those who could not appreciate its potential mothballed it. Sympathisers in America managed to 'liberate' this unfinished test-type, and myself and others then strived for years to source the parts needed to finalise its construction, along with the esoteric fuel it requires to operate. In just a few weeks we had planned for it to make its maiden voyage into the distant past." He paused, and then his voice turned cold. "But now everything I have sacrificed to make this happen is on the verge of failure, because you refused us daily access to the container."

"I… I didn't know…" Abercrombie's mouth flapped like that of a guppy that has just seen a shark hove into view.

"Jabril!" someone shouted, and the two of them turned and gazed up. Someone was calling down towards them from the ship's superstructure.

"Wait here!" Jab said curtly, and he quickly crossed to the side of the ship to peer upwards. Benjamin Khan was standing on the ship's open bridge wing, calling down to them.

"We're coming up on those other ships!" Jab heard him cry. "They're only a few minutes away. The woman says we'll have to stop to avoid suspicion."

"Have her keep going until we're among them, and then stop the ship! We want our behaviour to appear as normal as possible!" Jab shouted back up. Khan waved to signify his understanding and turned away.

"It's the Titanic Memorial Fleet. Mr Abercrombie, I'm going to need someone to pose as a ship's officer on the radio…" his voice trailed off.

He had been so focused on the troubleshooting of the *Liberty Bell* that he had gotten careless. His gun had been left resting against the container.

And now it was in Abercrombie's hands.

"Don't… move…" The M&B Holdings representative had a panicked look in his face, but, alarmingly, he had managed to release the FAMAS's safety.

109

Slowly, cautiously, Jab raised his hands in surrender.

*

As the launch to the *Anatoly Sagalevich* pushed away from *Oceanic,* Pip looked around. The many vessels surrounding them dotted the horizon like stars, filling in for the heavenly bodies lost behind the rainclouds.

A White Star Fleet.

Just as the thought crossed her mind, the various ships began to spit fireworks, each rockets shooting high into the air before bursting in cascades of white sparks.

She chuckled for a moment, and then with a sibilant hissing the rain intensified, and the sea began to spit and roil like fat in a pan. When the pilot announced they'd first be stopping off at the USNS *Rescue* en-route to the *Andrei Sagalevich*, Pip checked her watch.

11.35pm. Just a few more minutes until Titanic struck the iceberg, just a few minutes until the six seconds of slithering contact that sealed the fates of fifteen hundred lives one hundred years ago.

A cheer went up from somewhere above her aboard *Oceanic,* fireworks continuing to burst all around, as if in mocking parody of *Titanic*'s distress signals. Thinking back to her earlier comments on death worship, Pip felt worried thoughts churning around in her mind.

*

"Now, we're all going…" Abercrombie paused to wipe the rain out of his eyes, now directing the FAMAS into the container. "To very calmly, turn off the time machine, and then hail one of the other ships."

"What are you doing, Adrian?" Jab took a step forward, and halted when the other man suddenly swung the gun back at him. "We had a deal…"

"You were going to shoot me!" Abercrombie hissed, readjusting the gun so that the butt sat square against his shoulder. "And our deal was just to transport a 'device'. You never mentioned that it was a fully working time-machine!"

His teeth were now bared in a manic grin, and Jab mentally berated himself for having intimidated the man into violence.

"We were not going to shoot anyone!" he protested.

"What about the captain's toy-boy, huh? You shot him!"

"That was in self-defence."

"Yeah, and I can say this was too…" Abercrombie's eyes glinted as he tapped the barrel of the gun. Jab had seen the same light in the eyes of mercenaries. "And then I'll take that *thing* in the container in lieu of payment. I'll bet some of your friends in Syria or Iran will pay good money for it, even if it is stolen goods."

"You want to sell it!" Jab said in disbelief. "The most awesome device ever crafted by the genius of man, and you want to sell it for money!"

"Everything is for sale…" Abercrombie grinned. "Loyalty, integrity, and now eternity…"

The man was mad.

"We wanted to use it for peaceful purposes!" Jab hissed back at him, while realising he sounded like some despotic head of state defending his right to possess enriched uranium. "As a means of saving the world, not eradicating lives!"

"That's real sweet, altruistic even. Too bad I've never had time for selflessness, when its money and self interest that has kept the planet merrily spinning around for centuries, despite what all the beatniks like to believe. So at the very least, you've saved my own little world. Thanks for everything, Jabril," Abercrombie finished, steadying the rifle.

Jab did not even have time to close his eyes before a bright rocket leapt up from ship's bridge, trailing brilliant white sparks. The firework burst with a crack overheard, and Abercrombie swung round in surprise, clenching down on the trigger.

The FAMAS spat rounds like a chain gun. He must have had it on full-auto. Jab flung himself to the deck as the shots drew a line across the *Liberty Bell's* container, hearing simultaneous retorts coming from ahead as more rockets were launched. It was the fireworks display every ship in the memorial fleet carried, synchronised to local timers.

Winded, he looked up. Abercrombie was struggling with the rifle, trying to adjust the fire-mode selector, when someone threw themselves out of the container and tackled him. It was Nash.

The gun fired. Again, and again. Groggy, his world spinning as if he had been drugged, Jab dragged himself to his feet and lurched forward.

Abercrombie lay on the ground, struggling to lift Nash off of him. Forcing his hands to steady, Jab knelt down, grabbed the rifle, and smashed the stock into Abercrombie's face hard enough to knock him back down. The man screamed in pain and rolled aside, clutching at his nose, but remained down.

"Help! Venez M'aider."

He spun. From inside the container, sparks were flying. Pierre Fontaine was on his feet, tapping frantically at the controls on the side of the *Liberty Bell.*

"What happened? What's wrong!?" Jab yelled.

"He hit one of the capacitors, and our bypass on the safety meant the surge triggered the firing sequence before we were ready! Our destination is set, but we hadn't programmed the aperture radius, it's locked at full dilation and cycling itself to discharge! I can't shut it down!"

Behind him the immense bulk of the *Liberty Bell* had gone ominously quiet, and the machine's hull was glowing with an eerie pearlescent sheen.

"Don't cut the power!" Jab stammered. "Whatever you do, don't shut off the pow-"

BANG!

Without warning, a spent ammo casing launched itself off the deck and flew straight at the *Liberty Bell,* adhering to the machine's hull. The sound of the impact echoed ominously in the constrained space.

"Oh, no…"

Now fragments of the machine's hull casing began to fly through the air, drawn by an invisible energy field, and Pierre's head whipped around with horror as the container groaned ominously. Spinning, he dove to his knees, closed the lid on the laptop and shoved it hard, sending it sliding across the deck to Jab's feet.

"Get out!" Jab shouted, ignoring the computer. *"Run!"*

The walls of the container suddenly pulled in with a sickening crunch. Pierre vanished in a crush of mangled metal, and Jab fell to the deck in shock, before turning and dragging himself over to Nash.

"Nash, Nashat! We've got to…" Jab grabbed the young Bosun to pull him to his feet, but then stopped in horrified dread.

Blood was pouring out down the length of the deck. And it was not Abercrombie's.

God above, what have I done?

An alarm was sounding. Through the deck, Jab felt the ship shudder, the engines grinding horribly as the propeller shaft was pulled up against its bearings. Ringing like explosions, other containers began to buckle, some immense, immeasurable power crushing them like drinks cans.

Metal was ringing and struts twisting. Bolts exploded from joints and buttressed girders, hurtling through the air like deadly shrapnel. Jab's belt buckle tore away and he clenched his mouth shut to hold into his fillings. Crawling over the deck he positioned himself over Nash, shielding the younger man, who was struggling to stem the blood pouring from his gut.

From stem to stern, the *Seguin Laroche* began to shudder and scream…

*

"Ladies and Gentlemen!" a magnified voice bellowed across the water, the source hidden from view by the rain. "It is now exactly two minutes until eleven forty pm! The moment everyone has been waiting for!"

Project401.net >> Ships & Teams >> RV Anatoly Sagalevich >> Live Stream

Pip, still riding the launch, which was making heavy going of the rising waves, had her laptop out. It had quickly picked up the Wi-Fi connection for Project 401, a local network sharing server space on all the ships. Setting it down on the bench in the centre of the launch she turned the screen so that the other passenger, Doctor Akira Oshiro, could also see it. The bookish Japanese native nodded with polite thanks, and the two of them turned their attention to the live video stream from aboard the *Anatoly Sagalevich*.

Despite the heavy rain, the far end of the ship was clearly visible, lit by bright halogen lights. The camera was mounted behind the ship's bridge, facing aft over the partially-submerged centre deck of the ship. Orange floats marked where the huge section of *Titanic*'s double-bottom rested. Surf broke over the deck, momentarily revealing a flashing glimpse of dark, rusted metal in the troughs.

There was no sound, though Dean Simmons could be seen filming his own segment for the BBC in the background.

"I thought you would have wanted to be there, Doctor?" Pip said softly. "This is your moment of triumph."

"Not quite," his speech was curtly clipped. "This is just a press junket. My triumph was when that piece of flotsam took flight from the seabed."

Despite his dispassionate tone, she could see his eyes were bright with interest behind the half-moon spectacles he wore owlishly, but before she could comment she was distracted by a burst of static that flickered across the screen. In the bottom corner the connection strength bar was plummeting.

"Damn signal…" she adjusted the laptop's position so that the wireless adaptor was pointed straight back at *Oceanic*, and the image stabilised a little. "This is it, look!"

In the distance the two of them could hear someone counting down on a loudspeaker, faint voices on the various ships acting as a chorus. Pip joined in, noticing Oshiro's lips also moving as he silently observed the last few seconds till eleven forty pm.

"Three… two… one! Arise!"

The camera on the *Sagalevich* jumped as the ship purged its ballast tanks, hefting its well-deck out of the sea. Like mythic Atlantis revealing itself, the waters broke apart and revealed the huge chunk of wreckage. Despite all of her brooding over the ethics of the expedition, Pip could not help but smile.

"That's going to New York," she said softly. "There's a new museum being built on the Hudson there at Pier 59, the old White Star Line terminal."

"It is an impressive achievement," he replied. "I've followed your blog at length. I must say that your enthusiasm is… admirable."

"Thank you…" she replied, feeling more accustomed to people's praise now that she had a few flutes worth of champagne fizzing inside of her. But before she could attempt to coax more compliments out of him, something caused him to sit forward.

"Something's wrong."

Pip looked, and then scrunched forward. The signal was once again fading; the image reduced to stark greys and whites, but on the *Sagalevich's* deck, people could be seen pointing off to one side, expressions of shock on their faces. One figure, whom she recognised as Captain Gorbachev, ran up the stairs below the camera and silently shouted something into the wheelhouse, and the image began to vibrate as the ship's propellers bit into the water.

*

"Is that the bridge?"
"Yes, what have you sighted?"
"An iceberg, straight ahead!"
"Thank you."

*

"Listen!" Oshiro held up a hand. Pip cocked her head. Somewhere out across the water, a foghorn began to blow, loudly and with great alarm. And then she pointed to the laptop's display.

"Look!"

Onscreen, people were running away from the *Sagalevich's* starboard rail, becoming pixelated blobs as the signal collapsed.

From the angle the deck on screen was forming with the water, Pip realised the research ship was turning hard. Then, just before the feed dissolved into white noise, Pip saw something massive come tearing into the left-hand side of the screen.

It was the bow of a speeding ship, travelling almost parallel to the *Sagalevich*. The camera shook as the two ships sideswiped each other, sparks flashing brightly…

And then they lost the signal.

*

"Stop all engines, hard a'starboard!"

*

Pip and Oshiro looked towards each other, and then turned their heads to the open window. Out in the dark could be heard the scream of metal grating on metal. The Coast Guard plane, invisible in the dark, roared overhead suddenly, making its first flyby and ignorant of what was happening below. Pip suddenly felt very small, a china doll adrift in the open sea, blind and helpless.

"What do we do?" she said towards the launch's helmsman, who ignored her, staring out into the rain. The foghorn was rising in note, getting louder, and over the fizzing sound of the rain another sound could be heard, the growing rush of a ship pushing a huge bow-wave ahead of it.

"Civilian launch, civilian launch, this is the USNS *Rescue!*" the radio suddenly squawked. "Turn from your course immediately, over."

The pilot snatched up his own hand set. "This is the launch *Traffic*, please repeat that, over."

The voice on the on the other end was now more drastic, breaking through the mask of static by sheer volume. "Dammit *Traffic*, move fast or you're in danger of being run over. That thing that just tore past the *Anatoly Sagalevich* is bearing down on you from astern, over."

The pilot turned and stared past Pip, eyes wide as he peered into the murk beyond. And then Oshiro suddenly bolted upright from his seat, pointing.

"Kamisama!"

*

"The engines are slowing sir!"
"Is the helm hard over!?"
"She's hard over to starboard, Mr Murdoch!"
"She's turning, good... good... blast! The stern's going to slam into it."

116

"Sir?"

"We're going to have to port-around Mr Moody, to swing the stern clear. Prepare to reverse the helm…"

*

Out of the dark loomed an immense bow, coming straight at them from astern. Pip stared up at white lettering stencilled on the forest-green hull towering over them: *Seguin Laroche*.

"Holy shit!" she heard the helmsman shriek, and the deck pitched up as he slammed the throttle forward and spun the wheel over. Pip saw her laptop sliding off the bench and instinctively jumped forward to catch it, her life's work, and then pushed it into the waterproof enclosure of her bag, struggling to keep her footing as the engine beneath the deck of the launch roared away. Waves and bursting spray obscured the rear windows, but the rush of the oncoming ship's bow-wave was still growing in volume. Pip, her bag clutched to her chest, felt it pick up the launch and fling it away like a child's toy, spinning them around until they were slammed against the ship's hull.

As windows smashed she latched onto a handrail; then one of her high heels twisted out from under her on the canted deck and she slipped down with a shriek into water that was rushing in through a rent in the hull. She looked up as the launch spun around again, the stern section grinding against the green wall sliding past them. Doctor Oshiro lay beside her, eyes half closed and a gash on his head trailing blood from where he had been hurled against an upright. But his chest still rose and fell. Kicking her heels off, Pip grabbed hold of his arm and pushed off the curved wall, pulling him back into the centre of the compartment as they continued to bang down the side of the passing ship, spinning around like rocks in a crusher.

*

"The bow's swung clear. Hard a' port!"
"Hard a' port, Mr Hichens!"
"Turn, turn… this is cutting it fine."

117

"Hard over!"

"She's hard over sir."

"I heard, James... no, no we're coming too close- wait, do you feel that?"

*

From somewhere above there was a bang and a strangled roar, as if a pressure-cooker had just exploded. Dull red light lit up the half-submerged launch like a distress flare, and Pip saw rivulets of molten metal dribbling down the side of the ship, smouldering like hot wax where they landed on the launch's polymer hull. As sky and sea whirled dizzyingly, she momentarily saw the Coast Guard Hercules pass right overhead, body lit up from underneath by the glare of the explosion.

Then the molten slag ate its way through into the launch's engine compartment. The deck exploded upwards on a ball of fire, something struck her in the forehead, and sweet blackness carried her away into oblivion.

*

"She's struck it! We've hit."

"I'm closing the watertight doors and sealing the compartments!"

*

"Civilian launch *Traffic*, turn harder!" Jordan Jones had screamed down the radio on *Rescue's* bridge. Then from outside he heard a dull thud, and rushed out on deck to see the razor-sharp bow of the *Seguin Laroche* tear into the tiny boat like a shark taking a bite out of a surfboard. Almost torn in two, the launch wheeled away to port; until the larger ship's hydrostatic wave sucked it back in for further punishment.

"All hands, prepare to rescue survivors!" he called out. "Run out the emergency boat!" Then the drone of turboprop engines drew his attention to the sky and he shouted towards the radio operator. "Cameron! Warn the Coast Guard plane that there's something wrong. They need to keep well clear in case of..."

Before he could finish speaking, the stern of the runaway container ship was engulfed in a huge explosion, an upthrust of flame so dense it was practically solid energy, piling up on top of itself to swat at the Hercules aircraft swooping overhead. As Jones stared in horror, the blast wave hurled him into *Rescue's* bridge, and the back of his head collided hard with one of the consoles.

"*Ah!*"

Through the disorientating sense that his brain was now dribbling out his ears, he wondered if they could collect a piece of wreckage from the burning container ship, maybe mount it on a plaque…

The launch! The plane!

Woozy, but determined, he pulled himself back to his feet.

"Captain, you're bleeding."

"Never mind that now!" Holding a hand to stem the flow of blood from where he had hit his head, Jones dragged himself back to reality and clawed his way into a standing position. Out in the pouring rain he could see that the crew were doing their duty to the best of their ability, and already *Rescue's* steel-grey emergency motorboat had been swung out on its gantry. He turned his eyes to the heavens, and through the rain dimly made out the Hercules, flames trailing from one side.

"*He's got engine fires!*"

Rescue suddenly shimmied hard as she took an obstacle on the nose, and Jones saw a navy-blue shipping container glide past in the dark, thrown from the *Laroche's* deck by the force of the blast.

"Captain!" he heard someone shout.

As the motorboat dropped free from the lifeboat falls and powered out into the dark, he turned to find himself staring straight into the boyish face of his Lead Salvor.

"What is it Kai?"

Kai Alinka pointed across *Rescue's* bow. "I think they might need our help too."

Jones turned and came face to face with the awesome sight of the *Seguin Laroche,* several hundred yards off and motoring past at full speed, her stern a flaming pyre.

"She's heading straight for *Oceanic*!" Alinka shouted.

"No, someone's still in control, look!" Jones replied. Sure enough, the *Seguin Laroche* was swinging away, turning north in a wide arc to avoid the immobile bulk of the *Oceanic*, kicking up a huge sideswiping wave of foam as she went. In the light of the fire he saw a figure rush out onto the ship's high bridge wing.

"Kai, get me the loudhail-"

A sharp crack ripped across the gap, as the figure on the *Laroche's* wing lifted what was unmistakably an assault rifle into view and fired. Jones and Kai dropped to the deck just as a bead of gunshots tore their way into the bulkhead behind them, the rifle roaring away. Jones rolled on his back, and stared up at *Rescue's* mast, where the antennae and dishes were suddenly sparking with blue fire. High above them, the sky growled, as if pouncing to strike.

Rolling back onto his knees, Jones clutched at his side, and with his breath whistling between his teeth, hobbled over to kneel beside Alinka at the gunwale. The random gunfire had stopped.

"Is he out of range?"

"No sir," Alinka replied, his eyes wide and his voice quiet with awe. "He's probably staring at the same thing I am."

Jones peeked over the gunwale, and felt a finger of ice travel down his spine.

"Holy Mother of God!"

The *Seguin Laroche* was engulfed in white light, spectral ribbons streaming off the metal like smokeless flame. Steel screamed and distorted as forces Jones could not even name shredded containers like confetti, the cacophony rising over a pulsating whine, like something mechanical was coming up to speed. Black figures ran to and fro on the deck, dark scabs against the light, and they and the ship seemed to be *twisting* around some invisible axis, flickering in-and-out of sight like an image on a badly-tuned television.

As he stared at the metamorphic vessel, Jones felt like his eyeballs were itching.

His radio, still clutched in his hand, vomited static, before suddenly latching onto a clear frequency.

"Capacitor drive opening," intoned a synthesized voice, cool and emotionless against the chaos. *"Aperture dilation set for max: fifteen hundred metres. Injecting graviphotons. Injection ratio exceeding*

seminal, exceeding nominal, exceeding critical. Gradient fluxing. Device 'Liberty Bell' will fire in ten seconds. All personnel shield eyes now."

"Full astern!" he heard himself screaming. "Get away from that ship!"

Too late.

From life experience Jones knew that perception of time often slowed down in crisis situations, but it seemed that the order had no more left his mouth when the *Seguin Laroche* shed its coat of white fire like a dog shaking water from its back. *Rescue* lurched sideways as the front struck her, knocking most of the crew down. Jones, holding onto the rail with both hands, looked up just as the ethereal glow around the *Seguin Laroche* shattered with a blinding flash, exploding into shards of brilliant spectral light that seemed to stab deep into the back of his skull like white-hot knives. He screamed in pain, bringing up his hands to shield his eyes even as they burned in their sockets. Then he felt Alinka tackling him to the deck, the younger man throwing himself over him as if to shield him. Unable to see, Jones could only focus on the terrifying roar that seemed to engulf the ship, a howling, noisome bellow, like immense engines pushed beyond their limit.

There…

…was a moment when every atom in his body seemed to fly apart and then collapse back upon themselves, as if he had just exploded from within, soul going supernova. Beneath his clutching fingers the deck felt like flexing rubber, soft and malleable, before suddenly springing back into alignment like the crack of a whip. A wave of silence washed over them, so absolute it felt tangible. For a moment, he seemed to float in a serene darkness…

…and then the world came crashing back upon him.

"…like nothing I've ever seen!" Alinka was yelling. Jones struggled to his knees, his vision reduced to dots of colour that burst brightly on an inky black sea.

"Kai…" he hissed, lungs struggling.

"…she's disappeared into the rain, can't even see the glow from the fires. The Coast Guard plane's turning away too, flying off west, back towards land!"

"Kaikaina…" he rasped again. Against the pain he forced his eyes to open, and saw nothing. Gingerly he felt for his face, fingers brushing against blisters forming around his eye sockets.

"…must be due north of us now, and getting further away. There's fog forming too, just boiling up off of the sea."

"Crewman Alinka!" he shouted, his voice quavering unfamiliarly. *"Shut UP!"*

When he finally sensed he had his lead salvor's attention, he turned in what he hoped was the right direction to be facing him. "Kai, I think I'm blind."

His chest heaved for several seconds as he mentally flailed in panic, before he composed himself and extended a hand towards Kai. "Now help me up, and let's find out what just happened to us."

With no vision with which to see, Jones' mind scrabbled for any sense to latch onto. His ears, searching, dimly heard the soaring note of the *Seguin Laroche's* foghorn, as the ship vanished on into the night. Blind and reeling, he shivered.

Suddenly the night feels a lot colder…

*

"Mayday, Mayday, Mayday. Air Station Elizabeth City, this is Coast Guard Flight 401 declaring a mid-air-emergency. I repeat, Mayday, Mayday, Mayday. Hello? Hello? Fuck!"

"Commander King, what's wrong sir?"

"I can't seem to raise anyone, Ramirez. The radio's out."

"Not just the radio, look at the nav display, sir. Everything's dead."

"…the hell? Okay, let's not panic. First of all, which way are we pointed?"

"South west I think, sir. The compass is spinning, but I'm pretty sure we were about to turn back over the fleet when whatever that was happened."

"Alright then, then we maintain this course. At the very least it'll take us back towards the States. Lieutenant, I want you to go aft and try and locate whatever damage was done to us by either the explosion or that pulse of light…"

"One more thing sir, we appear to be losing fuel…"

"Shit. Alright, we'll fly this course as far as we can. If we lose so much that we can't make it home, then we turn north and attempt to reach Newfoundland instead... Lieutenant, are you listening to me?"

"Gareth... look at the sky!"

"What do you mean by... Oh, my God. Is that... is that an Aurora!?"

ACT TWO

A NIGHT TO REMEMBER

CHAPTER SEVEN

Jack Thayer paused in buttoning up his nightshirt. Something was wrong. Something had changed.

From his bed he quickly inspected his cabin; everything appeared normal. His steamer trunk was still standing open in the corner and the tuxedo he had worn to dinner was hung neatly on the closet door. From the bedside dresser his pocket watch ticked away, as steady and constant as the thrum of the ship's engines.

Wait, now he realised what was missing. The cabin was completely still, his berth did not tremble beneath him like a hammock, and the cut crystal glasses on the washstand no longer tinkled gently in time to the propellers. The engines had stopped.

*

"Reverse engines, bring her to a halt."

"What just happened, Mr Murdoch?"

"It was an iceberg, Captain. The lookouts saw it dead ahead and I attempted a port-around, but we came on top of it after I reversed the helm."

"I see. You stopped the engines?"

"Aye sir, and closed the watertight doors as well."

"Well, that should contain any flooding for now. Where did she strike?"

"Starboard side Captain, for'ard of the mast as much as I can judge."

"Hmm. I can see we've picked up some ice from it too. Mr Olliver, locate the Carpenter to assess our draft. Now, William, come and show me from the wing where you believe she made impact-"

"Captain, Mr Murdoch. Apologies for my absence. Mr Moody's informed me of the situation."

"Ah, Mr Boxhall. Send a steward to call on Mister Andrews. We might need his expertise to sound the ship and effect repairs."

"Captain, sir. I think she might be worse off than just damaged."

"What do you mean, William?"

"Sir, before the turn swung the stern out, the 'berg had came right up alongside the bridge, and we were rubbing against it the whole time. And just look at the inclinometer. She's already down two degrees at the head and listing a degree to starboard."

"Oh, my God."

*

Thoughtful, Jack did up his last button and crossed to the porthole. He had left it half-open to freshen the cabin. Now, however, the air was still and a deathly, suffocating silence seemed to press in through the porthole in place of the breeze.

The ship was motionless. Thinking back, he tried to connect this development with some cause. An iceberg maybe? Mr Ismay, the head of the shipping line, had shown his family an ice warning just a few hours ago, so perhaps they had drawn up on the edge of field ice, or maybe even bumped into something? He had felt the ship shudder softly just before he noticed the absence of the engines, as if something massive had slithered under the hull…

"What the-"

A flash of light, brilliant and faceted with colour, had erupted outside his porthole, its source somewhere out of sight, far off astern. Like a gigantic flare, it momentarily lit up the ocean for miles, and Jack saw that the ship was indeed surrounded by icebergs, gaunt and ghostly in the harsh light, and then he turned his head away, blinded and pressing his hands to his face to blot out the colourful spots dancing in his vision. They whirled around the dark after-images of the icebergs like fireflies in the Pennsylvania woodlands.

Eventually the mass of light and shadows composed themselves into the pattern woven into the rich burgundy carpet. Jack found he had slumped down on the berth with his head hanging towards the floor. He checked the time: eleven forty-two, eighteen minutes to midnight. From outside his cabin he could dimly perceive other passengers leaving their cabins, voices raised in curiosity, some laughing, others inquisitive.

Far off, a long, echoing growl, like slow rolling thunder, undulated wearily across the water.

*

"What the devil?"

"A bright light on the stern quarter off to the south, Captain. It might have been lightning."

"Captain!"

"Yes, Mr Hichens?"

"Sir, the compass on the binnacle is spinning!"

"What!? – you're relieved from the wheel, run aft and check the standard compass."

"Yes sir!"

"An electrical storm perhaps, sir?"

"Nonsense, there's no hint of thunder in the air. But it will certainly rouse the passengers, which is the last thing we need. Who's coming now?"

"It's me, sir. What was with that flash?"

"Ah, Mr Wilde. I can't give an answer there, I'm afraid. You have news?"

"Bad news I'm afraid. There's air hissing out of the anchor locker, she must be shipping water in the forepeak. What's going on? Captain? Will? You've both gone white as sheets…"

"We struck a berg, Henry, and on my watch I'm afraid."

"We'll have time for recriminations later, gentlemen. Right now I wish to sound the ship."

"Sir, should we make preparations to evacuate? Run the boats out?"

"No, there's no need as of yet, and the last thing we need is a panic. Still… Mr Moody, go rouse the other officers, and then assist them in mustering the crew, just in case. And pass word to the Chief Engineer to keep up steam and ensure the auxiliary dynamos on D-Deck are ready should we have need of them. Mr Boxhall, please work out our position in the event we need to put out a distress call. Meanwhile, the rest of us must move quickly to assess damage from the ice. Chief Wilde, go assess the lower decks amidships. Find out how far aft she's shipping water, if at all. As soon as Mr Andrews arrives he and I will go for'ard and do the same. Mr Murdoch, you have the watch. Summon me if things look in the least doubtful."

*

Grabbing his overcoat, Jack crossed quickly to the short corridor that linked the two bedrooms in this shared suite and rapped a knuckle on the dividing door before pushing it open.

"Mother, Father," he said, seeing his father, Vice-President of the Pennsylvania Railroad, sitting upright in bed, and his mother at the dresser preparing to retire. "Something's happened; I'm just going up on deck to see what's what." He paused and laughed. "Wouldn't want to miss the fun, would I?"

But as he left the cabin and moved forward through the ship Jack found his humour flagging, spotting other passengers clustering together in knots, accosting stewards and demanding explanations.

"Why have the engines stopped?"

"What was that flash of light?"

"I heard an explosion. Is the ship damaged?"

Like Jack, most were dressed for bed, hastily-donned overcoats and dressing gowns draped over nightshirts and robes. Others were still in their dinner dress, and as he climbed the ornate grand staircase to A-Deck a group of such men emerged from the First Class lounge, admiring a chunk of ice that a tuxedoed youth was passing around.

"Are you certain?" one man asked.

"Positive," was the answer. "There are great chunks of the stuff all along the ship's foredeck. I'm telling you, we struck an iceberg!"

The first man casually swirled his highball while another shaved fragments of ice into the drink with his penknife. "From the looks of things, it seems the berg came off worse than us."

Jack was about to ask if anyone else had seen the cause of the flash of light, when the ship heeled slightly, groaning as she did. As the portside lifted, the starboard side fell away, and before the ship righted herself he was reminded of a descending elevator. It had not been a big movement, more like riding over a small swell, but it was singularly unexpected in still, calm seas. Shocked silence was broken by the clanking of the hull and the merry tinkling of crystal chandeliers. As if by mental agreement, the small crowd exited out onto the starboard promenade.

*

"Did we just take a wave? Is this the reason the ship stopped?"

"Ah, Mr Ismay, and Thomas. You're just in time. And no sirs, I am afraid the situation is considerably more severe than a mere wave, whatever that was."

"What is the trouble, EJ?"

"The ship has been in an altercation with an iceberg. She's shipping water, and I fear she's taken heavy damage. Thomas, would you please accompany me below to assess the situation?"

"Certainly, but how bad was this supposed collision?"

"Well, according to Mr Murdoch…"

"Captain!"

"Yes Mr Boxhall, do you have our position?"

"No sir, and my apologies for interrupting, but there's an issue. I have a rough idea of our position from dead reckoning, but I can't take a star sight to confirm it."

"Why not?"

"Sir, the stars have vanished…"

*

Outside more people were heading forward, where Jack supposed the iceberg must have hit. The air was now strangely warm and moist, as if a rainstorm had just passed. Crossing to the rail, he looked down; the ocean was rising and falling in small waves, but the surface was curiously smooth, silky, with no whitecaps or rollers. Wisps of vapour rose towards him like steam off of coffee.

Jack looked back down the length of the ship, towards where he believed the flash of light had originated from, and as his eyes adjusted to the dark he found himself looking into a foggy shroud that blotted out the horizon on all sides. Sea, sky and stars were all hidden, and the icebergs he had glimpsed from his porthole had vanished into the night.

*

"This is a proper Grand Banks fog, yes indeed, but where did it come from? Mr Murdoch?"

"No idea rightly sir, but twenty minutes ago I was seeing whiskers of ice around the lights, and now I'm sweating."

"You're right, the air is warmer, and a breeze has struck up... strange. Well, that's beside it. Mr Boxhall, work out our position as best you can. Thomas, we'd best get below..."

"Captain!"

"Mr Wilde, what's the situation below decks?"

"I'm afraid it's severe sir. She's flooding freely in two of the boiler rooms, and water is already rising into the squash court on F-Deck."

"I can add to that!"

"Mr Hutchinson, why the rush?"

"Captain, the forward compartments are also filling with water!"

"...let's go, Mr Andrews; we'll start with the Mail Hold."

*

"Thayer!" a middle-aged man called out, circumnavigating the crowd to meet Jack at the rail. "Did you see that wave? Took us properly broadside and raced away into the dark."

"Milt, hello," Jack replied, pumping Milton Long's offered hand. The two of them had met over coffee earlier in the evening, and despite over a decade's difference in age had struck up a quick friendship. "A single wave, out on the open ocean. That's a bit strange."

"Not so strange as what they say is up front. Let's go see!"

As the two of them walked briskly along the deck, Jack wondered at everything. The flash of light, followed by a short, wide wave of water and the sudden appearance of this enshrouding fog; surely all three events were connected? He suddenly envisioned an avalanche of stones crashing into a lake, throwing up waves and vaporised water. "There was a bright flash of light and a bang!" he called to Milt. "Perhaps a meteor hit the ocean somewhere south of us? Like that event in Siberia."

"Maybe, maybe. It got my attention, that's for sure," Milt excitedly replied. "But you'd be hard pressed to explain everything!"

The further forward they went, the thicker the crowds became, passengers gathering together where the promenade wrapped around the front of the ship's lily-white superstructure, overlooking the tapering bow. Jack supposed that, were it not for the burst of light and the thunderous roar that had accompanied it, many of these people would have slept through the soft jar that he had felt through the floor, which he supposed was the ship coming into contact with the unseen iceberg. Trying to put an explanation to it, he thought back to his family's recent travels in Europe. At one point whilst attending a consulate party in Berlin, he had been regaled along with several others guests by a Russian attendant's fantastical account of events near Lake Baikal:

"A bright burst of light, so great as to tear a hole in the sky, and a roar like all the Tsar's cannons and artillery firing in concert, setting trees ablaze even as the blast laid them low by the million."

Despite being localised to some distant Siberian backwater, witnessed only by Tungus peasants, the story from the Podkamennaya Tunguska River had inspired a sense of dread and awe in Jack. Now he felt the same grim excitement as Milton led him down to a second promenade on the deck below. Beneath them now there was only the well deck, an area of deck space shared between the Third Class and cargo-handling equipment. Immigrant steerage passengers were having a game of knockabout soccer with blocks of shattered ice, flitting like ghosts in the mist between cranes and hatches. Milt, however, pointed upwards, and Jack felt his sense of dire elation rise as he saw the ship's masthead was crowned with a spike of blue flame, eerie specks of light fizzling on the rigging and wireless antennae.

"Saint Elmo's Fire!" Milt crowed. "I've not seen a sight so grand since I witnessed the Northern Lights on the Alaskan passage, when I was shipwrecked aboard the SS *Spokane*!"

Jack winced as a few bystanders reacted nervously to Milt's ill-chosen words. Other passengers, those not caught up in the Third Class football match, were also admiring the phosphorescent light beautifying the ship's upper works. Through the fog that entwined the mast, the dancing flames cast a diffused glow like a halo. But gradually they began to fade, though strangely the hissing Jack had associated with the blue fire seemed if anything to be getting louder.

Slowly, he turned and crossed to the portside rail. Following the sound to its source he peered out into the murky blackness. Even through the thickening fog, he felt he could perceive a shadow deeper than the dark, and a curl of white foam breaking at its base.

"Jack, what is it?" Milt came beside him as Jack pointed. "Another iceberg?"

"No," Jack intoned with rising dread, as a dim green glow became visible high above the shadow's white bow-wave, and the hissing escalated into a full-throated roar.

"Green light to port!" a voice cried, and the bell in the crow's nest rang out in alarm.

"Full astern! Main engines full astern!" came a shout from the bridge, above and behind them. Jack heard the sound of panicked feet on the deck and the clamouring of engine-order telegraphs, as the shadow pierced the veil of mist and revealed itself to be another ship, converging on their own. Underfoot the floor began to pulse as the engines rumbled into life, frantically working up into a roar that set the deck bouncing, even as the oncoming leviathan closed to less than a quarter mile, slicing the glassy ocean like a knife through soft cheese. Their own ship's voice suddenly made itself heard, brassy whistles booming in warning in an attempt to sound the runaway off, and Jack reeled.

Milt's hand landed on his shoulder, and he felt his friend tug him back from the railing. "Jack, move away, quickly. If she strikes us it's going to be here that takes the worst of it."

Jack staggered in Milt's grasp, his mind trying to comprehend the impossible size of the dark green bow forging towards them, leaden feet seemingly rooted to the deck as he was dragged away. Other people were moving as well, and the two men suddenly found themselves in a crush of panicked people fleeing to the starboard side. His hand brushed against a rail, and the cold shock was like grabbing an electric wire.

"Jump for it, Milt!" he shouted, before throwing himself over the balustrade, landing on the drum-like motor house of one of the cargo cranes. Milt followed, lost his footing on the slick metal, and slid off onto the deck with a sickening crunch. In trying to catch him, Jack himself slipped, landing with a pained gasp atop the crane's jib, and held on for dear life as it bounced underneath him to the beat of the panicked engines. When he at last found a handhold that would bear his weight, he lowered himself down onto the actual well deck, once again managing to botch the landing and knock the wind out of himself.

"Oh!" he hissed, a hand moving to cradle ribs that had caught the jib in his fall.

Wheezing and hurting, he rolled over and, sprawled on the deck, stared upwards at the other hull now looming over them, but slowly beginning to swing clear. A collision narrowly averted, the name of the giant briefly hove into view, before its wake seemed to swat them off.

"Seguin Laroche," he whispered, not recognising it as the moniker of any vessel he knew of. As the other ship powered away into the dark, Jack caught a brief glimpse of a long deck piled high with multicoloured metal blocks the size of houses, followed by a towering white superstructure that rose like a castle from towards stern of the vessel, capped with an emerald navigation light. Darkened bridge windows glared down on frightened passengers and crew like judgemental eyes, and a single squat funnel belched a strange bluish haze. More of the large metal blocks were stacked behind the wheelhouse, and through the pain blurring his vision Jack started as he saw many had been crushed together, crumpled and mangled, while others had burst into a fiery conflagration. Raised voices and shouts of alarm rang across the water between the two ships, as matchstick figures ran back and forth against the flames, armed with fire extinguishers.

And then the stranger was gone, vanishing into the night. Seconds later their own ship's whistle blared again, roaring impotently as the last of the fire's glow was swallowed up in the fog. Jack slumped back onto the deck, breathing deeply and his heart pounding away like a piston. He laughed nervously and found salty tears streaking his face. Feeling a sudden shame at the unmanly display, he wiped his eyes dry and tried to compose himself. Other passengers might see him, people he knew as friends and acquaintances.

"Mr Thayer, are you alright?" someone enquired. "Up you come, lad."

A hand was offered and Jack grabbed it. The man who pulled him upright was a tall, dark-haired fellow, whose look of concern was shaded with a wry amusement. Jack recognised him quickly. "No damage done Mr Andrews, thank you."

Thomas Andrews, the ship's designer, nodded curtly, and turned as the unmistakable figure of the captain approached. Jack had the vague recollection that the two of them had run onto the well-deck from one of the forecastle doors, just after he had fallen off the crane.

Why would the captain and the ship's architect be below decks at a time like this? the rational part of his brain enquired, drowned out by the overwhelming cries of the rest of his mind, demanding answers to more immediate questions.

"Mr Murdoch!" The Captain shouted upwards towards the bridge. *"All stop!"*

"Aye, Sir!"

As the commands were tolled out again on the engine telegraphs, the captain directed his attention back to the man standing closest to them.

"Thomas, where on earth did that brute come from?" he demanded, mental train of thought seemingly running on parallel lines to Jack's. "I thought we were aboard the largest ship in the world, but she was a speck against it."

The deck was rolling softly in agreement with his words, the ship riding the larger vessel's wash like a rowboat.

"I don't know, captain," the marine engineer replied. His expression darkened, and Jack swore he saw the light go out in his eyes. "But I think we need to try signalling her immediately on the wireless. She might be the only ship near enough to help us, even if she seems to have trouble enough of her own."

"Is that so?" the Captain's voice was grim, but matter of fact. Jack and several other passengers had gathered around, and the white-bearded seaman took note, carefully taking the Irish shipbuilder by the elbow as if to lead him away. "Well, we'd best discuss it on the bridge."

Away from panicky passengers, his eyes seemed to silently add.

"Boat in the water!" someone yelled from several decks above, and Jack, the engineer and the Captain all looked up in unison to see one of the ship's officers waving down towards them, pointing overboard once he had their attention. "Captain! She dropped a lifeboat as she passed!"

Turning on his heel the Captain strode to the rail, and Jack followed, eyes wide. A robust boat, bright orange and totally enclosed except for a small glass dome that rose from its back like a pimple, was bobbing in the rough waves left in the wake of the intruder.

"Mr Wilde!" the Captain yelled up towards the wheelhouse. *"Take men below to open the forward companionway!"*

The party atmosphere that had been building had now died a quick and merciful death. As Jack looked around people were now talking amongst themselves, passing on what little they could suppose from the two men's attitude. What was it that the captain would rather not discuss in front of them, and why did the ship's designer feel they needed to signal another ship for help? After all, this ship was unsinkable. Should not the mind behind it be aware of that?

Jack fumbled in his pocket, and found his watch. The time was eleven-fifty-five. Coming into the lee of the cargo-crane he had landed on, he found Milt curled up, moaning softly as he clutched at one of his legs. Instinctively Jack knelt beside him and checked for signs of a broken bone or other serious injury, just as he would on the sports pitch back home. Thankfully, Milt seemed to just have a sprain. Jack, however, could feel his mind spinning. In just ten minutes the world had been turned on its head. And now, looking around, he noticed that the ship had developed a definite list, and was down at the head.

If he did not know better, he would think the RMS *Titanic* was sinking…

*

The *Seguin Laroche*'s lifeboat was of the freefall variety, designed so that the crew could evacuate quickly were there any danger of the ship rapidly sinking or developing a list that might hinder the launch of a conventional lifeboat, always a risk on large cargo vessels.

The concept was simple; the lifeboat, a sealed and watertight pod, was stored on an inclined track that protruded over the side of the main deck. The crew boarded, closed up the pod, and then released the mooring clamps, causing the boat to slide down the track and off the edge of the deck, plunging in a swan dive thirty feet into the water below.

Adrian Abercrombie knew that much, and when things had gone wrong on the *Seguin Laroche* he had made for the safe refuge that was the lifeboat, once he had pushed through the blinding pain from where that bastard Jabril had mashed him in the face and left him rolling on the deck, his pained moans matching the screams of the *Liberty Bell*. The Arab had not even noticed when Abercrombie had gotten up and fled the scene, so concerned was he for the Bosun, Nash.

Get to safety. Hide. Find a way to defend yourself, and don't stick your head up until everything's blown over…

Reaching the lifeboat, Adrian had intended to launch it and get the hell away from the ship. But climbing aboard he had found the control panel locked out, requiring a key to launch the boat and start the engine.

Then something had exploded outside. What had followed was chaos. The damage the *Liberty Bell* was causing must have set something alight, because flames were spreading across the ship's rear deck, engulfing several of the containers. Jabril's mutineers, or terrorists, or whatever they were, had then released the ship's deck crew to fight the flames, and in the chaos someone had fired a gun, setting off a mad fight between the two groups that Adrian himself only avoided by hiding in the lifeboat as the ship swerved to dodge the immobile bulk of the *Oceanic*.

That witch Captain Jo might be a tool and a pain in the neck, but damn if she doesn't know how to handle a ship, he had thought to himself, face pale and hands clenched to an upright as the *Seguin Laroche* slalomed at full power around the nose of the ocean liner, *Oceanic*'s pointed prow coming within a few feet of the reinforced porthole through which he was staring.

Seconds later the *Liberty Bell* must have blown up or discharged, because *something* had filled the inside of the lifeboat with brilliant white light. The whole world twisted itself up into a knot, tangled around him, before everything suddenly whiplashed back to what he would call 'normal'. Stunned, he lost his balance on the inclined deck and tumbled down the length of the lifeboat into the darkened nose, breathing heavily as his heart pounded fearfully.

What the hell is happening here?

He had still been lying there winded, unintentionally hidden, when someone had climbed up to the hatch and helped another person into the boat. At the sound of one of them moaning, Adrian had peeked up to find none other than the bastard Hab Allah helping Nash into a seat and strapping him down. Neither seemed to notice him. The Cadet Officer said something reassuring, and then scrambled back up out of the boat, leaving one of the assault rifles for the younger man to defend himself with.

Relieving him of it had been easy, a good punch being enough to stun the already injured Nash. Climbing back up into the lifeboat's pilothouse, and now armed, Adrian had found that Hab Allah had brought along the key for the control panel and inserted it into the dashboard, unlocking the controls. He gripped the helm, and the small wheel turned freely in his hands. Outside the flames were still roaring, but from the shouts he could hear it seemed that the crew had stopped killing one another and were working together to douse the flames.

Then the *Seguin Laroche* had abruptly canted as it and another vessel began bellowing at each other. To his ears the other vessel's foghorn had sounded like an antiquated steam whistle, but that was impossible.

Unless we moved in time... he thought, but before he could give further shape to those thoughts he had heard someone shouting.

"We're passing another vessel!"

"Get to the lifeboat, abandon ship, quick!"

The figure of a man appeared in the hatchway, and Adrian's finger clenched down on the trigger of the FAMAS he had taken from Nash, not caring who it might have been. Screaming, the dark figure fell back down the access ladder, and before anyone else could climb in Adrian slammed the hatch shut, slung himself into the pilot's chair and yanked on the release lever.

The boat lurched forward down the launch ramp, and he felt a momentary swell of triumph, followed by a moment of horrified realisation.

I forgot to strap myself in...

He clung to the wheel, body rigid with fear and eyes staring forward through the windows as the lifeboat tipped over the end of the track and fell.

The water rushing up to meet him looked like a solid black wall.

*

"Right everyone. It's been fifteen minutes since... the anomaly. Where are we at?"

After Kai Alinka had helped Jones to his chair on *Rescue*'s bridge, the captain had shunned medical attention, instead ordering that the medics first assess the rest of the crew. Within a few moments the good news came that his were the worst injuries, the remainder of those hurt being due to broken bones or bruising. He had been the only one looking directly at the ship when that light had gone off in his face, and though a few others had suffered temporary loss of sight his seemed to be the only permanent case.

After that, Jones had fought off the urge to crawl up and cry. He knew *Rescue*'s bridge by heart, and even without the use of his eyes could turn and point directly at the ship's crest on the rear bulkhead, complete with her motto: **For I Am Full Of Spirit And Resolve.** In the past he had spoken to the crew at great length on taking that creed to heart, and he was not going to be the first to crack.

Eventually, though, he knew that he'd need to find somewhere to be alone and take a page out of Kai's book by indulging in some self-contemplation; but not before they had ascertained what had happened. Even *Rescue* seemed anxious at the turn of events, the hull rising and falling restlessly beneath him as the salvage ship rode the swells.

The first order of business was the rescue of survivors from *Traffic*, the launch that had been run down by the *Seguin Laroche*. Despite the smaller boat being half-flooded with water, its inbuilt buoyancy tanks had kept it afloat long enough for the helmsman and both passengers to be rescued, along with some of their possessions. Aside from minor exposure, cuts, and concussions, they were all well, and had immediately been provided with the use of a shower and a change of clothes each.

Second priority was to ascertain damage to *Rescue*. Reports quickly demonstrated that although the hull was sound, the ship had lost the use of one of her twin propellers due to a burnout on the electric motor that powered it. Several windows had blown out and there was also some mild superficial damage to the superstructure, but after consulting with the rest of the senior crew, it was apparent that *Rescue* was in quite good condition; with the exception of certain electrical anomalies that people were finding hard to explain...

"We're not receiving any data from the GPS downlink, or on any satellite systems. Even the TV in the mess is just showing static if you try tuning it to an outside channel. Radar and radio appear to be working, but we're getting a lot of data we can't understand."

"Explain," Jones grunted, drawing his sunglasses from his jacket pocket and donning them to mask his blinded eyes.

"Well, we appear to have lost most of the Memorial Fleet. Radar shows many small contacts on all sides but only two other ships in close proximity, which we've identified as the *Oceanic* and the

Anatoly Sagalevich by radio contact. Both took some superficial damage from that wave of light, the same as us, and the *Sagalevich* got sideswiped by the *Seguin Laroche*, but Captains Waters and Gorbachev say they've only suffered a handful of casualties. As for the *Seguin Laroche* herself, she's vanished among all the smaller radar returns, we can't get a visual fix on her due to the fog, and even if she is picking up our radio signals I doubt she'll return them."

"And the Coast Guard plane?"

"Gone. Last saw her flying away west. We tried hailing her on the radio but she didn't reply. I think their equipment may have taken a battering when they flew through that explosion."

"Humph. I see. Well, good luck to them. Here's hoping they make it home safely. Now back to these problems with the communication systems. Is it possible that this is just interference from the aurora I'm told has appeared overhead?"

"No sir, it's a bit more complicated than that," someone said, and Jones had to focus for a second to put a face to the voice; radioman Cameron. "I thought something, like maybe the aurora, had seriously thrown the radio for a loop because I kept getting what I thought was heavy pulses of interference across a wide band. But then I realised it was Morse code. Someone out there is Morsing away at high speed. They're identifying themselves with the callsign 'MGY', and they just put this out."

He cleared his throat and read aloud. "*'To merchant vessel Seguin Laroche, we are sinking by the head and require immediate assistance. Our position is 41.44N 50.24W...'* And then he repeats it."

"Sounds like they might have had a run-in with that monster, like the *Anatoly Sagalevich*," suggested Lieutenant Miller, the XO. "I mean, they evidently saw her, and now they're sinking, so I'd be surprised if the two events were somehow not connected."

Jones himself was wondering the same, and then he heard the rustling sound of a chart being unfolded, before another voice spoke up. "Just one problem. Our position is 41.39N, 49.56W, right over the wreck of the *Titanic*. If MGY is where he says he is, the *Laroche* travelled fourteen miles in less than fifteen minutes. Someone's got the wrong co-ordinates and I don't think it is us."

"And who is MGY?" Someone else piped up. "None of the ships in the fleet used that as their callsign."

"That's irrelevant," Jones coughed. "A ship is out there calling for help, so we're going to go answer. Slowly head north in the direction the *Seguin Laroche* took off in, and Cameron, inform MGY's Captain that we're coming to their aid."

"Well, that's the problem sir. I've tried hailing them by voice and Morse, and they're not responding. It's like they can't hear us. Also, I think we're stamping on their signal, because they were just squawking about atmospheric interference."

"So, they don't know we're here? We can't even ask them for a corrected position or an estimate of the number of persons they have aboard?"

"No sir, unless…" Jones could imagine the radioman screwing his face up in thought. "If we're jamming them, maybe I could use that as a Morse signal. Hold down on the radio key to create static in their ears, and then use bursts of that instead of dots and dashes.

Clever boy. "Good thinking, try it. Meanwhile, we'll start heading north. While we do, I need you to obtain a full assessment of their situation, and tell them we're coming fast. And since they're evidently lost, but nearby, have them sound out their position by foghorn, and we'll home in on that."

"Aye Captain."

"Also, notify the *Oceanic* and the *Anatoly Sagalevich* that we're going to the aid of one of the fleet. If they ask if they can do anything to assist, request that they stand by until we can assess things."

The sound of running feet assured Jones that the radioman was not hanging around. *Rescue*'s engines below deck began to growl, and he felt the familiar surge of the ship as she started forward and dug her bow into the sea.

As she stirred into motion, Lead Salvor Alinka spoke up. "If this MGY is sinking, we'd best get the appropriate equipment on deck for quick setup when we arrive."

"What would you recommend?" another voice asked. "We've got equipment onboard to deal with practically any injury a ship could take. Do you want welding gear, or the foam guns, or even the wetsuits?"

"We'll definitely be using collision mats and pumps to stem flooding. Get both of the portable high-capacity units out of the holds, and ready the hoses so we can run suctions between the other ship and our intake manifold. And get the boom cranes unchocked, rouse the operating crews!"

As various voices hammered out a plan, Jones sat back in his chair, for the first time feeling useless. But it was comforting to know that the crew could handle things now that he'd set the wheels in motion.

CHAPTER EIGHT

The bulbous orange lifeboat spun like a top in the churning waters beside *Titanic*. For the third time, Chief Officer Henry Wilde lit a green flare and waved it over his head, trying to draw its attention, while privately wishing he had the freedom to light himself a cigarette.

"Ahoy!" he shouted, punctuating his calls with shrill blasts on a silver whistle. "Over here, make for my light!"

The boat just turned its nose away, rolling ponderously in the light swells. Cursing to himself, Wilde blew again on the whistle.

"Unidentified lifeboat, start your engine and make for the ship!"

It was a random guess, but from the absence of oars Wilde supposed the strange craft had to be fitted with some kind of motor. Finally, with a chatter of exhaust, the boat seemed to come to life, billowing spray churning from its rear as an unseen propeller thrashed at the water.

"At last!" he exclaimed, before turning to the men assisting him. "Ready to take aboard survivors?"

"Ready Mr Wilde," confirmed Quartermaster Hichens, one of the three deckhands deputised to assist him. The four of them had swung open one of the E Deck Reception's gangway doors, and were now struggling to direct the lifeboat dropped by the *Seguin Laroche* towards them.

"Hey Officer, there's water coming in here!" someone shouted, and Wilde turned to see a passenger attired in priestly vestments come struggling up the stairs from the next deck down, his sodden robe trailing water behind him. He was one of a steady stream of people evacuating the bow, and Wilde recognised him as a Catholic gentleman whom he had seen several times in Second Class. The man seemed to have taken it upon himself to come below decks and help lead the steerage passengers to the boat deck.

"Please wait on the next deck above this, Father," Wilde replied mildly. "Preparations are being made to evacuate the ship."

Nodding, the priest joined a steady trickle of steerage passengers migrating either up towards the forecastle or back along the length of the ship, ushering families with small children along with him. Wilde momentarily thought of his own sons and daughters back home, and his late wife. Then he swallowed, repressing painful memories of her recent death in the winter of 1910, just after the loss of their newborn twin sons...

First Richard and Archie, and then my dear Polly...

He choked off that train of thought abruptly. There were more important matters to worry about now. From up above he could hear the chatter of the lifeboat davits, and hoped to himself that the Captain and his fellow senior officers, Murdoch and Lightoller, were keeping a tight grip on affairs. The Captain he knew well, as he did Will Murdoch, and both were good, experienced seamen. The Second Officer however, Charles Lightoller, was a bit of a stranger to him, and he had concerns that the cavalier Lancastrian had not quite grasped the peril that the ship was in.

The *Titanic* was sinking. From Mr Andrews' testimony he had reason to understand that the Atlantic could claim the ship within as little as an hour. And here he was, trying to encourage people to come *aboard* her, even as the water rose higher and higher towards his open perch. Normally this door was more than ten feet above the waterline; already the ship had settled low enough that the people on the boat might be able to climb aboard without the aid of a ladder.

"Mr Hichens," he said to the quartermaster beside him. "As soon as we've brought any wounded aboard from this boat, I wish to fill her with as many of our own passengers as possible. You'll be in charge, is that understood?"

"Yes sir," the wiry crewman nodded, his face pallid. Wilde understood his unease; until the Captain had relieved him, Hichens had been manning *Titanic*'s helm. The poor fellow had been the one who executed Will Murdoch's orders to avoid the iceberg, and both he and Wilde himself had been on *Titanic*'s bridge when that monstrous ship, the *Seguin Laroche*, had barrelled past them in the dark.

Please let her be close enough to help... he thought – no, prayed. *We've not enough lifeboats for even half our complement. If no-one else arrives to take our passengers onboard, this will be a disaster.*

And yet, a second train of thought added ominously, *is it wise to accept help from a strange ship about which we know nothing?*

As if in acknowledgement, Wilde's hand drifted down to a Webley revolver holstered under his greatcoat. *Titanic*'s complement of small arms, for defence and shipboard security, were stored in his cabin, and when the Captain had ordered him down here to take in the mystery lifeboat, he had appropriated one of the handguns for himself.

When I get back up top I'll suggest distributing them to the rest of the senior officers. One can't be too careful...

"Hello!" a voice shouted from the boat, coming nearer with short bursts on the engine. "I'm injured and am having difficulty controlling the boat!"

Wilde relaxed slightly, recognising it as an English voice. "Bring the stretchers forward," he ordered to the crew assisting him. "And pass me a boat-hook."

With each of them wielding a hook, Hichens and Wilde managed to grab hold of a mooring-eye on the nose of the boat, and grappling against its weight and the motion of the water they held it to the side of the ship. But the boat's free end still swung loose, pointing out into the night.

"Turn your helm away from the ship!" Wilde heard himself shouting, even as he felt his muscles strain and his face flush with the effort of trying to keep the craft moored. "And then motor forward in small bursts!"

Someone must have heard him, because after a few seconds the boat obediently swung its tail towards *Titanic*, smacking lightly against the larger vessel's iron hide. Then, with Wilde again providing direction, it edged slowly forward under its own power until the hatch at the stern came up to them. Stepping over, Wilde crouched and stuck his head inside, extending a hand in greeting.

"Hello there, I'm Officer Wilde. Welcome to *Ti...*" His words trailed off, unfinished, and his expression hardened. "What's the meaning of this?"

The interior of the lifeboat was all but empty, except for two men, both injured. One was Arabian or Persian, quite young and pallid, breathing shallowly and in evident pain. He was seated before the lifeboat's helm, while an Anglo-Saxon gentleman menaced him with a strange, bulky rifle, evidently to solicit his cooperation. The face of the gunman was considerably bloodied, and one of his arms hung limply at his side, forcing him to clench the stock of the rifle under his remaining arm to steady it.

"Hello…" he said with an air of affected politeness. "My name's Abercrombie. Forgive me if I don't shake your hand, but I'm a bit indisposed. This animal here was one of several crewmen that tried to take my ship."

Wilde studied this 'Abercrombie' dubiously. Despite the blood covering his face, he was dressed as a well-to-do man of business might be; but there was a savagery to his demeanour that Henry found unbecoming in a Briton. And he was obviously no seaman, from how he had evidently forced a wounded lad to take the helm of this boat in his place. Against his better nature, Wilde found his sympathies drifting towards the alleged pirate.

"Is what he says true?" he sternly asked of the struggling youth. "Mutiny on the high seas is a serious crime."

He got no answer, but even if the young man had any desire to defend his reputation he was in too much pain to show it. One hand was cradling his lower abdomen and his skin was covered in sweat, his breathing becoming more laboured with every second.

"Do you speak English?" Wilde asked, softly, suddenly reminded of Polly's final hours. The youth nodded with some difficulty. "Alright then, I don't know what it is you've done, but we'll get you to our ship's doctor immediately. Hold on, son."

He directed his attention back to Abercrombie. "Your arm sir, is it broken?"

"Yes. I got thrown around when the boat was launched."

"Where's the rest of your crew?"

"Still aboard our ship. The raghead here…" he jabbed the barrel of the gun at the younger man. "Took me hostage and launched the boat prematurely. I was able to get the gun away from him."

He was lying, through his teeth, with sickening shamelessness. And from the look of utter loathing that the younger man was now directing at Abercrombie, Wilde was not the only one who knew this.

"Very well," he said calmly, bringing one hand down to rest on his Webley. "We'll have that splinted in just a moment, but I'll have to ask you to relieve yourself of your weapon before you come aboard the ship."

Reluctantly, Abercrombie surrendered the lethal-looking rifle, which Wilde handed across to Hichens. The quartermaster took it uncertainly, before slinging it over his shoulder. Then, with the boat made secure, Wilde and another crewman helped lift the young man over onto *Titanic*, laying him out flat on the deck with his odd, fluorescent lifejacket wadded up to support his head. Finally, Abercrombie was allowed to depart the lifeboat, though Wilde had every intention of delivering him into the custody of the Master of Arms until such times until he divulged the truth of his story.

In the whole affair it had slipped his mind that *Titanic* was sinking, until Abercrombie stepped up to the lifeboat hatch, gazed up at the liner for the first time, and all but fell back in surprise.

"Welcome to *Titanic*, Mr Abercrombie," Wilde said, feeling a momentary twinge of pride in the man's reaction to his ship.

"*Titanic…*" Abercrombie said, staring up towards the distant boat deck with an expression that Wilde realised was more horror than awestruck disbelief. "Fucking hell, the damn machine worked after all!"

Wilde frowned. "There's no need for language sir."

Abercrombie looked at him with what could only be described as open disgust, his lip curled. "That's rich mate. You're all dead already; you just don't know it yet."

Wilde had had enough and, with his not inconsiderable strength, grabbed hold of the other man and hefted him onto the *Titanic*. "I've had it up to my ears with you, Mr Abercrombie," he hissed. "Your ship nearly runs our own down, you lie to me about having shot an otherwise harmless young man, and now you play games with me when it is evident that you know something."

Abercrombie stared into Wilde's angry face with a serene beatitude, before craning his neck to look down the staircase to F-Deck, up which water was rapidly advancing. "Fuck you," he

147

said softly. "Your ship is sinking and there's nothing you idiots can do about it."

There was a quiet '*click*' and Wilde froze, feeling something long and blunt pressing into his gut. Abercrombie had reached over to Wilde's belt and drawn the Webley revolver from its holster.

"But there is something you can do for me," Abercrombie continued, his expression suddenly as cold and unfeeling as a serpent. "We're going up to the bridge, and you're going to order this ship catch up to the *Seguin Laroche*, so that I can get home to where I belong!"

Wilde slowly looked over his own shoulder. Hichens and the other crewman were focused on trying to tend to the man brought aboard with Abercrombie, lifting him onto a stretcher. Behind them, concerned Third Class passengers were heading up and aft. None of them were positioned to see the gun in Abercrombie's hand.

"No," he growled lowly, turning back and trying to force the other man to see reason. "You said it yourself, this ship is sinking. Moving her now will only accelerate the flooding, and prevent us from evacuating passengers in the lifeboats. You're mad if you think I'll let you endanger them any further than we already have."

"I am not going to be trapped here, in the fucking Dark Ages, because of more idiots who prize their damn morals over common sense," Abercrombie seethed, his eyes flashing with a mad focus behind the lenses of his glasses. His words might have been nonsense, but that seething gaze gave Wilde the entire context he needed. "I need to go back to the *Seguin Laroche*, and unless you take me to the bridge right now, I'll shoot you and find someone who will!"

Wilde's heart was pounding in his chest, with such force he could feel the blood pulsing through every part of his body. He looked back again. The crew were struggling to prevent the other man from bleeding to death. That Abercrombie was capable of firing the gun without any feeling was evident. But so was the fact that the man's insanity would kill everyone on board this ship.

Henry Wilde thought of his surviving children...

Jane, Harry, Arnold, Nancy. Forgive me...

He drew himself up tall, and saw sudden fear in Abercrombie's eyes.

"Mr Hichens!" Wilde bellowed as he lunged forward. *"Defend the ship!"*

The gun fired, the Webley roaring like thunder and the bullet flying wide as Wilde hurled himself at Abercrombie, throwing his weight on the man's broken arm. Abercrombie screamed in pain, but with a vicious motion brought his own knee up into the soft tissue of Wilde's stomach, shoving *Titanic*'s Chief Officer back towards the open door in the shell plating, and giving himself room to bring the revolver to bear. Wilde saw the muzzle of the gun flash once…

BANG!

…and before he even registered the sound of it firing something punched him in the chest.

All the warmth drained from him as if he had just plunged into ice water. He staggered for a moment, the world spinning, and looked down in disbelief to see a patch of red glistening on the front of his greatcoat. Something hot and wet was trickling down his back; was that why he felt so cold?

Someone was yelling, and people were screaming.

"I… I've been shot," he tried to say, but all that came from his mouth were dumb gasps. Deafened by a roaring sound in his ears, he saw a second flash, and now a fiery pain burned in his neck. He tottered on his feet for a moment, trying to understand what was happening, but all he could think of was Polly lying cold and white on her deathbed one Christmas Eve.

Then his legs twisted out from him and he slumped sideways through the door, glanced off the lifeboat, and toppled overboard.

The shock had killed him before he hit the water.

*

Father Thomas Byles had been leading a crowd of Third Class passengers in prayer, making good use of an open space on D-Deck, when he heard men's voices shouting from below, cutting short his group's whispered devotions. After a moment's silence there followed a sharp bang from the direction of the stairs, and instinctively he headed towards them, his vestments flapping about his feet and the beads of the rosary in his clenched fist clacking together. It sounded as if a cable had snapped, or perhaps some piece of cargo had fallen free. Then a second retort sang out, followed by an alien *rat-a-tat-tat*, a vicious staccato he realised was gunfire; and for a second he was confronted by the horrific notion that some beast had somehow brought a Maxim or a Vickers gun onboard.

Then there came a chorus of screams, heralding the flight of a human multitude up out of the E Deck Reception.

*

"Shots fired below!"

"Man overboard – I can see him in the water – it's Mr Wilde… Oh Lord, I think he's dead!"

"No, Henry!"

"Mr Lightoller, take arms and secure the ship!"

From *Titanic's* Boat Deck, Major Archibald Butt, United States Army, had heard the unfamiliar gunshots, followed by crew's shouts and the sudden, panicked screams of passengers. Reflexively his hand travelled to his side, where he felt the comforting weight of his service revolver, concealed beneath his greatcoat.

"The arms cupboard is locked, Captain, and Mr Wilde had the keys on him!"

"Then break it open man, or find Mr Lowe, he has his own pistol!"

"Blast!" His feet moving ahead of his thoughts, Butt headed for the nearest companionway, pushing against the flow of people fighting their way up through the ship. From speaking with the captain at dinner he understood that the ship's fifth officer, Lowe, had brought a Browning semi-automatic pistol onboard, but could the young Welshman wield it against another man?

No… he thought to himself. *Such things are best left in the hands of professionals.*

The sounds had come from down below. As he descended the grand staircase, Archibald unbuttoned his overcoat and left it in the upraised arms of a carved cherub, giving him free access to his revolver. He had donned the weapon on his person when he noticed the activity outside his cabin, and now he drew it, nerves steady with years of trained discipline.

*

Hands trembling, his glasses lost in the madness, Byles slowly descended the stairs to E-Deck, emerging into a horrific scene. A young foreigner was laid out upon a stretcher on the deck, clothes around his stomach red with blood. To one side two members of the crew were attempting to apply pressure and reduce the bleeding, while a third sailor was on his feet, a lethal-looking rifle in his hands.

"Do you even know how to fire that thing?" taunted another voice, and Byles turned to see another man, this one armed with a more familiar revolver. "You probably just wasted half-a-clip because you had it set to full-automatic fire. I should know, I made the same mistake myself once."

Byles drew a sharp breath. The man with the revolver had a hostage, a small boy from steerage class that he was pinning to his chest with the same arm that held the gun, putting the child between himself and the other man's weapon.

"Pulls hard to the side, doesn't it?" the man continued. "I mean, you held down on the trigger for all that time and not one bullet connected with me. But then, you know all about how hard it is to steer something, don't you? Yeah, I heard your name, Mr Hichens."

Then his voice became cold. "Now drop the gun…"

The sailor named Hichens, one of the ship's Quartermasters from what Byles could see, swallowed and looked from side to side. He had brought the gun up to his shoulder like an old-fashioned musket man, eyes sighted along the barrel.

"Let… let the boy go first, Mr Abercrombie," he replied.

"No… no, I need something to leverage Captain Smith with," replied the man, Abercrombie, tousling the boy's hair with the butt of the gun. "Beside, this little brat is probably going to die tonight anyway. I think only one in three Third Class kids survive the sinking. But then, that's why they're steerage class, aren't they?

Lovely idea that, drives home how perfectly expendable they are. No modern rubbish about 'big society'."

"What are you talking about?" Hichens demanded, lowering his own gun slightly, and Abercrombie whipped his arm around with deathly speed, firing the revolver again. The gun flew out of the quartermaster's hands as he was spun around by the impact of the bullet, before his body crumpled up and collapsed down the stairs to F-Deck. Seeing the broken man's shattered form, Byles felt something in him snap, and as if a dam had come down he felt himself possessed of a burning, righteous rage.

"Three bullets down, three left!" Abercrombie was saying, all but bouncing on his feet with a demented energy. "And hey, you should be thanking me. One less useless, can't-steer-for-toffee sailor means one more space in a lifeboat for some other piece of scum."

The cheeriness of the words was deplorable. Byles breathed deep, remembering all he had ever taught his students in the Ongar boxing club about restraint. Stepping to the bottom of the stairs, he slowly raised his hands and coughed, trying to make himself seem harmless, while also fighting back against the fury welling up within him.

"If the boy's so worthless, why not trade him in for someone more valuable…"

Abercrombie looked up, and smiled. "Oh, how sweet, a brave priest coming to save the little boy. My, my. How things have changed in a century."

"You keep talking about 'time', and things that are 'going' to happen," Byles said, slowly walking sideways around the edge of the room, forcing Abercrombie to move as well. "What is the meaning behind that?"

"I don't know, Father, do you believe in predestination?" Abercrombie smiled nervously. "Because I've got two words for you that will sink that idea like the *Titanic* herself!"

As if protesting at her name being taken in vain, the ship groaned, and Abercrombie grinned mockingly. "See, even the boat is curious."

Byles stopped circling, and Abercrombie, dragging the boy behind him, stopped as well. He was now standing at the top of the stairs down to F-Deck, up which water was beginning to rise, the inrushing sea claiming the body of the dead quartermaster, trickles of his blood floating on the surface like red veins of oil.

This is He that came by water and blood; Jesus Christ; not by water only, but by water and blood. The words of the Mass Byles had recited only that morning churned in his memory unbidden, even as Abercrombie grinned devilishly, the gun in his hand extended towards Byles' own chest.

"And what words are those?" he asked, managing to maintain an even tone.

"Time travel, Father!" Abercrombie crowed. "Time travel! So all that shit you types like to spout about destiny and faith and the Grace of God, well you can take it all and shove it where the sun doesn't shine, because I'm the face of your future, and let me tell you, the twentieth century is a real shithole!"

"Your fault…" someone wheezed in accented English, and Abercrombie's attention shifted sideways from Byles to the young man on the stretcher. The dropped rifle had landed within reach of his arm, and despite his pain the injured man had taken it up and now had it levelled neatly at Abercrombie's head. "Your fault," he said again, struggling to form the words. "Your fault, that we're trapped here…"

Abercrombie's mouth moved silently, repeating the word 'trapped' and his face suddenly twisted up in a scream.

"Don't say that, DON'T SAY THAT!"

In that moment Byles threw himself forward in a sudden blur of motion, shifting his weight from foot to foot in best Marquess of Queensbury style to build up momentum. His fist flew out in a right hook, connecting cleanly, and Abercrombie's head snapped back, but he still held onto the gun. Byles grabbed the child by the shoulder and threw himself down into the flooding staircase well, pulling the boy with him.

*

"Shit!" Abercrombie sprang back and turned to flee up the long corridor that led aft, at which point a bullet buried itself in the bulkhead beside him. A man in a tailored suit was standing in the corridor, a handgun calmly braced in his hands and aimed at him. A neat moustache twitched as he spoke.

"Do not move," said Major Archibald Butt, his voice full of authority.

"Oh, great…" Abercrombie laughed, lifting the Webley towards the older man. "Another hero without the balls to shoo-"

Butt's gun fired once, the retort deafening in the confined space, and Adrian Abercrombie slumped onto his knees, staring in shocked disbelief at a bloody hole in the centre of his own chest. His revolver clattered to the deck and Butt picked it away as he strode past.

"I am a professional soldier, not a hero."

*

"Nicely done, father!" someone said approvingly, and Byles found a solidly-built gentleman assisting himself and the boy out of the flooding stairwell. As they dripped in misery, their rescuer tipped a nod to the young man on the stretcher. "And to you, young man…"

Nodding in gratitude, the olive-skinned youth sighed and fell back into the stretcher, clearly finding it a struggle to breathe. Relieved at this ordeal's end, Byles released the small boy, who immediately ran off without a word of thanks, hurrying up the stairs; no doubt in search of his family.

Then Byles turned his head, hearing a pitiful whimpering sound. The man named Abercrombie had folded up on the deck like a collapsed tent, chest heaving with an obscene sucking sound. The man was visibly on the threshold of death. Byles slowly limped forward, wincing where he had struck his leg in throwing himself down the stairs, and knelt beside the dying murderer. For some reason he now felt hollow, the frothing surge of rage and bile having passed him.

Abercrombie was crying, his mouth moving in inaudible words as his last scraps of life slipped away. Pulling him upright into a seated position, Byles held the dying man and prayed fervently, unsure of why he was trying to win such a broken soul forgiveness, but feeling the same fire of faith that had brought him to the Church.

154

To err is human, to forgive divine…

That was why. He had no idea who this man was, or the world that had shaped him, and never would. Only the Lord on high did, and if there was any shred of hope for this man, then he would pray for him. Hot tears trickled down his cheeks, blurring his vision. In his arms Abercrombie heaved several times, his last breaths emanating as a series of frightened whimpers, and then he fell limp with a final sigh, the part that was his immortal soul fleeing with that dying exhalation.

Where, in what country, in what time, did this life originate? Byles thought as he laid the man's body down to rest, just as a stampede of footsteps heralded the arrival of late reinforcements. One of the ship's officers, armed with a handgun and supported by several other crewmembers, was running towards them down the subtly sloping deck.

*

The young man on the stretcher was quickly removed to the ship's hospital for treatment, along with the bodies of Abercrombie and Quartermaster Hichens. Byles and Butt stood to one side, watching intently as Third Class passengers were loaded into the strange orange lifeboat and the external door in the ship's hull levered shut from the outside, just before water rose to its lip. The ship groaned as she sank further.

"Did he really say he was from the future, Father?" Butt asked softly.

Byles checked his watch. It had been not even ten minutes since the first gunshot, yet it seemed like it might have been hours. Time seemed to be flowing like water. "I find it hard to believe…" he said lowly. "And yet, what else might explain these events?"

Taking up the unfamiliar rifle, Butt quickly found the button that released the magazine, which slid out of the body of the weapon with a smooth click. A few more moments of experimentation allowed him to eject the unspent round in the firing chamber, after which he finally looked closely at the gun, and laughed faintly. "I have never seen a weapon comparable to this. And nor have I seen a man so flushed with madness or desperation, even during my service in Cuba."

Byles stared at the deck for some time, before kneeling and picking up a pair of thin-framed spectacles, which he returned to his nose. "I think, Major," he said at length, "that none of us have ever seen a night such as this."

The ship creaked loudly at that juncture, and Byles straightened up. "He said that only one in three Third Class children would survive, and I doubt that bodes well for their mothers and fathers. If you'll excuse me, Major Butt, I need to see if I can do something to change that statistic."

They shared nods, and Byles excused himself, leaving Butt to explain how they had pacified the situation to the crew.

Best not to mention time-travel, the Major thought to himself. *Would not do to confuse the situation further.*

But for his part, Archibald Butt felt calmed. He had been touring abroad in order to try and reconcile a conflict of loyalties to two of his friends, a conundrum which had left him stressed and wearied. Now, however, there was just the quiet certainty of a situation that required action.

"Mr Lowe, I presume?" he greeted the officer armed with the Browning. "I understand that the ship is sinking and that there are strange deeds afoot. How might I be of assistance?"

*

Safe aboard *Rescue* and struggling to make sense of her situation, Pip Paik gingerly felt along the dressing that had been wrapped around the crown of her head; she could feel a fresh crease about two inches over her left ear. *"Ah!"*

"I wouldn't press too hard on that, you might pop those sutures they put in your head," said Doctor Oshiro, like herself dressed in a heavy sweater, tan shirt and thick trousers. The clothes Pip had been given to replace her ruined dress were all allegedly in her size, but she still had to roll up the sleeves and tighten the belt as much as possible to avoid drowning in fabric.

"I know what I'm doing," she lied, wincing at the stinging sensation as she applied too much pressure. Red began to seep through the white bandages. "Shit, I'm bleeding again."

"I did warn you," Oshiro chided gently, standing alongside her and holding a wad of gauze to her temple. "Here, keep pressure on it. Now sit down, and try to conserve what blood you've got left."

He pressed down on her shoulder, gently but insistently, and a dizzy Pip sank onto a padded bunk. After the medical officer had sewn her head up, she and Oshiro had been asked to remain in the Doctor's cabin until sent for. Trying to stomach down another bout of wooziness, Pip drew her feet up onto the bed and watched as her companion rummaged around in stowage spaces, sorting through various belongings until at last he produced a baseball cap and handed it to her. Pip stared blankly at gilt lettering woven into the navy blue fabric.

T-ARS-54
USNS *Rescue*
Military Sealift Command

"To hold the dressing in place," he explained.

"Thanks," Pip muttered, and pulling back her hair she slipped the cap on and allowed her short locks to hang through the gap above the strap. As promised, the cap held the dressing in place, and hid the rest of her bandages.

"That might also keep you from scratching yourself," he added as he settled into a chair that faced her. For a short eternity they sat in silence, studying each other.

"I notice that we've not been formally introduced," he said at last, extending a long hand. "Akira Oshiro, IJN Ishiyama Shipyards."

"Phillipa Paik," she replied, reaching out to shake his spiderlike hand. "Texas A&M University."

Another uncomfortable pause followed; seeking to break it, Pip began to rummage through what belongings had been saved from the wreckage of the launch. Amazingly, her laptop looked alright, and she set it to one side for further evaluation. The dress, however, was ruined, the fabric spotted with blood and saltwater.

"Marilyn's going to kill me," she groaned in self-depreciation, momentarily wishing they'd never make port if only to escape the wrath that would ensue.

"I beg your pardon?" Oshiro enquired, and Pip raised her head from where she had tried to bury it in her knees. "My sister; she said that this dress was worth seven hundred dollars, made me promise to take good care of it."

"Well, to be fair, I doubt she foresaw you wearing it while being run down by a ship."

It was meant in good humour, but the offhand comment, instead of bringing a smile to Pip's face, instead reminded her of the elephant in the corner of the room.

"Oh, yeah…"she said softly, drawing her knees came up to her chest, while questions and emotions broiled inside of her. "What happened out there?" she finally asked.

"Honestly, I do not wish to guess," Oshiro's mouth twisted uncomfortably. "What do you suspect?"

"There was… an explosion, on the ship, and fire. The launch was burning… *the sea was on fire!*" Pip shuddered at the perverse memory of flames flickering on the water. "And then, someone was pulling me from the launch, and then… then…"

"Something else exploded," he finished for her. "Very loudly, and with a lot of… energy. The brightest light I have ever seen."

"Yes, but it felt… it felt like I was a piece of toffee being stretched, or a rubber band. That's not normal, is it?"

"Feeling like you are a passing fancy flying down a neuron in God's mind? No, that's not normal."

His calm overstatement made her laugh softly, and she smiled properly for the first time since before she had left *Oceanic*. "So what was it?"

"I suspect… though I am not sure… that something very powerful was being transported on the ship. Yes, very powerful, and profoundly dangerous," Oshiro murmured, lapsing back into silence. His expression was dark, but his eyes were bright with thought as he seemingly retreated to some deep inner laboratory. Unable to coax a further word from him, Pip grabbed hold of her laptop and cautiously booted it up. Thankfully it seemed the heavy-duty casing had protected it from impact damage, and the waterproof satchel had seemingly protected it from immersion in seawater, unlike her dress.

Testing it, she opened one of her media folders and clicked on the first file: **VID DIARY 001.**

"So long New York!" her voice shouted, tinny through the speakers. *"Seeya in a month!"*

Footage she had filmed on her handheld camcorder jumped around shakily, shot from the upper deck on the *Anatoly Sagalevich* as they set sail from New York, symbolically retracing the unfinished part of *Titanic's* maiden voyage. The ship's horn blared multiple times, and cars and trucks on the Manhattan shoreline bleeped and roared in response, though it was more likely that they were simply expressing their frustration at the gridlock.

"There, there's Pier 59!" her recorded counterpart said, as the camera zoomed in towards the nearly-finished *Titanic* Metropolitan Museum, sticking out into the river, before the whole field of reference spun so that she could position herself between the lens and the pier. *"That's where Titanic should have docked! And in a month and a half, part of her will complete that voyage! Isn't that amazing!?"*

Blurring again, the image finally stabilised as camerawoman-Pip rested her elbows on the ship's rail, forming a crude tripod. Now individual faces could be made out among the crowds sending off to the ship, and the video focused in on one of them, a young woman in a tailored business-suit, beaming and waving goodbye.

"Bye Mari!" Pip's voice shouted. *"Thanks for the dress! Keep an eye out for me on the news!"*

Marilyn Paik's mouth could be seen to move, but her words were drowned out among the roar of the crowds and the sudden din of a tannoy announcement.

"Ladies and Gentlemen. Project 401, the Titanic Centennial Expedition, is now underway!"

The cheers of the crew on deck were enough to blow out the camcorder's microphone. Far below, Mari, still the focus of the shot, jumped up and down, both hands raised in Victory-Vs as she cheered her sister good luck and goodbye.

Watching it, Pip smiled fondly, and then her expression grew serious. Marilyn would have been watching one of the live newsfeeds back home, and probably saw part of that runaway ship's near-collision with the *Anatoly Sagalevich*.

She must be worried sick.

Leaving the video to run, Pip minimized the window and opened her email client.

'Dear Mari,' she typed. *'You might hear on the news that things have gone crazy out here. I actually got run down by a ship half an hour ago, but don't worry, I'm alright, just got a little hurt on my head, but I think the expedition might be cut short.*

Need to rest now, but will keep you in the loop.

Love, Pip

PS: The dress got ruined. All my sorries'

Dragging the cursor to 'send', Pip clicked, feeling a bit of relief at having gotten that off her chest. She closed her eyes, exhaling, only for them to snap back open again when the laptop chimed to signify an error.

MESSAGE FAILED TO SEND: NETWORK UNAVAILABLE

"That's weird…" She glanced towards the signal bar; it had automatically picked up *Rescue*'s own extension of the Project 401 wireless network, the security key and password for which she had committed to memory. She should have internet access.

Licking her lips in a moment of nerves, she tried to open her web browser, and got a blank screen for her efforts, not even a '404' Error Message or a *'server could not be found'* write-up. It was as if the entire internet had vanished…

Okay, no worries… there's probably just something wrong with the ship's antenna…

Saving the message as a draft, she returned to the video diary. New York onscreen had now receded to the horizon, a forest of skyscrapers shrinking into the distance as the *Anatoly Sagalevich* passed under the Verrazano-Narrows Bridge.

"There it goes…" the diary concluded. *"It's not the first time I've been to sea, but I've got to say, it's always a bit frightening to see your home fading into the distance like this. But hey, in four or five weeks we'll be back, bringing an entire ship's worth of treasures with us."*

The camera swung around so that Pip's own face once more filled the screen, smiling cheekily.

"And I'm going to bring you guys watching online along, every step of the way! From the Anatoly Sagalevich, on the first day of the Titanic Centennial Expedition, this is Philippa Paik, signing off. Seeya all soon!"

Feeling suddenly uneasy, Pip closed the laptop's screen and tried to relax. Lying back on the bunk, the warmth of the thick clothes she had been leant finally began to displace the cold that had seeped into her bones. *Rescue*'s engines growled comfortably away below decks, the cabin tilting as the ship manoeuvred through a turn. She began to feel quite cosy, and the bunk was surprisingly soft...

...suddenly feet were scurrying on the deck above her head, and she could hear the sounds of machinery stirring into life. Was *Rescue* in trouble now? Or going to the aid of another ship? She suddenly feared for her friends on the *Sagalevich*; had that monster ship done more than blindside it?

"I'm going out," she announced, with confidence that surprised herself. Doctor Oshiro, who had not stirred once while she had been using the laptop, grunted in answer, his mind parsecs away in deep space for all she knew. Stuffing the loose ends of her trousers into the open top of a pair of boots loaned to her, Pip quickly laced up, pulled on a bomber jacket with *Rescue*'s badge emblazoned on the shoulder, and exited the cabin, quickly finding the main deck. It seemed the rain had stopped, though a thick fog had sprung up, shrouding the work lights.

Directly overhead however, shining through the murk like rays from heaven, were wispy rays of multicoloured light. An aurora.

Staring in awestruck wonder, Pip's eyesight gradually adjusted, and in the dim light coming from the sky she began to make out black objects drifting past in the water. Were they shipping containers dropped by the runaway *Seguin Laroche*, like a trail of breadcrumbs? No, the shapes were too irregular. Then one ground slowly down the side of the hull, glowing pale white in the ship's lights, shimmering with crystalline reflections.

Ice. They were giant chunks of ice. Even as her mind asserted that the weather was too warm for ice to have reached *Titanic*'s wreck site, Pip inhaled a fiercely cold breath of air, and sharp pain cut into her mouth like toothache. Well, that explained where the fog had come from; warm, rain-moistened air had run into this sudden cold front.

And it was cold, she now realised, freezing even, as if the temperature had dropped by tens of degrees in a matter of minutes.

Ironically appropriate on tonight of all nights. They said it was incredibly cold... the lookouts were told to maintain a keen watch for small ice and growlers... survivors described the night air near the ice field as having a strange, earthy smell to it, and that when the sun came up, those in the lifeboats could see pack ice on all sides, and the bergs lording over them like white mountains.

Amazed, she watched the first mini-iceberg, a growler, vanish astern. Then, peering around, she spotted other dark objects just beyond the reach of the lights, craggy shapes that faded in and out of sight amid the drifting fog. And yes, now that she looked for it, she swore there was a strange smell in the air, like freshly turned soil, or the scent of Dad's vegetable patch, back before he and Mom...

Icebergs, she realised. *These are actual icebergs, as described on the night of Titanic's sinking!*

Suddenly, *Rescue's* foghorn boomed out, and even as Pip dropped to her knees and covered her ears to block out the din, she found herself turning to look forward, tingles of fearful anticipation running across her skin, waiting for whatever was out there to respond.

When it did, she felt like she had been punched in the stomach.

CHAPTER NINE

As Managing Director of Harland & Wolff, Shipbuilders of Belfast, Ireland, Thomas Andrews' profession was ships; the designing of ships, the construction of ships, the operation and improvement of ships. They were his life and livelihood.

But when he followed Captain Smith down to inspect *Titanic*'s lower decks, he quickly realised that his entire life might be defined by the loss of this ship.

The *Titanic* was going to sink.

He had not noticed the collision with the iceberg, nor had he seen or heard the explosive flash of light that had allegedly followed. But he had felt the engines stop, and almost immediately a steward had arrived with the message that the captain urgently requested his presence on the ship's bridge. Andrews had grabbed a set of general arrangement drawings bound up with string and followed immediately from his cabin, up the grand staircase, and through the officer's quarters to the chart room. Along the way he had been joined by Bruce Ismay, President of the International Mercantile Marine and General Manager for the White Star Line, and the two friends and business partners had shared a silent conversation marked out only by the terse tread of their feet on the deck as they climbed through the hull. Thomas had still been dressed when summoned, and had simply thrown on his overcoat. Ismay, however, had been in bed, and now wore a dressing gown over his pyjamas; he was pacing along in burgundy slippers.

As they passed the wireless room, Andrews saw the door open and Harold Bride, the junior of the ship's two Marconi operators, had run past them, still clad in his nightshirt. As the door swung shut the senior operator, Jack Phillips, had yelled after the younger man to check the antennae and try and "find out where this dratted interference is coming from."

Thomas added it to the growing list of concerns silently accumulating in his mind. But he had reassured himself that the ship was built to the highest standards possible, and over-engineered to withstand the worst damage imaginable.

The shipbuilding press might be putting out exaggerated claims of Titanic being 'practically unsinkable', but she is still a sound ship, perhaps the safest afloat. If she has taken on water, our much-vaunted watertight door design will contain any flooding to the damaged compartments.

But he still felt a chill of unease when he arrived on the bridge and was informed that the ship had struck a berg. A simple glance at the inclinometer confirmed that *Titanic* had developed a list to starboard, and was down slightly at the bow. After the initial damage reports had arrived from Officer Wilde and Carpenter Hutchinson, he had joined Captain Smith to make a second inspection. Thomas had felt familiar buoyancy calculations whirring in the back of his mind, numbers dropping into place. *Titanic* was designed as a 'two-compartment' ship, able to remain afloat should a collision compromise her right on the bulkhead between any two of her watertight compartments, but the reduced volume in the tapering prow meant the ship could stay afloat with the first four of her sixteen compartments flooded. It was with that knowledge in mind, as he and Smith descended the stairs into the depths of the hull, that Thomas had assured himself that there was no scenario that could damage a hull along three hundred feet of its length.

When he saw the mail hold quickly filling to the roof, sorters hauling up sodden bags of letters to higher decks, he found himself proved wrong. Quickly corroborating the reports, he realised to his horrified disbelief that the ship was stricken, fatally. The pumps were keeping incoming water down in Boiler Room 5, but Boiler Room 6 and the three holds ahead of it were filling with water. Wilde's report of air hissing out of the ship's anchor-chain locker at high pressure suggested that even the forepeak compartment, reinforced to withstand head-old collisions, was open to the sea.

Six compartments flooding freely, five of them lost causes.

By the time those five filled to the tops of the bulkheads, cool formulae informed him, *Titanic* would have taken on nearly fifteen thousand tons of water. And then, as the bow went down and the water came up, it would slop over into Boiler Room 5 and overwhelm the pumps there.

Like dominoes falling, the mechanics of what would happen etched themselves into his mind. The ship would settle slowly at first, as if bedding herself down to sleep. But then the flooding stability curves would pass through the moment of equilibrium and turn negative. At that point she would begin to dive, until the fatal moment was reached where the hull took on more water than it could displace. *Titanic was going to sink.*

Mockingly, in an almost sing-song voice, the presence at the back of his thoughts pointed out that the twenty lifeboats aboard were sufficient to hold twelve hundred people, at most.

Twelve hundred, against a total passenger and crew allowance of over three thousand and five hundred people.

He knew the ship was not full to capacity – sailings in April rarely were – but for a brief moment he wanted to pound his head at the fact that the she carried only enough lifeboats for one in three.

All of this was processed in the few moments it took for the swirling water to submerge the mail deck. At the captain's shout Thomas backpedalled up the staircase, water lapping at his shoes. Electric lights burned a luminescent green below the surface.

"What's the verdict, Mr Andrews?" Smith had asked, his voice level, but his eyes grim. "How badly damaged is she?"

"I… I…" Tom's mouth had moved wordlessly; already he had jumped beyond the knowledge that the ship was going to sink, instead trying to calculate how long she had.

An hour or two maybe? How long before the weight of water overcomes her remaining buoyancy?

He could not see her remaining afloat long after the pumps in Boiler Room 5 were overwhelmed. Would the crew even have enough time to launch what few lifeboats they did have? And what of the people left to freeze in Arctic waters?

She can't sink, but she can't float!

165

The distant blast of an unfamiliar foghorn blew away those thoughts like warm summer wind. Thomas spun on his heel and saw the same light in Smith's face. Another ship was nearby, one that might volunteer to serve as a single gigantic lifeboat for all of *Titanic*'s passengers and crew.

As they had rushed up the stairs, Smith surprisingly hale and nimble for a man of sixty-two, Andrews had paused. Should he warn the fireman quartered here in the bow that they might have less than an hour to live? He halted at the top of the spiralling staircase that connected the stokeholds to the firemen's quarters. Such an announcement might cause a panic, which they would need the least at a time like this.

The sounds of gurgling far below snapped him out of his reverie, and he glanced down; black water swirled tempestuously at the foot of the stairs. Grabbing one of the men, Andrews quickly passed on the message to get the rest out of bed. As he followed Smith out onto the open well deck, he suddenly felt the hull trembling beneath his feet, could practically hear the frames and hull girders jumping in their bedplates; the ship had gone into full reverse; something else was wrong.

Screaming voices cut into him as sharply as the cold night air, and his first thought was that an unwise word had sparked a panic among the passengers. But as *Titanic* roared warnings again from her triple-note whistles, he saw the captain staring up in disbelief, and turned.

What in blazes!?

Titanic had appeared to be backing into a dock, sliding past a vertical wall of metal that towered over the well deck like the terminal jetties on New York's Hudson River. Then the liner was heaved aside on a wave of displaced water, and Thomas realised he was looking at another ship, a ship larger and more massive than he had ever conceptualised. He saw the burning decks, the figures fighting the flames, faintly shouted words rising over the roaring fire. None were in languages he could understand.

As the intruder raced on into the dark, Thomas caught a glimpse of her name and port-of-registry. The words SEGUIN LAROCHE, MAJURO, stamped themselves onto his mind, and then the ship's flat transom vanished into the night...

Looking back now it seemed surreal, a dream made all the more strange by the swirling fog now wreathing the ship. He had helped a First Class passenger, young Mr Thayer, to his feet and finally, having removed the captain from a rush of curious bystanders, confided in him that his command was quickly floundering.

Smith took it better than Andrews had expected; the shock broke over him like a wave on the shore, alarm flashing clearly on his face but receding before the indefatigable bulk of experience and protocol.

"We'll run the boats out, at once, and try to convince that beast to return and take on our passengers…"

Now, however, the news that a madman from the *Seguin Laroche* had murdered two of the crew, including Chief Officer Wilde, almost felled the Captain.

"Good Lord… it was by my request that he was onboard with us, Thomas, and now his four small children are orphaned…" Smith said, aghast, before finding some superhuman reserve of strength and setting to mucking in alongside his crew in Wilde's place, directing the swinging out of the boats.

Andrews helped too, demonstrating how to operate the new design of lifeboat davit installed on *Titanic*, his shouts almost drowned out by the sound of the steam escaping from the funnels. Through the chaos, he had briefly caught a glimpse of Bruce Ismay, still in his pyjamas, cranking away at one of the windlasses with a crewman.

He then considered going down to begin assisting in rounding up the passengers, but word of the strange events, near-collision and death of two crewmen had circulated quickly, and passengers were making their way up to the boat decks without prompting, the first of them standing nervously to one side in their white lifejackets. The mustering power of rumour was so thorough that stewards were having to direct people back down to the public rooms in order to leave enough room for the men to work. Tom, Bruce and Smith had all agreed that it was essential that a panic not be spread in the event that the mystery ship, the *Seguin Laroche*, did not return in response to their distress signals, but confusion among the passengers threatened to become anxiety.

"Third Class passengers are refusing to stay below decks!" reported one steward. "They're gathering on the stern castle and in the aft well deck, demanding to be let up to the boat deck."

"There's no room!" Smith replied. "If all the passengers from all three classes rush the boats at once, we'll not be able to get a single one launched safely."

"What can we do, EJ?" Tom replied. "A madman was running around with a gun in their part of the ship, and water is already rising into their accommodation. They know better than most that the situation is dangerous, and have just as much a right to fight for their lives."

Smith's mouth had hung open for a second, as if the growing tragedy was overwhelming the man, and then his expression had steeled as he laid eyes on the ship's eight musicians, striking up lively tunes outside the First Class entranceway.

"Mr Hartley!" the Captain called to the bandmaster. "Take your lads right to the aftermost part of A-Deck, overlooking the Third Class deck space. Play whatever it takes to keep the steerage passengers calm!"

And so, ironically, the band provided for the entertainment of the millionaires and the bourgeoisie in First and Second Class had relocated to a spot where they could be seen and heard by all the immigrant passengers threatening to swarm the upper decks. After a few lively renditions of popular numbers they had started taking requests from the mass of people gathering below, and when Thomas passed by, he spotted a young couple in the crowd dancing happily to the tune of a waltz, unaware of the shortage of lifeboats that might very well mean whether or not they lived or died.

The Captain's suggestion was perhaps a cruel delaying tactic, but a smart move.

Let's just hope the boys in the Marconi Room can get that monstrous ship to return to us, he thought to himself. *God willing, the rest of her crew are not gun-wielding maniacs!*

In possession of the knowledge that a ship was nearby and potentially able to help, he found himself unable to leave the boat deck. Instead, he gratefully accepted a pair of binoculars provided by Second Officer Lightoller and stood on the bridge wing, scouring into the dark fog for any glimpse of a light. It gave him time to think, and aside from revising his estimated sinking time for the ship upwards to sometime around 2 o'clock in the morning, he worried about what to do were a ship to respond. How could they transfer several thousand frightened people off of *Titanic* while not endangering whatever vessel came to their aid?

And of course, such thoughts drew him to the unsettling nature of the *Seguin Laroche*...

She's obviously in some distress herself, that much is true. Perhaps there has been a mutiny, but even taking that into consideration, her very existence is inexplicable!

As one of the world's leading marine architects, Thomas was unaware of any facility in Christendom where something the size of the *Seguin Laroche* could have been built.

Next month Blohm and Voss in Hamburg are going to launch their 52,000 ton leviathan Imperator, which will comfortably outstrip even Titanic's prodigious size, but the Seguin Laroche seemed to be at least 30,000 tons in excess of even Imperator. Who would have the funds to build such a ship, and where, and why in secret?

There was a blinding flash that tore him from his musings. Beside him a pair of quartermasters had arrived bearing a box of signal rockets, and under the instruction of Fourth Officer Boxhall they were beginning to fire them from a vertical tube mounted in the rail beside the bridge; when they pulled a lanyard fitted to the shells, an explosive charge shot the powerful flare out of the stumpy tube like a cannon, to explode high overhead in a shower of stars.

"Launch them closer together," he reminded Boxhall, who seemed to find a way to be doing several jobs at once. "Remember, they only signify distress if fired at one-minute intervals."

The young officer flushed at being chided, but complied with a nod. To Boxhall's credit, he was the only one who had thought of using starbursts to try and draw the attention of any ships nearby, but Thomas wondered if even the socket shells would be enough to penetrate the fog that still pressed in on them, the fume now so great as to hide even what was allegedly an incredible aurora overhead.

And where did that come from? And what caused the St Elmo's fire that was sighted on the ship's rigging before we encountered the Seguin

Laroche? More and more questions, but when do we deserve to get some answers!?

He was still standing at the rail, sweeping the binoculars from side to side and wreathed in cordite smoke from the shells, when Harold Bride, the junior Marconi-man, found him.

"Mr Andrews! You're needed in the wireless room," the young man declared, outwardly calm, but his words curtly frustrated. "A ship nearby is requesting technical particulars that we can't provide."

Thomas wondered if the two radio operators were aware of the severity of the ship's position, but followed with a nod. Inside the telegraph room, Jack Phillips was bent over the wireless key, banging away in quick bursts and then listening with a hand to his headphones for agonisingly long breaks. With his other hand he scribbled down incoming messages.

"Thank you for coming, Mr Andrews," he fumed, shouting over the ever-present roar from the safety valves as he pushed the slip of paper towards Tom. "Please take a look at this. I don't know who this idiot is, but his spark is terrible and he doesn't even know shorthand. And then the bugger went and started asking idiot questions of me!"

Ignoring the coarse language, Thomas scanned through the message.

MGY, request details of your damage and rate of flooding, please stand by for assistance

"Is this from the *Seguin Laroche*?" he enquired, turning the paper over in the hope of finding words more on the reverse side.

"No, some fool calling himself *Res...* hold on," Phillips held a hand to his ear as if struggling to hear and scribbled down more words, snorting as he did. "Now he's insisting the position we sent him is wrong, and asking us to sound our whistle instead."

He ripped loose the sheet from his pad. "Here, Harry, pass that to the captain."

As Bride left the cabin with the scrap in hand, Thomas used the stub of a purple pencil he used to annotate diagrams to scribble down *settling at the head, taking water in forward six compartments, estimated 2000 tons in first five minutes.*

Then he focused his attention on Phillips, a sense of relief rising in him. "This ship thinks he's close enough to hear us?"

"Must do, he's certainly close enough to blow my ears off. Said he saw the *Seguin Laroche* himself not that long ago, and that they're tracking north to meet us…" Bride trailed off as he began to Morse what Thomas had scribbled down.

Thomas' own burgeoning relief began to settle warmly in his stomach as he strained his ears, listening for a response. He never drank himself, but he suspected this was what whiskey was meant to feel like. "How big did he say he was?"

"That's the thing, he didn't say! I only get short messages from him, and he sounds like a rinky-dink ship – listen!" Bride removed the headset for a second to massage his ears, and Thomas held one of the speakers to his own. Instead of the sharp buzzes and clicks he associated with Marconi equipment, he heard a series of screamed tones coming in stuttering bursts.

"See what I mean?" Phillips frowned wearily. "And it's stamping on all my other signals. I've had the *Californian*, the *Frankfurt*, *Mount Temple* and even *Olympic* on the line, but that idiot slams the door on them every time he transmits. The stooge on the *Frankfurt* is bad enough, but at least he can format messages. It's the worst spark I've ever heard, and I think the operator is drunk."

Without even taking the headphones back from Thomas he began to bang away at his key again.

"*Rescue*, keep out, shut up, I'm working other ships."

"*Rescue?*"

"That's what he keeps calling himself. USNS *Rescue*," Phillips replied. "But I've never heard of a ship with that designation before, and there's no '*Rescue*' listed on the North Atlantic Wireless Charts. I asked for his call sign and he replied with a bunch of gibberish."

The headset began to click in Tom's hand with familiar Morse tones, and Phillips took it back quickly.

"*MPA*… that's the *Carpathia*… he's asking me if I've got interference! See, he can't have heard anything I put out before… '*did you know Cape Race has traffic for you*', bloody hell…"

He began to signal back in a machine-gun staccato. "Come at once! We have struck a berg! It's a CQD old man!"

Thomas checked the clock over the Morse equipment and left the cabin as Phillips continued to bang out their position.

It was 12.15am, thirty-five minutes since the collision. Feeling somewhat dazed, he came back out onto the boat deck. Steam was still gushing at high pressure from the safety valves on the funnels, and glancing up towards the source of the noise he saw the silent whistles mounted on the forward faces of the towering structures. Then, with new life, he ran towards the bridge.

He found Bride and Captain Smith in the wheelhouse, the younger man gesturing at the piece of paper in Smith's hand. The Captain shook his head in disbelief and Bride spoke up as he saw Thomas enter.

"Mr Andrews, you were there sir! Tell the captain what *Rescue* said."

"Thomas, Sparks here claims there's a ship close enough that she wants us to sound our whistle; is this true?" Smith intoned, his voice grave.

"Yes, Captain. Mister Phillips doesn't think much of her operator, but the *Rescue* says she saw the *Seguin Laroche* not long before we did; she must surely be nearby."

"Nevertheless," Smith growled, eyes drifting towards the whistle cord that hung from the roof. "I'm disinclined to sound a signal; the passengers are already becoming distressed, and they might interpret it as a sign of distress. We need no further cause for panic, or we may find ourselves saving no lives instead of some."

As Thomas struggled to find a counter-argument, a long, sustained note reverberated from out beyond the ship. If it was a whistle, it was the flattest, ugliest sounding one Thomas had ever heard. But to both him and the Captain, it was a message straight from heaven.

"Maybe it might give the passengers hope, EJ."

With the certainty of another ship close at hand, Smith nodded, and as Thomas ran back out to the railing, Lightoller's binoculars thumping against his chest, *Titanic*'s triple-bell chime whistles bellowed; a rich, brassy tone so different to the blare she was answering.

Seconds later, the stranger replied, its voice undulating like the drone of thousands of angered bees. It was like no whistle Thomas had ever heard, and in light of how much the *Seguin Laroche* alone troubled him, he felt a sudden dread at what might emerge from the fog.

The baritone blast that echoed out of the dark ahead was like a trumpet call from out of the dark of history. Even distorted by the fog, Pip recognised it straight away.

She had heard it before.

As if dreaming (was she dreaming?), she began to move forward along the deck, until she was standing below *Rescue's* bridge, overshadowed by red emergency fenders slung under the superstructure. Voices clamoured from above her, while the crew's shadows flitted about like ghosts in the mist. Dead ahead she could see a milky light made hazy through the fog, growing brighter as they slowly edged closer.

"They've heard us. Make for that whistle!"

"Five hundred yards and closing."

"I've cleared the radar up, sir. It shows at least seventy contacts within two nautical miles. I think there are only three ships out there, and the rest are all icebergs, but I've got no idea where they could have come from!"

"Reduce speed to five knots, minimum steerage."

"Kai, we've got the pumps out of the hold, the hoses too."

"Sir, MGY finally gave me his ship's actual name-"

"Not yet, son, we'll see soon enough."

"But Captain, it's got to be a joke. He says that he's aboard the-"

"Ship ahead!"

"Oh my God!"

The three simple words were not enough to convey Pip's feelings. Slowly she sank to her knees, clutching onto the rail tight enough that her knuckles turned white, as *Rescue* pierced the veil of the fog.

"Stop all engines, right full rudder."

As they drifted forward on the ship's momentum, Pip stared.

Rescue was coasting straight at a vertical wall of black metal, studded with glowing portholes. The mystery ship's hull was not smooth, but made up of overlapping metal plates, hobbled together with rivets. Pip had seen it before, through the tiny window of a submersible. But this was not a cold, decaying corpse buried at the bottom of the ocean; the paintwork gleamed with new life, and from every window, every deck, hundreds of faces stared at the strange interloper.

Their faces were white, their eyes wide as black pits. They looked like they had seen a ghost.

Rescue was now turning, and as they came parallel to the other vessel Pip's eyes slowly travelled upwards, past the black hull, to a pristine white superstructure trimmed in gold. Wooden lifeboats hung like children's toys from davits on the uppermost deck, and towering overhead were four tan funnels, their tips neatly picked out in black. Steam vented from valves on them with a deafening roar, and as *Rescue* came past a wheelhouse that was so terrifyingly familiar, the other ship roared again with its main whistles, bellowing a thankful welcome to the smaller ship.

She trembled, knowing what was coming next, and looked forward. There, incised into the other vessel's bow in letters four feet high, was a very familiar name. She mouthed the three syllables to herself, struck dumb by what she was seeing, just as an equally hushed silence fell over *Rescue*, punctuated by low murmurs, until at last a gruff voice asserted itself.

"Dammit, what's happened? I can't see, remember."

Pip suddenly felt life return to her, and without thought she scrambled up the first companionway she saw, shouldered her way through a door, and burst onto the bridge. Crewmen stared at her, while a slender youth she guessed to be the radioman was struggling to put into words what they were all seeing to a figure seated in the centre of the room, expression masked by a pair of aviator sunglasses.

"Who are you?" someone asked. Pip ignored him and crossed to the radioman, a boy who still stood an inch taller than her.

"Did he say he was MGY?" she demanded, pointing through the windows at the impossible ship.

"It's the girl from the launch," another man muttered.

"Did he say he was MGY?" Pip repeated, almost ready to shake the answer out of the radioman.

"Miss!" the man in the chair yelled, the single word layered with command. Pip paused in her attempts to choke the unfortunate youth into giving her the answer she needed, and looked towards him. Despite the sunglasses, his disapproval was evident.

"Sorry," she muttered, suddenly abashed. "It's just, a bit much, you know."

"That is all well and good, but given that my subordinates have suddenly swallowed their own tongues, would you please explain what has happened?"

Pip drew herself up straight and tried to compose herself; remembering her presentation from earlier, she drew a breath and felt a wave of calm certainty wash over her. Facts, she could repeat facts fearlessly.

"MGY was the radio call sign of the RMS *Titanic*."

"*Excuse me?*"

*

Thomas felt the warmth in his stomach curl and die, drowned in ice.

The newcomer, small but determined-looking, had come alongside *Titanic*, turning with an agility that he could not explain. Manoeuvrability was not the only thing about her that perplexed him, however. Her lines were fiercely sharp and angular, and from her waterline all the way to the strange spires and spikes that adorned her mast, her form and construction spoke of an origin and purpose that defied his understanding. He held the binoculars to his eyes and focused on a nameplate affixed above the wheelhouse door.

"*Rescue*."

"Mr Andrews, sir?" asked one of the quartermasters, unable to keep a note of fear out of his gruff voice. "What kind of a ship is that, sir?"

"I don't know, Mr Rowe," Thomas replied as he slowly lowered the lenses and looked around. He had expected the arrival of a ship to create a sense of euphoria, but passengers who had kept their calm now murmured with confusion. Crewmembers paused in the middle of swinging out lifeboats to stare. Others were looking around for some figure of authority to explain the situation. A sinking ship was a certainty, but the arrival of an inexplicable, threatening vessel was not something they were mentally prepared to deal with. Thomas could feel the urge of panic pressing at the fringes of his own mind, a primitive response to the unknown and uncertain.

Shaking himself, he crossed to the already loaded distress mortar and yanked on the cord.

*

There was a sudden flash from beyond *Rescue's* bridge, and seconds later a sharp crack. Through the windows Pip saw white stars drifting down from a point in the sky, lighting everything up as bright as day; a distress rocket.

One of the distress rockets.

Her eyes drifted down to the lowest row of portholes she could see on *Titanic*, and with a chill she realised that they were pitching down into the oily black water. Two entire decks were already submerging. Glancing around, she looked up and saw the bridge clock; the time was fifteen minutes past midnight.

It's almost a perfect match, but then we had the fleet's clocks synched to local time…

Dimly, she realised that the captain was speaking. "Miss, are you suggesting that…"

She looked straight at him. The cap that Doctor Oshiro had appropriated for her suddenly felt heavy on her uneasy head. The captain wore the exact same design, enhanced with gold leaf and the title of '**Captain J Jones.**'

"The *Titanic*, Captain Jones; your ship has come to the aid of the RMS *Titanic*. And at this point, she has just over two hours left to live."

Slowly, Jones turned to face in the general direction of a subordinate. Pip recognised the younger, bronze-skinned man from Dean Simmons' newscast. Kai Alinka.

"Is what she saying true?"

"Sir, it sounds crazy, but I can't deny what my eyes are telling me," came the reply, moderated with a quick addendum. "No offense intended, sir."

"None taken," Jones muttered. He began to slowly massage his temples, and turned his head towards the rear bulkhead, as if blindly visualising it. Pip followed with her eyes and saw the ship's crest branded onto the steel, along with *Rescue*'s motto. **For I am full of Spirit and Resolve**.

"Cameron!" Jones suddenly whipped around to the radioman, snapping orders. "Contact the *Oceanic* and the *Anatoly Sagalevich*. Inform them of this development, and ask for them to come immediately. We're going to need their lifeboats."

"And what do we do, sir?" asked the man who had tried to remove Pip from the bridge.

"We continue as planned, Mr Miller," Jones said, his voice firm, if tinged with stunned disbelief. "Prepare to lend pumping assistance to the *Titanic*."

*

The double bang and flash from the socket shell Thomas had launched seemed to break the spell, and after another minute of confused but relatively calm murmuring amongst the passengers, Captain Smith emerged from the wheelhouse with a metal loudhailer in hand. The sight of the venerable master in his impeccably pressed uniform, medals bright on his breast, helped restore a sense of normalcy as he crossed the wing to where Andrews stood. The two of them exchanged an uncertain glance, before Smith hefted the loudhailer to his mouth.

"Vessel '*Rescue*', this is Captain Smith of the Royal Mail Steamer *Titanic*; thank you for responding to our hails."

There was a long silence, and then Andrews saw movement on the bridge of the other vessel. Hefting the binoculars to his eyes revealed a young man in a tan uniform emerge with a device that resembled Smith's loudhailer, only thicker and made of an unfamiliar white material. He held it to his mouth, and Thomas winced as it produced a shrieking whine for several seconds, before emitting a majestically enhanced voice.

"*...dammit. Testing, testing. Hello? Captain Smith! This is Lieutenant Miller of the USNS Rescue, attached to the Military Sealift Command. I speak for my commanding officer, Captain Jones.*"

The accent was American, his rank pronounced phonetically instead of the '*lefthenant*' expected from a British officer. As Thomas struggled to recall if he had ever heard of a 'Military

177

Sealift Command', Captain Smith replied. With the opening niceties dealt with, negotiations could now begin.

"Lieutenant, please request your captain to swing out your boats and prepare to receive our passengers."

Thomas saw Miller lower his own loudhailer, which he had now decided was somehow mechanically or electronically amplified, and turn towards the dark interior of his own wheelhouse. Seconds later a second figure joined him, a diminutive form in a similar uniform. A minimalist cap obscured the newcomer's face as they made several pointed gestures towards *Titanic*, before Miller turned and shouted back at someone who Thomas presumed was Captain Jones.

"…well, can I tell them?"

"Yes, but don't confuse things…"

Miller shrugged and finally returned his attention to *Titanic*. *"Captain Smith! I have been informed by an expert that if unaided your ship will sink completely within two hours. Our travelling companion Oceanic is coming to provide lifeboats, but Rescue is equipped for marine salvage and we believe we can best assist by keeping your vessel afloat as long as possible. We have hull repair equipment on board and a pumping capacity of 7,500 tons per hour."*

The words hit Tom like a sledgehammer, even as his inner voice enquired if Miller's figures were in imperial or metric. He looked at Captain Smith, who was equally stunned, his open mouth a dark hole amidst his finely trimmed moustache and beard. Passengers began to shout at the confirmation of *Titanic*'s remaining lifespan, and someone fired off a gun to silence their cries. After an agonising moment when Thomas feared the Captain had finally been rendered insensible after all of the past hour's madness, Smith whipped the loudhailer back to his mouth.

"Thank you *Rescue* – please raft alongside to port and have your equipment ready!" He lowered the device and whipped around to address the officers and senior crew, his eyes burning.

"We have to act quickly. This *fool* has possibly prompted the same panic we tried to avoid, but he's offering us more than we asked for... Mr Pitman, please take Purser McElroy and the other junior officers and continue lowering the starboard boats only. Someone find Mr Lightoller and direct him to go below to supervise opening the port and starboard gangway doors – we'll need to run suctions through and transfer passengers to other ships' boats. Mister Murdoch, please issue arms to all the officers in the event of further attacks on our ship, and then co-ordinate with *Rescue* to bring her alongside."

As his staff began to disperse on their missions, relief at having something definite to focus on showing on their faces, Smith looked at Tom.

"Mr Andrews, if we're to receive pumping assistance, we'll need you and your boys from the guarantee group to bring your technical expertise to bear below. I can't order you to do down there, but it would be appreciated."

"It's not a problem Captain; we'll do the best we can."

"Thank you, Thomas," the Captain nodded, laying a grateful hand on Tom's shoulder. "If need be, ask Chief Bell to lend you assistance from the engineering staff."

Thomas nodded and took his leave to round up the Harland & Wolff staff onboard, the guarantee group sent to assist with any teething troubles on a ship's maiden voyage. Despite the air of optimism given off by the officers, he feared that Smith was deluding himself. It may already be too late to save his ship, and all of the 2,200 souls aboard.

*

"Come up quick!" Pip said, pushing her way into the cabin with mad abandon. Doctor Oshiro, still sitting thoughtfully in his chair, looked up at the sudden interruption.

"What is it?"

Pip was frantically pushing her laptop into its carry bag, and paused to stare at him in disbelief. "You didn't hear? People shouting back and forth across the centuries with megaphones and you didn't hear a word?" With the laptop now slung over her shoulder she grabbed hold of his wrist and pulled him upright. "You wanted to know what happened when that ship exploded, come and see!"

He shook himself free of her grasp, but followed without complaint as she retraced her steps back onto the deck. Scurrying up the last staircase she threw open a door onto the deck with a massive smirk on her face, arm outstretched towards another ship, which *Rescue* was drawing alongside of.

"Ta-da!" she proclaimed. "Doctor Oshiro, I give you the *Titanic*, whisked a hundred years out of her time to join us in the twenty-first century!"

Akira lowered his glasses as if to confirm the ship was not just some giant smear on the lenses. "Unbelievable," he whispered quietly. "It's undeniably *Titanic*... but how do you know that..."

He turned his head, to find his excitable companion had already run off into the fog. His breath misted slightly in the cold.

"...that it isn't *we* who have moved in time," he finished lamely. With no-one present to answer him, he began to walk forward, eyes fixated on the riveted hull that rose sheer from the sea across from him. A light pall of smoke lingered in the air, and he waved his hand through it, watching particles of ash and uncombusted coal dust whirling in its wake. He took a deep breath, tasted the chill on the air, and considered the fog.

"Welcome to 1912," he said at last, before being overwhelmed by an urge to curl up and weep. He resisted it, barely, and then spun around and strode towards the aft deck, determined to fight off those feelings with action.

His polyurethane recovery techniques had already refloated one part of the *Titanic*. Now he was faced with a new challenge.

To save the rest of her.

CHAPTER TEN

Rescue's eighty-ton boom crane whined mechanically as it swung out, cradling a high-capacity pump from its tip. Powered by its own internal diesel engine, the pump was encased in a yellow protective steel cage. Kai Alinka had secured himself to the side with a carabiner harness, feet on the lower lip of the cage as he now flew through the air towards *Titanic's* forward well deck.

"Ten feet, down, gently," he called through a walkie-talkie, guiding the crane operator.

Several of *Titanic's* crew had already gathered at the point he was aiming for, and as the pump came low enough they grabbed hold of the frame and helped swing it into place alongside a cargo hatch. Two double racks of coiled six-inch diameter pipe had already been lifted aboard, and as the pump touched down Kai released himself and stepped onto the wooden deck.

He had half-expected everything to explode in a dimension-splitting paradox at the moment of contact, but the absence of all life unravelling as every molecule in his body disintegrated suggested reality was not about to come screaming off the tracks. After a moment's silent awe, he pounded his fist on the hoist's quick-release mechanism and the crane swung free, returning to *Rescue* in order to take hold of the second portable pump.

"I'm aboard *Titanic*," he said with surprising calm into the walkie-talkie. "Setting up now."

The crewmen were quick to grasp what he was directing them to do, using a portable length of pipe to connect the pump to one of the piping racks whilst several others removed the canvas cover to one of *Titanic's* cargo hatches. The dark shaft below echoed with the rushing sound of rising water. Quickly, Kai directed the crew on how to unreel the rack's twin suctions down the hatch, before he turned away to prime the diesel motor, which turned over with a snarling roar. Several of the contemporary crew jumped at the sound, but carried on working.

"Commencing pumping now," he dictated into the walkie-talkie, and slowly let out the clutch. The pressure gauges kicked upwards as the drive engaged the motor to the turbine-pump, and then fell back almost to zero, the engine nearly stalling under load before he increased the fuel flow and steadied out the revs. As the needles rose to full capacity, the pump's outlet port gurgled once, and then spat a thick tube of dirty water onto the deck, the splashing liquid flowing with the ship's slight list to cascade through the starboard scuppers into the dark Atlantic.

"Hello!" someone shouted, and Kai turned to find a tall man in an overcoat and fly-collar striding across the deck to him, hand extended in nervous greeting. "I'm Thomas Andrews."

The man's face was haggard, but he had a relieved smile cutting through the premature stress lines. And his eyes were attentive, lingering first on the pumps, and then on Kai's Polynesian complexion as the two of them shook hands.

"Pleased to meet you. I'm Kaikaina Alinka," Kai responded warily, thinking back to what little he knew of *Titanic*, mostly gleaned from the movies. "Thomas Andrews... you're this ship's designer, right?"

"One of them. I can't take full credit," was Andrews' equally guarded response. "Are you an engineer yourself Mister, ah, Alancar?"

"*Alinka*," Kai corrected, reminding himself that Andrews was not the first person to mispronounce his name, and that both of them were out of their depth. "And yes, I have a Masters in Marine Engineering and Naval Architecture. Five years study at the University of Newcastle."

"You're a Tynesider by adoption?" the Ulsterman responded, and seeing a smile curving at the corner of his mouth Kai sighed in internal relief. "That's a proud legacy to uphold, Mr Alinka. How might I help? Do you need any assistance in setting up your equipment?"

"We will!" Kai replied, now having to shout over the mingling roar of the motor and discharging water. He pointed to port, where the second of *Rescue*'s two portable pumps was being swung aboard under the crane. "These two pumps between them shift about fifteen hundred tons an hour. That's about a fifth of our total lift capacity, but they're limited by priming distance."

"The vertical height they have to pump the water?" Andrews asked in confirmation.

"Yes sir, so we're just trying to buy time with these two so that *Rescue* can get her main dewatering pumps running amidships. We'll need you to direct us where best to take the water off from!"

The second pump came down with a rough bang, and he saw Andrews wince as several deckplanks splintered under the weight, but still received a nod of acknowledgement.

"Mr Alinka," Andrews explained, striding to the cargo hatch. "This shaft leads to cargo-hold three, but the ship has a better chance of survival if we can pump out the next compartment astern, Boiler Room Six."

The crew, having done the same task once before, were setting up the suctions without Kai's assistance, leaving him free to set the pump running. As they had, Andrews started in surprise as Kai depressed the ignition switch.

"This is a fuel oil engine, yes?" he asked, and Kai nodded, wondering where this would lead. He observed Thomas studying the gauges on the control board; keen eyes running over the engine output and pump capacity.

"Where did the US Navy obtain these machines? I've not seen ratings this high without use of a reciprocating steam pump."

As the second pump began to discharge an equal amount of water to its sibling, Kai directed his attention to Andrew's, seeing in his face genuine curiosity, mingling with confusion and trepidation; he suddenly felt saddened for a man considered to be an expert in his field, thrown so suddenly out of his comfort zone.

"And though I'm familiar with the campus in Newcastle, I was unaware that it has seceded from the University of Durham..." Andrews added, every observation loaded with silent interrogation.

Deciding it was best to cushion the inevitable blow, Kai hedged his answer carefully. "We can talk about that later I suppose, sir, once we've gotten the ship stabilised."

"Do you honestly think you can achieve that?" Andrews probed harder, turning back towards the comforting truths of engineering, of tonnages and displacement. "Or are we just trying to draw out her sinking as much as possible?"

"Honestly sir, that depends on what we find when our divers have inspected the hull."

Andrews' face collapsed into an expression of stunned shock, and Kai mentally cursed himself for giving away something so revolutionary; it had slipped his mind that freediving had not been invented until after World War One.

"This isn't a joke?" the other man pressed, his voice taking on traces of a thicker accent as his emotions made themselves known. "You have the ability to inspect the hull from the outside..."

The unspoken words *who are you people?* hung in the air, and then Kai's walkie-talkie crackled, breaking the silent standoff.

"This is Rescue, moving aft now, can you meet us at the portside gangway doors down on, ah, is it E-Deck, Ms Paik?"

"Yes, aft of the fourth funnel and two levels below the first continuous deck..."

As the off-screen conversation continued, Kai glanced down at the communications device, and Andrew's eyes moved with him.

"That's another interesting device you have there," the marine architect said at last, yielding his position and motioning to a set of stairs. "We can reach E-Deck through the Third Class companionway."

Kai waited a moment to pass a second walkie-talkie to a quartermaster, instructing him to hold down on the button and call for help if the pumps began making strange noises or suddenly lost suction, and then followed Andrews below decks.

Immediately down the first flight of stairs was an open space, one crowded with people being instructed to remain below by the stewards. The reason for their concern became evident as Thomas and Kai went down another level; this far forward E-Deck was already awash, the water lapping at their feet, and as he was led up and aft along the noticeably tilting deck Kai, questioned whether it was possible to save this ship. The words *The Titanic, you're trying to bail out the* Titanic! kept bouncing around in his head, insisting that it was not only futile, but *wrong* to try and keep her ship afloat, an insult to history.

Still wrestling with himself, he followed Andrews up out of the water and into a long corridor, thankfully empty of passengers who had already fled astern. The shipbuilder eventually stopped beside an open hatch in the metal wall and indicated inside. Lighting his torch, Kai stepped inside and found himself atop a metal gantry in a cavernous open space. Vast uptakes led upwards towards the ship's foremost funnel, and a ladder extended down from the gantry into black water that swirled just a few feet below his perch.

"This is the escape trunk for Boiler Room 6!" Andrews yelled over the commingling roar of water, pumps and ventilators. "When the water rises to this deck, it will quickly flood aft over the bulkhead and into Boiler Room 5. Once that happens, the ship is beyond all hope of recovery!"

Kai shone his torch down. In the time they had been talking the water seemed to have risen at least several inches. Black coal dust floated like ashes on the surface, which steamed slightly with the residual heat of the submerged steam plant. That was another complication; they'd need wire-mesh guards on the suctions to prevent the pumps becoming clogged with debris.

"What time do you make it?" he called, and checked Andrews's fob-watch against his own watertight dive watch. They matched almost exactly, 12.30am. He saw more questions burning in the other man's eyes at the sight of the digital display, but Andrews kept his mouth shut.

"Where can we get a pipe in on this deck?" Kai asked, guessing that at most they had only minutes before the water rose to their level.

Andrews pointed aft. "Your crewmates must have seen the forward gangway door was already submerging; reopening it would only risk flooding this deck faster. The next door aft is several hundred feet in the opposite direction, alongside the main engines."

"Well, fuck!" Kai cursed, uncaring for any wounded sensibilities. "I doubt our main suctions will reach that far, and even if they could, we'd lose capacity due to the increased distance we'd have to pump from."

Fuming, he turned his head sideways, looking into the open door of a large bunkroom. Over the door a sign described it as *'waiters' accommodation'*. It was a glory-hole, and a cramped one at that, a tiny space lit and ventilated mainly by a series of portholes along the outer wall.

He pointed at them, fired with sudden inspiration. "What's the diameter on those ports?"

Andrews' face lit up, mirroring his own. "Twelve inches; what's the diameter of your pipes?"

"Smaller than that!" Kai called as he ran aft, pushing open doors as he went. Every room had access to at least one porthole. "*Rescue* can come alongside here, where the ports are still above the waterline – we bring suctions through opened portholes and drag them straight across the corridor and down the hatch; if the water level keeps rising, we disconnect the pipes and seal the ports shut again."

"Brilliant," Andrews nodded, as he began hurrying aft, the tails of his coat billowing behind him. "Quick, your colleagues need to be informed; they'll be at the aft gangway by now."

As if in perfect time, several figures entered into the corridor from the far end. Thomas saw the tall figure of Second Officer Lightoller acknowledge him with a distant nod before leading a team of seamen into an alcove where he knew there was an access door intended for use by the ship's engineering staff when docked. Coming around the corner, he found the men undogging the hatch and working to swing it open.

"Mr Lightoller!" he panted, Kai following him. "What happened to using the aft gangway door?"

"Many of the third cabin passengers are gathering in the public spaces aft," Lightoller replied, his lip curling. "Several cowards among them tried to jump ship onto this gentleman's vessel when we opened the door, so we shut it and came forward."

Thomas nodded his understanding, and as the door swung open took a deep breath of fresh night air. If they could keep *Titanic* afloat, he really needed to improve the ventilation in the lower decks. He saw *Rescue* was drawing alongside, steaming (or was it motoring?) slowly astern to raft her transom side-to-side with *Titanic*'s hull, while a gangway was extended from the side of the smaller ship towards them. Backtracking into the E-Deck corridor, Thomas peered forward and saw the water was beginning to relentlessly advance towards them, already lapping around the open escape trunk hatch. Turning back, he saw Lightoller's men grab the proffered end of the gangway and drag it over the lip.

"Quick," he heard Alinka call as the other man strode onto *Rescue*'s deck. "Drag the suctions aboard *Titanic* and then spin her around! Put *Rescue*'s bow here alongside the door and from her stern we'll connect up through the portholes forward of here!"

As the other man took charge of his colleagues, Andrews finally got an opportunity to pause and examine the other ship. Beside him, he heard Lightoller click his tongue in disapproval. "She's quite the piece of work, isn't she?"

"Definitely," Thomas agreed, admiring the craftsmanship with which the salvage vessel's hull had been welded together, with not a rivet in sight.

"Not the boat," corrected Lightoller, shaking his head and pointing. "Her!"

Thomas was tempted to laugh at how the second officer had disparaged the size of their rescuer, but obliged him and followed his hand. Alinka and the other salvors were working to manhandle lengths of pipe over to *Titanic*, but another uniformed figure was advancing down the gangway, almost unnoticed amid the chaos. Thomas realised it was the crewman he had seen arguing with Lieutenant Miller from the Boat Deck, but as the arrival turned to one side and reverently laid a hand against the edge of the doorway, he saw silky hair hanging down through the back of *her* cap.

A woman! he realised with a start, an Oriental apparently, and yet carrying herself with a buoyancy and energy that made him think more of the younger workers in the shipyard. Before he could make sense of her, the creature in question turned to face him, eyes bright with a strange wonder, and her face lit up in delight.

"Thomas Andrews?" she beamed, and leapt forward to shake his hand. "Oh my gosh, it really is you!"

Thomas had enough time to process that her accent was American when he suddenly found his arm being pumped as if the ship's survival depended on it. When the woman – girl, really – composed herself she stepped back abashed.

"Ah, sorry, but it's just an honour to meet one of the men who designed the *Olympic*-class liners."

Thomas managed a grin that was not quite a grimace as the feeling returned in his wrist, eyes flicking to her name *'Rescue'* embroidered on her cap and jacket. "It's a pleasure to be recognised so enthusiastically, Miss…"

"Paik, Phillipa Paik, student of underwater archaeology."

Over her shoulder, Thomas saw Lightoller roll his eyes at the girl's forwardness, before the three of them had to step back into the corridor to make room for Alinka and his team as they came through, carrying ten-foot lengths of non-collapsible steel-belted pipe.

"The E-Deck working corridor, main thoroughfare for Third Class and crew," she breathed, peering in amazement along the length of the companionway. "Named 'Scotland Road', for a working-class residential street in Liverpool…"

Before Thomas was able to question her on why she found an access corridor so fascinating, a voice cut in through another one of the portable speaking devices, this one clipped to her belt.

"Ms. Paik, can you please locate Titanic's captain; the more time you fawn over the ship now, the less time you may have to enjoy it later."

Snatching the device to her mouth she replied with sudden seriousness. "Sorry Captain Jones, I'm heading up now." She turned between the two men. "I need to speak to Captain Smith immediately. *Rescue*'s master has approved me to speak on his behalf and try and explain our situation."

Lightoller indicated aft. "You'll not have much luck using the Second Class stairs, it's bedlam out there."

Thomas glanced between the girl and the men heading forward with the pipes, making a decision. "Mr Lightoller, can you assist Mr Alinka's team here, and I'll take Miss Paik up through the D-Deck galleys. If you require my aid, please summon me through one of these pocket-wirelesses."

Lightoller nodded, evidently happy at the prospect of not having to liaise with the young woman. With a courtly nod indicating that his new charge should follow, Thomas headed up a side passage, the girl following alongside as they climbed the stairs.

Quickly they reached the galleys for First and Second Class on D-Deck, the next level up, and Thomas headed forward through the kitchen spaces into the First Class dining saloon. The girl, Miss Paik, stalled when he held open the double door for her, mouth agape as she gazed around the vast room that reached right across the width of the ship, polished tables already being set for breakfast.

"Oh, my…" her hands covered her mouth, and Thomas had to urge her forward to the reception, though he was touched by her awe and added with some pride that the saloon was *"the largest room ever to go to sea"*.

He did not like the somewhat pitying look she fostered on him in response, however, as if she was laughing at some personal joke.

"Is something funny?"

"No Mr. Andrews. It's just that… all this," she waved around at the room. "Well, it's so strange to see it in person, if you understand."

He did not, but chose to not comment as they continued forward to the D-Deck reception and the Grand Staircase. Her awe at the sight was once again evident, and yet it was tinged with a bizarre familiarity. He almost felt like he was watching someone seeing the pyramids for the first time, a sense of amazement at encountering something only known heretofore from books and other accounts. Perhaps she had followed the construction of *Olympic* and *Titanic* through periodicals, but he was certain that she had never travelled on a ship before, at least not in First Class. Paik and Alinka both felt to him more like second-class passengers, examples of the admirable young professionals who oiled the wheels of the world, rather than the *'figures of note' who* claimed to shape the actual clockwork.

After all, evidence of intelligence and vitality does not, regrettably, translate automatically into social standing.

The same principle was in evidence by the reaction of other passengers to his companion's presence and demeanour. As the two of them climbed the four flights to the Boat Deck, he noticed that she increasingly drew the attention of passengers. Judgemental expressions on all sides conveyed a clear disapproval or disbelief of a woman so mannishly dressed, not holding onto the arm of an escort, brazenly striding up the stairs two at a time and lovingly running her hands over the balustrades and woodwork, especially the relief carving on the topmost deck, depicting two nymphs laying a laurel wreath atop a clock.

"Honour and Glory, Crowning Time!" she exclaimed, before staring at Thomas with an expression approaching fanatical adoration. "You have no idea how legendary this ship is to become, Mr. Andrews, the most famous vessel of all time."

And then, amazingly, she had *taken the lead*, exiting onto the Boat Deck and climbing over the railing to the officer's promenade with no hesitation. As if this was not enough to cap a night's worth of increasingly unexpected events, Thomas found himself having to run to keep up, weaving among passengers made massive by their cumbersome white lifejackets. It was like trying to chase down a street urchin, and at last catching up, he sacrificed his status as a gentleman by grabbing her shoulder and stopping her before she barged onto the bridge, his actions drawing as much disapproval from the surrounding passengers as did her outlandish attire.

"My apologies, Miss Paik!" he cringed, catching hold of one of the funnel stays as he caught his breath. "But it would be best if I introduced you to Captain Smith, rather than presenting yourself."

Smith was in the small cab on the outermost extension of the portside bridge wing, loudhailer in hand and watching with a professional eye as *Rescue* orientated herself for the pumping operation. Although lifeboats were only being lowered on the opposite side of the ship, Andrews noticed that a considerable crowd had gathered here just to gawk at the other vessel.

"Thomas," Smith had regained a familiar twinkle in his eye as he noticed his presence, the edges of the elder mariner's moustache twitching upwards in a smile. "Can you please tell me how this tiny ship is able to dance around as if she had an entire tugboat fleet to assist her?"

Thomas spared a glance. Sure enough, *Rescue* was now spinning on a point around her long axis, in order to nuzzle her pumping manifolds alongside the appropriate portholes. Then his eyes flicked to her bow, where the unmistakable wash of a propeller could be seen foaming the water.

"Ingenious!" he marvelled. "Auxiliary engines in the bow that help to manoeuvre the ship!"

An alarm suddenly sounded and a pair of bright red fenders deployed from below *Rescue*'s bridge, splashing into the water and allowing the two ships to buffer up, the action of *Rescue*'s bow engines holding her against *Titanic i*n place of ropes. He could only shake his head at the engineering involved, and again the mystery of how such a ship could be built and outfitted without anyone at Harland & Wolff learning, or being informed as a professional courtesy, nagged at him.

"So…" Smith's eyes turned distrustful as his gaze slid from Tom's fascinated face to something behind and below his shoulder. "Is this our envoy?"

Thomas turned, and saw Miss Paik had come up behind him, clutching her satchel to her stomach nervously. She was staring up at the sky, however, where the stars were just coming into view through the dissipating fog.

"Yes sir." Thomas shook off his sense of disquiet, a sense of wry amusement igniting in him as to how events would now proceed, and he coughed to draw their guest's attention away from the heavens. "Miss Philippa Paik of the *Rescue*, might I introduce you to Captain Edward John Smith, Commodore of the White Star Line."

The young woman seemed more intimidated at being in Smith's presence than she did Andrews, to the extent that she made a shallow curtsey, the motion bizarre given her attire in trousers, sweater and jacket.

"It is a supreme pleasure, Captain Smith," she said faintly, all of her previous enthusiasm having apparently vanished, before turning with wide eyes to greet the third man present. "And you, First Officer Murdoch."

Smith and Andrews exchanged raised eyebrows, and Thomas briefly considered that she was attracted to Murdoch, a tall and well-built Scotsman. Then he reconsidered; Miss Paik was not only surprisingly aware of Murdoch's name and station, distinctions he doubted few of the passengers could have made, but from her transfixed and somewhat fearful gaze, she was *intimidated* by him. Again he was reminded of someone being introduced to a national monument or celebrity, and remembered how vigorously she had pumped his hand and praised his creation.

Murdoch was beginning to blush as the young woman continued to stare at him, as if trying to read his inner thoughts, and the silence was becoming uncomfortable. As discretely as possible, Andrews brought a hand to his mouth and coughed once more.

"Ahem. Miss Paik, I believe you had a message from your captain, yes?"

Seemingly remembering why she was here, the young lady straightened up and composed her awestruck face into something resembling professionalism.

"Sirs, I'm here on behalf of Captain Jordan Jones of the *Rescue*, and have been asked to provide you with a means of communicating with him." She held out the device she had until now carried on her belt, and Smith cautiously took it. "It is a two-directional voice wireless," she clarified. "Hold down the button on the side of the device to transmit, and release it to receive."

Smith once again could only cock an eyebrow, but having seen numerous confusing scenes in one night, he seemed to take it in his stride and pressed the button, holding the grilled panel on the front of the object up to his mouth as if it were a telephone.

"This is Captain Smith; do I have the pleasure of addressing Captain Jones?"

The button depressed with a click, and seconds later his counterpart replied.

"Captain Smith, the pleasure is mine. How is your evacuation proceeding?"

"We're ready to begin lowering boats. Is the other ship you spoke of ready to lend her assistance?"

"Yes sir; Captain Waters of the White Star liner Oceanic is somewhat dubious of our reported situation, but should be with us in several minutes. We show her as approaching on our starboard side. Until they arrive, please avail yourself of Ms. Paik for further information."

Curiouser and curiouser, Thomas mused; he was familiar with the former White Star flagship named *Oceanic*, but when he had last seen her, only four days ago, she was laid up in Southampton, and not due to sail. And even if she had departed at the exact same time, it would be impossible for her to catch up to the sleeker, faster *Titanic*. And he was certain that there was no 'Captain Waters' in the employ of White Star.

From Smith's dubious expression, he was asking himself the same question. Unlike Thomas, however, he voiced his opinion, calmly but with a cold tone in his voice that demanded compliance.

"Miss Paik," he began, lowering the speaking wireless from his mouth. "Short of striking an iceberg, much has happened tonight that I would not expect after twenty-five years at sea. We have been all but run down by a ship of impossible size, and assisted by another the likes of which I have never seen. Mr Andrews, a master shipwright, expresses admiration at the unconventional design of your vessel, which seems to possess exactly the facilities and skills required in our hour of need..." a causal hand motion served to include the two pumps still thundering away on the foredeck. "Now I learn that apparently the *Oceanic* is coming to relieve us of our passengers, despite currently being interned at Southampton due to a lack of coal, and that *Rescue* is somehow able to detect her approach despite being as blind in the fog as we are. Now throughout this whole affair, one thing that no-one has been able to do is explain to me is this: *what is happening?*"

Throughout Smith's polite but frustrated tirade Andrews could see Paik's calm beginning to crack, replaced by a mix of excitement and...

...apprehension.

With sweat on her brow, she began to speak. "Captain, what I am going to say will sound impossible, but I beg you to hear me through. An event has occurred, the likes of which has not been documented in human history. You might call it an incursion, *in time...*"

She paused, as if allowing them to draw their own conclusions, and indicated the satchel she carried. "If you would care to allow me to follow you to the chart room, I can provide evidence of what I'm describing."

Thomas could feel his own veneer of professionalism beginning to fall apart, a madness pushing up from within. In the corner of his eye he could see Smith's lower jaw hanging open slightly, his eyes a million miles away, while Murdoch had relapsed into a form of stoic muteness.

"Miss Paik," he trod carefully. "Are you suggesting… *time travel?*"

She nodded. "Yes, Mr Andrews." Slowly she turned to take in every aspect of her surroundings; the abandoned portside lifeboats swung out on their davits, the last wisps of excess steam pressure whistling from the funnels, passengers in elegant clothes and lifejackets. He could see her biting her lower lip to keep it from quivering, and suddenly realised that beneath the excitement, she was afraid.

"The stars are wrong…" he heard her whisper softly, and he felt a fresh chill.

"Preposterous!" Smith exclaimed, indicating towards the device in his hand. "It's a poor joke to assume that a few marvellous toys can convince us of what you're saying. I can accept perhaps that your ship is somehow more technologically advanced than our own, but to suggest that you are from the future is ridiculous!"

"The future!" she laughed weakly and turned upwards to scan the heavens as the fog continued to clear, revealing the still-shimmering aurora. "Your future was my present! I first thought *Titanic* was moved forward in time to us, I was imagining the heroes' welcome you'd receive as you sailed into New York Harbour, a century late but triumphant…"

She laughed briefly, eyes still turned to the sky. Thomas saw tears staining her cheeks.

"…but the stars are all wrong, the air's too cold, and our fleet is missing…" the fear in her eyes was now very real, and Thomas could see Smith's expression shifting at the convincing sense of loss infusing her words. Inside, he was still holding on to the scraps of the world he knew, hoping beyond hope that this girl was simply hysterical, or mad.

Slowly, she looked back down to the three of them. "I was born on November 7th 1992, and in the world I knew no-one came to help you tonight. *Titanic* sank in two-hours and forty minutes, and nearly one thousand, five hundred people went with her. A century later, it is the most famous, *the most infamous,* shipwreck in history. Ask any child of the twenty-first century to name a famous ship, and they will say '*Titanic*'. The ships around us, and those coming to your aid, had gathered over this spot to commemorate the centenary of what transpired on this night, when *something* I don't understand saw fit to bring us here."

No-one spoke as she gazed imploringly from one face to another, desperately willing them to understand. "You think I'm mad, don't you, a hysterical female…"

Their silence surely condemned them, and her face screwed up in disgust as she jabbed a finger at them. "Right! In the world I come from, a black man is President of the United States, gay love is accepted, and I have the right to vote! If you want proof, I'll give you proof!"

Hands moving quickly, she unzipped the shoulder bag she carried and produced a shiny black device that resembled an oversized hardback book. "This contains photographic documentation of *Titanic*'s wreck taken by submersible cameras! So you can take your preconceptions and shove them straight up your self-righteous asses!"

Thomas recoiled at the language, while Murdoch blanched, but Smith drew himself upright.

"*Young lady!* I am the captain of this vessel and *you will moderate your tone!*"

Even standing many yards away, beyond the officer's promenade, Thomas could see several passengers react to the captain's outburst. Smith and Paik glared daggers at one another, before the captain's voice softened a tad.

"But… it would not be right to dismiss you out of hand, without first having a look at this 'proof' you have brought with you."

He turned to his First Officer. "Mr Murdoch. Please take Miss Paik to the chart room and provide her with whatever facilities she requires. Myself and Mr Andrews will join you momentarily."

"Yes Captain," Murdoch dipped his head, and then, uncertainly extended a hand. "Miss, if you'd care to step this way."

"Thank you," she sighed, relief glowing in her face as Murdoch led her into the bridge. Thomas saw her direct another of those marvelling glances towards the brass telemotor that supported the wheel before she and Murdoch vanished aft into the chart room. Smith seemed to visibly deflate, his shoulders falling in the aftermath of the confrontation.

"If you told me anyone of this age could raise such an obstinate girl I would not believe them," he growled. "Perhaps that serves to confirm her story."

"Do you believe her, Captain?" Thomas gently inquired.

"I wish not to," he replied. "But honestly, Thomas, I can't conjure an alternate explanation, no matter how much her story rebels against common sense. But at the same time it sounds incredible!"

"That *Titanic* could sink?"

"No, heavens no; you and I know both that ships are man-made constructs, and so feeble against the work of God and nature. But that a century hence an event like this should be remembered, let alone commemorated, sounds beyond the pale."

"Perhaps…" Thomas slowly began, allowing logic to carry him on as surely as it would in the design of a ship. "We should look at it not from her perspective, but from ours."

Smith slowly turned to face him, and Thomas could see the gears resisting in his mind. He pressed harder. "EJ, imagine the reaction around the world if this ship does go down tonight; the largest vessel on Earth, sunk on her maiden voyage with some of the most notable celebrities imaginable aboard. It would be traumatic; there would be boards of enquiry, investigations, demands as to how this happened, and how it could be prevented."

Thomas was gaining speed, following the idea to conclusion like one beam riveting itself to the next. "It would be a historic moment, comparable to the Battle of Waterloo or Trafalgar… if we remember Nelson and Napoleon a century after either's death, surely the great events of our era will be remembered as well."

While he talked, they had slowly crossed into the bridge; glancing aft, Thomas could see Murdoch standing upright in the chart-room, his face glowing a pale blue as it reflected a strange artificial light. Curiosity worried away at him, and yet he was fearful of what he might see.

As if the universe was determined to open his eyes that he might see, a new foghorn echoed out of the lingering mist to starboard, and captain and shipbuilder exchanged a hesitant glance. In the same mind, they continued forward onto the starboard wing.

Lights stirred in the trace remnants of the murk, as something impossibly large moved slowly alongside them. He could hear voices, breaking water, and a rising thrum, as if of a vast engine running smoothly at an incredible number of revolutions.

"Well, Tom, what's coming next?" a new voice interjected wearily. Bruce Ismay, now changed out of his pyjamas into a subdued suit and tie, had come forward to join them.

"Apparently, the *Oceanic*," Captain Smith said quietly. "Or, if what we've been told is true, a ship from a hundred years hence, one bearing the same name."

Ismay nearly snorted a laugh, but at the deathly serious expressions on the faces of the two men, trusted colleagues both, it died before passing his lips. "These ships are of the future?"

"So I hear," Thomas conceded, his eyes focused forward. Ismay turned to watch with them, and before their eyes, and the eyes of hundreds more, the curtain of mist lifted, revealing the new arrival.

It's only got one funnel was, strangely enough, Tom's first thought, the only observation able to assert itself over the numerous voices suddenly screaming in his mind. He felt Smith inhale slowly beside him, and Ismay breathed a stunned "Bless my soul".

Oceanic III – and what else could it be, given how the name was written beneath that single, raked funnel in illuminated letters – was a giant, a floating Brobdingnag against *Titanic's* miniscule Gulliver. Even that other strange vessel, the *Seguin Laroche*, would have been dwarfed by it.

It could swallow Titanic whole, funnels and all!

Slowly, his eyes roamed from the high, angular bow, so much like the elegant prow of a clipper ship, to the towering superstructure, the many rows of balconied cabins lit up with lights, continuing all the way to the rounded stern. A long row of brightly-coloured lifeboats awaited action along a promenade halfway up the height of the ship, at the same level at *Titanic's* boat deck.

In length, he estimated it was twelve hundred feet long. In terms of mass, it was easily three times the size of *Titanic*. The part of his mind devoted to shipbuilding immediately began to fantasize about the lavish interiors he could prepare with so much space to hand, ballrooms and restaurants and cabin suites more spacious than anything he had ever accomplished in marine architecture.

It was Captain Smith, however, who spoke the obvious.

"We've been outclassed in every way."

As *Oceanic* drew alongside about a quarter of a mile off, she reversed her engines and bellowed a greeting.

Tom's whole world was torn apart with that thunderous roar, and the calm certainty with which he had once imagined his future collapsed like a house of cards, fragments fluttering away into chaos.

And yet, another part of him, the part he regarded as the greater part of his soul, piped up, demanding to be heard.

You still have your work, your family, your life back home in Belfast. You have so much to live for, and so many new possibilities that might have been cut short this night. But these people have lost everything. Homes, families, lives, an entire world. And, despite all of this, they're trying to help.

"Those poor people," he heard Bruce Ismay say.

*

Adrienne McKinn felt the first aid kit she was holding tumble out of her grasp as she gaped, mouth wide open, at the ship across the water, her other hand clutching at the rail of *Oceanic*'s Pilothouse Lounge. Positioned directly above the ocean liner's bridge, the lounge's external balconies extended out atop the projecting bridge-wings, allowing passengers a stunning view of the open ocean. But now those passengers, and Adrienne herself, seconds ago focused on tearing strips of silk from her skirt to supplement the kit's supply of bandages, were all staring at the vessel now emerging out of the fog.

"It's so small…" she whispered to herself. "I'm higher up than even her funnels…"

From her elevated position she could see hundreds, possibly thousands of people swarming the other liner, crowding around a pitifully small contingent of lifeboats.

The Titanic… I'm looking down on the Titanic's Boat Deck, watching as her passengers prepare to die…

It was like some perverse blood-sport, as if more than two thousand people had been thrown into the Circus Maximus for the entertainment of Rome, with a commandment that less than one in three of them would be allowed to live. It was by that logic that Adrienne had never really enjoyed movies and TV dramas that trivialised historical disasters, but her imagination and years of immersion in the history of the *Titanic* could furnish up a multitude of scenes to fill in the gaps normally occupied by Hollywood exaggeration.

Ida and Isidor Straus, the Jewish owners of Macy's of New York, who both refused a place in the lifeboats so that they could die together...

Benjamin Guggenheim and his valet Victor Giglio, donning evening wear so that they could meet their end in the best spirit of chivalry...

Wallace Hartley, Titanic's bandmaster, who with his fellow musicians all played on until the ship went down, and died to a man...

Thomas Andrews, the shipyard's senior representative, giving up his life jacket to a stewardess before departing to the First Class Smoking Room, where he was last seen gazing wistfully at a painting of Plymouth Harbour...

Father Thomas Byles, one of many clergymen who were offered seats in the boats, but instead remained aboard to lead steerage passengers to the Boat Deck and administer the Last Rites to those who were about to die...

Chief Engineer Joseph Bell and his engineering staff, by popular myth killed at their posts in those torturous final moments when the ship broke apart...

And dozens upon dozens more fatalities, fifteen hundred all told, and about to repeat the whole spectacle before her very eyes, and the eyes of everyone else now crowding onto the balcony beside her, voices raised and faces white.

Some of her fellows were donning orange lifejackets. Turning her head, Adrienne saw even more people crowding onto *Oceanic's* promenade deck far below, pressing against barriers set up to hold them back as the ship's crew readied several lifeboats for launch.

"Ladies and Gentlemen!" boomed the public address speakers. *"Please remain calm. At this point there is no call for alarm!"*

What a joke.

"Mrs McKinn!" someone shouted. "Where's Adrienne McKinn!?"

She turned and found Catherine Vickers, *Oceanic's* Safety Officer, forcing her way through the crowd towards her, bellowing her name.

"Here! Cathy, here!" she waved. Sighting her, Vickers drew near and sighed in relief.

"Quick, Addy, come with me. The Captain needs to speak with you down on the bridge."

Hitching up what remained of her skirt, Adrienne followed, back through the Pilothouse and against the flow of passengers trying to find a rail or window to see for themselves, all shouting and talking.

"…you heard what they said!"

"The *Titanic*, it's the *Titanic!*"

"…not telling us!"

"What about us…"

"Is the ship sinking?"

"…running out our lifeboats!"

"What's happening!?"

Among the chaotic babble some people were crying, lending a note of tragedy to the scene, and Adrienne shivered, feeling a sudden connection with those across the water on *Titanic*.

"Through here!" Vickers directed, leading her through a discrete passcard-secured door and down a flight of stairs to a corridor that opened onto the bridge, which was crammed with crewmembers just as confused as the passengers they were responsible for.

"Hold this position, all stop!" shouted the familiar voice of Lloyd Waters as he strode across the room and caught her eye. "Adrienne, come with me!"

Not pausing in her own stride, she turned and kept pace with him out into the bridge wing, towering over the shorter man. "Tell me what's happening, Lloyd."

"It's bedlam here!" he said gruffly. "People are scared, we've lost almost all contact with the outside world, and we've several fatalities on our hands!"

"Oh no, who were they?"

"One elderly passenger had a heart attack, two more people got trampled in a panicked crush, and several got thrown around bad enough to break their necks or backs when the ship suddenly heeled to one side during our transition of… whatever it was that brought us here!" He sighed, and pinched his nose, eyes screwed up. "Worst of all is that Ingrid is among the fatalities."

Adrienne felt her mouth clench, just like her gut. Ingrid Rutherford was a wonderful woman, the soul of wit, and not even thirty-five. She was also *Oceanic*'s resident Doctor – *or had been.*

"I know, right?" Waters sighed, the same grief mirrored in his own eyes. "She got knocked over a banister and fell three stories, never stood a chance. Tony Jackson the Assistant Doctor has taken over her duties, but the hospital is struggling to keep up with all the injuries we've sustained."

Then he pointed out at the other ship. "Either way, we are facing an utter disaster, and now we're also confronted with *that!*"

Adrienne shook her head, mouth hanging open slightly as her head slowly turned to peer out into the night as he continued speaking. "Is that what my eyes tell me it is? But my head says is impossible! Captain Jones of the *Rescue* has been saying for the past ten minutes that we've been knocked about in time, but I thought he was just *twp*, crazy!"

"He's not mad, Lloyd…" Adrienne replied. "That's the *Titanic.*"

"Iesu Grist," he hissed in Welsh, before his shoulders slumped. "I feared as much, but I wanted to hear it from your mouth, Addy. She's trimmed down by the head badly, sinking fast. Jones says his team are going to try and keep her afloat, but he wants us to take aboard her passengers and crew."

Her head swarming with conflicting voices, thoughts and questions, Adrienne did not answer. Instead, struck by a sudden realisation, she was squinting hard into the distance, beyond *Titanic.*

Where are you? Stanley Lord, where are you?

"On top of that," continued Waters. "If we have been thrown back in time, we've no hint or clue as to whether this is temporary, reversible, or permanent. How do I explain that to the passengers without raising an even worse panic?"

"Get them involved. Make them feel like heroes," she replied automatically, still peering out, still trying to spot the dim lights of another ship she *knew* was just a few miles away. "When I got on the ticket for Congress we ran a grassroots campaign in every major town in Montana; got local youth involved who sold the idea to their friends. Won by a landslide because we convinced all the cynics of the truth that their contributions matter, that they can make a difference in history..."

"Well, I was going to put out a call for volunteers to assist in the hospital and lobby, so that's a start."

Every difference matters, every action has weight. As long as we act, as long as we don't stand still!

"Lloyd!" She spun around, suddenly galvanised, and grabbed his hands. "Can you show me your radar? It's vital that I know what other ships are in the area!"

"OK," he answered without question, and as her heart soared he led her across the bridge to the navigational suite, where one of the officers was plotting every radar return on a monitor. There were dozens of green dots, spread out all over the map, except for a perfectly circular patch of open water over a kilometre across, as if a section had been removed with a cookie-cutter.

"The dots are ice and other ships and so on," said Waters, before pointing to the vast open pool. "But I think that hole is a sign that not just our ships were moved in time, but also a massive spherical chunk of sea and sky from 2012 as well, and that huge wedge of reality has traded places with an equal volume of air and water from here, 1912. So back home, in the future, or whatever, we've vanished and a few dozen hundred-year-old icebergs have appeared in our place."

"That explains the fog..." Adrienne murmured, her eyes fixed on the display. "The weather was close and humid back home, so the several billion tons of water we must have brought along with us would be warm as well. Now it's mingling with this native water, which is at freezing temperatures, and the result is a mini-weather front."

"Yeah, and for all we know we've given the Labrador Current a heart attack..." Lloyd muttered blithely. "And perhaps the Gulf Stream too. What is it you're looking for, Addy?"

"Can you eliminate which of these targets are ships?" she asked, and after a few moments study he nodded and pointed.

"This is us and *Titanic*, more than a mile north of 'the hole' and our point of arrival, well up among the ice."

202

Adrienne frowned, wondering how they could have appeared two miles south of the sinking *Titanic* when *Oceanic* had been stationary directly over where the ship had sunk.

Was going to sink, Adrienne... she corrected herself. *After Captain Smith stopped Titanic's engines, the ship would have begun to drift south with the current, until she finally broke apart and foundered some distance from where she actually hit the berg.*

"The *Anatoly Sagalevich* is about a mile off and slowly coming up from behind," Waters continued, interpreting the radar plot. "And *Rescue* has gone around to the far side of *Titanic* from us, which is hiding her from our radar. Them aside, there are only two other contacts I'd profile as showing the right return to be ships, about five or six miles North-Northeast."

He jabbed his index finger onto a pair of glowing dots that were in close proximity to one another.

"One of them is almost certainly that runaway bastard the *Seguin Laroche*, but she's stopped and superimposed over this faint haze, which I think means she's actually run into the pack ice. The other is much smaller, and is slowly moving closer to the *Laroche*, and I've got no *dratted* idea who she is."

Yes! Good show Captain Lord! Thank you, sir, thank you!

"Can you ID that ship for me, Addy?" Lloyd pressed. "Do you know who she is?"

"It's the SS *Californian*," Adrienne said firmly. "She's a six-thousand ton freighter belonging to the Leyland Line."

"Indulge me by jogging my memory," Lloyd said wearily, rubbing at his face. "Isn't that the ship that stood still?"

"Yes. She's captained by a man named Stanley Lord. On the night of the sinking, this night, she was stopped on the edge of the ice field, maintaining minimum steam, some distance away from *Titanic* but just near enough that the two ships could dimly make each other out. *Titanic* tried to draw *Californian's* attention with wireless, signal lamps and rockets, but *Californian's* only wireless operator was off duty, neither ship could make out the flashing of the other's Morse lamp, and a mistake made in launching the rockets meant they were not recognised as distress signals. By the time *Californian's* crew realised their mistake, *Titanic* was long sunk. Both the British and American boards of inquiry made Captain Lord their scapegoat, saying he could have saved everyone onboard the Big T if he had made the effort."

"Bullshit," *Oceanic's* master breathed. "There's enough ice between them and us that, even if he could make full speed, he'd not get here within less than ninety minutes, not without radar... but I tell you what, Addy. Whatever they did before, they're not standing still now. That blip is almost right on top of the *Seguin Laroche* and turning to come alongside her."

He was right. As Adrienne watched, the radar needle swung around again, and the dot representing the *Californian* shifted slightly closer to the luminous green blot that was the *Seguin Laroche*.

"Captain Lord's investigating. Good for him," she said softly, before straightening up to her full height. "Lloyd," she implored. "Don't let *Oceanic* be the ship that stands still this time around. Launch our boats, and bring *Titanic's* passengers to safety. Project 401 has the people and skills to liaise with them, and hell, I'll take responsibility for their conduct if needed..."

"I accept your aid, Addy," Lloyd said firmly. "But responsibility lies with me, and my first concern must always be the safety of *Oceanic* and those lives already aboard her. However, I can't ignore what's going on before my eyes..."

"Captain," interjected one of the officers. "We've already got four thousand panicked people onboard; can we really take on half as much again? And what about the damage this will do to history; I mean, those people out there are *meant* to die..."

Everyone on the bridge turned to face their small group as Captain Waters brooded to himself, before looking up sharply at the dissenting officer.

"Your opinion is noted, and overruled. Alright, everyone listen up, because I'll only say this once! You heard Mrs McKinn. Our colleagues aboard the good ship *Californian* are taking action instead of sleeping out the night. History has already changed, and they, as do we, have a clear and present moral duty to assist a ship in distress so long as we do not endanger our own. Miss Vickers, what's your assessment of the situation?"

"Conditions could not be better," the Safety Officer replied. "Visibility is improving, the sea is perfectly calm and *Titanic* is settling at a sedate rate with no indication that she'll suddenly do something unexpected. So long as the hotel manager affirms his staff can house and sustain several thousand additional passengers, I see no hazard to ourselves or *Oceanic* by moving to assist. I've already sent instructions to run out five of the portside boats and merely await your order to begin a passenger transfer."

"Very good; then you have my blessing, Ms Vickers. Proceed to the Promenade Deck and oversee the lowering of those boats, with instructions that they should make for *Titanic!*"

"And our own passengers?" asked Adrienne, as Vickers strode away purposefully. By way of answer, the Captain strode over to the shipboard security console and held down on the microphone switch for the Emergency Public Address System.

"Ladies and Gentlemen, this is the Captain speaking. I understand your distress and can now inform you of our situation. Amazing as it sounds – but as you can already see – we appear to have been thrown back in time, and are preparing to render assistance to the RMS Titanic. At this time our attention is focused on rescuing her passengers, but once that task is complete I assure you that all efforts will be made to understand our situation and future course of action. Until then, please remain calm, give the crew the space they need to work and do not interfere in the launching of the lifeboats now being deployed to bring aboard Titanic's passengers. Volunteers with useful skills such as medical training or fluency in foreign languages are asked to gather in the Belgrave Square Lobby on Deck 2 where the crew will direct you to where your skills can be put to use. To any individuals with detailed knowledge of Titanic and her complement, please gather in the Grafton Ballroom where your expertise can be coordinated under the direction of Mrs Adrienne McKinn. Further details on our situation will follow. On behalf of myself and the companies of the Royal Mail Ships Oceanic and Titanic, we thank you all for your patience and fortitude."

He released the switch. "There. Now they know as much as we do. So let's get to work, we have a ship-to-ship transfer of passengers about to start…"

As the silence on the bridge erupted into activity, Adrienne beamed with pride, before a whooping siren drew her back out into the bridge wing. Below, strobes were warning people to keep clear of the edge of the Promenade Deck as two of *Oceanic*'s motorboats smacked down into the pristine black water, turned, and then powered at full speed towards *Titanic*.

"Alright," she breathed to herself, before turning and striding off into the heart of the ship. "Let's do this!"

CHAPTER ELEVEN

Charles Groves stared grimly up at the green bow that towered above him, almost lost in the night sky. The beam of light from his powerful handheld torch illuminated where the name SEGUIN LAROCHE had been picked out above the anchor alleys, and the ship was dusted with a light hoar frost that sparkled coldly, in chill harmony with the aurora flashing brightly in the skies.

The huge vessel was stationary, her stubby bowsprit embedded deep into a treacherous briar patch of field ice and small icebergs. No lights shone in the distant wheelhouse, and the sterile silence was disrupted by not so much as a whisper.

Beneath Groves' feet, the tiny freighter *Californian* seemed to quail fearfully from the giant obstacle.

"Halloo!" he called out. "Vessel '*Seguin Laroche*', this is the Leyland steamship *Californian!* I am hove to off your starboard bow! Can anyone hear me?"

Echoes of his voice fled into the night, and Groves turned to a man standing above him on *Californian*'s open bridge, one whose face was weathered and deeply-lined despite being only in his mid-thirties. "No response, sir."

Like Groves, Captain Stanley Lord's attention was focused on the looming ship. For a few moments the tall, dapper man quietly rubbed his gloved hands together as if to warm them, deep in thought. Then he crossed to a speaker tube and signalled for minimum revolutions on the ship's only engine. With a slow, plodding rhythm, *Californian* slowly stirred forward, advancing down the side of the *Seguin Laroche*'s elongated hull. Groves saw the letters CML branded in twenty-foot letters midway along the length of the other ship, ghostly white against forest green, and wondered what they stood for. Climbing the stairs to the bridge, he was amazed to find that, even from this elevated position, he could only just see onto the other vessel's main deck.

"It's gigantic," Lord spoke quietly, his austere voice tinged with an awestruck reverence that seemed out of place for his normally taciturn demeanour.

"Lloyd's of London will get a shock at this," Groves added glibly. Lord arched an eyebrow, his thin lips pursed together in disapproval, and an abashed Groves tried to explain his joke. "The insurance sir, if this thing sinks."

"Indeed," Lord humourlessly intoned, before glancing back towards the *Seguin Laroche*'s bow. "She seems to be listing a touch to starboard; I suspect she was holed when the ice brought her to a sudden stop."

Groves nodded in agreement. The colossal ship must have ploughed like an icebreaker into the obstacle that had stopped her, mangling her hull below the waterline in the process. "But if she is sinking, then she seems to be doing so very slowly."

The sound of footsteps on the stairs below heralded the arrival of the ship's Marconi-man, Cyril Evans, a long-faced and bespectacled man only a few years ahead of Groves in age, who arrived on the bridge in a whirl of activity.

"Master Ship's Marconigram, sir!" the Irish wireless operator announced, touching a hand to his cap as he addressed the captain. "From the *Titanic*. She says she's still sinking, but that at least one ship has already arrived to assist her. She's asking for other vessels to not risk trying to run the ice on her behalf."

"Very well," Lord nodded, signing the telegraph docket. "Please wish them luck and inform them that we have located that mystery ship of hers. Further details will be given once we have uncovered them, and unless *Titanic* requires further assistance, we'll stand by here until daylight."

While Evans noted down the captain's message, Groves mused on the strange events that had transpired so far, and they universally bothered him. Earlier in the night *Californian*, a cargo ship belonging to his employers, the Leyland Line, had come to a stop when ice had been spotted ahead. Captain Lord, aware of potential hazards and acting with overt caution, this being his career's first encounter with ice, had placed extra lookouts in the ship's bow beforehand, and rang down for an emergency stop as soon as water was sighted breaking ahead against an unseen obstacle.

"We'll hold until morning," Lord had decided. "Not even making up the time we've lost is worth the risk of wading into that mantrap."

In his role as Third Officer, Groves had been standing watch with the Captain at the time, but with *Californian* drifting safely south in company with the ice, he'd had little to occupy himself with until about an hour ago, when he had seen the lights of a ship creeping up over the horizon, travelling parallel but far to the south of their own course. He and the Captain had debated the size of the newcomer, with Lord leaning towards it being a vessel similar in size to *Californian*'s diminutive six thousand tons. Groves, however, based on what he had gathered from spending time with Evans in the wireless shack, believed it to be a much larger ship, maybe even the fabulous *Titanic*, boldly ploughing the waves on her maiden voyage. For a second he had entertained the happy thought of someday serving aboard such a ship; having gained his second mate's certificate after just six years at sea, and now serving as *Californian*'s Third Officer at the age of twenty-four, it seemed possible that some day he might himself captain a grand liner, entertaining illustrious guests at his private table in the dining saloon, turned out in best evening dress.

Yes, Captain CV Groves has a pleasant ring to it.

His fantasised ambition had been broken, however, when the unidentified ship suddenly went dark.

"She's put her lights out for the night, to encourage the passengers to turn in," he'd opined after a minute's consideration. The captain had moved to reply, just as *Californian*'s bell sang once to mark a watch change.

For Groves, that single clang rang in a new world. As soon as he had registered the sound of the bell striking, a bright, silent flash of light burst on the southern horizon, somewhere beyond the mystery ship, and both he and the captain had averted their eyes with a cry of alarm. Seconds later, a rumbling roar reached *Californian*, the sound rushing past and dying away in a series of peals, like a train thundering into the distance.

When his vision recovered, Groves glanced off to the south. Instead of blending into the stars, the masthead light of the mystery ship now stood bold and brilliant against an inky black curtain that veiled the sky in that direction. Quickly the spreading blackness shrouded her from view, and some minutes later, born on strangely warm winds, a few faint wisps of fog reached *Californian*. They flitted around the ship like wraiths, but never grew any thicker, quickly beginning to disperse. Groves had crossed the Atlantic before, and seen his fair share of the infamous fogs that could bewitch this part of the Grand Banks off the coast of Labrador, but this behaved in no way that he could explain. Even harder to comprehend was the incredible lightshow that followed, great waves of colour washing across the sky like running watercolours.

The Vikings held that this part of the Atlantic was cursed, he thought with a supernatural tremor of awe, *but this is something else…*

While the image was fresh in his mind, Groves had grabbed paper and pencil from the chart room and began to scribble a sketch of *something* that he had seen in the flash of light, reckoning it might later prove useful, or at least make for an interesting story for the day when he achieved command of his own ship. By the time he had finished, the paper was covered in black smears except for a perfect half-circle of white in the centre, rising over the horizon and spreading out in a blurry corona. In the middle of that splash however, silhouetted against the light, were several black shapes. One was the other ship, which Groves now felt had not extinguished her lights, but instead had hidden them by swinging bow-on to *Californian*, and surrounding her were a series of jagged spurs, extending up from the horizon like the upper pinnacles of a mountain range rising through a cloud bank.

"Icebergs," Lord decided when Groves showed him the scribbled sketch. "Our visitor must have swung to avoid one, and ended up pointing straight at us."

"Do you think she saw what caused the light?"

"Quite possibly, but I'm more concerned with whether or not she hit that berg," Lord had said, tapping at a craggy mass adjacent to the mystery ship in the sketch, before beckoning towards the wireless shack. "Go rouse Evans and see if she can be contacted."

In their own way, it turned out that both of them were right. Groves himself had accurately guessed that the ship was the *Titanic*, and it seemed the Captain's grim but pragmatic concern was correct too, as despite foreign interference stamping on the signals, Evans had managed to catch fragments of messages. Piecing them together, they reported their findings to Lord. *Titanic* had struck an iceberg, and minutes later had nearly been rammed by a vessel named the *Seguin Laroche*. When Evans managed to get through for a second, he found *Titanic* was banging away in Morse trying to locate that ship, and requesting anyone else listening in to come to her aid.

"She says she's sinking, sir," Groves had concluded.

Lord had immediately rung below for the boilers to be charged with fresh coals and for Chief Engineer Mahon to ready the engines. Then, after consulting a chart and dismissing the *Titanic*'s reported position, he instead decided to head towards her by dead reckoning. When the engine room reported that they were ready to set off, *Californian* had swung her nose around and began to follow the fringe of the ice field south, making three knots and desperately trying to recover sufficient pressure to go full ahead. The Captain estimated that at most they were ten miles from *Titanic*, and at maximum revolutions could reach her within the hour, but the need to mortgage the boilers and evade large pieces of ice had slowed them considerably.

The nearer they got to *Titanic*, the denser the lingering fog became. And then, out of the dark, they had stumbled upon the immense bulk of the *Seguin Laroche*. It was as if they had suddenly run upon Land's End, as the alien vessel was darkened from stem to stern, with not even navigation lights to her name.

Now, Groves found himself staring up at the enormous ship's bridge, which rose from the hull like a white castle in the air. The strange instruments on her mast particularly drew his eye, and while Lord mused aloud on what had caused immense damage to the stern of the vessel, where metal was torn, blackened and smoking, Groves wondered at the function of a dish-shaped object that was raised to the stars. Above, more and more of those stars were becoming visible as the last vestiges of the fog burned off, revealing the heart of the strange aurora, which seemed to radiate out from a single point in the sky, burning like a giant eye glaring balefully down on where *Californian* hugged against the other ship like a pilot fish to a shark.

"Well Mr Groves," Lord said. "We'd best find some way to board her and determine what she is, and where she came from."

"That might be the best way, captain," said Groves, pointing to where a long gangway ladder hung at a drunken angle from the side of the other ship. It appeared to be normally stored on deck next to the railing, but something had knocked one end free; now it hung from the end still fastened to the ship, partially extended and dangling towards the water.

"Get some of the crew," the Captain agreed. "We'll try and snag the free end with our cranes."

One of *Californian*'s main cranes was quickly deployed, the winch engine panting breathlessly as they swung the jib to and fro, eventually hooking onto the dangling gangway and dragging it onto the Leylander's deck.

Climbing it towards the other ship, torch in hand and with Mr Stewart, the Chief Officer, leading the way, Groves felt the gangway bouncing beneath their step. It seemed to be made of aluminium, a very springy and yet surprisingly strong metal, which he also knew to be very difficult and *expensive* to produce. Further wonders awaited them on the main deck, the first of them being a lifebelt hanging from a peg. Unlike *Californian*'s it was bright red, and from the seams along the side it seemed to have been cast from some form of resin, not fabricated from wood. As Stewart oversaw securing the two ships lightly together, Groves stepped up to the lifebelt and rapped on it with his knuckles; it rang dully.

Maybe it's made from that new stuff... Bakelite, is it?

Then he swung the torch around, noting the absence of rivets in the metalwork, and instead how all the major structural members seemed to have been fused neatly to one another. It was welding, he realised at last. *The entire hull was held together by welding.*

"Chief, this is incredible!" he said aloud. "Why haven't *Shipbuilder* magazine run an article on a vessel so beyond the state of the art?"

"I don't know…" Chief Stewart nodded towards an open doorway. "Let's find the wheelhouse. If we're going to find any answers, they'll be there."

As the two of them climbed the stairs, other odd details began to scream out. By the time they reached the higher levels of the superstructure, each had accumulated a small collection of trophies. Stewart's torch had been replaced by a tiny one from an open cabin, which threw an amazingly bright and concentrated beam of light despite being small enough to toss like a pencil, while in his free hand he held what appeared to be a copy of the ship's manifest, French annotations scribbled across the surface with a device attached to the document by a loop of cord; it was much smaller than a fountain pen, but when drawn across the surface of the paper, it left a neat black line of ink, devoid of any blotting.

Groves, however, had found an incredible treasure. A dim glow through an open door had drawn his attention, and inside he had found a small yet comfortable lounge. The source of the light was a device that had been sitting on a mess table. It was small, about the size of a thin book or pamphlet, and was made of the same rigid material as the tiny torch and the lifebelt. But when he had picked it up, he found that it was inlaid with a glass window, on which a cinematograph film was being projected from within, in amazingly bright colours. A wire led from the side of the device to a pair of buds that resembled the earpieces of a Marconi headset, and holding one to his ears, he heard the sound of laughing voices and music. They synched neatly to the footage on the glass pane, depicting what appeared to be some kind of comedic act.

Talking cinema, in colour, and compact enough to be carried around casually! His inner child was jumping for joy at the discovery, and the more academic part of his brain, the part of him studying for his Marconi operator's license, wondered what other functions the device could perform. Feeling around he had found a single illuminated button on the thin upper edge of the device, which seemed to break its power circuit, and with it shut down he had slid it into one of his inner jacket pockets for later investigation.

Coming back into the corridor, he found Stewart kneeling beside a dark streak smeared along the floor. Directing the deceptively tiny torch on it, the two men started as they realised that what looked like wet paint was actually *fresh blood*.

"Oh good God…" Groves heard himself whisper.

"Easy, Charlie," cautioned the chief, his words laced with a soft Merseyside accent. "Don't go losing your head."

"He did!" Groves replied, jabbing at the streak of blood. "Maybe."

Stewart directed a withering glance at him, and the younger man calmed himself. Following the trail of blood, they found the body of a man slumped in a corner, clad in a thin buttonless shirt and heavy corduroy trousers. Despite the man's glazed, sightless eyes and the bloody mess that had been made of his stomach, Stewart checked for a pulse as Groves tried to suppress the rising sense of horror. He thought of the happy figures on the tiny cinema's screen; had this man been watching the film, laughing along, only to be suddenly gunned down in cold blood and left to die?

Why?

Still kneeling, Stewart closed the dead man's eyes and sighed. "This place is a grave."

"Halloo! Help!"

At the sound of a voice calling faintly from somewhere above, the two officers stood bolt upright. Groves suddenly wished for a weapon of his own as they climbed the final flight of stairs and arrived on the highest level. Trilingual signs in English, French, and some form of Dago-speak directed them towards the ship's office, the captain's quarters, and the wheelhouse.

"Hello, is anyone there?" Stewart called out.

"Oui!" the unseen person replied. *"Come untie me!"*

The voice was feminine, but roughened and ragged. Following her cries, the two men found themselves on the *Seguin Laroche*'s darkened bridge, their own torches providing the only illumination. Waist-high metal-and-glass cabinets flanked a tiny metal helm, to which a woman had been lashed, her wrist handcuffed to the wheel.

She must be a passenger, or a stewardess, Groves thought to himself, before noticing that she was wearing the same heavy work-trousers as the dead man. *But why is she dressed in so unladylike a manner?*

214

"Oh, *merci*. Thank you!" she called, peering over her shoulder. "I've been bound here for hours."

Looking around, Groves saw to his revulsion a corpse lying on the floor, hands folded over its chest.

"Careful!" the woman said. "There's a gun lying on the floor there, but I think it's empty; the bastard using it wasted all his bullets and threw it aside when he ran off the bridge."

Warily sidestepping the body, Groves soon found the gun hurled into a corner; like everything else aboard this ship it was like nothing he had ever seen – short and blunt, with a curving metal bracket extending from underneath the stock. There was a strap attached to it, and he used it to shoulder the weapon, careful to keep his finger away from the trigger guard.

"The key," the woman was imploring Stewart, weakly tugging at her wrist. "The spare key to the cuffs are hanging on the wall in the ship's office."

Nodding, the chief headed aft, and she turned her attention to Groves.

"You're English?"

"Yes Ma'am," he replied. "Officers Stewart and Groves, of the Leyland ship *Californian*."

"Leyland?" she replied wearily, massaging her bound wrist with her free one. "I've not heard of you. Are you a new company?"

He blinked, more surprised by her abrupt demeanour than from her ignorance of Leyland's status as the largest cargo-handling company on the North Atlantic; after all, what would a woman know about the maritime industry? "No miss, far from it. Leyland celebrates its fortieth anniversary next year, and I've been employed by the line for six years myself."

At that moment Stewart returned with a keyring, and quickly located the right one to undo her handcuffs. As she expressed gratitude he made a gentlemanly dip of his head. "Are you alright, is there anything we can do for you?"

"No, don't worry about me, but what about my crew?" she looked from one to the other, and then to the third figure present, spread out in eternal repose on the deck. "Marc…"

Her lip trembled, before she scowled and turned abruptly back to the two of them. "There was a mutiny onboard, and it devolved into violence. Are there any other survivors?"

Steward and Groves silently exchanged a glance, wondering how to best break the news and so avoid any hysterics. And yet something in her words struck Groves as strange.

Did she say 'her' crew?

"We've only found one other body so far, miss," ventured Stewart, picking and choosing his words. "However, we've not seen anyone alive since we came aboard. But rest assured, we'll do all we can to assist…"

"There were members of my crew fighting the fires alongside the mutineers, and there must be someone alive below decks," she interrupted sharply, looking around at the darkened bridge. "The engines were shut off after we collided with the ice, and it wasn't done from here. They must have pulled the circuit breakers at the same time, to kill the electrics."

Before either man could react, she vanished into the darkened rooms aft, and Stewart took a step to follow her. "Miss, wait, are you a passenger? Where's this vessel's captain?"

"Mr Stewart!" Groves called out, kneeling to pick up an object that had fallen to the floor beside the helm. It was a navy blue 'baseball' cap, a few long hairs clinging to a tacky material on the strap line. He turned it over so that Stewart could read the lettering on the front, and see for himself the 'scrambled egg' oak leaves woven into the bill. "I think she *is* the captain."

"Impossible…" Stewart had enough time to mutter his head in disbelief before the woman, the captain, returned, a black object clenched in her fist. She was speaking quickly in French, and at first Groves thought she was talking to herself, until she released a button on the side of the device and another voice replied through it. Through the string of words, he heard '*electrique*', and after a few seconds, the interior lights came back on in with a series of bangs, followed by a rising symphony of whines and hums as various devices on the bridge stirred into arcane life, the glass panels around them illuminating.

"The engineers are all safe," she said with a sigh of relief, lowering the device from her mouth. "They were herded into the air conditioning room, but got free and shut down electrical power. Then they barricaded themselves into the engine room to await help." She paused, and her expression darkened to serious

216

concern. "Those who survived the violence on deck are in the ship's hospital."

"Miss..." Stewart stepped forward, the hat Groves had found in his hand. "You said 'your crew'. Are you this vessel's captain?"

"Yes, Capitaine Joanna Laroche," she answered matter-of-factly, brushing her hair back from her face and, taking the cap back off him, setting it on her head. Then she offered a hand. "Mr Stewart, Mr Groves, thank you."

Uncertain of proper etiquette, they returned her handshake, Groves marvelling at her upstart confidence. He had not failed to notice the connection between her surname and that of the ship, and suspected that she was a member of the line's owning family, cocky or misguided enough to believe mere ownership qualified her as master of this vessel. He could not help but pity the crew compelled to serve under such a 'captain'.

"Miss... Captain Laroche," Steward began slowly, his discomfort evident, and his mind evidently coming to the same conclusion as Groves' own. "What happened here?"

Her pretty face darkened. "Some of the deck crew vanished in Tripoli a month ago; these men took their place. During the voyage they revealed themselves to be Islamic terrorists, or smugglers, or something..."

As she continued to talk, Groves could see a perplexion on Stewart's face that mirrored his own.

"...they took the ship, and murdered my First Mate. One of them decided I should be tied to the wheel, and his henchman made me hold course at gunpoint, right until we nearly ran down several members of the Memorial Fleet. After he ran off the bridge I tried to steer us into open water, and nearly hit another ship, before eventually crashing into this *unforecasted* field ice..."

She frowned momentarily, and then looked up, expression concerned. "Were there any ships in the fleet dressed-up to resemble the *Titanic*, because that second ship I nearly hit looked almost like a fully-working replica!"

Groves was about to say that she had by all accounts nearly collided with the *Titanic* herself, confused himself as to what this 'Memorial Fleet' of hers was, when Stewart spoke up. "I don't understand. Are you describing an act of piracy? And you said these men were Mohammedans, so are they affiliated with the Ottoman Empire? Why did you even have *ethnics* in your deck crew?"

She stared at the man as if he had suddenly sprouted a second head, opened her mouth to reply and then paused, breathing deeply.

"I smell smoke – is the fire at the stern still burning?"

Pushing open a sliding door she crossed onto the bridge wing. Unwilling to move, Groves reverently picked up the black handheld device she had left on a table top and turned it in his hand.

"Mr Groves," Stewart coughed. "I don't think she's quite all together; and I can't understand how a female can believe herself qualified to master a fishing-smack, let alone a vessel of this size. Perhaps Captain Lord should take command of the ship on behalf of her owners, this woman's family, assuming she doesn't sink."

Barely paying attention, Groves crossed to the rows of the upright cabinets, and realised that the windows sunk into their upper surface were cinematic devices, like the contraption in his pocket. One machine in front of him was displaying a chart of the North Atlantic. All the annotations were in French, but in the bottom corner he saw a small icon of a tricolour, and depressed a button next to it. Images of several flags of the world filled the screen, each annotated accordingly. Français, Español, Deutsch. His finger settled on the comforting image of the Union Flag, and with a chime the screen reverted back to the previously-displayed electronic chart, but with all the text now appearing in English. The words *'Connection Lost'* and *'Last Known Position'* blinked in the corner, along with a pair of co-ordinates and the time and date. Reading to himself, Groves slowly felt the jumbled pieces of information sliding together in his mind, leading to an incredible conclusion.

"Mr Stewart…" he trailed off. When no-one replied he looked up and saw that the Chief Officer had exited after Laroche, and he followed after them.

Out on the wing, the woman was staring down in disbelief at the *Californian*, smoke from the smaller ship's funnel wafting up towards them. Far below, he could see Captain Lord's pale face turned up towards them. He saw Laroche take an unsteady step back from the rail, watched her clench a trembling hand and take several deep breathes.

"Your ship… it's a relic, steam-powered…" she looked levelly at Stewart, her eyes narrowed. "Please tell me that you're a preservation society, and that down there is your museum ship?"

"No, Captain Laroche," Groves interjected, keeping his voice carefully neutral. "She was launched only eleven years ago."

There was the sudden confusion of footsteps, and turning they saw that other members of the ship's crew were joining them on the bridge, two of them armed with weapons similar to the one Groves had slung over one shoulder. He was surprised at how clean the engineering officers' overalls were, used to seeing men slaked in oil, sweat and coal dust.

"Could someone please explain to me what is happening?" Stewart interjected, the normally calm man beginning to express deep-running frustration.

"Chief," Groves slowly replied. "This ship is so different to *Californian*, so much more advanced, in ways we've never seen…" he paused, and looked at the other arrivals, hesitant. "And the clock in its wheelhouse thinks the year is 2012… Sir, I think this ship has travelled through time, from a hundred years in the future."

He expected Stewart to dismiss the idea, or snort a laughing objection, but the Chief Officer simply stared off forward along the many high-stacked steel containers racked on the long deck. "Incredible…"

The other men were beginning to murmur loudly, until Laroche cut them off in their native tongue. Groves could not miss the immediate deference the crew showed her, nor the fear in their voices, even if the words were double-Dutch to him.

Amazing… she really is *their captain. And they respect her!*

Several of the men crossed to the rail and gazed down on the ship rafted alongside, from this elevated vantage appearing like a child's toy boat on a millpond. And he saw in their faces that they immediately recognised it as being from a school of design as antiquated to them as Sir Francis Drake's fleet would be to *Californian's* crew.

"*Californian…*" she rolled the name in her mouth, then her eyes widened. "You're the ship that stood still!"

Those words struck a strange note of horror in Groves as she checked her watch and then scanned the surrounding fog. "*Mon Dieu!* Then that means that ship we just avoided was not a replica at all! The *Titanic* is sinking right now! You've got to tell your captain to go to her side, aid her passengers!"

"It's alright," Groves said, taking a breath and raising a hand to calm them both, though a voice in his mind cautioned him from actually attempting to restrain her. "We were travelling to meet with *Titanic* when we found you. We've already been assured that help has arrived without us."

"Is that so?" she asked. "Then maybe we're not alone…"

Biting her lip, she spun around and returned into the wheelhouse. Groves followed, seeing her brush her hand over one of the cabinet displays, where ghostly green afterimages lingered on a black field.

"*Le radar fonctionne…*" she whispered aloud, before pointing sharply at one of the engineers. "*La radio! Confirmer la situation de Titanic, et si quelqu'un peut nous aider. Vite-vite!*"

"*Oui, capitaine!*" was his immediate reply, before the man in question disappeared back into one of the rooms astern. Pausing for a second, Laroche seemed to relax. Groves himself released a held breath, and then everyone present tensed as the ship groaned softly.

"Chief, we're listing…" he heard Laroche say in her accented English. She was leaning on the helm, mouth pursed in obvious grief. "What's our damage, Thierry?"

"It is not good, Joanna… whatever forces 'moved' us also shook the hull up badly. The reserve fuel tank below the aft deck got compressed and ruptured explosively – that's what started the fire. She's sprung leaks in the shaft alley and engine room, the main generators flooded out about ten minutes ago, and I think our rough halt in the ice probably ripped open the forward thruster tubes and one of the holds. We've on the emergency circuit for lights and instruments, but there's not enough power to run the bilge pumps…"

"*C'est des conneries!*" the Captain spat, clutching at her brow for a moment before drawing herself up straight and pointing at

Californian's representatives. "What about these men? Can their ship help dewater us?"

The engineer took a single glance towards the Leyland officers and shook his head. "The *Seguin Laroche* is flooding forward and astern, *capitaine*… she is going to sink, in a few hours or so, if she doesn't roll over like a whore before then."

"My girl's no *pouffiasse*, Thierry, and you know it," Laroche said firmly, gripping the helm and squeezing it. "She'll fight to stay alive as long as she can retain buoyancy…"

Her shoulders sagged. "But if you say she's sinking, then I've got no choice but to believe you."

A call from astern heralded the man she had sent on some mission. From the scrap of paper in the man's hand, Groves guessed he had returned from this ship's equivalent of a wireless cabin.

"You were right, *capitaine*," he sweated, hand shaking as he read aloud from the sheet. "We have moved in time. Monsieur Cameron on the *Rescue* confirms that they are standing by off *Titanic* and providing her with assistance. But *Rescue* and the other ships are needed there, and cannot aid us."

"*Putain de merde!* Did you inform them of what we have onboard, of those *bastards'* cargo?"

"No… I, uh, I didn't want to broadcast that. Wasn't sure who might be listening."

"Alright, that was sensible," she nodded, hissing wearily. "And so is their decision to remain with *Titanic*. She's carrying over two thousand lives; we number less than twenty and already have a ship at our side… so we've got to take care of things on our own."

She tipped her head and beckoned to *Californian*'s officers. "Sirs, please come with me."

Confused, but drawn along by the force of her command, Groves and Stewart followed her and some of the ship's contingent down to the stern. That there had been a fire was evident from the blackened steel boxes stacked here, given how many were twisted and deformed, spilling their contents across the decks.

"Viens m'enculer…"

And there were more bodies, many burned and blistered horribly, laid out on fire-scorched decks. Overwhelmed by the gruesome sight and the smell of cooked flesh, Groves staggered through a hatchway to be sick, only to find his nostrils assailed by the reeking stink of blood. His stomach reacted violently.

When he was done being sick, he looked around, hoping there was something other than his sleeve with which to wipe his chin. He seemed to be in a small service space, one that had been used as a makeshift surgery judging from a small pile of bloodied bandages in the corner. Other than grotesque reddish smears on the deck and wall, the space was silent and sterile, untouched by the blaze that had consumed the aft decks.

Groves stood a step forward to steady himself against the foul metallic stench, and felt his foot kick against something lying on the deck. Kneeling, he found it to be another electronic device, like the one he now carried in his pocket, but larger and bulkier, hinged in the centre like a book. Opening it he saw another illuminated screen, on which reams of information was being displayed, all relating to something called the '*Liberty Bell*'.

Closing the lid, he turned the device over and found a label on the underside. Most of it was in French, but he discerned what he took to be a name.

Nashat Abu Shakra. Well, that sounds like the kind of name Johnny Turk would give himself. And she said that the rebelling crewmen were Mohammedans…

"Mr Groves?" someone called from behind him. "Are you alright?"

It was Captain Laroche, and from beyond her he could hear the sound of men getting to work. Keeping his back turned so that she could not see the machine he was holding, Groves nodded. "Yes, captain. Just… a little queasy, is all."

"I know how you feel…" she said sadly, before her tone of voice hardened. "Could you and Mr Stewart please introduce me to *Californian*'s captain as soon as possible; if the *Seguin Laroche* is going to sink, then it's imperative that we transfer one particular piece of cargo off of her immediately."

Still facing away from her, Groves slowly placed the device he had found down on the deck and slid it out of sight beneath a workbench, before rising and turning to face her, mimicking more sickness than he now felt. In truth, he suddenly felt as if he had been given the keys to the universe.

"Of course, Captain, but what item of cargo might that be?"

She smiled grimly and, leading him back out on deck, indicated towards one particular 'container', one that appeared to have been crushed in the fist of an angry deity. "Whatever's left of the time machine that brought us here."

CHAPTER TWELVE

Thomas Andrews was standing on the roof of *Titanic*'s officers' quarters, assisting some of the crew. With their backs to the forward funnel, they were working to release a stowed Engelhardt life raft, and all he could see was the wood-and-canvas body of the 'collapsible'. It filled his vision, blocking out what his overwhelmed mind could not comprehend.

After *Oceanic* had arrived, he and Ismay had followed Smith into the chart room where Murdoch and Miss Paik were waiting. Murdoch himself was uncharacteristically dazed, and did not even acknowledge their arrival, transfixed by the device Miss Paik had placed on the chart table.

She had called it a *'laptop computer'*, and described it as an advanced, electrically-powered variant of Charles Babbage's theoretical thinking-engines, capable of many useful tasks. To illustrate, she had set in motion a presentation much like an epidiascope slideshow, but in full colour.

He had laughed to himself when he saw that the title was *'Titanic's Heirlooms'*, but the images she had shown them of *Titanic*'s wreck, lying broken on a future seabed, had destroyed both his momentary humour and any last reservations he had had as to the veracity of her story. The presence of the *Oceanic* confirmed her jumbled account of time travel, but it seemed incredible, impossible even, that this was all connected to the sinking of his ship.

He shivered as he recalled the image she had called up of this very spot, the deckhouse rent where the expansion joint had torn open, causing the forward funnel to collapse to starboard, the action of the wall peeling away exposing the porcelain bathtub in the captain's suite of cabins. Smith himself had been particularly struck by the sight of his personal toilet facilities submerged two-

and-a-half miles below sea level, but as if seeking assurance that the wreck was indeed *Titanic*, the captain sent for the wireless technicians. Phillips and Bride had been shown Miss Paik's images of a Marconi spark distributor, allegedly recovered from the wreck, and confirmed it was *Titanic*'s, the only one of its kind in the world.

It had been a convincing show, but Paik's behaviour had been even more illuminating. Thomas swore that she was analysing all of their behaviours and mannerisms, taking mental notes as if adding to a personal historical record. It leant weight to her assertion that she was a student of *Titanic*'s history, granting him an uncomfortable vision of future historians and academics extrapolating the events of tonight from eyewitness accounts and the evidence provided by the wreck; it was frightening to consider.

And it begged the question: *what about me?* What conclusions had history reached on his own life and character? Paik had attempted to skip through certain parts of the presentation, but all of the gathered men had caught a glimpse of an upright lifeboat davit on the starboard side of the wreck, annotated with the words *'Officer Murdoch's Last Stand'*. Beside him, Thomas had felt the man in question tense, before the Scotsman made a quiet excuse and left the room.

The inference was clear. Murdoch had died 'tonight', and from the scrutiny Paik had given to the Marconi-men he was also left wondering if both of them had survived. And when she had been introduced to Bruce Ismay, her handshake had been chillingly curt, leaving Tom in mind of the gospel of Matthew.

He will separate people one from another as a shepherd separates his sheep from the goats, and He will set the sheep on His right hand but the goats at His left.

Judgement; she was judging them based on accounts of their past lives, and was treating them accordingly. He was not sure what had happened to Ismay, but it had evidently not left him a particularly strong place in history. Her awe of Murdoch, and delight at meeting Thomas himself, was far more ambiguous. Had he lived, or died, and as what kind of man had he done so?

So when Officer Pitman had come to the chart room requesting aid in releasing collapsible life rafts A and C, so that they could be launched together with the starboard boats, Thomas had volunteered, in order to drown out the debate raging in his mind.

"That's the last of them," the leading quartermaster said eventually. With his hands raw from where they had struggled with cold metal, Tom took several steps aft until he was standing alongside one of the Findley trunks, ventilation intakes for the boiler rooms. To port, he was able to make out *Rescue*'s arcane upper works. He could hear the raised voices of her crew as they rushed to connect suctions fed through portholes along E-Deck to her intake manifold, and from further forward he could also hear the two portables roaring in full chorus.

Titanic's own pumps were singing away as well, removing water at a rate of seventeen hundred tons per hour. *Rescue*'s two portables had almost doubled the ship's pumping capacity, and once the salvage ship's main pumps came online, the combined figure would rise to more than nine thousand long tons of pumping force per hour. Although at first he had estimated that water was entering the ship at a rate of two thousand tons every five minutes, the inflow had decreased as the pressures inside and outside the hull equalised; he was beginning to believe it possible that *Titanic* could be held at a point of equilibrium.

The sinking could be drawn out to allow as many people as possible to survive, or even be averted altogether.

Did he dare hope?

*

Boiler Room 5 seemed virtually dry, except for some water flowing up through the floor grates at the forward end, but *Titanic*'s pumps, racing away smooth and constant, showed how she was barely keeping ahead of this compartment's water intake alone. Aside from the looming boilers, the room was practically empty, almost all the firemen having climbed the escape trunks after closing down steam production by drawing the fires. But the residual heat was stifling, made worse by the suffocating blackness caused by the fusing of the lighting circuits after the collision.

"Where's this injured man?" Charles Lightoller, *Titanic*'s Second Officer, called as he reached the foot of the escape ladder.

He drew from his belt a torch that Kai Alinka had given him and marvelled as its beam cut through the murk like a blade of white fire. Charles decided that Alinka's description of the torch as being like a *'lightsaber'* very apt, assuming the analogy referred to some piece of future technology of which he had no possible conception.

The future? Yes, the future. After Andrews had left with the girl, the islander named Alinka had broken the truth quite bluntly.

"Officer, here's the deal. You've got questions about our ship, our practices, and ourselves. The answer to all of them is that we're from your future, and we're trying to make sure *Titanic* doesn't sink. Nothing else matters beyond that."

Charles had found it all a bit hard to take in, and observation of the *Rescue*'s crew had only compounded his turmoil. He had assumed that Alinka, as a Polynesian, was subservient to the whites among the crew, but was surprised to find them deferring to him as a leader. And that young woman who had come so cocksure aboard the ship was also some kind of Oriental, a race for which he had never had much of an opinion.

"You're a man who finds it easy to hold others in contempt, Lights," he had been told once. Now he was honestly confused as to which caste stood in command aboard *Rescue*. Yet there was a clarifying solace to be had in that these people he was working with were Americans; he supposed the finer qualities of being raised in a predominantly Anglo-Saxon society had smoothed out their ethnic idiosyncrasies, so he should treat them as he would any other intelligent, civilised person.

And then he realised that he'd gone round in a circle and ended up back where he started, but given how quickly *Rescue*'s crew were setting up their hoses under Alinka's direction, there was little for him to do except wonder at the strangeness of these 'time travellers'.

The news that someone from *Titanic*'s crew had broken their leg was a genuine relief, providing him with an outlet for his energy. Now that he was down here in Boiler Room 5, he could see how easy it would have been for someone to get hurt; the atmosphere was thick with smoke, and the lifting of numerous inspection plates to assist with pumping operations had created gaping holes that were all but invisible in the dark.

The injured man, an engineer named Shepherd, had been brought over to the pump room, an enclosed space at the back of the boiler room. Charles had quickly established that the man was incapable of walking, let alone climbing a ladder, and promised to return with help, instructing Barrett and Harvey, the two men attending the pumps, not to try moving Shepherd into another compartment.

Climbing back up to Scotland Road, where Alinka and his team were feeding hoses down into Boiler Room 6, he went aft and gained access to *Rescue*'s gangway through a cramped door intended for offloading bags of ash when in port. He knew he should not leave *Titanic* without Captain Smith's permission, but needs must, he rationalised.

Besides, he wanted to get a quick look at this queer ship, if only to satisfy his own curiosity.

"Hello!" he called. "We've a hurt man below, he needs help!"

One crewman, seeing his officer's uniform, saluted and immediately called for a first aid team. While they made themselves ready, Charles had crossed the deck to a workstation, upon which books had been hastily strewn about. An electrical device whirred softly, a glowing glass screen filled with text, but he had instead focused on an open book, pages turned to reveal a glossy reproduction of a painting. The vibrancy of the colours and quality of the print was stunning, but that was not what had caught his attention.

The illustration depicted *Titanic* sinking under a slew of stars, her bow submerged and lifeboats floating in the foreground. With a morbid fascination, he began to flick through the pages, pausing every now and again.

There were more pictures, artistic impressions of *Titanic* departing Southampton, *Titanic* moored alongside *Olympic* in the Belfast shipyards, and *Titanic* tearing in two. The last was a grim image, metal rending as broken fragments of machinery were vomited from the breach, the ocean boiling with steam and splashes. An inset panel showed the ship's bow beginning a long plunge to the seabed.

Shuddering, he turned another page, and discovered an image of a figure in a seaman's sweater standing atop a capsized lifeboat. Inky black darkness surrounded the fragile wooden island all around, while countless people clung to its side, struggling to pull themselves up onto the boat's curved back.

'*Second Officer Lightoller coordinates passengers aboard Collapsible Lifeboat B*', read the caption.

The officer in the image was heroic, reaching out to drag someone to safety, mouth open as he yelled words of command. Again, there was an inset panel, of a face Lightoller knew well; his own.

Charles Herbert Lightoller; 30th March 1874 – 8th December 1952.

Quickly he skimmed over the abbreviated biography printed below, before closing the book and inspecting the cover. *Titanic Century* by Adrienne McKinn, illustrated by Janice Patton. Gracing the frontispiece was an image of the ship in the final moments of her sinking, the stern rearing high into the air, lights ablaze from every port and window. Clean, bright, sterile and terribly beautiful against the stars.

His eyes moved from the book to the actual *Titanic*, noting streaks of black grime from where she had taken on coal at Southampton, the patches of rust already forming in the creases of metalwork, the darkened cabins that had never seen occupants, the dim glow of the electric lights scattered infrequently along the decks.

As he tried to come to terms with what was or was not happening tonight, one of *Rescue*'s crew, wielding a rigid red backpack emblazoned with (strangely enough) the Swiss flag, called out to him.

"Mr Lightoller, is it? We've got our gear, sir."

The bag turned out to be an ingenious collapsible stretcher, large enough to take a man. Back in the boiler room its function was quickly demonstrated, and engineer Shepherd was quickly secured into the stretcher. Then, using ropes threaded up the escape trunk to Scotland Road, they had begun to slowly lift him out of the bowels of the ship.

Charles himself had been at the bottom of the ladder, keeping the foot of the stretcher steady, when a sharp **bang** broke over the rhythm of the pumps.

Like the canon at Fort Denison, he had time to think, remembering a prank he had pulled on a voyage to Australia, and then he heard the sound of inflowing water increase in volume.

"That sounds like it came from the coal bunkers!" he called to fireman Barrett. "Are they open to the sea?"

"They bloody well are," the leading stoker replied, anxiously wiping coal dust and sweat from his brow. "When we hit I was in Number Six; saw the plates open as if she'd busted a seam, and that damage extends past the bulkhead into this room's for'ard bunker, so I had the stokehold doors closed to contain the worst of it."

Charles attempted to wet his lips, but the air was too dry. "Wasn't that the bunker in which coal caught fire back in Belfast?"

"Yup," Barrett nodded. "We've been emptying it through the voyage, got the last of the smouldrin' coal out yesterday, but the bulkhead itself was black from the heat." His expression became concerned. "You don't think that the bulkhead might collapse under weight of the water on the other side, do you?"

"I don't know..." fretted Lightoller, still clinging to the escape ladder to stabilise Shepherd's stretcher. "Run forward, quick. Try and judge if water is coming through from Boiler Room 6."

Nodding, Barrett vanished through a gap between the boilers, and after a tense few seconds broken only be the hiss of steam and the thrum of the pumps, Charles heard him shouting back.

"I can't see into Boiler Room 6. The water on that side has covered o'er the inspection peephole, but there's water spilling out 'round the stokehold doors on our side!"

Then that bunker has flooded completely, Charles thought intently. *The firemen were ordered to empty it to combat the fire... which would leave a massive void for the water to fill, with the door acting as a crude dam...*

"Get back!" he shouted. "Mr Barrett, come back to the escape-"
CLANG!
Something broke, he heard Barrett cry in alarm, and then with a hungry roar, a huge wave of dirty green water flooded aft between the boilers. At the foot of the ladder, Charles saw a limp figure being carried back on the flow like a twig in a current, before the wave broke over the stoker and pulled him under.

Without thinking, he threw himself into the flood in an attempt to reach Barrett, who was drifting face down just a few feet away, but every time Charles tried to get to him, the rising water just swept the fireman up and smacked him back against the boilers.

"Lightoller! Hey, *Lights*!" Kai Alinka shouted from above. "Help! We can't hold him!"

Charles looked up to see a terrified Shepherd swinging like a pendulum, and then glanced back towards the motionless Barrett, little more than two arms-lengths away.

He made his choice.

*

Tom Andrews heard a sharp bang reverberate up the Findley trunk from the Boiler Rooms, just before a blast of air roared up the shaft and swatted him back off of his feet. Unable to stop himself, he rolled awkwardly from off the roof of the officers' quarters, bowling over several passengers as he landed on the Boat Deck. Despite the cushioning provided by their thick lifejackets, Thomas lay prostrate for several seconds, winded.

He could feel the deck quivering beneath him, subtle groans reverberating up as the ship's nose took a dive. Passengers chattered nervously as he and those he had landed upon struggled to their knees. Then, with an effort worthy of Samson or Gilgamesh, he got to his feet and hobbled forward, his right ankle protesting every time he put weight on it. He found Smith on the bridge, trying to reach someone on the engine room telephone.

"Thomas, what's happened?" the Captain demanded, hanging up the phone as soon as he laid eyes on him. "Why's the ship suddenly pitched herself forward?"

Thomas quickly furnished an answer, and reached an unwelcome conclusion. "It's because of that bunker-fire! A surge of air came up the ventilation trunk from Boiler Room 5, so the heat-damaged part of Bulkhead E must have given way!"

"If another compartment has flooded, we'll have to move our own pumping operations back to Boiler Room 4 and hope for the best, yes?" Smith postulated.

"It's worse than that," Thomas sighed. "If the bulkhead between them is compromised, Boiler Rooms 5 and 6 are now one massive free-flooding compartment, and as the water rises in both its weight is going to pull the ship down rapidly by the head; there's no way we can keep her afloat now."

"*That's not true!*" an increasingly familiar voice butted in, and Philippa Paik introduced herself to the conversation. "I'm sorry, I should have remembered that Boiler Room 5 would flood beforehand, but it's not because of a collapsed bulkhead!"

"Miss Paik," began the captain. "Mr Andrews knows the ship better than anyone-"

"Yes Sir, but with all respect, I know the testimony of tonight's original survivors better than either of you!" she said decisively. "Fred Barrett, a stoker down below, is a witness to this. He said that he saw a wave of foam come tearing through between the boilers and that he then jumped for the escape ladder, not that the bulkhead collapsed! He ran before actually seeing where the water was coming from!"

She turned to Thomas. "Mr Andrews, at the enquiry into the sinking, Edward Wilding from Harland & Wolff testified that the fire would not have had sufficient power to compromise the bulkhead's watertight integrity, that at most..." she paused, as if searching through her memory, and then spoke aloud, as if quoting; "*it might weep a few bucketfuls an hour, that could easily be handled by the pumps.*"

Thomas listened carefully; Edward Wilding was his assistant back at the shipyards, and so would knew *Titanic*'s particulars as well as he did, and would have had access to further reports and information in the aftermath...

Ed was testifying in your place, does that mean that-

He discarded that train of thought as Ms Paik implored again. "Sir, you're a marine architect. Even if the fire did heat the bulkhead up, you know that they were over-engineered to handle extreme loads; with the benefit of hindsight we believe that the coal bunker flooded *by itself*, and that one of the stokehold doors gave way under the weight of water trapped behind it. *That bunker's* where the wave witnessed by the men came from, not Boiler Room 6, which means that the ship's watertight subdivision *has not been compromised.*"

Tom licked his lips, glancing from her to Smith, who stepped forward.

"Thomas, if you believe that pumping can help the ship stay afloat a while longer, I'll trust your judgement; if not, we need to launch the portside boats to speed the evacuation, and that will require *Rescue* to cease pumping and stand off to allow us to lower them to the water."

"Keep pumping as long as possible, captain," answered Tom, breathing deeply to calm himself. "I trust Ed Wilding's judgement... or at least what he'll later conclude; if Ms Paik is correct, and she has been so far, then the ship has a chance, but I need to go below and assess the current nature of the flooding..."

Smith nodded, acknowledging him. Thomas turned and began to head aft, his stride broken by the protests of his ankle.

"I'm coming with you," Paik announced, matching him with shorter, quicker paces. Her thinking-engine, the oracle she called her 'laptop', was carried under arm, and she looked up at him with a calm seriousness. "You don't know what damage the ship took when she hit the ice, Tom, but I might... I've spent years sifting through conflicting theories, from what commands Murdoch gave during the collision, to whether she broke bottom-up from the keel or top-down from the expansion joints."

His legs failed him, and he stopped at the vestibule to the grand staircase. "The ship is going to break in two?" he repeated, stunned. His imagination had been vague as to how *Titanic* would finally sink, but he had not expected her to go down in anything less than one piece.

He saw her blanch and struggle to hold back a curse.

"I'm sorry; I gave too much away..." she looked at him and bit her lip, before checking her watch. "This way..."

With her providing support, they descended the first flight of stairs to the lifts. Thomas closed the sliding grate and jammed the lever into the down position, the bellboy who should have attended this station having vanished.

As the lift started down, she turned to him. "Around 2.15am in the original timeline, the ship tore herself apart somewhere around the third funnel. We argue about the mechanics, but the simple truth is that the fore and aft thirds of the hull ended up half-a-mile apart on the ocean floor, with everything in between scattering itself across the bottom. But that doesn't have to happen tonight, Tom. Boiler Room 5 flooded exactly an hour after the collision in my time, and that deadline passed *twenty-five minutes ago!*"

She held up her watch, another marvel with a numeric display; sure enough it was five past one.

"We're changing things Tom... it's, it's like a clock winding down, the beats are coming further apart, and might stop altogether."

The lift jolted as it reached the lowest level and struck the stops. Thomas pushed open the grate to E-Deck.

"Carry on – you say you've heard theories on the iceberg damage, what's the consensus?"

"It's divided," she replied, placing herself under his shoulder to help take the weight off of his ankle. "Edward Wilding estimated that the damage to the ship was at most twelve square feet in size, spread over the first six compartments, but until the wreck was found popular opinion was that only a single enormous gash could have sunk the ship."

Thomas repressed a mental snigger; damage of that magnitude along three hundred feet of her length would have caused *Titanic* to founder in minutes, possibly even capsizing as she did. The implications of Ed's calculation were incredible, though – twelve square feet was an area not much larger than the average door.

"The two biggest theories," Paik continued, once Thomas had directed her to an emergency access that opened onto the forward part of Scotland Road, "are that either the iceberg popped seams and rivets as the ship scraped alongside it, causing water to come in through gaps between the hull plates, or that *Titanic* grounded briefly on an underwater shelf of the berg, damaging the double bottom and twisting the hull; again causing the strakes to part."

Thomas paused at the door, leaning onto the frame as she pulled it open. "Like twisting the ends of a banana in opposite directions, causing the skin to split," he clarified. She shrugged, heaving on the door while Thomas continued to think aloud.

"If *Rescue*'s crew have the equipment, and if the pumps can buy time, it might be possible to rig collision mats along those compartments we know have sidewall damage, like Boiler Rooms

5 and 6 – if we could limit the water coming into those two, it might be possible to keep her head up."

She came towards him to help him along, but he stopped her, holding up a hand.

"I saw water coming up into the fireman's tunnel," he began, slowly, thinking aloud and judging her response. "The tunnel's too far inside the hull for ice to penetrate from the side. That would support your notion of damage to the double-bottom. *But*, if you're right about the hull being racked during the collision, then the tracks for the watertight doors separating Boiler Room 6 from the end of the tunnel might have deformed, jamming the doors open; that would mean a second source of water into Boiler Room 6, separate from damage to the boiler room itself, and maybe the cargo holds as well, if the access doors that connect them with the tunnel are open."

"Would you believe," she said, smiling wistfully, "that you're practically quoting Brown and Stephenson's paper on the subject?"

The names meant nothing to Tom, but straightening up he motioned from the two of them to proceed. "I need to talk to someone who was in Boiler Room 6 when she struck, someone who saw the damage."

She positioned herself under his shoulder again. "I mentioned Fred Barrett earlier; he was on duty in Number 6 during the collision and saw water coming through the side of the hull, and will have escaped up the ladder out of Boiler Room 5 when the water came through just now. He's the man to talk to."

They turned into the corridor. Further forward, Kai Alinka and Lightoller were helping to lift a figure shrouded in a black jacket out of the escape trunk for Boiler Room 5. Slowly the two of them approached as some of *Rescue's* team lifted the body onto a stretcher. Thomas felt Pip stiffen his arm as they drew close, the girl whispering a horrified "oh, no."

"Philippa," Thomas said slowly. "When the bunker door gave way, was there anyone unable to escape from Boiler Room 5?"

"I… I don't know. Some accounts say engineer Shepherd broke his leg and couldn't climb, but they were regarded as having been made up or exaggerated…" she trailed off.

"Is this man… engineer Shepherd?" Thomas enquired, as two men took up the ends of the stretcher. Charles Lightoller and Kai Alinka, both sodden, stood off to one side, the contemporary officer's turtleneck sweater hanging off of him like the fleece of a drowned sheep.

"No, Sir," Lightoller shook his head. "We evacuated Mr Shepherd safely. This poor soul is fireman Barrett."

Tom felt Philippa Paik go rigid under his weight, a horrified squeak escaping her lips.

"I just killed the witness!"

*

Turning his back on Barrett in favour of trying to save Shepherd, Charles Lightoller had gotten a booted foot up and pushed off from one of the cooling boilers, before half-swimming, half-struggling his way to the foot of the ladder. The first few rungs were hard-going, but once above the level of the water he had taken hold of the bottom of the stretcher and used its weight to stabilise both himself and the unfortunate Shepherd, who was wailing like a child in distress. Then, slowly, with Alinka and the others hauling from above, they worked their way up to where the ladder bent back onto the slanted face of the funnel uptakes, allowing the stretcher to slide easily up the final push to the escape trunk hatch.

With Shepherd safe, Charles had scrambled back down to the turn of the uptakes and shone his torch into the void. Barrett's body drifted below, seeping rich red blood from a head wound. The water was no longer surging around the compartment in waves, and carefully Charles and Alinka climbed back down to check the body for a pulse.

Nothing. Frederick Barrett had been dead for some minutes. They brought the body up immediately, using a length of rope tied under the corpse' armpits. It was only now, as they were placing him on a second stretcher, that they realised they had company. Charles repressed a groan at the sight of Paik, the brazen young female who had come aboard from *Rescue*, and then started in surprise when she cried out in despair.

"I just killed the witness! He was meant to testify at both of the Enquiries!"

Her horror at the sight of Barrett's shrouded body was evident, but when Andrews instinctively moved to comfort her, Charles inexplicably saw her push him away.

"Frederick Barrett was meant to live…" she softly groaned. "And I've gone and *killed him!*"

Andrews opened his mouth, but she threw up a flat black object like a shield, pushing it into his hands. "Don't waste time talking to me, just try and save the ship!"

Then she covered her face in her hands and slumped against the wall. "The program you need is '*Titanic* 3D'."

"But, I don't know how to operate this thing…" Andrews said, gingerly holding the device like it might shatter.

"I can use a laptop," Kai Alinka butted in. "Bring it through here into the steward's quarters."

Andrews, conflicted, looked between the salvor and the girl now sinking into a sitting position at the foot of the wall. Seeing his discomfort at leaving her alone, Charles put his most manful foot forward. "Go save the ship, Mr Andrews. I'll take care of the young lady."

"Thank you, Mr Lightoller," Andrews replied, before following Alinka into the other room.

"You did not kill Mr. Barrett," Charles said quietly, crossing over to the girl and squatting down beside her.

"I knew that BR5 would flood, and I forgot to mention it to anyone," she replied, her voice flat and emotionless. "I as good as killed him."

Sad as it was to admit, it was a pretty definite sin of omission. Charles struggled to put words to his thoughts. "Life and death are illusions, a dream from which we awake to the reality of hereafter. He's not dead, but merely, set free."

She looked up at him, a slightly amused grin on her face. "Charles Herbert Lightoller, Christian Scientist. I forgot that you had a strong sense of faith." She closed her eyes. "Again, something I should have remembered – especially since I read your autobiography, Lights."

He had written an autobiography? Charles' first thought was to whether or not there was a copy floating around somewhere on one of these time-ships.

"Funny, though," she suddenly laughed in self-depreciation. "The tale of someone drowning in Boiler Room 5 was said by the experts to have been impossible, another popular myth, like the collapsing bulkhead. Barrett went straight up the escape ladder when the water rushed in, and Shepherd, despite his broken leg, had been moved back into another compartment for his own safety. *Shows what we know!*"

Charles froze, feeling the comforting grin on his face freeze into place like a mask.

Harvey and Barrett kept Shepherd where he was on my orders... and because of that, Barrett was unable to climb the ladder at the critical moment because I was there steadying Shepherd's stretcher. My God, what have I done?

Suddenly the image of himself in the book, of Second Officer Lightoller riding atop a capsized lifeboat like a heroic cowboy, seemed like a mirage, a promised reward that had now been snatched away from him.

If there is anyone here now guilty of accidentally taking a life, it is myself...

Miss Paik was looking at him now, visibly longing for comfort, but he found himself unable to speak.

Tell her, Charles. Tell her that it is your mistake, not hers, that killed Barrett.

But the bitter words lodged in his mouth like sackcloth, and instead he lay a hand on her shoulder and spoke with a treacherous semblance of calm. "I would say that things never happen the same way twice, Miss Paik. Things are going to change now, regardless of whether or not we try to guide their outcome. Even if the rest of tonight's events unfold as your histories say they should, I still have the freedom to choose my own course, and the awareness that things have changed only convinces me of that freedom. And so do you."

"But what good is that? What can I accomplish? I'm just a student intern, a *Titanic* enthusiast who talked her way into this situation."

Now struggling to deal with his own guilt, Charles' racing mind jumped aboard a familiar chain of thought, ironically one that he himself was now struggling with: self-respect.

"Look at yourself," he said solemnly, as if addressing a slovenly junior officer. "You have the power of command, an authority conferred upon you by that uniform you wear…"

She looked down at herself and held out her arms, as if noticing her attire for the first time. Then, slowly, she took off her cap and touched a finger to the embroidered words **USNS Rescue**, before laughing. "Cute, but I'm not a member of that ship's crew."

Charles shook his head sternly. "To anyone aboard *Titanic* who does not know better, you are. And haven't you come aboard a sinking ship determined to save lives, bringing with you knowledge and experience that has convinced us to trust you?" He took the cap from her hands and placed it back on her brow, pulling it straight with a final tug. "I am certain that *Rescue*'s captain would be honoured to count you among his crew."

He felt like the world's biggest hypocrite at having talked her up instead of simply revealing that she had no part in Barrett's unfortunate death, but the words of praise drew a smile from her, and she slowly looked aft.

"*Oceanic*'s boats will be here any second," she said softly. "They might need someone to help load passengers, someone who knows about the demographics of *Titanic*'s complement."

"Then hop to it, sailor!" Charles instructed, rising to his feet and pulling her up as if she were an idle cabin boy, suddenly wanting to be rid of her and the feelings of shame he now felt for denying her the truth. "On your way and be quick about it."

Nodding, she turned and began aft along the gentle uphill slope of the Scotland Road corridor, at first uncertain, but gaining in confidence with each step and looking all the more like a young officer ready to take command.

Charles managed a chuckle, calling out with a final snippet of wisdom as he did. "Remember lad, women and children only."

She stopped, and then turned to face him, shaking her head sadly.

"No, Lights – the order is women and children *first*," she corrected, her smile limp but fresh fire in her eyes. "I'll make sure everyone learns from that mistake, at least."

And then, turning away, she strode away up Scotland Road with her hands balled into fists.

What lesson? Charles thought to himself, before shaking his head and trying to shrug off the sudden burden of guilt that had come upon him. Water was beginning to flow into the steward's glory-hole, and inside were Kai Alinka and Thomas Andrews, their faces lit by the glow of the device Ms Paik had left in their custody. On its screen Charles could see a representation of *Titanic*, which was being dragged around and expanded as the two men tapped away at the machine's controls.

"...the flooding in the Forepeak will be contained by the Lower Orlop Deck so long as we don't sink any further," Thomas Andrews was saying, gesturing to the screen to illustrate his words. "The portable pumps are already fighting the water in the cargo holds, and the rest will be coming online in seconds. With three of *Rescue*'s suctions in Boiler Room 6, and one in Boiler Room 5 to assist *Titanic*'s own pumps, I think we can do it!"

"Gentlemen," Charles intervened, the fighting language appealing to him. "What are we doing?"

Andrews looked first to Alinka as if seeking approval, and securing a nod from the younger man, turned his attention to Charles. "We're going to try and save the ship, Mr. Lightoller. Not just slow the sinking, but completely refloat her, and if possible get her into safe harbour!"

He held up one of the futuristic 'talkie' devices and spoke into it. "*Titanic* to *Rescue*, all suctions are in place..."

CHAPTER THIRTEEN

"...begin pumping NOW!"

Jordan Jones had been nearly six years old on the day when his father was killed in a mining disaster. Early one morning, when it was still dark, he was woken by an explosion which shook the house from deep underground. He had stared at the amazing sight of flames gushing hundreds of feet into the air from the shafts in the hills above his hometown, innocently loving every moment of it, unaware that at that very moment his father was choking to death deep beneath his feet.

At the time, he could not understand why his mother was so desperately trying to phone Daddy at work. And when Llewellyn 'Lion' Jones was not among the men who escaped, Jordan had stubbornly refused to accept it, believing that he was still alive, holding out underground, alone, without a light or candle, waiting for the rescuers to find him. When he finally gave into the truth that his father had died down there in the sunless tunnels, Jordan and his mother had cried together for hours, clinging desperately to each other.

Unsurprisingly, most of his childhood nightmares involved blindness. In moments of introspection he privately suspected that he'd chosen a life afloat to ensure he'd always have an open sky over his head.

And now the nightmare had come true, and his world had been reduced to darkness and noise. Without eyes to see, he sat in his chair beside *Rescue*'s helm and listened intently to the ship around him, a walkie-talkie clutched in his hand like a lifeline. Over the tinny sounds of voices repeating orders and reporting on the salvage operation, he could hear first-hand the roar of steam and the clatter of lifeboat davits from high above. Unable to confirm the salvage's identity with his own eyes, it was almost possible to believe that he was sitting outside the open door of a cinema, listening to the work of sound effects artists.

But he knew disasters first hand. Not just from his childhood, but from catastrophes like the Sendai earthquake. He and *Rescue* had been there, attached to the US 7th Fleet in Yokosuka, ship and crew struggling together to save lives, fighting on through the screams of panicked, fearful civilians.

The cries he could hear right now were no different, and from them he *knew* he was listening to an unfolding tragedy, but the stubborn little boy inside him still refused to accept a traumatic truth.

That they had travelled in time; that they were rafted beside the *Titanic*.

And then the handheld radio crackled in his hand, and the voice of a man claiming to be no less than Thomas Andrews spoke again through the static.

"Rescue, I'll say that again. All four suctions are in place. Please commence pumping."

This was insane. He had accepted that there was a ship here in danger, but for it to the *Titanic*, of all things…

But then he thought back to the moment when the *Seguin Laroche* had given off a pulse of light bright enough to blind him, and he had felt himself and his ship twist like corkscrews.

Something happened at that point. Is time travel so hard to believe?

"Captain Jones!" the voice called again. *"The water is about to rise to the tops of bulkheads A and E. If her head goes down much longer we won't be able to counter the additional flooding in the Forepeak and Boiler Room 5. We must act now!"*

"Roger, Mr Andrews, acknowledged. *Rescue* over and out," he responded at last in clipped tones, before releasing the radio's 'speak' button and turning to Lieutenant Miller. "Sam! Bring both main engines to maximum power!"

"Yes sir. Bridge to Engine Room, the captain's calling for max power on the main engines."

Well, it was some comfort that even 'Stoic Sam' Miller seemed to be sharing in his madness.

Below his feet he could feel *Rescue*'s power plant revving up, the twin Rolls-Royce Bergen diesels roaring in turbocharged harmony. Unlike the quadruple-Caterpillar installation of her *Safeguard*-class predecessors, they were not coupled directly to the propellers, but instead to a bank of generators that powered all of the ship's systems. Despite being more complex and maintenance-intensive, the advantage of this arrangement was that in a situation like this, *Rescue*'s full power could be devoted to her arsenal of pumps.

In his mind's eye he could see it all, despite the impossibility of what they were allegedly moored up against. Thick, non-collapsible pipes would have been strung between the two vessels, leading to *Rescue*'s main manifold. Deep in the hull, the engineers would be standing by in the pump room, poised before a vast wall of gauges.

"Engine room reports she's developing 4 Megawatts, Captain. Max power, as you ordered."

Jones already knew. The deck was quivering in a way he had grown very familiar with, as if *Rescue* was trembling with professional zeal, the excitement of a NASCAR driver itching to break out from behind a pace car. Feeling the output of the engines plateau, he motioned for Miller to hand him the comm., and took a steadying breath before speaking with forced calm into the mouthpiece.

"Pump room, begin dewatering *Titanic*."

It was the strangest order he had ever given in his career, and now he was convinced he had taken leave of his sanity.

Well, we might as well indulge our mutual delusion, he thought to himself.

The ship bucked hard as the main valves were opened, and Jones envisioned the needles on the pressure gauges soaring as the pumps bit. After several long seconds, the mighty growl from below decks harmonised with a thunderous outfall as water removed from *Titanic* was regurgitated back over the side of *Rescue*'s deck into the Atlantic.

Sweet Jesus. We're salvaging the Titanic.

"Pumping has commenced sir," Andrews said through the radio. *"It's looking good from this end."*

"The pump room reports that they're working her up to full capacity, sir," Miller confirmed. "They're confident that once there, she'll discharge six thousand tons of water every hour. Add in the two portables plus *Titanic's* own pumps and that makes…"

"…Nine thousand, two hundred tons, yes Sam…" Jones finished for him, the walkie-talkie held under his chin in contemplation, waiting for some sign that this was not some deranged hallucination. As if answering his silent pleas, the radio suddenly stuttered back into life.

"Captain," Andrews said. *"There's a man here who wishes to speak with you."*

"Put him on," he acknowledged, carefully keeping his voice neutral. After a few seconds of scuffled sound, in which he heard Thomas instruct whoever it was to *"hold this button down, like I'm doing"*, a new voice made itself heard. It was a man.

"Hello Captain. This is Charles Lightoller speaking, Second Officer of this ship. I just wanted to express all our thanks for the efforts you and your crew are making on our behalf."

Despite the fact that it had no effect on his vision, or lack thereof, Jones squeezed his eyes shut for a moment, struggling to put a face to that name.

Lightoller? Isn't that the officer the movies portray as either a saintly hero of the British Empire or a toffee-nosed snob?

As if in defiance of those expectations, this man speaking to him had a roughness in his voice that suggested a factory town upbringing, and Jones felt a moment's kinship. It seemed he wasn't the only one present who had run away to sea. "You're quite welcome, Mr Lightoller. How is your ship holding up?"

"Mr Andrews might say otherwise, but in all honesty Captain, unless your boat's pumps can get ahead of the flooding I cannot see *Titanic* staying afloat beyond a couple of hours."

Did he just refer to Rescue as a boat?

"Challenge accepted, *Charlie*," he replied, to his own surprise feeling a smile blooming on his face. "My *ship* is capable of towing *boats* like *Titanic* across entire oceans at a speed of twelve knots. I'm sure we can tackle a little flooding."

A laugh came from the other end of the conversation. *"Well then sir, I look forward to your success. Godspeed and good luck."*

"The same to you, Mr Lightoller…"

The transmission ended and Jones indulged in a full-blown grin, feeling like himself once again. "This entire thing's a load of bull, but damn if *Rescue* isn't pumping away at something. Sam, I require a favour from you, please."

He explained what he needed and Miller quickly used one of the bridge computers to see if *Oceanic*'s wireless network was still in place. Finding a strong signal still showing up, he accessed the Project 401 database and, at Jones' direction, located the archive for one Charles Herbert Lightoller.

"He survived, sir," Miller confirmed. "When the ship plunged at the end he was washed off the deck, and swam to a capsized lifeboat. He and a load of other men balanced on top of it until help arrived in the morning."

Jones heard the sound of keys being tapped, and then Miller cleared his throat and gave a grunt of satisfaction. "And years later he gave an interview to the BBC. There's a sample here."

Shifting forward in his chair, Jones listened as Miller double-clicked…

"Up to the time of getting away the first few boats, no-one believed that the ship was actually in any danger. I'm afraid my own confidence that she wouldn't, or couldn't sink, rather conveyed itself to others…"

It was like being punched in the face. The voice coming out of the speaker, although wizened with the passage of time, was the same one Jones had just been holding a conversation with. They shared the same cadence and pace, and the same accent that he found hard to describe.

That confirmed it. This was real. But what was noticeably different was that, compared to the old man he was now listening to, recalling his past adventures from a recording studio, the Lightoller to whom he had spoken had sounded *afraid*. There was no doubt that his confidence now was that the ship would sink.

"…frankly I'm never likely to forget the sight of that cold, greenish water, creeping step-by-step up that stairway. Some of the lights were shining down on the water, and others, already submerged, were giving it a sort of ghastly transparency…"

He could see it. Like a painter's brush filling in a canvas in front of him, Jones could envision exactly what was being described. Suddenly the fearful cries from out in the dark had something to be afraid of in his imagination, not just a special-effects trick rearing up on a cinema screen, but the relentless weight of water, and a hungry ocean.

"Alright Sam," he said, turning to Miller. "Find volunteers from the crew who have SCUBA experience. Issue them with dive gear and instruct them to swim through the inside of *Titanic*'s flooded bows. They need to locate any open portholes below the waterline, and close them."

If that green onslaught of water was what he was fighting, then he was going to bring every weapon he could find or improvise to bear.

At that point the radio crackled again, and he heard Kai Alinka spluttering. *"Captain, are you there?"*

"I am, Kai," he replied. "What's happened, you sound like you've just dunked your head in a bucket of water."

"Pretty much. I brought a dive-suit and face-mask over to Titanic with me, and I just made a quick inspection of the forward boiler room, number six."

"Smart kid, what did you find?"

"There's damage down the compartment's starboard side close to the floor; I can feel water flowing in there, but even more seems to be flooding in from further forward, through what Tom here calls the Fireman's Tunnel."

"Well, fuck me…" Jones massaged his head. "Are we thinking alike Kai?"

"Yes sir, I think we are. Can you get the gear we need over here ASAP?"

"Way ahead of you," he replied, waving to get his XO's attention. "Sam! Find Doctor Oshiro and his team; ask them to get the DRP gear ready for an emergency field test! And request Captain Gorbachev on the *Anatoly Sagalevich* to approach *Titanic*'s starboard side and stand by. We might need his help in plugging some holes!"

*

People were beginning to panic. Like ripples in the stock market, outward stability masked turbulent emotions beneath. Once someone cracked, others would quickly follow.

Jack Thayer and Milton Long descended the Grand Staircase together, shepherding Jack's parents along. John Thayer was

246

holding onto his wife's arm with a grim tenacity, while she was the model of perfect composure.

"Are you sure about this, Milt?" Jack probed, as they reached the reception room on D-Deck and continued to descend; below this point the stairs were far more austere, the woodwork less intricate, and the crowds denser.

"Definite, Jack," his older friend replied, striding along with confidence. "That huge ship *Oceanic* will send its boats across to us, and they'll have to load through this deck; we just need to make our way aft."

Jack glanced over his shoulder. His father was still maintaining a firm grip on mother's arm, and his face was drawn.

"Father will insist on putting mother on the boats alone," he said quietly. "He won't leave the ship unless all the womenfolk have been evacuated.

"None of us would contemplate that," Milt replied. "But the sooner we find where they're loading the boats, the better chance all of us have."

They reached E-Deck and Jack glanced right, towards an open service door, the contrast between the well-varnished reception room and the white-painted corridor beyond striking. Through it he could see shimmering ripples of light playing on the metal walls; the water had reached this level already. Shouting voices echoed distantly over splashing water and the sounds of powerful machinery at work.

"Wait here," he said, as he crossed to the door. Before he could stick his head through, however, a short figure strode through and turned straight into his chest, knocking them both to the floor. Jack's hands came up and grabbed hold of a thin but surprisingly slick material, like vulcanised canvas; the person was wearing a thick padded jacket that resembled a less bulky version of the life preservers that each in his party wore.

"Ah, shit!" the person exclaimed, and as their head came up the duck-billed cap atop came loose. Dusky black hair spilled across the floor, and Jack found himself looking down at the pleasantly delicate face of a young Oriental woman. He was suddenly very conscious that he was lying on top of her, his hands pinning her own arms in an outstretched position, and that despite their thick clothing he was pressing against the gentle swell of her chest.

247

"Could you please get off?" she said, a little shocked.

"Ah! Oh good Lord, I'm sorry!" Jack replied, whipping his head around and struggling to think of some way to remove himself from his current position without causing any further embarrassment.

"Oh, no rush…" she rolled her eyes, which were very large and almond-shaped. "It's just that, you know, the ship is sinking."

"Ah, erm, yes…" Mortified, Jack shuffled to one side and got to his feet as Milt, laughing openly, came forward and offered the girl a hand up. Blushing, Jack grabbed her fallen piece of headwear and saw the name '*Rescue*' stitched into the fabric; she must have been a crewmember from the strange boat that had come alongside. He supposed it explained her shamelessly masculine attire.

"My apologies, Miss," he said, offering the hat back to her and bowing at the waist, practically prostrating himself for having dishonoured a young lady. "That was extremely discourteous of me."

"No problem," she replied, affecting an airy tone despite a slight blush that had risen to her cheeks. "Are you looking for *Oceanic*'s boats?"

"I suppose we are," Milt offered. "I'm Milton Long, and this is the Thayer party. Would you happen to know which route we are best advised to take?"

At the mention of their names, the woman cocked her head, looking from Jack to his parents and back again. "I don't believe it…" she smirked. "John, Marian, and Jack, correct? I'm Philippa Paik."

Her mouth twisting as if she was struggling not to laugh, she gestured past the staircase and twisted her hand to indicate aft. "They'll probably load the boats through the Second Class reception aft on this deck. I'm heading there myself; this way."

She started walking forward with bold strides. When she heard no-one move to follow her, however, she paused and turned to see the four of them still standing in a loose knot at the foot of the stairs, and she looked back.

"What now? Not willing to follow a woman?" she said, her tone guarded, but suggesting a amused resignation born of frustration.

Jack slowly looked to the rest of his party, an uncomfortable silence ruling until his father took a single step forward and politely cleared his throat.

"Miss, pardon our hesitancy, but you seem to have a remarkable awareness of us, which given recent events raises many questions. No less than three strange ships have appeared in less than an hour, crewed by people the likes of which I have not met in my life. Forgive my bluntness, but who are you?"

Jack felt a swell of pride, seeing in his parent the very model of a gentleman. In response, the face of the woman named 'Paik' softened, the taut creases at the corners of her mouth and eyes smoothing out to leave behind an expression of sadness and... pity?

"I'm sorry for raising my voice. Honestly, I'm a bit overwhelmed myself. I'd like to take the time to explain, but it would only raise more questions for you than answers. Please believe me, however, when I say that we are here to help, and that I can lead you to the boats."

Jack considered her words. Despite her outlandish appearance and uncouth manner, she spoke eloquently and with an informed attitude, an impression reinforced by her uniform, and her appeal to their trust seemed honest. He was also, to be frank, extremely curious. Gathering up his courage, he stepped forward, putting himself at the front of the group. "Please lead on, Miss Paik."

She nodded in gratitude. "Thank you. Mind your footing in Scotland Road, there's water everywhere."

Jack ducked through the open door behind her, and saw that even though the water had not yet flooded this far aft, the passage of multiple persons had dragged large quantities of it up from the forward part of the corridor. One such group were hurrying past as he stepped into the corridor, carrying large yellow cylinders on their backs. Pausing by the door, he held out a hand to assist his mother through, and found the girl taking up the same position on the other side of the doorframe, each of them taking one of Marian Thayer's hands to help her over the raised lip.

"Thank you, Miss Paik," she said genteelly, and Jack recognised in her voice the cheery but slightly mocking tones she used in the company of his friends from university.

"Please, Mrs Thayer," the strange girl replied. "Miss Paik is my grandmother; I'm just Pip."

Marian pursed her lips in clear response to the decidedly masculine abbreviation, and Jack himself cocked an eyebrow, uncertain as to whether or not his mother approved. As Miss Paik – Pip – nodded and continued to lead them aft, Jack found himself watching her closely, noting how the baggy jacket and workman's trousers failed to hide the sway of her slender hips, and how her short hair, stuffed through the back of her cap, bobbed with each step.

"Careful, Jack," warned his mother quietly, her hand lightly held in the crook of his elbow. "She's an interesting young woman, to be sure, but a complete unknown."

Jack nodded in silent agreement, and glanced over his shoulder at the sound of a repressed laugh. Behind him, Milt was holding a hand to his mouth, and from the tight-lipped expression on his father's face, the two of them were sharing some private joke at his own expense.

*

John Jacob Astor stood some feet from the open companionway door, hemmed in by other passengers that were filling the compressed space of *Titanic*'s Second Class reception. Holding his young wife to him, he stared out over the shoulders of attending crew at the gleaming *Oceanic*, lighting up the horizon a quarter-mile off. The ocean surface was as still as a pool of water, and it seemed to him that the two ships were frozen on a field of black ice, motionless and firmly set in place.

A slight quiver of the hull and a far-off groan shook him from that illusion, as did the sensation of his wife's hand clutching tightly at his elbow. Smiling gently he turned to lay a kiss on her forehead, letting his own hand rest lightly on her own in a gesture of comfort.

"Now don't be afraid, Madeleine; the boats are on their way, see."

Madeleine, slight, dark haired and radiantly beautiful in the flush of her youth, not even nineteen years old, leaned close, her head pressed to his chest so that when she whispered, only he could hear.

"Don't leave us alone, John."

He felt her swelling belly pressing against him, and through it a faint kick. "Don't worry," he replied softly. "I'll stay with you as long as possible."

It was a half-truth. John's plan was simply to get Madeleine aboard a boat and ensure the safety of her and their baby; if he was barred from taking a place with her, then he supposed there was nothing more to it.

Over Madeleine's shoulder, he could see that the first of the *Oceanic's* orange, capsule-like lifeboats was drawing alongside *Titanic*. They were right in the liner's stern, and he could already perceive that this end of the ship was beginning to heft itself out of the water; normally the gangway was a few feet above water level, but now evacuating passengers would have to be helped down onto the roof of the enclosed lifeboat, descending into the interior via open hatches at the side. The water surrounding them looked black as death, and cold as the grave. He shuddered slightly, and raised his eyes to the *Oceanic*, filling the horizon and drowning out the stars with her blazing radiance.

"Never saw anything quite like it, did you JJ?" a larger woman to his right interjected, her casual words layered with awe.

"No, Maggie," he agreed, his own tone more measured. Margaret Brown, the wife of a lucky-strike gold miner, had been a good friend of his for many years, and one of the few to have not shunned him during his recent divorce and remarriage. He was glad that at the very least she might end up in the same boat as Madeleine; should he not find a space it would at least mean his wife had a shoulder to lean on, and Maggie was as good as any man when it came to will and strength of character.

The thought gave him some cause for hope, even as he heard *Titanic's* own lifeboats splashing down into the water, felt the deck trembling beneath his feet as if the ship was caught in protracted death tremors.

"JJ!"

He turned. Being the wealthiest man on this crossing had its privileges, but also disadvantages; being constantly picked out

251

of a crowd for one. A group of people had just entered into the reception, one of them raising a hand as they made their way through the crammed space, quality clothes standing out against the plainer, coarser garments worn by the surrounding Second and Third Class passengers. As the group came close enough to distinguish, John straightened up to receive them as if at home welcoming guests, an airy smile coming automatically to his lips.

"John, Marian, Jack," he addressed each, nodding once to a fourth man with whom he was unfamiliar. Before he could say anything, however, he was politely but firmly nudged aside by a shorter figure bedecked in strange clothes, who squeezed past him and Margaret to the ship's officer manning the gangway. John stared after her, amazed at the sight of a woman dressed as a man. Quizzically he turned his attention back to the Thayer party, and young Jack managed a sympathetic smile.

"Our guide. Don't try to understand her, she defies all rational thought."

*

Bruce Ismay was not a sailor, by any measure, but the sea was in his family blood. His father, Thomas Ismay, himself the successful son of a shipbuilder, had purchased White Star Line from its bankrupt founders late in 1868, when Bruce himself had just been a six-year-old boy. As he had grown older, he had seen his father build what had been a failing concern into one of the foremost shipping lines in the world, Bruce coming into his own maturity alongside the business. Thomas had poured much love, time, energy and money into developing the firm, with his family having to be content with what little he had left to give at the end of each day. Despite the mix of fear and awestruck reverence Bruce felt towards the man, it stood to reason that he himself should take a position in the firm; sentiments which eventually saw him succeed an ailing Thomas as Managing Director. Yes, it was fair to say that he had grown up with the White Star Line, and the ships it owned and operated.

So now, as he stood aboard *Oceanic*'s bridge, despite a century's advances in technology, he could still recognise helm and engine controls, and hazard a guess at the function of some of the others.

"Mr Ismay," directed the officer who had led him up from the lower decks. "Captain Waters will be with you in a few minutes. Please make yourself comfortable until then."

Nodding, Bruce had crossed over to the protruding bridge wing, where he found a small lounge, two sofas facing one another over a coffee-table. A potted plant stood to one side, providing a splash of colour.

Make myself comfortable, while Titanic sinks. Good God, is this real?

Finding himself sweating in the warmth, Bruce quickly pulled off his overcoat and draped it over one of the sofas, but remained standing, unable to sit. There was so much to see, and gazing back into the glass temple of the bridge he observed crewmembers in short-sleeved shirts moving amidst glowing screens, consulting in low voices. It was a stark contrast to *Titanic*'s bridge, where right now Smith and his officers would be bundled up in greatcoats against the cold, shouting to make themselves heard over the roar of the safety-valves and the clattering lifeboat gear. He had been there too, trying to make himself useful, when Captain Smith had asked him to board one of the first lifeboats to leave the ailing liner, requesting that he cross to *Oceanic* and open a dialog with her captain. But now that he was here he found himself once again unsure of what to do. It was an unfamiliar and unwelcome sensation, and brought back unpleasant memories from the years after his father's death.

Thomas Henry Ismay had died in 1899, having lived his entire life within the reign of Queen Victoria. Not two years later, Bruce had been approached to sell White Star to the International Mercantile Marine, a trust financed by the American monopolist JP Morgan. With his father barely cold in his grave, Bruce had resisted selling the family silver right up until Morgan offered a sum four times greater than White Star's takings in what had been a very strong business year, at which point the line's Board of Directors had capitulated gladly. Bruce, despite his misgivings, had felt a certain sense of relief; having been hand-groomed to take over the firm from his youth, the chance to part ways with White Star in favour of a destiny of his own making had been enticing.

It was not to be. IMM quickly burned through its funds and fell into financial difficulties. Bruce, looking forward to fishing, spending time with his family and perhaps dabbling in another industry, such as railways, had suddenly been head-hunted by Morgan to take over the presidency of IMM and reorganise all its subsidiaries, including White Star. It had seemed like some cruel joke, and Bruce had argued with himself at great length as to whether or not he should accept the position, all the while feeling that the restless spirit of his father was hovering over his shoulder, pouring poisonous advice in his ear.

In the end, fearing the shame he would feel if he allowed IMM and White Star to collapse at the expense of so many people's livelihoods, and lured in by the promised salary, he had accepted, and reshaped Morgan's ragtag collection of shipping lines into a going concern. And Morgan's money, funnelled through IMM, had enabled Bruce to develop White Star in a way in which his father could have only dreamed, funding ever-larger and better ships for the line. Ships like the *Celtic*, the *Cedric*, the *Baltic* and the *Adriatic*, which were all soon renowned for their comfort and stability. This process of aggrandizement was meant to reach its zenith with the marvellous *Olympic* and her sister *Titanic*…

Titanic, now reduced to a collection of lights slowly floundering in the near distance.

Unable to watch any further as the legacy he had strived to secure gradually sank into the Atlantic, Bruce turned and peered aft along the side of *Oceanic*. The bridge wing protruded from the side of the ship, giving him a perfect view down onto the promenade deck far below, over which the ship's strange, bulbous lifeboats were stored in elevated racks. To Bruce's eyes they were ugly things, their bright colours and immense size doing much to spoil the vessel's dashing lines. Several were even stored directly in front of cabin windows and balconies, denying those passengers a decent view of the sea. It was a poor design choice, and brought to mind an argument he had had during the construction of *Titanic* and *Olympic*…

"Alexander, we've no need to clutter the upper decks with superfluous lifeboats that will never be needed. After all, you designed these Olympians to be their own lifeboats…"

It had been one meeting, one among hundreds, with Alexander Carlisle, head shipwright of Harland & Wolff, until he retired and was succeeded by Thomas Andrews. Thinking back to that day, while staring at these strange lifeboats, left Bruce uneasy. Much like he had felt when debating whether or not to take Morgan's offer of the presidency of IMM, a feeling of pre-emptive guilt was beginning to rise within him.

"No ship can be truly unsinkable, Bruce. If we send them to sea as they are, they'll carry more than the number of lifeboats to satisfy the law, yes, but that won't be enough for even a third of the total number of people they'll be designed to carry..."

Feeling momentarily light-headed, he reached out and grabbed a rail with one hand.

"And how would you accomplish it, Alexander? Those same laws require lifeboats to be carried 'under davits'. We can't just go piling them onto the deckhouse roof like those collapsible life rafts we've allowed you to add..."

"Captain!" someone called. "The safety officer wishes to launch more boats from our port side."

"Very well. Tell Ms Vickers that she may lower away immediately."

As Bruce watched, the order was repeated into a small device, and moments later one of the orange lifeboats swung out on mechanical arms to the level of the promenade.

"That's the beauty of this new design of davit that Axel Welin has come up with, Bruce. Their arms can swing inwards, meaning a second set of boats can be fitted inboard, and a third can even be carried on top. Three times as many boats can be carried with no modification to the ship herself..."

On deck, crew members in bright lifejackets and what looked like protective helmets were scrambling into the lifeboat. Then, with a smoothness that indicated some mechanism at work rather than an army of deck hands straining at the falls, the boat descended rapidly into the dark, splashing down into black waters almost ninety feet below. The whole process, from the order being issued to the boat entering its natural element, was less than ninety seconds.

Hrm… Titanic's own winch motors can only be used to winch boats back up on deck… he mused to himself. *I'll need to have words with Thomas Andrews to modifying the design…*

Thought of Thomas, however, only led him back round to that meeting with Carlisle…

"There will be no change to the specification, Alexander. Yes, the legislature is twenty years old, but that is so as not to provide owners with an excuse for poorly maintaining their ships. Improved watertight subdivision is the path to greater safety, not this. The objective is to make the ship her own lifeboat; these little boats are merely there to ferry passengers to rescue vessels. And besides, if we place thirty boats or more on Olympic and Titanic, when we already carry more than the Lusitania or the Kaiser Wilhelm der Grosse, people will think we've got something to hide, that the ships are less safe than those of our rivals. I will not make passengers question their faith in White Star…"

The thought trailed off as he thought of countless other passengers and crew struggling to stay alive on *Titanic's* decks right now. He clutched at the windowsill, fighting back unfamiliar depths of emotion. Far below, the freshly lowered boat pulled clear of the ship and set off towards *Titanic* at what he guessed to be a remarkable five or six knots, throwing up a meaty wake as it ploughed through the water with a purposeful solidity.

"Besides, you and I both know that the North Atlantic is no place to be in a wooden rowboat… we're better served by making the ship as unsinkable as possible, rather than condemning our passengers to a miserable death in a thirty-foot skiff…"

He was now being forced to eat his own words. As the boat powered away it went past another returning to *Oceanic*, one that had several of *Titanic's* own tiny boats in tow, like little ducklings following on after their mother. The contrast in size was staggering, especially when the boat reached one of *Oceanic's* gangways and quickly unloaded what he guessed to be over one hundred persons, maybe closer to one hundred and fifty.

"Alexander. Sometime within the life of these ships, perhaps quite soon, the legislature will change, and then we must graciously submit, at the same time as our competitors. That is why I approved the use of these new davits, as a future investment for the day when we must

provide boats for all. But until that day, we will reap the rewards of open, uncluttered decks offering perfect vistas of the sea..."

Bruce shuddered, suddenly feeling sick. Why hadn't he tried working with Carlisle, challenged him to come up with some new way of storing boats without taking up valuable passenger-space, or suggested improvements to the lifeboats so that they could withstand the tempestuous moods of the North Atlantic, and thereby justify their provision in greater numbers? Had his self-confidence really led him to the brink of such hubris?

"You've made me soft, Bruce... were we not friends, and were White Star and IMM not the yard's best customers, I would fight you over this tooth and nail. Fine, have your sixteen boats, but I pray that it does not take a disaster of terrible proportions to open everyone's eyes to this danger..."

It had indeed come to that, in another life, or so it seemed. He and the rest of the world were now simply catching up to Alexander's doom prophecy.

In the bridge window, Bruce's dim reflection stared back at him with darkened, judgemental eyes. Unable to meet its gaze, he lowered his head and rested it against the cool glass, forcing himself to breathe deeply. How had it come to this?

"Mr Ismay, I presume?"

The voice that interjected was calm, considered and professional, laced with a soft Welsh accent that poured oil on the troubled waters of his thoughts.

Bruce looked back up to see a second reflection in the glass beside his own haunted visage, a dark figure looming like some grim hobgoblin. Turning, he found himself facing a stocky man in an officer's uniform, and noted with some relief the crest of the White Star Line on his cap. In a deviation from the uniforms of his time, however, the familiar red pennant was also embroidered on the breast of the man's jacket. A gold and silver badge pinned just below it declared him to be Captain Lloyd Waters.

"Indeed I am." he took the offered hand and shook it, forcing himself to maintain a firm grip. "Do I have the pleasure of addressing the commander of this fine ship?"

"You do, sir. Lloyd Waters, at your service. Of sorts."

Despite the warmth of his voice, Ismay had the very distinct impression that Waters was studying him intently; the Captain had the same focused look in his eye as Thomas Andrews had when explaining the finer points of a new idea. It had been just the same as when he had been introduced to the strange young woman, Philippa Paik; her gaze had been that of someone sizing up a meal, implying that she already knew of him, had weighed his balance in her mind, and found him wanting.

The thought frightened him.

"How do you mean, of sorts?"

"White Star Line, as you know it, was bankrupted in the nineteen-thirties," Waters said bluntly. "It could never fully recover from the sinking of *Titanic* and was eventually forced into a merger with Cunard Line. As such, I don't know which chain of command I might potentially fall under."

If it wasn't for the fact that Waters was still clutching his own hand, Bruce would have stepped back. His father's company, his own life's work, amalgamated with their most personal rival?

"Complicating things further," continued Waters. "After the collapse of timetabled passenger shipping, Cunard itself was eventually purchased by an American company specialising in the pleasure cruise market. With the purchase, that firm inherited the goodwill and house flag of White Star. This vessel, the improved sister of Cunard's current flagship, is in truth a giant marketing stunt specifically to commemorate the centennial of the world's most famous maritime disaster."

Bruce silently repeated the last words to himself, his mind reeling. Waters, expression composed, seemed to be waiting for his response, and when none came, prompted again with another question.

"So, Mr Ismay, do you have any orders for the captain of your new superliner?"

Bruce swallowed, possibilities racing through his mind, and then shook his head. "You are the captain, Mr Waters. At sea, you operate entirely on your own judgement."

Waters nodded, and finally released Bruce's hand. "I hoped you would say that. Please, take a seat."

He waved towards the small lounge, and the two of them made themselves as comfortable as possible. Bruce, somewhat put out, was now trying to find the upper hand.

"First of all, thank you for coming to our aid. Captain Smith extends his own thanks as well," he said quickly. "Although we are receiving aid from the *Rescue*, he and I both agree that we must operate on the worst case possibility that *Titanic* will sink tonight, in the event of which all her passengers and crew must be transferred to this vessel."

"Agreed. We are already preparing the public rooms for use as dormitories, and sourcing blankets and clothing for those who need it. Our ship's hospital is also preparing to receive any wounded…"

They continued to explore the minute details of how exactly *Oceanic* was to house and care for over two thousand additional guests, and Bruce was able to focus his thoughts on managing this disaster, and away from *Titanic*. Between her and *Olympic*, with a third sister now beginning construction back in Belfast, it had looked as if White Star was finally ready to assert its superiority on the North Atlantic. When they had set sail from Southampton, he had felt he could finally step away from the firm and hand control over to his subordinate and friend Harold Sanderson, content that he had gone far beyond what might have been expected of him. The future had seemed bright.

But now, deep down, he doubted that he would ever be free of what might transpire this night.

Somewhere, Bruce Ismay suspected his father was laughing at his expense.

*

"It's good to see you're all safe," JJ Astor collected his thoughts as he addressed the Thayers. "How did you get below?"

"We came down the First Class stair and along through the bowels of the ship," Jack replied. "How about yourselves?"

"JJ figured that the boats would come along here," Maggie Brown answered for him. "So we climbed the rail from the First Class promenade and came down the Second Class stairwell."

"Oh," Marian Thayer sounded somewhat amused. "Wonderful use of initiative, Mr Astor."

"Somewhat unsporting of me, I know, Marian," John replied, friendly words masking his seriousness. "But if it means Madeleine is guaranteed a seat I'll do whatever is necessary."

"Yes, how is her condition?" the refined lady pressed, but with somewhat more tact. "Still somewhat 'delicate', I trust?"

From the corner of his eye, John had seen Madeleine observing Miss Paik, the young woman in men's clothes now arguing pointedly with Fifth Officer Lowe, who despite his obvious distaste was obviously conceding some form of authority to her. At Marian's words, Madeleine now turned to face the other woman with a winningly sunny smile on her face. "Still pregnant, if that's what you mean, Mrs Thayer." Her hands came down to cradle her belly, and for a moment John knew he had married the most wonderful woman in the world.

"Wonderful to hear, as always," Marian Thayer replied, a wry light in her eye as if approving of the unexpected force underlying Madeleine's retort. "Take good care of her, JJ."

John nodded, yielding the last word to the Thayer matriarch, who led her elegantly composed husband into a more secluded spot in the lee of a fire extinguisher. He knew that John Thayer had apparently suffered some mental mishap recently, so he supposed that rumours that the family had taken a European tour to give him space and time to recover were justified. That said, he himself had done something similar; when he had announced his intention to remarry, the public scandal had driven him to whisk Madeleine off on an extended honeymoon, only returning now that her pregnancy had forced his hand.

"JJ." the lowered voice of Jack Thayer drew his attention back to present affairs. "A word if you don't mind?"

John checked towards the gangway. The officer named Lowe was now allowing female passengers to board the bright orange lifeboat, his face glowing in the light reflected from the tiny craft's luminescent hull. The crude queue in which he and Madeleine stood began to shuffle forward slowly, but it would be some time yet before she would have a chance to board. "Very well, Jack, you have my attention – what do you need?"

"You know more of science and philosophy than me; and you've written on the subject. '*A Journey in Other Worlds*', correct?"

He was referring to a novel penned about fifteen years previous by John, who was gratified that the younger man was at least aware of it.

"I wrote a romance of the future Jack, a work of fiction – but yes, I've dabbled in the sciences."

"Well, do you think it's possible that these ships, these people, are… alien?"

"You mean from other worlds, or other realms?"

"Not from here; not from this time."

John's first reaction was to chuckle, but his laughter fell silent as he considered Jack's idea. It was a fantastical notion, but bait for his imagination, and he looked up, moustache twitching. Paik, the girl who had led the Thayers here, was standing across the way from him, calling down at the people manning the lifeboat.

"How many seats do you have?"

"Room enough for a hundred and fifty apiece. But this isn't some joke right, this is THE *Titanic*?"

"Believe me, it's true. RMS *Titanic*, warts and chauvinism and all."

"But that means that…"

"Yeah, assuming we can't go back, this is home now, but keep it quiet."

Their words were guarded, as if they were skirting some issue that would derail the entire conversation.

"Well, John?" Jack pressed. "Tell me if that is not an emancipated woman, transplanted from a world where society regards her as the equal of a man?"

Was it possible? HG Wells had penned an excellent story on the notion of a time machine, and John's own fiction had sent men soaring far into the boundaries of space by the power of harnessed gravity, or *Apergy*. He had envisioned a world of the year two thousand where the march of science had elevated mankind to a position second only to God's own angels, but he had not considered that such an era would bring such societal change as a woman content to act the part of a man. Did that discredit the idea of time travel, or simply place a black mark next to the scope of his imagination?

Again he found himself drawn to the *Oceanic*, impossibly vast and bright compared to the dim and slightly grubby *Titanic*. Sleek and brilliant, it certainly seemed a ship that could voyage across oceans of time as well as space.

The more he considered it, the more it seemed probable; not only a possibility, but the only explanation that satisfied as an answer to all the events of the past few hours.

"Jack," he said quietly, resting his hand on the younger man's shoulder. "I think you've hit on the answer without need of my help."

"Thank you, JJ."

As Jack slipped away, back towards his own family, John looked around. Both Madeleine and Maggie Brown had overheard his conversation, and as he returned to them both looked to him for clarification.

"John, if they're from the future, then what do they want with us?" Madeleine's eyes were impossibly huge and fearful, dark pools in which John might drown if he let himself.

"Hush yourself, Maddy," Maggie kindly if brashly soothed his wife when John, deep in thought, failed to answer. "If they had any intent that was dishonourable, I'd think we'd have seen more evidence of it by now."

"They said that they had expert advice that *Titanic* would sink soon," John thought aloud, carefully keeping his voice low so as to not carry further than the three of them. "Maybe they've come back in time to avert a disaster? Perhaps their history books recount that ships arrived from the future to provide aid, and so they have worked to bring that fate into effect."

Both of his companions fell silent at that, but even though he himself had suggested it, the idea sat wrongly with John. If such a loop in time was possible, then it meant that everything that was to happen tonight was foretold and fixed, making it impossible for the outcome to change. In a sense, it would prove that free will was a lie, and that events were forever governed by destiny.

"John," Madeleine tugged at his shoulder to stir him from thought, and he realised that they had reached the front of the queue for the boats. "It's our turn."

"Mr Astor," Officer Lowe said by way of greeting. "Women and Children first I'm afraid, sir."

John nodded mutely, watching as Maggie stepped down from the doorway onto the roof of the lifeboat moored below. Feeling Madeleine clutching at him, he looked at her and saw the silent plea in her eyes, and struggled to find his voice.

"Mr Lowe," the girl in outlandish clothing butted in. "Mrs Astor is pregnant…"

John held up a hand to stop her. "Thank you, Miss Paik, but I can answer for myself." He looked around, seeing entire families waiting behind him, many clutching their few meagre possessions in their hands. Many frightened faces returned his gaze, including desperate men trying to secure places for their wives and children among them.

Gently, he pulled his hand free from Madeleine's grip, and held her hands in his own. "Madeleine, I'll follow on; there are surely enough boats between both ships, so I'll be along as soon as the women and children have been taken off."

Slowly his wife looked up at him; he felt her hands wriggling in his grasp, and then she nodded. "Come back to us soon, John."

"I promise," he lifted her hands to his mouth and kissed them to seal his word, and, noting how cold her skin was, handed over his own gloves to help keep her warm. Then he stepped back alongside John and Jack Thayer, who had placed Marian in the line behind Madeleine.

As Madeleine took the outstretched hand of a crewman from the lifeboat, John noticed the strange girl standing to one side, shaking her head at him, her mouth working as if she wished to argue his decision. He considered approaching her for answers to his questions, when he heard Madeleine scream, the sound cutting deep in him.

Whipping around he saw his wife's feet slipping out from under her, unable to find a grip on the slick surface of the lifeboat. With a second shriek she landed on the curving edge of the roof, and as multiple hands reached for her, slid backwards into the sea between the boat and *Titanic*, glancing off the ship's hull as she did.

Even before he heard the splash, John was fumbling with the straps on his life-jacket, trying to pull the bulky article off so he could jump in after her, when he was shoved to one side by Jack Thayer, who, with coat already discarded, pushed past him and jumped feet-first from the gangway door. Following behind him, John reached the opening and peered down into the black water. Madeleine, buoyed up by her jacket but head lolling to one side, was bobbing in the water, motionless, while Jack, gasping and breath steaming, ploughed hand over hand towards her.

Not thinking anything beyond the urgent need to get down to their level, JJ jumped forward and landed atop the lifeboat, very nearly going into the sea himself until two men caught him. Pulling free, he went down onto his knees and swung himself into the open side of the boat, where he could reach down far enough to touch the water. Jack now had Madeleine, and was towing her the small distance towards the boat, while passengers and crew grabbed boathooks to fend the tiny craft off from the ship, so as to not crush the two people caught between them.

"Jack, here!" John found himself shouting, and grabbing hold of Madeleine's sturdy lifejacket hauled her bodily into the boat with the aid of several others. Laying her out flat on a raised line of benches he felt for her neck, and to his relief found a pulse.

"Madeleine, darling..." he whispered, seeing her eyes flutter. Behind him he could hear Jack being dragged into the boat, men slapping him on the back in praise.

"John..." she replied. "I'm so cold..."

"You're safe now," he smiled in relief, holding her hands in his. "Both of you."

Smiling, but shivering, she brought her free hand to her belly. "The baby..." she cooed, and then suddenly screamed, her back arching as she tried to sit upright. John started back but then reached out to catch her as she flopped backwards, panting furiously.

"Madeleine, what's wrong?"

Her mouth opened and closed wordlessly, and then suddenly she shrieked again, her face screwing up with the sudden pain.

"The baby... our baby's coming!"

If he had not already been on his knees John would have fallen down in shock. As it was he could only hold Madeleine's hand as other passengers covered her in greatcoats to keep her warm.

"Is there…" he gasped, struggling to speak, "…is there a doctor, or a midwife here?"

No-one answered, and he turned to look up through the open side of the hull at people crowding in *Titanic*'s companionway door.

"My wife's gone into labour!" he cried, fear giving him sudden voice. "She needs a doctor!"

Lowe stepped back in surprise, but the girl kneeling beside him went pale with horror.

"No!"

John focused on that word, pulling himself upright and as close as possible to her across the gap.

"What is it?" he demanded, all his previous questions cast aside "What do you know?"

Like himself, she clearly had difficulty in mustering an answer, and he motioned for her to come over and kneel on the edge of the deck where he could look up into her eyes. He saw tears threatening to spill from them, and felt his fear grow deeper. "Please, Miss Paik, I've deduced the origin of your ships and yourselves, now what do you know about my wife's condition."

When she replied, her voice was a strained yell. "John Jacob Astor the Sixth wasn't supposed to be born until August of this year; *he's four months premature!*"

Her words were spoken loud enough for a few to hear, and instantly further voices took up their implications, adding to the hubbub. None of that mattered to John however, who took an ashen-faced step back. "So there's no hope…"

"No! Jesus Christ JJ, no!" she replied, and he looked up in surprise at the unexpected blasphemy. Undaunted the girl ploughed on. "You were meant to die tonight, JJ, but right now you're alive. If you've got a chance, then surely your son does too…"

"Then we've got to go now!" he heard Jack Thayer assert himself, and turned to see the young hero, soaked except for a donated fur coat, addressing the boat's helmsman, seated in an elevated cupola like a railroad caboose.

"We've got to take on as many people as possible before *Titanic* sinks," the man replied.

"Heaven's sake, man!" Maggie Brown rose up like some dragon out of legend to stand beside Jack, lapsing back into western vernacular in her passion, and seemingly ready to drag the helmsman down from his perch. "You've got boats aplenty coming and this ship doesn't seem ready to give up fighting for its life just yet. But there's a baby coming fast, and if there's a chance of a decent doctor aboard that fancy floating palace of yours…" she pointed at the *Oceanic*. "Then you've got a responsibility to get Madeleine to him, or else that's one innocent life lost already."

As she wrapped up her tirade John pulled himself to his feet, hands already rummaging under his jacket as he crossed to the foot of the elevated wheelhouse. "Please sir, if there's any chance you can save my wife and child, I beg you to take it." He produced the money-belt he wore under his jacket and held it out to the man. "I'll pay you now to take us straight back to your ship!"

Philippa Paik, still looking down from the *Titanic*, was peering intently at the belt in John's hand, and then shouted towards the helmsman. "That belt was found to contain $2440 when the *Mackay-Bennett* recovered it with Mr Astor's body. He's offering you the 2012 equivalent of *fifty thousand dollars* to save his family."

John, Jack and Maggie's heads whipped round at her words, exchanging silent glances. The helmsman looked at the proffered money and gently pushed John's hand back down, before reaching to a small device connected to his controls by a coiled wire.

"Boat 6 to *Oceanic*, we're returning to ship immediately with a woman in childbirth," he spoke into it, before pushing on a small lever. Immediately, John felt the forward end of the boat rise up as a hidden motor surged powerfully forward. With his small wheel right over, the pilot swung them away from *Titanic* and into the dark that separated the sinking ship from the brilliant glare of *Oceanic*.

"Good luck!" Paik called down from the ship as they pushed away, and JJ raised a hand in what he hoped was an expression of gratitude.

"Oceanic to Boat 6, the ship's hospital is asking for details," crackled the helmsman's device, some kind of wireless telephone.

As John got back on his knees and held Madeleine's hand tightly, he saw the helmsman reach down to offer Maggie the speaking device.

"Er, hello, this is Margaret Brown, aboard Boat Six. Please tell your doctors that Madeleine Astor is giving birth four months premature," she said cautiously.

From the other end of the conversation a multitude of voices exclaimed loudly.

"…did she say Astor?"

"…isn't he the richest man in this world?"

"…was that the unsinkable Molly Brown?"

Still holding Madeleine's hand as she caught her breath, John looked up at Maggie, who had a startled look on her face as she held the small black device in one hand. Finally a new voice asserted itself over the others.

"Boat Six, the ship's hospital will make preparations to receive Mrs Astor, but get her over here as quick as you can. Oceanic over and out."

John sighed in relief as he looked towards Madeleine.

"The year 2012?" she asked, breathing heavily in a moment's respite between contractions. He nodded wordlessly.

Can they keep our child alive, even four months premature? Would a ship's hospital even have the facilities to?

The bloom of relief he felt in his chest suddenly imploded on itself and died, leaving a cold weight in its wake. As he struggled to comprehend, Madeleine raised a hand to young Jack Thayer's.

"Thank you for saving us…" she murmured, somewhat deliriously, before shrieking again and arching her back, the deck bouncing as Boat 6 bounded across the open sea towards the gleaming *Oceanic*.

Bitterly, John realised that he had the answer to his unspoken question from aboard *Titanic*. The girl's words plainly stated that he would not have survived had the arrival of the time-travellers not changed the course of events, and thus offered an assurance that he was still master of his own destiny, but it was foul irony that this could be demonstrated by his witnessing the birth and death of his son in a single night.

Standing alongside Philippa Paik in the door in *Titanic*'s hull, Milton Long followed Jack's boat speeding away. Then suddenly he felt himself being shoved forward, dangerously close to the edge of the deck, beyond which was just thin air and the long fall to the sea.

"Hold back, hold the line!" Officer Lowe was shouting, ordering his seamen to push back against the crowds filling the Second Class Reception, but it seemed more and more of the First Class passengers were forcing their way down into the Second Class quarters. Milt, Paik and the senior Thayers found themselves pressed into a tiny window of space between the inner and outer hull doors, John holding Marian protectively against the wall and shielding her from the crush.

"Go back! All male passengers, get back!" Lowe shouted, firing his gun out into the night to try and restore some order. But there were too many people coming down the stairs to contain, forcing the crew and the Thayer party ever closer to the open gangway door.

"You've got to let them onto the boats, all of them!" Paik was shouting, her tiny form pressing back against the crowd alongside Lowe. "Otherwise the crush will become too big to control!"

Order and decorum are all coming apart... Milt realised, whipping his head between the desperate faces inside the ship, and where another of *Oceanic*'s boats was coming alongside. *Surely there's a solution besides allowing anarchy to run its course?*

A pressure wave flowed through the crowd as they surged forward, and one of *Titanic*'s crew was forced through the door, toppling overboard and plunging into the lifeboat with a cry.

Unless these people are evacuated now, the chance of injury or death becomes too great to risk.

"Come on!" he shouted, and threw himself across the gap, landing on the roof of the boat, gritting his teeth. "Mr Thayer, yourself and your wife must come over immediately!"

"My wife, yes!" John Thayer shouted over. "But not me or yourself, young sir. I would sooner die a man than flee the ship ahead of the women!"

"We don't have that luxury any more; if we are to be truly men, now we must sacrifice our honour rather than our lives, not out of cowardice, *but out of necessity!*" Milt pleaded, before turning his gaze to the attending officer. "Mr Lowe, do you honestly have the option of separating men from women in this mess? I know it's distasteful, but hundreds of men struggling back up those stairs to the Boat Deck will just add to the chaos!"

Lowe, braced against the crowd, pistol in hand, stared grimly down at him.

"We'll take them all!" called one of the boat's time-displaced crew. "We've room for a hundred and fifty people per boat, and we don't care if they're men or women!"

"He's telling the truth!" Paik said firmly. "The separation of families when the *Titanic* first sank shook the world up to the pointless chivalry of women and children only! Families left without husbands and fathers to provide for them, children orphaned, newlywed women made widows! You're only going to hurt the survivors by denying their men a chance to live!"

Milt and Lowe exchanged a glance, and then the ship's officer pointed to John Thayer. "Sir, get over onto that boat immediately, your wife as well."

He turned to the girl alongside him. "You too, Miss Paik."

"No!" she said defiantly, straightening the cap on her head. "I'm staying to help ensure we evacuate all the passengers."

"Fine, have it your way!" Lowe snapped, his patience exhausted as he spun and shouted into the crowd. "Alright, let them through, two and three at a time, men and women together, whether they like it or not!"

The boat began to fill quickly. John and Marian Thayer were the first, the two socialites coming across with all the graceful ease of a bull elephant at a soiree, and then Lowe began to send more passengers over. Most came aboard without complaint, but whenever a man protested and insisted that he be allowed to return to the ship, having safely seen his wife or children placed in a seat, two burly crewmen grabbed him underarm and threw him across the gap into the boat with the rest of his family.

"There's no time to waste! Fill the boats, fill the boats!"

Finally, fully laden, the boat pushed off, allowing another to take its place, into which more passengers were quickly lifted, directed and hurled, like some macabre circus act. Milt watched from his own boat and felt a mixture of pride and shame. He rationalised that the benefits of lives saved outweighed the cost of lost chivalry, but for the first time he was beginning to feel a distinct sense of concern at the effect these 'time-travellers' were having on him.

Already we are being changed by their presence, and I am not sure that I like it.

Then, from further along *Titanic*'s length, where her own boats were being filled and lowered on the starboard side, multiple voices *began to scream...*

CHAPTER FOURTEEN

The sound of screams drew Archibald Butt running to the starboard side of the Boat Deck, and leaning over the rail amidships he saw the cause of the commotion. One of *Titanic*'s lifeboats, Boat 13, had been lowered into the water beside the ship's condenser outlet, and the rushing outflow of water discharging through it from the ship's pumps was pushing the fragile craft aft underneath Boat 15, which was being lowered *on top of it*.

"Stop lowering!" he turned and yelled. "Stop lowering 15!"

But his voice was inaudible over the din, and between him and the lifeboat station there was a solid mass of passengers. Horrified, Butt threw his upper body over the rail and stared aft. Some of the passengers in the trapped, overloaded lifeboat were trying to prop up the one descending onto them with the oars, while others attempted to cut the ropes shackling them to the ship. One of *Oceanic*'s motorboats was coming alongside, possibly to try and tow the smaller boat free, and seeing it passengers began to throw themselves into the water, abandoning the effort to cut through the falls and instead attempting to swim for their lives.

A few people, paralysed with fear, were still seated petrified in the boat when number 15 came down on it with a splintering jar, crushing the other craft and pushing it over, spilling the passengers into the water. White-knuckled hands gripping the rail, Butt saw one unfortunate bob back to the surface, body mangled and lifejacket dyed red, even as willing hands began to pull survivors into the sturdy orange boat that had attempted to pull the lifeboat free from disaster.

"Help me! Somebody please help me!" someone screamed, and he saw a seaman in the water, entangled in the shattered boat's falls and being dragged under by the weight of the tackle. Butt watched

271

with horror as the poor sailor was sucked under the surface, and then he turned away, face pallid and sweating.

I should have drawn my revolver! he berated himself. *A few well-aimed bullets would have spared that poor man the agony of a death by drowning!*

Suddenly he felt the ship tremble, the groan of stressed metal reverberating up through the decks. Deck timbers shivered underfoot as some passengers continued to flee towards the boats and others to the Second Class staircase, fighting their way down through the crowds to where *Oceanic's* lifeboats were being laden.

"It's starting to fall apart," he said to himself, feeling strangely light on his feet. Turning into the flow of humanity, he began to push his way forward, drawn downhill by the trim of the deck and the weight of the gun holstered on his belt. No-one impeded him as he strode down the Officer's Promenade and came to the forward rail, overlooking the bow. *Titanic's* forecastle still stood above the waterline, and below his vantage point the two pumps brought aboard continued to thunder away, dirty water gushing from them with unimpeded confidence...

...and yet the ship continued to settle.

"Major Butt!" someone shouted, the words seeming distant and far-off to his ears. Again they called his name, and dumbly he turned to find Father Byles leading a group of steerage passengers through the darkened wheelhouse towards him, ignoring the protests of a single dissenting sailor. On pure instinct, he extended his hand, and Byles clasped it in his own.

"What's the situation, Father?"

"It is utter madness below decks!" the English priest shouted. "So many people are crowding into the stern passageways that there's a danger of injury in the crush."

Butt's eyes drifted off of Byles, to the group he had been leading. They were mostly women, children and families, scared and hesitant. The Father must have led them up with hope of loading them from the boat deck or promenades.

"It's no better here," Butt managed to say. "People are attempting to flee the ship in a mad panic, and the crew are hard-pressed to contain them."

Byles nodded, but before he could answer the sound of a plunging scream snatched at both of their heads, drawing them to the portside rail, looking for the source. Byles saw it first, and pointed down towards *Rescue*, still moored alongside *Titanic*, jets of water spraying high from her pump outlets. Butt blanched at the sight of a man's broken body lying prone atop the smaller ship's deck, arms and legs splayed out like some deformed crucifix. He was surrounded with a red halo of his own blood, and two of the salvage tug's crew surrounded his remains, frozen in shock at the gruesome sight.

"He attempted to jump for it," Byles said softly, before whispering a prayer of absolution for the unfortunate man. For his part, Butt suppressed an ungentlemanly curse and instead bit his own lip. From the taste of copper in his mouth, he must have drawn blood.

"Be calm, Major," said Byles, raising a hand towards him in gentle admonition. "All these pumps are surely making headway against the floodwaters, and we seem to not be sinking that fast. The passengers will soon realise that."

"That's of no consolation to those already dead, Father, or those who may soon follow if this escalates into outright panic. Were it not for the arrival of these 'time-wrecked' ships, we might have an ignorant calm by which to evacuate as many women and children as possible. But instead, that fool with the loud-hailer has given us a date of expiration, and so like rats people are simply focused on jumping ship."

"So what is the solution, Major?"

As he spoke Butt had been regarding *Rescue* with a grim gaze, and Byles now stepped back in alarm as he drew his gun and snapped open the firing cylinder. "You can't mean to…"

"Be calm, Father," Butt said quietly as he began to draw the rounds out of the cylinder. "Just as people might hear a doom prophecy and assume a sinking ship from it, they might see a gun wielded in the hand of a confident man and assume it is loaded."

He closed up the now-empty cylinder, and held the gun up as if ready for combat. From Byles' gasp, he guessed the priest understood that it would be impossible for anyone to tell that the weapon was not loaded unless he was to pull the trigger.

"So you intend to bluff your way aboard the *Rescue?*"

"I do, Father. The crew of that boat know better than us how long this ship has to live, and perhaps the passengers will listen to them if call is made for calm. Let us find ourselves some answers."

Butt glanced over the pocket of passengers around them. "Ladies, would you be so kind as to allow us to escort you to safety?"

*

"Get them on, give them some air! Keep them warm with blankets!"

Reaching over the edge of *Gallic*, the sturdy tender lifeboat that he and the Thayer parents had boarded, Milt Long found another person's lifejacket in the dark and, pulling with both hands, dragged them up out of the water. "I've got another!"

John Thayer Senior jumped to his side, and between the two of them they hauled a coughing, middle-aged man over the gunwale and into the boat. The second he slapped onto the floor like a fish pulled from the stream, they turned back in the hope of finding more survivors from Boat 13, shouting out into the dark and praying to hear a reply.

None came. For several minutes more *Gallic* motored back and forth slowly, until the pilot despaired of finding any more souls in the water. With *Titanic*'s Boat 15 tied onto a cleat, over-packed but under tow, they began the short trek across to the waiting *Oceanic*. The lifeboats and tender-launches from the larger ship were looping back and forth between it and *Titanic*, delivering passengers to *Oceanic* before heading back to the floundering liner, forming a continuous chain. Observing it all, Marian Thayer sat primly on *Gallic*'s centre row of benches, face composed even as her eyes flashed with worry for her absent son.

"Mr Long," she said at last. "Would you be so kind as to help this poor man up?"

"Certainly, Mrs Thayer," Milt replied, cursing himself for having not acted without prompting, and pulled the spluttering person who had been plucked from the Atlantic into a sitting position. After several seconds, the man finally got his breathing under control and thanked them for their assistance. His accent was English, and the words carefully enunciated.

"Lawrence Beesley," he gave his name as. Milt and John shifted apart on their seats to make room for him, and Milt fished a cigarette and a box of matches out of his pockets. Offering them around, and finding no takers, he lit one and took a long hard pull, the smoky warmth in his lungs bringing a blessed relief from all the chaos of the past few hours. Many who knew him had commented on his delicate refinement and innate calm, but he sometimes wondered how much of his was due to his fondness for smoking.

His lit cigarette in hand, Milt finally turned towards the *Oceanic*. At Southampton he had been impressed by how *Titanic* had towered over the docks, like some be-pillared temple rising out of the River Solent, but to look at *Oceanic* was to gain the impression that several Manhattan city blocks had seceded from America and taken to the high seas. The ship glistened with brilliant lights, which reflected perfectly in the still water, lending her the air of a vast Christmas decoration afloat on her own reflection. The single buff and black funnel rose overhead like the summit of a mountain, or Atlas holding up the dome of the heavens. It was a vision so bright and radiant that the very stars were drowned out in its glare.

"Jessica, look how the floor of heaven, is thick inlaid with patines of bright gold," he heard Lawrence say in a low voice. Like him, the unobtrusive Englishman was peering towards *Oceanic*. From the whispered words on his lips – Shakespeare, Milt supposed – the other man was a either a teacher or student of the classics.

Tiny as a bright goldfish beside a whale, the lifeboat came into the shadow of the immense ship. A small jetty had unfolded out of the side of *Oceanic*'s smooth hull, and as they approached Milt could see that another boat was already pulling away and heading back towards *Titanic*, leaving a space for them to moor at.

Voices shouted orders and a pair of ropes were tossed across the gap and looped around several bollards, holding the boat in place. Before any of the passengers could disembark, however, a tall, dark-skinned man in uniform stepped aboard, as resplendent as any maitre-d' Milt had ever seen. And yet he had the bearing of an officer.

"Ladies and Gentlemen!" the man said aloud, raising a hand to quell their voices. "Welcome to the Royal Mail Ship *Oceanic*. No doubt many of you have questions about ourselves and our ship, so to save time, please allow me a moment to explain the salient points, and then we'll bring you all aboard as quickly as possible."

The curious murmurs bubbled softly as he took a breath, before continuing.

"*Oceanic* is from the future. We do not know exactly how, or why, but we and several other ships have been displaced into what is our past, your present. At this point we're not exactly sure when, or if, we can return home, and so are working on the assumption that we cannot."

He paused to allow time for his words to sink in, and then, just as the first passenger opened their mouth to field a question, cut them off. "*Oceanic*'s passengers and crew together number over four thousand persons, all of whom are just as confused or frightened by this situation as you are. We are preparing the ship's public rooms as dormitories, but keeping our contemporaries separated from yourselves is impossible. In fact, it is the wish of Captain Waters that people from both eras interact. However, this may also lead to some conflict, due to different social norms. As such, the Captain has made it clear that any attack, verbal or otherwise, on any persons, yourselves included, on any grounds, will not be tolerated."

He let the point hang in the air for a second, before standing back to clear the gangway. "If that is understood, feel free to come aboard, and make use of our hospitality."

Looking around and seeing hesitant faces surrounding him, Milt rose to his feet and put his best foot forward. As he passed, the man he nodded politely and with a few quick strides stepped over onto *Oceanic*. The side of the ship rose above him like a sheer wall, dotted with lights, and directly ahead of him was a brightly illuminated doorway.

"Name please, sir?" enquired another member of the ship's crew. In his arms he carried a folding device which glowed softly. A second man stood ready with what appeared to be a ridiculously tiny camera.

"Milton Clyde Long," he replied quickly, and with a nod the first of the two tapped on several lettered keys, and the fellow with the camera held it up to capture Milt's likeness. Suddenly feeling like he was being registered as a felon, but remembering the warning towards taking offence, Milt simply accepted it. John and Marian Thayer followed him in kind, the diligent husband taking his wife's arm in his own, and Marian holding onto the hem of her billowing skirt to enable her to step off of the gangplank. Then Beesley and over a hundred other persons began to file past the checkpoint. Sticking close to the Thayers, Milt took a deep breath, flicked the stub of his cigarette overboard at the sight of an illuminated *No Smoking* sign, and stepped aboard.

All the while, the sense of unease in his gut only grew worse.

*

"It's Doc Oshiro on the line for you, Captain," Miller said aboard *Rescue*'s bridge, holding his hand over the mouthpiece of his two-way radio. "He says we've not got enough of the DRP supplies aboard for a job of the scale Kai is planning."

"Send out our motorboat," Jones replied. "I asked the *Anatoly Sagalevich* to stand by for a reason; they've got more of the polyurethane mix and water glass aboard than we do. The boat is at Oshiro's disposal – get him over to the *Sagalevich* to ask Captain Gorbachev directly for his help. Anton's not returning most of our calls, but he and Oshiro respect one another…"

"Yessir!" Miller replied, before adopting a more guarded tone. "And what about the *Seguin Laroche?*"

"Cameron said Jo Laroche's got matters in hand over there, right?" Jones replied, shifting warily in his seat. "Did they pass anything else along?"

Like whether or not they know anything about what the fuck brought us here…

Before Miller could reply, there was the sudden sound of commotion from outside. For a moment Jones was struck with the horrific thought that another person had thrown themselves off of *Titanic*'s deck and so splattered themselves all over *Rescue*, but there was no sick 'thud', no scream cut short. Instead, Miller faded away in a series of footsteps, only to return seconds later in a rush.

"Captain!" he reported sharply. "Two men are demanding we take aboard a party of *Titanic*'s passengers. One of them is wielding a gun."

Jones sat in silence for a second. "How big is their group?"

"About twenty, all families apparently. They're also demanding to speak with you."

The recorded interview with Lightoller continued to loop in Jones' memory as he considered his options…

"*…I remember one young couple, evidently not long married, walking up and down the Boat Deck. I asked the girl, she was only a girl, from the western States I should say, if I should put her in a boat, but no, she wouldn't be parted from her husband. "Not on your life!" she said. "We've started together, and we'll finish together." Brave girl, but she didn't know how near that finish was. Certainly I didn't…*"

"Bring these people over," he said firmly.

*

Archibald Butt made sure he held the revolver in as convincing a manner as possible as he stared down one of *Rescue*'s officers, but also attempting to disguise the fact that the firing cylinder was actually empty. Dividing the two of them was an open gap of eight feet, strung with the pipes and ropes that intertwined *Titanic* with the smaller vessel. Far below open water churned in the trench between the two hulls.

Butt, Byles and the group of steerage passengers were standing in the First Class entranceway on D-Deck, one level above where the pipes had been fed through several portholes, directly alongside the mysterious ship. Forcing one of *Titanic*'s assistant pursers, at gunpoint, to unlock the portside gangway door had proven disappointingly easy.

"You say this ship is sinking!" he spoke, repeating his earlier demand. "We have women and children here who are unable to find a boat to take them off, and yet you sit here directly alongside us and deny access. How dare you, sirs."

Another one of *Rescue*'s officers suddenly came out of the bridge and uttered a few quiet words to the junior officer. The subordinate turned away in relief and vanished below decks as his superior turned towards Butt. The two regarded each other, and Butt recognised him as 'Miller', the fool with the megaphone.

"Captain Jones says you're welcome to come aboard!" Miller said suddenly, though his face radiated disapproval. "The gangplanks are being fetched now! But first you must relinquish the gun!"

"Gladly, sir!" Butt nodded, tossing the gun and catching it by the barrel to present the handle towards Miller, a gesture more suited to his friend Theodore Roosevelt. "It was not loaded anyway."

"Smug bastard," the officer muttered, before two other men pushed a gangway across to *Titanic*'s door and he stepped over to relieve Butt of the weapon. "I'm Lieutenant Sam Miller, welcome to *Rescue!*"

"Go ladies, go!" Byles encouraged, and one brave mother with her children in tow strode straight over the extended walkway onto the deck of the future-built ship. While Byles and Miller saw to helping passengers across, Butt walked back over to *Titanic* and propped open the entryway doors.

"This way everyone, *Rescue* is taking aboard passengers!" he shouted.

"I say, Major!" someone called in reply. "Is everything quite alright?"

Butt looked up. Standing on the stairs was a dapper, but somewhat bland-faced gentleman in evening dress, a glass of brandy in hand. Accompanying him was his valet, also immaculately turned out, but incongruously smoking a cigar.

"Mr Guggenheim," Butt nodded in recognition, noting that the New York businessman's French travelling companion, the singer Mademoiselle Aubart, was absent, hopefully already in a lifeboat. He gestured to the open entranceway door. "This ship *Rescue* is taking aboard anyone who wishes. Would you and your man please come across quickly?"

"No, no I think not," Benjamin Guggenheim replied pleasantly, his face serene as smoothed marble. "Giglio and I intend to wait out events until the end. I'm sure this is just a matter of repair, and that in the morning *Titanic* will be underway again."

"It's no joke, Ben," Butt said firmly. "These people have come from the future, and they tell me that *Titanic* is likely to sink."

"And as I said, Archibald, we intend to remain dressed in our best and ready to die as gentlemen," Guggenheim replied, as calmly as if they were discussing the time of day, not events of world-changing magnitude. "Once everyone else is safely off the ship, then we will consider removing ourselves. I will not shame my good wife back home by not doing my duty as a man."

As Butt tried to reconcile that statement with the fact that Guggenheim was openly travelling with the latest of several mistresses, the philanderer in question drained his glass and set it down. "However, since it seems many are fleeing either to the upper decks or further aft, as far away as possible from this place, the two of us shall see to it that people are informed that this '*Rescue*' has opened her doors. Giglio, stub your cigar out and come with me. I believe we shall start on the Promenade Deck..."

With that same inscrutable calm in the midst of crisis, the two men disappeared up the Grand staircase, Guggenheim's top hat bouncing jauntily as he led the way. Butt shook his head in both admiration and disbelief before grabbing hold of a few more passengers willing to listen. Only when he had cleared the area around the foot of the stairs did he follow his own party over onto *Rescue*.

On the ship's bridge, Byles was being introduced to a man seated in what was evidently the captain's chair, and seeing Butt approaching, the Englishman extended a hand.

"Captain Jones, might I introduce you to Major Archibald Butt, Military Advisor to the President of the United States."

"Really?" Jones asked, expression masked by a pair of tinted glasses. "I'd almost say that's good luck, a personal envoy to the current President."

"You have information you wish to share with him?" Butt asked guardedly.

"A whole century's worth, Major."

"So it is true?" Byles asked, and Butt supposed he was remembering the madness expressed by Abercrombie. "These ships really are from... the future?"

"Take a look around you, gentlemen," Jones waved his arm in a circle. "Does this look like a ship of this age?"

Byles and Butt both glanced around, seeing arcane electrical devices and glowing displays. Either this ship truly was from the future or they were standing in the centre of a mass delusion.

"Very well then, Captain," Butt said. "Earlier your Lieutenant Miller announced to all of *Titanic*'s passengers that our ship is going to sink, and the result has been a panic. The both of us insist you retract your statement or assure our passengers that their lives are not in danger."

"No," Jones replied levelly. "*Titanic* is still sinking, and I'd rather people be motivated to try and save themselves rather than wait like lambs for the slaughter. My men are working right now to save the ship, but if those efforts fail, then I have no idea how long we have before she goes under."

Butt thought back to Guggenheim, so calm in the face of his possible death that it seemed unreal, and wondered how much of his behaviour could be explained as courage, and how much was ignorance. Regardless, it was a dangerous combination. "Very well, Captain, then please allow us to bring as many persons aboard your ship as possible."

"That, Major, I will gladly acquiesce to," Jones nodded. "Mr Miller, open up all the unoccupied cabins, the mess and the lounges to accommodate passengers, ready our infirmary to receive any wounded and order the galley to prepare hot drinks by the bucket; we've got plenty of room, just keep the working spaces and the rear decks clear. Nothing interferes with the pumping operation!"

As Jones continued issuing orders, Butt turned and peered off forward. Even with *Rescue*'s pumps running, *Titanic* was beginning to nose forward with an increasingly noticeable list, and he feared that this night's ending was preordained.

And then he straightened up and excused himself, striding back over to *Titanic*. Benjamin Guggenheim was just descending the stairs, a gaggle of nervous people in tow, and quickly the elegantly dressed New Yorker directed them over onto *Rescue*.

"Ben," Butt nodded as he passed the other man, before heading down the stairs to E-Deck.

"I say Archie, where are you going?"

"I'm following your example by searching for anyone who is unaware of how close rescue is at hand," he answered as he reached the bottom of the stairs and headed aft.

Titanic might be sinking, but his part in the evacuation of the ship was still not done.

CHAPTER FIFTEEN

Akira Oshiro blanched slightly as the Zodiac motorboat he was riding came up alongside the pearly-grey hull of the *Anatoly Sagalevich*. Given that his last little voyage had climaxed with him being run down by a container ship, it was easy to justify his nervousness at getting into what was little more than an inflatable tyre to which an outboard motor had been strapped.

Still, he had found the courage to make the short trip over to the Russian research ship, and now he had to accomplish something far harder; bartering with her captain.

"*Zdravstvuyte, Gorbachev-senchou;* may I come aboard?" he called out as he climbed onto the deck, trying to sound casual and instead lapsing into a pidgin-mix of English, Japanese and basic Russian.

Anton Gorbachev, dressed in overalls, was waiting for him beside the massive section of *Titanic*'s hull that had been recovered back in 2012. The huge construct now lay on its back like the shell of some massive iron turtle, and the *Anatoly Sagalevich*'s master was regarding it grimly, burly arms folded and expression solemn. He was an impassive man with the size and bearing of a bear, hailing from some Siberian waste on the far side of the Urals. When he turned to greet Oshiro, the *Sagalevich*'s work-lights threw a brilliant glare over him, underscoring his craggy features with deep shadows.

"*Dobriy den', Gospodin Doctor,*" he greeted, before transitioning into English, in which they both had some degree of fluency. "This is truly happening, *da?*"

"See for yourself, Kapitan," Oshiro replied, adjusting his glasses as he waved across the water towards *Titanic*, still settling by her bows.

"I saw, and I heard…" Gorbachev rested one hand against the decayed chunk of wreckage lashed to his deck, and then held up a walkie-talkie, his mouth drawn into a thin line. "And I do not like."

"Kai's almost ready to dive into Boiler Room Six," the handheld device crackled. *"But we've only got two portable tanks of DRP mix left. Does anyone know when Doctor Oshiro will be back from the Sagalevich with more?"*

"Earlier on radio I heard little girl from my ship, Pippa Paik, running all over *Titanic* and being very excited," Gorbachev intoned, face dark as clouds. "Is sweet girl, but stupid to treat history as game."

He pointed at Oshiro. "You stupid too, maybe. Are normally smart man, Akira, have you thought on what this mean?"

"That saving *Titanic* might alter history, so that if we go back to the future, we might find a very different world?" Oshiro said, his voice clipped. "Yes, I have thought about it."

"Or maybe changing history makes it impossible for us to go home. But you still here, asking me for help with DRP supplies?" Gorbachev said, pronouncing the acronym as '*derpy*'. "Why?"

Akira struggled to put his own reasons into words, wading through a conflicting tangle of feelings, and suddenly reached back and grabbed hold of his short ponytail, holding it to the side of his head so that Gorbachev could see. "You remember why I never cut my hair, Anton?"

"Yes…" the man-mountain replied, his voice softening. "In memory of family killed in last year's tsunami."

In so many words, the man was right. It had been a family reunion, at his sister Ami's house in Minamisanriku, a small coastal town north of Sendai. Akira himself had been running late, and was twenty kilometres away and crossing the Kitakami River when the initial earthquake struck. The following tsunami took out the coast roads, and so he'd detoured round through the back hills of the Miyagi Prefecture, eventually arriving to find Minamisanriku a desolate wasteland. Most of the town, including Ami's house and everyone in it, had been completely washed away; the only sign that they had ever existed were the broken remains of her husband's imported Mustang, swept off the concrete driveway into a nearby ditch.

"It's not because I grieve," he explained, stomach clenching. "If that were the case I would have shaved my head. No, I made my peace with their deaths months ago. But the reason that I was delayed that day was because I'd stopped in Sendai to get my hair cut. Were it not for that, I'd have been killed with my family in Minamisanriku. I've kept my hair long since as a reminder that I was lucky, when they were not. And to remember that even the smallest decision can have massive consequences…"

"I too have lost many, in bad ways…" Gorbachev nodded, his own expression guarded. "I know this pain too, Comrade Doctor."

"Yes, well…" Akira turned and pointed out towards *Titanic*. "Right now, we are those people's good luck. Whatever the *cause* of the accident that brought us here, the *reason* for it must surely be for us to save them."

"Hrm. So, you believe in fate?"

"No, I believe that random encounters aren't just chance, but present opportunities. Having your life saved by a haircut does that to you. And the odds of a time machine being in the right place at the right time to bring exactly the right people and technology needed to the side of a sinking ship, surely means there is a higher purpose at work here…"

"Very poetic," Gorbachev said, his voice growling. "But I do not believe in such things. No fate, no high powers. Just people, in struggle to live, wherever and whenever. And back home are family, our people, who if we do not return must now suffer and grieve more."

Then the Russian smiled grimly. "But, if getting back to future mean letting thousand and thousand of these people die, *I say is price not worth paying.*"

He gestured, and Oshiro turned around to see some of the Russian crewmembers coming forward with tanks of the DRP admixture, polyurethane, oils and sodium silicate, which they began loading into the *Sagalevich*'s own rigid-hulled launch.

"Ever since first heard of *Titanic*," the Slavic man rumbled plainly, "I have despised cowards who sat in lifeboats and listened to people scream for help after ship sink, but not go back. I will not be like them when faced with same choice."

"It was a complicated night, long ago, Anton. And the people in those boats would have been afraid…" Oshiro said softly.

"No, is tonight, not yesterday. And I am not afraid," the captain of the *Anatoly Sagalevich* growled, jabbing the smaller man lightly in the chest. "And neither are you I think, *Gospodin* Doctor."

He hefted the walkie-talkie and spoke rapidly into it in his native tongue, far too quickly for Oshiro to follow. There was a bang of mechanical locks disengaging, followed by a deep mechanical whine, and the Japanese engineer peered forward past the Kapitan. On the starboard side of the ship, a massive metal hangar was opening up, revealing one of the ship's submersibles, Mir-3, gleaming brightly in the lights.

"What transpire to bring us into the past, or why, I do not know," Gorbachev mused. "But if Kapitan Jones, good man, needing ask for help, and Comrade Akira Oshiro say it right thing to do, then help we will. We have been prepping '*Tolya*' for launch this past hour..."

"You're deploying the Mir-3 to assist?"

"*Da*, search for iceberg damage below *Titanic*'s waterline, plug with derpy foam," he turned back to the fragment of the original *Titanic*'s hull and gestured at where the expanded DRP foam used to refloat it emerged from the ruptured ends of the cellular double-bottom. "No holes, no flooding water."

His expression darkened. "Would send second submersible too, except '*Saga*', Mir-4, was left behind in future, diving on *Titanic* when time broke. Am wishing their safety..."

Mir-3 was quickly swung out above the water on a dedicated crane, the action ironically similar to the deployment of a lifeboat. As the crew worked the *Anatoly Sagalevich* was herself manoeuvring closer to *Titanic*, closing the distance, while more and more of the ship's complement came out on deck, cameras and mobile phones snapping pictures of *Titanic*.

"As I say," Gorbachev brooded, grimly observing their curiosity. "Is like we are playing game. But is not game anymore, is history, new history, and if trapped here, then course to shore ahead is hard, rough, with many dangers to pass."

"We've been playing the game of history all our lives..." Oshiro replied, suddenly feeling the weight of two eras pressing down on him. "The only difference is that we now have an idea of how it all plays out..."

"Hrm. You know what word 'Mir' means in Russian, da?"

"It means '*world*' doesn't it."

"True, but also means '*peace*' as well," Gorbachev smiled, a touch of hope in his voice. "We are in position, be launching submersible in a few seconds!"

Reversing engines, the *Anatoly Sagalevich* slewed round in the water as she came to rest just off of *Titanic*'s sinking bow.

"*Ispodvol' i ol'khu sognyosh…* now we fight against time."

*

Kai pulled himself upright, shouldering the weight of the oxygen tank on his back. Around him men worked quickly, some setting up racks of gas cylinders and *Rescue*'s limited reserve of the DRP ingredients, while others, including Officer Lightoller, were laying down sandbags to contain flooding, both in the corridor called Scotland Road and its counterpart on the starboard side of the ship, Park Lane.

Suddenly *Titanic* groaned mightily, metal flexing and banging somewhere aft as the hull girder was bent under the weight of water pulling her down at the bow. The lights flickered momentarily, causing the men to pause.

"This is the balance point!" Thomas Andrews shouted over the noise. "If Boiler Room 5 can be drained, and the levels kept down in Boiler Room 6, then we can hold the ship in this position."

The water in Scotland Road had risen slowly by several feet since Boiler Room 5 flooded. As Kai and Andrews had decided, one of *Rescue*'s four main suctions lines was deployed down the escape trunk used to rescue Shepherd, while the other three struggled to keep more water from flooding up from Boiler Room 6 and spilling aft. *Titanic* was now flooding in her forward seven compartments, and more water was apparently now rising up from beneath the floor grates in Boiler Room 4 as well, implying an eighth had sustained some small amount of damage. The sinking was still progressing, slower but no less relentless.

"What if we can't stop the sinking, but just slow it?" Kai asked, trying to establish the odds in his head. "How long do you give her?"

Andrews was again fixated on Pip Paik's laptop, hesitantly scrolling through a .pdf document file Kai had scrounged up from the Project 401 network.

"At first I thought she would last for no more than an hour after the collision," the Ulsterman replied. "I underestimated her resilience. But if this structural analysis from your time is correct, we have at most until Boiler Room 5 floods to the level of this deck and begins to slop over into BR4; at that point the stresses on the hull will become so great she'll begin to rip herself apart!"

Kai stuck his head into the escape trunk for Boiler Room 5, and saw that the water had flooded to a depth of about ten feet above the floor grates. The next compartment forward, BR6, was within minutes of spilling over into Scotland Road. He trusted that the pumps were up to the task of dewatering the ship, but they were fighting a rearguard action unless the amount of water coming aboard could be reduced.

He tested his rebreather, and felt the familiar rubbery tang of the diving gear's mouthpiece. Clad in a full-body neoprene suit, the black seals and material glistening in the light, he must have looked as if he had been dipped in tar.

"Are you up for this?" Andrews enquired of him, looking at the equipment brought across from *Rescue*. A heavy wadded package tied with straps was propped against the wall, and laid out on the deck were two of the foam guns, connected by rolls of piping to the foam tanks. "It's going to be dark down there, and filthy."

"Doesn't matter," Kai spat out the rebreather and tested the LED lights built into his mask and hood. "Got no choice, otherwise the ship sinks."

Andrews seemed to be wondering if he was either incredibly brave or foolish. "Well, good luck to you," he said at last, before turning to their other companion. "Mr Lightoller, are you alright to oversee things here?"

"I'll be fine here, Mr Andrews," the lanky officer said briskly, waving a handheld radio. "But you need to get up top and help in setting up the collision mats. If I need you, I'll give you a call on one of these marvellous 'talkies'."

Kai saw Thomas's hand drift to an identical device clipped to one of his waistcoat's fob-pockets. "Understood."

With that the engineer nodded and started forward, Pip Paik's laptop carried in the crook of his free arm. As he vanished from view up the Third Class stairs, Kai scrambled through to the escape trunk from Boiler Room Six, now so flooded that water was swirling around his ankles.

"Mr Alinka," Lightoller called out. "I'm not given to speeches, but God be with you."

"Thanks," Kai returned a handshake. "I think."

Then he drew up his mask and, with the wadded package underarm, and a DRP gun strapped to his back like a harpoon, stepped off of the escape trunk platform and into the dark depths of Boiler Room Six.

*

When Thomas reached the forward well deck he found *Titanic* and *Rescue* engaged in some gigantic game of 'pass-the-parcel', transferring collision mats from the smaller vessel. With *Rescue* now moored amidships, her main crane was unable to reach far enough forward, so *Titanic*'s largest cargo derrick, normally secured upright behind the mast, had been swung out to hoist up the mats, each one a wooden frame covered in thick canvas. Even after a hundred years, the basic principle was no different from than that from the days of sail; the mats would be placed alongside the damaged section of hull, and the water pressure would suck the canvas onto the wound like a poultice.

As a scratch crew of men from both vessels received the mats and laid them out, Thomas set down the laptop on a ventilator and unfolded it. On the screen glowed the wonderful three-dimensional elevation of *Titanic* that Miss Paik had directed him to. Using it as a reference, he had sketched out in his ever-present notebook the outline of a master plan to keep the ship afloat as long as possible. While collision mats were used to stem the intake of water along the side of the ship, Mr Alinka would dive into the flooded compartments and use his own equipment to try and squeeze off as much as of the inflow as possible from within.

"This is exactly where you need to be!" he called out over the discordant roar of the pumps, while tapping the screen with a pencil. His audience, a pair of men armed with large industrial clamps, watched attentively. "The A-Deck promenade underneath the first funnel; the water is coming in directly below there through Boiler Room 5's bunkers."

Once he had sent them on their way, he turned to the team manning the two portable pumps. "We need to relocate these suctions soon. There's no point any more in trying to keep the water down in the cargo-holds; it's in the boiler rooms that we'll win or lose the ship. Be ready to withdraw them at a moment's notice."

He grabbed one of *Rescue*'s crew, easily identifiable in his uniform. "Mr Alinka says you have tools that can cut through steel plate; we need them up here immediately."

As the man nodded and headed below, Thomas turned to the handful working with the first of the collision mats. It was about six feet long and four feet high, fitted with eyes for wire cables at top and bottom, to which a sturdy line from the small electric crane on this side of the ship was being fixed, along with a second pair of long wires. Thomas followed them with his eyes leading up and aft along the side of the hull, to the enclosed promenade that ran below the boat deck. With the glass panes smashed out, the far end of the wires had been clamped onto the bottom of the window frames, and men with ratchet windlasses were levering out slack.

"Right, she's hooked up!" the leading quartermaster shouted, waving an arm at his contemporary manning the crane controls. "Swing her out."

The powerful electric motor engaged with a desperate whine, and after a moment's manhandling, the mat was lifted off of the deck and shoved over the gunwale, swinging in the flow of water still gushing over the sides from the portable pumps.

"Play out the line, slowly!"

Again the motor hummed, and as the long wire ran out through the jib hoist, the mat, suspended from the two wires secured to the promenade, slowly swung back and down, like the hand of a clock approaching the bottom of the hour. Two further cables hung from the bottom eyes, trailing in the water, and as the mat reached the bottom of its swing, one of *Rescue*'s motorboats buzzed into place to take hold of them, a pair of divers flipping backwards into the water and disappearing into the dark. For a second the lights behind their masks glimmered green in the still water, and then they vanished as they headed for the bottom of the hull.

Thomas envisioned what they might see as they descended along the hull, using the laptop display to add detail to his thoughts; the riveted hull, steel plates locked together like a collage of scales, painted black above the waterline, red umber below. Deeper still, almost at the turn of the bilge, the very bottom of the ship, and then… what? An ugly mess of mangled plates, twisted and deformed from where the iceberg had scraped over them? Or a series of thin, surgical slits where the strakes had parted?

He turned away from those thoughts and focused on the actual task. The hawser from the crane had been freed and wound back in, and the men manning the clamps on the promenade were now racketing out their lines, allowing the mat to slowly sink below the surface. Once it was at the right level, the divers would signal electronically to stop lowering, and then would dive deeper, fastening their own clamps onto a uncompromised piece of hull so that the mat could be drawn tight against the breach, sealing off a small part of *Titanic*'s wounds.

"Mr Andrews?" asked the man he had sent below, now returned with two others, carrying what looked like monstrously sharp handheld rotary-saws. "Where do you need us to cut?"

"Right here!" he paced out across the deck and pointed beneath the darkened porthole of an empty First Class cabin. "Break through the deck here and then down another level; that will put you through to E-Deck and the Scotland Road corridor, and we'll be able to drag these suctions through to meet with their fellows at the boiler rooms!"

The men immediately set to work, breaking open junction boxes on *Rescue*'s two portable pumps and linking their tools up to what was presumably the equipments' onboard electrical supply. Moments later, with an ear-splitting roar like an angered swarm of bees, sparks showering over the wet deck, the handheld saws began to scythe into the light steel of the ship's upper superstructure, cutting through like a knife through butter.

Tom stepped back, hands pushed into his pockets to relieve them from the cold, and then heard someone calling his name. *"Mr Andrews! Thomas!"*

He looked up to see Captain Smith standing out on the bridge wing, pointing down off to the starboard side of the bow. "There are lights in the water!"

Stunned, Tom turned and ran to the rail. Sure enough, something was lighting up the water from underneath, submerged lights casting an eerie green light below the surface. He squinted, and could just make out a small, dark shape, bulbous form resembling one of *Oceanic*'s lifeboats. Some sort of miniature submarine?

"Do not worry," a heavily accented voice suddenly announced through the talkie radio. *"Speaking is Gorbachev, Anton Petrovitch, of the Shirshov Institute of Oceanography, Kapitan of research ship Anatoly Sagalevich…"*

"Captain Gorbachev, welcome to our flotilla…" Andrews heard Smith respond through the radio, as he looked up and got his first proper view of the Russian vessel. An unfamiliar flag flew from her mainmast, and his eyes narrowed as he spotted something dark and huge lashed to her rear deck…

He started, feeling a sudden chill that had nothing to do with the cold night striking deep in him.

No… that can't be possible…

Instantly galvanised, he turned and began scrambling up out of the well deck, coat-tails flapping behind him; doglegging up two flights of external stairs to the Boat Deck, he came out onto the Officer's Promenade, alongside the bridge.

Smith was there, still listening to the radio, through which Gorbachev was speaking at length.

"…object you are seeing in water is named Tolya, Mir-3. Is scientific manned submersible for deep-ocean research missions, and is studying your hull; with intention of patching holes."

Winded, Thomas paused and spun around, searching for a pair of binoculars. On deck *Titanic*'s officers were focused on launching the last of her starboard boats as the bow sunk lower, and below he could see more of *Oceanic*'s boats taking off passengers from the stern gangway doors, but masses of passengers were still crowding the boat deck, pressing in on the lifeboat stations.

"Keep back, keep back!" Murdoch was shouting, he and other crewmembers working to prevent a rush on Collapsible C. "More boats are arriving from *Oceanic*, maintain calm!"

He fired off his gun several times into the air to make his point, and Smith whipped round at the sound.

"*Blast*, we're on the verge of madness! Thomas, what's wrong?"

"Captain!" Thomas panted, flushed from his run up the deck. "Captain Gorbachev must turn the stern of his ship away from us immediately!"

"Why?"

"*EJ, just look at what he's carrying!*"

Smith quickly obtained a set of binoculars, and at Thomas' direction pointed them towards the *Anatoly Sagalevich*.

"Yes, there is something on her rear deck. Looks like a piece of salvage, from the wreck of a…" his voice trailed off.

"*…the wreck of a very large ship,*" Thomas finished for him.

Smith's face looked both horrified and crestfallen, and he suddenly turned and pressed the binoculars into Thomas' own hands. "Heavens above man, take a look and tell me, is it a part of us?"

Through the powerful magnifying lenses Thomas could clearly see that the object was indeed a massive piece of ship, a port-to-starboard section of double-bottom about thirty feet long, and ninety feet from side-to-side, so huge as to require being stored lengthways on the ship's deck.

"Well?" Smith pressed. "Is it a fragment of our own hull?"

Thomas' throat was dry as he tried to further focus the image. From his angle he could see the object was painted with red copper-oxide anti-fouling paint, but heavily decayed and covered in so many rusty growths and tendrils as to make it hard to distinguish detail. But despite all that it still bore certain unmistakable identifiers: the cellular double-bottom, tapering elegantly together at the turn of the bilge, marked by a protruding section of stabilising bilge keel.

"It is, EJ…" he said at last. "That is a wedge of our own double-bottom."

Smith was breathing heavily, as if about to faint, but he collected himself quickly and took up the talkie again.

"Captain Gorbachev, please turn your ship's bow towards us *now*. I have just been advised that you are carrying a piece of temporal salvage, and I do not wish to arouse further panic in my passengers should they catch sight of it."

"Understood Titanic, we correct immediately."

Smith closed the channel, and lightly dabbed at his brow. "If I had not seen it with my own eyes…" he said shakily, before directing his attention back to Thomas. "Please, Tom, do all you can to prevent that from coming true. The mangled condition that object was in suggests a horrific end to tonight's proceeds that we must avoid at all costs!"

"I understand, Captain," Thomas replied, but then a weak smile came to his face. "On the other hand, it suggests that these time-travellers might indeed have the technological muscle to make a salvage attempt possible."

"So I see from the metal fish scurrying around our prows," Smith pointed down from the bridge. Following it, he again saw the lights of what Gorbachev had called the *Mir-3*, moving slowly along the length of *Titanic*'s bow, below the waterline. Then his gaze shifted slightly to the forward well-deck, where men were rushing to-and-fro with the methodical chaos of an anthill; cutting, pumping and patching. *Titanic*'s crew worked with a professional haste, but the time-travellers were powering along like men possessed, faces set and eyes burning with silent intensity.

Glancing up, he caught a last glimpse of the immense piece of wreckage carried on the *Anatoly Sagalevich*, now disappearing from view as the ship turned on a point. How much time, effort and money had it cost to raise what was an otherwise worthless chunk of metal? Why do such a thing, and to what purpose?

Not for the first time, he wondered why *Titanic* meant so much to people distant by a hundred years.

*

The water now filling Boiler Room Six was warm and black. Kai's lights picked out the curve of a boiler, and as he descended past he reached out a gloved hand to stroke the casing, black metal roughed by just the slightest down of rust. Clean, pristine, brand new. And, just like when on any other salvage job, he felt buoyed up by a sense of adventure that was in stark contrast to his professional concerns.

When he had stepped off the E-Deck platform into the water, the instinctive urge to panic had come quicker than usual, the light from his mask showing only suspended specks of coal dust on all sides as he sank deeper into the compartment. Not even his hand on the escape ladder had been visible, and when he reached the turn on the edge of the funnel uptakes, he felt like he had plummeted off of a submerged cliff into the abyss. Now, his exhaled breath bubbled faster, ringing in his ears.

With a muted thump, his flippered feet landed on the grated floor of the boiler room. Carefully he threaded the foam gun through one of the escape ladder's rungs in order to keep the pipelines straight and free of tangles, and turned left, the weights on his belt holding him to the floor as he waded forward. The heat was noticeable, and with the drysuit pressing in on him, he felt like he was drowning in a sauna.

A jet of hot water gushed from somewhere above him, and directing his mask-light up revealed bubbles of steam and milky water seeping from a long crack in one boiler, where sudden contraction had split the pressure vessel like over-ripe fruit.

They drew the fires over an hour ago, he thought to himself. *But the boilers are still charged with steam; they could explode or implode at any time.*

Stepping as far away from the hulking plant as possible, he approached the portside hull, the wall of metal which separated him from the dark Atlantic, and followed it as far towards the prow as possible. Out of the void a bunker-door loomed in the dark, opened like a monstrous mouth. He had arrived at the forward bulkhead.

Andrews said to turn right here, and find the door to the fireman's vestibule… the watertight door should be closed…

Rebreather wheezing, he slowly walked down the open space between the bunkers and the towering boilers. The entombing water was thick with dust and fragments of coal, ash settling like snow underfoot and mingling with rust and grime to form a slick sludge. Overturned wheelbarrows, dropped shovels and scattered coals made going difficult, and he once again had to be cautious not to allow the pipes to get snagged or tangled in valves, gauges and stanchions. Glancing either side he could pick out open bunkers and furnaces gaping wide on either side of him. It was like sailing down the perilous gap between two galleons, cannon-ports open to fire. The heat was growing almost unbearable; the water leeching warmth from the cooling boilers as it circulated through their tubes and fireboxes. Kai felt as if he was slowly melting inside the drysuit, sweat running down and clinging between his skin and the inner layer of the suit.

There it is... the passageway to the fireman's vestibule.

The watertight door was a giant slab of grilled metal that was meant to drop like the blade of a guillotine, sealing off the passageways through the bulkhead. Cumbersomely, as if walking on the moon, Kai slouched closer, and stopped, his eyes going wide behind the mask as he felt a flow of cool seawater strike him.

Andrews was right! It didn't shut completely!

It was obvious to him what had happened. The racking of the hull had pushed the bulkhead door's guide-rails out of alignment; when the gravity-operated door came down it had consequently jammed when only part-shut, leaving an open gap of at least three feet between the bottom of the door and the lip of the frame. The resulting flow of water from compartments forward was constant and even, the current pushing Kai back as he tried to hold his position. Unable to swim against it, instead he scrambled onto the door, his head orientated towards the floor and belly pressed against the steel. Then, spider-style, he dragged himself under the lip and through the open gap.

The change in temperature was instant and vicious; not the sharp shock of jumping into a cold pool on a summer's day, but the bite of arctic ice, a fluid cold armed with teeth and daggers that cut and hacked at the slivers of skin the suit left exposed around his mask. Not daring to try and adjust it for fear of blinding himself with water, Kai bit on the rubber mouthpiece to relieve the gnawing pain and shone his lights around; at least in here, up-stream from the boilers, the water was clear and the visibility improved.

He was inside the fireman's vestibule, a small room within the bulkhead, hemmed in on two sides by coal bunkers. Directly opposite the gap that Kai had crawled through, a second watertight door was jammed open. Flanking it a pair of conventional doors hung from their locks, their hinges having sheared in the collision. They flapped limply in the current like broken wings.

Those doors lead to Cargo Hold Three, the next compartment forward, he thought to himself, before shining the light through the larger opening. *And that's the tunnel to the stokehold crew's quarters in the forecastle; the tunnel where Andrews said he saw water coming in.*

He shook his head. Thanks to the fireman's tunnel, at least three major compartments all shared access to this one small room; it must have been the main trunk through which water had so quickly flooded the ship during the sinking.

Stop thinking in the past tense, he then scolded himself. *This ship is sinking right now.*

As if to confirm his precarious situation, he checked his depth gauge. It showed him as being nearly fifty feet below the surface, well below *Titanic's* design draught of thirty-something feet. As he watched, he swore as the tiny needle progress a little further along the dial.

Slowly he kicked forward, half-swimming and half-walking, until he had wedged himself into the open watertight door. The fireman's tunnel stretched away beyond the range of his lights into the dark. He thought he could hear the sound of bubbling water.

Something settled on his shoulder and he moved to flick it away, only to find his fingers entwining with someone else's. He looked up and yelped, backpedalling with arms and legs as he saw the corpse of an unfortunate crewman wedged up towards the ceiling, one arm hanging towards him in supplication. The dead man's eyes were wide and staring, his neck twisted at an unnatural angle.

Kai shuddered, imagining the horror of dying alone in this underwater tomb of metal.

Reaching up he grabbed hold of the body and, with as much respect as possible, pushed it into the fireman's vestibule, before picking up the package that he had carried through the boiler room. Unlacing the straps around it, he unfolded a heavy nylon bag that had been wrapped around a tank of compressed gas. Holding the bag in front of him and bracing himself, he turned a valve on the tank. With welcome speed, the folds of canvas began to inflate and transform into one of *Rescue*'s heavy-duty salvage balloons, normally used to lift heavy objects from the seabed...

...but excellently suited to plugging a hole.

As the teardrop-shaped float continued to expand, blown up on a single extended breath, Kai manhandled it into the doorway between the tunnel and the fireman's vestibule. With it now trying to rise towards the ceiling he found it difficult work, until at last the expanding sides snagged in the doorway, the parachute bag puffing up around the clenching frame like a malignant growth. Shutting off the gas feed so as to not overstrain the rubberised fabric, he saw to his satisfaction that it served to plug almost all of the open door, leaving only gaps in the corners.

Now to seal it up, he thought, taking hold of the long 'gun' strapped to his back, the delivery system for Doctor Oshiro's DRP system. Mounted to a cumbersome stock, it took the form of a stainless-steel tube, a series of intermix chambers and atomisers that came together in a deviously complex rotary nozzle that Captain Jones always referred to as the 'spinneret'. Long pipes leading back the way he had come connected the gun to supply tanks in Scotland Road, and the indicator light on its fuel cell glowed green.

A flip of a switch started the 'spinneret' into motion, multiple nozzles whirring around a fixed point. Directing it away from himself, Kai pulled the trigger to test the equipment. The DRP gun 'kicked' in his arms, extruding a gooey jet of what looked like runny caulk from the tip. Immediately, however, it began to froth and expand into a mass of grey and gold bubbles, a semi-colloidal mix of chemical gasses and natural oils, trapped in a syntactic matrix of polymer reinforced by glass micro-balloons.

Releasing the trigger, Kai kept his distance, counting under his breath as the foam continued to expand and set, rising towards the ceiling as it did. Designed to be used in mass quantities to displace water from sunken wrecks, DRP was chemically engineered to be as environmentally-harmless as possible, but it was still not the kind of stuff you'd want to get all over yourself. Not even the use of non-isocyanate based polyurethanes could completely mitigate the toxicity issues, and even the heat of the polymerisation reaction could cause blistering if the goo got on any exposed skin.

By the time his count he reached thirty seconds, the clump of foam had solidified, becoming a pumice-like mass that bobbed against the underside of the ceiling. Now that the reactants had consumed themselves, it was chemically inert, and safe enough to handle that Kai kicked upwards to prod at it, finding to his satisfaction it had set as hard as resin or cement.

With everything working as it should, he lashed himself with a carabiner to one of the deformed door-guides, leaving both of his hands free to steady the gun in the feckless currents around the edges of the plugged door. Secured, he got into a position and squeezed the trigger, seeing foam shoot from the tip. Instead of trying to direct it against the flow into the gaps, he instead sprayed the adhesive substance over the surrounding walls, building up a 'foundation' to which larger wads could 'anchor', building a skeleton-grey coral reef that eventually swelled to seal the aperture, leaving him free to move on to the second opening.

By the time Kai had finished, thirty minutes after he jumped into Boiler Room 6, the door from the fireman's passage was completely sealed up, and for good measure he had caulked up the openings around the two service doors leading to Cargo Hold 3, to prevent water flowing through them. If Thomas Andrew's damage estimation was correct, then at least this should have restored the integrity of the ship's watertight subdivision, isolating each compartment and allowing them to be tackled individually.

Finally done, he checked his depth gauge. *Titanic* was still settling, but slowly.

*

They were losing the fight, Charles Lightoller feared. As he had played out the line that connected Alinka's foam gun to its supply tanks, the hull had continued to creak and groan around him with ever-increasing volume, the ship bellowing in pain as her frame was stretched in ways it had never been meant to endure.

Well, this won't be the first time I've been shipwrecked, he thought, remembering when he and several crewmates had been had been marooned for more than a week on a desert island after their ship, the *Holt Hill*, was demasted in a storm and ran aground. Charles had been just a lad of fifteen then, serving aboard the second ship in his career at sea. Now here he was aboard an artificial island, Second Officer of the largest ship of her age, a ship now sinking into the sea like mythic Atlantis punished by the gods for unbridled hubris.

No, stop that! he berated himself, remembering how the mercy of the Almighty had seen him through many hardships in his life. *If Titanic's sinking was punishment from on high, then the Lord would not have sent ships to our aid right across the gap of a century.*

But the presence of hope is by no means a guarantee of salvation, a treasonous part of his mind suggested. *After all, Abraham need only have found ten righteous men in Sodom for that city to be spared the Wrath of God, and his hope was met with failure.*

With ironic timing, a fountain of sparks suddenly scattered from the ceiling further along Scotland Road, streaming down to sizzle in waist-high water like falling stars sent upon some condemned city. Andrews' men were cutting through from above, and would soon be arriving with more suctions.

Are you a righteous man, Charles Lightoller? Are you deserving of rescue tonight, to find your place on that upturned lifeboat, while so many others cling to a sinking ship, or freeze to death in frigid waters?

I am deserving of nothing... it is by Grace alone that men are saved, not by their works...

Says the man who cast his burdens upon an innocent slip of a girl, a man unable to admit his own failings? Confession is good for the soul, Charles... why did you choose to not partake of it?

He did his best to ignore such thoughts as he continued to feed the line out to Alinka, but he could not help but think back to his encounter with Miss Paik. Having acted to save the life of another, Charles did not feel guilt as such for the death of Frederick Barrett, but instead at having not had the courage to tell Paik the truth. The cost of his own accursed pride shamed him deeply.

Not for the first time tonight, he uttered a prayer of deliverance.

As if in answer, he suddenly heard the tramp of running footsteps, and turned to see several men running down Scotland Road towards him, carrying more tanks of DRP polyurethane mix. Several he recognised as crew from *Rescue*. This must have been the team sent over from the Russian ship by the Nipponese gentleman, Doctor Oshiro.

"Quickly," one shouted. "Plumb those tanks into the supply lines."

As they worked, water sloshing around their ankles, Lightoller gave over responsibility for the supply lines. Rising, he strode several dozen yards aft and peered down into Boiler Room 5. Even with one of *Rescue*'s suctions dropped down the trunk, the water below was still so high above the floor plates at the deeper end that even a well-built man's head would have trouble breaking the surface at the shallow end.

Well, Charles, you might not be a righteous man, but you're certainly a tall one.

Focusing on the additional tanks of DRP materials now being connected up to a portable manifold, he followed a second line of piping to a spare foam gun, standing against the wall like an umbrella.

That'll do...

Grabbing the gun, he stepped over the elevated lip of the escape trunk and began down the ladder into the steaming chamber, endeavouring to not draw unwanted attention as he did. Torch held between his teeth and the gun strapped over his shoulder like a hunting rifle, he stopped at the swirling surface and took a breath. He could see water swirling in and out of the nearest firebox, and hear the sizzling of hot metal. Alinka's jaunt into the fireman's vestibule came with the advantage that Boiler Room 6 had been flooded for an hour, but even with the fires drawn and the Atlantic applying itself to the task of cooling the steam plant, this compartment was still far hotter.

I survived swimming in the bloody Atlantic in another life; this is just going to the other extreme.

Placing the soles of his shoes on the ladder uprights, he slid down into the hot water, and cried out at the heat. It was not scalding, but close enough, be damned! Gritting his teeth, he forced himself to swim hand-over-hand forward around the boilers, the waterproof torch adding hellish contrast to venting steam and smoke as the elements fought for dominance. His feet, weighed down by his boots, struck against the bottom, and every time they made firm contact with an object he kicked off, fighting to keep his head above the water.

The bunkers, which reached right into the ceiling, were arranged against Bulkhead E, the solid wall that divided this compartment from Boiler Room 6, and stacked full with coals that trickled down by force of gravity to the shovelling plates. Although all of the stokehold doors were submerged, he could determine which one had collapsed from where water was mushrooming up to the surface. With a deep breath, he dove under and kicked for the bottom, until he had a handhold on the floor plate. The open bunker door was just a darker void in the black water, ash and dust burning in his eyes, but he squeezed them shut, thrust the muzzle of the gun toward the flooded coals, and held down on the trigger.

*

"Hello, hello. Calling Thomas Andrews. Is Tom Andrews there, over?"

"Andrews speaking. Go ahead."

"Sir, the collision mats you needed suspended alongside the forward boiler rooms."

"Yes, what of them?"

"Sir, there's been a complication…"

*

Kai dragged himself up the ladder, chest heaving at the effort and his breath coming in bubbling gasps. Finally he dragged himself into Scotland Road and slumped forward, lying on his side in blessedly cold salt water. Coming back through the boiler room had been like voyaging through the flooded depths of Hell.

Something mechanical shrieked harshly in the near distance, the sound tinny as he tried to recover. For a few seconds he lay in the water, breathing deeply as he pulled off his diving gear.

Eventually he rolled into a sitting position and checked around him. The sound of cutting metal was coming from the team trying to break through into the corridor from above. Dismissing it, he looked the other way; the suctions from *Rescue* were still strung between the escape hatches and the portholes, and several of his fellow crewmen were gathered around the door to BR5's escape trunk, charged DRP cylinders in their arms, but Lightoller was missing, as was the spare foam gun...

Suddenly alert, Kai pulled himself onto his knees, and then shakily to his feet, staggering forward into their midst, and saw for himself the piping trailing down the escape ladder.

"Oh, shit!" he cursed, guessing at what had happened. "The fucking idiot, how long has he been down there?"

"Three minutes or so," one man replied. "We noticed he'd gone it alone about a minute before you came back up."

"The dumb bastard's wearing nothing but his deck clothes! He'll *kill himself* in there!"

Pulling himself forward onto his knees, and then struggling to his feet, he threw himself into Boiler Room 5, gazing down from the escape gantry and coughing in the rising fumes as the water smothered the red hot detritus from the fires. But there was something else in the smoke too, a familiar chemical tang...

"Lights!" he called out. "Are you alive down there?"

No-one replied, but he could hear the click and hiss of the valves on the polyurethane mix tanks as they discharged. Someone on the far end was still holding onto the trigger.

"...Scotland Road, this is Thomas Andrews speaking... Scotland Road, hello..."

Kai spun in response to the call, and his legs twisted out from under him. For the second time in as many minutes he found himself hitting the deck hard. The walkie-talkie he had left with Lightoller was clipped to a pipe on the wall, and he pushed himself upright to grab hold of it.

"Scotland Road here... the fireman's vestibule is sealed up tight, but Lightoller's gone down into Boiler Room 5 with the second DRP gun... I think he's trying to close up the bunker."

There was a long pause, and then Andrews quietly asked. *"Will that work?"*

"Why?" Kai's eyes opened wide. "Tom, what's happened up there? Has something gone wrong with placing the collision mats over the holes flooding the stokeholds?"

"The... your divers say we've done too good a job in reducing the inflow there: the mat is in place, but isn't being drawn tightly against the hull because the pressure differential is insufficient for a clean seal over the protruding strakes and rivets..."

"Tom, we need those mats to close off the damage to her broadside – even with what's been brought over from the *Sagalevich*, I don't have enough DRP kit to seal up the entire starboard side damage to BRs 6 and 5."

"Your people say they're going to try welding the frames of the collision mats directly onto the hull. Is that possible?"

"Geez..." Kai groaned, weakly dragging himself to the ladder as he tugged his dive mask back into place. "Yes, it's possible, but it will take time to scrape the paint off and prep the hull to receive the patch."

"So what can be done?"

"Stupid as he's acted, Lightoller's got the right idea. We're fighting the water's rise in BR6, and BR5 is mainly flooding through the compromised coal bunkers. If the bunker door that collapsed can be plugged then that might buy enough time to get the collision mats welded in place. I'm going down to assist. Scotland Road, out."

Hanging the walkie-talkie on the gantry railing, he took the ladder in his tired hands and made his way cautiously along and down the sloping top of the uptakes. Far below and forward he could see the flicker of a torch through the haze, shining on the forward bunkers, and heard the sound of a man coughing heavily.

His feet protesting at every rung, Kai swung himself off the ladder and crossed his arms over his chest as he dropped the last ten feet. The drysuit muted the shock of the hot water, but it was still enough to jolt some life back into him, and as he swam through water too deep for him to stand in, his heart fluttered painfully in his chest.

"Hey! Lightoller, are you there!?"

"I'm alright, just finishing up," was the surprisingly merry reply, even if Lightoller's voice cracked as he called out.

Titanic's Second Officer was a dark spot in the acrid fumes, thanks to his navy blue sweater. He was holding onto the release mechanism for one of the bulkhead doors, awkwardly clutching onto the purloined foam gun at the same time. His other hand was holding the neckline of his sodden sweater over his mouth to filter the air. As Kai swam up he saw the other man properly, and hissed in sympathy. Lightoller's face was a blotchy mash of red and purple. One of his eyes was swollen shut, and his other was bloodshot. The man rubbed at it with his sleeve, trying to clear out the motes of ash and DRP that covered him like swarming flies. Kai could see blisters forming on the officer's hands, and was in no doubt that some of them were chemical in nature.

"What did you think you were doing?" he all but yelled, attempting to not choke on the befouled air.

"I thought I'd buy a few more minutes and try and close up this gap in the bunker," Lightoller called hoarsely, before wincing and bringing his free hand up to grab at an upright. "I succeeded, I think. Take a look, would you?"

"Alright, but then we need to get you out of here and into a decontamination shower!" Kai reprimanded him, before taking a breath and diving underwater. Waving his hand around to clear away debris, he quickly saw Lightoller's handiwork. Expanded foam and coals blocked the open bunker door like a giant sponge pudding, loose tendrils of the stuff waving around like seaweed.

Surfacing with a gasp he nodded in approval. "You plugged it alright, should hold fine; polyurethane sets like asphalt." His feet brushed the floor. "And it looks like the water level's already falling in here."

"That's as may be!" Lightoller acknowledged, "But what happens when the bunker fills again? Look!"

Quickly he pointed upwards before latching back onto his handhold. Kai looked and saw how, with its drainage point through the stokehold door now blocked-off, the bunker was evidently beginning to fill with water again, evidenced from how it was beginning to jet from the seams in the metal face, rivulets dribbling down from around the rivets.

"Then we do what we can," he answered.

"Will it be enough, Kai?"

"I don't know, Lights… I don't know."

CHAPTER SIXTEEN

"Pull, pull! Together now!"

As the quartermaster bellowed, Thomas Andrews heaved hard. He had discarded his jacket and was working alongside three other men dragging the portable suctions up the cargo hatches. With the collision mats useless until *Rescue's* crew could prep *Titanic's* hull for welding, it was all the more urgent that the pumps be put to best use.

The hand-saws had continued to grind away through the deck planking and supporting steelwork until they broke through into an empty cabin, number C4. Aiming to have as straight a path as possible for the pipes, the men had then dug down through the floor towards E-Deck, but found their speed hampered once they entered the main hull girder, finding themselves up against steel stronger than that of the ship's lightweight superstructure. Cursing himself for having not foreseen this, Thomas had been surprised when *Rescue's* crew had produced two portable oxy-fuel welding sets, miniaturised versions of equipment developed less than a decade ago by the engineers Fouché and Picard. Having seen a limited amount of welding employed experimentally in *Titanic's* hull, Tom had been stunned to see how the resulting jets of flame had cut through the ships' battleship-quality steel like a soldering iron plunged into a block of chocolate.

Now, after twenty minutes' effort from the angle-grinders and cutting torches, they were through to Scotland Road. Thomas just hoped that Alinka and Lightoller had stemmed the flooding enough to keep the ship afloat.

The time was now a quarter to two in the morning. Two hours and five minutes since the collision, and eighty minutes since they had first started the portable pumps.

"No slacking, heave!"

The tip of the pipe came up over the lip of the cargo hatch, and the men immediately broke into a shambling run, dragging it forward to the first hole in the deck and passing it through.

"Below, below, now!"

…now running forward, down into the Third Class open space on D-Deck, water flooding up from beneath. Stairs to E-Deck submerged, quick forward to the hole cut in the rear wall into cabin D6, floor ripped open and carpet shredded, down through the next hole via a quick-rigged ladder, grab pipe. E-Deck cabins, Third Class, plain white wood smashed by ladder, water waist high, cold, so cold, turn left into corridor, through rough-cut door into Scotland road. Uphill now, water shallower, dragging pipe to escape trunks and forcing it down, quickly…

"Start the pumps!" Thomas heard himself yelling into the radio. "Start them now."

A distant roar, the lines jerking at their feet, drawing water powerfully, the men pause, stunned, uncertain: what next?

Tom tried to catch his breath, pinched his eyes to squeeze the sleep from them.

"Help!" called out one of several men gathered aft around the escape trunk from Boiler Room 5. "We've got hurt men here!"

Moving fast, Tom and several other dragged two bedraggled figures up against the water now cascading down into number five through the hatch. They were Kai Alinka, wheezing and brandishing a foam gun like a spear, and Lightoller, the poor man looking half-broiled.

"Give them room, let them breathe," someone shouted, rolling the two men onto their backs, showing red blotches all over Lightoller's face and arms. "Get help for this man."

Lightoller was quickly put on a stretcher, forced to lie very still as one of *Rescue*'s medical staff injected him with something, before they carried him rapidly away. Kai Alinka, still clad in his slick black drysuit, dragged himself into a sitting position against the wall, his chest heaving.

"What happened?" Thomas asked, dropping to his knees. "What were you two doing down there?"

Kai wheezed, his head lolling from exhaustion. "Lights… went below, gummed up the bunker with the gun," he coughed, stealing hacking breaths and visibly struggling to calm himself. "He's minimised the flooding into Boiler Room 5."

Thomas started. 'That might buy us the time we need to get collision mats in place!'

Getting to his feet, he strode forward into the floodwaters, coming alongside the half-submerged escape trunk to Boiler Room Six. The water was still foaming up the shaft, but seemed to not be rising any higher. He knelt and, using a grease pencil, drew a mark on the wall just above the waterline.

For a long minute he stared, daring the water to submerge the pencil mark, as more men dragged the second set of suctions through from the portable pumps and dropped them down the hatches. The gap between the line and the surface was a few millimetres. Then he blinked and wiped his eyes.

Yes!

The gap had become a centimetre, and was increasing further still.

It's working. Her head's coming back up!

Slowly, as if in a dream, Thomas staggered aft onto the dry part of the deck, until he found the escape trunk into Boiler Room 4. It was closed. Numb hands fumbling with the latches, he heaved it open and shone a light down below; there was no sign of water. Though the bottom was out of sight, the sounds of murmured voices could be heard over the roar of the induction fans feeding air to the boilers, which were still under pressure and supplying power to the pumps and lights. The Boiler Rooms were truly *Titanic's* heart and lungs.

"Thomas Andrews here," he said into his 'talkie' wireless, which he had taken pains to keep from getting wet. "What's the situation down in Boiler Room 4?"

Static crackled for a few seconds, and then a voice replied.

"Engieschr Brle haer, sitathfsn ith unsenghef."

It was Chief Engineer Bell, though heavily distorted, and Thomas laughed to himself for a second, feeling strangely giddy. When had someone given Joe Bell a talkie?

"Joseph," he replied. "Hold the device away from your mouth a little. All I can hear is your moustache rubbing against the grille."

After an abashed silence he heard Bell's voice responding, clear and calm.

"Sorry about that, Thomas. The situation is unchanged in Boiler Room 4; our own pumps are going steady and keeping the water down. How are things forward?"

"I think they're improving…" Thomas smiled, feeling another belly laugh threatening to burst up from inside him. "*Rescue's* full pumping capacity is now deployed in the forward two boiler rooms, and Messrs Alinka and Lightoller have cut off much of the flooding in both of them. We may be able to pump her dry…"

Then there was a bang from somewhere forward, followed by a roaring gurgle, and shouting voices.

Thomas spun so fast he struck his hand against the railing and the talkie flew out of his grasp, falling out of sight into the depths of the boiler room. As it did, a second, louder bang reverberated through the corridor, the ship's frame trembling as it did. Clutching his hand and holding back a pained curse he stepped out into the corridor, where the men were crowding back around the hatch to Boiler Room 5.

One of them was Frank Parkes, a twenty-one-year-old apprentice attached to Thomas' guarantee group from Harland & Wolff. As Tom approached, Parkes turned to face him, eyes wide. "Something broke down in there, Mr Andrews. Water's rising fast."

"It's worse than that!" shouted Kai Alinka from just forward; he was leaning breathlessly against the door to Boiler Room Six. "The level's falling in this compartment."

"God above, no!"

Thomas ran up to Kai, and saw to his dread that water was indeed retreating down the escape shaft like the flushing action of a toilet.

"Damn it!" he banged his clenched fist against the fall, heedless of any obscenity. *"God damn it!"*

"Another bunker door must have given way, sir," said Parkes.

"Yeah, and all the water drained out of the bunker back into the boiler room," Alinka added, pulling himself upright, "causing Bulkhead E to *actually* give way."

"I... I don't understand..." stuttered young Parkes, who was casting his eyes about fearfully as *Titanic* gave another bellowing shudder. The water about their feet surged, languid waves forming as the ship noticeably adopted a gentle list to port.

"Bulkhead E was already weakened by the bunker fire, Parkes," Thomas said leadenly, cradling the hand that he had smashed against the wall. "Each time that the water drained rapidly out of the bunker it would have created a void, exerting an extra load on the bulkhead as it tried to hold back the weight of water on the other side, in Boiler Room Six. Between the fire, and the two occasions that the bunker has abruptly emptied, the hydrostatic load overcame it, causing it to rupture."

"So now both of these boiler rooms have a direct connection, causing them first to equalise, like they're doing right now, and then they'll flood at the same rate," Parkes, an apprentice plumber, said in sudden understanding, his eyes opening wide.

"Great..." Kai sighed, before turning and viciously kicking the wall with a yell. "*Shit!* Our whole strategy was to keep the level constant in Number Six and drain Number Five dry. We can't do either if they're both flooding freely!"

"And the free surface effect of the equalisation is playing merry hell with her stability..." Tom added grimly as *Titanic* tried to right herself, struggling to pull herself back onto an even keel. "She was already adopting a list to port; if we try too hard to keep her in this position, the action of water slopping around in the conjoined boiler rooms might even increase that list to the point that she rolls over onto her beam."

"Fucking hell..." Kai hissed, now holding himself up on the frame of the escape hatch and glaring down into BR6. Thomas looked down at the scratch he had made with his pen; now the water was bobbing just below it, a small wave rising to lick at the black smear.

Struggling to deal with the rapid reciprocation of his emotions, he laid a hand lightly on the apprentice's shoulder. "Parkes, head out fast and try and find yourself a place in a boat. Find the other youngsters from the Guarantee Group and take him with you; poor Ennis Watson's only nineteen..."

"You think it's that bad, sir?" Parkes's eyes were wide and white as saucers.

Thomas' answer was a grim squeeze on the shoulder, before he gently shoved him aft towards the bottom of the First Class stairs. "Go."

As the youth ran, *Titanic*'s designer focused on the roar of the pumps and suctions, matched against the sound of crashing water within the two boiler rooms. No collision mat, no magical expanding foam could fight this now. The bulkhead between Boiler Rooms 5 and 6 was the front line of this battle, and its collapse would cost them the loss of both compartments, and the ship with it.

He looked at his pocket watch; it had stopped.

"You said she sank at about twenty past two," he spoke to Kai. "I think we've won her another hour, maybe a little bit more, but then she'll almost certainly roll over or break up completely. Except now there are sufficient ships at hand to evacuate the remainder of our company."

Squatting in the water, he clenched his eyes shut. "Thank you for everything, Mr. Alinka, but I think this is as far as we can go. Both our ship's pumps are going full blast, but they're not holding the water back. Please inform your Captain Jones that he may have to be ready to stand off of *Titanic* in a hurry."

"The hell he will!" Alinka laughed harshly, and Thomas looked across to him. *Rescue*'s lead salvor was holding a hand to his head, grinning bitterly. "You don't know squat about the captain. His dad died in a mining explosion when he was six, but they couldn't get the bodies out because of fires and cave-ins, so the Captain held onto this hope that his Dad was still alive, and needed rescuing. A week later, his mother found him *digging a hole* in their back yard, trying to get down there and save him!"

Thomas stared, trying to match the image of an obstinate child with the courageous mariner who would surely have command of a ship like *Rescue*.

"And you know shit about me," Alinka added darkly. "After I got my salvor's qualifications I basically ran away to sea, to get away from the 'tropical paradise' of Hawaii, and all the tourists and fawning surfer girls and crap. I'd barely seen my mother while I was studying for my Masters in England, and once I joined the MSC I basically broke off contact with her for six years, even though I knew she was living with my brother and on her last legs. It was Captain Jones that made me realise what a selfish bastard I was, and convinced me to go be with her at the end."

Kai rolled forward onto his knees now, fire in his eyes. "*Rescue* saves people! Jordan Jones saves people, even if it's from themselves! So don't you dare even imply that he's going to just stand by and watch this ship sink if there's the slightest possibility that letting that happen will endanger even a single life!"

The young man paused in his diatribe, chest heaving. "We just… we just need to find a way to make that happen."

Then he fell back against the wall as if he had expended all his energy in one burst. But his words had given Thomas a moment's stunned clarity in which to think.

"Let them flood," he said softly.

"Say what now?" quizzed Alinka.

"Let Boiler Rooms Five and Six flood, right to the bulkheads!" Thomas said, his own thoughts pushing forward now. "The ship is designed to stay afloat with any two compartments completely full of water. We've lost the fight here, yes, so let's make a strategic retreat, and continue pumping out the three forward cargo holds."

He rose to his feet now, mind racing. Kai Alinka was staring up at him, a faint smile on his face.

"Yes, yes, yes!" Thomas continued, hands spread like a preacher. "One of the *Anatoly Sagalevich*'s little submarine-boats was working at that end of the ship and has possibly closed off some of the flooding there, so let's relocate all these suctions forward, drain the forward holds and focus on keeping the ship's nose up!"

"Now that's the Tom Andrews I saw in all the *Titanic* movies!" Kai laughed. "Oh you should see yourself from this angle, man, it's crazy heroic! Legs astride, sleeves rolled up, defying the waters like King Canute." He pulled himself up, accepting Thomas' help. "But you know what? I think you might just succeed where His Majesty failed."

"Thank you," Thomas replied, trying to force as much gratitude as possible into his voice. "I need to inform Captain Smith. Where's your talkie?"

Kai pointed, and Thomas turned to see it hanging from a wire. As he stepped forward to reach it, it crackled as if anticipating his actions.

"Mr Andrews... Thomas?"

Even at a moment like this, he could not repress a smile at how Captain Smith had not made Bell's mistake; remarkable, given the captain's full moustache and beard.

"I'm here, EJ..." he said after taking up the talkie, biting his lip. "There have been some setbacks, Captain, but there's still a chance if we can redeploy the suctions to the forward holds."

There was a pause, and then Smith cleared his throat.

"How long will it take to accomplish that? Do you even have enough time to do so?"

It was an unknown, but Thomas tried to take all that he had seen and learnt and heard in the past hour and channel that knowledge. He glanced down into the compromised Boiler Rooms, and estimated how long it would take the water to rise to their level.

"At most, we have twenty to thirty minutes before no amount of pumping can save her."

"Right! Very good!" Smith replied, sounding strangely smug, even jovial. *"Don't fret about moving those pipes and pumps around, leave them where they are. Instead, please request those futurists to take their cutting tools quickly amidships. There's additional assistance coming alongside to starboard."*

"The *Anatoly Sagalevich?"* Thomas asked, feeling his heart jump and then falter, unwilling to commit after so much peril and promise.

"No. Some other ship from out of time, like nothing I've ever seen before. Just move fast, lad. By your own account we don't have much time."

"I'll do that sir."

"Thank you, Thomas," Smith ended the call with a polite curtness that Tom felt was punctuated on the other end with a nod.

"What was that?" spoke up Kai, now on his feet. Tom barely heard him, and simply muttered "This way" as he began to retrace the trail of holes that had been sliced through the ship. The younger man followed with little protest.

Initially Thomas thought the well deck was deserted, except for a single man at the controls for the two pumps. Then he realised that all the crew had gathered at the starboard rail, water from the

313

pumps sloughing around their feet. They stared off into the dark, murmuring incredulously.

What could be happening now? he thought as he crossed to stand beside them, curiosity tempered with indignation. This one night had already thrown so many wonders at him, that he was doubtful anything else would astound him.

He was wrong.

Something black moved in the dark, visible only by the glow of a red navigation light and where a sleek, tubular form broke *Oceanic*'s brilliant reflection. At first he thought a whale was broaching alongside *Titanic*, but then the approaching vessel began to sound a booming siren, clearing itself a path through the lifeboats scurrying between the two passenger liners. Spotlights flared in the dark, glistening on a tall tower that rose from the stranger's cigar-shaped hull, and Thomas realised that once again he was looking at a submarine, one more massive he had thought possible. It would have dwarfed the tiny Mir-3, and he suspected it was larger than many of the ships he himself had helped to design and build.

But he was familiar with the primitive Holland submarines under trials with various navies, and had heard debates over their potential as weapons of war, and quickly grasped that he was witnessing that concept carried through a hundred years of refinement.

This is a warship, a submersible dreadnought!

Now he could see men scurrying on the long deck behind the vessel's navigation tower, pouring up through opened hatches. Flying over them from a stubby mast was a red St. George's Cross on a white field, a proud Union Flag rampant in the canton.

He recognised it with a thrill of pride; the Royal Navy of the future had arrived.

"Attention!" called out another electronically-amplified voice. *"To the Captain of the Royal Mail Steamship Titanic; this is Her Majesty's Submarine Viking! Prepare to receive pumping assistance!"*

Looking for answers, Tom looked towards Kai, and paused in surprise. The other man's olive face had paled to an ashen grey, and he was staring at the submarine with a mixture of awe and horror.

"Oh, fuck... she's a *boomer*, a ballistic missile boat!"

Ballistic missiles? But are not all missiles and projectiles 'ballistic' in nature? What makes this submarine so evidently fearsome?

Thomas opened his mouth to speak, and then Kai turned upon him and made eye contact, his lips pressed together in a firm line.

"Don't ask, Tom. Honestly, it's better that you don't know."

Stunned, Thomas mouthed a quiet "alright then" and turned, finding his voice. "We need to make preparations to take her suctions aboard. We need the power tools brought below and enough manpower to drag them over."

As the men stirred and headed below, some with more urgency than others, Thomas heard the sound of a snarling motor, and glanced past Kai's shoulder; *Viking* had launched a small motorboat, which was flying over the still sea beside *Titanic* faster than any motor-launch he had ever seen. Several men sat upright in it, and for a moment he swore he saw the black muzzles of rifles glinting in their hands.

And then they vanished off into the night.

*

Off to the south, Stanley Lord could now see the gigantic blaze of light that surrounded the *Oceanic*, the fog having evaporated some time ago. It seemed incredible to him that such a ship could manoeuvre in a harbour, let alone traverse the open sea with no fear from wind or storm. The futuristic liner looked so top heavy that he swore it should capsize at any second, and so prodigiously long that her back ought to snap the first time she took a heavy sea on her bows.

And yet there she was, in defiance of his expectations, still halted alongside the allegedly sinking *Titanic*. As for what was happening over there right now, he could not say.

No sense in worrying over that now. If she's gone she's gone, in the flash of an eye. There's another stricken giant to consider here.

Acknowledging that, he turned to regard the immense vessel that still loomed over his *Californian*. The *Seguin Laroche*'s rear decks were a tangled mess. Steelwork had been bent like a giant had sat upon it, and many containers had tumbled over into a higgledy-piggledy pile, the unbalanced weight only worsened by the ship's distinct list to starboard.

Bodies lay broken among the wreckage; many of them burnt horrifically, having died in the act of fighting the fires. Fortunately their efforts had borne fruit, and thanks to some unknown hero's decision to use fire hoses to swamp the aft deck in water, the blaze had apparently not penetrated into the ship's superstructure. Indeed, it had burnt itself out before *Californian* had even arrived on the scene.

Despite their role in the disaster, the remains of both crew and mutineers were collected and respectfully sheeted over until it could be decided how best to dispose of them.

Captain Lord watched quietly, interjecting with an order when necessary, as his ship carefully manoeuvred against the larger vessel's stern, men working *Californian* along with ropes and assisted by brief nudges from the engine. It was fortunate that the weather was so calm, as the flat seas made possible manoeuvres that normally he would not attempt unless in a harbour with the assistance of tugboats. He also had the assurance of the other ship's crew that the calm conditions would last until morning, at which point they warily believed a chop would stir up.

Another advantage of time-travel, he thought, shaking his head as one of the Leylander's cranes was swung out, the hook on its end reaching the deck of the *Seguin Laroche*. This ship was from the future – it boggled his mind, and yet he found himself accepting it with surprising calm. The sheer size of the other vessel compared to his own, and the technological marvels that Stewart and Groves had described, left him with little room for an alternative explanation.

One of those wonders was currently clipped to his belt, a handheld speaking device. Monitoring the situation he took it in hand and held down the button on the side as he had been instructed.

"Slacken off aft, over."

Another voice quickly replied, and from aft Lord heard the sound of one of the winch engines playing out the stern lines, keeping *Californian* from swinging in too tight against the *Seguin Laroche*'s flat-faced transom. Regarding the name painted on the giant hull, his eyes travelled higher, and he spotted a petite figure in a green jacket and navy cap approaching the other ship's jackstaff. He frowned, recognising the disquieting quandary that was Joanna Laroche, and shook his head. From a brief meeting, he had been unimpressed with the woman that claimed to be master of the *Seguin Laroche*, finding her to be shrill, shrewish and unfit for command.

Yet he still watched with interest as she quickly unrolled a package bundled under her arm and tied it to the cleats on the flagpole. Lord saw a flutter of blue, white and red fabric as she pulled on the line to raise the flag, before she stepped back and stood to attention. Her gaze drifted down towards him, and she nodded respectfully, as one captain might to another. Hesitantly, he responded in kind, and then felt a moment's stunned confusion when Laroche saluted him, her palm held downward just as he would expect to see in the Royal Navy.

Pride, Stanley Lord realised. *This woman is proud to command her ship, and knows enough of the ways of the sea to honour me with a proper Navy salute.*

Swallowing, he smartly came to attention and returned the gesture, for a moment seeing beyond the feminine exterior of Joanna Laroche, and understanding the mariner beneath, his *sister sailor.*

A slight breeze stirred, lifting the limp flag, and the familiar tricolour of the French Republic flew proudly from the *Seguin Laroche*'s stern. Lord nodded to himself; it was reassuring to see that despite the differences in technology and attitudes, at least one thing had remained consistent over the course of a century.

At the same time, *Californian*'s 'Red Duster' stirred, and he felt a moment's pride at his having decided to fly the ensign of the British Merchant Navy when they had first approached this alien vessel. Once again he felt a kinship with Laroche, whose attention had returned to her own standard, her hand still raised in salute, but palm turned outward.

Then she briskly lowered it, nodded down at him, and strode off to assist her crew. Lowering his own hand, Lord silently watched her cross the *Seguin Laroche*'s aft deck, cluttered with the shattered ruins of countless 'shipping containers'. Men

317

with tools had cut open the crushed fuselage of one particular container in the heart of the wreckage, and now the free end of the line from *Californian*'s crane was being attached to something within. Several men shouted out calls that it had been made fast, and Lord gave the order for the crane's winch be started, slowly drawing in the line.

The time machine… he thought uneasily. *What manner of device is powerful enough to move several ships one hundred years out of their time?*

When revealed, manhandled from out of the container by mechanical and human effort, the time-engine was deceptively small. About the height of a man, it had a domed top and a widely flared flange at the bottom, and looked like an enormous bell, trailing several loose pipes and conduits. In the directed light from torches and deck lamps, the device gleamed mercurial silver.

Most chillingly, despite the way the container had been crushed in around it and set ablaze, the time machine itself appeared utterly unscathed, the only sign of its traumatic experience being a grotesque red splash across its hull.

Lord had heard how one of the *Seguin Laroche*'s engineers had been unfortunate enough to be inside the container when it imploded, and realised that he was looking at blood. *Human blood.* He suppressed a shudder, experiencing as he was a first-hand demonstration of this device's power, and the thought of what uses it might be turned towards left him cold.

I'd have rather dumped it two miles overboard, but all hope of these people returning home is bound up in the blasted thing… and the Seguin Laroche is sinking, albeit slowly…

With the crane jib visibly flexing under its weight, the time engine soon was lowered into *Californian*'s hold, snuggled up against bales of woven cloth.

"Ahoy!"

Lord turned at the sound of a new voice and peered off to the south. One of the lookouts sprang forward, holding to the rigging as he gazed into the dark. *"Captain, skiff in sight!"*

'Skiff' was the wrong word. The tiny craft motoring up out of the night seemed more like some nicety created by a balloon artist, an air-filled tube bent into the shape of a hull and strapped to a tiny motor that made up for what it lacked in size with raucous noise. The man hailing Lord was standing hunched in its bow, holding on with one hand and brandishing a loudhailer with the other.

"Ahoy to the cargo vessels Californian and Seguin Laroche, we wish to come aboard!"

Despite the man's polite tone, his words were underlined with an unspoken threat, and from his elevated position Lord could see that the men in the tiny raft, boat, whatever, were all armed. He remembered every story he had ever heard of pirates, and for a second entertained the notion that he might have to repel boarders.

"Ahoy again! This is Lieutenant Scott Thresher of the HMS Viking, do you hear me?"

So this man was an officer in the Royal Navy? The whole affair seemed preposterous.

Then again, half an hour ago I would have thought it preposterous that a woman could command anything more than a rowboat.

He stepped up to the rail and called out in greeting, adopting what he hoped was a relaxed smile. "Lieutenant, feel free to come aboard. On behalf of myself and Captain Laroche, welcome to our ships."

As he lowered his hand, smile frozen on his face like the cold grin of a skull, Lord cursed the strange cargo he had just taken aboard. He understood that the device had to be removed from the ship rather than be lost when the *Seguin Laroche* sank, and that *Californian* was the only vessel to hand fitted with cranes (the absence of any kind of loading equipment aboard Capitaine Laroche's command struck him as very strange), but Stanley Lord had a sinking suspicion that his ship had just become the most vulnerable vessel in the world.

CHAPTER SEVENTEEN

On *Titanic*'s F-Deck, cantilevered out over Boiler Room 5, was the ship's swimming pool, exclusive domain of the First Class passengers. Located between two protective bulkheads, it was still mostly dry, despite the fact that the portholes that provided dim illumination were already submerged. One of the first heated swimming baths to go to sea, the room was austerely furnished, the tiled floor and white-painted metal walls giving it the air of an industrial meat-locker.

And now men with power tools were tearing it apart, sparks and jets of flame lighting up the room in lurid flashes as they fought to cut holes through which additional suctions from *Viking* could be forced into the Boiler Room beneath. Thomas Andrews was there, working in a team of men all armed with long-handled lump-hammers, smashing through the tiled bottom of the empty pool to expose the metalwork.

Further aft and down a connecting corridor, Kai Alinka was in the opulent Turkish Baths, another first of its kind onboard a ship. But the elegant furniture and exquisite wooden carvings were now covered in dust and filth, some items shattered into pieces, as he and other men created a thoroughfare to bring the pipes through into the swimming pool.

Kicking aside broken chunks of wooden panelling to give himself a better footing, Kai brought the searing flame of an oxy-acetylene torch to bear against the steel hide of Watertight Bulkhead G, cutting through the tempered metal with agonising slowness. Other men were slopping buckets of water about, trying to keep flying sparks from setting the ruined spa on fire.

It did occur to Kai that if they failed to save *Titanic*, all these acts of vandalism would actually help to speed the ship's sinking, providing convenient bypasses by which floodwaters could flow easily from one compartment to the next.

But still he kept cutting, driven on by the mad belief that they could keep the ship afloat.

Finally, he opened up enough of the wall to make a hole big enough for a man to scramble into, and abandoning the tools he climbed through and entered one of the two Third Class Dining Saloons, a low-ceilinged space simply panelled in white painted wood; a far cry from the lustrous finish the Turkish Baths had possessed when he first entered them.

Running up the sloping deck, he came to where *Viking*'s own engineering crew had cut an opening in the side of the hull's shell plating, the cold night air dispersing the odour of heavy food and human sweat that already seemed to have permeated the saloon. The submarine's crew were already at work here, hauling aboard lengths of pipe.

"Down there!" Kai pointed forward to the hole he had just made. "That leads through to the swimming pool, and from there you can get your pipes into the Boiler Rooms!"

Nodding, the men began to drag the massive suctions down the length of the room. Kai moved to help them, but felt his strength fail him and sat down on the edge of a dining table, dizzy and exhausted. Inside his chest his heart was racing away like a turbocharger, struggling to circulate blood through him at a sufficient rate to keep up with his limbs and thoughts.

Feeling lightheaded, he put his head between his knees and breathed deeply. His mind however was still far away, juggling variables.

Titanic, Rescue and Viking; their cumulative pumping capacity has got to be enough, surely?

No, it wasn't, at least not for him. Once he'd caught his breath, he'd slug down some water and go back into the fray, and he wouldn't stop until the ship was secure...

"Hallo! Hallo, is anyone be hearing?" something screeched electronically, and looking up Kai spotted an abandoned two-way radio half-hidden in a coil of hosepipe. Forcing his legs to steady themselves he staggered over and picked it up.

"This is Leading Salvor Kai Alinka, aboard *Titanic*, over…" he said.

"Thanking goodness," came the reply, barely audible over the roar of pumps and the screech of power-tools in the hull. *"This is Captain Gorbachev, with urgent news. Tolya has encountered severe problem."*

"*Tolya*? You mean Mir-3, right?" Kai clarified, remembering that he had last seen the submersible fluttering around *Titanic's* bow, searching for the fabled damage inflicted by the iceberg.

"Yes, has gone underneath hull of Titanic and found many holes, but is unable to get DRP foam in place, due to robot vehicle becoming stuck. Is asking for diver to go down and be helping."

Kai's vision was flecked with little white spots, and he blinked and shook his head to clear them away. Where had he left his dive gear? It was still in Scotland Road, right?

"Tell Mir-3 that I'll be there ASAP," he said with a firmness that arose from some reserve he did not know he possessed, and ended the call.

Rescue saves people, Jordan Jones saves people; and so do I, full of spirit and resolve.

*

"Hello! Hello, is anyone here!?" Pip ran through *Titanic's* emptying corridors, banging on doors and calling out to any persons still present. "There are more boats coming! Everyone needs to get to the E-Deck reception right now!"

Already she had found several immigrant families who, despairing of being able to fight their way through the earlier crush, had retreated to their cabins to await the end. Following the mental map of the ship she had assembled in her mind over the years, she had also located the Italian staff attached to the ship's A-la-Carte restaurant. Being neither passengers nor crew, but hired-in contractors looked down upon by *Titanic's* own company on account of their race, they had been overlooked during the 'original' sinking and all lost. Pip's Italian might have been limited to *"Cosi! Cosi!"*, but she had managed to get them to follow her down to E-Deck and into another of *Oceanic's* motorboats.

She was certain that of the two thousand, two hundred persons onboard, nearly three-quarters had been evacuated, an estimate that included not only the majority of the passengers, but also the ship's domestic company and the better part of three hundred firemen. The last of *Titanic's* starboard boats had gone, and the deck crew were now trying to lower those portside boats that did not overhang *Rescue*.

Coming round a dogleg bend into the main part of Scotland Road, she momentarily stopped and blanched. Just a few feet ahead of her was where her neglect had cost Frederick Barrett his life. His body would have been brought out right through here…

No, remember what Lightoller said; I'm a part of Rescue's crew, by adoption if not by assignment, and I have a job to do.

Rousing her resolve, she proceeded forward; then she spotted one man dragging himself up a flight of stairs from the Third Class dining saloon below and ran to help, only to realise from his dress that he, like her, was a time-traveller. It was one of *Rescue's* crew, the Hawaiian salvor from the news, Kai Alinka. He looked exhausted and bedraggled, his face and neoprene dive suit smeared with oil and other stains.

"I'm alright, get off me!" he said when she tried to get under his shoulder to support him, instead directing her towards a set of SCUBA breathing gear resting against one wall. "If you want to do something, help me carry this!"

"You're going back in the water?" she asked, dubiously eyeing his worn-out posture and his face, which was blotchy with minor scalds.

"I've gotta. Mir-3's having trouble patching up the holes in the ship," he grunted. "You're the expert, right? What can I expect to find down below?"

She repeated what she had told Thomas Andrews about conflicting theories as to the damage that sank the ship, and he scowled.

"Great, so if she grounded, I might have to go right under the hull. That's forty or fifty feet down…"

"Why not get someone else? You look like you've done enough already."

"I'm the only one who responded. All the other divers are trying to weld patches to the hull, and the Royal Navy crew are busy modifying their sub's ballast purge systems into a giant bilge-pump."

Straining, between them they dragged the bulky SCUBA gear down to where *Viking* had made a hole on F-Deck. The submarine had come up alongside *Titanic* at this point, with her propeller pointing towards the liner's bow, and a simple wooden gangplank connected the two vessels. Pip eyed Britain's ultimate defence of the realm uneasily, and her mind drifted towards words she had earlier heard exchanged between Captains Smith and Jones over the walkie-talkie radio loop.

Someone boarded this ship with a gun… someone from the freighter that ran Doctor Oshiro and me down. He was babbling about time travel before Rescue had even figured out 'where' we were, let alone 'when'…

Jones had cut Smith off before he could divulge much further, apparently not wanting to exchange critical information on an unsecure channel. But Pip had heard enough to determine that whatever had brought them to 1912 was an act of man, not God, and that one of those men was currently under observation in *Titanic*'s hospital.

The addition of a nuclear 'boomer' to the situation only threatened to complicate things further, but she forced herself to focus on helping Alinka into his diving apparatus, remembering to focus on salient facts, not crude hypotheticals.

"This says you've only got enough oxygen left for twenty minutes of dive-time," she blurting, catching a glimpse of the air tank's pressure gauge. "Is that enough to get down there and come back up with decompression stops?"

"What do you know about diving?" he asked, seemingly in as much curiosity as annoyance.

"I study Underwater Archaeology, of course I've trained as a diver! And I know how easy it is to screw up. There's been deaths on expeditions to the *Andrea Doria*, *Empress of Ireland*, and even *Titanic*'s sister *Britannic*, all because people miscalculated how much air and time they would need to come back up without suffering from the bends!"

"Decompression sickness," he corrected her, but not even the sterile parlance was enough to drive away the grisly visuals used to illustrate the dangers of surfacing too quickly after a dive, of how blood saturated with compressed gas could suddenly boil inside the human body as pressure decreased, causing horrific cramps, internal injuries, even death. "Don't worry. This is a shallow dive, and I'm not going to be down long."

"How do you know that?" she demanded, but he did not answer, simply inserting his rebreather and stepping backwards into the gap between *Viking*'s hull and *Titanic*'s tapering bow, splashing down into the water.

*

Straight away Kai felt the change in temperature despite the insulation provided by his suit, and the comparative coolness was almost pleasant, salving his stinging skin and clearing his mind like a cold shower. Kicking his flippers, he struck down and forward, slowly descending as he swam down the gap between *Viking* and *Titanic*, one hand running along the ship's curving hull, fingers bumping over hull joints and countersunk rivets, the metal gleaming in the light thrown by the LEDs fitted to his mask.

Through the murk he could see flashes of light coming into view, and without pausing he swam over two teams of divers working to secure collision mats to *Titanic* by welding brackets to the hull outboard of Boiler Rooms 5 and 6. It would take them time to finish the job, and he even doubted that it would be possible to weld to *Titanic*'s steel, uncertain of its exact metallurgical composition.

But if the pumps were to get ahead in the boiler rooms, then the collision mats needed to be in place, and time could only be won for that by reducing the inflow of water to the other compartments. Leaving the welding teams behind, he pressed on, angling down steeper now until he came to the turn of the bilge, the angle formed where the ship's side and bottom met, and swam alongside it towards where he had last seen Mir-3. Seeing the identical construction to the huge chunk of wreckage he had

325

helped bring aboard the *Anatoly Sagalevich* only a few hours ago, he shivered. That had been not long before dusk on April 14th 2012, and now here he was in the small hours of the morning, April 15th 1912, swimming underneath the *Titanic*.

It was enough to make him feel ill. Beneath him the black depths of the North Atlantic gaped wide open, and he was reminded once again of the old legends of Milu, the underworld. The current was still pushing the ship south, and right now they should be approaching the spot fated to be *Titanic*'s final resting place, 41.43'N, 49.56'W.

But soon they would pass right over those co-ordinates, and if he had his way the surrounding ocean plains would never feel forty-five thousand tons of steel come crashing down onto them.

Focusing on that, he kicked hard and made for Mir-3, which was cautiously hovering further along, just off the turn of the bilge, lights directed upwards. Evidently, despite the circumstances, the submersible's pilot was wisely refusing to risk taking his craft underneath an overhanging obstruction, especially one that might at any minute sink on top of him.

Swimming right up to the sub he waved into one of the tiny portholes, seeing the face of Doctor Oshiro squinting back at him, before the Japanese engineer nodded in recognition and jabbed a finger forward and up towards *Titanic*.

Forming an '*OK*' signal with his hand, Kai manoeuvred himself forward and followed a fibre-optic wire that extended from the front of Mir-3 and led off underneath *Titanic*. The cord tethered Mir-3 to '*Aelita, Queen of Mars*', a little ROV, or Remotely-Operated-Vehicle, to which the submersible acted as a mothership. Each of the Mir craft was fitted with one of the little robots, which had been invaluable workhorses during the centennial expedition's dives to *Titanic*, retrieving artefacts like the Marconi apparatus and using mounted DRP guns to pump refloatation foam into larger objects like the double-bottom section.

Now, one was being used to save the *Titanic*.

Aelita, about the size of a largish dog's kennel, was painted red with neon pink highlights, the colours serving to visually distinguish it in dim environments from the absent Mir-4's silver and blue ROV *'Metropolis'*. Gradually, it emerged from the dark, and Kai saw that the blocky little robot seemed to have impaled itself at an odd angle in the bottom of *Titanic's* hull. Coming closer he shone his lights up and stared, air boiling from his rebreather as he gasped in surprise.

Oh, shit…

The tiny craft was wedged inside of a horrific graze that had eviscerated the liner's starboard underbelly and exposed the guts of her double-bottom. The ROV's shielded propellers whirred in desperation as Oshiro evidently tried to pilot it free.

As he swam closer Kai considered trying to pull *Aelita* out of the gap, before realising he would not be able to get enough purchase. Instead he swam around to the front of the craft, forcing a hand up into the hole so that he could wave for the benefit of the ROV's inbuilt cameras, signalling for Oshiro to 'stop'. The man must have gotten the message, because *Aelita* immediately stopped shimmying around, allowing Kai to make a better inspection.

The hole in the bottom of the hull must have been caused by the ship grounding on a shelf protruding from the iceberg, stripping away the skin of the outer hull and delivering massive shock damage to the cellular structure of the double bottom. It was damage that the ship was designed to withstand, but under the presumption of suddenly grounding on a wreck or shoal, while operating at reduced speed close to shore or within a confined waterway. Out here in the open ocean, *Titanic* had been forging ahead at full steam, and had ran over the ice with all the grace of a Lamborghini hitting a speed bump at sixty miles an hour; *her underside had buckled…*

Something tugged at Kai's limbs. There was a current trying to draw him up towards the hole, signifying that this indeed was a point where water was entering into the ship. Swimming around to the side of *Aelita*, he immediately saw the source of the problem. The robotic vehicle had been using its mounted DRP gun to try and fill in the hole in the hull when the current must have sucked *Aelita* itself in as well, lodging it firmly in place.

Now that he understood the situation, he could see the solution. Trying to pull *Aelita* out of the hole was impossible, but if someone could get *inside* they could brace themselves against *Titanic's* inner hull and push the ROV off with their legs. Cautiously he swam up into the void and found himself inside the hull, separated from *Aelita* by a large section of webbed framing. Getting his arms through one of the gaps was easy, but when he tried to pull his body through as well the oxygen tank proved too big to fit.

And so comes the moment where I bravely discard my oxygen, sacrificing myself to save the ship, he thought sarcastically. *Not yet.*

Carefully, he removed the tank from his back, and then, while keeping a firm hold on it, pushed it through the hole in the girder before squeezing through himself. Replacing the cylinder to its proper position, he braced himself, placing one foot either side of *Aelita's* main camera array, no doubt giving the guys back in the submarine a wonderful view of his crotch. The men in Mir-3 were either desperate to get away from such a view or smart enough to understand his intent, because as Kai pressed down hard with his legs, the plucky little robot re-engaged its propellers, which spun away in full reverse. Finally, with man and machine working together, the craft finally dropped free, Kai sinking out of the hull to come to rest beside it.

Affectionately he gave *Aelita* a pat as it if were a pet, just as the speakers mounted inside the hood of his mask suddenly crackled.

"Kai, can you hear me?" said Jordan James. *"Ms Paik tells me you've gone under Titanic, and your gear's uplink to Rescue shows you've got less than half your air remaining. Now, Doc Oshiro has reported that you've freed the ROV, so well done. Now get the heck out of there and come back up."*

Pondering, Kai re-orientated himself in the water so that he could examine *Aelita* and the hole. With the ROV no longer plugging part of the opening, the current was noticeably stronger, and he swore *Titanic* was visibly sinking towards him. Shaking his head, he tapped out a quick message on the waterproofed keyboard attached to his arm.

alita 2 big to fit in hole but im not.

He heard someone on the other end repeat the message for the captain, who responded with an emphatic *"No!"*

If hole not plgged titnic sink, he typed back, and then as the Captain shouted in protest swam over to *Aelita* and unclipped the

DRP gun from its side. A set of pipes trailed back to the distant Mir-3, supplying the agents and additives that reacted in the gun's intermix chambers.

"If you don't leave right now you're going to either run out of air or be forced to do a rapid resurface and risk yourself serious injury before we can get you to Rescue's decompression chamber!"

i m full f spirit an resolv

"Don't cite the ship's motto at me, Kai! I'm not letting you drown yourself or destroy your lungs trying to prove something to me!"

u new

"Of course I knew! You've been hard on yourself ever since I called you out over your mom, trying to make up for one mistake. Well you can quit it right now. You're a damn fine salvor and there are many people up here who owe you their lives. Get out from under there and let us focus on trying to save as many of them as we can before the ship sinks."

no he typed back, checking his dive watch and oxygen meter. Wasting time arguing had cost precious minutes **not wen possibl to sav everone -rescue saves lives, so do i**

As Jones continued to beg with him to not play the fool to the end, Kai took the gun in both hands and swam upwards into the double bottom. It was impossible to see exactly where the water was getting through into the inner hull, but squeezing the gun's trigger released a small bit of foam which was quickly sucked along by the current, showing him the way.

Following it along, he eventually found a spot where the action of running over the berg had crushed and mangled the cellular webbing beyond recognition, and wrestling the gun in as deep as possible he held down on the trigger. Within moments the grey foam expanded to fill the space, and he was suddenly reminded of how as a child he used to pressure-inject spray-cream into Twinkie Bars. He smiled around his mouthpiece, indulging in the warm memory…

…no, that was the first signs of the oxygen deprivation starting to kick in. He had to stay on course. His oxygen gauge was red-lining now, an inbuilt light flashing red warnings that he was eating into the emergency supply of air.

I won't be able to surface at this point; not without killing myself slowly and painfully. Might as well make it a worthwhile death…

It was amazing how easily he made the decision, and even the captain seemed to understand, having falling silent.

Kicking his way down out of the hull, with *Aelita* trailing after him, Kai followed the damage along the mangled double bottom until he felt another fitful current tugging upward, and again forced foam into the crush of metal. His breathing was coming faster now as he patched a third area before dropping the gun, his vision growing dim and his lungs hyperventilating in an effort to squeeze more air out of the dive gear.

And then he felt the respirator valve click in his mouth as the tank ran empty. He almost swallowed his tongue as his body screamed for air, chest clenched up as his lungs burned.

From his training he knew drowning to be a surprisingly subdued affair, devoid of all the thrashing that was seen in movies. Instead the body usually went into a reflexive action of trying to roll onto its back in an effort to float, the limbs moving in weak little motions as if swimming and the victim's mouth hanging open fearfully as they struggled to breathe.

But this wasn't drowning; there was no water in his lungs. Instead he was being *suffocated* by the rebreather, flailing and spasming wildly as he instinctively tried to break free of the invisible attacker that was smothering him.

Then someone grabbed hold of his shoulder and spun him around. Through the red haze of pain darkening his vision, Kai fearfully tried to fend them off as they ripped away his mouthpiece and, before he could swallowed a lungful of water, forced something else in between his lips.

Air flooded into him, sweet and clean; he breathed deeply and his chest expanded as if punched from the inside. Going suddenly limp in the water, he saw lights shining onto him. Looking up, he saw one of his fellow divers from *Rescue* floating in front of him, a secondary mouthpiece trailing from her tank to Kai's mouth, sharing her air supply.

Too weak to swim, his tortured lungs content to respire in peace, Kai allowed the other diver to guide him to *Aelita*, which slowly pulled the two of them away. Dazed and confused, all he could think of was the irony of it all; that despite being submersed in the Atlantic, he had nearly died of asphyxia…

On *Rescue*'s bridge, Pip watched intently as Jordan Jones held a radio to his ear. Someone spoke through it and the captain's shoulders shook. Pip bit her lip, fearing the worst, and then her heart leapt in her throat as he gave a laugh of relief that could almost have been a sob.

"They've got him! He's alive."

Uncertain of what to do, Pip reached over to squeeze his shoulder, at which point the blinded captain spun around in his chair and enveloped her in a solemn bear hug.

"Thank you for warning me of what that idiot had gone and done. That stupid, brave idiot. You're both heroes, the pair of you."

Unable to think of anything to say Pip simply returned the embrace.

"Captain!" called Lieutenant Miller, lowering his own radio. "*Viking*'s Captain and Senior Engineer say they're commencing pumping!"

"And not a moment too soon!" Jones replied, breaking away from Pip and staring towards *Titanic* as if able to peer through her hull to the submarine drawn up against her opposite side. "Looks like Kai might have brought us just enough time to save the ship, the fucking idiot!"

But he was smiling, even as he said it. Miller was smiling too.

"There's one more thing, sir," Miller added. "Our infirmary is preparing to receive Salvor Alinka, but they've also had a request from *Viking*'s medical officer – he's going over to assist in *Oceanic*'s hospital and is asking if we can spare some of our synthetic pulmonary surfactants for a patient who requires specialist treatment. What should we do?"

"Share and share alike, Sam, but make sure we've enough to maintain our own emergency stocks; the same with any other medical supplies *Oceanic*'s hospital needs. What's the status of Mr Lightoller?"

"Stabilised enough that we can release him back into the care of Doctor O'Loughlin on *Titanic*…"

"You want to send him back to their shipboard hospital, Sam?"

"Yes," nodded Miller, and Pip saw him look towards her briefly. "Officer Lightoller has been washed, salved and bandaged and now just requires observation. Sending him back 'under escort' allows us to free up a bed for any other critical cases…"

He trailed off, eyes flicking back and forth between Pip and the captain. Guessing Miller's unease at her presence, she politely excused herself and strode out of the wheelhouse.

He wants someone watching over the man already in Titanic's infirmary, she thought as she descended towards the aft deck of the salvage ship. *Sending Lights back is a decent excuse to keep an eye on whoever came aboard from the Seguin Laroche as well…*

The realisation should have unnerved her, but the events of the last hour had left her feeling strangely resilient. As she negotiated the aft deck, making for *Titanic's* gangplank, people from this era gazed at her respectfully, one seaman in a White Star Line jersey even saluting her as she passed, and she returned the gesture a little uncertainly.

She felt *strong*, stronger than she ever had. The uncertain girl who had dreaded giving a presentation aboard *Oceanic* suddenly felt like a stranger. And it wasn't just the clothes she wore that had empowered her, but the sense of responsibility she had suddenly developed for everyone on *Titanic*. Charles Lightoller had been right; she had a mission to perform, a duty. Every other concern was secondary to that.

"Benjamin Guggenheim," she said firmly, entering *Titanic's* D-Deck Reception and coming face-to-face with a dapperly-dressed gentleman at the foot of the Grand Staircase. "It's time to leave this ship, sir."

Guggenheim looked down at her, and then around at the empty room, before nodding. "Very well, young Miss. Would you kindly lead the way to the boats; *Rescue* seems a mite busy to my eyes."

"I'd be glad to," she said, indicating that he should follow her. As they passed through the ship, they found almost all the corridors empty except for salvage workers and assisting crewmen. No screams or cries of alarm could be heard from above, nor could they hear the sound of hundreds of feet pounding on the decks, fleeing in a panic from advancing floodwaters.

Pip's pace quickened, her excitement rising. And when they came into the Second Class reception, her heart soared to see two elderly figures arriving down the stairs. The husband, a dignified and bearded gentleman dressed in a thick fur overcoat, was arm-in-arm with his wife, who was slightly plump and radiated the wonderful warmth of a loving grandmother.

"Ah, Mr and Mrs Straus!" Guggenheim greeted, doffing his top hat in greeting. "I'm glad to see that the both of you are alive and well at the end of this remarkable ordeal."

Isidor and Ida Straus, the legendary couple who had been offered a chance to escape in *Titanic's* lifeboats, but who chose to stay on the ship, undivided until death, smiled graciously, and suddenly Pip suddenly felt eyes dampen with unshed tears.

"Mr and Mrs Straus, it's been far too long," she said reverently, bowing slightly at the waist as she addressed them. "Please, come this way. There's a boat awaiting you both, one's that been waiting for a hundred years."

Bemused, but still maintaining an air of relaxed calm, the two allowed Pip and Guggenheim to help them board the safety of the launch, Ida producing a blanket that she spread over their legs to keep out the cold as they sat together.

Smiling at the sight, Pip grabbed hold of the handrail to pull herself back up onto *Titanic*, but found her way blocked by Harold Lowe, the Fifth Officer.

"Ah-ah, no Miss," the Welshman said. "This time, I must insist you leave with all the other passengers."

She opened her mouth to protest and Lowe held up a hand. "It's Captain's orders. No-one who has entered a boat is to come back aboard."

"But what about all the other passengers!?" she protested. "I swore I would not leave the ship until I had ensured the safety of everyone aboard."

"And you have," he said plainly, but smiling. "You in this boat are among the last. Congratulations on a splendid piece of work."

He reached over and shook her hand, before calling out to the helmsman. "Alright you, push off now!"

Holding on tight, Pip remained standing in the entryway as the launch turned away from the hull, peering along the length of the ship. *Titanic* rested at ease beneath a perfect starry sky. On station to her starboard side was *Viking*, numerous pipes strung between the two vessels and the water around the submarine churning softly, suggesting vast amounts of water being discharged through her ballast ports. High above, not a single lifeboat was to be seen on the starboard side of *Titanic*'s Boat Deck, the outreaching davits looking naked and forlorn.

And then Pip's heart caught for a moment. To the side of *Titanic*'s bridge, watching their boat pull away towards *Oceanic*, stood Captain Edward John Smith, gazing towards her with his hat raised in salute. Beneath his feet his command stood proud in the water, still trimmed down a little at the head, but afloat.

Pip checked her watch. The time was 2:30am.

Ten minutes ago *Titanic* would have finally sunk, had they not arrived. At this moment, in another time, the wreck of the ship's bow would be crashing onto the seabed two-and-a-half miles straight down, coming to rest at the end of her final voyage but ploughing into the ocean sediment as if forever underway, a ghost ship doomed to never make port.

The stern section, tumbling as it fell and ripped apart by the forces of air and water pressure, would be landing a short distance away, a broken carcass surrounded by spilled innards, forming a debris field that told the violent story of the ship's final demise.

And there, at the bottom of the Atlantic, *Titanic* would lie in a sleep of living death for seventy-three years. But then eyes of a man, Doctor Robert Ballard, would light upon her again, and like Sleeping Beauty roused by a kiss *Titanic* would awake into new life, into a world so in love with her that their passions threatened to destroy her, hungry eyes and hands ripping her apart in search of her secrets.

Even Pip had been guilty of that possessive obsession. But that was all in another life now. Less than three hours after striking the iceberg, *Titanic*'s passengers had been evacuated, and the ship was now being made sound.

Feeling the emotions boiling up inside her, Pip punched the air with a whoop of joy.

"Congratulations, Captain Smith!" she called across the open water at the top of her lungs. "You made it! And *Titanic* has never looked finer!"

She was certain that Smith was smiling beneath his whiskers, because he then turned and called something into the wheelhouse, and moments later *Titanic* roared, her whistles shattering the night with jubilant noise.

The cries of the whistles seemed to resonate through Pip's frame, bringing fresh tears to her eyes. She wiped them away as the boat came alongside *Oceanic*, and standing in the door of the launch she began to assist the Straus couple, Benjamin Guggenheim and forty or so others in their first steps towards the twenty-first century.

"Want Trevor..." a little voice cried out, and amongst the passengers Pip spotted a First Class woman carrying a toddler.

"We'll find them now, Loraine, there's a good girl..."

"Want Trevor!" the little girl repeated with greater volume, and her mother shushed her nervously, clearly struggling to maintain a stoic facade. Some part of Pip's mind strung together salient factoids from the sinking, and she gave a little gasp of recognition.

"Mrs Allison," she called softly as the mother and child came past her. "Is everything alright?"

Hearing her name being called, Mrs Bessie Waldo Allison turned in surprise. Her daughter, Helen Loraine, hiccupped nervously in her mother's arms. She was not even three years old.

"My family..." Mrs Allison whispered hoarsely. "Can you help me find my family?"

It was one of the greatest tragedies that 'would' have occurred tonight. Having already become separated from her husband after *Titanic* struck the iceberg, Mrs Allison had been unable to locate her eleven-month old son Trevor. Unwilling to leave the ship without the baby, she had removed herself and Loraine from a lifeboat just before it was lowered, unaware that Trevor had already been safely evacuated from the ship in the company of his nursemaid. The infant would be the only family member to survive tonight.

Right now, they'd be in the icy grasp of the North Atlantic, dead or dying as hypothermia set in, Pip realised grimly. *Major Arthur Peuchen claimed to have witnessed their final moments... he said they boarded Collapsible A on the starboard side... but 'A' got half-swamped when the forward Boat Deck submerged beneath it, and*

335

most of the people in it were thrown back into the water when it nearly
capsized... the Allisons included.

It was a doubly cruel fate, to twice find a seat in a lifeboat and still die, especially for a kid. Gathering herself together, Pip smiled and nodded. "I'm quite sure we can locate your family, Mrs Allison."

Gently taking Loraine into her own arms so that Bess could rest her weary joints, Pip guided the two of them through processing, and then up into *Oceanic*'s Belgrave Square Lobby, which had been transformed. Tables had been pushed together to form a circular helpdesk at which people were making enquiries, and against one wall a series of screens and digital projectors had been set up to display a copy of *Titanic*'s crew and passenger manifest. Most of the names upon it had been ticked off in green, and Pip felt a surge of pride and relief.

I helped do that...

And all over the room, filling it with life and activity were passengers and crew of both eras. Bouncing Loraine in her arms, Pip could see several of *Titanic*'s bellboys manning the Lobby's elevators, their uniforms gleaming with gold trim and brocade as they pressed the buttons on behalf of passengers. Stewards and stewardesses in wildly contrasting styles of dress shimmered about, tending to people's needs and taking requests for hot drinks and blankets.

And everywhere that Pip looked she could see families standing together, holding hands or hugging one another as husbands and sons were reunited with wives, children, parents and fiancées, their happy laughter complementing the light and golden tone of the vast room. She was suddenly reminded of Marilyn and her foster parents in New York, and her own bright mood trembled on the brink of an emotional abyss. But she forced herself to hold back tears, knowing that her family would want her to be strong.

"C'mon then," she said to the little girl she was carrying, managing an encouraging smile. "Let's go find your baby brother."

Turning to catch her bearings, she saw Adrienne McKinn at the centre of the ring of tables, directing operations like a general masterminding a campaign. Bruce Ismay was working away beside her, and she felt a moment's shame at how coldly she had treated him earlier.

"Addy!" she called out, making a mental note to apologise to Ismay sometime later. "I've got half of the Allison family here! Do you have the rest of their party?"

Spotting Pip, the former congresswoman beamed, and came forward to meet her. "You found them! Oh, well done!"

"Madame, do you know where my husband and son are?" Bess Allison demanded, equal parts hope and dread lacing her words.

"Yes indeed," Adrienne nodded graciously, a glance towards Pip suggesting that she had taken an especial interest in the welfare of the Allison family. "They arrived in two separate groups. Your husband is safe, and young Trevor was brought aboard by his nurse."

"Oh, bless you all!" Bess's hands came to her mouth as she stifled a cry of relief, and the Congresswoman turned away to call out to Ismay. "Bruce! Is there someone free who can lead these ladies to the rest of their family?"

Looking up, a somewhat haggard-looking Ismay nodded, and gestured towards another assisting volunteer, a young man in an ill-fitting modern suit.

Pip felt another breath catch in her throat. It was Jack Thayer.

*

Scotland Road was silent now, except for the thrum of the pumps and the sloshing of Thomas Andrews' feet as he slowly walked down into deeper water, searching for the pencil mark he had made on the wall earlier. The shipwright's wavy hair was matted and slicked back with a combination of water and grease. Dirt and grime had worked into the fabric of his suit, as well as all the wrinkles and creases in his face. He wagered said wrinkles had a few new fellows to join them following the stress of tonight.

After a minute's searching along the starboard side of the corridor, he resolved that the water must have washed the mark away and started back uphill.

Then his eyes narrowed.

Wait a moment…

He ran forward several paces and knelt. There, two feet above the waterline, was the unmistakable smear of a grease pencil.

337

Thomas turned to look aft; the flooding was receding back along the length of the corridor, leaving a scattering of filth and debris all over the floor. A number of sodden sandbags denoted the high-water mark.

The distance between the two cardinal points, the tide-line and the current water level, was at least twenty feet, and growing with every second.

"Practically unsinkable, indeed," he said softly, a smile blooming on his face, as *Titanic* once again roared the news of her survival.

*

The sound of *Titanic* shouting triumphantly from her whistles echoed deafeningly down the long, hollow tube that was *Viking*'s hull, eventually reaching Robert Furness in his bunk, where he had been trying to catch a few moments' contemplative peace and examine his options. Further aft, the submarine's nuclear power plant was whirring away mightily, and all around could be heard the sound of flowing water as the submarine pumped aboard flooding from *Titanic* and immediately discharged it through her trim tanks.

If I had to describe this sound, I would liken it to being trapped inside the bowl of an eternally-flushing toilet.

Viking, her crew, and a number of other ships had travelled in time, that much was certain. Equally certain was that a time machine similar to those described in Dossier 7000 was at the heart of the affair.

I wonder what Scott has found off to the North... should I have sent another officer to secure the device?

Reflecting on the past few hours, his thoughts came back to Scott Thresher. The young officer was gifted and competent, but incredibly spontaneous. It had been him who had sent them hurtling off in pursuit of the *Seguin Laroche* 'back' in 2012, and after a violent disturbance that had thrown *Viking* around underwater like a tin-can in a tumble-drier (which Furness now supposed to be their transference through time), the XO had wanted to surface immediately and establish where and *when* they were.

Scott, who the hell do you think we are? We're sailors of Her Majesty, not superheroes!

Robert had not shared that enthusiasm. Some kind of high-energy event had certainly happened above them on the surface, but he needed to first eliminate all other possibilities before assuming that they had travelled in time, such as an air-burst nuclear detonation. Following convention, he had instigated the procedure for determining what the international situation was in the event of a nuclear war, and so *Viking* had been brought to within a few feet of the surface, and lurking there hidden from sight the submarine had opened up all her many ears and listened hard.

Nothing; no incoming orders, no emergency broadcasts, civilian or military – not even BBC Radio 4.

The only radio traffic they could pick up in the area, aside from the ship-to-ship conversations of the equally confused Memorial Fleet, were an infuriating series of dots and dashes that quickly proved to be Morse-encoded distress calls from a ship designated 'MGY'. When he had chanced a full sweep on the sonar array, Bob had been shocked to find they were surrounded with obstacles, which the navigational suite quickly identified as icebergs. There were still a few other ships out there, however, and so he had left the rescue of this 'MGY' to their discretion, rather than give away *Viking*'s presence.

Heh, shows what I know. Now we're moored up alongside her, keeping her afloat while she trumpets her invincibility.

Focusing on their own responsibilities, and growing increasingly concerned, Bob had broken the Number One Rule of missile subs by ordering his radiomen to send out a few cautious encrypted broadcasts, trying to reach any Royal Navy ships, stations or bases. He had even tried to raise the Admiralty on *Viking*'s satellite phone. When that failed, he had tried his wife, and then his sister-in-law and nephew. No-one picked up, but even worse, no answering machines clicked in, and no automated message informed him that the person he was calling was unavailable. There was not even a dial tone. It was as if the United Kingdom and the rest of the world had ceased to exist. Gone in a flash.

Has someone dropped the bomb? he had asked himself at the time as he laid down the phone, a cold chill washing over him. Even as he began to hope that it was themselves who were lost, and not the whole of Britain, he began to take emergency actions. Guided by years of training and procedure, he had convened the senior staff, and – using the various keys issued to them – they had opened the secure safe and retrieved the folders that contained the codes to arm and launch 'Sherwood Forest'. Without a command structure to report to, it was required that he assume direct responsibility for the disposition of the nuclear launch systems.

"A lotta people running and hiding tonight, a lotta people won't get no justice tonight. Remember to kick it over, no one will guide you come Armagideon Time, oooh-oooh…" he hummed briefly to himself, before snorting grimly. *I've been spending too much time listening to George Montgomery playing his LPs.*

Back when he was first offered command of a *Vanguard*-class submarine, Bob had asked himself how he would react if he found his career ending in a nuclear exchange, instead of an honourable retirement ashore. He knew that he was not the most even-tempered of men, and had fully expected himself to be full of rage, ready and willing to lay down thermonuclear vengeance for friends and family, crown and country. But instead he had found only icy calm in his heart as he picked up the folders that would hand him the keys to Armageddon, and retired to his cabin to secure them in his own safe.

Already got one world-shaking dossier in my possession, what's another?

Returning to the bridge, he ordered *Viking* to proceed several miles to the west, diving deep to avoid the submerged mass of icebergs all around them, before surfacing outside of the region of fog that had suddenly sprung up, hiding in the lee of several bergs to avoid the radar suites of the other ships in the area. Then, bundled up warmly, sextant in hand and breathing fresh air for the first time in eleven weeks, he had attempted to take a series of star fixes and work out their position with the navigational officer.

But the stars were all wrong… Polaris is still broadly in the same place, but the rest have… wandered.

It was at this point that the radio conversations carrying-on back and forth between the other ships had taken an unusual turn, and as Bob and Thresher had listened in, they finally got their answers as to where they were in time and space.

"Mayday, mayday, mayday, this is USNS Rescue transmitting in the blind guard. All ships who can hear this message please check in."

"Captain Lloyd Waters, RMS Oceanic. Go ahead Rescue."

"Research Vessel Anatoly Sagalevich, Captain Gorbachev, Anton Petrovich speaking."

"Captains. Rescue has followed the track of the Seguin Laroche about two miles to the north, and we have come alongside a ship in distress; we're declaring a general SOS on her behalf..."

"Did that monster hit someone? Who's the casualty?"

"SOS? What happen? Are they sinking?"

"Please let me finish. The ship is... well, she's the Titanic, and yes she's sinking. From hitting an iceberg. Captain Jones has asked those of you who can to come here immediately and to prepare your lifeboats to take Titanic's passengers aboard."

"If you think this is funny joke, is very bad taste in mouth."

"We'd like to speak to Captain Jones directly."

"Speaking."

"Jordan, are you aware of the drivel your man Cameron was just putting out?"

"Captain Waters, Lloyd... yes, it sounds ridiculous, but he was not making it up. We are currently coming alongside Titanic and getting ready to pump. My crew tell me they can practically count the rivets in her hull. Either this is real, or someone has pulled an immense trick on us all..."

The conversation had then degraded into a series of recriminations and arguments. That sense of cold weight settling in his chest again, Bob had slowly taken the earphones off his head, and laid a hand on the radioman's shoulder, the younger man's clenched lip a sign of inner anxiety. Then he looked at Thresher, and to his shock saw that the Lieutenant-Commander's normally bright and enthusiastic expression had been replaced with one of mute horror, and that his face had paled to a sickly grey.

That ship really was carrying a time machine… But the presence of Titanic would mean we skipped exactly a hundred years into the past… a Ballistic Missile Sub in the time of the Dreadnought Race.

"Round up the senior officers, Doctor Montgomery, and the leading engineer for an emergency meeting. We'll meet in the Officer's ward room, in five minutes," he had ordered. "And get the second engineer to see if we can kludge the ballast system into a giant bilge-pump."

"You want to assist *Titanic*, Captain?"

"We've got nothing to lose if we do. There's nothing in this era that can hurt *Viking*, and heaven knows we'll have to show our faces eventually, if we're going to try and get ourselves and those other ships back home…"

For ninety minutes, he and the senior crew had debated their position, while trying to assemble an exact sequence of events. The resumed broadcasts from the *Seguin Laroche* had clarified the situation somewhat, but it was only when *Titanic*'s situation had become desperate that the decision had been made to go to her aid.

Should we have let her sink? Bob wondered. *Scott's enthusiasm is one thing, but now we're running roughshod over history. Perhaps we should rename the boat HMS Cavalier?*

Now he lay still and silent in his bunk, listening as *Viking*'s pumps, relentlessly powered by her nuclear plant, continued to bail out the *Titanic*.

Maybe she'll not sink at all. What's that going to do to the flow of time? If we've changed history are we going to start fading out like Marty McFly?

As with the documents now locked in his safe, it was a circumstance he did not want to dwell on. There were too many variables to consider.

The intercom system chimed, and Robert picked up the mouthpiece on his end. "Captain Furness speaking."

"Sir, we have Lieutenant Commander Thresher on a secure channel, he wishes to speak to you."

"Very well," Bob grunted, pinching his nose. "Patch him through."

The channel clicked over and Thresher began to speak. As Bob himself had instructed, the Lieutenant-Commander had taken an armed security team out north in one of *Viking*'s Zodiac motorboats, charged with confirming the situation of the *Seguin Laroche*. Apparently she had dug her nose into pack ice and was shipping water.

"Has she sunk?" Bob wanted to know. Assuming that the time-machine could function bi-directionally, their only help of getting home was if that ship remained afloat.

"No sir – well, not yet, but I don't think she'll make it much beyond sunrise. The explosion and flooding is one thing, but her cargo is beginning to shift, and her metacentric stability with it."

That got a nod of agreement. Container ships were notoriously top-heavy and needed to be carefully balanced during lading. "Is she beyond rescue?"

"Yes sir. She dinged her bow badly and is flooding through her thruster doors, but she's also taking on water astern from several leaks. The resulting list has unbalanced the container stacks enough that their weight will eventually pull her over, even if we could get her bone dry. I can confirm though that the contemporary ship assisting her, SS Californian, had come alongside and was transferring the... sensitive piece of cargo off the Laroche as we arrived."

He nervously paused, and Bob waited for him to continue, sensing what was to come next.

"Captain, it's one of those Apergy devices, the Project Lesterpack ones. It's currently stowed in Californian's hold."

"You got some men guarding it?"

"Yes sir, two petty officers, both armed."

"Very good, and one of our men and another from the *Rescue* are standing guard over the mutineer in *Titanic*'s hospital..." Bob replied, and Thresher coughed.

"There's one more thing, sir. I had an idea while aboard the Californian, but due to all the radio chatter at the time I was unable to check with you to get permission..."

"...so you took the initiative and did in anyway?" Bob finished for him. "Well, what did you do?"

"Sir, I extended an offer to the captains of the Seguin Laroche and the Californian to come back in the Zodiac with me; I felt it was the only way that we could co-ordinate whatever we do next."

343

Bob agreed with the logic of it, once again marvelling ruefully at his XO's ability to improvise. "Where are they right now?"

"Captain Laroche of the Seguin Laroche is currently overseeing the recovery of anything useful from her ship before it sinks, and although Captain Lord of the Californian has had to stand off of the Laroche *because of her list, he's lowering his lifeboats to shuttle men between the two vessels."*

"Alright then. We'll see all of you in the morning. *Viking* out."

As he ended the call Bob considered Scott's idea. Getting all the various captains together would be a good chance to work out a plan of action, and pooling ideas and knowledge was better than having all the different ships gossiping away...

Gossiping...

Struck by a sudden realisation, he swung his legs off the bunk. Opening his safe, he removed one sealed envelope from a separate compartment, stuffed it in his pocket and strode out of the cabin.

"I have the Conn!" he announced as he entered the control room, taking command. "Navigation, any more contacts?"

"None close at hand, Captain, but a ship called the *Mount Temple* has come up on the other side of the ice field and stopped, about eleven miles off to the west. Other ships seem to be keeping their distance, with one exception."

"Would that be the passenger liner *Caronia?*" Bob answered, trying to recall what he knew of the *Titanic's* sinking.

"She's identifying herself as *Carpathia* sir."

"Yes, that's it. What's the story on her?"

"She's coming on at just shy of fifteen knots, guess that's her top speed, and hasn't stopped since we first picked her up. She should close the gap in about ninety minutes, tops. We're also picking up her Captain's wireless messages – both he and *Mount Temple* are in visual range of *Oceanic*, and describing her to anyone who will listen."

"Very well. Communications, extend all the radio antennas and follow ECM protocols, I want you to run interference on all radio transmissions within thirty nautical miles."

"Captain?"

"At the moment ourselves, *Titanic, Oceanic, Rescue,* the *Anatoly Sagalevich, Seguin Laroche, Californian, Carpathia* and possibly the *Mount Temple* are the only ones who have any idea of what's happened here tonight. That's eight vessels all in possession of potentially compromising information, and I want them all radio-jammed with *Viking's* Electronic Counter-Measures suite before they can all start running their mouths off to the outside world about time travel. If definite word of this reaches the mainland then there'll be a global panic that might spiral out of control before we can figure out where we lie. Now shut them up!"

"Aye sir, establishing ECM shroud!" the ensign said in a fluster, before his hands began to dance over the keys in front of him. Radio jamming was technically illegal, but also a necessary component of *Viking's* ECM defences, and Bob had every confidence that his command's operators and computers were more than capable of scanning all the active frequencies and 'squelching' any transmissions.

Am I the only one looking at the bigger picture here? he thought. *And how much longer can we keep this all under wraps?*

Well, that left just one last issue to take care of for now. He might as well go up and see what had become of the *Titanic*.

Steeling himself, he scrambled through the hatch to the top of *Viking's* sail, and turned to gaze up at the elephant in the corner of the room, or off the starboard beam, that until now he had been trying to ignore.

A great wall of metal loomed over them, crowned with a white superstructure. Pipes from *Viking's* engineering spaces hung between the two vessels, threading through holes in the hull and flexing confidently as they pumped more water. High above he could see sparks flashing from where men were welding a set of cables in place, leading down to where a final collision mat had been placed below the surface.

Surmounting the ship, four Doric funnels glowed warm tan in the dim illumination of the deck lights. Coils of smoke curled lazily from the black caps of two of them, a few puffs of steam woofing from the safety valves in random bursts.

Bob's eyes travelled down her hull to where a lick of red paint, slightly scuffed from contact with one of the hundreds of icebergs lurking out in the dark, peeked just above the surface. It marked the ship's natural waterline. She was trimmed levelly, her nose was back up, and not a single porthole was submerged below the waterline. Clad in wires and collision mats like a patient in traction, bearing the holes wrought by power saws and blowtorches like proud battle scars, the ship sat in triumph on the ocean surface, victoriously building steam for whatever came next.

It was 3.30am on Monday April 15ᵗʰ 1912. In just two hours the sun would rise, and *Titanic* would have lived to see another day.

Bob's hand travelled to his back pocket and withdrew the envelope he had removed from the safe in his cabin. There was one just like it carried on each of *Viking*'s sister *Vanguard*-class missile boats, and unlike the Roswell files, they were not the subject of jokes, but were instead treated with a deathly reverence.

It was the 'Letter of Last Resort', the secret order issued from the Prime Minister instructing Britain's nuclear arsenal of what to do in any war scenario where the Government was wiped out before a counter-strike could be ordered. There were four basic variations that Bob was aware of, with each Prime Minister choosing the option that best suited their own tastes. Three of those potential choices would be to order him to either fire back against the enemy, do nothing, or place himself under the command of an allied power.

But in Bob Furness' opinion, it was the fourth option which was most frightening, which called on him and his fellow V-Boat captains to independently decide what course of action was best. It was either the most considered approach, allowing the captains to react according to the situation as it was, or just a cop-out by which the PM could dodge making the decision for themselves.

Now, fearing what he might find, Bob found himself to be in a situation that evoked the spirit, if not the word, of the scenario for which the Letter of Last Resort was intended. Cut off from command, he needed a concrete footing on which to stand regarding launch authority. Wetting his lips, he unsealed the envelope. Then, alone on the top of *Viking*'s sail except for the mournful sighs of a light swell now breaking against the hull, he read the two short paragraphs hand-written on the sheet of paper within.

His shoulders fell and he bit back a curse. The letter from the Prime Minister was couched in fine language, but its point was crystal clear.

"Fuck, shit and damn!" he swore, before rereading the orders again, as if hoping it would change before his eyes. But the facts of the situation were beyond question.

The *Titanic* was afloat, and *Viking* was now the deadliest weapon on the face of the Earth, and himself the world's most powerful man, by virtue of all other competitors having being left behind in the future.

And, if it proved impossible to reverse the phenomenon that had caused this, they were stuck here.

So many variables to consider; so much uncertainty.

He wanted to cry.

ACT THREE

PASSENGERS AND TRAVELLERS

CHAPTER EIGHTEEN

John Jacob Astor sat in a profound silence in the waiting room that adjoined *Oceanic*'s small hospital. Madeleine's lifebelt was lying over his legs and with slow, mechanical scribes of a pen-knife he was cutting through into the cork padding that gave the device its buoyancy. His watch, a golden one studded with diamonds, relentlessly ticked away the minutes as he waited.

About an hour after they arrived aboard the ship, the sounds of Madeleine's cries and the doctor's urgent calls for her to push was drowned out by the horrifying sound of a faint, frail shriek. John had been ready to push his way into the improvised delivery room there and then, and would have done so, had not Maggie Brown threatened to lay him out on the deck if he went so much as an inch closer towards the door.

"You'd be a hindrance, John; leave them to do their work. The best thing you can do now for Madeleine and the baby is to pray, and that's work that can be done from here, there or anywhere."

Slowly he continued to cut away at the cork, making a small stack of tiny cubes. He had not felt much like praying; he had said several hasty devotionals, and pled the case for Madeleine and the child with the Almighty, but after some time the words had begun to ring hollow, tainted with a lingering anger. Only recently, the mouthpieces of the same deity to which he was begging had condemned his marriage at the age of 47 to a girl young enough to be his daughter, with most of them taking umbrage at the fact that he had divorced his first wife. The twin peals of scandal and condemnation had rung from pulpits and high-society galas alike.

Small wonder, then, that he had taken Madeleine away from New York in an attempt to escape all of that.

From beyond the doors to the waiting room, there was a steady buzz of traffic through the rest of the ship. He imagined that

Oceanic must be packed to the eaves after taking on all of *Titanic's* passengers and the better part of her crew; even the hospital, tucked away in part of the below-decks rabbit warren, was kept busy with a constant outflow of patients being admitted for minor injuries, hypothermia or shock. When Jack Thayer had been discharged after his dunk in the Atlantic, Maggie had immediately taken him off to locate his parents. The fact that neither of them had returned yet suggested to John that it was easy to get lost in a ship this large and crowded. That was another reason why he had not left the hospital in the hours since arriving; he was uncertain of being able to find his way back.

The watch continued to toll away the seconds, piling them upon hours of agonised waiting. There had been no sound from Madeleine's room since the first weak cries of his son. Since then several other members of the crew had come through with odd pieces of equipment, and further doctors had arrived as well, or so he had been assured. He did not know whether to be relieved or alarmed; a moot point anyway, since he suspected he was too spent to feel either emotion, if any at all...

"JJ Astor?"

He came to his feet with a speed he had not believed possible, fragments of cut cork spilling across the floor. A nurse was standing at the door, smiling.

"You can come see them now."

Dazed, forcing each foot to step into place, John half-stumbled, half-walked into the room. Madeleine was propped upright in a bed, her chest rising and falling gently and a peaceful smile on her face. Her eyes were closed, and immediately his hand drifted to her own, fingertips lightly brushing over her skin. Someone had changed her out of her wet garments into what must have passed for hospital wear in the 21st century.

"She's alright..." he whispered. Glad and relieved, he turned to the table beside her, and slowly drew closer.

It was an improvised *'couveuse'*, an infant's incubator. A large box made of some rigid translucent material had been stripped of its lid and contents and turned upside down, acting as a container to shield a bundle of blankets in which a tiny child had been wrapped, outstretched arms flexing weakly as he slept.

John knelt weakly, as if at prayer, the better to see through the smooth sides of the box. The newborn, his son, was so incredibly small that he was tiny enough to be held in a single hand. His skin was a mottled red, and a breathing tube was secured to his mouth by bandages. A second tube was bound to one of his arms by a wad of gauze.

Then someone's feet scuffed against the floor, and John realised that he was not alone in the room – two men and a woman were standing against the wall, waiting for him to have the first word. He opened his mouth to speak, and found the words coming with difficulty; his throat was dry and his mouth parched, but turning his head away he managed to shape his tumbling thoughts into a single question.

"Will he live?"

The woman, short-haired and dark-skinned, exhaled and looked to the senior of the two men, who wore a blue pullover over what looked like a pared-down navy uniform. Taking the lead, he took a step forward.

"Mr Astor, I'm Doctor George Montgomery, HMS *Viking*… we estimate your son was between twenty-three and twenty-five weeks developed when your wife went into labour. In our time, this is the absolute threshold at which point a child is viable-"

"Will he live!?"

The volume of John's voice surprised even him, and he leaned forward until all that separated him from his son was the side of the box, his forehead resting against the surface.

"John…" someone called out faintly. He looked up and saw Madeleine gazing down at him from the bed, one hand reaching out to him, lips curling lovingly. His shout must have woken her. Staring into her soft eyes he felt something stinging at his own, while droplets of salty moisture trickled down his face and into his moustache. As he took her hand and clasped it tight, the doctor began to speak again.

"Sir… none of us are trained as paediatricians, and we've had to improvise given the lack of facilities available, but we think your son has a thirty-to-forty percent chance of surviving. There is the concern of infection, but if he makes it safely through the next month, then those chances will improve."

"When we checked the information available to us, we learned that he lived to the age of seventy-nine in his first life," added the woman. "So as far as his health is concerned he's potentially very strong..."

There was a long silence, and then John's shoulders collapsed into a series of tremors as he wept in relief, looking up at them with tears running down his face.

"Thank you... thank you..."

"Mr Astor," Doctor Montgomery spoke again, his voice solemn. "You need to be aware that children born this premature may also develop lasting disabilities that afflict them for the rest of their lives."

"It doesn't matter..." Madeleine whispered through her own tears. "He'll never want for care or doctors... all that matters is that he's alive, thanks to you good people."

Montgomery swallowed uncomfortably, indicating to the man on his left. "Doctor Jackson here is *Oceanic*'s only remaining doctor, he oversaw the crew in preparing the incubator; and Ms Terri Patton to my right is a passenger certified as an emergency nurse; she did most of the delivery work. Captain Jones of the *Rescue* has also supplied us with respiratory surfactants from his ship's dive supplies, surfactants which at this point are essential to your son's ability to breathe. If you need to thank someone sir, thank them... I arrived last."

"Thank you," John stated again, now with more control over his voice. He looked back at Madeleine, and basked in the warmth of her smile. "From the both of us."

*

Watching the millionaire, who she had heard was possibly the richest man in the world of 1912, weeping over his family in a moment of raw humanity, Terri Patton smiled softly.

He's a lucky man, to live to see his son born, she thought to herself, and then her mood blackened. In her career as a nurse she had seen many pregnancies, though she had participated in only a few deliveries, but every time she had witnessed the miracle of birth she had treasured it. *If only Jan and I could biologically have a baby...*

It was something she and her newlywed wife had given much thought to during their engagement; whether one of them should bear a child through artificial insemination, with sperm from an anonymous donor, or possibly adopt.

The important thing, however, was that they wanted to have a family. Terri particularly longed to raise a child in the loving, supporting environment her own parents had denied her.

But now, looking at the small miracle they had accomplished in keeping the Astor baby alive, she felt a new possibility tugging at her mind.

Mom and Dad hated me for my sexuality, when I came out to them. How many other kids have suffered like that, are going to suffer over the next hundred years...? could we do something about it right now? And not just for gays, but for blacks and all other minorities...

It was a compelling idea, especially in the light of her mixed heritage, but one that would mean staying here in the past, even if it turned out that a return to the future was possible.

And that would mean living in an age of bigotry and misogyny, and all the pain and suffering that life would bring. Could she do that?

Could she ask Janice to do that? To not only suffer the slings and arrows of outrage, but take arms against those troubles and by opposition, end them?

Certainly nobler to challenge bigotry than to run away... she pondered, turning over half-remembered scraps of Hamlet. *For who would bear the whips and scorns of time, the oppressor's wrong, the proud man's contumely, the pangs of despised love, the law's delay...*

Her mind arguing over the pros and cons, she headed off into the ship as soon as Doctor Jackson determined she could be spared for an hour. When the call for volunteers had gone out, she had immediately offered up her nursing skills. Now, she was wondering if she should volunteer her entire life to a new cause, and whether or not it was worth giving up the chance to have a family of her own...

*

353

Jack Thayer slowly stirred from a restless sleep in which angels and demons warred over a dark ocean like grotesques out of an engraving by Gustave Dore. Lights, far too bright to be comfortable, were shining into his eyes, and he found himself to be slouched deep in the leather embrace of what felt like an armchair. Groggily rubbing the sleep from his eyes, he sat upright and slowly took in his surroundings.

It had not been a dream. He was aboard the *Oceanic*, in one of her opulent public spaces. An elaborate red-carpeted staircase filled a cavernous void several decks deep, free-standing artworks and plants dividing up the landings to create smaller, cosier spaces. The armchair in which he had found a few hours sleep did not have the benefit of such privacy, and was right against the rail looking down into the stairwell. The light that had woken him was that of the ship's own internal illuminations; beyond the windows there was only the grey haze that preceded dawn, indicating that he had only slept two or three hours. Around, above and below him, people were sleeping, finding spaces wherever they could find them on floors or furniture, and the rumble of machinery deep in the hull was matched only by the soft sound of low voices and multiple people breathing, some snoring. The Jewish couple, Ida and Isidor Straus, sat opposite him, leaning against one another on a couch, slumbering contentedly.

Shifting his weight, he winced; something with a sharp edge was digging into his side. Pulling it from a pocket, he produced an object about the shape and size of a playing-card, coated in a thin transparent varnish or lacquer. A colour photograph of his face (and was that not a marvel in of itself?) had been printed on it, along with his name; a 'boarding pass' that had been issued to him when he came up from the ship's hospital. Slowly, he turned the object, holding it between two fingers; on the reverse side was printed a detailed legal disclaimer, along with a reflective black strip that ran down the full-length of the card. The officer who issued it had explained that the card would render payment for food and drink in the ship's eateries, but Jack was left to wonder at the specifics of its function.

Eventually he returned it to his wallet, momentarily considered the money he carried on his person, and then looked around. It seemed he was not the first to wake, but from the many figures still sleeping, not the last. Many of those resting were, from their familiar manner of dress, his contemporaries. Others, he could only assume, were among the time-travellers.

Oh brave new world, that has such creatures in it, he thought, admiring (with a touch of shame) a young woman walking past, the hemline of her dress high enough to expose not just her ankles but her calves and knees. He had to admit to not having much knowledge of the female form – at least, not from direct experience – but from what he could see (and at the moment, he could see a lot), the fairer sex had much to be proud of.

Then something shifted beside him and he turned his head.

Oh my...

It seemed that he was actually seated in a couch, not an armchair; while there was a well-stuffed arm to his right, on his left there was actually a somnambulant young woman in decidedly modern dress. She slept leaning against him with arms folded, with a thick padded jacket wadded up behind her head and a cap marked USNS *Rescue* drawn down over her eyes.

Miss Philippa Paik, he remembered, blushing slightly as a host of memories came flooding back to him.

*

Milton Long had found himself unable to sleep. He had seen Jack Thayer reunited with his family, accepted John and Marian's thanks for his companionship, and with a glib promise that he would see them later he had set out to explore this extensive vessel, *Oceanic*.

What he found by turns delighted and appalled him. At first, he had found the ship to be an expansive playground, and had felt himself to be as a child running around at his leisure, exploring at a glance, or pausing as if in an art gallery when something drew his attention further.

His first observations were that *Oceanic*'s passengers enjoyed a surfeit of luxury. The ship was appointed with ballrooms, restaurants, promenades, bars, swimming baths, a fine library and even a theatre and observatory (or so he understood from the hurried explanation given by a harassed steward of what constituted a 'planetarium'). He even understood the theatre had the ability to exhibit motion-pictures, and made a mental note to avail himself of this at the nearest opportunity.

In travelling the length, breadth and depth of the ship, however, he had come to his second and far more serious realisation; there was an almost total absence of class. This was not so much an observation of *Oceanic*'s passengers; in matter-of-fact, they all appeared to be people of good breeding and education, even the more scandalously-dressed among them. No, what unnerved him was that the ship seemed to have no provision for separating out *Titanic*'s passengers according to their ticket price. Steerage families were being billeted in the same spaces as the social elite, and the absence of servile decorum on the part of the crew unnerved him, as did the potential for thievery, impropriety and other such vices. He had assumed, however, that the ship was intended primarily as a luxury liner for the conveyance of the wealthier element of society, and simply had no capacity for storing the lesser classes separately.

But it was when he enquired about this curiosity that he came to his most revelatory findings; the attitude of these travellers towards him, upon learning about his class-related concerns, was one of contempt.

Musing on this, he spotted two young ladies talking intently together, alone from the crowd, and out of concern approached them and asked if they required an escort. The first stared at him in disbelief, before the second sneered, called him *"a creep"*, and suggested that he *"get lost"*.

Milt glanced at her; judging from her coffee-toned skin, she was either a mulatto or some form of Negro. From the attire she wore, a sort of pale green smock, he supposed she was the personal maid or assistant to her companion, a white woman. Biting back a word of reprimand for her impertinence, he politely but firmly stated that he was simply doing his duty to herself and her mistress as unaccompanied ladies.

"Excuse me?" the two had shared a look of incredulity, and Milt had the sudden fear that he had completely misjudged the situation. "Are you suggesting that I'm Jan's... slave?"

"The safety word is still *banana*, Terri," the other young woman, 'Janet' or 'Janice' he supposed, snickered quietly, only for her darker-skinned companion to direct a glance at her that instantly killed her laugher. When 'Terri' returned her attention to Milt, her dark eyes seemed to smoulder like angry coals about to ignite. Milt fought against the instinct to step back.

"My apologies, ladies…" he said haltingly, struggling to keep up with the situation. "I seem to have made a poor start."

"Start? This is finished!" she had replied sharply. "Who do you think you are, forcing yourself on two girls as if you were God's gift to women?"

Milt's collar suddenly felt uncomfortably tight. The young woman was getting increasingly agitated and he looked to her companion for assistance.

"Miss, would you please tell your coloured friend to see reason?"

"Coloured?" the pale girl's grey eyes became as cold as ice, and she took a step closer to her companion in what he realised was a show of solidarity. "You've got thirty seconds to apologise to my wife, right now."

Apologise, for what? He struggled for a second to assert himself, and then swallowed, mentally pacing himself. Gradually, the qualifying word in her statement sunk in.

"*Wife…* that's impossible."

"Take that back," the blonde-haired woman said, her voice steely. The other one, Terri, was trembling, her fists clenched. He supposed they were heading towards hysteria, and laid a hand on 'Jan's' shoulder in order to calm her.

"Miss, you must be labouring under some form of delusion…"

"Let go!" She tried to pull away and he tightened his grip, temper fraying.

"Please, constrain yourself!"

"Get off of her!"

Before he could finish, Terri had grabbed hold of him with surprising strength, and before Milton had time to comprehend what was happening, she had positioned herself under the curve of his back. Momentarily he caught a glimpse of a wedding ring on her hand before she heaved, flipping him head-over-heels.

"…"

Milton Long suddenly found himself face-down on the floor, breath knocked clean out of him. Stunned, he felt someone seize his arm and twist it painfully behind him, forcing his submission.

"Right, *you little tit*, first bit of advice from the twenty-first century. Don't ever put your hand on a girl unless she gives you her permission. Second…" and now she paused, and from the deep breaths she was making, Milt suddenly realised she was crying. *"Never tell me who I can and cannot love!"*

Wheezing, blinking back his own tears, Milton had merely been able to nod his head in response.

*

After coming aboard *Oceanic*, Jack Thayer had at first been taken to the hospital in case of any possible injuries sustained from his impromptu swim, then a change of clothes had been provided to him (but not shoes) and he had been turned loose.

And despite all the mysteries of the 21st century lining up to reveal themselves to him, after locating his parents and Milt Long, he had found himself unable to stray far from the ship's lobby. He had immediately observed that all people coming aboard from *Titanic* were being brought through here for what was somewhat coldly called 'processing', and realised that if he remained in this space he stood a high chance of meeting with Miss Paik again.

As to why he was so enthralled with the young Oriental-American, he could not say. It occurred to him that she was the first person of similar age he had met among the time-travellers, and it made sense that any questions he had regarding the future were best directed at someone with whom he had at least one thing in common…

…but that would be vanity, a prideful attempt to justify what was in truth a very primitive motivation; when he had first come into contact with Miss Paik aboard *Titanic* he had been struck by her exotic charms, not only in appearance, but also in demeanour. Honestly, he wished to know more about who this woman was, in an attempt to better understand why he felt such a childish attraction to her.

"Be warned Jack, attraction has a habit of becoming infatuation," Milton Long had laughingly warned him, before heading off to explore the ship on his own.

"Attraction, Jack?" Marian Thayer had asked, eyes askance. Jack had felt himself blush, but had remained steadfast in his decision to stay in the Belgrave Square Lobby, awaiting Miss Paik.

"At the very least," he had explained. "It will allow me to apologise for the ungentlemanly manner in which we met."

That seemed to have satisfied his parents, who had bid him adieu and left to "take the measure" of *Oceanic* and her complement, leaving Jack to wait, uncomfortable in his borrowed clothes. Eventually, however, his constant presence had drawn attention from a person named Adrienne McKinn, who seemed to be in a position of some authority, and somehow he had found himself assisting her in welcoming more contemporaries of his own aboard and trying to set them at ease, ridiculous given his own conflicted feelings. Observing Mrs McKinn had also given him some inclination of the world that had produced Miss Paik. From observation, both women seemed to be confident, self-assured, and remarkably capable given that neither seemed to have the support of a husband or father.

Is it possible that they have moved beyond such a need? Is everything I understand about women based on a fallacy, mistaking social mores for weaknesses in the female character?

In truth, Mrs McKinn rather reminded Jack of his mother, not least for a remarkable ability to see through bluster and pierce to the truth of an individual's character and motivations. When he approached her on the matter she had expressed amusement, explaining that such skills had been honed during a career as a respected stateswoman, which had led Jack to wondering what might happen if his mother turned her considerable intelligence and social skills to a political platform. The thought was rather intimidating, and once again left him questioning the traditional concept that the domestication of women was essential to ensuring the stability of Western Civilisation.

But those questions had been foregone when he had finally come face to face with Miss Paik, a situation which had seemed to come as a not-unpleasant surprise to her. Their conversation had been stilted, however, until he had noticed her looking with somewhat tearful eyes at the couples around her, and suddenly realised his foolishness; for all her evident independence, it was obvious that Miss Paik surely had a family from which she had now been parted. Whilst this would be the same for almost everyone aboard these time-displaced ships, surely it would be a burden the younger among them would find harder to bear.

Feeling a sudden urge to embrace and protect this lost girl, he had offered her his company, and to his pleasure she had accepted.

And so he found himself, resting here with the strange young woman to his side, feeling a strange contentment.

"Good morning..." someone said, and Jack turned to see Miss Paik opening her eyes, large and expressive and a very pretty shade of hazel-green, unusual in someone of her race.

"Good morning," he replied, wondering what this day would bring.

*

"You were married in Springfield, Massachusetts?" Milt said quietly. The spoon in his hand shook slightly as he stirred a cup of tea, one of many which were being handed out by crewmembers to anyone who needed them. His hand was trembling, his nerves shaken.

"Yes, why?" Terri and Janice were sitting opposite him. The two were holding hands, resting them lightly on the table.

Milt nervously sipped his drink. "It's my home town. My father is a judge there. I'd hesitate to think what he would make of..."

Terri's eyes flashed, and he swallowed.

"...of all this."

The tea was hot and sweet, and seemed to steady his resolve. "I'm... sorry for what happened. My actions were not those of a gentleman, but I was taken off guard at meeting two..." he paused, blushing, "...two female homosexuals."

"The word is 'lesbian'," Janice laughed softly, seemingly delighted at his reluctance.

"Yes, well. I am sorry – I just find it hard to believe that the two of you are... wife and wife."

360

"Go on…" Terri said darkly. "Keep digging."

They had sat in uncomfortable silence in a champagne bar called The Magic Stick, which due to all the furniture permanently fastened to the floor was one of the few spaces not being used to accommodate *Titanic*'s passengers. After Janice had convinced her partner to release her hold on Milton, the two parties, feeling a mutual abashment, had agreed to sit and talk.

But conversation had been limited, both himself and the two women mostly sipping their drinks, inserting an occasional question or making some trivial observation when the silence became overtly oppressive. Mostly, he had just observed them, trying to get the measure of their character. Throughout, Milton noted several shared glances between the two wives, and how they continually held hands, as if clinging to one another.

They are afraid… he concluded at last, just before Terri abruptly rose and pulled the hem of her green smock straight.

"Well, that's my hour almost up, they'll need me back in the ship's hospital so that the next poor person can come out on break and mingle with high society," she said, shooting a venomous glare at Milt before kissing her wife farewell. "Be safe, Jan, I'll talk to you about my idea later."

As she left, Terri made a strange hand gesture, pointing with two fingers to her own eyes, and then directing the gesture back at Milt. Janice Patton had left a few moments later, seemingly every inch a glamorous, refined young lady, but he could not forget the quiet anger he had seen her exhibit when he had brought up the issue of Terri's race.

With the grudging soiree at an end, he slowly paced around the interior of the ship, thinking and observing.

Yes, they are afraid. And they have every right to be.

From what he had gathered, the word of 2012 was much different from his own, so far as the lives of women and blacks were concerned. Both of the two girls were economically independent, sexually liberated (a curious idea, but he could see the definite appeal), very much in love, and politically emancipated. Indeed both had apparently voted for a Negroid President named Obama. They were also used to social criticism for openly expressing their... perversions, affections, in public, and had learned to find solace in a circle of friends, and one another.

Now, they were on their own, in a world hostile to their plight. Although he had not finished his course of study at Harvard, Milton could think of few courts in the United States that would recognise either's' alleged right to vote, much less sanction a marriage between the two. They were more likely to end up in a penal institute, or confined to an insane asylum in order that their Uranian tendencies might be treated. He also, reluctantly, acknowledged that Terri would have limited options for employment as a mixed-race woman, and that her being in a relationship with a Caucasian would only inflame anger further. There were already cries, back in the States, for the lynching of the Negro boxer Jack Johnson for his marriage to a white woman; he could not imagine the affronted cries that would resound from pulpits in response to two *women* of different races being married.

Yet, as much as he sympathised with them, it being hard to demonise two beautiful women with whom one had shared tea and made polite if strained conversation, while the two of them shared looks of such soft and warm affection that it was evidently love, not lust, felt between them, Milt could not help but feel offended. Their blasé attitude to how radical their behaviour was only seemed to intensify his conflicted feelings. How dare they challenge his values so brazenly, so casually?

And he was equally dubious of what would happen when they reached shore. Slowly, he came to the lip of a balcony and gazed down on the crowds filling the ship's lobby. Two firebrands alone could set a whole country ablaze with scandal. But what could several thousand do, coming from a society a century distant from the one in which they now found themselves? It would be inhuman to ask them to give up all they knew in order to fit into the world of 1912, and equally impossible to ask 1912 to accept them without protest.

What would be the impact of the same questions now tearing him apart, writ large on the canvas of America or Europe? The backlash from those too closed-minded to see the *future perspective* could even rebound on innocent blacks and women, which would further aggravate the malcontents of society against their 'oppressors'.

Was it madness to envision a second Civil War?

Milt clutched the balcony rail tight; his hands trembled uncontrollably. Until now, he had kept his calm through all the madness that had befallen them this night. The prospect of *Titanic* sinking under his feet had not done so much as caused him to blink.

But now he too was deathly afraid.

*

"Yeah, my eyes are a bit weird, but they run in the family. Apparently one of my distant ancestors was a Dutch trader who bedded a Hanyang girl during the age of the Korean Empire, hence this little aberrant gene... she and her baby were disowned by her family, or so I'm told."

Jack Thayer and Philippa Paik casually made their way along the *Oceanic*'s crowded promenade, the young girl holding court while Jack marvelled at the expansive view. Not a mile off, he could see *Titanic* drifting with them in the current, the few figures on her boat deck at the same height as himself. Then he turned and looked towards the many decks of cabins arrayed above him, and shook his head in disbelief. This ship defied definition; in size, in comfort...

In class, he thought to himself, as a pair of children ran past him to the rail, their parents chasing after them. The small family was dressed in plain, sturdy clothing with little decoration. He supposed they were from *Titanic*'s Second Class, or maybe Third, though honestly he could not tell. There had been no attempt on the part of *Oceanic*'s crew to separate the survivors according to social rank, and for the first time he was beginning to wonder why.

"...then after Japan annexed Korea in 1910 my family escaped to America, finally settling in New York round about now. My sister Marilyn and I are third-generation Korean-Americans..." Pip continued, becoming more subdued. "But then our parents were killed when I was a girl, and we were taken in by friends of the family..."

She paused, and then laughed softly. "The Paiks have always been nomads, I guess, moving from one place to the next, always a bit unwanted…"

He could not help but feel she included herself in that statement, and frowned.

"May I ask what is troubling you?" he asked, at the exact same moment as she blurted out. "So what do you make of the 21st Century?" They both trailed off, and Jack subconsciously scratched at the back of his head. Philippa had sunk back into a brooding silence, and he very carefully began to speak.

"So far, I'm enjoying myself. This ship is a marvel, and the people are pleasant, if somewhat… abrupt."

She sniggered, and as he looked curiously towards her she arched an eyebrow. "Go on?"

Jack shrugged. "It's hard to say, but everyone seems ready to ask me how I am, if they can help in any way, all approaching without any sense of proprietary or decorum. You all seem to have no sense of ceremony when interacting with each other."

"You've not seen the fundraising events NOAA throws," she laughed softly. "Everyone's bowing and scraping then, clamouring after investors with false compliments and acts of obsequiousness. I suppose it's little different to a Philadelphia social function."

"It sounds pretty much the same," he murmured, looked around at the people mingling in a sort of 'beer garden' outside of the Red Pennant Inn, strangers exchanging conversations and jokes across a century, while others hung at the edges in stony silence. Gradually, two eras were beginning to emulsify together. "All your peers seem so relaxed, not what I would expect on an Atlantic crossing."

"Two world wars and a hundred years of civil rights demonstrations can really wear down people's self reserve," she shrugged. "But this ship isn't like the *Titanic*, or the *Lusitania*, or the other great liners of your age, Jack, ferrying the immigrants and powerbrokers between the great cities of the world. Where we come from, air travel has taken over the majority role of conveying people internationally for business or pleasure. Everyone aboard *Oceanic* is essentially here to experience an ideal of shipboard life – they were on holiday."

Jack shook his head again, thinking of the primitive aircraft he knew were under development in America and Europe, and then imagining the descendants of such machines. What was it like to look down on the Earth from dizzying heights, soaring effortlessly above the clouds?

"My little foster-brother wants... wanted, to become a pilot," Pip suddenly said, and he saw that once again her gaze had drifted away. "I remember... remember when the Concorde was retired; no-one expected a nine-year old to be so torn up over a plane as Jimmy was – cried for days at the thought that he'd never get to fly a supersonic airliner."

The context of her words was alien to Jack, but her melancholia required no explanation. "I can't imagine what Marilyn and my family are going through right now... for all they know, I'm dead."

Jack felt his stomach twist, its contents curdling in empathy.

"Look around us, Jack," Pip extended a hand, waving it around idly. "Tell me what you see?"

He obliged her, and turned on a point, taking in the whole of the surrounding section of the ship.

"People laughing, socialising," he said at last. "Mostly comprised of your contemporaries, or at least I assume so from the clothing. There's a handful of *Titanic*'s First Class, and quite a few of her Second and Third. Some people are drinking alone though, or in small groups; they're quiet, mournful..."

"Like me," she finished for him. "Like I said, most of these people were on holiday; what happened last night was a grand adventure... *'we helped to save the Titanic'*, and all that. But gradually they're going to realise that their children, parents, relatives back home, are completely cut off from them. For all those we've left behind, these ships just vanished from the North Atlantic, as thoroughly gone as if they were atomised to dust. Thinking of my family having to suffer through that, with no answers or explanation..."

Her words broke off in a sob.

"I'm not depressed Jack, just ahead of the curve. When people realise what this means, the entire ship is going to feel it..." she snorted. "We might have rescued *Titanic*, but in truth, we're refugees. Cut-off, stateless, friendless... alone."

Her shoulders had become hunched, and her hands were balled up and trembling. Slowly, fearful of the social norms he was breaching, and hoping that it was considered respectable behaviour in her time, Jack reached over and took her hand in his. Her skin was warm and soft and quivered like a frightened mouse.

"Not entirely alone," he found himself saying.

He felt her hand steady for a second, and then she abruptly snatched it away as if scalded, turning her back to him. "I appreciate the sentiment Jack, but I don't need it right now."

Was she crying?

"Tell me about it," he offered uncertainly, trying to take her mind off the difficult issue of family.

"What?"

"Tell me about your world." He pulled a slightly damp handkerchief from his pocket and proffered it; taking it she dabbed about the hot moisture pricking at her eyes, which he could see were heavy, dark-lined with unshed tears.

"I want to know about it," he said firmly. "I want to know everything."

She nodded. "Alright. Come to the ship's library and I'll show you."

As they headed forward, the sun slowly began to rise; pink-tinted clouds in the sky gaining a filigree of gold as it did, throwing light on the gathered ships.

Glancing to the North, beyond *Titanic*, Jack spotted another cluster of vessels in the distance, two steamships nuzzling up against an immense green hull that was settling deep in the water.

CHAPTER NINETEEN

The wheelhouse of the *Seguin Laroche* was all but empty, the corpse of Marc Pètain having been committed to the deep with the ship's other dead. Joanna Laroche herself had rung eight bells as the bodies were slipped overboard, in salute to sailors whose watches had come to a close.

Now she stood alone on the bridge, squinting as the first light of dawn streamed through the salt-encrusted windows. Slowly she made her way around the room, running an affectionate hand over the switches and control panels, saving the helm for last. Outside, the sunrise leant a fiery cast to both the crisp icebergs drifting on the ocean surface and the soft, diaphanous clouds that were streaked across the sky. The surface of the water was just beginning to whip up into small waves, except for around the listing container-ship, where air seeping from the hull had become so churned up in the water that it formed thick foam, breaking apart the surrounding pack ice.

They had been thrown back in time. Joanna had to accept that, but she found it a surprisingly easy pill to swallow. The quiet, internalised rage that had almost become a part of her these past few years was gone, and instead she just felt sad, as if that was the only emotion left to take the place of the anger that had been cut out of her.

And she was sad because the *Seguin Laroche* was sinking. The wallowing ship's deck was already listing heavily to starboard, although the downward slope towards the bow was negligible. It almost seemed that she had achieved a kind of balance, but from experience she knew that container ships and bulk carriers could be notoriously unstable when flooding. At any moment they might suddenly roll over, or rear back in the water and sink by the bow or stern.

The sound of tearing metal drew her gaze briefly forward. As the ship's roll had increased, so to had the containers stacked five high on the foredeck deck begun to tip. Although several had simply fallen straight into the sea, the majority were still connected top-to-bottom, and like sedimentary planes in a fault were folded and crushed together, those closest to the edge tipping out over the water at forty-five degrees. Now the load evidently became too much to bear, and as she watched, ten or more of the huge boxes cleaved away like an iceberg birthing itself from a glacier. They plunged overboard in a solid mass, followed by a colossal avalanche as dozens of suddenly unsupported containers toppled, fell and tumbled after them. Bolts and fasteners popped like gunshots, the entire vessel shuddering as she shed hundreds of tons of cargo.

Joanna watched dispassionately as the landslide of steel smashed down into the frothing sea, the Atlantic's surface bomb-bursting with each impact, spray and water erupting high into the air. All she could hear was the *Seguin Laroche*'s agonised groans, the ship heaving and shaking as she struggled to adjust for the sudden shift in mass. The end could not be far off now. The tannoy system had been repeating recorded warnings for hours, instructing crewmembers and any passengers to don lifesaving equipment and abandon ship immediately.

But at the same time, they were endeavouring to save anything of value; in complete defiance of evacuation protocol, duffels and backpacks had been dragged out of cabin lockers and were being stuffed with keepsakes and knick-knacks. The faster-thinking men had roped some of Captain Lord's men into liberating as much of the ship's library as possible, realising that each book, even something as mundane as *The Child's Guide to the Sea*, was potentially worth a fortune 'nowadays'. One of the engineers had personally emerged from below decks armed with a pair of bolt cutters with which to cut through the anti-theft chains securing the TV and VHS player to the lounge bulkhead. Joanna had considered suggesting that he not waste time with the DVD/Blu-Ray player, too advanced and complex to reverse-engineer, but then shook her head and decided that anything that could be carried was worth saving.

Still mulling on the past few hours, she came to the ship's helm. Resting a hand on it, she suddenly remembered the first time she had been brought onto the bridge of one of the family's ships. The *Aux Cygnes Laroche* had been invited to New York to participate in the Liberty Weekend, celebrating the centennial of the Statue of Liberty. That was in 1976, when she would have been four years old. Her father had been the captain. A framed photo of him holding her up so that her tiny hands could grab the spokes of the then-flagship's wheel still hung in the company offices at Le Havre…

"Had hung…" she said to herself, feeling fresh tears pricking at her eyes. Trying to blink them back, she turned away from the helm, only to confront where Marc's blood and brains were still splashed across the rear bulkhead, the red smear now dry and flaky. She began to cry, unable to hold her emotions back, and her tears flowed hot and wet.

"*Capitaine?*" someone spoke. It was Thierry Mallard, her former Chief Engineer and an old friend of the family. She had sent him to recover as many of the ship's blueprints and technical documentation as possible, and he had just emerged from the corridor to the ship's office to see her crying. Satchels stuffed with manuals and engineering drawings were slung over his shoulders, but in his hands he held something else.

The *Seguin Laroche*'s bell.

Wordlessly he held it up, and Joanna stepped forward and ran one finger along the inner lip of its mouth, feeling her name stamped into the metal, along with those of every member of her family who had ever been baptised in it.

"Are you alright, *petite-Jo?*"

"I'm fine, Thierry," she lied, keeping her head turned away as she tried to wipe away the tears with one sleeve. "*Génial.*"

He opened his mouth as if to speak, and then seemed to think better, and turned away with a cough.

"Another ship has arrived," he said softly. "The *Carpathia*. Her captain is another *anglais*, a man named Rostron, and he has sent some of his own boats over to assist *Californian*'s. The crew are loading the last of our treasures now."

She nodded, and he left.

The famous Carpathia. Another ghost out of the murk of history.

But the most terrifying spectre of all was *Titanic*... a ship to which Jo long suspected the Laroche family held a personal connection. Now the truth was just a few nautical miles away... and she was terrified as to what she might discover. Emotion threatening to overwhelm her, she stood in silence for a few seconds, hand still pressed to her face and shoulders shaking as she tried to control herself. The ship was beginning to shudder as well, slowly slipping into its death throes. Then she sniffed deeply, inhaled, and lowered her hand, eyes dark.

Jabril Hab Allah...

That man, the man who had shot Marc (for some reason, the word 'murdered' now eluded her). She had not seen his body amongst the dead, and while lashed to the wheel was certain that she had heard his voice shouting from out on deck during the fire, after the lifeboat had been launched.

Crossing to the office with new purpose she grabbed a fire-axe and smashed the padlock on the armaments locker, swinging it wide open.

He's got to still be onboard.

As she selected a SIG Sauer pistol and loaded it, the deck continued to tilt under her feet, the ship slowly rolling over onto her beams.

*

Charles Groves, carrying a large duffel-bag, made his way stealthily along *Californian*'s starboard boat deck. All of the crew were gathered to port, watching the giant *Seguin Laroche* sink, and this side was abandoned.

Eventually he came to one of the lifeboats and loosened the tie-downs for the watertight tarpaulin that shielded it from the weather, before heaving the duffel-bag inside. Then he tied the tarp back into place, hiding the bag.

Inside it were various objects from the *Seguin Laroche*, but most importantly the two electronic devices he had found on the ship, which he now understood to be called an 'iPad' and a 'laptop computer', respectively. Both, he knew, would be valuable,

370

and the computer, he had determined from brief examination, contained priceless information on the time-machine now stored in *Californian*'s hold. He had turned them off, to conserve what he understood to be a limited battery life, but both were still functional.

The benefits this technology and knowledge would bring to Britain were boundless. All he had to do was get them to the appropriate authorities in England.

*

Joanna ran down the length of the heeling *Seguin Laroche*, keeping to the higher side of the listing hull so that she might not be suddenly crushed by a falling container. Angry thoughts directed towards Jabril Hab Allah were blurring in her mind with memories from her life, frothing together into a raging maelstrom of betrayal and vengeance. The only constant was the purposeful weight of the SIG Sauer in her hands, and the fire burning in her mind behind the font of emotion, holding back the worst of the dark flood with its cold light.

Yesterday morning Hab Allah had been helping Nash to inspect the chain locker. He might still have the key.

Reaching the front of the cargo deck she took the stairs up onto the forecastle three at a time, her legs working like pistons. Under her feet was the Bosun's locker, the ship's store of tools and equipment. But forward of that was the chain locker, into which the anchor chains retracted while the ship was at sea. It was a well-hidden space that could only be accessed through a hatch that opened onto the deck right up in the prow of the ship, and as she came running up she saw the padlock that normally secured the hatch was missing.

Joanna drew the SIG Sauer and fumbled at the safety, drew the slide to chamber a bullet. Swallowing once, she put her foot under the rim of the hatch and kicked it open, pointing the gun down the stairwell with both hands gripping the butt.

"Come forward with your hands up!" she shouted down in French, before repeating the order in English. No-one replied. She strained her ears. Over the soft hush of the rising sea, she could hear wet, laboured breathing.

"Whoever's down there, identify yourselves now!"

Silence. Her nose wrinkled as a reeking, metallic smell wafted up the hatch, born on a wave of hot air. She recognised it from the night her grandfather died; it was the smell of blood and impending death.

"Right, I'm coming down, and I am armed!"

Slowly, keeping one had free to hold the pistol, Joanna climbed down the ladder into the chain locker, keeping the gun facing out into the centre of the room. It was a triangular space, tapering towards her end, and consisted solely of a wide catwalk flanked by two deep pits, in which long coils of chain were tangled up like twin snake nests. Air displaced from the flooding compartments below was jetting up through ventilators, adding an appropriate angry hissing to the scene.

In the dim light shining up through the anchor alleys, she could see two figures on the small spit of decking, one on his knees resting next to the other, who was prone on his back. Slowly she came closer, both hands gripping the gun and breathing through her mouth to stem out the growing stench of blood. As she came up beside them, her stomach attempted to offload her last meal.

Lying at her feet was the young Arab who had threatened her on the bridge, his chest rising and falling slowly, despite the fact that his stomach was a torn mass of flesh and muscle. The bright pink and red contrasted sharply with the deathly pallor of his skin. In the chill air the exposed contents of his abdominal cavity were steaming softly, and from the amount of blood on the catwalk, he had bled out copiously. Fighting back a wave of nausea she glanced again at his broken stomach, and saw that oil and grease had impregnated the jagged wound. He was not going to survive; either blood loss or infection was going to kill him.

Kneeling beside him, holding the dying youth's hand, was Hab Allah, softly murmuring in Arabic. As she approached he paused, and without looking up, addressed her. "His name was Benjamin Khan, born in Birmingham, England. His father taught music, and his mother was beaten to death by white thugs when he was a boy. He sailed on the British oil tankers, and when the demonstrations began in Egypt he jumped ship and joined the crowds protesting in Tahrir Square. When I was looking for qualified sailors who could help me unify the Arab awakenings, he was the first to volunteer."

He turned his face to her, and Joanna suddenly felt as if she was looking down from heaven on a man in despair. Tears had matted his beard, and he almost seemed to welcome the sight of the gun in her hand, barrel turned towards him. "Another young life on my hands…"

He seemed to be silently begging for his own death, and she bit her lip deeply, struggling to hold onto the anger now slipping away from her. "What happened?"

"Friendly fire…" he said bluntly, still holding onto Khan's hand. "Someone shot him when he tried to board the lifeboat. I think it was Abercrombie." He spat the representative's name as if it was poison, and Joanna felt her own mouth twitch in a momentary snide grin. Then Hab Allah looked down at his forearms and her smirk died; they were covered with Khan's blood, as were numerous bloodied rags and strips of cloth scattered around.

He must have been futilely trying to clean the wound… she thought, before realising that aside from the mess that had been made of his stomach, the rest of the young man's body was spotlessly clean. *No, he was preparing him for death…*

Slowly, keeping the gun held carefully between both of her hands, she crouched down into a squat. Khan's eyes were open, and he was staring at the ceiling, blinking slowly, his gaze distant. The blood-loss had almost claimed him.

"We're sinking," she said quietly to Hab Allah. As if to support her statement, the listing ship groaned loudly and the room tilted, settling forward. Even with both of them crouched or kneeling, it was a struggle to stay balanced as the *Seguin Laroche* started on her final voyage. Not looking him in the eye she tilted the gun towards Khan. "Can we move him?"

"He fell out of my arms climbing down the hatch," Jab said dully. "The fall injured his spine, and hastened the collapse of his system. Trying to drag him to safety would only worsen the injuries."

The unspoken words *not that he's got long left to live, anyway…* seemed to hang in the air between them. The hissing from below decks was getting louder now, and with a sudden bang an inspection hatch was forced open by the air pressure. As if a balloon had burst, the ship seemed to lurch downwards, and now the sound of gurgling water made itself heard. Carefully Joanna scooted sideways and looked down into the anchor pit on the listing side of the ship. Sure enough, white, turbulent water was foaming up around the chains. She looked up the sloping deck, and saw Jab holding the unconscious Khan in place.

The dark-haired Arab turned his piercing gaze towards her, specifically to the gun in her hands. "I killed your first officer and fiancé. That you've come to avenge him is obvious. But if you are to kill me, please put the boy out of his misery first. Drowning unable to swim is no way to die."

Carefully working her way back up to him, Joanna tried to latch on to the flame of anger that had burst into life and temporarily filled the hole in her heart. But she found nothing. Trembling, she brought the muzzle of the pistol to the boy's head and pressed it against his temple. Her finger hovered uneasily over the trigger and she breathed deeply, willing herself to pull on the innocuous little lever.

Then she lowered it. "I can't…"

"If you cannot bring yourself to do it, then I will try to relieve you of the gun and do it for you, *capitaine*."

She looked at him, incredulous, and suddenly wondering if this was all part of some sick game on his part. Either she took this boy's life herself, or relinquish her only means of protection so that he could do it…

Something brushed against one of her fingers, and she cautiously glanced down. She had placed one hand on the deck to stabilize her crouch, and it was very close to Khan's own hand, which was slowly flexing, as if trying to clasp hers.

Just like grandfather had wanted to hold my hand as he died…

She made her decision. Setting her jaw firmly she held the gun up and thumbed the magazine release button. The clip dropped to the deck, and she kicked it away. A splash suggested that it had landed in the free-flooding chain well.

"There's one bullet already chambered," she said, extending the gun in her hand. "You can shoot me, or him, but not the both of us."

Slowly, he reached forward and rested his hand on the gun, his face unreadable. Then he snatched it out of her hand with remarkable speed. "Thank you, capitaine…"

Joanna squeezed Benjamin Khan's free hand, and closed her eyes.

The sound of the gun firing was deafening in the confined space.

*

Arthur Rostron, Captain of the Cunard Royal Mail Steamer *Carpathia*, was not a man given to blasphemy. Indeed, his quiet piety was well-known to those who frequently served under and travelled with him. But as he held onto the rail of *Carpathia*'s bridge and gazed across to the listing *Seguin Laroche*, his lips moved against his will in a silent profanity.

The green-and-white ship was now hard over on its side like the carcass of a whale, waves gradually eating their way up the long cargo deck. With every second that passed, more and more of the strange cargo boxes, once stacked neatly fore and aft of the superstructure, slid or tore free from their racks, tumbling down over their companions in their eagerness to drown themselves like lemmings. Some floated, but most sank quickly, and he wondered what treasures of future technology within were being lost to the sea.

He quickly discarded that notion as irrelevant. In the here and now these 'containers' posed an immediate threat to the small wooden boats still offloading whatever detritus the *Seguin Laroche*'s crew had piled up on the aft deck. *Carpathia* and the smaller *Californian* were both keeping a wary distance as the last of the flotilla of lifeboats came up alongside the ailing vessel's superstructure. The ship's list had now brought the lip of the deck almost down to the waterline, and men were hurling boxes and bags into the boats like stevedores, before eventually throwing themselves on top of the pile. It was a farce, and yet one with which he could not help but sympathise.

A bubbling roar heralded a momentous blast of spray that burst up from somewhere within the submerging hull, which visibly surged down. For a second the ship seemed to right herself, but then the bow nosed forward again, and this time did not stop.

"Right, that's quite enough," Rostron said aloud, and called for *Carpathia* to signal the boats back. In response to his orders the ship's whistle bellowed several times, a clear message to anyone in the water that the ship they were loitering beside might turn over on them at any moment. They quickly heeded the order, turning back towards the two steamships...

Except for one lifeboat, whose crew were keeping hard up alongside the *Seguin Laroche*. Again Rostron signalled for them to come back, yet they continued to ignore them.

"My glasses," he snapped out, and someone obligingly presented him with a pair of binoculars. Pressing them to his eyes, he spun the focus dial and a white-on-blue blur resolved itself into the image of his First Officer, Horace Dean, standing upright in the boat and waving wildly up at the plunging ship. Rostron turned slightly and saw the figure of a man, his face brazed as a nut and swathed in a thick beard, scrambling along a promenade on the ship's wildly canted superstructure. A second figure in a padded green jacket was following him. Dean was evidently waiting for them. A brave man, if somewhat foolish.

"Wait, what are you doing..." he suddenly heard himself shouted aloud. Instead of heading down the stairs towards Dean's waiting boat, the person dressed in green was instead going up, towards the level of the *Seguin Laroche*'s bridge, even as the sea completely swallowed the forecastle and the ship's stern began to lift up out of the water. The bearded man paused, as if torn between the boat and his companion, and then turned away and fled after her. Although Dean's voice was inaudible over the surf, Rostron could see his first officer's mouth open in shouts, no doubt demanding they come to him immediately.

For the second time that day, *Carpathia*'s captain found himself suppressing the urge to curse.

*

"Capitaine Laroche! The ship is sinking; we have to abandon it now!" Joanna heard Jabril shout, but she ignored him. Her free

376

hand, the one not holding onto the rail, fumbled in her pocket until it found her keyring. With it held tight in her hand, she fought her way up to the bridge and climbed onto the roof of the wheelhouse. The open horizon spread out around her, tilted crazily as the ship began to thunderously shed more containers. Water spilled down across the deck, leaving a thin, oily sheen on the metal, and as she tried to climb towards the radar mast her feet slipped uncontrollably. Falling forward, she bit the keyring between her teeth and crawled on all fours, pulling herself up to the foot of the mast, and got an arm and a leg around the base, straddling it like a child on the branch of a tree. Pulling the keys from her mouth, she forced one into the lock on the box that container the ship's good-luck totem and twisted it. Pushing open the plastic shield, she grabbed the small silver disc within and clutched it close to her chest.

"Come on!" someone shouted, and she turned to see Hab Allah standing below her, clinging to the top of the ladder. The sea roiled angrily behind him. "You have what you came for, now let's go!"

Nodding, Joanna rolled onto her back, and let go, sliding down the now near-vertical deck towards him and the rail. As he caught her, the *Seguin Laroche* finally rolled right onto her side, the green hull crashing down into the water and throwing up a white wave that rushed away from them with a foaming roar. With their feet on the rail and their backs against the deck, the sea lapping at their heels, she saw the tiny white lifeboat that they had nearly boarded was still lingering nearby, rising over the wave and plunging back down into the swirling water on their side. The officer in charge was shouting to his crew, who heaved at the oars with powerful strokes, coming closer. Then Joanna heard the Arab gasp as his attention turned towards the parent vessel of the antiquated craft. *Carpathia*, with her bluff bows and single funnel casting a pall of smoke, looked like some wreck that had raised herself from the seabed and come to their rescue. *Californian* lingered beside her like a smaller sibling.

"*Allahu Akbar,*" he breathed softly. "It worked."

"Your 'nuclear device'…" she replied sarcastically. "Your *time machine?*"

"Yes… it was called the *Liberty Bell.*"

"Nice name," she said, unable to keep a mocking tone out of her voice. "Very American."

He waved his hand to brush her sarcasm aside. "When are we? What year have we landed in?"

Her mouth worked silently for a second as she struggled to explain, and then she pointed off to the south, far to the right of the *Carpathia*. "See for yourself."

Looking where she indicated, she saw his eyes widen. Joanna had had the exact same reaction when she had first looked in that direction hours earlier. There, proud against the dawn sky, rose the iconic profile of a four-funnelled steamship. Though still down a little at the bows, the proud and balanced lines of the vessel showed no signs of sinking any time soon.

"It's the morning of April 15th, 1912, and the *Titanic* is still afloat. Your *Liberty Bell* has saved fifteen hundred lives."

His eyes closed for a second, the lips of his mouth pursing together in dismay and hurt. And then he smiled as he once again beheld history's most famous ship with his own eyes. "God be praised."

The lifeboat from *Carpathia* finally pushed up to them, and the officer held out his hand. Grabbing it Joanna stepped over, followed by the Arab.

"Push off quickly!" she shouted. "The ship displaces over 80,000 tons, when she goes down the suction will be immense!"

The officer needed no prompting, and with a shout he put the tiller over with a snap as the crew heaved at the oars. Spinning on a point, the tiny lifeboat pulled free as the ship gave a final bellowing groan. Only the superstructure and aft deck stood high of the water now, like a besieged castle teetering over an abyss. Joanna watched as the stern came high out of the water, exposing the rudder and propeller. As the ship dived, it corkscrewed, turning until the name painted on the transom came into view.

SEGUIN LAROCHE, MAJURO

She clung tightly to the medal in her hand. It had been her grandfather's. The *Seguin Laroche* had been launched just a month after his funeral, and she had been riding on deck as the ship had slid down the ways, scattering his ashes from a cold metal urn. It had been a slow, painful day of mixed feelings.

And now she was again bidding farewell to something dear.

"Captain Laroche?" she turned and found the officer in charge standing. "First Officer Dean at your service, of the steamship *Carpathia*. My commiserations for your loss."

He touched his hand to his cap in respect, and she returned it, her own cap still perched atop her head. "Thank you Mr Dean, but please…" She paused and glanced down at Hab Allah, pulling away at an oar beside one of *Carpathia*'s crew, who was regarding the swarthy man dubiously. "…I'm not alone in my loss."

"I understand, Captain," Dean turned and directed a wary eye at Jab as well. "And this gentleman is…?"

"Jabril Hab Allah," she answered, like him cautiously regarding the man in question, who gazed evenly back at her as she wrestled with herself. Quickly she came to her conclusion; "Mr Hab Allah is my Cadet Officer, and a trusted member of my crew."

"Very well," Dean nodded, mouth screwed up as if debating whether or not to question her words. "If you have no objection, we will return to *Carpathia* immediately."

"Thank you…" she replied dully. Standing in the prow of the boat, she looked back as the stern of the *Seguin Laroche* hoisted itself up with a cavernous mechanical bellow, the sea at its foot boiling. The ship hung in the sky for a second, and then with surprising speed it fell down into the waves, like the foundations had been pulled out from under it. The tricolour at the stern fluttering bravely, the after end of the ship ploughed down out of sight. There was a last flash of colour from the flag, and then the ship was gone. Only a patch of bubbles and several sinking containers remained.

But the *Seguin Laroche* was gone, erased. Like her family, and CML. Her whole world had been washed away and rubbed clean.

She opened her palm, and looked down at the small medal. On the reverse side it carried her grandfather's name, and was edged in a French inscription.

"Whoever saves one life saves the world entire…" she read silently, thoughtful, before turning away from where the ship had been, and taking up an oar to help carry the lifeboat forward.

Towards *Carpathia*.

Towards the future.

"Well, there she goes," Margaret Brown said aloud, as the after end of the *Seguin Laroche* sank from view. She sighed in disbelief. "God Almighty, is this really happenin', JJ?"

John Jacob Astor observed his friend. In the light of dawn Maggie's face seemed to glow with a ruddy red light, and her compact, stocky frame trembled with suppressed energy.

"I daresay that it is, Maggie," he replied between sips of his coffee, before kneeling to stroke the head of a small Airedale Terrier whose leash he held. Kitty, his darling pet, had been brought over from *Titanic*'s kennels in one of the last boats. He hoped one day to see his son playing with the dog on the floor of their New York home, and the thought made him smile, doing just as much to ease the worst effects of his sleep exhaustion and emotional stress as his cardboard cup of coffee.

"Here, Maggie," he said, rising to offer the drink to her, and as she took her own swig continued to muse aloud. "The question is what do we do next?"

Her attention was clearly still fixated on the spot several miles away where the other ship had sunk. Then eventually she turned and regarded *Titanic*, floating in the middle distance.

"That was one of the largest ships in the world, built with the advantage of a hundred years developments in ideas and materials, and it sank in just a few hours. So, could it really have been us instead that went down last night?"

"I don't doubt it…" JJ answered, drawing his coat tight about him. Despite the biting cold out here on *Oceanic*'s long promenade, the crowds that had gathered with morbid curiosity to see the cargo ship sink were quite large, and he nodded at one cluster. "These are good people, Maggie. They've already performed a miracle for my family. Now I feel they need our help to survive in a world not their own."

Maggie's eyes softened, their internal fires damped down, and she smiled wearily. "We're just a few, JJ, and there are several thousand of them. We can't be expected to hold all their hands once we dock, wherever that may be."

"No," he admitted. "But perhaps we can help in presenting them to a new world, and put an acceptable face on their… oddities.

And maybe ease the blow of their loss. The duty falls to us, not merely as a responsibility of our position, but an obligation for the help they have offered us freely."

"You've never been one for following convention, JJ…" she pointed out, and the two of them smiled affectionately. "But you're right, of course…"

She glanced around, as if searching for inspiration, and then her attention fell on one of their contemporaries. He was a young man, accompanied by a woman JJ presumed to be his wife, and from their smart but unostentatious clothing were presumably Second Class passengers from *Titanic*. More importantly, he was cranking away on the handle of a portable cinematographic camera, a varnished wooden box resting on a collapsible tripod. JJ had been aware of his presence throughout the sinking of the other ship, preserving a filmic record of the event. Now, however, he seemed to be demonstrating the function of the camera to one of the time-travellers, who was watching with rapt fascination and holding up a tiny device of his own. From where they were standing, the two onlookers could see an open panel on one side of the device, upon which a tiny cinema image was projected from within. Like the Second Class passenger's bulky apparatus, it was a camera.

John Jacob Astor saw Margaret Brown's face light up with impish glee. It was a look that suited her. "Tell me, JJ, have you seen Danny Mervin about since we came aboard?"

"The kinematographer?" he saw the first sketchy lines of her notion, and smiled in admiration. "I've not ventured far from the ship's hospital, Maggie, but if I had to warrant a guess he would be in the vicinity of the ship's theatre, which I understand is also used to show moving pictures."

"Well that's just grand…" replied the indomitable Margaret Brown, as Kitty yelped happily.

*

Oceanic's library was a two-storey space situated in the front of the ship's superstructure, as evidenced from the curved and be-windowed bulkhead that made up one wall. The other walls were all hidden behind wooden bookcases, each full of new editions. Jack Thayer almost expected the shelves to creak under the weight of future knowledge, and the thought must have occurred to someone else, for a member of the ship's crew was standing guard at the door, granting free access to the library, but ensuring that no-one walked off with any of the books, any one of which might be enough to transform the world.

"Alright!" Pip called out from an upstairs balcony, smiling confidently. Down below her, Jack turned his attention from the bookcase he was browsing, and saw that she was holding open what appeared to be an encyclopaedia. Clearing her throat, she began to read aloud.

"The largest volcanic eruption of the twentieth century occurred between June 6ᵗʰ and June 8ᵗʰ 1912, in what is now the Katmai National Park, Alaska. During the sixty-hour-long event, over three cubic miles of magma were expelled, leading to the collapse of the summit of the neighbouring Mount Katmai. The eruption ended when the vent was blocked by the extrusion of a three hundred foot high lava dome, later named 'Novarupta'."

She snapped the book shut, a triumphant smirk on her face. "So let it be written, so shall it be done."

Her enthusiasm was a welcome relief from her earlier melancholy, but in exploring the library she seemed to be swinging to a new extreme that unnerved Jack. Beginning to regret that he had asked to come here, he thoughtfully rubbed at the tufts of hair on his chin and slowly turned to take in the surrounding books with new eyes.

"This is a gift of prophecy," he said aloud, suddenly realising the potential carried in this one room.

"Exactly!" Pip replied, almost skipping down from the level above and crossing to the indexing board. "Human history might change as a result of tonight, but natural history, earthquakes and natural disasters operating on a level beyond our influence will continue unchecked. And if Novarupta still forms in a little less than two months, then that proves it!"

Jack's fist clenched on the table, providing him with a better support on which to rest his weight. "So, are you saying that there will be more events like the 1906 Earthquake?"

He was referring to an event of just a few years previously, when San Francisco had been all but levelled by a devastating earthquake. Only hours later gas from broken pipes had set what remained ablaze, and the city had burned.

But just imagine if people were given a forewarning, years in advance, of the exact day when tectonic forces would rip their city apart. Would they have prepared, or never even have settled in that area to begin with?

"Yes," she said evenly. "There'd been enough quakes and tsunamis and hurricanes in just the last few years of my time to feed all manner of bullshit stories about the world ending in 2012. The worst have been undersea earthquakes in the Indian and Pacific Oceans. Thousands died in Japan alone from the most recent. But now they can be warned years in advance! Build a storm wall there; don't ignore that bulge on the side of that volcano, build your nuclear power station with better safeguards…"

Jack's head was spinning. The room was going out of focus. Leaning forward he rested his head against a shelf and found himself staring at the spine of a history book entitled *The Last Great Quest: Captain Scott's Antarctic Sacrifice.*

Scott, the great British explorer? he thought wearily, forcing himself to reach up and seize the book in question. *He's meant to be journeying back from the South Pole as we speak…*

Gripping the edge of the table with one hand, he flipped open the book as Pip talked away, eyes scanning through the foreword. His heart rapidly sank. It was widely known that Scott's quest to be the first to reach the South Pole had failed, with the recent announcement that the Norwegian explorer Amundsen had attained that lofty goal sometime before Christmas. But the book claimed that Scott and his team had frozen to death on their return trek, roundabout March 29th 1912.

That was barely a fortnight ago… he thought, stunned. *But this says their bodies will not be discovered for another eight months!*

His eyes slid to other volumes he had already pulled from the shelves, darting from text to text. *The Second World War; Moonshot: The Inside Story of Mankind's Greatest Adventure; Nineteen Eighty-Four.*

It was too much information, coming all at once. Ships fated to sink, innumerable conflicts and disasters looming in the wings, international heroes obituarised before their deaths were even known…

"Stop…" he uttered weakly.

"And that's just scratching the tip of the iceberg, pun intended…" Pip continued obliviously, her enthusiasm overwhelming. "Atomic physics, that's another thing entirely!"

"Stop, please…"

"This reference section contains information on species not yet discovered, and other advanced science this age has not yet touched on. Bequeathing all this information to the early twentieth century might just set off a second renaissance-"

"*Shut up!*" Jack yelled.

Silence fell as swift as a guillotine. Pip, eyes wide, stared at him from across the room, her arms filled with books. Jack felt his chest heaving, and he fell back against the wall for support. "You travellers are going to upset every apple cart from here to Timbuktu. Dumping ideas on someone without context is just… knowledge without wisdom. I don't even know what a 'nuclear power station' is, but I already suspect that it's extremely hazardous, and now you wish to rush us into building one?"

He cupped his face in his hands and laughed sardonically. "You people… you really are from the future. I thought it was impossible, but there is no possibility that such a wild-child could have been born of this era."

As he spoke his knees folded under his weight, and he slowly slid down against the wall into a seated position, his burdens and emotions pouring out in a flood he could not stem. "What manner of animals raised you to be so uncivilised…" his chest heaved. "Romulus and Remus might have suckled from the teats of a wolf, yet gave us the bastion of culture that was Rome. But you people are just dangerous, so very dangerous."

For a moment blissful silence reigned, and then with a sound like falling trees, the books she was carrying were scattered over the floor as she clenched her fists, arms trembling.

"My parents," she said at last, teeth gritted and eyes wide with anger, "are dead! But they loved me, and supported me, and my uncle and aunt are just as wonderful!"

The force of her sudden rage struck him like a blow. Rebounding from it, he felt his own ire rise, and he pushed himself to his feet, the room coming back into focus.

"Are you implying that my own family is somehow lacking?" he responded. "That they are less deserving of respect and affection?"

"Maybe!" she shouted. "My father wasn't a railroad tycoon, and my mother had to go out and work two jobs to supplement his income. But they worked so hard that by the time they died, they'd saved enough money to pay for Marilyn's and my college tuition, and they never said a word of it in their lives, because they did not want us to feel burdened by it. That is beautiful! That is love!"

"What would you know of love?" he responded. "You're a blot among masses lacking in temperament and bearing, seemingly incapable of any subtlety of feeling! But I have three dear siblings back home who I care for deeply!"

"Do you!?" she all but screamed. Her hair was almost standing on end, and her face was drained of all colour. "Then where are they? You and your family have been touring around in Europe for months, leaving your brother and sisters to *what*? Totalitarian boarding schools; where they live in fear of strict housemasters and matrons who will beat them on a whim? How is that love!?"

She paused for breath, and when she restarted, her voice resounded with something he had not expected to hear. Disappointment.

"You people are seen as *monsters* back home," she hissed. "Your class has become a... a *Downton Abbey* stereotype! Cold, reserved, uncaring, unthinking, and so devoid of humanity that it's amazing we're of the same species!" Then she laughed cruelly and threw her arms wide. "But at the same time, you're refined and exotic and so *beautifully* elegant that we find you unbearably *romantic* as well! And I wanted to believe that there was some depth to all of you. But no, what do I get? You! Jack Thayer, the fascinating, eligible bachelor that most women who study the *Titanic* would die to know in person, and you turn out to be a snob who assumes anyone without an upmarket address is somehow less in intelligence, feeling or dignity! You people are dangerous, and all the wars looming on the horizon, all the greed and the hate? *IT'S ALL, YOUR, FAULT!*"

Jack's whole body seethed. How dare she, *how dare she!* Their eyes remained locked together for a long moment, and then he said, very carefully, "This is an age of tumultuous change and progress. But it would be a blind man who could not see that the working and middle classes are gaining in strength and power, and require a delicate touch if they are to be uplifted to the respect they demand so much. These are new ideas, new territories, and we are doing as best we can to not lose our way on an unsteady course. And then you burst out of the sky, invade our minds and insist that we go faster into the icebergs, that we immediately live up to your standards, with no consideration of deigning to meet our own. Have you considered that parading yourself in this manner is more likely to set back the cause of female emancipation, by providing fuel for the arguments spouted by all who oppose it? You, Miss Paik, are acting in a manner rude, judgemental and uncivil; the very definition of the female hysteric."

Rolling on momentum now, he concluded coldly. "It will be argued that your foster family should be glad that they're never going to see you again. Yes, this accident has done them a favour by ridding them of you!"

No sooner had the words left his lips than he felt a sudden void in him, as if the boiling rage had been vented with them, leaving his mind unclouded. Trembling in front of him, clad in a borrowed uniform a size too large for her petite frame, was not a monster from out of the chaotic mists of time, but a human being who had just lost everything she held dear. All she had left to connect her to the world she knew were these books and her memories, and he had just shunned one and insulted the other.

"You bastard!"

He was both shocked and unsurprised when she balled a fist and struck him across the face with deceptive strength. Even then, however, she did not have the body mass to do more than force him to step back, a hand rising instinctively to his cheek. He would have a shining bruise come the evening.

"I... I am..."

"Save it, Jack!" she replied, eyes burning with a passion he had never witnessed before. "It's just words. It's all you ever were to me, words!"

Dropping to her knees, she grabbed hold of a slender volume and all but pushed it into his face. "Your own words, Jack! Now eat them!"

His eyes slid to the title.

The Sinking of the S.S. *Titanic*, by John B Thayer Jr

God above.

"I read this when I was twelve, and then I read it again," Pip fumed. "I thought, underneath the writings of a bitter, frustrated man who the world had left behind, that I could see a wide-eyed optimistic teenager, who despite his wealth and privilege had been chewed up and spat back out by the twentieth century, who had suffered the same as every other person. You fascinated me, Jack; you were my first crush!"

Jack opened his mouth to protest, but she flung the book at him and, while he fumbled to catch it, she left the library. "Good luck with the twentieth century," she shouted over her shoulder, voice hard as newly tempered steel. "And the best of luck in not fucking yourselves all over again!"

He stood paralysed for several seconds as she slammed the door, and then felt life return to his legs. The crewman outside glowered at him darkly through the glass, having watched on and not intervened, but Jack was bothered by neither his unspoken reprimands nor his hypocrisy in not carrying out the peacekeeping promised when they had boarded the ship.

"Miss Paik!" he cried out. "I'm sorry! I spoke out of turn!"

Dropping the book, he threw himself after her, pushing the door open to find himself in one of *Oceanic*'s grand lobbies, bustling with confused and disorientated passengers from both ships.

Philippa Paik had vanished in the crowd. Not knowing exactly why he did so, he called out her name several times, and then climbed to a higher point on the stairs in the hope of catching a glimpse of her.

Nothing. She was swallowed up in the press of humanity.

CHAPTER TWENTY

"Gentlemen," Captain Smith said, slowly turning from where the *Seguin Laroche* had just foundered, hands folded behind his back. "We have much to be thankful for, but at the same time, much to consider."

His remaining officers – Murdoch, Pitman, Boxhall, Lowe and Moody – stood at a form of nervous attention, their backs to the wall of *Titanic*'s navigation bridge. Bride and Phillips, the two Marconi operators, were also present, but off to one side as silent observers. Apart from the eight of them, the bridge was deserted, Smith having dismissed the two assisting quartermasters.

"First of all, we are most fortunate that ships were to hand in our hour of need last night. However, that does not excuse the errors of navigation that led to our collision with the iceberg…" He held up a hand to ward off any possible responses. "Responsibility for that error lies with me as much as anyone else, but none of us can ignore where the course of this ship's maiden voyage would have led were it not for what I can only describe as a miracle on par with divine intervention. Mr Boxhall?"

"Yes, sir…" replied the ship's fourth officer, a bright twenty-something who Smith favoured for navigational duties.

"Have you prepared the materials I requested?"

"I have, sir."

"Very well, this way gentlemen…" Smith beckoned and they all proceeded through the wheelhouse into the navigating room, where Boxhall had laid yesterday's chart out for inspection.

"Now, as I recall," Smith continued, "on Friday evening, we received a Marconigram from the French Line vessel *La Touraine*, warning us of ice in this vicinity, and I see that the co-ordinates they gave have been duly noted on the chart…" he indicated towards a pair of pencil marks, but then brandished a handful of additional messages. "In the two days between then and the collision, however, we also received warnings from the *Rappahannock, Caronia, Noordam, Baltic, Amerika, Mesaba,* and twice from the *Californian,* all indicating the presence of large icebergs and field ice drifting much further south than might be expected on the Atlantic in April... and yet none of those warnings were plotted on the chart. Not one man here, senior officer, junior officer, or captain, saw fit to tally the information freely provided to us by other ships."

He produced a pencil and held it towards Boxhall, who cringed, as if it were a sword and Smith was demanding he throw himself upon it. "Mr Boxhall, please now update the chart."

Nodding, the fourth officer quickly set to work. As he did, Smith glanced aside at the two Marconi-men, Bride and Phillips. Several of the ice warnings Boxhall was now making reference to had not even made it to the bridge, and had only turned up, buried amongst private messages for the passengers, when Smith himself had personally made an inspection of the wireless cabin just an hour ago.

It's not their sole fault, he reminded himself, even as he struggled to retain his composure. *They're servants of the Marconi company, not the Line, servants whose first appointed task is the revenue-earning business of relaying private messages... the wireless was introduced to ships as a passenger convenience and novelty, with its aid to navigation being but a happy circumstance...*

But look at how useful it might have been, were the will there... whispered a second, mocking tone from the dark reaches at the back of his mind. *And look towards the 'talkie' devices and these ships from 'up-time'. They've harnessed the power of wireless telegraphy into the absolute service of safe navigation and inter-ship communication, with no such divisions of labour, duty and loyalty...*

So true, so absolutely true. Evidently the power of 'radio' was a vital tool in the arsenals of his non-contemporaries. He suspected such mastery of the ethers was also the secret science behind which *Oceanic* and her peers had the ability to 'see' icebergs in the dark of night.

By comparison, Titanic's wireless suite is a crass afterthought. It is sixty feet or more aft of the wheelhouse – as far as the Officers of the Watch are concerned, it might as well be on the moon! And beyond relaying messages by hand, there is no means by which vital information might be readily and conveniently forwarded to the bridge... thus when the wireless operators are busy, such essential navigational aids get brushed aside or buried in the backlog... blast it all, the Purser's Office is three decks down and has better communications with the Marconi Room, a direct pneumatic tube no less!

Behind his back, where the other men could not see, Smith's hands were clenched and trembling. The casual negligence being carried out right under his nose, the negligence of the entire system and philosophy of maritime practice, the negligence *of which he himself was a part*, once revealed, was shocking.

"I've finished, Captain," Boxhall said at last, and stepped back so that the other men assembled might see. As Smith stared at the chart, trying to stem the involuntary quiver of his hands, he heard Moody, a quiet, observant type of fellow, inhale softly. In the corner of his eye he could see Murdoch's jaw clench.

It was easy to understand their discomfort. Once tallied, all the reports of ice, which Boxhall had joined up with ruler-straight lines, formed a deadly wall right across the path of *Titanic*'s projected course. Silently, Smith measured the area demarked against lines of latitude and longitude; correctly scaled, they indicated a vast region of ice approximately sixty miles long by ten miles across.

"This, gentlemen..." he waved a hand over the chart, as if trying to erase the new evidence with a magician's wand. "This is the region into which we steamed last night at over twenty-two knots, the highest speed we attained during this voyage. Were the ship empty it would be bad enough, but entrusted to our care was not only *Titanic* herself, but all who sail in her, some two thousand and two hundred lives."

Turning on his heel he strode back out to the bridge, this time exiting onto the starboard wing. From decks beneath could be heard the clamour and cries of men at work shoring up the ship, and moored directly off to *Titanic*'s side was the dark hull of the *Viking*. His eyes fell upon the looming *Anatoly Sagalevich*, ghostly grey in the dim light, spotlights picking out the wreckage carried on her aft deck as she manoeuvred towards a bulbous orange boat caught in the swell. Recognising it as the lifeboat dropped by the *Seguin Laroche*, Smith felt another pang of guilt; in the chaos of last night he had completely forgotten about the little craft and the quotient of the *Titanic's* passengers she had been laden with after Mr Wilde had been… murdered.

Further off, *Oceanic* brooded like a sleeping colossus. And all around them were icebergs, some of the smaller growlers interposing themselves between the various ships, while their larger cousins formed a seemingly impenetrable wall to the north, south and west. A patch of open sea to the south marked the area that had been transposed with 2012, but only to the east did open water stretch as far as the horizon, a deceptive channel through which *Titanic* had steamed into this inlet of the ice-field. Had she not collided with that fatal berg last night, she surely would have chanced upon another within minutes.

"The facts speak for themselves…" he declared to the gathered men. "Yesterday evening I ordered a slight adjustment of our course, hoping to skirt the little ice we believed we might encounter. But that only led us deeper into the heart of this graveyard. Had any of us bothered to tabulate the warnings we had been given, we would have known to swing many miles further south, thus safeguarding our ship, our crewmates, and our precious human cargo. As it is, our mistakes have led to much loss of life, including our dear friend Henry Wilde, yet it is but a small sampling of the tragedy that might have been…"

He spun around sharply. "We cannot chance that there will be further ships adventuring out of time to save us from our next mistake."

As if to strike a note of accord, *Oceanic* suddenly blasted a proud note on her horns, and *Titanic's* deck crew turned. The other White Star liner, a century out of her time and looming over the surrounding ice like a sea monster, was calling their attention as something strange began happening on her uppermost deck. A noise like a rapid-firing engine could be heard, and then a tangle of machinery that Smith had thought to be part of the other vessel's complex superstructure separated from the deck and, amazingly, flew upwards, born on what seemed to be a swirling set of quick-spinning wings.

"A flying machine…" he heard William Murdoch say aloud, and turned to see the First Officer staring upwards in stunned disbelief. Quickly the craft ascended even higher, until it was just a shining speck in the crisp blue sky, poised over a thousand feet above the smoking, fuming funnels of the gathered ships. Then it began to slowly fly in a wide circle, weaving its way about high above the icebergs.

Moments later, a second, larger craft took off from the *Anatoly Sagalevich*, joining its fellow in patrolling the skies over the ice field.

"What are they doing?" Pitman asked, squinting hard to try and make out the now tiny craft.

"They're scouting…" replied Moody, one hand cupped to his chin in contemplation. "Trying to plot the fleet's course out of this maze of ice."

"Bloody impressive…" Lowe said, before coughing to cover his language. "Apologies."

"None taken, Mr Lowe," Smith replied, waving away any indecency. "It *is* impressive." He slowly looked around at the marvelling officers and wireless operators.

"It is certain to say that, had this ship sunk, there would have been investigations on both sides of the ocean…" he began, speaking carefully. "From them would arise new recommendations to prevent a disaster such as this from being repeated. But now that there has been no wreck, it is altogether possible that such enquiries will not be deemed necessary, or that they will focus on our guests, their journey, and the world from which they hail. As such, it falls to us to conduct our own investigation, to determine what needs to change in maritime navigation to ensure that last night's events are not repeated again, lest we wait until another disaster at sea shakes the world to wakefulness. Our failings bring upon us this responsibility, do we agree, gentlemen?"

"We were charging into ice…" Murdoch said by way of answer, eyes narrowed in thought. "Because we believed it safe to do so and that we could see any obstacle well in time to turn, that greater speed on the engines would increase the ship's manoeuvrability and make dodging any obstructions easier… those assumptions must change."

"Worse than that, Mr Murdoch," added Moody, his words blunt. "We were complacent. We travelled at speed in wilful ignorance of any dangers. Could any of us have foreseen a collision with that iceberg, so shrivelled were our imaginations with hubris and false confidence?"

"Our side was vulnerable," put in Lowe. "Her bows and stern are reinforced to deal with head-on-collisions, but we were struck on the beam. Double hulls or greater strength in the shell plating would safeguard against that."

"Better wireless procedures," suggested Pitman, briefly casting an eye at the abashed Phillips and Bride. "We should not for any reason disregard messages pertaining to navigation, nor should commercial traffic between ships, shore and passengers be given priority. And twenty-four hour wireless watches should be mandatory, so that every ship so equipped has her ears open night and day."

"And more lifeboats…" Boxhall said at last. "Enough for everyone on board, and carried in such a manner than they can be launched with a minimum of fuss. We did well last night to launch the number that we did, but there needs to be a revision of lifeboats in general; at the very least additional craft might have floated off the ship and provided artificial islands for people in the water to cling too."

As the officers continued to put out ideas, Smith's eyes focused on the flying machine orbiting overhead. Some international organisation, equipped with such airborne craft or fast, light oceangoing vessels, should exist to monitor ice drifting into sea lanes, and report on the hazards they might pose to navigation, which would dovetail nicely with Moody's thoughts on wireless traffic…

"Excellent…" he nodded, directed his attention back at them. "You are all qualified mariners, gentlemen; continue to think on the mistakes made by ourselves and our colleagues, so we might endeavour to right those shortcomings. Document every recommendation you might come up with, no matter how trivial it might seem."

"And yourself, Captain?" Murdoch probed gently. "What do you plan upon doing?"

"I intend to finally meet with these time-travellers," Smith replied. "They have come a great distance to our aid, and I believe before any further decisions are made that we must arrange a gathering of minds to decide on our course of action. Quartermaster Wynn!"

"Yes, captain?" came the reply from beyond the bridge.

"I understand that our wireless is currently inoperable for reasons beyond my understanding," Smith continued, also casting an eye towards the equally perplexed Marconi-men. "Therefore, please man the Morse lamp, as I wish to put out an invitation to the Captains of all the gathered ships. All are invited to join us this afternoon for a light luncheon, a discussion of our current situation and planning a common course forward from this point. Ask them to RSVP."

The light laughter that followed from the gathered officers added a strange touch of gallows humour to the conclusion of the meeting. Smith found himself smiling, too, as he and Murdoch headed off to begin a full inspection of the ship.

But lurking underneath it all was the fear that none of this would be enough to make amends for everything he had gotten so horribly wrong.

*

The interior of the tiny Mir-3 submersible was not exactly spacious. Thomas Andrews squatted uncomfortably in the corner, feeling another bit of metal jab into him. A small fan whirred away within the casing that he had banged into; he supposed it was some sort of air purifier. He shifted around awkwardly in the unfamiliar overalls he had been given to wear, Cyrillic lettering stencilled over his breast, and then with a thud his head came roughly into contact with a low pipe.

"Blast it."

"Stop fidgeting," a deep voice whose accent hailed from somewhere west of the Urals interjected. "You only make it worse if you try and make more room. *Tolya* is submersible, not... erm, how is it you say in English, 'gin-palace'."

Thomas stared at Captain Gorbachev, the Russian with the big voice lying prone beside him inside the tiny space. "Gin palace? I don't understand."

"You know, luxury boat. Yacht."

"Ah!" Thomas's mind cleared. Yes, on reflection, 'Gin Palace' seemed a good way to describe some of the private yachts he had been on in his life. And then his face darkened.

The captain noticed and turned on his side. "I say something wrong?"

"Oh no... Gin Palace sounds right," Thomas laughed humourlessly. "No it's just that... my uncle, Lord Pirrie, is recovering from surgery right now, and he's gone on a voyage to the Baltic to recover, on his own yacht, *Valiant*."

"Your uncle... he is close to you?"

"Yes indeed. But he owns Harland & Wolff shipyards, so he's also my employer."

"Hmm... he would have taken news of ship sinking badly then?"

The thought of someone coming to the aging William Pirrie with the news that his latest and greatest ship had sunk, taking the nephew he was grooming to succeed him with her, chilled Thomas. They might as well have put a gun to the poor man and shot him where he lay.

He turned onto his own side. "Captain Gorbachev... did you have family back, back in the future...?"

Anton Gorbachev punched silently at a few buttons for a second, and nodded. "Da, a brother and two nieces, three cousins. No wife or children, but big family. Much love between us."

"I see..." Thomas replied, but not really, as he looked through one of the tiny portholes off to his side. Technicians and sailors scurried like ants on the decks of the *Anatoly Sagalevich* as they prepared to launch the submersible from the deck of the research vessel. Like Gorbachev, his own family was also massive, and he had several brothers, each raising their own brood. He could not see them responding to his own absence with anything other than distress. But Gorbachev was so calm that he seemed to felt nothing. He looked towards the other man with pity in his eyes.

"You cry for me?" the heavyset Russian grunted, before smiling sadly. "Is no need. The family already lose my father and first brother, fighting in Afghanistan. We survive their loss, though sad for it, but we survive. We survived Stalin's purges in days of my grandfathers, hardships of perestroika when the Union collapsed... we will always survive..."

The words meant nothing to Thomas, but he understood the tone. Before he could ask any questions, though, the deep-voiced captain suddenly smiled, beaming widely in a manner that made his ears rise like engine governors. "Besides, we may yet go back, find world not changed... like film, *'Ivan Vasilievich Changes Profession'*."

The dim light from the open hatch above suddenly vanished as a third person climbed down the hatch. Thomas half expected it to be Miss Paik, based on the excitable girl's ability to find her way into any place she desired, but instead it was Kai Alinka. Gorbachev gestured for the Hawaiian to take the third place, and Thomas shifted aside his notepad and pencil to make room. He winced as he got a clear view of the other man, however; Kai's face was red and shiny, from a mixture of burns and an antiseptic salve that had been spread over them.

The younger man made eye contact with him and shook his head, rasping lightly. "Feel bad for Lightoller, not me; he dived into that boiler room without anything to protect him other than his clothes."

Thomas had heard; Lightoller was still under observation in *Titanic*'s hospital. "Don't sell yourself short, Mr Alinka; I heard what you did for the ship, and the price you nearly paid."

"Yeah, well I was a bit of an idiot about it," Kai replied softly. "The captain's chewed me out for it already, told me to rest up... but I can't, I've got to keep moving, fixing, doing. So I thought I'd come along in the Mir and take notes for you."

"Well, I appreciate it. Thank you."

There was a deep thud as Gorbachev, now on his feet, pulled shut the interior hatch and folded the access ladder into place, before getting back in his prone position behind one of the tiny fish-eye portholes.

"Mir-3, ready for launch."

Within the sealed space all outside sounds were muffled, but Thomas could still hear the whine of the external motors and winced. Moments later, the cabin lurched upwards as the submersible was hoisted up out of its cradle. Freed from the deck, it began to softly swing to and fro. Through the porthole he could see the green Atlantic waters swirling in the wake of one of the Zodiac motorboats, churned up as if by sharks circling a dangling morsel.

And then they dropped into the sea.

*

When he was a nine-year-old boy, Nashat Abu Shakra's family had taken the *Hajj*, the sacred pilgrimage to Mecca. After six laps around the courtyard of the al-Haram Mosque, circling the sacred Kaaba, the House of God built by the hands of Ibrahim and Ismail, the heat and sun had overwhelmed him, and Nash awoke to find himself ashamed and dehydrated in a hospital ward, his mother holding his hand as he vomited into a bucket.

Now a grown man, he once again woke from blissful oblivion to feel his head reeling and nausea racking his body. Instinctively he rolled to one side and found someone holding a pan for him to vomit into. Gratefully he accepted their offer, his chest expunging great hacking breaths until only a few thin trails of spittle hung from his mouth. He tried to bring up his hand to wipe them away, only to feel it stop suddenly, held in place by some restraint. He flexed his arm again and heard the soft clinking of chains drawn tight. His left arm was handcuffed to the bed.

"Here... hold still," someone said in English, the voice suggesting no room for argument as they held a cloth to his face and rubbed away the last of the filth.

"Thank you," he grunted, still trying to get his bearings.

"You're welcome," the voice replied; male, English-speaking but not British-accented, maybe Irish, elderly, authoritative. Possibly a doctor... "Well, I'll notify them that you're awake."

Hunched on his side, all Nash could see was the back of his host's uniform jacket as the man crossed to the door, shutting it behind him. This side of the door was painted white, lying flush with the plainly-panelled wall. His roving eyes turned towards the floor; black and white tiles laid out in a geodesic pattern.

Too weak to hold himself in his position, he lay back and stared upwards. An electric light in a plain fitting stared down at him, unlit, and the airy room was illuminated by brilliant light streaming in through an open porthole. The faint scent of antiseptics lingered in the air.

He was in a ship's hospital, handcuffed to a gurney. Thoughts of torture swam blurrily in his mind and he pounded them into silence, noting that he was attached to a blood-pack on an IV drip; from his experience, jailors tended to not care as to the well-being of their subjects.

But how had he gotten here? He thought back, remembering the sirens and alarms emanating from the *Liberty Bell*, and how he had tackled Abercrombie… then there had been a lifeboat, and a ship… for some reason the identity of the ship seemed important, but he couldn't focus through a dull pain in his abdomen.

He looked down slowly, and gingerly felt at his abdomen. He was heavily bandaged there, and through the fog dulling his thoughts he could remember a pain, a hot pain like a superheated knife jammed into his gut.

He had been shot. Abercrombie had shot him.

Whatever vessel he was now aboard, that ship's resident surgeon had evidently sewn him up and put him on a blood transfusion. He tugged lightly at the cuffs securing him.

Yet they still see fit to restrain me.

Once again he looked around, trying to spot some clue as to his situation. Despite the lingering smell of disinfectant, the room looked brand new, all the paintwork gleaming with a lustre that suggested this was a new facility. And yet aside from the stainless-steel IV stand he could not see any of the pieces of equipment he would associate with a hospital, not even a computer on the small desk at the foot of his bed. It was downright primitive.

He looked in the other direction, and tensed. A second bed was set against the wall opposite him, and lying on the sheets was another man, heavily bandaged below the neck and breathing slowly.

"Hey…" he said, and the other man nodded. His face was bright red and glistening with antiseptic salve, but as best as Nash could tell, the man was not one of the *Seguin Laroche*'s crew, which begged the question of how he had gotten so badly burned.

What else had happened while he had been unconscious?

The sound of feet on the deck brought his attention back to the present, and he pushed himself backwards, despite the pain in his belly, managing to get himself propped up against the wall before the door opened.

Four figures entered the room, two of them men dressed in severe navy-blue uniforms. He tensed, and then realised that these men were surely merchant seaman and not members of the armed forces, as neither of their caps featured a fouled anchor in the badge; instead both of them depicted a raked pennant adorned with a white star.

The design looked familiar to him, but before he could scrounge through his memory, he recognised the other two people who had just entered the room, and felt himself tense with sudden confusion and fear.

Capitaine Joanna Laroche and Jabril Hab Allah.

"Captain Laroche, is this man part of your crew?" the eldest of the three men enquired of the woman. His neatly trimmed white beard and the medals on his uniform seemed as familiar to Nash as the emblem on his cap, but he could not say where from.

"Yes, Captain Smith; he was my Bosun." She met Nash's gaze and for a moment they exchanged a thousand words, before his attention shifted to Jabril, who despite his serious demeanour winked surreptitiously.

Seeing that, Nash felt himself relax, and as if letting the tension go his thoughts cleared, and suddenly the things he had noticed came together in his mind.

"We travelled in time!" he said, trying to sit upright and immediately regretting it as the pain in his stomach reignited.

"Easy, lie back down," soothed the second man in uniform, an elderly gentleman with a kindly disposition and a magnificent handlebar moustache, who Nash supposed was the doctor who had stitched him up. "You were quite badly torn up by that shot."

Nash nodded and caught his breath, but persisted in speaking. He knew where they were, and needed to voice his realisation aloud.

"This is the *Titanic*…" he gasped, pointing at the bearded officer. "You're Captain EJ Smith."

"Bright lad," Smith nodded, smiling, before directing his attention to the other figure in the bed. "Hello, Charles; you're looking a bit worse for wear from last night."

The man grunted once in reply, and Nash saw Smith's eyes twinkling with mirth as he explained aloud how he was injured. "Mr Lightoller is one of my officers; he courageously swam through a boiler room full of hot water and chemical fumes to help repair part of the ship."

Lightoller merely grunted again, lifting a hand as if indicating that it was nothing.

"And my utmost thanks to you as well, young man," Smith continued, turning to Nash and bowing formally. "I understand from Captain Laroche that you were instrumental in the events that have resulted in the saving of my ship; furthermore, my officers have confirmed that you aided in subduing the gentleman responsible for both the mutiny aboard your ship and the murder of two of my crew."

Abercrombie? Nash's eyes flicked to Laroche and Jabril as his mind turned over at maximum revolutions. *You've pinned everything on him? Why? And how are we on the Titanic, and what's this about other ships?*

"…the bullet from this 'assault rifle' that struck you was almost certainly a ricochet," the doctor was explaining. "Despite the apparent severity of the wound, the shot did not have the kinetic energy to penetrate deep into your abdominal cavity or inflict massive trauma. You had a lucky escape, however – the round narrowly missed your stomach and ended up nicking your abdominal aorta – it was only the presence of the bullet itself plugging the hole that kept you from bleeding out. Now, I've not got much experience with gunshot wounds, but I've treated enough casualties from engine-room accidents to know a bit about how to get shrapnel out and stave off infection, so you're alright for now. But once you're safe enough to move, we'll be

400

getting you onto one of the other ships so you can have the best care available…"

Nash nodded his understanding, and Captain Smith motioned towards the door. "Well, with Doctor O'Loughlin's permission, he and I shall leave the three of you to get reacquainted."

He tipped his cap towards Nash, Jabril and Laroche, and made his exit. As Smith pushed the door open, however, Nash observed two men outside in uniforms of the twenty-first century, each carrying an assault rifle much like the F1 that had made a mess of him. Then the door was swinging shut and Captain Laroche was advancing on the bed, a small metal object glinting in her hands; he realised that it was the key to the handcuffs restraining him to the bed frame.

"They must have feared you'd try to escape from the hospital," Jab said breezily as the two of them released his bonds and helped him sit up in the bed. "With your stomach sewn up as it is, trying to leave unassisted might have killed you."

The context of the guards, however, laced his words with massive context. Evidently the *Seguin Laroche* was not the only vessel to have come back in time, and though the people of 1912 were no-doubt ignorant of 'modern' politics their contemporaries were probably making speculative theories connecting the French container ship and her Arabian crew.

"Well done for what you did last night," Laroche said aloud, with surprising conviction. "Jabril tells me that you and Pierre almost forestalled this entire mess, though as you saw, the people here are very glad that the *Liberty Bell* fired as it did."

So that was the framework they were building, was it? Well it would certainly dovetail with Captain Smith's perception of him being a hero.

"What's the status of the *Bell* now?" he replied, massaging his wrist where the cuffs had chafed it.

"Intact and operational," Jabril replied briskly. "It was salvaged before the *Seguin Laroche* sank."

"Sank?" Nash's head spun towards Capitaine Laroche, who held up a hand.

"Please, don't offer commiserations. I'm coming to terms with it on my own, and it makes it easier if everyone isn't expressing their sympathies for the loss of my ship."

"What about the crew?" he asked, and winced at the sudden pained look that flashed across both of their faces.

"Benjamin Khan and Pierre Fontaine are dead as a result of the mutiny and subsequent fire," Jabril said at last. "Along with almost all of the *Seguin Laroche*'s deck crew. The survivors from the engineering staff are being hosted aboard the *Carpathia* and *Californian* until a course of action is decided upon by the masters of the fleet."

Nash moaned softly at the devastating loss, but didn't voice his grief at the failure of the plan, aware of the chance that the room was being monitored, even by as low-tech a means as a guard pressing an ear to the other side of the door.

"Then, what is our situation?" he ventured at last. "What's this about a fleet?"

"We were not the only ships moved in time to the present day – which is 1912, by the way – four other vessels came with us into the past, including a British missile submarine," Jabril said darkly, before his tone moderated. "That said, her doctor provided the necessary equipment and supplies that helped keep you alive; blood groups and transfusions have only just been discovered in this day and age."

"Oh, I was a complete idiot!" Nash said, lightly banging the back of his head against the bedrail.

"It was nothing of your doing that brought us back here," Jabril said soothingly. "Adrian Abercrombie bears responsibility for bribing members of the crew to steal the *Liberty Bell*, and he has paid his debts…"

Nash frowned at that statement, and then Captain Laroche caught his eye and nodded subtly towards Lightoller, still lying in the other bed.

Their cover story is coming together… he understood. *And the Capitaine is helping to deflect responsibility onto Abercrombie. But still, why?*

Clearing his throat, he carried on, trying to keep his own words aligned with their apparent scenario.

"Well, I know Abercrombie is to blame, but it is still my fault that we got shunted into the past. You charged me with rendering the *Liberty Bell* safe, *capitaine*, but I did not resolve the fault in time."

"What brought us here, Nash?" Jabril asked, radiating intensity of purpose. "You said that the internal clocks were out of alignment; fighting with each other, but how did that take us to the side of *Titanic*?"

"Because the difference was exactly a hundred years, right down to the second. One set of clocks had the right day, Saturday April 14th 2012, but the other thought that it was Sunday, April 14th 1912."

"Wait a second," Laroche interrupted. "Are you saying that everything that went wrong, the reason we ended up in the past, was the '*Millennium Bug*'!?"

"Yes!" Nash laughed, and immediately regretted how the action tore at his tender abdomen. "Some of the older software dated from 1994, and never received a Y2K patch, but the remainder came with those updates by default, along with a leap-year rectifying patch. The result was a conflict that caused the system to crash repeatedly and threw us back precisely a hundred years…"

"I don't understand," a new voice broke in. "What is this Millennium Bug?"

*

Charles Lightoller's mother had died when he was just a baby, and his father had run away to sea during his childhood, leaving him parentless. However, he had possibly inherited some of his father's wanderlust, because eventually Charles too became a sailor, seeking his fortune on the high seas. After his apprenticeship he had plied sailing ships between England, Australia and South America, and eventually graduated to steamships. But it had not proved enough to satisfy his thirst for adventure, and so he had abandoned the sea and in 1898 went prospecting for gold in the Yukon.

In less than a year he was bankrupt, and so had travelled as a 'gentleman tramp' across the length and breadth of the Canadian railway system, with the goal of making it back to Great Britain, taking work as an itinerant cattle-handler along the way to pay for his sea-passage.

The man who had set first foot back on the docks in England was one who had not a penny to his name, but who at the time had endured enough adventure to satisfy a lifetime of tall tales. Yes, 1899 had been a rollover year for him, and in January of 1900 he had started anew, taking a position with the White Star Line as fourth officer on the new SS *Medic*, a choice that ultimately led him to meet his beloved wife Sylvia aboard the *Suevic*, she a passenger, he a well-regarded officer of the line.

So now, lying in *Titanic's* hospital with nothing better to do than listen to the three people's technical double-talk, his ears pricked up when he heard them make reference to the turn of the twenty-first century, and wondered if it had held the same relevance to them as the dawn of the twentieth had to him.

"Well... the Millennium Bug is hard to explain..." began the youth named Nash, who had been shot by the same man who had killed Henry Wilde. "I don't know if you've had any contact with our future technology, especially our 'thinking machines'..."

"I am quite familiar with the concept of a 'computer', if that is what you mean," Charles replied grandly, thinking back to the device Miss Paik had brought aboard.

"Alright..." Nash replied, before clearing his throat. "All computers have an internal clock which keeps track of the time and date all year round. In 1999, many people came to believe that at Midnight on New Year's Eve, many such clocks would reset to January 1st 1900, instead of January 1st 2000, causing widespread chaos. That is what happened here. The *Liberty Bell*, apparently left in storage for over a decade-and-a-half, ended up confused over what the base year was."

"So someone built a 'time-machine', that was unable to tell the time," Charles smirked, before chortling to himself. "Hilarious."

"Quite," Nash replied dryly, before Charles saw him look back up at his two superiors. "Last night I was trying to get the *Liberty Bell* to safely discharge by making it carry-out a one-second jump into the future, and the mis-configured clocks interpreted that to mean a 100-year jump to 1912. Before I could work around that problem, Abercrombie shot me."

After a moment's pause he gave an inarticulate shout of frustration and beat one fist against the rail of the bed, before falling into a gloomy, pained silence.

"There's no point in crying over 'what ifs' now," Laroche said briskly, and Charles was impressed at the professional composure of the female mariner. "We're here, and we still have the *Liberty Bell* – for the moment, at least."

She and the ethnic gentleman named Hab Allah left shortly after, leaving Nash and Charles to rest, recover and heal, but neither of them seemed able to simply lie down and sleep.

He could not say what it was that troubled his fellow patient, but for Charles, his flippant comments masked a deep wellspring of questions that had first been tapped last night when he realised his culpability in the death of Fireman Barrett, and then withheld that information from Miss Paik.

Who are you, Charles Lightoller? You've already seen one world's history call you a hero, but what about this new world? That lad Nash made his mistake over this 'Millennium Bug' sound like a schoolboy error, something that should have been caught and noticed from the very start. What similar mistakes might we on Titanic make now, or have committed already?

And, as before, his thoughts came back to a single worry.

Are you a righteous man, Charles Lightoller?

Unbeknownst to him, across on the other side of the hospital ward, in the opposite bed, Nashat Abu Shakra was worrying about something less spiritual and more temporal in nature.

What are Jabril and Laroche planning?

*

As Mir-3, or as Gorbachev kept referring to it, '*Tolya*', descended along *Titanic*'s hull, Thomas forced himself to bide his time, instead turning to a piece of paper slipped inside his notebook. It was a diagram of *Titanic*'s forward hull, amazingly duplicated from one of his blueprints by the researchers aboard the *Anatoly Sagalevich*. With his pencil, he began to neatly mark down each of the main uprights for the hull, numbering the frames from bow to stern.

"Mysta Andrews," the Russian captain softly growled, like a purring engine. "We are here."

He indicated for Thomas to lie down on the mattress on the opposite side of the cabin, and indicated towards a pair of monitors that stood to one side of the small porthole. "Is live feed from camera on end of the manipulator arm. You say where you need it pointed, and I do."

Thomas nodded, and all but pressed his face to the screens and port. *Tolya* was coming alongside the *Titanic*'s hull, where the ship's bottom rose up to form the bowsprit. Even without the light from the submersible's cameras, the diffuse light from the surface was enough to lend the hull a pale blue glow.

Directly below the ocean shaded to black, and he tried to not visualise that he was now hovering over a two-mile deep abyss, not carried safely on top of it aboard a ship. He forced his attention back to the vessel beyond their fragile hull, comparing his own view of *Titanic* through the port with that on the monitors. The detail was so crisp that he could see the first barnacles making their homes on the metal. Thoughts of indignation were quelled, though, as he spotted several mangled plates just a few feet back from the bow, a black line showing between them as if to underscore the damage. Visually, the two buckled plates and the open seam looked like a leering mouth.

"Kai, can you take notes?" he called, receiving a confirmation grunt from the other man. "Two deformed plates and an open seam, about nine inches in length, five feet aft from the bowsprit. It looks like this is what flooded the forepeak tank. I estimate it was caused by the ship coming back against the berg when Mr Murdoch tried to swing the stern clear."

Kai's pencil scribbled for a few seconds, and then paper rustled as he checked against some notes. "That conforms with the findings of the 1996 Expedition."

Thomas nodded, and indicated for Gorbachev to take them further aft along the ship's hull. One of the remarkable adjustments he'd had to make in light of recent events was how much work had gone into determining the damage inflicted upon *Titanic*, research conducted by people yet to be born. The notion that eighty-four years hence, someone would use a device called 'sonar', harnessing sound itself, to search for evidence of iceberg damage on *Titanic*'s wreck was incredible.

Strangely, he had already reconciled the fact that *Titanic* had truly sunk in another time with what he currently was looking at. Having been able to touch the massive chunk of wreckage on the *Anatoly Sagalevich*'s rear deck, and match it to his memories of constructing that part of the ship, had finally convinced him.

So here he was, amazingly examining his ship from the outside, in the middle of the open sea.

The 1996 expedition's findings listed six intermittent wounds in the hull, extending over 249 feet of the ship's length, he thought to himself, refreshing his memory with information gathered aboard the Russian research vessel. The problem he faced now was determining which of these holes were caused by the iceberg, and which were created when the sinking hull crashed down onto the Atlantic floor, compressing like an accordion as it did.

"There is next hole," Gorbachev slowly intoned, and Thomas hissed. Unlike the first wound, a 'trace' entry, what he was now looking at was like an ugly scar that refused to heal, extending out of sight. Again, consulting with his plans and counting the frames, he dictated the damage to Kai, observing how clean the break between the plates was.

It's like the two plates pulled apart like a portcullis sliding up, guillotining the rivets at their necks.

By the time they reached Boiler Room 5, however, he knew that there was something that they were missing. Although the collision mats placed alongside the Boiler Rooms hid the damage there, he estimated it confirmed with the 1996 expedition's finding of a 45-foot-long shear between the plates, and he had found a sixteen-foot-long tear broaching Cargo Hold 3, which collision with the seabed in the first timeline had split open to become the thirty-two-foot gap observed on the sonar graph.

But that left no obvious source of flooding to Cargo Holds 1 and 2.

Thomas rapped his pencil thoughtfully against the glass of the hull, tapping out a tune in his head. Kai's near death experience last night had shown that there was significant damage to the underside of the hull; now he needed to confront the degree of that severity.

"Captain Gorbachev, please take us lower."

Obligingly, Anton made tiny adjustments to his controls and *Tolya* sank deeper. Again, Tom's eyes drifted down to where the blue water faded into the dark below, and shivered at the thought of *Titanic*'s wreck, lying shattered on the ocean floor like some pagan ruin, succumbing to time and tide.

I am Ozymandias, king of kings. Look on my works, ye mighty, and despair...

With Shelley's words hanging over him like a brooding presence, he leaned forward, watching the video feed as Gorbachev deployed the ROV named *Aelita* and directed the little vehicle's cameras up at the bottom of the hull.

"Oh dear God..." Thomas quietly blasphemed. "It filleted her like a fish."

Underneath the fireman's staircase, where he had seen water coming in, the bottom of the hull was crumpled in on the starboard side, exposing the subdivided tanks that made up the ship's double bottom. Some of the internal bracing was mangled and deformed, but the outer hull itself was just gone.

Here and there, patches of expanded DRP foam could be seen, where Kai had sealed up several points of entry for the water, and turning to the Hawaiian Thomas expressed his appreciation, which was quietly deferred.

Then *Tolya* motored slowly moved forward and he counted the exposed frames. The damage extended forward along the starboard underside from frame number 111 right along to 132, exposing nearly fifty feet of the ship's double bottom to the sea when she grounded on the ice. The damage was not uniform, however. Here and there the plates were still intact, but bent and mangled from running over the ice. Elsewhere, they were simply gone, peeled from the hull like slivers of soap.

"Is incredible," Gorbachev praised quietly. "How did she not sink in minutes with such big hole?"

Again Thomas thought of Ed Wilding's twelve square feet. "Because this damage only flooded the double-bottom. It was designed to protect the ship in case she ever ran aground or hit an underwater obstruction. But I never imagined anything on this scale…"

He paused, and then waved a hand in explanation. "When the bottom was mangled like this, the iceberg broke through the inner hull in places, either by direct contact, or from where the shock displacement of the outer hull travelled through the internal structure and deformed the inner shell." He shrugged. "Water pressure did the rest."

Kai had become very silent, and Thomas suspected he was thinking of that poor crewman whose body he had discovered inside the fireman's tunnel. He wondered what the man had seen, or felt; a grinding jar, followed by thin jets of water spurting up through the floor with incredible force? Or maybe the deck had actually jumped up underneath him, throwing him down the stairs and into an awkward landing… no, he shouldn't focus on that.

The main issue was clear; Harland and Wolff's design, *his design*, had failed to protect the ship. It had come close, but in Tom's estimation, close was not good enough.

Coming to the forward end of Cargo Hold One, they found where *Titanic* had first come onto the ice. Where the hull rose up in an elegant curve to the base of the bowsprit, the double bottom was staved in, as if someone had punched the ship right in her vulnerable underbelly.

Thomas spent a long time staring at the impact, eyeing with some concern its proximity to the keel, the backbone which gave the hull its strength. The damage flirted with the immense girder throughout its whole length, and in places the keel had been scuffed and gouged; and yet it still seemed to be straight and true, not pushed out of alignment.

"Well?" he heard Kai Alinka say, the younger man leaning forward to stare at the damage on the screens. "Do you think it's safe to move her?"

Again Thomas rapped his pencil against the hull, aware that he was probably letting it develop into a nervous tic.

"I think that, if we could perhaps fill some of this damage with the last of the DRP foam supplies, then yes, she should be able to make way again."

The other two men nodded, and Thomas looked down at the sheet of paper before him, on which he had begun to sketch out a diagram, crowned by four scribbled words.

WE MUST DO BETTER

*

"You still haven't told me why you haven't had me locked up as your Head Mutineer, Capitaine…" Jab Hab Allah said softly, as he and Joanna Laroche walked along *Titanic*'s A-Deck Promenade, killing time. "You did not out me to the crew of the *Carpathia*, introduced me as your trusted Cadet Officer, invited me to come over to *Titanic* with you, and even released Nashat from his restraints."

The sun was passing its zenith now, and the teak decking seemed to glow with fresh varnish.

"Don't for a moment assume it's because I've forgiven you," she said, striding along with fists clenched. "I might be handling the loss of the *Seguin Laroche*, but your little game of 'smuggle the time-machine' cost the lives of all my deck officers and many others. Nor have I forgotten how you unloaded a gun at point-blank range into my fiancé's head!"

He nodded slowly as they turned a corner, completing a full lap of the deck. "Which is even more reason for exposing me. Yet you've even convinced the surviving crew of the *Seguin Laroche* to not denounce Nashat and myself, despite the evident suspicions of our British and American contemporaries."

"No, Cadet Officer, you don't get off that easily…" she hissed sibilantly. "All that's keeping me from that recourse is a realisation that you don't appear to be a terrorist, and the fact that we're all in enough trouble as it is without confusing things with twenty-first century politics."

He shrugged as they turned a corner, completing a full lap of the deck and starting on a second.

"As it is," she continued, "to the people of this era you're simply my senior surviving crewman, and I'm fine with letting them believe that. I'll even defend your character should anyone from forward in time bring up the coincidence of an illegal device being transported aboard a ship that had a considerably large number of Arabs onboard. I doubt that man Lightoller picked up on the subtext of our conversation in the hospital, and all I'm going to tell the crew of *Viking* and *Rescue* is that neither you nor Nash knew what was in that container, and Abercrombie and his cash-bought mutineers forced an attempt to fix the *Liberty Bell* at gunpoint when it malfunctioned."

"And if evidence arises that I led the attack…"

"*It won't!*" she cut him off, pausing in her step. "The only survivors who witnessed what transpired on the bridge are the two of us. And I've already won the crew's complicity – they'll back up my story…"

They had come out to the rear of the promenade now, where *Titanic*'s mainmast sprouted from the deck like a leafless tree, and now she leaned against it, arms folded, awaiting what he would say next. Jabril glanced around and confirmed that there was no-one within earshot before leaning in close to her.

"You would not go to all this effort without some reason other than simply keeping the peace," he said in a low voice. "You mentioned survivors, consider this; of my team only Nashat and myself are still alive, and neither of us are much of a threat. We could be both confined to the hospital or pushed overboard and I doubt anyone would notice."

"Nash is a kid who did not once attack anybody last night, and you cried over the body of a thug who wanted to do something obscene involving my mouth and the business end of a rifle," she replied bluntly. "Neither of you seem to be the stereotypical radicals who fly planes into buildings or walk into supermarkets wearing C4 waistcoats. You wanted to use the *Liberty Bell* for something, but I doubt it was the destruction of the state of Israel or the usual fundamentalist *merde*."

He snorted and walked past her to lean on the rail. "I am an Arab Nationalist, Capitaine Laroche; I very much wish to see the abolition of Israel and the establishment of a great unified republic reaching from the Mediterranean to the Himalayas." Then he paused and sighed. "But I would not want to see it accomplished with needless war and bloodshed. I may despise Israel's existence, but I have no quarrel with its citizenry. And a state founded on blood will die by that blood – there is no future in mindless *jihad*."

"Well, that's a contradiction."

"So says a descendant of the French Revolution?" he replied sarcastically. "Those who instigate bloody reigns of terror are more often than not hoist by their own petards. Your Monsieur Maximilien Robespierre comes to mind, executed with the same guillotine that he wielded against the French aristocracy. Compare such men to the example led by America's venerated founding fathers, or even their 'Great Emancipator', Abraham Lincoln, who trumpeted a righteous cause and did so with civil legislation as much as armed conflict."

"So now you're comparing yourself to slaveholding hypocrites and a man who ruled as a tyrant, by wartime fiat? And need I remind you that, by modern standards, those men were all racists."

"You know your history, I grant you. But remember the complexity of those times, and remember what those flawed men still achieved. And look to the true exemplars such as Frederick Douglass or Thaddeus Stevens. The firebrands and champions of righteousness and justice, the men unafraid to speak against the age and administer potent and unwelcome medicines to cure evils other men championed as holy. I saw the *Liberty Bell* as the gateway to such a medicine."

"So what, you wanted to be the Martin Luther King of the Arabian Gulf?"

"No," he said without pause. "I am a man who has killed brutally and without mercy in the past, who surely has lost all favour with God. Place me in power and I will be another Saddam Hussein or Osama Bin Laden, ruling without divine or civil mandate. But the riots and uprisings of recent years, in Tunisia, Libya, Egypt and Syria, have shown that there is a thirst in the Middle East for democracy and the rule of law. But such men as I once was will turn this popular movement to yet more chaos and conflict and theocratic tyranny, unless a great leader such as He who first founded Islam can be found to unite the people."

"So you wanted a Prophet, or a great legislator, or a champion of democracy?" she tapped the toe of her boot thoughtfully on the deck, gazing out towards the horizon. "There could be men or women who fit that bill anywhere out there right now, but it's a funny thing with life that you can't tell if someone was destined for greatness until they've already done their work and died. History is all about weighing the lives of individuals in retrospect."

"Not when you have a time machine…" he said softly, waving his arm towards the various ships floating serenely on the open sea around *Titanic*.

When she did not respond he turned around, to find her staring off across at the stately, silent mass that was *Oceanic*. "Captain?"

"There's a family named Laroche over there…" she said at last. "They would have been evacuated from *Titanic* during the night. Perhaps they're on the promenade deck right now, looking back at us…"

She paused, as if expecting an answer, but Jab did not know what to say. Tapping her foot once more on the deck, she glanced at him and sighed, speaking in a voice that sounded pained.

"They *might* be my family… distant cousins. I'd long wondered if that was the case, and because of your same time machine, I might have the chance to know them… but going over to *Oceanic* and getting my answers would mean giving up on… on the bigger picture."

Now that was interesting…

"The bigger picture of history at large?" he ventured. "And how we might alter its course?"

That seemed to break the spell of melancholy resting over her, and although she still reclined against the mast, the *capitaine* now seemed to radiate an aura of triumph. "Exactly, Cadet Officer."

She extended one hand out, reaching for the horizon. "This is a new world, and one that I think we're responsible for, you and me. After all, it was our actions that created it."

"Don't get above yourself, Capitaine. There is but one Creator, and all things proceed according to His will."

"Alright, well that should make you agree with me even more. If this is all proceeding by divine mandate, then we're here for a reason, and I think that reason is to take responsibility for the course of history, now that we've already interfered. All the mistakes that gave rise to our own world's troubles, all those poisonous politics, they're going to be repeated here if we run away. Now I've got nothing back home, so one way or another, I intend to stay, and try to put right what once went wrong."

She smiled again, with that same bright confidence that bordered on arrogant, and yet which he found quite winsome. "Call me conceited to assume I can change history, but I can't do anything less than try."

"I will confess, I feel the same way too," he said at last, curiously mimicking her posture, leaning against the mast. "So you have a plan, Capitaine?"

"No, but I can suggest a shared objective."

She held up one hand, showing him the small silver medal she had retrieved from the *Seguin Laroche* just before it sank. The inscription upon it threw her entire proposal into context for Jab. He considered the open sea for a long minute, and then nodded.

"Alright, you have my support. But we'll need the co-operation of one of the contemporary Captains."

"They're all be gathering soon for the conference. I'll stay quiet during the meeting, observe their reactions, and if one seems a good fit, I'll approach him afterwards."

"And what do you want of me in the meantime?"

"I want you to focus on the *Liberty Bell*," she replied. "Complete Nash's work and get it into serviceable condition, so that those who don't want to stay here can go home."

"Why not ask me to sabotage it so that no-one can take us back against our will?"

"Because fixing the *Liberty Bell* is the condition by which my crew's silence about your actions was bought – they want to go home. From what you've told me, the only way that can happen is through the *Liberty Bell*, and you won't be able to get it working from inside a cell aboard *Rescue* or *Viking*... that's the deal that keeps you your basic freedom of movement, so you *need* to fix that time machine. And if we want to try and put wrong the mistakes of history, we need to get as many of our contemporaries as possible back to the future."

He raised a questioning eyebrow, and she stepped away from the mast and faced him, feet planted firmly on the deck, a captain giving instructions to a crewman.

"I'm not God, Cadet Officer, you said it yourself. History is going to change from this point on whatever we do, but introducing several thousand people and all these ships into the mix is going to be too many variables for historical inertia to absorb. If you and I are going to have any influence over how events proceed through the twentieth century, we need the basic course of history to not deviate too far from the baseline, at least until we're ready to intervene on a grand scale. Getting all those other people back to where they belong not only reunites them with their families, but removes them from the equation."

She folded her arms and looked him in the eye. "Fixing the *Liberty Bell* is not just an act of mercy. It's damage control."

*

Rescue's mess was deserted when Akira Oshiro entered. Drawn by the soft sounds of running water and metal clinking against metal, he crossed to the galley and softly knocked on the door.

"Hello? It is Doctor Oshiro here, may I come in?"

"Feel free, Akira," someone called over the continuing sounds, now accompanied by a sudsy sloshing which reminded him of the mixing vats for the DRP solvents back at IJN Ishiyama. Striding into the galley, he made his way through gleaming stainless steel avenues of storage freezers and cooking facilities, pausing at the familiar sight of a Zojirushi rice heater resting on a workstation. He lightly tapped the device's plastic lid, wondering how long *Rescue* had spent stationed in Japan for the crew to have picked up a taste for the local cuisine.

"Five years," someone answered, as if reading his thoughts, and Oshiro turned. Captain Jones, his shirtsleeves rolled up and a towel hanging over one shoulder, was standing at a massive sink, clumsily washing dishes. The now ever-present sunglasses hid his blinded eyes. "Five years in the Pacific theatre, attached to the US Seventh Fleet in Yokosuka."

"Yes, I saw this ship on the news last year…" Oshiro replied, removing his hand from the rice warmer. "How did you know I was thinking that question?"

"Lucky guess…" Jones paused in washing dishes and groped for the towel to dry his hands. "I suppose you're thinking the same things as me. Are we ever going home, are we ever going to see our families again, that sort of thing."

Oshiro shrugged, not willing to comment on a matter so personal. "Excuse me, but why are you washing dishes? Do we not have galley staff for that?"

"I guess," Jones's face wrinkled up. "But I needed to do something with my hands, and decided it was better than lying in bed and trying to force myself to sleep."

"That sounds like something Kai Alinka would say."

"I know, and I very much regret that he nearly got himself killed trying to impress me," Jones sighed. "Even right now he can't stay still. He's off in one of Anton Gorbachev's subs, helping Andrews to inspect the damage to *Titanic*."

Oshiro nodded, and then undid the cuffs of his shirt and rolled up his own sleeves. "Do you need some help?"

"I wouldn't mind it," Jones replied, picking up a scrubber with which to attack a caramelised layer of grease in the bottom of a pan. Oshiro took the cloth off of him and began to dry glasses and cutlery, laying them out neatly so that he could later hunt for their appropriate storage space.

"You know the story of how my father died, right?" Jones said eventually.

"Yes, it was in the Farmington Mine Disaster. I'm very sorry that you had to lose him so young."

"Me too…" Jones replied, his lips pursing for a moment. "Well, after the initial collapse the mine was sealed to try and strangle the flames. At the time I thought my Dad was still alive down there, and that the rescuers were giving up on them… a week later Mom heard me wailing in the back yard; I'd begun digging a hole in the ground in an attempt to get down to him, but after three feet of topsoil I hit bedrock and couldn't go any further. I started desperately trying to smash through the stone by swinging the blade of the shovel against it, right up to the point where it rebounded and hit me in the face, which is why I was screaming…"

Jones smiled wanly.

"I managed to knock out several of my front teeth. Mom and I cried together for hours after I was released from hospital. That was when I accepted that my father was dead, and about a year later they opened the mine up again and began trying to get past all the cave-ins to recover the bodies. My Dad wasn't found for another five years; but when they found him it looked like he had been leading a group of men towards an air shaft when the fumes from the fire overcame them, fighting to the last second to stay alive."

He sighed and then laughed softly. "I inherited my father's stubbornness, and somehow I seem to have passed it on to Kai. I just hope now that he's learned the same lesson I did as a kid; that there's a difference between doing your best to save the lives of others, and stupidly throwing your own life away."

"I was watching the whole time… from Mir-3," Oshiro replied. "His courage was exceptional, Jordan; he did you proud."

"I guess he did…"

Seeing Jones feel for more pans to wash, he sank back into the rhythm of drying. Working in silence, the two of them listened to the distant play of waves against *Rescue*'s hull, and the ever-present growl of her engines below decks, powering tirelessly away at the dewatering pumps.

"How did this happen, Doc?" the Captain asked at last.

"We leapt through time…" he replied matter-of-factly.

"Yeah, but how?"

"I don't know," Oshiro answered at length. "Flux capacitor, warp drive, darkmatter butterflies, any number of possibilities. I'm an engineer, not a quantum theorist. My field has always been that of working with what is known to be possible; not speculating on what might be possible…"

He laughed lightly, regarding a carving knife he had dried to a brilliant shine. "Shows how short-sighted I am."

His own face looked back at him from the surface of the knife. In the corner of his vision he could see Jones slowly turning towards him, eyes unseeing but listening intently. Then, reaching over his shoulder, Oshiro took hold of his ponytail, lifted the knife behind his head, and cut the short braid off, wincing at the sharp tug on his scalp. He tossed the several inches of hair into the trash without a glance.

"You'll need to clean that again," he said as he placed the knife's handle into the captain's hand.

He had worn his hair long as a reminder of his luck in Sendai. Now it seemed he had a new path to tread, and he was not going to live in the past anymore.

Metaphorically.

CHAPTER TWENTY ONE

Father Thomas Byles was both surprised and delighted to discover that *Oceanic* was provided, amongst her many public rooms, with a small non-denominational chapel, a welcome change to *Titanic*, where he had made use of rooms such as the Second Class lounge to perform the Holy Eucharist to eager passengers. *Oceanic*'s chapel was, or so he understood from the crewmember who had led him there, intended primarily for the purpose of conducting acts of marriage while at sea. It was a notion that struck him as both sweetly romantic and somewhat garish, but regardless the chapel would serve nicely as a makeshift sanctuary and place of worship.

What he had not expected was to find several priests and ministers crowded into the small space, along with a considerable number of laity passengers. Many of the clergy present were figures he recognised as fellow Second Class travellers from *Titanic*, but there were a lesser handful of strangers as well, and all of them were speaking or listening to passengers from all eras, people who must have converged on the chapel in the hope of spiritual counsel. The sight of a Baptist minister holding the hand of a weeping woman, next to a Catholic priest who was sharing his rosary with an elderly man, fired the same flame of faith within him that had compelled him to pray over Abercrombie in the dying man's last moments.

In times such as this, when discord between Catholics and Protestants is forever reported in Ireland and further abroad, it is no small miracle to find men of all faiths called to a Universal Church, he thought.

Inspired to immediately join his brothers in their good work, Byles had entered the adjacent anteroom to set down a carry-bag he had brought over with him from *Titanic*, only to stop in abrupt surprise, the bag falling from his hand and scattering its contents over the floor.

Hanging on the wall opposite was a portrait of *himself.*

"How the-!?" he gasped. "What in Heaven's name!?"

It was a painting in oils, depicting him and two other priests speaking to a crowd on the stern of a sinking ship. Byles himself, recognisable by his thin glasses, was clinging to a capstan for support as the deck canted ever steeper, while his free hand was extended in a gesture of benediction. The light of a sole functioning deck light cast a profound luminosity on his painted doppelganger, lending him and the two other figures an almost heavenly aura.

Stunned and searching for explanation his eyes fell to the caption inscribed on the frame of the painting.

Fathers Thomas Byles, Josef Peruschitz and Juosaz Montvila administer the Last Rites on Titanic's stern, moments before the ship finally sinks. Donated to the Chapel of Oceanic by artist Janice Patton.

He shook his head, feeling both humbled and proud at the saintly image the painting gave of him. It was an idolatrous indulgence, and ashamed of himself he turned away, trying to stem back vain thoughts, only to find a young woman seated in the corner, eyes fixed on him intently. He got the distinct impression that she had been waiting for him.

"Father Byles…" she said at last, rising at extending a hand. "It is a pleasure to meet you at last."

At last? Byles thought, and his confusion must have reflected in his face, because the woman then smiled and bobbed her head towards the painting.

"Oh…" he laughed mildly and smiled as he took her hand in his. "I fear the artist may have overplayed any possible heroism on my part."

"Oh really?" she returned the smile, enjoying his own confusion. "I do apologise then."

He blinked, and then turned to consider the name on the painting's dedication plaque. "Ah, do I have the pleasure of addressing Miss Janice Patton?"

"Yes, I'm *Mrs* Patton…" she said, a touch of worry entering her voice as she corrected him. To Byles' eyes she seemed suddenly nervous, as if expecting criticism of her work, and he put aside the bevy of questions that rose to mind and instead smiled appreciatively.

"Well then, you have my thanks for a very... flattering portrayal."

"Factual as well, according to the testimony of those who stayed on the ship to the end..."

She left the end of the sentence hanging, prompting him to respond. Byles considered her words, weighing them carefully.

"If you came to hear the tale from the horse's own mouth, as it were," he said slowly. "Then I am afraid I have nothing to say. I'm struggling to understand the context of these past few hours, let alone any possible fate of my own last night..."

He trailed off before his thoughts ran adrift into musings on free will and predetermination, instead focusing his attention on Ms Patton, who was suddenly wringing her hands, and yet with apparent relief.

"Actually, Father, I came to ask for some guidance. I wanted to know what you had to say... about courage."

Interesting. Byles drew himself up a chair and bid her sit herself back down in her own. "First of all, may I ask if you are a Catholic yourself?"

"No. Protestant, United Church of Christ."

It was not a denomination he was familiar with, and he said as such, to which she smiled wanly.

"I don't think the church has even been founded yet, which makes me possibly one of only two members left in this new time..." she fell silent, and Byles shifted his weight. Again she had made a statement and then stopped speaking, as if demanding he ask the obvious question.

He suspected however that he would not get the answer he expected.

"You say one of two. Might I assume that this other practitioner of your faith is your husband?"

"Yes... and no," she said simply, before pausing as if to gather her strength, before calmly stating "She's my wife."

Byles inhaled sharply, and he felt his hands twitch as he suppressed the urge to jerk away from her. He suddenly wondered if this was how Cortez felt when he first brought the Catholic faith to the shores of Latin America, only to find the natives practicing the most deplorable of sexual perversions, and for a moment visualised himself as calling down God's own wrath on this, this…

Harlot?

Whore?

She-Devil?

And then he saw her flinch at his reaction, and felt a wave of shame at how he had treated someone who had evidently sought him out. So he forced himself, as he had advised Major Butt, to be calm, and held up his hand in a gesture of contrition.

"Please, indulge me with a moment to gather my thoughts…" he said, eyes closed and head bowed. When comforting Abercrombie he had decided that, knowing nothing of the future that had shaped the life of the murderer, he had no right to deny him succour. So now, why should he act any differently?

Christ might not have approved of the actions of the prostitutes and tax-collectors, but He did not drive them away with curses and condemnations. No, He invited them into his company, which the Pharisees took umbrage with…

Oh Lord in Heaven, let him not be a Pharisee to these emissaries, these lives delivered miraculously unto them by an act of divinity…

"Please…" he said evenly. "Tell me more."

And so she told him the tale of two young women, who from an early age both realised that there was something 'different' about how they felt towards the boys and girls in their class.

One of the two, Janice, who lived just outside of Manchester, New Hampshire, had explained her feelings to her parents, one an agnostic and the other a long-lapsed Calvinist. They had told her that this was simply who she was, and that there was nothing to be ashamed of. They had explained that some people would hate her, and judge her, and pressure her to act against the feelings that were natural to her, and that she should never listen to such people.

Most importantly, they told her that they loved her, and that they would support her, all the days of her life.

The other little girl, Teresa 'Terri' Fisher, was the daughter of a mixed-race Minnesotan family deeply involved in a minor

Midwestern church, a congregation that preached a doctrine of hate against all *"queers, dykes and homo faggots"*. When she realised that she might be one of those sinful 'brutes' she was too afraid to speak to her parents about her growing desires, fearing how they would react. So she had prayed, prayed for God to intervene in her life and take away the evil inside of her.

As she had grown older, Janice had, like all kids, wanted to start dating, but found it hard to identify a girl at school who, like her, was gay. So, when a massive new romantic movie came out starring Leonardo DiCaprio and Kate Winslet, she had gone to see it with her mother, and not, as she had hoped, a girlfriend. But it was one of the best trips to the movies that mother and daughter had ever had, both of them crying their eyes out for a tale of doomed love on an equally doomed ship, the *Titanic*. But what had moved Janice the most was a scene towards the end where a brave Catholic priest, his voice choked with emotion, had promised frightened passengers that *'God shall wipe away all the tears from their eyes'* and that *'there shall be no more death'*.

Afterwards she had gone to the town library, and found a book that revealed that the man whose courage was so moving was not a fictional character at all, but one of several clergymen who had all refused places in the *Titanic's* lifeboats, staying behind to lend strength to people still trapped on the ship. For the first time, she had felt that maybe there was something to religion after all.

Terri had seen the movie too, on a date her parents had arranged for her with a *"nice, God-fearing young man"* from church. He had later complained that she *"didn't put out once during the whole night"*, and that marked the last time she ever saw her mother come running to her defence. But the movie itself had been a revelation, and she had felt a certain empathy, as well as a shameful attraction, to the female lead, trapped in a situation that was slowly strangling her spirit.

And so her first mental barrier came crashing down.

Janice's parents, at first alarmed by their daughter's sudden interest in religion, had indulged her with a visit to the local church, a branch of the United Church of Christ, and had found, to their delight, an environment where gay members were openly welcomed and where Janice could be with children like herself.

And gradually, the church became a greater part of their lives, first in little things like helping out with the parish bake-sale, and then in more subtle ways, until one day Mum and Dad started describing themselves as Christians. And Janice had found her first ever girlfriend in the church, the minister's own daughter.

As with all the other children at her family's church, Terri was told to hate and despise anyone who spoke out against *"the Truth of God Almighty"*. So, hoping it would add strength to her prayers, and make God love her enough to save her from herself, she had started bullying the children at school who were openly gay, organising 'faith squads' that would hunt these kids down during recess and hurl them into the dumpsters behind the school boiler room, or shove them over on the playground. She would point and jeer in the corridors, and call them horrible names, and go home at night to be praised for her righteousness.

"Junior Crusaders," she and her friends were called by the pastor. Terri was so proud with herself. But still the feelings grew, the wicked desires making themselves felt in her dreams.

It was at this time when the two girls' paths first crossed, when all of America was shocked by a spate of child suicides in the Midwest, all from the same school.

Terri's school.

Five children took their lives in just one year, all of them students who had been bullied and harassed for their sexual orientation by Terri and the other *Junior Crusaders'*. Janice's parents had held their crying, frightened daughter tight and whispered support in her ear as they watched the situation unfold on national television. Terri's mother had given an interview, ranting about how these deaths were not due to bullying or persecution, but stemmed from the *"disgusting mental illness"* that was homosexuality.

Terri herself had been there when her mother was speaking to the cameras, hoping that if she was simply *'sick in the head'*, then maybe she could get better. That night she had summed up her courage and confessed to her parents her fears, her fears that she too was a *'fag'*.

They had shouted, screamed, and sent her crying to her room. They never once hit her, but they might as well have struck her with a two-by-four, so harsh was their shift in attitude.

In the summer of 1998, both girls went away to camp. Janice went on a church-funded trip with all her friends up into the hills out past the Merrimack River, where the children were encouraged to explore their hobbies and passions. She had learned to tie knots, read a map, and row a boat. But most importantly, during an arts and crafts session, she had learned to paint. She had dabbled with crayons and then charcoals in school, but it was out there, seeing how the light sparkled on the surface of Lake Winnisquam, that she realised how much she loved to make art. It was another turning point in her life. That Christmas, she received a complete set of watercolour paints and a collapsible easel from her parents.

Terri's camp was focused on one thing; to *"pray the gay away"* through a focused course of bible study, constant supervision, and group counselling. And bullying, and harassment, and institutionalised self-denial and self-loathing.

When her parents left her at the camp, Terri's mother said to her face that she prayed to come back to find her sweet, submissive, straight little girl waiting for her, and not the wicked devil that had taken possession of her.

It didn't work, and with each day at the camp what was left of little Teresa Fisher faded away almost completely. For the first time, Terri was experiencing what she had made other kids suffer, and she did not like it. Guilt for the bullying and empathy for her victims preyed upon her mind day and night, and deepened the cracks already splintering her paradigm. It was a slow process of breaking down many internal doors in her mind, but eventually she had realised that *this was not right*.

When she expressed those doubts, the supervisors had confined her to her room for a week, with no books or reading material except for a King James Bible. It was in those seven days that the final deconstruction came about, and Terri's metamorphosis was complete. She had lost the love of her family, the certainty of who she was, and finally she lost her faith.

There was no God, no Jesus. No loving creator could make one of his children suffer like this.

And so, as her mother had hoped, the girl that came back from the camp was a completely different creation. Outwardly, Terri played along, faked a complete recantation of her sexuality. But secretly she planned her escape, and eventually convinced her parents that she wanted to become a nurse, so that she could help bring the practices of *'sexual reorientation'* to the Godless, mainstream medical world. They had practically jumped up and down in delight and cried Hallelujah.

And so it was that the two girls' paths crossed once again, at the University of Minnesota, but the choice of campus was made for totally different reasons. For all their declared support, Terri's parents wanted her to stay in the same state where they could drop in at will to keep an eye on her, while Janice, wanting some independence and distance from her immediate family, took advantage of the fact that she had relatives in Minneapolis, who happily agreed to let her live with them while she studied art and found her feet in the wider world.

By this point the two of them had been diametrically opposed individuals. Janice, loved, assured and well-adjusted, made friends easily, was involved in extracurricular activities and was dating. Slender, blonde-haired and with the natural grace of a dancer, she turned heads wherever she went. Terri, meanwhile, had become quiet, isolated and angry, so very angry that she began hitting the gym outside of classes to burn off some frustration, and tutors had expressed alarm at her aggression and curt manner towards other students, the faculty and even the patients. And even as she grew into the lithe, well-toned, short-haired stereotype of an angry lesbian, she resolutely kept her sexuality a secret, not wanting to be hurt again.

It was right when Terri was in danger of being kicked off the course, and ending up back in the clutches of her parents, that a cinema just off of campus had announced a limited re-release of a certain movie about star crossed lovers amid maritime disaster. Both girls had gone alone to a scarcely-attended screening late one October evening, Terri still dressed in her nursing tunic and Janice on her way home after a drama club meeting. Both had noticed the other during the film.

As the credits rolled and Celine Dion sung her heart out, Janice exited the cinema and caught sight of Terri walking away into the night, head bowed and hands deep in her pockets. As she called out to the nursing student to offer her a lift in her car, a mugger come out from an alley beside the cinema and attempted to steal Janice's bag. Hearing the other student's call, followed by her screams for help, Terri had turned, seen the situation, and before the man could react, had run up, balled her fist, and decked him with enough force to lay him out on the asphalt.

Janice had been too shaken up to drive home, and had spent the night at Terri's student accommodations. A week later Terri had been invited out to a meal with the Pattons of Minneapolis as a thank you gesture, something she had never expected and almost turned down.

And then, somewhere between desert and coffee, someone had mentioned that Janice was a lesbian. It was the first time in Terri's adult life that she had been in contact with someone of her own sexual orientation, free of the constraints of her childhood, and after dinner she had abashedly asked the other girl if they could stay in touch. It still took her several weeks before she came out about her own sexuality, but when she did, both girls admitted that they felt a certain attraction to the other.

From there, the two strands of their lives, which had crossed once before and snagged one another on the second pass, became tightly woven into a single thread, which had proceeded from friendship to love, and then to something more than either could have hoped.

"We seemed to complete each other," Janice said, as she began to wrap up her telling of the story to Byles, who had sat in silence throughout. "I introduced Terri to yoga classes, sort of like an exercise session that promotes mental and physical discipline, which helped her control her frustrations and saved her place on the medical course. In return, she me gave everything she was, everything she had. Her love, her strength, her heart, and she had so much of it to give, as if all the years of emotion she had been unable to express suddenly found its outlet in me."

She rubbed at her eyes with the back of one arm, holding back tears. "When her parents became suspicious that something was happening, Terri invited them up to Milwaukee, to the same restaurant where we first connected, and began to explain everything that had happened in her life. The plan was for me to come over from the bar when the moment was right, to show just how serious she was, and how much we loved one another."

She paused and laughed sadly, leaving Byles hanging expectantly on her next words.

"What happened?" he asked softly, wondering at what point he had become so emotionally involved in this tale.

"They left…" Janice said, pained and outraged at the same time. "Their own *daughter* was pouring out her very soul to them and they left before she had a chance to introduce me. Wouldn't even hear her out as she begged for them to come back…"

"Afterwards…" she sighed. "They cut her off completely. My parents stepped in to help finance Terri's education when her own abandoned her, and she became part of our family. She was so scared when she came home with me for her first Thanksgiving with us, but that holiday proved to be the happiest time she had ever had in her life. My parents loved her like a second daughter, she helped with my little brother's baseball team, and when we talked her into coming to church with us for Thanksgiving, the warmth of the welcome she received overwhelmed her."

She was weeping now. Not with grief, but with happiness so profound it must have hurt. "I found her crying in the church restroom, repeating over and over again her thanks to God, Jesus, or whoever who was listening, for delivering her to me, and I started crying too. We just hugged each other, bawling out our hearts because we both felt that we'd found the soul we were made for, the person God had always intended as the partner right for us. When she came back out with me into the church, she sang beside us with so much love and joy that I thought she might suddenly grow wings and transform into this… this… angel of light, this gift from Heaven that I did not deserve."

Janice was gazing off past Byles now, chin resting on one hand and smiling tenderly as she retraced the steps of her memory. Thomas's own arms were tingling with goosebumps, and he dabbed at his eyes to hold back a dampness he felt there, moved as he never thought he might be by the spiritual testimony of one so different to himself.

"We moved in together at the university, and went home to Manchester at the end of each semester. Then one day my mother came up to me and asked me, with this sly little smile on her face, when Terri was going to become 'a *Patton in name as well as spirit?*"

She laughed sweetly. "We all sensed that one day Terri was going to take our name, and so cut her final ties to her parents, but we wanted to do it properly, and she needed time to heal. So we graduated, got jobs, saved and worked to rent a small condo in Springfield, went to church and built a life together. She worked at the hospital, coached Little League Baseball, and I painted portraits and opened a small gallery. And then one night, while watching 'our' movie, curled up together on the couch, Terri must have felt that the time was right to seal our relationship, because she whispered in my ear if she could please become my wife."

She turned over one hand so that Byles could see the wedding band she wore. "It was a bit late coming, because I suddenly landed the gig to do the artwork for a book called *'Titanic Century'*, but we were finally married two weeks ago."

Byles stared at the ring, and felt the flame burning brightly again inside himself, calling him on in defiance of what he had long thought to be acceptable standards of morality.

"I am so happy for you Ms Patton, truly I am..." he said at last, clasping his hands over her own. "And I am humbled by the trust you've shown in speaking to me like this, and grateful for your insight on a part of God's church that I have so far in my life overlooked. I might not understand your desires towards other women, but I cannot doubt or deny the depth and sincerity of your feelings."

"Thank you," she said, sniffing once. "So, you don't condemn us."

"You know so much about me... do you know why I was travelling to America aboard *Titanic*?" he answered with a question of his own.

"Ah, yes, I think so..." she replied. "Your brother had emigrated to America, and asked you to come to America to officiate over his wedding."

The miracle of time travel was truly far-reaching.

"Yes indeed," he nodded, adjusting his glasses. "And what I see here affirms what I've been contemplating during the voyage, struggling to prepare a sermon for that happy day. Until now I had always considered 'same sex relations' to be an affront to God, and in truth I still can't help but react to them as unnatural… but if what you tell me is true, then yourself and your wife Teresa were specifically made for one another, in body, mind and spirit. To deny the either of you the other, to withhold that completeness and love, instead demanding celibacy and the denial of these wholesome emotions, would be cruel and inhumane, and the truer affront to all that is divine in this, oh-so-large and beautifully complex universe…"

"Sound like you've got a good lesson written out right there already," she said, smiling.

"I assure you, you've given me enough inspiration to fill twenty sermons," he laughed kindly, laying one hand on her shoulder. "And I am honoured, that it was my own life's story, a past life's story, which inspired you to such courage."

"Not so much my courage…" she whispered in a voice so low that he almost missed it, before speaking up again. "Father, in our life together, it's always been Terri that's been the beacon of strength, the one brave enough to face her parents and offer them an olive branch, and to not give into grief when they passed her by. But now she's in pain again, and I don't know how to help her…"

"Please, tell me."

"Terri has been volunteering in the ship's hospital, and earlier, after helping to deliver a baby, she had an idea, but she couldn't explain it to me because another passenger interrupted. But when I went to meet her on her next break, she was crying her heart out in our cabin…"

She paused and swallowed. "There's rumours going about the ship that we might be able to go home, but Terri feels the right thing to do is for the two of us to *stay* here, in this time, to speak out against the prejudices that shaped her own life. But at the same time she's torn, because that means giving up all we had back in the future. Our family, our home, and the life we had built…"

Hearing this, Byles was suddenly reminded of Luke 9:61.

Still another said, "I will follow you, Lord; but first let me go back and say goodbye to my family". Jesus replied, "No one who puts a hand to the plough and looks back is fit for service in the Kingdom of God."

By now, Janice had turned her head away. "I didn't know what to say to her. I had built so much hope on us being together in the future, of maybe starting a family, that I hadn't even considered the possibility of us staying here. I turned and ran out of the cabin, unable to look her in the face. Now that I've thought about it, I think she's right, but I'm so scared at what it means… to take up this cross and travel with her, wherever it leads…"

Abruptly she turned back and stared at him. "I need to know how to be strong for her, to help her. You're the man brave enough to refuse a seat in a lifeboat, to stay behind on the *Titanic* and conduct a final ministry on a sinking ship. Tell me, how can I be as strong as you?"

"It…" Byles sighed, feeling renewed sympathy for both of these women. "It is not my place to tell you what to do, child. But it is clear to me that the Lord is calling the both of you, as surely as he called his disciples…"

"Don't say that…" she mumbled. "We're hardly perfect."

"None of us are," he said softly. "But when I was young I felt a powerful urge to not only convert to the Catholic Church, but to take Holy Orders and do God's work in this world. I think the same light is burning brightly in the two of you now, to show this love you feel to the world, and open blinded eyes as you have mine… but that decision, that commitment, is like the question your Teresa asked of you while watching that 'motion picture' account of *Titanic*. It is a choice that can only be made by the two of you, as wife and wife united."

"How can I go back? I left her in the cabin when she needed me…"

"Go to her, you silly goose!" he replied firmly. "You said yourself that she is your wife. She knows how lost and scared you are right now, she feels the same herself. Go to her and tell her the truth of your feelings, as a good wife should. Only then will the two of you will find your answer."

"Are you sure?"

"*Let those whom God have brought together, let no man put asunder.* Of course I'm sure!" he said, smiling in what he hoped was a wise manner, before gently folding his arms around her and holding her as perhaps her own father might once upon a time, providing support to a lost child.

"Thank you, Father," she said, returning the embrace. "God bless you."

"No, thank you, for this most potent blessing you've conferred upon me," he replied, before nudging her towards the door. "Now go, quick. There's someone who needs you."

She went with a spring in her step, and Byles smiled, before directing his attention to recovering his spilled artefacts. Amongst them was a pocket-mirror he used when preparing himself before services, and looking into it he sternly regarded his own reflection.

God has brought more than two lives together tonight; he has united two whole worlds in a sacred tryst… the question is, to what purpose?

He sighed. If he was any judge of character, those two bright young women were going to be the font of an unprecedented ministry, a rock upon which a church might grow.

But he still had duties of his own to attend to…

Very well, here we go…

He straightened his cassock and, feeling the same conviction and weight of commitment as he did on the day he was ordained, stepped out into the Chapel, ready to offer his services before God and this new, time-lost flock.

CHAPTER TWENTY TWO

Oceanic's main venue was named the *Mayflower Theatre*. It was an opulent auditorium, the saffron seats and furniture contrasting pleasantly with walls patterned in alternating panels of light and dark wood. The carpets were thick, mustard-gamboge in colour, and felt deliciously soft under Milton Long's weary feet. During the night it had been pressed into service as sleeping space for several hundred people taken aboard from *Titanic*; now it was filled with curious contemporaries and time-travellers who had been promised *'a revue of great twentieth century cinema'*.

The first film scheduled was called *'The Great Dictator'*. Taking his seat, Milt's eyes curiously scoured the program of entertainment he had collected from the lobby as he found a seat. The starring actor and director were billed as 'Charles Chaplin', a name that sounded vaguely familiar, though he could not precisely remember where he had heard it.

His thoughts were disturbed by another passenger politely enquiring if he could borrow the program. It was Lawrence Beesley, the passenger from the lifeboat who Milt had guessed was a teacher of some sort, and handing over the playbill he observed with interest the man's reaction as he read a brief description of the film aloud.

"Praised by the American Film Institute as the 37th funniest film of the 20th Century, 'The Great Dictator' is widely regarded to be the ultimate achievement of comedian and filmmaker Charles Chaplin. Produced just prior to America's entry into the Second World War (1939-1945), it details the parallel lives of the insane dictator Adenoid Hynkel and a humble Jewish barber whose people suffer the wrath of the self-styled 'Emperor of the World'. Both parts are portrayed by Chaplin, and while his physical antics as the Jewish Barber draw upon the rich traditions of vaudeville slapstick, it is his megalomaniac

turn as the neurotic Hynkel (a pastiche of genocidal dictator Adolph Hitler) that makes 'The Great Dictator' both hilarious comedy and a cautionary tale of the tragedy of fascism, and an evil that in real life would leave over eleven million dead."

It read, in truth, more as an excerpt from a schoolbook than an entertainment brief. For his part, Beesley paused and gazed off towards the screen, eyes distant.

"Merry and tragical!" he said at last, once again quoting Shakespeare. *"Tedious and brief! That is, hot ice and wondrous strange snow. How shall we find the concord of this discord?"*

"I imagine we are about to discover that for ourselves, Mr Beesley," Milt replied, as the lights dimmed and the murmurs of the audience was drowned out by a swell of bombastic trumpets. The flickering light of the projector began to shine on the screen, and they were instantly absorbed into the narrative of the film, marvelling at the astonishing fusion of sound and moving pictures.

*

Maggie Brown lingered near the back row of the theatre, watching first with curiosity, and then with rapt fascination as the film progressed. Seated with her were the two men she had approached. Both were passengers from *Titanic*; Daniel Mervin, a youth whose father had founded the Bibliograph film company, and William Harbeck, a freelance kinematographer. At first the two had whispered between themselves as the credits played out, marvelling at the depth and clarity of the image onscreen, and the synchrony of film and sound. But quickly they fell silent, and were soon laughing along with the audience at both the hapless folly of Chaplin's unnamed barber attempting to fly a plane upside down, and then the impassioned antics of the deranged dictator Hynkel, spouting nonsensical Germanic gibberish to an adoring crowd of sycophants.

Then Maggie realised she was laughing along as well.

After about forty minutes, someone came in through the back door and knelt in the aisle beside her.

"Mrs Brown, We're ready to see you now."

"Thank you Mr Hume," she turned towards her two companions. "This way boys."

For a moment, she thought that Mervin and Harbeck could only be removed from the spectacular film kicking and screaming; but, eyes shining bright with possibilities, they followed her immediately. Hume, a thin, bearded crewman, led them out of the theatre and through a discrete door into one of the crew passages that ran behind the scenes of the public decks. Molly's formal dress and overcoat suddenly seemed very ostentatious in the stark white corridor.

Up a flight of stairs they went, and then through a door marked 'Media Production Suite'. Inside was what seemed like an arcane laboratory to her eyes, but from the looks on her companion's faces, was obviously an Aladdin's cave of treasures. Off to one side stood what was surely a projector, throwing a cone of light through a glass panel out into the theatre beyond; but she saw no film-reels or canisters, just gleaming glass screens on which a multitude of images were playing, and in so many colours.

"Do you like it?" Hume said, smiling proudly as he turned, hand extended to encompass his domain. "We started with *'The Great Dictator'* because it's black and white, but gradually we'll work on up to full colour films. By the end of the day we'll be handing out 3D glasses for the *'Titanic'* rerelease."

"3D?" Mervin paused, thoughtful. "Do you mean stereoscopy, the ability to project images in three dimensions?"

"Yes indeed," Hume beamed. "I can't wait to see the reactions. But sorry, where's my manners? Please, take a seat." He gestured towards several chairs set around a table, and served coffee from a machine as they made their introductions. The coffee was, like the one Maggie had been offered by JJ Astor, cheap, bitter and nasty, but the conversation was stimulating enough to make up for it.

"This is the hub of *Oceanic*'s media services" Hume explained. "We control the cinema, planetarium and theatre stage from these rooms, and produce and edit our own television and radio programs that can be broadcast on the internal systems or transmitted to other ships. We even print a daily newspaper, *'The White Star Commutator'.*"

As he continued to explain what his duties entailed, Harbeck and Mervin posed their questions about film and cinema in the 21st century, while Maggie watched them interact. Her two contemporaries were both full to bursting with ideas as to how this technology could be applied, and though Hume was candid about his conflicting feelings of loss and excitement, he was also possessed of a vision as to the opportunities now open to them.

"...modern filmmaking as I know it does not exist here in 1912. There's no sound, no colour, and the scope of the films produced is limited. Georges Mèliès, the French director, has laid the groundwork for editing and special effects, and the idea that you can use the medium to do incredible things, but film is nevertheless still a novelty for many. Where I come from, it's irrevocably tied up in people's lives. We have television channels that broadcast news reports continuously all day round; that alone would be revolutionary in this day and age. But we can make it happen in just a decade or more, if the technology can be reverse-engineered."

"Actually," Maggie cut in lightly. "We aim to make it happen right now."

Hume paused and looked at her in disbelief. Maggie beamed winsomely. "What we came to ask, Mr Hume, is if you would help us to create a cinematographic account of what is happening on this ship right now? We've seen people wandering around with those amazing cameras of yours, but what if we could... you used the words 'broadcast', yes? Yes, broadcast interviews and people's opinions, throughout the various ships. It would help to ease tensions between the two times, and create a historical record of an event that will define the world."

In the aftermath of her proposal, Hume and the two other men exchanged inquisitive glances. Then he turned and looked around at the equipment whirring and whining and thinking all around them.

And finally, he smiled.

"Well, you're not lacking in vision, Mrs Brown. Let's see what we can put together."

*

"Jack, my boy!" called John Thayer from across the *Olympic* Restaurant. "Over here!"

In a dream, still trying to comprehend what had happened in the library, Jack turned to see his father motioning that he should join him at a table for two. His feet responded automatically to the summons, as did his other limbs, and Jack found himself returning John Thayer Senior's embrace, before sitting as bid.

"Where's mother?" he heard himself asked, mind distant.

"Ah, she has joined forces with a gaggle of other ladies and gone off to have a small soiree. This charming woman named McKinn seems to be their nominal ringleader. How about yourself, how was your day?"

"Troubled," Jack replied, finally coming around to the situation. After he and Philippa Paik had parted ways under the worst of circumstances, he had scoured the ship in the hope of finding her and apologising, with no success. Now he was tired and sinking into a pit of despondency and self-despair.

"It's a shame that you were not around in the main atrium an hour ago," John's face crinkled into a smile. "You missed quite a show when Cosmo Duff-Gordon finally tired of the company of all these "*uncouth, uncivilised louts*" and demanded he and his wife Lucille be transferred to another ship."

"I can't imagine that went well," Jack replied. "Isn't Sir Gordon an *Olympic* athlete?"

"Yes, a fencer, but without a sword in his hands it seems he's not much good for anything," John laughed. "The crew simply ignored him until the point that he became so indignant that Lucille had to beg him to calm down for the sake of keeping face in front of '*the guests*'."

"By which I suppose she meant all of the time-travellers?" Jack said, rubbing at his forehead.

"Yes…" John's face became pensive, and he shifted a little closer to Jack, as if huddling forward to confide secrets. "What do you make of these people?"

This was hardly something Jack himself wanted to dwell upon. Lack of sleep combined with the turbulent events of the past few hours had left him with what felt like an eternal headache, and he availed himself of a glass of water, poured from a convenient decanter.

"Honestly father, I don't know what to make of any of them. I managed to cause great offence to Miss Paik, and when I ran into

Milton Long earlier he informed me that he had actually been subdued by a woman who thought he was trying to assault her… her female spouse."

"Remarkable," John shook his head in disbelief. "Well, I saw Miss Paik leaving for *Titanic* with several other crew members some time ago, on the same boat that Cosmo Duff-Gordon attempted to board. She seemed in a black mood, and if you are to blame for that then I can hardly say I'm proud. But you seem to be punishing yourself enough as it is without me berating you. But to other matters…"

He suddenly produced what appeared to be a very thin softcover book or a form of magazine, the cover bordered in yellow. "I've wanted to share this with you for some hours. I found it in a magazine rack in the lobby, and discovered something of great interest inside. Have a look for yourself to get your mind off of things, and then I'd like to hear your thoughts on a *notion* of mine."

The atmosphere suddenly felt chilly. In the near distance Jack could hear the lonesome chords of *Oceanic*'s organ, the melancholy sound drawing a shiver up his back. Slowly he took the publication and began to browse through it, recognising it as a less-ornate edition of *National Geographic Magazine*, bold and simple in presentation. But while idly turning the pages, he lit upon a spot his father had marked with a slip of paper.

It was a two-page map of the District of Alaska (though the text described it as a *state*, which was interesting). The article to which it was attached was on an issue evidently being discussed in the Congress of 2012, on whether or not to drill for oil in something called the *'National Arctic Wildlife Refuge'*. Jack's father had circled several spots on the map, all along the northernmost coastline of Alaska, and underlined several pieces of information printed on the map.

Milne Point, Endicott, Lisburne, Point McIntyre, Prudhoe Bay.

Next to the last, Father had drawn a thick line beneath the words *'25 Billion Barrels, 1968'*.

Oil reserves, Jack realised, and the shock of realisation momentarily banished though of Philippa Paik from his mind. According to this innocuous publication, massive reserves of oil apparently existed in Alaska, reserves which so far as he was aware were *currently undiscovered*.

From this 'Prudhoe Bay', John had drawn in a long, unbroken line, striking south through Fairbanks and into Canada, extending past Dawson City and across the mountains to join with the Grand Trunk Pacific Railroad, thence onward to Vancouver and Seattle. Next to it were several tentative names;

Trans Alaska Railroad?
Pennsylvania Railroad of Alaska?
American Arctic Railroad

"It is trade that will save the world," his father said, and Jack looked up at him. Pensively they stared at one another for several seconds, and then the Vice-President of the Pennsylvania Railroad leaned towards his son as if drawing him into a conspiratorial circle.

"From this article Jack, I have gathered that Alaska contains reservoirs of oil twice the size of those already being exploited in Texas." He reached over and tapped at the map. "In the world that was, they built a pipeline through which fuel flowed freely for four decades. It was only at this ship's time of departure, in 2012, that it began to seem that the wells were becoming exhausted. Imagine the benefits this could bring to the Union."

It was a striking vision, and yet singularly terrifying.

"Is this right, father?" Jack asked quietly. He turned the pages to see colour images, bright and glossy, of ugly pipes striding on piers across starkly beautiful tundra. Moose and elk roamed beneath the structures. "Aren't we cheating? Could this be declared Insider Trading on a grand scale?"

"Perhaps," his father shrugged. "But I plan to share this information openly with anyone who will listen, Jack. Charles Melville Hays of the Grand Trunk Pacific Railroad was travelling onboard *Titanic*, and I know for a fact that he is somewhere aboard this floating colossus; his company have a mandate from the Canadian Government to build a line North to Dawson City, which would be the ideal jumping-off point for this grand scheme of mine, the 'American Arctic Railroad', an enterprise which can bring nothing but good to both the United States and Canada. I mean to approach him and win his support."

Jack felt very unconvinced, but still found himself responding in kind, contributing observations.

"Father, from my time with Miss Paik in the ship's library, it's clear to me that oil will be the currency of the next century. Tapping these wells now could well indeed enable America to stand free and independent of bloody crusades that will sweep over Persia and Arabia in a quest for black gold…"

"Exactly," replied John. "We can keep our hands clean of such strife. Indeed, we would have so much lucre to spare, that we could easily sell most of it to foreign powers. When someone is trading with you, it becomes less likely that they will go to war with you."

"And if war does come," Jack continued for him, his face dark, one hand clenched to his chin. "Then the nation that wins is the one that is best fuelled."

"*Exactly,* Jack. The American Arctic Railroad will be the outlet for this treasure, and the means by which men and materiel enter Alaska to tap those resources, and so bring prosperity both to the Union, and to this region. Something which, I might add, this pipeline failed to do for Alaska in the world that was, once the boom of construction had finished."

John's hand drifted south across the map, to the vicinity of the Prince William Sound. "While JP Morgan fights to monopolise control of the coal and copper reserves in the Wrangell Range, so greedy for profit that he will surely exhaust those mines in just a few years, further North we will lay the cornerstone of a new American Century. *Just imagine it, Jack.*"

"I am Father…" Jack said, a smile curling at his face. "I suddenly feel like a boy playing God with his model trains."

John Borland Thayer Senior chuckled, only to stop as his son's voice turned frosty.

"But at the same time," Jack reached out and pressed a finger to the Bering Strait, the narrow bottleneck of oceans that separated continental America from Siberia. "What if things go wrong? What if we prevent this 'First World War', and so prop up a corrupt Russian autocracy, that might decide it wants Alaska back?"

His hand swept from the strait east across the expanse. "All this would become the front of a new war in the Arctic."

"That's the beauty of the railroad; it will enable troops to be brought in at an instant to repel invasion. Indeed…" Jack's father reached over, pen in hand, and with one bold motion drew a line from Fairbanks directly across to Nome and Barrow, on the coast opposite Russia's Cape Deshnev. "We could even run a branch out to tap the mineral resources of the Bering region, as well as prepare for any hostilities. Again, this is where the American Arctic Railroad covers every eventuality."

"It can't!" Jack lifted his voice, staring with awe at how easily the sweep of a pen might decide the course of history. He looked across and stared into his father's eyes. "It's a grand scheme, Father, bold and brilliant, but we cannot even begin to imagine how all this will play out."

His mouth searched for the right words, and eventually he gave up. "I don't know. I'm no businessman, and if you think this will do a service of good then please drive these rails into the wilderness, to this Prudhoe Bay. But do not be so arrogant to presume that a glimpse of one possible future enables us to puppeteer history from this point on. Even with this new wisdom, we are like specks of dust, caught in winds that may hurl us wherever they choose."

John, abashed, stared at the floor for a long moment, before looking up, tears in his eyes. "My boy…"

In those two words he conveyed such shame and pride that Jack thought his own heart might burst with feeling.

Slowly, John reached out and rested a hand on his shoulder. "You are so wise beyond your years. Yes, it is trade that will save America, but men such as yourself that must be her conscience."

Taken aback, Jack turned and looked down at the map. For a moment, he saw in his mind long trains of oil tankers snaking their way through the wild forests and open plains, and of new towns and communities springing up when none had before, in this world or the last. Maybe one of them would be named 'Thayer'.

Or better yet, he amended his fantasy. *They might honour someone more deserving. The township of 'Philippa, Alaska' has a nice ring to it.*

His hand clenched over the map. How might he be expected to be a voice for good in the future of America, if he had been so pig-headed as to drive away a charming, vivacious woman who had come to them in the spirit of friendship?

Stomaching down his shame, he looked to his left, through the broad windows to where *Titanic* floated serenely on a midday sea, the water so blue and cold it sparkled like ice.

He had to make amends.

And somehow or other, he had to get back onto *Titanic*.

CHAPTER TWENTY THREE

Arthur Rostron straightened his uniform jacket as he stepped aboard the bright orange launch that had been sent to pick him up from *Carpathia*. The craft's attending officer, unfamiliar cut of his uniform made slightly more recognisable by the White Star Line badge sewn on his breast, saluted with what seemed to Rostron exaggerated respect.

"Captain Rostron sir, the other captains thank you for joining us."

"I am honoured to accept their invitation," nodded Rostron. "May we proceed?"

"Right away sir," the man acquiesced, gesturing that he should head aft. Rather than take a seat in the dark interior of the launch, Rostron climbed a short flight of stairs to the tiny craft's upper deck, which was fitted with a number of benches. Holding on with both hands at the forward railing, he was afforded a first-rate view as they pushed off from *Carpathia*. Passengers and crew on her deck honoured him with a small round of applause as the launch pulled away, and when he raised a hand in response a stronger cheer went up, as if he were the King reviewing the Fleet.

He regarded his ship with a wry smile, gaining an unusual perspective of her in mid-ocean. Small compared to the other giants attending this unusual gathering, he nevertheless felt that her long, low profile compared favourably with the hulking *Oceanic*. And he was unspeakably proud of what his crew and command had achieved in the course of the night, dashing headlong to the aid of the sinking *Titanic*, braving the ice field and pushing the engines close to their top speed.

It was a strange relief to reach the given coordinates and find that their efforts had been unnecessary.

Thoughtful, he turned his attention towards *Titanic*. The stricken ship was several hundred yards off to starboard, a yacht in comparison to the *Oceanic*. The *Anatoly Sagalevich* and the *Viking* were still moored alongside the White Star liner, the submarine's slick black hull broken where the vessel had sprouted several antennae, which he suspected was the source of whatever signal was jamming all wireless transmissions in the vicinity, forcing the ships to break out the Morse lamps and signal flags in order to communicate. While he doubted *Viking* had sinister intent, the piratical measure of blocking all communication with an outside world surely crying out for news of *Titanic* sat wrongly with him. Indeed, the entire situation screamed 'wrong' to him, and he was sure he was not alone.

The launch was now coming alongside *Oceanic*, and Rostron marvelled at the sight of a hinged door opening like a drawbridge from the side of the hull, forming a sturdy jetty. Regardless of these people's intent, their technical skill was beyond compare. But he wondered if this was anything more to them than mechanical marvels.

No sooner had they come to a halt than a new figure made himself apparent, golden braid on his cap and jacket marking him as the superliner's master. The surprisingly short figure crossed to the launch at a brisk pace, accompanied by a young Oriental who to Rostron's eyes seemed somewhat under the weather. As if in confirmation of that suspicion, only the Captain climbed to the upper deck of the launch to meet with him. Drawing themselves up, the two men saluted smartly before shaking hands.

"Lloyd Waters, *Oceanic*."

"Arthur Rostron, *Carpathia*. I must say, Captain, your ship is a marvel."

"Not so fantastic as your ship is to my eyes," Waters smiled openly. "From where I come from, we look back on this as a golden age at sea."

Rostron paused. "So the words that have been bandied around by the crew are true. You are all from the future?"

"Yes," Waters said, his previously bonhomie suddenly shrouded. "But I'm sure the full details will come out in the assembly."

"Indeed," Rostron looked down at crewmembers carrying several pieces of electrical equipment aboard the launch, while a handful of additional passengers waited to board. He recognised one among them instantly.

"Bruce Ismay?" he asked. "The President of the White Star Line is attending?"

"It was felt he had the right," Waters explained. "*Titanic* is his company's ship after all, and we are convening in part to determine what to do next in light of her damage."

Rostron glanced up at the WHITE STAR legend emblazoned in red on the down the side of *Oceanic*'s superstructure. "And establishing a pecking order, I assume."

Waters' answer was to shrug noncommittally, donning another affable smile in the process. Rostron had yet to get the measure of the other man, but he suspected *Oceanic*'s master was far from being as easy-minded as he presented himself to be.

"So will anyone else be joining us for this Council?" he asked. "I understand it is to be mostly comprised of ourselves and our counterparts."

"So I'm told, though we're apparently accommodating some experts in various fields. The young lady who came aboard with me is one."

"That Asiatic youth?"

"Yes," Waters replied, tone a little cooler. "She spent most of last night aboard *Titanic*, helping with the evacuation…"

*

"Miss Paik," someone said softly, "I must express my thanks."

Pip turned away from where she had been morosely gazing at the swells. "Oh, Mr Ismay."

Bruce Ismay was looking somewhat worse for wear, though strangely Pip could not muster much sympathy for the man, or anyone else as a matter of fact. Her experience with Jack had been… if not traumatic, then certainly enlightening. She had always known she viewed the world through stained-glass windows, but the way she felt now was as if someone had put a brick through them; all that was left was an empty frame.

She shook her head slightly to clear her thoughts, one hand pressed against her temple. "I'm sorry, I was miles away there…" she lied, simply not having much strength left to care. "You're more than welcome, it was nothing."

Evidently she was not giving off the right signals, because Ismay lapsed into what sounded like an age of platitudes; probably from the heart, if she was feeling charitable. But she wasn't.

It's just reality catching up with you, a pernicious little voice whispered in the back of her thoughts.

Shut up...

Except for Adrienne and a few friends on the Sagalevich you're all alone in this upside-downtime world, well except for that monied boytoy Jack...

Shut up.

...I mean, the way you sought each other out after that little 'meet cute'. Ha, as if you were trying to make the Disney stereotypes come true. Well, take a reality check Pip. Lily-white Thayer isn't going to fall for a half-breed Chyong... or would he just call you a Chink out of ignorance?

Shut. Up.

I mean, what did you think was going to happen, that the two of you would fall head over heels in love, as if this whole world-shaking affair is just a platform for your life to turn into a time-travelling riff on the lyrics of Uptown Girl?

Shut Up!

Uptime Girl, she's been living in an uptime world, always dreaming of a downtime guy, though she never thought she'd get to try...

SHUT UP!

She must have clenched her fist to quell the treason in her head, because Ismay suddenly broke off his thanks and took an alarmed step back from her.

Wow, well done 'Uptime Girl', you're creating a new stereotype for TV Tropes: 'The Angry Time Traveller'. And see that real fear in his eyes – imagine what you look like to him; an alien enigma wrapped up in a military uniform that doesn't even belong to you – he can't decide if you're going to throw a punch or just ignore him.

Feeling a tiny pang of guilt, she took an actual look at what today had made of the White Star President. It was a pitiful sight; his elegant attire from last night was gone, and now he was dressed in an ill-fitting uptime shirt and jacket, looking surprisingly small, almost shabby.

"What happened to your clothes?" she asked, making an effort to relax her posture, choosing instead to slide her hands into her bomber-jacket's pockets, where they could clench and unclench to her heart's content.

Ismay flushed a little. "Ah, I had a little accident this morning aboard *Oceanic*. Nothing to concern yourself with, Miss Paik." He stepped away, suddenly looking like a caged ferret trying to tear itself an exit from its confines. "Once again, my utmost thanks for your service last night."

And then he was gone, limping as he went, leaving Pip in the unwelcome company of her own warring thoughts.

So make way for this uptime girl, she's gonna' take on this whole white bread world, as much as any girl with hot blood can, but she's still thinking of that downtime man, that Thayer man...

*

Passengers and cargo stowed at last, the launch pushed off from the side of the mammoth ship and made for the *Titanic*. It was the first opportunity that Arthur Rostron had to view the famed ship from up close, and he was suitably impressed, but he could hear Waters' breath catching as the liner sounded her whistles in greeting.

To his surprise however, it was Waters who presented the question already forming on his lips. "Captain Rostron, what does *Titanic* mean to you?"

Momentarily stumped at having become the schoolboy called to task, rather than the master presenting the challenge, Arthur Rostron had to pause and think for a while, before whetting his lips and essaying a wary answer.

"I think that she is a beautiful ship, a product of sound engineering and a triumph to admire. But I do find the constant touting of platitudes in her favour somewhat tiresome."

"Now that is fascinating." Waters now sounded very interested, resting one arm on the rail. "Is it because of the vainglorious boasts attached to her?"

"In part, but I consider myself more jaded by the fact that one hears the same circus play out whenever a new ship is launched.

Consider the RMS *Cedric*; when she entered service just a few years ago all the press sung her praises and declared her to be the ultimate product of shipbuilding, and the maximum size to which a liner could ever be built. Not four years later the same hot air was spouted for *Lusitania* and *Mauretania*, and identical empty platitudes were heaped upon *Olympic* in turn. Give it but a few months before the Germans no doubt begin to brag about the size, speed and stability of their new *Imperator*. I find it incredibly cynical that a ship be presented to the public solely by how she 'outmatches' all competitors when she first enters service, when in truth she herself will be outclassed in a matter of months."

"So you're saying that *Titanic* is just a passing fad?"

"A fancy, yes. Once White Star puts their next ship in the water, I doubt anyone will much care for the *Titanic* save for her merits as a stable and comfortable vessel. And if a ship truly has a soul, I imagine a touch of humility will do hers a world of good – a ship earns her keep through years of reliable service, not through a few crossings' worth of celebrity fame."

"Under most circumstances, I'd be inclined to agree with you," Waters nodded, but then chuckled softly. "I suspect, however, that *Titanic* is a ship whose name will resound throughout time."

Considering those words, Rostron observed his colleague closer. Lloyd Waters was gazing at the nearing ship with a look of profound reverence; awe and self-abasement in the face of something greater. It concerned Arthur that something as temporal as *Titanic* should evoke so spiritual a response in the man; not only was it all too alike the worship of technology and humanity's alleged conquest of nature that so concerned him in this day and age, but it suggested that in a century's time the world had gone on to become even more materialistic.

His worried thoughts must have been all too evident, because Waters then turned towards him, smiling wryly. "Where I come from, Captain, *Titanic* is the most famous vessel of all time, not excepting Noah's Ark. Every child around the world knows of this ship, and its catastrophic sinking."

He chuckled again. "And even if she does not sink, I suspect she's set to acquire the same fame in this world too. '*Titanic* – the ship so great that time itself bent to her aid'. Sink or swim, I think she's always going to be remembered."

Rostron stood in silence, his concerns both confirmed and somewhat assuaged. "That's a little much to believe."

"It's quite true Captain Rostron," a solemn voice interjected. "*Titanic* was fated to become a disaster on the level of the sacking of Rome, or the destruction of Pompeii."

Arthur turned to find the new speaker; Bruce Ismay had come up the stairs and joined them, walking somewhat gingerly, as if it hurt to put weight on his left leg. The President of the White Star line was dressed in a suit of unfamiliar cut, underneath which he wore a light blue shirt without tie or cravat; Rostron could only assume that this was an example of future fashion, and then he looked Ismay in the face; the other man looked drawn and haggard, as if part of him had died.

Walking in that curious half-limp, Ismay reached the rail and stood alongside them, face turned up to regard *Titanic*. "Last night's events, if unimpeded, would have become a tale that will resound down through years to come, complete with great deeds, mighty heroes and capricious, craven villains…" He winced and shifted his weight to his right leg. "Or so my experiences on *Oceanic* would seem to suggest.

Ismay was now gazing up towards *Titanic*'s boat deck as they came into the lee of the other ship, and Rostron saw he was regarding the empty lifeboat davits that stretched along the side of the ship.

Perhaps I have been hasty… he thought to himself. *Even Titanic's owner seems to have been caught up in the spell that so clearly affects Captain Waters…*

Bruce Ismay had always been described to Rostron as a hard-headed businessman reputed for high confidence and an iron skin that deflected the world's critics. But now here he was, seemingly as self-abasing as the most penitent of religious converts. Clearly he had learned something aboard *Oceanic* that had brought about this sea-change in his attitude. Everything seemed to be turning upon its head, and Arthur suddenly wondered if this event might set off a similar metamorphosis across the world…

What humility might a man learn if cast into the harsh light of history's judgements, his works and deeds laid bare as vanity and pride? Might that man might strive to reinvent himself, to be born anew…?

The potential energy that lurked here, waiting to be released, was awe-inspiring, and he looked up at *Titanic* with newfound reverence, suddenly marvelling at what this ship's near-sinking might come to represent.

"Thank you for illuminating me, gentlemen," he said thoughtfully.

*

When *Titanic*'s sister *Britannic* had gone to sea as a hospital ship in the Great War, chartered on a mission of mercy to ferry wounded men back from the Dardanelles, an essential addition to her facilities, in addition to the various wards and surgeries, was a morgue. A white, sterile box of a compartment, it sat at the aftermost part of the ship, right out on the projecting shelf of the poop-deck, conveniently remote from the hospital spaces.

Titanic herself had no such facilities, and yet in the past few hours had taken on a considerable cargo of the recently deceased. Unwilling to commit the bodies to the deep, Captain Smith had ordered that one of the liner's refrigerated meat holds be emptied of provisions and made use of as a temporary mortuary store. Now over two dozen corpses were laid out on the deck and cutting slabs like choice cuts.

The corpse of Adrian Abercrombie was here, as were the two members of *Titanic*'s crew that he had shot dead: Hichens and Wilde. And standing over the three of them were four representatives of the living, their breath misting around them as they spoke.

"You know the truth about what happened," Joanna Laroche said without preamble. "I can't think of any other reason for you to request a meeting like this."

"That is correct, Captain Laroche," admitted Robert Furness. "At least, we know of the *Liberty Bell*." He turned his head, making a pointed expression at Jabril Hab Allah. "How and why it was aboard your ship remains somewhat of a mystery, although we have our suspicions."

There was a pause as the three of them leaned in and, working together, lifted Abercrombie's body up high enough that the

449

fourth person in attendance, Doctor Montgomery, could slide an open body bag onto the slab. As a warship, *Viking* was well-equipped with containers for the recently-deceased, and Furness had released enough of the zip-up shrouds to allow a temporary inhumation of last night's casualties. Montgomery himself, one of the older members of *Viking*'s crew, pointedly ignored the conversation going on around him, focusing instead on his duty of care to the dead.

"And frankly," Bob continued, once they had lowered Abercrombie into the bag. "I don't care to know the details, and I don't intend to bring my suspicions up at the conference."

He paused, and seeing obvious caution on their faces drew a hand back over his balding scalp. "What's important right now isn't how we got here, but how we move on; whether or not we can go home."

"It is possible to get us back to the 2012 we knew," Jabril replied without hesitation. "And if you are as knowledgeable about the *Liberty Bell* as you imply, then you knew that already."

"You're a sharp man, Cadet Officer, and yes, I had the advantage of some pre-packaged intelligence," Bob said, before handing over a bound sheaf of documents from a carry-case he had brought aboard with him. "I've had duplicates made of everything the Royal Navy knew about the *Liberty Bell* and *Project Lesterpack*, for distribution at the upcoming meeting..."

The two crewmates shot each other a look of surprise, and Joanna bit her lip. "That serves no purpose..."

"...unless you want to hide your knowledge of the machine's function, allowing someone else to come to the conclusion that a return to 2012 is possible," put in Jabril.

"Correct," Bob dipped his head in acknowledgement.

"So what should we infer from this?" Joanna probed. "Are you playing dumb, or simply trying to not wield your authority like a cudgel? *Merde*, you command the single most powerful arsenal on the planet. If you said 'jump', all any of us could ask is 'how high?'"

"What I command," he replied, turning her words back on her. "Is a light so bright that I'd rather hide it under a bushel than blind others with it, Captain Jo."

Jabril snorted. "This coming from the man who could rule the world?"

"Says the man who wanted to use time-travel to *change* the world," Furness replied without pause. "We need the help of the people of 1912 to get our fleet home as soon as possible. I'd rather do that with their consent rather than by force of arms... though I do aim to make clear that *Viking* is not a toy to be fought over."

"*Hnn...* I'm guessing you don't want the situation complicated further by bringing the politics of terrorism into the affair, otherwise we wouldn't be having this conversation?" Joanna surmised, receiving another nod of confirmation. "So what, you'll just keep quiet and let myself and the other captains take the lead?"

"Until such time that I can no longer follow. Better we have a consensus of equals than a tyranny of one."

"Alright then, whatever floats your boat, so long as it doesn't sink our own," Jo shrugged. She reached out and grabbed hold of the zipper on Abercrombie's body bag. "You clearly have your plans, and we have ours. But they don't have to be in conflict, and they both depend on us setting this situation right. So, do we agree to not interfere or undermine each other at this conference?"

"That is precisely what I wished for, Captain Laroche, on one proviso. You'll have my silence regarding the truth of the events aboard the *Seguin Laroche*, but I need something from you and your Cadet Officer in return."

Jo froze, hand gripping the zipper. "And what would that be?"

"I want the *Liberty Bell* jerry-rigged so that if a return-jump is made, it burns itself out in the aftermath."

There was a cool silence as the words sank in. Jo shivered, not entirely due to the cold, and tilted her head to one side, mouth puckering.

"They'll charge you with treason," Jabril voiced her thoughts, holding up the working orders included in the duplicated set of documents Furness had handed over. "Your instructions were to recover the device in operational condition, if at all possible."

"That's between me and the Admiralty, but right now I'm in a situational vacuum and have to act as I see fit," Bob Furness said firmly, no doubt showing in his eyes. "By involving *Viking* in *Titanic*'s story I've already introduced the concept of nuclear technology into the build-up of World War One; yes, I did it to save lives, but it's still a black mark against this new timeline's future history. I do *not* want to compound that mistake by dropping a functioning time machine into the geopolitical storms of 2012."

He paused and took a deep breath. "Ideally... I'd love to see the *Liberty Bell* disassemble itself down to the last atom. Taking it out of anyone's clutches probably won't stop the temporal arms-race that our return will almost certainly kick off, but it might delay it, might..." he laughed bitterly. "Might *buy enough time* for cooler heads to prevail..."

Jo turned and shared a long glance with Jabril. The Arab engineer clenched his jaw, and inclined his head in a tiny nod. "It can be done. The machine was designed to self-destruct if required, purging the hard-drives and crushing its core into a micro-singularity, putting the key technologies beyond recovery. It would require some effort to set those protocols back up, but we can ensure that the *Liberty Bell*'s next voyage will also be its last... and we can make its destruction look like an accident."

Furness seemed to shrink fractionally, and Jo realised that he had been holding his breath; now it was being released in a sigh of relief.

"That's fine by me," *Viking*'s CO said softly.

"Then we have a deal," Jo nodded, and at last she drew the zipper, closing the body bag over Abercrombie's face.

*

Captain Smith paused as he reached the foot of *Titanic*'s grand staircase and took a breath, struggling to compose himself while fighting off the sudden craving for a cigar. One hand nervously brushed at the medals on his breast, awarded for service in the Royal Naval Reserve.

He stood in the D-Deck reception room, a lounge-like space that fanned out around the stairs, alive with activity as crew from various vessels dragged pieces of equipment over the carpets and strung out great coils of wire, leading from portable generators up on the promenade decks, down the stairs, and through into the dining saloon that adjoined the Reception Room. He was reminded of the rush to get the ship ready to sail at Belfast and Southampton, of shipyard staff making the final fittings as provisions for the voyage were brought aboard. For a moment his thoughts jumped the rails, and he discretely rested a hand on the balustrade to steady himself. Had it only been a fortnight since he arrived in Belfast for *Titanic*'s sea trials? So much had happened since then that even the events of yesterday seemed distant and blurry.

He turned to face back up the stairs as the sound of footsteps on the deck drew his attention, and saw Pitman hurrying down towards him. The Third Officer's face was heavily lined, his eyes dark and sunken from lack of sleep; Smith realised that he himself probably looked no better.

"Sir, a message from Mister Murdoch," Pitman breathlessly began. "We've just received a Morse lamp message from *Oceanic*, and there's something that needs your attention; while the majority of our catering staff have agreed to stay over there to tend to the passengers, some of the stokehold and deck crew are refusing orders to return to *Titanic*."

"What, why?"

"They're concerned that the ship is unsound and liable to sink at any time. Some of our passengers are apparently volunteering to come over instead, to man the decks and stoke the furnaces in their place. Also, more ships are coming over the horizon and are attempting to signal us."

"Very well," sighed Smith, before comporting himself. "Allow those passengers willing to assist back aboard *Titanic*; we have little choice but to accept volunteers to make up our numbers, but ensure they are aware that they will be expected to work. As for these approaching ships, run up our quarantine flags, and suggest our companions do the same – the threat of contagion should ensure some measure of privacy."

That elicited a wan twitch of Pitman's moustache, and Smith struggled to return the smirk. "Inform Mister Murdoch that he has full command of the ship whilst I am in conference with the other captains, and that he is to encourage any further trespassers to keep their distance like the *Mount Temple* has. If they ask any more questions, he may instruct them to stand by for further details…" he looked forward through the doors into the dining saloon. "Hopefully we'll soon have worked out something to tell them."

Pitman nodded and began back up the stairs, taking them two at a time. Smith made a mental note to later chide him for such unbecoming conduct in the passenger spaces, but then reminded himself that the circumstances were exceptional.

The sound of voices murmuring reverentially drew his attention back to the reception room, and tugging the hem of his coat straight he stepped off the bottom stair of the Grand Staircase and turned to greet the last group of people to come aboard from the gathered ships. The first two, he was relieved to see, were dressed similarly to him, and he had only to check the cut of their uniforms to determine that one of them hailed from the same time as himself.

"Captain Rostron and Captain Waters," he said after introductions had been made and hands shaken. "Welcome aboard *Titanic*, and thank you both for all the assistance you've rendered us."

Over the new arrivals' shoulders he caught the eye of Bruce Ismay, lingering solemnly at the back. They exchanged a glance, and Smith noted that his employer seemed burdened with as great a strain as his own. Putting that aside as a question to raise later, he extended a hand. "This way, please; the galley staff have prepared luncheon."

He stepped smartly forward, leading the way. Rostron, Waters and Ismay followed, along with a handful of other persons the launch had collected from *Oceanic*, talking amongst themselves as a pair of stewards sprang into place to open the doors of the First Class Dining Saloon. Their murmurs became all the more louder as they entered the room, admiring the decor, much to Smith's satisfaction. He had sent down word for the victualling staff who had returned to the ship to ensure *Titanic* made a good showing for the guests, and it seemed they had done both ship and company proud. Despite the absence of passengers, all of the saloon's tables – well over a hundred in number – were properly laid for dinner, and the silverware sparkled brightly. In the centre of the room, white-attired stewards waited to seat them at the captain's table, as if for a formal party. Dimmed lighting lent a low lustre to the room's peanut Jacobean decor, working together with soft music to ease frayed nerves and create a more relaxed atmosphere than might otherwise be warranted.

The group that made themselves seated around the table were at distinct odds to the elegant setting and the immaculate stewards piloting trays of cold meat and baskets of bread into place. Smith's eyes were quickly drawn to the master of the late *Seguin Laroche*, a woman in a green jacket that very much resembled a foreshortened sou-wester, her thick hair spilling out from under a round-topped cap. Not far along from her sat a barrel-chested man he understood to be Gorbachev, the captain of the *Anatoly Sagalevich*, identified by a patch on his shoulder showing the angular profile of his ship.

Smith nodded in greeting to each of them; there were eight commanding officers present, nine counting Lieutenant Miller from the *Rescue*, representing Captain Jones. The other guests were a collection of passengers from the various ships, including Philippa Paik, looking quiet and withdrawn, and as Smith gestured for everyone to take their seats he noted that several extra chairs had been squeezed around the table in order to seat all sixteen persons.

Thomas Andrews had been placed next to him, though the seat was currently empty. Still squeezed into a sky-blue pair of overalls identical to Gorbachev's, the Ulsterman was following the stewards around the table, laying out a few bound sheets of paper beside each plate. Smith glanced down at the first page of his own copy; a list of the various ships' complements.

RMS Titanic; 1316 passengers, 908 crew (17 fatalities)
RMS Oceanic; 2950 passengers, 1310 crew (5 fatalities)
RV Anatoly Sagalevich; 85 crew/complement (2 fatalities)
MV Seguin Laroche; 22 crew (10 fatalities)
USNS Rescue; 34 crew (0 fatalities)
HMS Viking; 135 crew (0 fatalities)
Total; 6760 persons (34 fatalities)
Time Displaced; 4536 persons (17 fatalities)

The words were all neatly printed with exceptional neatness, except for where at the bottom some person had scribbled an additional line:

What might have been; 1514 lost, 710 saved.

Smith felt a sinister shiver run down his spine and carefully looked to his left, where Bruce Ismay was seated. The shipping magnate was quietly flexing a pencil between his fingers and gazing at the handwritten figures on his own sheet of paper with eyes narrowed, as if the numbers were staring back at him. Smith turned his attention back to his own sheet of numbers, and recognised the flowing script of the addendum as Ismay's own handwriting.

There was a rustling sound as Andrews took the vacant seat to Smith's right, the crumpled overalls he wore rustling like paper. Andrews' usually well-combed hair was matted with saltwater, and his face was smeared with grease. He was a far cry from the well-attired man who Smith had witnessed sitting down to dinner in this room only the previous evening.

"So then, Thomas," Smith spoke softly, so as not to be overheard amidst the quiet murmur of voices and the clinking of cutlery as the stewards began to serve food. "How badly damaged is she?"

"Under any other circumstances I'd call it catastrophic, EJ," Thomas Andrews replied in a confidential whisper, before slicking his hair back with his hands and briefly staring around at a room conspicuously free of seawater. "But I'll give a full report shortly, once the pleasantries are done with."

As they spoke, Smith noticed that the background sound of preparations for dinner had faded away, replaced with a quiet expectancy as the various guests turned to face him. The motions of hosting guests at this table came to him like easy instinct, and he rose to his feet.

"Ladies, and Gentlemen, welcome aboard the Royal Mail Steamer *Titanic*. It is my express privilege to thank you all, on behalf of my ship and her company, to thank you for the efforts you have made over the past night to assist us in our hour of need, and to recognise the sacrifices you have made in assisting us, as well as those we have all lost."

He had chosen the words carefully in advance, and while not outright saying as such, he was not just referring to the casualties. "As such, might I suggest a minute's silence before we proceed?"

In unanimous agreement, all present rose and adopted various postures. Some bowed their heads, whereas some, such as Captain Furness, stared into the beyond as if standing to attention on parade. As Smith dipped his own head, contemplating a suitable prayer, in the corner of his eye he spotted Philippa Paik on the other side of the table, wringing her hands and eyes wet with unshed tears. Seeing her grief, Smith felt words begin to pour from him, as if a dam had been unstopped in his mind.

"Heavenly father; to those entrusted to the care of this ship you have sent miraculous salvation, when we in her command failed to honour that trust. Those whom you saw fit to deliver through time, that they might deliver us from evil, now find they are alone in a world unknown to them. Please grant unto us the wisdom to learn from them, the courage to admit to our failings, and the strength and compassion that we might support them through this exile, recognising all that they have lost and sacrificed, that we might live. In thy mercy, God Almighty, who transcends all times and places, and to whom the hidden pain of lives and loves lost is known, please grant us thy peace and mercy. Amen."

Despite it being a spurious piece of prayer, cobbled together without thought, a few murmuring voices mirrored the 'Amen', and Smith opened his eyes to see some faces looking towards him with expressions of gratitude; while some others seemed surprised and even put out by his words, none said as such. Miss Paik's tears were now flowing in twin cascades down her face, but her mouth was propped up in a courageous smile. Smith felt his heart go out to her, and suddenly thought of his wife and fourteen-year-old.

As soon as possible I'll have Sparks wire a message home, and assure Eleanor and Mel that I'm safe and well.

Even as he thought that however, he realised with a stab of guilt that the comfort offered by a message home was a luxury not afforded to the four thousand people and more who he was now beholden to. Taking his seat again, he felt hot tears of his own beading at the back of his eyes, and dabbed them quickly away before his emotions made themselves known.

"To business, then," he continued, allowing a brief smile. "Please consider this as an invitation to my table. We have no formal agenda beyond making ourselves familiar with one another, but my hope is that by the end of this meeting we have come to an agreement on how we proceed in the light of these tumultuous events."

He extended a hand. "To commence matters, Mister Thomas Andrews of Harland & Wolff Shipbuilders has, with the aid of ships' carpenter Hutchinson and various experts among you, prepared a report on the condition of *Titanic*." Again he offered a flickering smile, his moustache twitching upwards. "However, I recognise that all here are somewhat famished, and I doubt he will object much if we eat while he speaks."

"Only if you don't mind my indulging myself as well, Captain", Thomas replied, and Smith saw that the engineer had buttered a roll of bread and stuffed several pieces of ham and cheese inside to form a crude sandwich. Waters, the jovial master of the *Oceanic*, jokingly commented on "dinner and a show", spurring a few nervous chuckles as people began to tuck into slices of tongue and cuts of meat.

Andrews, his own snack wrapped in a napkin, took up a position beside an upright screen that had been set up on the adjacent bandstand. Noting the absence of the musicians, Smith briefly wondered at the origin of the light string music drifting over the table, and then saw a small device besides Thomas which appeared to be playing recordings of light airs. Marvelling again at these new technologies, he dabbed a few crumbs away from his mouth as Andrews took up a small pointer in hand and clicked it. A machine similar to a slide projector, but connected by wires to the ever-present laptop that now seemed welded to the shipbuilder's arms, whirred softly into life, throwing a beam of light through the lens.

On the screen appeared a diagram of *Titanic*'s bow, seemingly extracted from the ship's own blueprints.

"Good afternoon, everyone," Thomas began, wiping a few crumbs from his mouth. "I'd like to present our findings. Now, to establish context, I've spoken with First Officer Murdoch, who was on the bridge at the time of the collision, and he confirmed that when the ship sighted the iceberg, he ordered hard-a-starboard, and that as the bow cleared the obstruction he had the helm reversed to port, in order to swing the stern of the ship out of harm's way."

Smith nodded; it was a straightforward 'port around' manoeuvre. He could see several of his seafaring guests nodding in agreement, and Paik was visibly hanging on Andrews' every word.

"...Mr Murdoch also ordered the engines stopped, so that in the event of the stern colliding with the berg, the starboard propeller would not be turning when it came into contact with solid ice. While a prudent measure in averting potential shock damage to the engines, reducing the ship's speed also sapped her turning power, with the result that she came close enough to the berg to run over a submerged, and consequently invisible, ice-shelf, with the following results."

Andrews clicked the projector again, and red lines overlaid the diagram of the bow, all lying below the waterline. "This is the result, a mixture of crushing damage inflicted on the double-bottom, and burst seams where the hull was lifted and flexed by the action of grounding on the ice…"

The next 'slide' showed the ship level, then advanced in a series of frames as she trimmed further and further down by the head, her stern correspondingly rising like a see-saw. In the corner comparative times blinked, advancing from 11.40pm until 2.15am, at which point the ship's propellers and rudder were rearing up out of the water.

"Unless assistance had come," Andrews concluded. "The ship would have broken up and gone down at about 2.20am. For the benefit of those unfamiliar with what might-have-been, I have here a… cinematic reproduction of the event, though I have been warned that the director of this motion picture elaborated events for purposes of drama."

Besides him, Smith perceived Bruce Ismay resting his hands on the table as if to hold on tight. His face was pale, a few droplets of sweat beading on the surface.

"I warn you," Andrews intoned. "That some of this footage is quite disturbing."

He clicked the pointer. For the next few minutes Smith sat in shocked silence as the film played, seeing his ship hefting up like a skyscraper at an impossibly high angle, hundreds clinging to her sloping decks. Suddenly the hull tore in two, the stern section crashing down on people writhing like drowning rats in the water below. Then, pulled down by the weight of the flooded bow, the stern rose to a vertical position, hung precariously for several long moments, and then with shocking speed sank below the surface. The final shot before Andrews ended the segment of film was of hundreds of doomed passengers thrashing in the icy waters of the Atlantic, their screams for help mingling into a horrific chorus.

When the film ended, Smith felt his hands trembling on the surface of the table; discretely, he moved them to rest on his knees, where no-one else could see them. Andrews' lips were pinched into a thin line, and Rostron and Lord were weathering the effect of the film with a stunned silence. Bruce Ismay had closed his eyes and was breathing shallowly, but the other guests were sitting in polite silence. He could only assume that they had all seen this motion-picture, and were inured to its effect.

"I apologise for that," Andrews said softly. "But it was felt best that we convey to everyone the gravity of the situation we would have faced, had the miracle of the fleet's arrival not saved us."

Somewhat harrowed, the engineer took a bite of his sandwich, and clicked his pointer again. "Moving on, this is the current situation. The collision mats applied by *Rescue* have managed to suppress all the water entering through the side of Boiler Room 5, and most of that entering into Boiler Room 6. The efforts of Messrs Alinka and Lightoller have also closed off the fireman's vestibule, allowing *Titanic*'s pumps alone to get ahead in those compartments. Injection of the last supplies of DRP foam has also dewatered the forepeak, giving the ship some additional forward buoyancy."

The final slide slowed the new water levels. Of the six compartments flooded, the forepeak and boiler rooms were all but dry. Thomas pointed again. "At this point, only the three cargo holds are taking on water. Cargo Hold Three is cut open along its side, and is a lost cause, but one and two are not as badly holed, and so *Rescue*'s two portable pumps are successfully keeping the water down in them. This has allowed divers to enter into the hull with underwater welding gear, locate some of the points where water is entering through the double-bottom, and close them up, further reducing the rate of water ingress in those compartments to a slow leak. With care, and one at a time, we have subsequently removed the suctions from *Rescue* and *Viking*, and now believe that between the efforts of her own pumps and the two portables, *Titanic* can remain afloat indefinitely."

Thomas slowly exhaled, and chewed on his lip for a second, as if to make a difficult decision. "And, if I am correct, she is capable of travelling under her own power. Boiler Rooms 5 and 6 were flooded-out for a time, and their plant is consequently unusable due to cracking from thermal contraction, but the remainder of her boilers are still serviceable. Chief Engineer Bell has also assured me that her auxiliary steam generation plant, the single-ended units in Boiler Room 1, have already been lit and will be up to pressure in just a few hours, ensuring an adequate supply of steam for the engines... However, this is all dependant on whether or not the temporary repairs hold when underway – should the hydrodynamic head overwhelm the patches, or a rough sea carry them away, she may flood again, and extremely quickly – in such an event, I cannot guarantee the safety of any persons remaining aboard, and advise against returning *Titanic*'s passengers to the ship."

Arthur Rostron raised his hand tentatively, like a child in class, and Thomas acknowledged him with a nod. "Captain Rostron, you have a question sir?"

"Yes, Mr Andrews – would it not be safer for one of the other ships to simply tow *Titanic?*"

"I agree," added Lieutenant Miller. "If it wasn't for the fact that we've been down one prop since transitioning the time-vortex, *Rescue* would be capable of towing a vessel of this size at a speed of about five knots, but I'm sure the *Oceanic* could also tow her with ease."

A few other voices assented their agreement and Thomas nodded, whilst still raising his hands to plead silence. "Normally, gentlemen, I would concur that the simplest solution is the safest, but at this time there is a risk that the forward part of *Titanic*'s keel and hull girder were either damaged in the collision, or strained immensely under the weight of the water in her leading compartments. Putting a tow line on her forecastle would further stress these structures, and exert additional dynamic forces on the temporary repairs we have put in place. Having *Titanic* travel under her own steam reduces these stresses to a minimum. Our only other alternative would be to attempt to tow her backwards by one of the stern bollards, but steering her while in reverse would then require a second vessel be put on her bow, which is exactly what we wish to avoid. Travelling forward, she will at least be able to use her own engines and rudder to manoeuvre."

"So your suggestion," Smith spoke up, "is that the other ships escort *Titanic*, whilst she travels unassisted, at a slow rate of knots."

"Yes, Captain," Andrews confirmed. "Reduced speed will also allow us to stretch out *Titanic*'s limited coal supplies long enough to get to shore; as such I would not recommend travelling much faster than ten knots, but even at that rate we should make New York within five days, and less time if we head to a nearer port, for example Halifax."

"No…" Bruce Ismay piped up to Smith's left. "I will not have White Star Line's newest vessel skulking off to a Canadian backwater as if attempting to hide our shame… the world's press will need to see *Titanic* limping up the Hudson in disgrace if the severity of our situation is to be understood."

"To be fair, Mr Ismay," Waters replied levelly. "Wherever we make port, I doubt the media will be doing anything but paying this fleet the fullest of attention, especially if *Oceanic* is following *Titanic* up the channel. I've personally got no objection to making for Halifax – *Oceanic*'s draught is shallow enough that she can fit in any port deep enough to harbour *Titanic*."

"That is big question, of course," Captain Gorbachev intoned, his voice grinding like steel in a mill. "Where are we headed, if even common destination in mind?" He looked around slowly, and shrugged. "Is easy mistake to make; most of us here English and American, with countries familiar enough in this time, but must remember that my crew are Russian, and in this time, the Rodina is still ruled by a despot, Nicholas Alexandrovich. The revolution is not due for four, five years, and I doubt any person claiming Russian descent while telling future truths will last long in company of the Secret Police… or be any more welcome within the 'worker's paradise' that is to come, ha."

Smith found himself leaning forward onto the table, subtly trying to support himself while drawing closer.

"Revolution?" he repeated in disbelief. "And the Tsar of the Russians remembered as a tyrant?"

Gorbachev coughed momentarily as the gaze of multiple eyes fell on him, but drew himself up proud. "Da. In our time, Russia is a democratic nation, the Royal family having been deposed during the Revolutions of 1917."

"…and ruthlessly executed." butted in another voice. "The entire Romanov family, children included, murdered on the whim of a man with even less of a mandate to govern than Nicholas. And what came out of that was a totalitarian government, one that murdered more people than Nazi Germany, and which conquered innocent nations in the aim of furthering its own sphere of influence…"

Everyone turned to see *Rescue*'s Lieutenant Miller ticking points off on his fingers as he rolled onwards. "…not to mention playing a major role in nearly drawing the world into a nuclear war, before becoming so corrupt and bureaucratic that it collapsed under its own bloated weight…"

He emphasised the last point by slamming his hand on the table, while Gorbachev sat in brooding silence, a simmering volcano in a uniform.

"The twentieth century was not a proud one for Russia, regardless of which regime was in power," another person said softly, "but America has much to answer for as well, when it comes to unbridled aggression and the use of nuclear arms."

Nazi Germany? Nuclear arms? It's almost as if these people speak an alien lexicon. With yet more questions bouncing around in his head, Smith checked against an annotated guest-list for the identity of the scholarly man who had quietly taken the spotlight away from Miller. *Doctor Akira Oshiro, Marine Engineer…*

"Well, if we're going to play the blame game, let's look at the big picture!" Philippa Paik said bluntly, interrupting both Smith's thoughts and the conversation. "It's 1912, so right now Britain is struggling with trying to finance its continued persecution of native populations in the Empire, while also being torn apart from within by the Irish Question, cries for welfare reform, and an ongoing arms race of *'who can build the most dreadnoughts'* with Imperial Germany, an investment in ships which will ultimately prove to be a complete waste, *because the submarine has already made them obsolete.* Kaiser Wilhelm's in much the same boat, except he wants to expand his own empire and so rouse up his citizen's nationalistic pride to distract them from their own domestic concerns.

"It's no better overseas. China is carving itself up for the highest bidders in order to finance a war of oppression against its own citizens, which appeals to the various European powers looking to colonise Asia and Africa. And to cap it all off, the United States and Japan are now just finding their feet as world powers, and following the example of the current players in Europe are doing so like overgrown kids asserting themselves in a playground."

She pointed around the table, from person to person.

"England, America, France, Russia, Japan… every one of our parent nations is currently contributing towards an international crisis, and none of them have the foresight to see beyond their own limited national agendas. Paris wants revenge against the ghost of Otto Von Bismarck, London wants Europe to hold to a status quo that died *long* before the Congress of Vienna. Saint Petersburg wants to modernise but thinks it can do so without reforming the court or uplifting the peasantry. Tokyo doesn't know if it wants democracy *or* militarism and all that indecision will accomplish is shifting government into the hands of those least capable of governance, while Washington DC wants to be the sole power in the Americas because its politics still cling to the spirit of Manifest Destiny. And as for Berlin – Wilhelm *wants a war*, wants a quick and clean conquest like in 1871, something that will rally the German peoples round the flag, cement Prussian militarism as the authority in the land, and win considerable prestige for the state and his own fragile ego.

"And none of these governments trust the others, and none of them can see the whirlwind they're sowing. Civilisation is being gambled in a poker game because the Great Powers keep drawing from the deck and adding to the pot – all of them think they've almost got a winning hand and just need that *one right card* to steal the game. But the deck is rigged and the table's legs are rotten – there's going to come a point when it collapses under the weight of the pot! No winners, just wasted bets, *and chips spilling out across the floor.*"

Captain Robert Furness, silent until now, his arms folded and eyes closed as if in deep contemplation, suddenly spoke out, his soft words nevertheless carrying across the table.

"She's right; we've been plunged into the twilight of the Age of Empire, and all these factions are about to throw the world into a century of disastrous conflicts. World War One to World War Two, then out of the ruins come turf struggles between the new world powers; Korea, Vietnam and the Cold War, which laid the unrest that will fester into the Gulf Wars, and the international War on Terror. Each following on from the other like a toppling row of dominoes."

Smith's mind was reeling, and he could see that Ismay, Lord, Rostron and Andrews were just as stunned, as Furness continued, rising to his feet as he did so. "And those are just the highlights, not counting all the other blood debts that children not yet born must pay for the sins of those now in power. The Falklands War, Grenada, bloody regime changes in Arabia and the Central Americas, and wars of succession and persecution as well. The Arab Spring, Apartheid, Palestine and Israel…"

Furness then directed a stern glare at, of all people, Thomas Andrews. "…and the Irish Civil War, which leads on to decades of innocents suffering and dying in *'The Troubles'*…"

He caught his breath and rested his hands on the table. "There's not been a bloodier century in human history than the hundred years we are about to enter. Tens of millions will die by the sword, if left unchecked. Consider that."

Then, as if spent, he sat back into his chair. Smith felt sweat beading under his collar; so far as doom prophecies went, this was incredible.

"I think that…" Bruce Ismay's voice broke the silence, "… that we may already have tasted some of the storm you say our generation sowed… the future you describe sounds like the events of last night writ large, pride and vainglory ripped apart, leaving behind a screaming tumult baptised in blood and fear."

There were a few hesitant nods, but then Miller leaned forward, shaking his head.

"It gets worse. What we've talked about so far are wars, which are still governed by rules, a kind of code of conduct. But atrocity has become a method of protest as well… bombings and terrorist attacks were commonplace in our time…"

"September 11th…" murmured Paik, and Miller waved attention back to her. "The worst example is September 11th 2001. Several aircraft, each large enough to carry hundreds of people, were intentionally hijacked and crashed into prominent buildings, two of which were over a thousand feet high. Several thousand people died when those towers collapsed." She shuddered slightly; "I was nine years old at the time, and my family lived on Long Island – you could smell burning paper and aviation fuel twenty miles from Ground Zero…"

An eerie silence fell as her voice trailed off, broken only by the distant sound of waves breaking against the hull and the soft twanging of the ship's structure. Smith could feel his heart pounding away in his chest. During the Boer War he had captained several ships transporting troops, and seen battle-weary soldiers carried away from the front. The girl had the same haunted look in her eyes, and he could not doubt the truth in her voice. He suddenly felt as if he was staring off into a great void, one ready to swallow the world whole and spit out a screaming, broken carcass.

People were looking to him to respond. Slowly, he balled his trembling hands and pushed himself upright.

"So, it would seem that we are standing on the edge of the abyss," he swallowed, searching for the right words, and remembered the spontaneous prayer he had conjured earlier. "If so, then the responsibility falls to us to try and prevent this turn of events. *However*, at this time, our first and only responsibility is to those specifically under our care. So far the seas have remained calm, but we cannot expect to continue to drift south in the current much longer before the weather turns, at which point we will be still among the icebergs; I would much rather we made our plans now, and were in motion soon enough that we can navigate clear of the ice by sunset."

Murmuring voices agreed with him. With their consent behind him, Smith rolled on.

"From the words of Mister Andrews it is apparent that *Titanic* will need extensive repairs, and only the Harland & Wolff shipyards at Belfast have a graving dock large enough to receive her. However, at reduced speed it will take us over a week, and closer to ten days, to cover the many thousands of miles between ourselves and Ireland, which will surely test both the endurance and provisions of our various ships, as well as greatly increase the risk of the temporary repairs made to *Titanic* coming undone. As such, I would suggest that we follow the earlier suggestion, and continue west towards Halifax, a safe harbour with the facilities to prepare *Titanic* for an eastbound crossing back to Belfast."

"Very good Captain Smith…" responded Waters. "I defer to your judgement. But if we are agreeing to continue our voyage, we also have to consider that at this time, *Oceanic* is carrying both our full complement and all of *Titanic*'s passengers as well, including those who came aboard *Rescue* during the night. So far the peoples of two eras are getting along, but the atmosphere onboard has become *interesting…*"

He then shifted uncomfortably, as if offended. "Some of *Titanic*'s passengers – mostly First Class, but not all – are also demanding they be transferred to contemporary ships."

Smith could only imagine the culture shock being felt. Part of him agreed with the sentiments of these uncomfortable passengers, wishing it were possible to segregate the two groups altogether and place *Oceanic* under effective quarantine. He nodded his understanding and addressed his two contemporaries.

"Captains Rostron and Lord. Your two vessels are under no jurisdiction here except your own. While I am in no position to demand your assistance, and given that neither of you have an obligation to be here, we would gratefully accept any help you can offer."

Rostron and Lord glanced warily at one another before the Cunard captain spoke up. "There is also safety to be considered. Even a vessel of *Oceanic*'s size could be said to be overloaded with more than five thousand people aboard, should another emergency emerge. While I feel it would be foolish to start transferring large numbers of passengers between the ships now given how the sea is becoming choppier, *Carpathia* would still be glad to keep pace with *Oceanic* in case developing events require a full evacuation."

"Thank you Captain," Smith nodded. Someone had mentioned that in the original train of events, Rostron had ultimately been rewarded for his efforts to rescue *Titanic*'s survivors by being made Commodore of the Cunard Line. He could see it was a deserving accolade.

"*Californian* will also stick beside you," added Captain Lord, as if running to keep pace with Rostron. "We've currently taken aboard some of the surviving crew of the *Seguin Laroche*, and the *Liberty Bell*. It makes sense that we do not part company from the fleet."

The words seemed delivered in good faith, but from the sharp glare directed by Lord at Captain Furness, sitting opposite him at the table, Smith wondered if the Leyland steamer's captain had much choice in his actions. Seemingly immune to Lord's unspoken criticism, Furness sat upright.

"*Viking* will keep company as well. If we aim to scare the world onto the straight and narrow path it stands to reason that we stay together; the more future ships arrive in Halifax escorting *Titanic*, the stronger the message delivered will be."

Gorbachev of the *Anatoly Sagalevich* quickly nodded his assent as well, but Smith's attention remained focused on Furness, wondering at what closed thoughts were playing out in the man's head.

"Therein lies the rub," a new voice cut into the conversation. "What kind of message do you aim to deliver, and in whose name?"

Smith turned in his chair and spotted a lantern-jawed gentleman steepling his fingers at the far end of the table, resplendent in the military uniform of an American cavalry officer. A finely-brushed moustache crinkled as the man's face twisted in concern. Smith recognised him as one of *Titanic*'s First Class passengers, a gentleman he had dined with himself yesterday evening, and who had intervened when Wilde had been shot.

Major Archibald Butt. Aide and military advisor to the President of the United States, returning home from Europe, where he delivered a

message to the Pope on behalf of the President, hence the uniform – and
the ceremonial sword…

"Major Butt," he responded. "You have a concern you wish to put to the rest of the table?"

"Yes Captain," Butt said, bringing his interlaced fingers down to rest on the table. "Most of us here might now be considered free agents, particularly the Russians, who themselves have admitted they will not brook to come under the jurisdiction of Tsar Nicholas. Although *Oceanic* and her complement can be said to be part of the White Star Line, they are also *persona-non-grata* to the governments of this day and age. *Viking*, however, is another matter entirely. She is a warship of a future Royal Navy, and as such the British Admiralty may claim she falls under their command. Can you deny this, Captain Furness?"

Furness' face twitched, and he folded his hands against his face, as if deep in thought. Smith felt a momentary pang of sympathy: like almost all White Star officers, he himself was a member of the Royal Naval Reserve, trained in gunnery and naval warfare, ready to serve in the Defence of the Realm should war break out. Furthermore, thanks to his voyages transporting troops to the Cape, he possessed first-hand experience of navigating the convoluted course of military hierarchy. He did not envy *Viking*'s commander, trapped out-of-time without a clear line of command.

With no response forthcoming from Furness, Butt continued on, directing the full force of his voice and personality against his naval counterpart.

"You speak of scaring the world onto the straight path, and do so with such confidence that you evidently have the means to back up such a threat. Well that scares *me*, Captain, especially given that *Viking*'s armament remains a mystery."

Smith slowly took in the reactions to Butt's hectoring, and while he saw casual curiosity in his contemporaries, the faces of Furness' fellow time-travellers were slowly turning towards dread, as if a dangerous variable had just presented itself.

"Not entirely unknown, Major," said Thomas Andrews quietly. "I'm sure all of the captains here are aware that for the past several hours, the only communication possible between our ships has been by Morse lamp and signal flags. All wireless technology, including the talkie-devices, has been jammed since shortly after *Viking* arrived last night."

It was the elephant in the corner of the room that no-one had wished to discuss. Furness opened his eyes, and Smith could see a profound sadness in them, a weariness he shared.

"Yes, *Viking* is the source of the radio jamming. We have a comprehensive suite of Electronic Counter Measures that enabled us to throw a shroud over this part of the Atlantic. I apologise for taking unilateral action without consulting anyone, but given our sensitive situation, I felt best that our 'Time Fleet', as it were, should be quarantined from the rest of the world until we could all meet up like this. There seemed too great a risk of panic around the world if rumours of time-travelling ships began to circulate before we could decide on a course of action."

Smith nodded. Furness might have acted over their heads, but the man's concern was justified. Even Butt rumbled a few words of agreement, before turning back to his original point.

"Given that, Captain Furness, what else is your command is capable of?"

Furness let out a weary sigh, though his eyes retaining a predatory alertness. "I had hoped to contain the secrets of this technology until mankind was ready for it; preferably never. Even the underlying physics behind it are still thirty years ahead of our current time."

Thomas Andrews was inching towards Furness, his interest evident. With his free hand he was making notes on the back of a scrap of paper as Furness continued.

"*Viking* is both armed and powered by the natural phenomenon of nuclear binding energy. It is the atomic force, the power that holds matter itself together, and under the right conditions certain materials can be induced to undergo processes that yield up that power. I wish you to imagine *Viking*'s reactor, which is the name for her main power plant, as a boiler containing enough steam to propel the vessel over great distances without need to refuel. In the twenty years she has been in service, *Viking* has racked up enough miles to circumnavigate the planet ten times over, all on her original fuel installation."

He paused, as if waiting to deliver the thrust of his argument. Smith mentally contrasted the amazingly efficient propulsion system Furness described with *Titanic*, which required six hundred tons of coal a day to fire her boilers. Clearly this 'nuclear energy' was a potent power indeed.

"Now please," continued Furness. "Imagine such a power-source reconfigured as a weapon, mated to a long-distance delivery system."

Smith's brow creased as he tried to visualise. In his mind he imagined *Viking*'s smooth rear deck opening to reveal a cannon, firing great shells tipped with this 'nuclear energy' many miles over the horizon.

As if thinking along the same lines, Major Butt coughed. "So you are saying that your submarine has the ability to lay down massive fire at ranged distances. How far inland can her salvos reach?"

"Salvos!?" Furness's mouth twisted and he laughed like a broken toy. "You're thinking too small, Major; *Viking*'s delivery range is in excess of *four thousand miles!*"

Smith saw Butt sit upright before the meaning of the words reached his own mind, and felt as if he had been struck by a battering-ram. Like the reverse of a flush, he felt a sudden chill as the blood drained from his face.

Furness, however, was still speaking, his initial laughter replaced with a cold, chilling certainty. "The current delivery system is a rocket called the Trident-II, fired at a speed of eleven thousand miles per hour. It delivers the weapons system to the fringes of space, at which point the rocket engine burns out, and the missile falls to earth under the action of the planet's gravity. As it falls, it spits out several small nuclear warheads, adjusting its trajectory successively, so that the warheads land in different areas. Each contains sufficient nuclear explosive to level a city centre. Collectively, *Viking*'s armament is equal to several million tons of conventional High Explosive."

Butt shoot to his feet and yelled something, words blurred and indistinct to Smith, whose own mind was reeling. He almost felt he was going to go over in a faint as he held onto the table for support. Opposite him he could see Rostron standing, trying to speak over Butt, who was turning red in the face. His eyes travelled to Joanna Laroche, and young Miss Paik, whose wide-eyed expression confirmed Furness's terrifying message.

"That's enough!" Smith roared, and the rage carried itself down his body like a bolt of lightning, grounding itself to the floor as he shot to his feet with such speed that his chair was bowled over backwards. The argument crashed into shocked silence as he struggled to keep his balance, the momentary flash of clarity racing away and leaving him wobbling on his feet like a marionette with cut strings.

"How…" he struggled, turning to the representatives of the future. "How could such a weapon have come into being? The power, the ability to rain down untold death on any point in the world, carried on projectiles travelling so high and so fast as to be immune to defensive fire? It is a diabolical concept."

Furness was on his feet as well, expression calm. "It was the only way to ensure our survival."

As if stepping up in Furness' defence, the Japanese engineer, Doctor Oshiro, rose and continued the lesson, voice quavering subtly. "My nation remains the only one in the world to have ever been attacked with nuclear arms, during the August 1945 atomic bombings of Hiroshima and Nagasaki. They were brutal attacks…" he said firmly, levelling his gaze across the table to Lieutenant Miller. "But they did cut short the bloody endgame of the Second World War, and prevented an invasion or blockade of the Home Islands, both of which would have resulted in greater barbarities. After the war, many nations built scores of such devices, as the only way to prevent anyone from using such a weapon was by ensuring they would take just as much damage in retaliation."

Oshiro then paused, his mouth working into a grimace. "Japan was one of the few after the war who had the means to construct nuclear arms but chose not to. Having seen two cities levelled, the victims burned to ash, and countless others slowly die agonising deaths from radiation poisoning, it was enshrined in our constitution that we would never contribute to the propagation of weapons that had the power to end human civilisation…"

"It was a madman's defence…" conceded Miller. "But the best we could do… and it worked. There were a few close-brushes, but since 1945 there has not been another worldwide conflict."

"*Non*," snorted Joanna Laroche. "Our 'Great Powers' have long favoured proxy wars or 'asymmetrical warfare'…"

Smith visualised the earth as an orange studded with explosive cloves, and shuddered. His eyes travelled across the faces of the time-travellers, and he wondered if the insanity that seemed to thrive in their time was contagious.

Butt's face was now returning to a normal pallor. During the voyage he had seemed contemplative to Smith, as if musing on deep inner conflicts, but now he was directing himself with great conviction and singularity of purpose.

"*Viking* might have been part of a madman's defence in your time, but here it is without equal, the most powerful weapon in existence. So again I ask: who do you answer to, Captain Furness? First Lord of the Admiralty Sir Winston Churchill perhaps, a man I would not trust to understand the potential of a submarine, let alone these arms you speak of."

In response, Furness drew an envelope from his pocket and carefully removed its contents, a single piece of paper which he carefully spread out on the table as he sat back down.

"While the prospect of serving under the greatest British hero of all time certainly excites me…" he smiled pointedly at Butt. "My crew and I are sworn to the Crown; now, while that august office is currently embodied in the figure of King George V, I am still in a position to exercise orders in the name of Queen Elizabeth II, thanks to a contingency implemented in the event of Her government ceasing to exist; if, in a nuclear war, the government were destroyed before it could issue strike commands to us, we are provided with a 'letter of last resort' written by the Prime Minister, outlining the course of action we are to follow, and I have chosen to interpret these events as being in the spirit of that final order."

He pushed the slip of paper forward, and it slowly made its way down the table, passed from hand to the other. Smith glanced at it briefly, and the few scant sentences burned themselves into his mind. As he handed it on to Andrews and the letter gradually progressed towards Butt, he turned to regard Furness, trying to get the measure of a man to whom such power was entrusted.

"This is…" Butt was reading the letter now, his face pale. "… preposterous. Your commander-in-chief released you from all responsibility, giving you the leniency to do as you wish?"

"Released from responsibility?" Furness said, his words now cold. "On the contrary, Major; the ultimate responsibility now falls to me, to determine how the weapon I command should be wielded. I'd gladly give up that task, except that would mean placing *Viking* in the custody of one of the nations of this world, and allowing her to be commanded by men with no understanding of the power at their fingertips. I *could* do that – the letter empowers me to align myself with a friendly world power – but which, of all the nations currently arming themselves for the coming century, would you describe as friendly? Who should I anoint as the sole superpower? Or would you rather I go from port-to-port dropping off a missile at each for safekeeping; Norfolk, Virginia, and then Portsmouth, then Hamburg? I'm sure the Tsar would love to close the missile-gap too, and of course I'd then need to make sure Tokyo has one as well, given their recent bit of mutual blood-letting with the Russians."

The Chinese would need a weapon of their own to defend themselves against the threat of Japan's colonial expansionism, Smith thought to himself, alarmed at what Furness was suggesting, albeit sarcastically. *And the Ottomans and Balkan states would not stand for the Russians and Austro-Germans having a device that would make either an invasion or resistance to an invasion a self-destructive tactic. It would be madness, and any nation left out of the 'nuclear club' would certainly begin attempting to duplicate the technology, and so the number of weapons would proliferate endlessly, beyond the control of treaties and ententes.*

Again the idea of an orange studded with explosive cloves came to mind, as Furness wrapped up his speech.

"…yes it would be a pleasant little world-cruise of gift-giving, *Atomic Christmas*, and once I'd dropped off the last, I could turn my rudder to the horizon, free of this burden, in my wake leaving behind a kick-started Cold War! No sir, I have once already seen the world suffer under the gun of a nuclear stalemate, and I will not be the man who starts another! I would rather *Viking* live up to the aspirations of the world she left behind and serve as an instrument of peace, even if is an enforced peace. For that, I would gladly shoulder the burden, for all eternity if need be."

"So you would retain control of these weapons, deciding by yourself alone how they should be used," surmised Butt, his voice clear even as his eyes widened in terrified comprehension. "No nation would support you, so how would you feed and supply your crew, except by holding ships to ransom? You'd be no better than Verne's Nemo, a vindictive butcher, or worse still – a pirate."

"A privateer, in matter of fact," Furness pointed at the piece of paper still in Butt's hands. "And that is my letter of marque, signed by no less than my Prime Minister, as representative of the will of Her Majesty; thus that standing order embodies the Crown to which I am sworn, ahead and above of King George."

"Gentlemen…" Smith said, forcing his tired voice to make itself heard, and miraculously he spoke at such a time that the two rebutting men had paused for breath, allowing him to draw their attention.

"We are not at war," he continued. "And we are not enemies. In matter of fact *Titanic* and all who sailed in her owe Captain Furness and his crew a debt of gratitude, given that without their aid last night, we would have sunk. In my eyes, every man-jack, and woman here, is a hero who gave all without question to come to the aid of this ship… there is no better way to spread word of the danger of these weapons, and the futility of history's current course, than by the world seeing *Viking* come steaming, if that is the right word, up into Halifax harbour as part of this great flotilla which has done us a service of peace, as an example of the madness which might have claimed us all…"

He turned to Furness. "Captain, might I be the first to welcome you to this twentieth century, and invite you and your fine vessel to sail beside us in a gesture of goodwill?"

He extended a hand and Furness uncertainly shook it, prompting a scatter of light applause. Repeating himself to extend the offer to the other arrivals seemed to cement the agreement, and the remainder of the meeting passed in relative calm.

That is, until Oshiro spoke his piece.

"Has anyone considered the possibility that we might be able to return home?"

CHAPTER TWENTY FOUR

"So, Mrs McKinn – I understand you have served as a lady of state?" Marian Thayer enquired, shuffling a deck of cards and beginning to deal four hands of thirteen each.

"That's correct," Adrienne replied. "I represented Montana for six years in the House of Representatives."

"You say it so casually…" commented a woman sitting to Adrienne's left. "I must say I envy the position you hold, Mrs McKinn."

The newcomer's name was Helen Candee, a dark-haired beauty who Adrienne would confess to envying for a near perfect complexion, despite the fact that they were of a similar age.

"To go out into the world and earn a living," Helen continued, her eyes bright. "It is not only the desire of all free-thinking women, but also the key to our emancipation."

She was an author, and an outspoken campaigner for female equality, and her excitement was infectious.

"Don't flatter me too much," Adrienne replied lightly, examining the cards she had been dealt. "Even after I won the election I had to deal with plenty of misogyny. Many of my opponents in Congress assumed that I would be a weak legislator."

"And what happened then?" said Marian, one eyebrow arched as if able to predict the answer, and Adrienne stifled a laugh at the other woman's perception.

"Well, ultimately I ended up chairing the House Committee on Ethics. We exposed several of my most ardent opponents as having taken bribes to pass acts favourable to business interests in their districts, and they quickly vanished into infamy. I even replaced one of them on the House Armed Services Subcommittee on Strategic Forces, and in his place helped accelerate the Trident Life Extension, an essential defence program. I even talked the

United Kingdom into participating in the project... a nation which, I might add, elected a female Prime Minister in 1979."

"How delightful, truly delightful!" Helen Candee's soft laugh and the clapping of her hands were lost in the general buzz. Around them, *Oceanic*'s Manhattan lounge, normally a private space for the highest-paying passengers, hummed with activity and bustle as passengers dined in the adjoining Liverpool and Southampton Grills, most exclusive of the onboard restaurants. With the influx of several thousand people, the doors of the ship's eateries had been thrown open to all, regardless of class, just to handle the numbers. The small group of ladies were fortunate to have found a table of their own at which to play a few hands of bridge.

"Would you not agree, Mrs Thayer," Helen addressed the woman sitting opposite her, her own cards forgotten, "that Mrs McKinn here is a shining example that women of this age should aspire to?"

"I for one do not," replied a fourth voice before Marian could respond.

Their eyes turned towards the fourth player, Ida Straus. Their senior by several years, her hair worn in a silvery bun, the Germanic lady's own eyes lightly sparkled with mirth as she laid her own cards on the deck, effectively ending the game before it could begin. "A woman's place should be at home, where we might better ensure our men do not go out and ruin the world."

Adrienne stifled a smile. "This is why I've long held a desire to meet ladies such as you. I wished to experience for myself the politics of suffrage, in an age where great men were backed from the shadows by equally powerful women."

The four of them had met by a mixture of chance and design. In her capacity as an informal member of *Oceanic*'s crew, Adrienne had positioned herself in the lobby to meet and greet those coming aboard from *Titanic*, mingling among the crowds and making small talk. Her formal dress, sufficiently similar to the passengers of 1912, had helped to set them somewhat at ease, and with a few words in the right place, she had managed to both ease tensions and establish her penthouse stateroom, the Majestic suite, as a focal point for the more prominent industrialists and society figures from both eras.

The results had been spectacular. Before they left for this little ladies' circle, Adrienne had seen one of her contemporaries, an African-American historian, engaged in a spirited argument with *Titanic* passengers Isidor Straus and Colonel Archibald Gracie over the ethics of the American Civil War. The fact that Isidor had run blockades during said conflict, smuggling guns for the Confederacy, only enlivened the debate.

Small wonder, then, that she had passed over an invitation to attend the conference aboard *Titanic*, and sent Pippa Paik in her place; the poor girl had needed to get away from *Oceanic* anyway.

"This is heavenly," she declared aloud, and her three companions turned their heads towards her in both surprise and interest. "In fact, it's better than heaven."

"How so, Mrs McKinn?" Marian replied, and not for the first time, Adrienne marvelled at the ability of this era's women to convey so much meaning with the very minimum of expression.

"I always dreamed," she explained. "That Heaven would be a place where you would be able to meet with the greats of history and learn directly from them, as I'm doing right now. Except unlike Heaven, these conversations will lead to actual changes in the world."

"You speak as if the dead man condemned to Hell has been allowed to deliver his warning to the friends he left behind."

"Well, why not?" Helen interjected on Adrienne's side. "Was not Marley's ghost able to gain enough of a reprieve to turn Scrooge from the same path?"

"Exactly Helen, thank you," Adrienne smiled, silently adding, *and thank you Charles Dickens.*

"I remain unconvinced," Marian responded. "How might the words of a few thousand people change the course of predetermined history?"

"Let me give you an example," Adrienne replied, ready to bring out her trump card. "Watch this."

She raised her voice and called out. "Service please."

A young woman in the uniform of a maid came over briskly, an antiquated lace bonnet bobbing atop her head. With the surfeit of passengers to care for, the majority of *Titanic*'s domestic staff had been pressed into service aboard *Oceanic*, the stewards and chefs having to come to grips both with their new ship's gigantic scale and the extravaganza of new technologies embodied within her.

As if to illustrate this, the nervous girl's uniform was contrasted by an electronic keycard hanging on a lanyard around her neck. She curtseyed subtly as she reached their table.

"Hello," Adrienne smiled warmly. "Please, take a seat."

The girl seemed ready to bolt, and as if on autopilot curtseyed again.

"That would not be appropriate, Ma'am."

"Oh, take a seat Violet!" interjected Ida Straus, a curiously knowing grin lighting up her weathered face. "Please my dear, consider it a reward for all your good service."

Hesitantly, the girl sat in the offered chair. She was at most in her mid-twenties, and her words of thanks were laced with a slight Irish accent. Despite her obvious nerves, she moved with grace and self-control, keeping her hands demurely folded in her lap. *Titanic* had less than thirty female crewmembers, Adrienne knew, and so any that did make the grade of serving on the White Star Line's flagship were surely a rare breed. But her mind was reeling at the name by which Ida had called the young woman, while at the same time giving an inner whoop of triumph.

"Miss, are you by chance Violet Jessop?"

"Yes I am," the stewardess replied, paling slightly. "But Ma'am, how do you know my name?"

They now had the full attention of the other ladies around the table. Adrienne thanked her good fortune.

"Violet," she said kindly. "Do you know where this ship is from?"

"Yes Ma'am, from the future. April 14th 2012, to be exact."

"Do not be so bashful, Violet!" laughed Mrs Straus. A touch of colour reached the stewardess' cheeks and she mumbled something under her breath.

Ida looked at her companions; the warmth of her smile was endearing. "This clever girl, like many of us, was told little of where *Oceanic* was from, such was the madness. But she went out and learned that you were marking the centenary of *Titanic*'s sinking, and came back with confidence to give us the very date from when you travelled."

Violet Jessop beamed in shy gratitude at the praise, and Adrienne went in to make the decisive blow.

"Violet, in the world I come from, you are a legendary figure amongst survivors of *Titanic*."

This time, the stewardess did not blush or shirk from praise, but instead looked straight at Adrienne, her grey eyes full of questions. "Why me? I am not a hero, nor am I important."

"Because you wrote down your memories of the sinking. *The Memoirs of Violet Jessop, Stewardess*, are a treasured work amongst *Titanic* historians who want to understand what it was like to work for the White Star Line in this period."

Adrienne's smile grew wider as she saw Violet Jessop's eyes open wide. "Indeed, Violet, it was only when I read a copy of your memoirs, a copy that my late husband gifted to me, that the legend of the *Titanic* took hold of my imagination…" She dipped her head. "If I had not read that book, none of us are likely to be here right now. Thank you."

"Well, you're quite welcome Ma'am. Thank you for sharing that with me." Violet replied, a flush of pride showing on her face now. She sat up a little taller, subconsciously drawing herself up to match the posture of the fine ladies gathered around her.

"Now, please tell me Violet," Adrienne continued, encouraging gently. "What do you think of *Oceanic*'s female crew?"

Violet opened her mouth immediately. "Oh they are so much happier than we were on *Titanic*, Ma'am. They smile gladly and laugh more often."

"And why is that?"

"Because they have not lost their dignity…" the stewardess replied. "Or rather, they have built themselves up." She glanced around as if looking for an example. "Do you see that lady at the entrance to the Southampton Grill?"

Helen Candee and Marian Thayer looked discretely. Ida Straus fairly bounced around in her chair to see, as if finding the situation a gigantic game. The woman in question was, like Violet, a stewardess, though there the similarities ended. She was dressed in a long, austere skirt, finely pleated, but there was none of the frilly encumbrances of a maid to her. Instead, above her beltline she wore a crisp white blouse, with a matching waistcoat that fit snugly around her. The gilt trim to her uniform seemed to shine like threads of gold woven into the fabric. And, as Violet had said, she was smiling broadly, greeting passengers and directing them into the restaurant. It was not just the effect of her uniform that made her stand out, however; she seemed to glow with pride.

"She is a Filipino named Carrie Fae," Violet explained. "She's the Chief Buffet Stewardess for the Southampton Grill, and she was kind enough to help me find my way around the ship. She let me sleep a few hours in her bunk while she worked, and when I woke up, I found she had returned and was crying. Today is her birthday, and she is spending it apart from her family, perhaps never to see them again."

Adrienne listened intently, wondering where this was going. Helen Candee had the studious look on her face of someone taking notes.

"If this was a ship like *Titanic*," continued Violet. "Carrie would have to deal with that grief alone. Few care about the handful of women in the victualling staff, and pretty much everyone in the crew looks down on us. But while I was trying to comfort her, some of her crewmates, men and women, came into the cabin and burst out singing 'Happy Birthday'. They hugged her, gave her presents, laughed and cried together. For all their loss, they are proud to be working together on this ship. And so welcoming to us…"

Violet tugged for a second at the apron that was a part of her uniform. "She… she has even promised to find me a uniform like hers," she said hopefully, face bright at the thought.

"And I'm sure you'll wear it well," Adrienne smiled, giving Violet's hand a squeeze before Ms Fae called out to Violet, and with a quick word of thanks, the young stewardess briskly went to assist her counterpart with preparing for the forthcoming dinner seating.

"Now would you agree, ladies," Adrienne postulated, beaming with gladness, "that Ms Jessop is a bright and intelligent young woman, who shows a lot of potential? Indeed, her words and memoirs, humble as they are, brought this situation into being." Her expression darkened. "Despite that, she is relegated to a position little better than a maid, with no options for advancement unless she attempts to seduce some wealthy passenger."

Marion Thayer coughed in surprise at Adrienne's bluntness, while Ida and Helen both laughed. Adrienne joined in, but then began to speak again, voice serious. "Why should Violet's intelligence and ability be squandered simply because of the accident of her gender? Why should she not aspire to be a great writer, politician, or person of business? And if the same goes for her, then why should it not apply to every woman in the world?"

Helen Candee looked ready to take up the cause Adrienne was describing straight away, while Marian and Ida looked less convinced. Before any comment could be passed however, a familiar voice was suddenly heard nearby.

"Good afternoon, to all aboard the *Oceanic*, I am Margaret Brown of Colorado, known to many of you as the 'Unsinkable Molly Brown'…"

Adrienne turned in her seat, and she saw Maggie Brown standing across the room with a young man she recognised immediately, speaking to a pair of film cameras held by two men in contemporary attire.

"With me is Dean Simmons, a professional tele-journalist previously in the employ of the British Broadcasting Corporation, and together with our colleagues Daniel Mervin and William Harbeck, we wish to take you all on a journey."

Adrienne stared in dumbfounded delight as Maggie, resplendent in the dress she had worn when disembarking *Titanic*, and conducting herself with the confident gusto for which she was remembered, turned to the youth beside her.

"Mr Simmons, would you care to explain?"

"Thank you Maggie. The journey that we're describing is one that will take us all into a past and future now fused into one present. We will be travelling the length and breadth of *Oceanic*, speaking with anyone who is willing to share their thoughts and views on what has happened this past night, and their hopes and dreams for what comes next. We don't care who you are or when you come from, except that you are open and honest in delivering your opinions on this most monumental of historical events."

The two of them were standing beneath a regal portrait of Alexandra of Denmark, for whom *Oceanic* was to have been originally named. Glancing up at the painting, Simmons seemed to be struck by sudden inspiration.

"On behalf of the 'Alexandra Press', this has been Margaret Brown and Dean Simmons."

Adrienne turned back to the circle of ladies gathered with her. "I rest my case... ladies, after my husband died and I retired from politics, I spent years trying my hand at any number of skills in the hope of finding a new outlet of for my passions. I have climbed mountains, qualified as a helicopter pilot, and prior to founding Project 401 briefly ran a baseball team, which failed spectacularly. And I am very willing to share those experiences with this entire ship, if it serves to broaden the horizons and opportunities of those onboard."

"I think..." Marian Thayer said, delicately wiping her lips with a napkin. "That would be an excellent idea, Adrienne, and I shall be glad to join you in that endeavour."

*

The debate that milled around the Captain's Table on *Titanic* stopped abruptly when Oshiro looked up from the duplicated documents brought aboard from *Viking*, and suggested the possibility of the time-travellers returning to the future. Smith's hand rose from a statement he had been penning on behalf of the group for broadcast by wireless, and he frowned.

"Please expand on this, Doctor..."

Prompted accordingly, Oshiro rose to his feet and took Andrews' place beside the darkened projector, adopting the manner of a man lecturing a room of bright (if disinterested) students.

"From this copy of Dossier 7000, kindly furnished by Captain Furness, I have some thoughts. Firstly, we can all say that the *Liberty Bell* device is indeed capable of transporting objects in time. However, it arose from an attempt to cloak warships to the human eye and electronic detection, an attempt which failed when a test on the cruiser USS *Eldridge* in 1943 displaced the ship in time and space."

He paused, as if waiting for them to draw the conclusion. "However, at the conclusion of the test, the *Eldridge* appears to have come back!"

A few gasps and sighs of understanding went up around the table, and Smith rubbed his eyes, half-expecting the conversation to descend into technicalities beyond his conception.

"Though Dossier 7000 does not directly *say* the ship returned, its supplementary data states that the *Eldridge* was many years after the Philadelphia Experiment sold to the Greek Navy and renamed the *Leon*, meaning that the US Navy must have recovered the vessel from where it was displaced in the time-stream. The folder also makes clear that the Americans' Project Lesterpack devoted funds and effort towards exploiting this phenomenon right up until the Project's termination in June 1994. In that time I believe they managed to duplicate the effect multiple times, with everything that was displaced in time returning to the point of origin on demand, crossing the boundaries between the original timeline and the forked event sequence."

"So in practical terms," said Captain Furness, with what sounded to Smith's trained social ear like feigned surprise, "you're saying that the US Navy created their time-machine entirely by accident?"

"Quite; indeed I suspect that was where their problems began, insofar as practical application of the effect went," Oshiro began, his face practically aglow with excitement, stumbling over his own words. "The US had a functioning time-machine, without a complete understanding of the physics behind it."

"Please explain, Doctor," Smith requested. "But please, in layman's terms."

"While temporal mechanics is only a theoretical field, one of the most basic principles in the universe is causality – cause followed by event. This is why many have theorised that going back in time is impossible, as any of the inevitable changes caused by a time-traveller would break or distort the sequence of events that produced the time machine in the first place, creating a 'paradox', a conflict of events. For example, if someone used the *Liberty Bell* to go back in time to prevent the American Revolutionary War, there never would have been a United States Navy to produce the device, which contradicts its own existence."

"Therefore…" began Joanna Laroche, following along. "It becomes impossible to change the future in the past… but that doesn't explain how we were able to prevent the *Titanic* from sinking. If that rule was iron-clad, Captain Smith would not be here right now, and this room should be sitting on the bottom of the Atlantic…"

Mentally Smith imagined being plunged into darkness, as if being clenched in a fist of ice, screaming silently in the abyss as the pressing oblivion poured down his throat, flooding his lungs…

It was a chilling thought of what his fate might have been. To his side, Bruce Ismay looked just as disturbed. Smith's hands felt out the elaborate carvings around the edge of the table, felt their solidity, and tried to take comfort from the hard reality under his fingertips.

Oshiro, meanwhile, had moved to the projector and flicked it on, throwing a beam of light on the screen. Then, pulling a translucent sheet from a small rack under the lamp, he laid it on the projector's surface and began to draw a crude diagram which was cast on the screen behind him, talking as he did so.

"For fifty years the scientists of Project Lesterpack might have attempted to play God with history, sending test subjects back in time with instructions such as *'assassinate Adolph Hitler while he's still a baby'* or *'prevent the death of Abraham Lincoln'* and the like, but I imagine they found *that 'the past is past'*, that the changes never seemed to carry forward. The termination document suggests the Project was shut down because no matter what they did, any changes made when they travelled back in time failed to manifest in the present, and any experiments sent forward in time refused to return. Their 'time-machine' became regarded as a failure, a curiosity with no practical application. But the fact remains that their experiments successfully reached the past and successfully effected changes – how can this paradox be explained? Thusly…"

He stepped back, and with the shadow of his hands removed they could see that he had drawn a crude stream, into which a rock had been placed, breaking the flow.

"This rock is us, time-displaced objects that have dropped into the flow of history. But time is fluid, and adaptable, and simply breaks around our presence, to form two separate currents, two courses of time. One is the original, where we never arrived, and the *Titanic* sank last night."

He tapped the flow on the left, and then the one on the right. "We however, are now in the second stream, a new timeline whose ultimate outcome is undecided."

Now his shadowed hand slid across the screen to a second crude sketch, of a rope unravelling into two threads. "Two timelines, A and B, drawing apart from each other as their event sequences diverge further."

He pointed. "We are here, in Timeline B. But right now in Timeline A, separate from us by only the breadth of a hair, *Carpathia* has collected the last of *Titanic*'s lifeboats, and is making her way to New York. *Californian*, shunned and disgraced, lingers behind in the hope of finding more survivors. *Titanic* lies broken on the ocean floor like the ruins of Atlantis, and elsewhere in the world events spiral towards war. That sequence of events is just on the other side of the veil from us, a veil composed of ripples and eddies in the quantum foam between two worlds, echoes from a might-have-been destiny."

Smith unconsciously clutched at his arms. A cold death in the depths had awaited him after sixty-two years of life well-lived? He could still feel the memory of the crushing dark playing around the edge of his thoughts as Oshiro drew a large spiral between the two streams.

"We also know, possibly thanks to these faint bonds still connecting the two timelines, that the *Liberty Bell* could take us back to our future. Like a stretched rubber-band, it retains a faint connection with our point and time of origin, and if we could but prompt it and supply enough power, it would return us all to April of 2012, in the timeline that we knew..."

He sighed. "You understand that I am speaking here as an engineer and not a theoretician, doing my best to make educated guesses. Conceptually, we could even bring *Titanic* and our other guests along for the ride back to the future of Timeline A, with the knowledge that it would be impossible to bring them home to *this* Timeline B; because any attempt to return to the past from Timeline A will simply create a new Timeline C, branching off from A..."

His timeline diagram now resembled a crow's foot, three forking lines surrounded by complex interconnecting arrows. "However, the longer we wait, the less chance we have of success, because as the changes between the two timelines accumulate, the further they diverge, the more we stretch the rubber band, which will ultimately *snap*, breaking the connection between realities..."

"A mathematical certainty," Thomas Andrews observed.

A hushed moment passed as people exchanged expectant glances. Smith spoke up, feeling as if he was speaking lines in a script penned by some greater hand.

"How much time?"

"Before so many changes amass that we time-displaced travel beyond the point of no return?" Oshiro slowly looked from his notes and Dossier 7000, to his diagram, and slowly turned around, taking in the elegant tranquillity of the dining saloon, dry and intact. "It's impossible to say; right now we are in a sort of bubble. *Viking*'s ECM shroud is keeping the outside world in ignorance of what has transpired here, and so the change in world events is for a little while mitigated. There'll be speculation and debate, just as there was in Timeline A while *Carpathia* slowly travelled back to New York with the survivors onboard, but I doubt those will translate into serious deviations from our immediate history for another few weeks, unless some nation decides to declare war spontaneously."

Smith held up his statement. "And would it be safe to issue this declaration to the world?"

Oshiro's lips thinned for a second as his mouth tightened, and then he nodded. "Possibly. From what we've discussed, snippets of these events had already leaked out into the world through various wireless transmissions before *Viking* threw up her shroud. So a controlled release of information, with a request for calm, might have the effect of slowing changes in the timeline, rather than allowing rumours and panic to fester and circulate among the nations."

"And it is the responsible thing to do, at least to give some comfort to those ashore awaiting news of their friends and loved ones aboard *Titanic*..." Andrews added.

Closing his eyes for a moment, Oshiro looked away from the diagram. "Like I said, this is guesswork. If possible, Captains Lord and Furness might allow the *Liberty Bell to* be transferred to the *Rescue* for study, where we would have access to modern tools, components and a steady supply of high-voltage electricity. Hopefully, it can be brought into working condition before we reach the continental Americas."

The two captains in question nodded, though Lord seemed more relieved than anything, and Furness had the faint traces of a hopeful smile playing around the corners of his mouth. Smith could feel something similar welling up in himself, and he stood to address the crowd.

"Thank you, Doctor; with that in mind, might I suggest the following course of action; that the *Liberty Bell* device be brought aboard the *Rescue* for examination, and the fleet as a whole informed of the possibility of the time-travellers returning to their own time. Meanwhile, all these gathered vessels shall set course for Halifax, remaining close together for mutual support and protection. In several days' time we shall anchor off of Nova Scotia, and reconvene again to determine whether or not we should proceed into Halifax Harbour, or transfer all contemporary passengers off of *Oceanic* and allow the time-displaced ships, and all aboard them, to attempt a return to their point of origin."

Heads around the table nodded in agreement, and Smith smiled in relief.

"To those currently lost in time, I'm sure you and your contemporaries will be glad to hear the news that they have a chance to return home. For the rest of us, we who've known no other world than that of the nineteenth and twentieth centuries, this has been a tremendous boon, a blessing of the kind not bestowed upon any man since the time of Christ. We are alive, where many of us should be dead. Our ship is afloat, and has the prospect of many useful years of service ahead of her. And we now have the hindsight of history and warnings of what is to come, as well as the freedom to stand apart from that destiny, separate and distinct from what we might have been. Friends, we have been given that most precious of things… a second chance…"

Major Butt spoke up, taking the last word. "And this time, we'll get it right…"

*

"As soon as *Viking* drops the shroud, send this off to Cape Race with instructions to circulate it," Smith said curtly, handing over a lengthy wireless message to Jack Phillips, who seemed somewhat overwhelmed to have been summoned to the First Class Reception. As his eyes ran over the lines of text crammed onto both sides of the piece of paper, Smith saw the pallor drain from the wireless operator's face. He chuckled softly and, in a rare gesture of familiarity, reached out and patted the young man's shoulder.

"I know it is a long message, but consider that your finger will be tapping out the first account of an event that will be remembered for all history. That is an honour few receive."

"Sir…" Phillips' face regained a little colour and he nodded. "Yes sir."

"Furthermore, there will be some new equipment coming aboard for installation in the wireless suite". Smith indicated for Phillips to follow him over to where some of the cases brought aboard from *Rescue* and *Oceanic* had been stacked. Another one of the time-travellers was lounging on them, and he came to his feet as Smith approached.

"Sparks," Smith began. "This is radioman Cameron from the *Rescue*. Given the losses to our crew, Captains Jones and Waters have found many of their people volunteering to fill positions on *Titanic*. Mr Cameron is also going to assist in setting up a two-way voice radio which will enable us to communicate directly with the other ships for the remainder of our voyage."

"Pleasure to meet you, Mr Phillips," Cameron said as the two men shook hands.

Phillips smirked. "So you're the drunkard who couldn't formulate a spark?"

Cameron returned the grin. "Those are fighting words, 'Sparks'. Help me get this gear in place and I'll show you the future of radio. Then we'll see who the master of the craft is!"

Smith left the two men to get acquainted and set up as he turned his attention to the rest of the dispersing guests from the conference. Off to one side he could see Butt and Furness

489

exchanging words, with considerable more courtesy than during their argument.

"…I'd be glad to accept your offer of a guided tour, Captain," Butt was saying. "So long as I not be required to censor myself in the aftermath."

"Far from it, Major," Furness smiled affably. "On the contrary, I'd wish for President Taft to receive as full a briefing as possible on *Viking* and her capabilities."

Butt nodded in gratitude, and Smith saw him turn away to mingle with the other guests. Elsewhere he could see Captains Laroche and Rostron in deep conversation. Stewards drifted through, unobtrusive bodies carrying various beverages. Curiously, and presumably for the benefit of the time-travellers, several boxes of various drinks had been brought over from *Rescue* during the night, and as a steward passed him, Smith snatched a flute of a dark, almost black liquid in which numerous bubbles fizzed merrily. He was reminded of champagne, and wondered if this was a black wine of sorts. Checking with the steward to assure himself that it was not alcoholic, he took a tentative sip, and was pleasantly surprised at the contrast between the sweet tonic and the bitter gas of the bubbles.

With his champagne flute of 'Pepsi' in hand, Smith slowly turned to gaze up the grand staircase, revelling in the light pouring down through the frosted glass dome above.

It was a new day, and he felt a nervous but hopeful spring in his step that he that he had not felt in many years, as if taking his first command once more.

"Captain," someone called. "The volunteer firemen are coming over now."

*

A crowd of men were clustered into one of *Oceanic*'s launches as it made its way across the gap between the modern liner and *Titanic*. Many were members of the liner's stokehold crew who had come over to *Oceanic* during the night when it still looked like the White Star flagship might sink.

The remainder were passengers who had offered to take the place of those firemen who had refused to return to the patched-up ship. Several were talking amongst themselves, praising each other for their sacrifice, while others stood aside and massaged their wrists and arms, limbering up for what would surely be hard labour.

Jack Thayer was one of those keeping to themselves, seated in a corner and hunched over, trying to edit a message of apology in his mind. He'd sworn to get himself back aboard *Titanic* in order to express his regrets to Philippa Paik, and if the path to salving his conscience led through the mighty ship's boiler rooms, then so be it.

Spotting something incongruous in the corner of his eye, he glanced up and noticed that there was a woman among the crowd. He frowned, recognising her as a famous designer of haute-couture ladies' fashion.

What's Lady Lucille Duff-Gordon doing here?

Then his eyes slid off the elegant fashion-designer and came to rest on her husband, Sir Cosmo Duff-Gordon.

Ah... that explains it.

Jack's father had mentioned seeing Cosmo get into an altercation with one of *Oceanic*'s crew, demanding he and Lucille be allowed off the ship, so he supposed the man had struck a deal volunteering his services in the boiler rooms in return for his wife being allowed back over onto *Titanic* with him.

Well, that's more than I would have given the man credit for. I wonder how much it cost him in bribe money... Jack mused, and then frowned. There he was, making spontaneous judgements on others again, without pausing to consider his own behaviour.

I would have thought my words with Miss Paik would have taught me that lesson already. Apparently not.

Still deep in thought, he was almost oblivious to the launch smacking up against *Titanic*'s hull, only coming to when the other volunteers began climbing aboard, entering through the same E-Deck reception that he had used to leave the ship. It formed a kind of symmetrical irony, he supposed.

"Welcome back aboard, gentlemen," Third Officer Pitman greeted them. "Thank you for volunteering your services at what is a difficult time; please proceed along the marked path to the D-Deck Reception, where Captain Smith would personally like to..."

Jack ignored the man's fawning platitudes and simply followed the other men through the corridors of the ship, wondered at how he was going to handle meeting Philippa Paik again. In his mind he went over the apology he had planned out, the words sinking into his memory like ink into paper, indelibly printing themselves onto the surface of his mind.

When he saw her standing halfway up the Grand Staircase, still dressed in her borrowed clothes and filming his group as they ascended into the D-Deck reception, those carefully prepared words were wiped away as cleanly as if the hand of God had struck them from existence. Seeing each other, they both stopped dead and stared for several seconds. Not for the first time, Jack wondered what the object of his frustrations might look like wearing a dress, before realising that he must look a sight himself, dressed for work in just his rolled-up shirtsleeves, braces and trousers.

Captain Smith at that moment stepped up to foot of the stairs to speak to them. As with Pitman, he thanked them for offering their services, and explained that shortly *Titanic* would begin navigating her way out of the ice field and proceed for Canada at reduced speed.

But after he had finished his speech, Captain Smith had introduced some representatives from the time-wrecked ships, including the Slavic giant named Gorbachev, and invited the volunteering passengers to spend a few moments conversing with them. Seeing his opportunity, Jack had approached the stairs and called out to Philippa Paik.

"Jack," she said at last, eyes narrowed.

"Philippa," he responded, trying to remember at what point they had progressed to first names. The uneasy silence hung overhead for several seconds, so oppressive that he half expected the staircase to collapse under its weight.

"I'm sorry," he blurted out. "What I said in the library, it was thoughtless and cruel and uncalled for and…"

"Don't," she cut him off, slowly descending the stairs. "Don't tie yourself in knots trying to apologise, Jack. We both said some stupid things."

"I…" he said, and then stopped, unable to express what he wanted to say.

"They say it might be possible for *Oceanic* and the other ships to go back to our future. So, I doubt we'll see each other again after this," she said, voice cool. "But looking back, I'd like to say it was an honour to have met you."

"You..." he said dumbly, mouthing hanging open, before he cleared his mind. "And you yourself, Miss Paik. Being in your company was an... eye-opening experience."

Before he could say anything else, an enraged bellow of anger drew his attention over to the far side of the Reception, where Captain Gorbachev was face-to-face with Sir Cosmo Duff-Gordon.

"What did you say?" demanded the aristocrat.

"I say," rumbled the Russian. "That you are the coward Gordon, Sir Cosmo Duff, who left *Titanic* in first lifeboat, and bribe crew to not return after ship sank, even though boat only have twelve people in, with room for almost thirty-other persons."

"I have not the slightest idea what you are talking about!" Cosmo roared, positioning himself as if to shield Lucille. "Our boat left the ship last night with every seat filled."

"Not last night, but *first time last night*, when *Titanic* actually sank. You paid lifeboat crew to not return to sinking ship, afraid of being swamped."

"How dare you!" Cosmo seethed, but Gorbachev just held up a hand and turned away, muttering in a string of Russian, leaving the Scotsman to fume.

"Is what he says true, Miss Paik?" Jack said, turning around to find that Pip had vanished. His shoulders slumped and, biting back a curse, he strode off to find his cabin and a pair of boots more appropriate for his coming work in the boiler rooms.

CHAPTER TWENTY FIVE

Archibald Butt climbed up the dark shaft in a fit of sudden terror, forcing himself hand over hand up the rungs of the ladder. Coming out into blessed daylight, he emerged into a small cavity atop *Viking*'s sail and breathed deeply of the late afternoon air, his chest heaving as if to purge his lungs of vile fumes. After some moments he caught himself and held a fist to his mouth, turning with a palatable dread to look back down into the black pit of the submarine's interior. The overpowering reek of human bodies and mechanical secretions, commingling sweat and oil, struck him in the face and he fought back the urge to wretch.

"How can man survive such confinement?" he asked, slowly stepping back to allow a second person to climb up and join him in the small space.

"Claustrophobia is something we fight with all the time," Captain Furness replied as he rested his weight on the rail and gazed calmly out across a boundless ocean littered with cold and bright icebergs. "The psych evaluations mean that only men who the brass hats think can endure the conditions onboard join the crew, but we are still only human."

Indeed. How can any soul come away from this black duty, if not shrivelled? Butt's thoughts rolled on as he saw the Captain's mild blue eyes taking in the view with a cool dispassion, his breath flitting around him like jets of steam.

"Three months at a time, we spend submerged on patrol," Furness said quietly, as if reading his thoughts. "The boat is as much our jail as our home."

"A jail…" Butt thought of the power plant he had been shown, the nuclear reactor, shackled with pipes and valves, captive-bound and double-ironed. Looking for some reprieve, he found himself staring aft along the sleek and venomous length of the submarine, a metal serpent aimed into the west, and shuddered again at the sense of raw, inhuman power that seemed to infuse every atom of the vessel. His eyes lingered on the missile ports, and he imagined the devices below, waiting to burst up like plants in bloom and scatter their deadly seeds across the Earth.

Power equal to millions of tons of explosive; ready to fire at any moment, and capable of reaching anywhere in North America or Europe in but thirty minutes.

"I can't imagine..." he paused and swallowed. "A conflict so dire that it would require the use of such weapons... but Doctor Oshiro said they have only once been used in anger, correct?"

"Yes – August of 1945 was when we became death, destroyer of worlds. We came close to using them several times again in the decades since, horrifyingly close to nuclear apocalypse, but we always held back from the brink."

"Why build such a stockpile of weapons, if their use would have been so cataclysmic to both sides?"

"It was the only way to ensure that no-one would fire; the threat of equal retaliation. Mutually Assured Destruction."

"But still, your governments would have burned the surface of the Earth to spite their opponents?"

"Well," Furness laughed. "There is a reason those letters spell out MAD."

"Who was the enemy? I gathered some details during the conference but-"

"Russia," Furness answered immediately, cutting him off. "You heard Miller and Gorbachev hinting at a revolution... well, in February of 1917 Russia's working classes are due to overthrow the Tsar, and a few months later, out of the ashes will arise a totalitarian communist state, one that in time will come to be governed by a supreme madman with paranoid aspirations towards any and all 'Imperialists' and 'Capitalists'. And America responds with equal fear and distrust, and anyone in between those two has to pick sides and arm themselves for a war that, if it came, would leave everyone equally dead, regardless of class or background or politics. Karl Marx's dreams wrought into a nightmare..."

"You were one of them, one of those 'Cold Warriors'?"

"Yes. I was born in the year of the Cuban Missile Crisis, and grew up in the shadow of Polaris and Trident."

The man suddenly looked extremely harrowed, and at the same time, relieved. "Despite everything that's happened, it's actually a relief to think that, *Viking* notwithstanding, this world doesn't have that burden resting on its shoulders, yet..."

"I'm sorry..." Butt said suddenly, his tone conciliatory.

Furness turned curiously. "Excuse me?"

Butt extended a hand astern, as if pointing into another world, or the future. "You say that the twentieth century is nothing but a procession of wars and atrocities, and I cannot feel that responsibility for such a drawn-out apocalypse falls at our feet."

"It's not your fault alone," Furness stood beside him. "If the finger of blame were asked to point at one generation to hold to account, it would give up."

Butt noted that, like himself, Furness naturally stood as if at parade rest, hands held behind his back and feet slightly spayed, and he rocked on them with the gentle rise and fall of the hull.

"There are war hawks in the twenty-first century, just as there are now. Even if the threat of full scale thermonuclear war has pretty much disappeared nowadays... *thenadays*, we still tootle around the Atlantic in the missile boats, ever vigilant to remind others of the cost of setting off the bomb, or just in case some fool builds themselves one."

"Is it really that simple?"

"Yes. In fact, with the right equipment, Pierre and Marie Curie could have made a sizable chunk of Paris uninhabitable. They did a good enough job of killing themselves, after all."

Viking bobbed slowly under their feet.

"And what of submarine warfare?" asked Butt, tapping his foot on the deck. "I cannot assume that we jumped from Holland boats straight to these nuclear engines and weapons, not without some... intermediate stages."

"Well, you tell me, Major," Furness snorted in amusement. "What do your contemporary military leaders make of new developments like subs and aeroplanes?"

Butt retreated within himself and considered the question. There was a man in the US Navy, a Lieutenant Nimitz if he recalled, who was very much in favour of the development of submarine warfare. Beyond that, he had devoted little thought to the subject, but Miss Paik's ominous words at how the growing dreadnought fleets were a waste of money left him wondering...

"They are undecided," he said at last. Some insist that these new technologies will make warfare as we know it obsolete. The majority insist they are merely novelties, or at best, useful tools to assist their fleets and armies."

Furness nodded. "I once read that at heart, every British sailor from this era harbours hopes to be the next Lord Nelson, commanding a great fleet into battle. That's why Britain and Germany are so set on building up their fleets – they envision a war that will be decided by the next Battle of Trafalgar..."

"Yes," Butt nodded in agreement. "To such traditional ways of thinking, the submarine is an affront."

"*Underhand, underwater and damned un-English!*" Furness chortled drily, and Butt raised an eye, recognising the quote.

"First Sea Lord Admiral Sir Arthur Wilson; he recently advised that all submarine crews should be hung as pirates."

"Yo ho ho!"

"Very droll, Captain – so your point is?"

"My point, Major, is that the battle, the next Trafalgar all those sailors so eagerly anticipate, from the greenest deckhand right up to the chiefs of the Admiralty, is a battle that will never come. The battleship is already obsolete, and the submarine's star ascendant. In the next war, and the one after, Germany simply attempts to starve Britain into surrender with her U-Boat fleets, raiding and sinking enemy merchant ships without let or hindrance."

"Impossible!" Butt all but roared. "No civilised nation could countenance such a crime!"

"The most successful submarine captain in history was a German officer who managed to sink nearly half-a-million tons worth of merchant ships in just three years. And his contemporaries all but climbed over each other in an attempt to equal him. When the *Lusitania* gets torpedoed, German citizens begin handing out commemorative medals."

The *Lusitania*, the great 35,000 ton Cunard liner, sunk by a submarine? Butt held on tighter to the rail, feeling faint and giddy as Furness continued to speak.

"And whether or not her sinking was a crime is still debated – she *was* being used to unlawfully carry ammunition – but it also helped to draw America into the war, which ended that conflict quicker. Over a hundred American citizens murdered by the Imperial German Navy made for good propaganda. But even after such a dramatic lesson, even after the *U-9* sails into Scapa Flow and sinks half the Royal Navy, the brass-hats refused to learn. Instead, they built more capital ships, more symbols of national strength and pride. Larger, grander, heavier, better armed and armoured…"

He caressed the smooth metal rail and smiled viciously. "And all that added mass and bulk accomplished was to make them easier targets for *Viking*'s forbears."

Butt's mouth was parched, and not just from the dry Arctic air, as Furness turned and all but prodded him in the chest.

"Everything's about to change, Major; so quickly that you won't believe it, even when it stares you in the face. Strategy, tactics, society and politics are teetering on the edge of history's abyss, and once they go over, you either run to keep up with the resulting avalanche or you get out of the way before it flattens you."

Viking's captain seemed like a man possessed, burning with an inner fire, and Butt was reminded of the nuclear reactor, or Aladdin's genie in the bottle; immense power trapped within a tiny space, begging and fighting for release.

"And that's only if history continues along the same path as I remember. But we've thrown it off the tracks, derailed it into the corn-fields, and it's starting to run amok!"

His arm swung wide, back to *Titanic* looming overhead. The last of the suctions were being withdrawn back out of holes cut in the side of the liner, like needles being withdrawn from a recovered patient.

"Who knows what chaos we're now setting in motion? The world was volatile enough as it is, but now new ingredients have been thrown into an already-curdling pot." The spirit seemed to go out of Furness, and he suddenly looked like a defeated man anticipating the gallows. "If we make port, all hell will be let loose."

Butt swallowed. "Can you not sink her now, scuttle her and be done with it?" he spoke lowly, under his breath. "Seal shut Pandora's box and drop it in the depths of the sea."

Furness' head came round, and Butt shivered at the sardonic grin he wore. "Do you mean *Viking*, or *Titanic?*"

"Sir!" Scott Thresher's voice echoed up the ladder, cutting off Butt's astonished retort. Unable to squeeze into the confined recess with the two of them, *Viking's* Executive Officer simply climbed up the ladder and stopped with his head at the level of the topmost rung. "It's time, sir."

"Very well," Furness nodded. "Sound three on the ship's siren, and instruct ECM to cease radio jamming at Captain Smith's discretion; await his own signal."

"Aye aye Captain," Thresher nodded, grabbing hold of the uprights and sliding out of sight down the hatch.

"Cover your ears, Major," Furness recommended, and Butt followed his instruction. Seconds later *Viking* bellowed once, twice, thrice, each blast resounding like a flat note in an orchestra, strident in the semi-silence of the ocean swells. As Butt lowered his hands he perceived Thresher scrambling back up to the head of the ladder, a portable radio in his hands.

"I thought you might want to hear when they start transmitting, Captain."

"This should be interesting…" Furness grunted as he set the radio on a small shelf and raised another speaking device to his mouth. "Officer of the watch, push us back from *Titanic*, give her some space to manoeuvre. Main engine slow astern, set speed five, starboard three-zero."

Butt held on tight as far aft *Viking's* single propeller whirred into life, churning the surface to foam and sending waves splashing over the afterdeck as she went into reverse, slowly retreating past *Titanic's* huge bow. Some distance off, he could see *Rescue* and *Californian* moored alongside one another, cranes at work as they transferred the *Liberty Bell*.

"Rudder amidships, main engine ahead half, set speed one-zero," Furness instructed again, and after a few seconds' hesitation the note of the submarine's distant engines changed and she stirred into forward movement, travelling parallel down *Titanic's* side, the ocean breaking over her nose and writhing white in the gap between the two vessels.

"Set speed one-five."

The deck seemed to leap forward under their feet; Butt glanced upwards to see a white-haired figure standing on the liner's bridge-wing, cap raised in salute, and Furness returned the gesture as *Viking* gained speed.

As the submarine whipped past *Titanic*'s high stern, Furness barked more orders into the device, and now working into her stride *Viking* swept into a wide arc, as if establishing a perimeter around *Titanic*, the rising spray forcing Butt to hold onto his cap as the submarine took the bit between her teeth.

"Officer of the watch, main engine ahead full, set speed two-one!"

"Aye sir!" crackled the talkie. "Setting speed two-one!"

The conning tower canted like a schooner taking the wind as *Viking* gained speed, powering through the sweeping turn. Butt braced his feet and turned to see Furness beaming happily, teeth bared as he held onto the rail like a jockey urging on his ride in the Kentucky Derby.

"Twenty-one knots in a submarine," he enthused to *Viking*'s captain. "Incredible!"

"It's rare that we get to put on a show like this!" he dimly heard the other man shouting. "Of course, we're faster submerged. Completely immersed in the water she'll make twenty-five knots!"

*

"Astonishing..." Smith breathed as he peered through his binoculars at *Viking*, now half a mile off and coming round to *Titanic*'s portside. He focused the lenses, and the sight of the White Ensign proudly streaming from behind the submarine's sail gave him a moment's pride.

"He's showing off for our benefit," Murdoch said softly as he stepped up beside him. "And perhaps demonstrating what he's capable of."

Smith nodded in response, suddenly feeling more than a little intimidated as his vision tracked from the flag of the Royal Navy to the two figures riding atop *Viking*'s sail, a pair of silhouettes against the glittering ocean.

Murdoch swallowed audibly. "Engine room says they'll be ready in a few minutes, sir."

"Very well, Mr Murdoch," Smith nodded, lowering the lenses. "Signal the fleet that we are ready to begin transmitting. Three blasts."

"Aye Captain," Murdoch nodded, his feet rapping smartly on the deck as he crossed into the shelter of the wheelhouse and drew on the whistle cord. *Titanic* sang out proudly, each blare resonating gloriously in the crisp air.

*

"Three whistles... *Viking* should have dropped her shroud," Cameron observed from a spare chair that had been wheeled into the Marconi suite for him.

Jack Phillips slowly turned the dial on the Marconi apparatus, phasing through static and conflicting transmissions until he suddenly stumbled across a strong spark, the signals bursting in his ears like electric fireworks.

"I have *Californian*," he called out. "And *Carpathia* too. Evans and Cotton are both putting out general notices to other ships, asking them to stand by. *Mount Temple* and a few others are stopped a few miles out demanding to know what's going on."

Cameron nodded as he hunched forward and adjusted his own equipment, the boxes that housed the two-way voice radios littering the floor of both the wireless office and the adjacent silent room, wires feeding between them and the open skylight, over which a portable antenna had been erected. "And I have *Oceanic* conversing with the *Anatoly Sagalevich*. Listen..."

He flipped a switch and immediately the sound of conversing voices filled the room.

"...many contacts all around, icebergs in every direction, except for the open patch of ocean around our point of arrival..."

"...yes, is like polynya, hole in ice, hole in the world."

Phillips sat for a moment in rapturous silence as Cameron fine-tuned the signal, eliminating static and interference until the transmission was as clear as if the two captains were chatting in the corridor outside. Then *Rescue*'s radioman held down on the speaker key and, with a euphoric grin, spoke aloud.

"Testing, testing. All stations stand by. Over."

Harold Bride, who had been evicted from the room by the other two men and their equipment, jumped down from the bunk bed in the adjoining cabin and stuck his head through the door. Philips pushed back the headset from his ears and listened as well. The speakers growled for a second, before the first response came through.

"Standing by. Will the transmitting station please identify themselves? Over."

Smirking, Cameron offered the speaking device towards Phillips, who shook his head and indicated over his shoulder. Instead, the *Rescue*'s radioman tossed the speaker on its wire umbilical to Bride, who caught it clumsily. Holding his hand up, Cameron mimicked holding down the key on its side.

"All stations, this is the steamship *Titanic*, transmitting on the agreed ship-to-ship frequency," Bride nervously spoke into the mouthpiece. "Over," he added at Cameron's mimed prompts.

"Titanic, this is USNS Rescue, message received, welcome to the club. Over."

"Is good signal Titanic. Over."

"The master and crew of Oceanic send their congratulations, Titanic. Over."

As the messages rolled in Bride stepped back as if drained, still holding the radiopiece. From his chair Phillips slapped him on the back with one hand as he scratched out a note on a scrap of paper.

Captain – Radio jamming from Viking has ceased. Speaking radio assembled and tested successfully. Ready to transmit prepared message – Phillips.

"Well done Harry," he said, sealing the message in an envelope and holding it out. "Can you deliver that to the bridge immediately?"

Bride, in a trance, tried to walk out of the room with the radio unit still in his hand before Cameron stopped him and relieved him of the device. Phillips chuckled as he adjusted his set, the lengthy message handed to him by Captain Smith spread out in front of him over two sheets of paper. As he twiddled the dial, however, he suddenly latched onto another signal and sat bolt upright.

"Wait a second... I know this spark – its MKC."

Cameron reclined in his own chair. "Who's MKC?"

"It's our sister ship, *Olympic*. She's calling out for us, asking if we're still afloat. Last I heard they were five hundred miles away and coming fast for us, but that was last night."

"Poor bastards must have been having kittens ever since *Viking* began jamming everyone."

"You can bet they are..." Phillips replied, listening to *Olympic*'s spark. "He says they're making 25 knots and have closed their distance to under two hundred miles. Captain Haddock must be driving her on like a racehorse..."

Resting his hand on the Morse key, Phillips blasted off a quick message.

"MGY to MKC – this is *Titanic* calling, stand by."

*

Thomas Andrews had heard *Titanic*'s signal as he anxiously stood opposite Chief Engineer Bell at the starting platform, the two of them facing each other across the bright brass wheel of the main pressure valve as if it were a chess board. On the adjacent steam manifold the gauges all held steady, and around them the vast engines hissed expectantly, the assembled engineering staff and the Harland & Wolff guarantee group waiting alongside. Over the hiss of hot water, he could dimly perceive the low rumble of distant boilers and the expectant panting of the starting engines.

Bell looked from side-to-side, eyeing the two telegraph dials mounted to the legs of the main engines, their needles pointing to 'Stand By'. Stiffening his lip, he looked to Andrews, and then suddenly winked in a moment of levity, and Thomas nodded in understanding.

"Mr Alinka..." he called, turning to a figure dressed in coveralls in the front row. "Would you care to do the honours?"

The bandaged Hawaiian reacted with surprise, but after a moment's prompting came and took his place beside the main valve just as the telegraphs swung, with a chorus of ringing bells, to 'Slow Ahead'.

"Ahead slow," Bell repeated aloud, and several of the engineers suddenly scattered, ready to disengage the starting engines, while the chief engineer gestured for Alinka to take a hold of the wheel with both hands.

"Starting main engines!" the Salvage Engineer called, and after a moment's effort spun the valve open. With a sigh like a gigantic exhalation, grease gleaming brightly on their rods and linkages, the engines stirred into life, and through the bedplates and footplates Thomas felt their growing rhythm, Olympian footfalls building into an easy trot.

Glancing upwards towards the ceiling, he suddenly spotted a lone figure standing on a high catwalk, filming them with a small handheld camera.

"Miss Paik!" he shouted, raising a hand in greeting, and she waved back, smiling in a manner that seemed rather sad, and Thomas wondered what was troubling her.

Then Hesketh, one of the assistant Engineers, produced a bottle of champagne from somewhere and popped the cork, drawing Thomas' attention; when he looked back up at where Miss Paik had been standing, the girl had vanished. Then his thoughts were drowned out as someone let out a cheer, which was taken up throughout the engine room as *Titanic* returned to life.

*

On *Oceanic*'s bridge, Adrienne McKinn was standing in the enclosed wing, basking in the sunlight. Out across the water *Titanic* drifted beneath a lazy pall of smoke, appearing to be dozing.

She turned and looked into the superliner's command-centre, where Lloyd Waters was speaking for the benefit of Margaret Brown's *'Alexandra Press'*, and she shook her head in laughter. It was a surreal image, one matched by the sight and sound of people clustered together on the promenade below. Then their voices were suddenly drowned out by a sustained, bellowing roar from *Titanic*, which was taken up in a symphony of sound as sirens, whistles and air horns all cried out in gleeful salutation.

Lloyd looked up from the cameras and caught her eyes, and two of them shared a warm smile before the Captain suddenly pointed past her shoulder.

"Look!"

She and the cameras all turned, and beheld *Titanic*. The coils of smoke from her central funnels were thicker now, bending back slightly, and where her heeling bow met the water there was a small but unmistakable dog-bone of foam.

Camera-crew in tow, Waters and Brown came over and joined her in the wing. "It's about as picturesque a scene as could be contrived," *Oceanic*'s captain said lightly. "Are you sure you didn't plan this?"

"No, Lloyd," she laughed. "I spent sixteen months working out Project 401, and you were there the whole time. I think you'd have noticed if I somehow slipped a request form for a time-machine in somewhere."

"*Titanic*'s moving, Sir," came a report. "Should we follow after her?"

"Yes, match her speed, and keep to her windward side – we don't want smoke from her funnels blowing across into the portside cabins."

"Yessir... Captain, *Titanic* just put out a quick radio message."

"Let's see it... excellent." Waters handed the slip of paper to Adrienne to read, and then gestured back into the heart of the bridge. "Would Madame care to do the honours?"

"I would be glad to, Lloyd," she replied, and allowed herself to be led towards the ship's emergency panel.

"That's the tannoy button, right there," he pointed. "Hold it down to speak."

Smiling by way of thanks, and with Maggie Brown and her cameramen filming, Adrienne leaned forward, gauged the distance between her mouth and the microphone, and then pressed her thumb down on the button indicated.

"Ladies and Gentlemen!" she said, hearing her voice repeating over speakers throughout the ship. "We have just received a transmission from Captain Smith aboard the *Titanic*. He has made the following entry in the ship's log: *3:15pm, April 15th, 1912. Repairs complete, now underway for Halifax!*"

A chorus of cheers erupted from the amassed crowds outside, and straightening up from the tannoy Adrienne felt a similar urge to roar aloud as the deck trembled and *Oceanic* started slowly after the smaller liner, they and the other ships slowly beginning to weave their way out of the ice field. It was if some great engine was stirring into motion, and moving them forward into an unknown future.

She could only hope it would be a happy one.

*

By the time the fleet had successfully navigated clear of the ice, it was late evening, just before dusk.

Even at reduced speed, *Titanic*'s prow cut forward into the swells with immense power, the spray from her bow-wave flashing brilliantly in the golden light. Holding on tight to the ship's bow rail, right up in the forecastle, Pip took the wind in her face, feeling her hair streaming back like a battle standard. Far ahead the sun was melting into the sea, and she glanced back to see *Titanic* putting her stern to the last of the icebergs, the seaborne mountains slowly beginning to fall over the eastern horizon.

And then she slipped from her perch on the cradle for the ship's central anchor, and winced.

James Cameron made this look so easy. He didn't show just how many pitfalls the forecastle deck is littered with.

She knew, from years spent browsing internet message boards where people heckled the inaccuracies of the blockbuster film, that passengers were forbidden from accessing both the forecastle and the bows of the ship, and evidently with good reason, but the part of her that wanted to indulge in some tragically romantic moping convinced her to head out to *Titanic*'s bowsprit and relish the moment.

Besides, it was not like she was the first. The author Helen Candee wrote that on the morning before the collision with the iceberg she had come out to this very spot, while it was still dawn, and indulged the same urges, so Pip could rightly say that she was following in someone else's footsteps. That was her story and she was going to stick by it. While she was at it, she was determined to get photographic evidence. If there was any chance that they could go back to the future, she had every intention of returning with first-hand images of *Titanic* as proof of their story, and perhaps finally settle some historical squabbles about minor details on the ship.

Pulling out her camcorder, she began to browse through some of the recent videos she had taken. There was Kai Alinka restarting the ship, footage of the immense reciprocating engines preserved for posterity. She had then gone down to the Turkish Baths, finding to her relief that the opulent Cooling Room at the heart of the spa was the one part of the suite to not have been destroyed in the race to run pipes through from *Viking*.

The Second Class lounge, the Smoking Room, the two Grand Staircases; she had wandered through the entire ship, building an archive. Now, pocketing the camcorder and producing her digital stills camera, she turned and quickly snapped a few shots off looking down the length of the forecastle, and then paused, noticing a severe figure standing between the anchor chains.

"Mr Murdoch..." she lowered the camera, seeing his disapproving expression.

"Miss Paik, I must ask you to leave this area immediately," the acting Chief Officer said curtly. "It's not safe."

"That's OK – I knew I was pushing my luck in coming out here in the first place."

"You've been pushing your luck since you came onboard," he replied, hands folded behind his back. "Please remember that you are a guest aboard this ship, neither crew nor a passenger. The Captain is a kind soul, and given to tolerate your antics, but I find your high-handed roaming of the ship intolerable."

Pip drew back as if stung, and then her fists balled in anger. "Oh great, you too? I've already had one indignant Edwardian blow up in my face, I'd like to avoid suffering through it a second time, Mr Murdoch! What's your problem?"

Murdoch drew himself up straight, and then beckoned aft, holding the gate to the well deck open for her. "Come this way, and I'll show you."

Up they went, climbing the stairs that bent back along the external walls of the passenger cabins to the boat deck, and then past the deckhouse that contained the Officers' quarters. Despite Murdoch's slow-boiling anger, he kept his voice level and held every door open, putting Pip slightly at ease.

Those feelings vanished when she stepped into the Officers' mess, and found her own laptop set up on the dining table.

"Mr Andrews placed this device into the care of the ship's officers when his presentation below ended," Murdoch said curtly. "He felt it would be unwise to take it into the environment of the engine rooms."

The plug on the end of the computer's charging wire was plugged into an extension cable that wound away towards the Wireless Suite, and onscreen was a familiar sight: Leonardo DiCaprio and Kate Winslet riding *Titanic*'s prow by the light of sunset, the very scene Pip had been recreating just a few minutes before. The playback of the movie was paused, frozen on the image of the couple, arms outstretched like a figurehead.

"So you know of this film?" Murdoch guessed, seeing her reaction. "I guessed as such when I saw you posing in the bows of the ship like that. Now..."

His hand fell to the keyboard and played over the touch-sensitive panels, scrolling the playbar of the movie forward. After fiddling around for a few seconds he found what he was looking for.

"Please explain this."

Chaos, people trying to fight their way into boats just before the ship dived. A po-faced actor in the role of Murdoch, looking almost like he was wearing a White Star uniform two sizes too big for him, was shouting commands, and then shoving a bribe back in the face of Billy Zane, the actor cast in the role of the film's villain.

Pip swallowed; she knew where this was going. The panic escalated into a rush, Movie-Murdoch's gun fired twice, and the comic-relief Irish immigrant character slumped to the deck, dead. The accuracy of the chaos on the deck to some of what the two of them had witnessed the night before was uncanny, eerie.

"Bastardo!" someone shouted, the word heavily accented.

Movie-Murdoch was staring ashen-faced at a trail of blood pointing towards him down the sloping length of the deck. Turning, he saluted to Henry Wilde's actor counterpart, and then pushed the Webley to his own temple.

"No, Will!"

She flinched as the bang of the gunshot blew out the laptop's speakers in a burst of static. Murdoch reached down and pressed 'pause', freezing the screen on a visual of his likeness face-down in the future. His mouth was tightly clamped shut, but his jaw worked with visible indignation, and after several furious seconds he finally composed himself and forced out a few words.

"I would *never* have committed suicide, not while there was still a boat to be launched," he snapped, face flushed, laying the sins of storytellers and filmmakers at her feet. Assaulted by his rage, Pip bounced back.

"Somebody shot themselves, why not you! And it makes good storytelling, Will! The incompetent officer who hit the berg, so overcome with guilt that he takes 'the coward's way out'!"

Immediately she caught herself and stopped, regretting the words.

"I'm sorry… that was wrong… look, too many first-hand accounts, too many to be ignored, say an officer shot himself at the end of the sinking, and the most likely candidates are yourself and Henry Wilde; most people don't even know Wilde existed, so in telling the story of the sinking, it makes sense to connect you with both the collision and the suicide. But I'm not one of those people! I know it's impossible to lay judgement on which of you it was, and I even described you as a hero for trying to launch the last collapsible right at the end…"

"Stop! Just… listen to yourself…" he breathed heavily. "You knew… that's my point. This… *film*," he spat the word out as if it was excrement, "portrays the Captain as a fool whose mind deserted him in a crisis, Mr Ismay as a greedy coward with not the least knowledge of ships, and Lights as a prig from the Home Counties. Now I accept you're not to blame for this, but you've admitted that this story has become the *fact* of the sinking to many; so how could you have come aboard the ship without *warning us?*"

She opened her mouth to protest and he held up a hand, stemming her before she could speak. "Haven't you wondered why Mr Ismay was so visibly limping when he came back aboard? Someone aboard *Oceanic* accused him of being responsible for the deaths of everyone aboard this ship and pushed him down a flight of stairs. Several other people kicked him in the ribs before the ship's crew came to his defence. And for failing to warn him of the crass judgements of your age, I do hold you responsible."

He pointed at the laptop. "I've worked my way through that story over the past few hours, in increments, and it makes most of us, and many of our passengers, out to be monsters. Now please consider how history will judge you for your part in that, and you might understand my feelings."

Then, with quick movements he folded the laptop screen down, bound it up with the lengths of charging cord, and pushed it into her hands.

"The captain tolerates your presence because he is a kind man, and we have done our best to be courteous hosts. You respond by demonising us in the crudest way possible. With that in mind, I'd like you to consider this; if we are as cruel and monstrous as you claim us to be, why have we not rammed *Titanic* into *Oceanic* already, so as to rid this world of your contemporaries and all the trouble you might cause?"

When she did not answer he did it for her. "Because we are people, not stereotypes or fictional characters who conform to the demands of a narrative, which is more credit than many of you give us, or so it seems to me."

He gestured towards the door, indicating that she get out.

"Kindly reflect on that when you get back to your world, Miss Paik."

Shaken, and on the verge of tears, Pip left, suddenly hating *Titanic* and everyone aboard her.

*

The *Liberty Bell* was humming softly, a susurration so faint that the constant sounds of *Rescue*'s hold often drowned it out. By the glow of the work lights strung up around it, the device gleamed with a silvery lustre.

Oshiro put his hand to the machine's hull and felt something inside quivering, trembling like a living thing. The source of the vibration might have been a pump, circulating the Apergy serum, perhaps a cooling fan, or possibly the backup power supply.

Then again, it might have been something else altogether. He tried not to think about what unworldly processes churned inside the heart of the machine, which despite their best efforts had not yielded up its innermost secrets. Privately, he was glad that the core housed inside the device had proved to be completely sealed; the thought of what might be restrained within the welds and reinforced plating frightened him in a way he did not think possible.

Opening an inspection panel in the Bell's hull, he found a darkened LCD display and a tangle of wires where the internal computers had been hastily bypassed on the night of the 14th back in 2012, and taking a long USB wire in hand he forced it into the appropriate port.

The screen flickered, several BIOS windows blinked open and shut in rapid succession, and then the machine gave a single chime.

"Internal clocks synchronised, Operating System established," he said to his colleague, before slowly glancing around the room. The guards from *Viking* watched them intently, assault rifles cradled in their arms. Yet for some reason, ever since they had started the *Liberty Bell*'s power-up sequence, Oshiro had begun to feel the unsettling sensation of eyes peering at him from every corner of the dimly-lit hold.

"The internal power reserves are almost drained," Jabril Hab Allah replied, standing at another open panel on his side of the device. "The needle on the master ammeter is about to flat-line."

Oshiro nodded and moved around to his side of the machine, where several other panels stood open. They had to complete the start-up now, or the *Liberty Bell* would become inert. As he circled the device, he had to watch his step; the deck was covered in flexible piping set up to circulate water from *Rescue*'s pumps through the *Liberty Bell*'s cooling systems. More thick conduits snaked away through the hold to electrical junction boxes.

"Ready?" Jabril asked, leaning around the machine to speak to Oshiro. One of his hands was gripping the *Liberty Bell*'s main power breaker, while the other hung at his side, clenching and relaxing repeatedly.

Oshiro quickly scanned his own controls, flipping rows of trip switches and opening up all the circuits. Dimly illuminated lines incorporated into the panel indicated the correct sequencing, converging at the top on a rotary dial that was set to **PRIME**.

"Ready…" he said, before Jabril pulled down on the knife-switch, and some mechanism banged inside the hull of the machine. As a klaxon began to scream, all the switches on Oshiro's side of the machine lit up. Simultaneously the integrated display was suddenly filled with popup windows, all running complex numbers, and from within the *Liberty Bell* a deep noise like grinding millstones began to emanate, layered with electronic pulses, spitting bursts of static and mechanical howls that quickly rose in volume. The two Royal Navy guards flinched, one covering up his ears to drown out the wailing, agonised mess of noise.

The hairs on Oshiro's own arms were standing up. Forcing himself to focus, he reached forward, grabbed the main switch on his panel and twisted it from **PRIME** to **CHARGE**.

All the sounds suddenly cut out, the klaxon silencing itself and the machine's animalistic growls settling down into a muted buzz, allowing him to turn his attention away to the display. On it, a single prompt blinked slowly.

STANDING BY

He pressed the 'return' key on a plugged-in keyboard; in the diagnostic window numerous checkboxes glowed green, along with the wonderful words **SYSTEM READY**.

Sighing in relief, he looked across the room.

"Mr Hab Allah, we have ourselves a working time-machine."

Jabril did not respond, instead remaining silent while rubbing thoughtfully at his beard, his eyes fixedly staring off into far end of the hold.

"Akira…"

Oshiro spun round, certain he had just heard someone call his name. With his back to the *Liberty Bell*, he peered in the same direction as Jabril, down a corridor flanked by secured salvage equipment. Something white fluttered in the gloom, and he squinted, momentarily thinking it was the shape of a woman in a flowing dress.

Ami, my sister Ami?

He blinked, and then the vision took off into the air and vanished through a partially open hatch. It had been a big sea bird, perhaps an albatross. Feeling suddenly light-headed, a horrible weight settling in his gut, he turned back to Jabril Hab

Allah, wondering what the other man might himself have seen. Behind them the two navy guards were rocking on the balls of their feet and nervously peering from side to side.

As if thinking in synchrony, they all looked towards the brooding *Liberty Bell*. The machine was idling now, gathering a charge and humming away like a sleeping volcano, whispering as internal pressures grew to a head…

Chikusho! he swore to himself, trying to put memories of Sendai out of his mind. Grabbing hold of the nearest available two-way radio he spoke into it quickly.

"This is Doctor Oshiro, aboard *Rescue*. The *Liberty Bell* is working, it is active, it is charging. Over."

He closed the channel and climbed to the main deck, breathing deeply of the night air. Darkness had fallen now, and the ship was stationary, rolling with the motion of the low waves, as *Titanic*, *Oceanic* and the *Anatoly Sagalevich* steamed by in the darkness. A few hundred yards off to *Rescue*'s side the *Carpathia* was slowly drawing up, while the *Californian* was stopped directly ahead.

"This is where we part ways, Doctor," Jabril Hab Allah said softly, coming up to Oshiro's side, pointing to a modern Zodiac motorboat that was coming across the water from the direction of the *Carpathia*. "Captain Laroche has made arrangements for her and me to stay behind."

Oshiro nodded in understanding. Numerous wireless messages back and forth between the ships had made it clear that *Titanic*'s sister ship *Olympic* was rapidly approaching from the west, and so it had been decided that instead of keeping pace with the other ships, *Carpathia* should turn back around and continue for Europe, bearing messages of peace and goodwill from the Time Fleet.

"I understand that the other survivors from the *Seguin Laroche* have been transferred to the *Oceanic*, but what do the two of you plan to accomplish by staying here?" he asked Hab Allah, as the motorboat drew up, piloted by Captain Laroche herself.

"Secure the future of this world, we hope…" the Arab said quietly, eyes turning towards *Oceanic* as she continued on into the night, taking what would almost certainly be his last glimpse of any part of the twenty-first century.

"You weren't an innocent party in this, were you?" Oshiro asked softly, keeping his voice low.

After a long moment Jabril nodded. "Yes, you're right, I was the one behind all of it, though our transportation here was a genuine accident."

"So why are you really staying behind?"

"Captain Laroche described it as 'taking responsibility' for a world of our making. Captain Rostron has agreed to take us on board *Carpathia*, and drop us off when he docks in Gibraltar. From there, we intend to disappear... and become ghosts in the flow of history, working to adjust its course where necessary."

"Well, good luck to you," Oshiro replied, taking the other man firmly by the hand.

"There is one last thing," Jabril said, his eyes glimmering in the dark. He held up a key. "You'll need to have this."

"What is it?"

"Captain Furness also worked out the truth of my culpability. He came to an agreement with the *capitaine* and myself. He does not want to see today's events repeated in the future, does not want to see another arms race when several thousand people return to 2012 recounting their adventures in time and space, with a functioning time-machine as proof."

Their gazes briefly slipped back at the open hatch to the hold. Oshiro felt himself swallow. "And that key?"

"It controls the *Liberty Bell*'s self-destruct. Once used for the return-jump, the machine will destroy itself. Don't worry – it's a clean process, no harm will be done to *Rescue* or her crew."

Oshiro eyed the key warily. "What, you're giving me the responsibility of arming it?"

"No..." Jabril shook his head. "It's already primed to implode. This is the disarming key."

"Why me?"

"You're the only person left with ready access to the *Liberty Bell* unbound by politics or military hierarchies. Keep this a secret if you wish, or reveal the truth to those you trust, whatever you choose. The *Capitaine* and myself felt it wrong to leave without making sure there was an alternative option in place, as insurance – you know... just in case."

The key, strung on a thin chain, was pressed into Oshiro's hand. He closed his fingers cautiously around it, as if it were a snake that might bite him.

"In case of what?" he asked. Jabril did not answer him, but simply shrugged, and stepped down the ladder into the Zodiac, which quickly pushed off towards *Carpathia*.

Oshiro watched as the boat vanished into the dark, and regarded the responsibility that had literally been placed in his hands. Then, hesitant, he slipped the chain around his neck and tucked it below his shirt collar, hiding the key from sight. Then, shaking his head, he climbed to *Rescue*'s bridge.

"Mr Hab Allah has left the ship," he reported, and Captain Jones nodded.

"It's a brave decision he and Joanna Laroche are making, to stay behind."

His tone was casual, but Oshiro suspected the Captain had come to the same conclusions as himself about the Arab's alleged innocence. There were few flies on Jordan Jones, even if the man had lost the use of his eyes. And despite the Captain being blinded, Oshiro suddenly felt naked, caught in the gaze of his mirrored sunglasses.

"Everything alright, Doc?"

"Fine," Oshiro lied, before nodding forward in an attempt to change the topic of conversation. "What's *Californian* doing?"

"We were struggling to keep up to the rest of the fleet on one prop, even with all the diesel engines devoting themselves to powering the drive-train. Now that some of that juice is being diverted to the *Liberty Bell*, Captain Lord has offered to put a tow-line on us and give us some assistance."

"So who is rescuing who?" Oshiro asked, failing in his attempt at humour, but still drawing a soft laugh out of Jones.

"Honestly Doc, I no longer have any idea."

In the dark night beyond the bridge whistles sounded, *Californian* and *Carpathia* bellowing in turn.

"And there we go," Jones said. "Mr Miller, half-speed ahead on the starboard engine, set our course for Halifax."

From far ahead Oshiro could hear *Californian*'s engine chugging away, and slowly the long tow-line between her and *Rescue*'s bow tightened until it formed a long parabolic curve between the two ships.

"We are now under tow, Captain," reported Miller, and Oshiro quietly exited onto the bridge. With her remaining propeller and *Californian* working in tandem, *Rescue* was once again underway, slowly drawing ahead of *Carpathia*, which was herself turning away and pointing her bow into the east, towards Europe.

Waving farewell one last time, Oshiro directed his attention into the west. Far ahead, across the sea, was Halifax, where they would eventually decide what to do.

He hoped that the *Liberty Bell* would have amassed enough of a charge by then to return them and all the other time-lost ships to the future.

And yet, as he stood on the *Rescue*'s bridge wing, he could not help but wonder at what else he might do, with all of time and space literally now at his fingertips. The disarming key, resting on his chest, suddenly felt as weighty as Atlas's burden of the sky.

If you could go to anywhere in time... if you had the power to correct any mistake, even if it only created a divergent timeline, rather than fixing your home dimension, what would you do?

ACT FOUR

VALHALLA

CHAPTER TWENTY SIX

Three bells sounded from the crow's nest, followed by a telephone call to the bridge.

"Lights ahead, multiple ships sighted."

Herbert Haddock gave the order to ring down for half-speed, and *Olympic*'s safety valves immediately lifted with a roar, as if the ship was wearily trying to catch her breath.

His pride in her was without measure. In the twenty-two-hours since they had first received *Titanic*'s distress calls, *Olympic* had raced tirelessly across the Atlantic, charging along in excess of her design speed by a substantial margin. It said volumes that even with the time they had lost in picking up the survivors of the crashed aircraft, they had maintained an average speed of over 23 knots. Chief Engineer Fleming even asserted that she had touched on 26 for minutes at a time, and the patent log record supported his claim.

The passengers, for the most part, had supported the choice to shut down the ancillaries such as heating and hot water, and so conserve steam for the engines. Those who protested had been placated somewhat when, during the course of the day, Fleming had found the boilers were producing steam faster than the engines could use it, and with Haddock's blessing had siphoned off part of the surplus pressure to restore some creature comforts to the cabins.

But a persistent faction of the ship's company had continued to berate his decisions, especially after he issued further orders saying that private Marconi traffic was temporarily suspended, so that the airwaves might be reserved solely for emergency transmissions. In truth, Haddock was simply trying to sit atop a genie bursting to be let out of its bottle, attempting to prevent any whispers of 'time travel' from reaching the passengers. About the only ones who appreciated the gesture were the wireless operators, who had been able to steal some hours sleep in the interim.

And so *Olympic* had continued to dash over the churning Atlantic, triple shifts of stokers working like machines to feed her immense appetite, while questions and wild rumours festered above decks like a boil threatening to burst.

It had been a relief when Bagot had suddenly come running with word that they were once again in touch with *Titanic*, and that she was putting out the most incredible transmission possible. At last, Haddock had the freedom to lance that boil.

And at dinner that night he had, standing in the centre of the First Class saloon to read aloud the whole of the message Captain Smith had put out, laboriously transmitted in longhand by his wireless crew.

"To all the peoples of the world.

Last night, at 2340, while travelling at reckless speed through a known region of ice, the RMS Titanic struck an iceberg and began to sink. Moments later, a bright flash of light was witnessed in our vicinity, whereupon several vessels emerged from said atmospheric phenomenon and immediately came to Titanic's aid. In the hours since, almost all of our passengers have been safely transferred to these ships, whose crews have also assisted in bailing out our flooded compartments and shoring up our damage. We are glad to say that, though there have been several regrettable deaths, the Titanic is currently afloat and proceeding under her own steam to Halifax.

However, this was almost not the case. We can say with the utmost certainty that were it not for the intervention of these ships that Titanic, flooding rapidly and equipped with enough lifeboats for only half of our total complement, would have sunk in less than three hours with a terrible loss of life.

We are assured of this truth by the very presence of the ships that came to our aid, as we may now disclose that these five vessels originated from the year 2012, having been moved a full century into their past by an accident of time-travel. More shockingly, prior to their unexpected voyage through time, these ships were gathered to commemorate the sinking of the Titanic, remembered in their era as a maritime disaster of historic magnitude.

Though at first we were sceptical, inspection of these ships and interaction with their passengers and crew have convinced us not only of the truth of their amazing journey, but granted us much insight into the world of their twentieth century. It is one defined both by incredible accomplishments and terrible catastrophe, one where man has eradicated many diseases, and developed technologies allowing the instantaneous exchange of knowledge across oceans. The aircraft has replaced the ocean liner as the means of long-distance travel, and the theory and practice of science has advanced so far as to reveal the first principles of the universe and life itself, and made possible journeys from the Earth to the moon, on which man first set foot on July 21st 1969. These are achievements of the highest order, and demonstrate the incredible potential of the human race.

At the same time, however, we must learn humility. Arrogance and nationalism, war and strife have left an indelible mark on these voyagers through time. The amazing technologies of which they speak were shaped by two devastating World Wars and countless other conflicts in which millions of lives have been lost. Hatred and prejudice have led to countless atrocities, appalling genocides, and boundless cruelty.

From these hard lessons, our guests have emerged much changed from ourselves. The roles in society of gender, race, and class have all been brought into question, as have definitions of morality, sexuality and liberty. In interacting with these travellers, we have found much that we take for granted challenged, and our first response was to either ignore these issues in the hope that they would go away, or to dismiss them as unimportant. This is folly. It is fear and pride that began this bloody waltz of war and revolution, and only by moving past such primal reactions can we hope to navigate a peaceful course through the hazards now ahead of us.

At present, the exact means by which this confluence of history was made possible is not fully understood. However, it is believed possible for the majority of these travellers to soon return to their time of origin, leaving us to contemplate our own actions in the light of history.

This night of April 15th 1912, the night of the Titanic Time Wreck, is a date to be commended to posterity, as the point in which two threads of time touched, launching a new voyage on which all of mankind are passengers, travelling together into a future which we now know to be of our own making.

As such, the responsibility falls to us, and us alone, to ensure we do not repeat the mistakes of futures past.

Signed

Captain EJ Smith, aboard the RMS Titanic."

The stunned silence that descended was then broken by the arrival of the survivors of Flight 401 in the dining saloon. Sequestered from the passengers until now, they had been furnished with spare officers' uniforms, their 'pilots wings' clipped to the jacket breasts in lieu of rank. As they entered from the outer reception, Haddock had presented them to the passengers, who responded with polite applause that gradually rose in intensity as the realisation that these people were actual travellers in time sunk in. Ramirez, startlingly winsome in men's clothing, had turned heads, especially when she thanked Haddock and gave a few words to the saloon in appreciation of the hospitality of *Olympic's* passengers and crew, ending with a salute and a promise to serve the peoples of this era with the same integrity and commitment they would their own, if called upon to do so.

Conversation over dinner, his guests a mix of time-travellers and carefully selected passengers, had been enthusiastic, Ramirez and her crew expounding on the history only hinted at by Captain Smith's missive, to the delight of Haddock's contemporaries. By silent mutual agreement on the part of all, however, the topic had always carefully skirted around issues of politics, race or gender, with one brief exception when Ramirez had corrected one passenger's mistaken identification of her as 'an Oriental'.

"No worries, I faced worse bigotry in basic training," she clarified. "And the ones putting me down then were often my commanding officers."

Afterwards, expressing the need for a cigarette, Ramirez had proceeded straight to the mahogany-carved snugness of the smoking room on the Promenade deck. By tradition this was the exclusive province of gentlemen passengers, and it had amused Haddock when he had later popped in to find her holding court to a crowd of interested young swells and even several women, the traditional inhabitants of the room watching on with grudging curiosity. The sense of calm, despite the abnormality of the situation, had been enough to set *Olympic's* captain at ease, as had the reassurance that his temporally-displaced guests might soon be leaving for their own world. Though the time-travellers were pleasant and professional company, he could not help but feel that the world now needed a long moment to catch its breath and contemplate the new gospel that had been bestowed upon it.

Now, as *Olympic* slowed to cautiously intersect the fleet steaming ahead of them, he felt both restless and uneasy. As if presenting his ship at a debutante ball, he took her right through a half-mile-wide channel in the open centre of the convoy, the dazzling show of *Oceanic*'s lights to starboard, and the more subdued glow of *Titanic*'s to port. The difference in size and aspect was stunning, and for a moment *Olympic* had straddled a century, passing by in the opposite direction. And then, helm reversed, they had looped back round and assumed a position on *Titanic*'s stern quarter. Moments later a telegraph message had arrived, courtesy of Moore and Bagot.

Captains Smith and Waters send their best regards to Olympic, it read. *And commend her company for their brave rescue of the lost aviators.*

That was one surprise that Haddock had the pleasure of bringing to the conversation, revealing to the flotilla that *Titanic*'s sister had herself flirted with future history. Rereading the message, and gazing around him at the strange fleet, his thoughts returned to Ramirez's circle in the smoking room. They had been gathered around the fireplace at the centre of the room, above which was set a painting in oils depicting New York Harbour. It was a view Haddock himself knew all too well from experience, the Statue of Liberty rising hazily through the morning fog, while tall ships and steamers crowded the harbour around it. In the foreground of the painting a stocky tugboat, dark against the sunrise, ploughed resolutely across the frame, presumably heading out to tow some unseen vessel safely into port, and observing the scene Haddock had suddenly felt a connection between the pugnacious little vessel and Ramirez.

The title of the painting had been equally fitting.

Approach to the New World.

*

Terri and Janice had booked the Cedric Suite for their honeymoon. Despite being one of *Oceanic*'s smallest 'named' staterooms, it had still cost over six thousand dollars apiece to book. But Janice had been flush with money from *Titanic Century*, and had produced the tickets as a surprise gift on the morning after their wedding. Terri had screamed with delight, and then thrown her arms around her newlywed wife and knocked her back onto the bed in a warm, ecstatic tangle of arms and legs.

And the tickets had been worth every penny. When they had boarded in Southampton, hand-in-hand and wheelie bags in tow, they had found their stateroom romantically prepared in advance by a thoughtful crew; pink champagne in an ice-bucket, sugar-dusted fruits and a selection of chocolate candies. The bed was a queen size, freshly turned down, and surrounded by soft gold and red drapes, forming a flowing silken curtain through which could be seen the door out onto their private balcony. There were even hibiscus flowers in the champagne glasses. After that first heady moment, and once the door had clicked shut behind their escorting steward, Terri had picked Janice up bridal style and laughingly spun her around. It had been a perfect moment, particularly after the jet-lag of the flight from Boston, one that rapidly proceeded into a repeat performance of their wedding night, which they got so caught up in that only the compulsory muster to a lifeboat drill stopped them.

After departing from Southampton, they had sat in silence on the balcony as dusk turned to night, slowly eating the hibiscuses and watching the lights of England receding into the dark. Another ship, only a half-mile away, had sounded its horn as it passed by into the night, and it had almost seemed as if it was saluting them and them alone.

And then it was gone, shrinking first to a distant cluster of lights, then a tiny dot that eventually sank over the invisible horizon, as *Oceanic* continued on out towards the immeasurable vastness of the Atlantic. Janice had trembled slightly as they peered together into the inky black void ahead of the ship, but Terri, smiling and confident and glowing with light and happiness, had squeezed her hand and simply said that there was nothing to fear, because they were together, and would never be parted again.

"You talk too much," Janice had replied, before taking her wife's cheeks in her hands and bringing them together for another kiss.

Now, backdated one hundred years, they were out on the balcony again, hands tightly entwined. *Oceanic* was slowly motoring on through the night, and across the water was another ship, *Titanic*, long and sleek and real.

Janice had come straight up after her conversation with Byles, and found Terri curled into a ball on the bed, weeping just as pitifully as she had on the night her parents had shunned her in that Minneapolis restaurant. Begging her forgiveness, Janice had crawled in alongside her spouse, and for several long hours they had simply held and comforted each other.

Standing on the balcony, Janice could hear Terri breathing deeply with forced calm, as she always did when struggling with her emotions.

"I'm... I'm scared, Jan," she said at last. "If we stay, then we're gonna be in so much trouble from the second we step ashore."

Terri's voice trembled, as she voiced her deepest fear. "I want to do this, but I need you... I can't do it alone, and what if they try to take us apart from each other?"

Janice squeezed her hand a little tighter. Terri was black, she was white. That was a problem right there, even before you touched on the issue of sexuality, or women's emancipation. If you could have created a checklist of issues which might light the ire of this era's social conservatives, and just as many of its liberals, the two of them might just tick every box. Race, gender, and sex...

...though come to think about it, those were all issues back in 2012, just by different extremes. Focusing on that, she took a deep breath.

"Terri, we're the daughters of Martin Luther King and all those heroes of the Civil Rights movement, the ones who marched and protested and triumphed over adversity. I'm not going to stand in their shadow and see you taken away, or forced into the back seat of a Montgomery County bus..." she said, carefully enunciating each word. "We're going to fight them, together. I'm not going anywhere, and no-one is going to be able to separate us, ever. Regardless of what anyone else says, we are married, and I love you."

Terri sniffed and rubbed at her eyes, gaining back some of her usual confidence and spirit.

"And I love you too," she affirmed. "Forever and always, till death do us part. And even if that bony bastard tries to get between us, he's going to have to fight for it."

Janice had always admired Terri's strength, the courage that had led her to first escape from parents that hated her for who she was, and then to try and build a new family with the Pattons. But now she would have to take some of that strength, and feed it back to Terri.

She gripped her wife's hand tightly. Whatever came, they were going to face it together.

*

There was no time to think in *Titanic*'s Boiler Rooms; there was just the Work, in the dust and gloom of the stokeholds. The ringing of shovels and tools, the heaving of coal to the merciless tune of the stoking indicators, and the solid wall of heat as the firebox doors were swung open. Jack had shovelled as demanded, firing the furnaces, then had 'cleaned' a dirty fire with a six-foot poker, breaking up slack coal and clinker that had fused onto the firebars and blocked the flow of air. When he had knocked away the last of it the sluggish fire had suddenly burst into new life, and at the same time a glow of pride burned in his chest. Then more fuel, placed where he was told, until the fire was a living, breathing mass of brilliant white flame that writhed over the black coals. The air sang with men's voices, rising over the howling fans and the roar of the fires, and as they laboured the pressure gauges swung upwards, and the thundering footfalls of the engines continued to beat away beyond the bulkheads, driving the screws that powered the ship.

For all that Jack had sweated and strained, limbs protesting, not having to think had been a relief. Several hours in, however, he had a moment's pause when he was sent to wheel a barrow of coal to a stoker firing away at one of the furnaces. The man in question was tall and strong-shouldered, and the sweat-drenched remains of a shirt and waistcoat hung limply on him as he shovelled relentlessly at the fire. Jack, saying nothing, had dumped the load of coal in a pile beside the man, who had then turned, as if reflexively about to offer him a tip.

The two of them met eyes and started, Jack more so, as he realised he was speaking to Sir Cosmo Duff-Gordon. The Scottish Olympiad's normally well-waxed moustache hung limply around his mouth now, dripping sweat from the tips. Gordon's face was ruddy and his eyes were watering from proximity to the furnace. Coal dust pockmarked his skin and was ingrained in his hair. If it wasn't for the way he still carried himself, Jack might not have recognised him, and he wondered how he looked to the other man's eyes.

"Master Thayer..." Gordon managed a gentlemanly nod, which Jack returned. With a look of contrition on his face, the Baronet then coughed. "I'm afraid I greatly underestimated conditions down here."

They both looked around, seeing the silhouettes of men toiling in the glow of the fires like damned souls. Jack tried to smile, but the action tore painfully at his dry, chapped lips, and he resorted to simply pursing his mouth as if in acknowledgement. "I think we all did, sir."

"Seeing men, living men, reduced like this..." Gordon struggled for words, "is humbling."

"And yet they take a pride in what they do..." Jack replied, seeing one man rearing back with a fire-ram in his hands, legs astride and arms raised like a Grecian god. "I don't think I truly understood that before now, that all men have their dignity..."

Before Gordon could reply, the bell on the stoking indicator beside his boiler chimed, instructing him to fire another furnace. Like an automaton he turned back to the job, lustily singing a few bars of the Eton Boating Song as he put his back into the endless struggle with the coals. Jack merely shook his head at how quickly even proud men could be laid low in this choking Perdition, and then someone called on him to dump a barrow of ash, and he slipped back into the trance that was the Work.

*

"What happens?" Bruce Ismay asked. "To White Star Line?"

"It goes down the toilet," Philippa Paik replied blithely, through a mouthful of pastry, not lifting her eyes from the screen of her 'laptop computer'. "It was a long and hard road, though, and eventually the line was sunk by a combination of the Great Depression and chronic financial mismanagement."

They were alone in *Titanic*'s Cafe Parisien, an exclusive part of B-Deck adjacent to the First Class à La Carte Restaurant. Two walls sectioned off part of the starboard promenade to create a small space decorated with ivy trellises and wicker furniture, from which passengers could dine elegantly while enjoying sumptuous views of the sea.

Or at least, that had been the intention. Having been aboard *Oceanic* and witnessed first-hand the sumptuousness of her appointments, Ismay now felt almost as if he was dining in a children's playroom that some kind parent had decorated for a party. And the child was himself, suddenly feeling very small and powerless.

"I want to know more," he said at last, pulling chunks of bread off a loaf that had been purloined from the galley. "I want to know what went wrong."

Blinking, she at last lifted her gaze to meet him, paused, and then nodded. "Alright."

He hung on her next words, and after pausing to sip at her coffee, she seemingly composed her thoughts enough to explain the circumstances of future history.

"Well, *Titanic* sank, for a start. And then the third member of the *Olympic*-class got requisitioned right out of the builder's yard for use as a hospital ship in World War One, before she struck a mine in 1915 and sank off the coast of Greece. Never sailed under the White Star house flag, never carried a fare-paying passenger. About as sad a fate as you could imagine for a ship. The line struggled on for quite a few years, and even regained its independence from International Mercantile Marine, but it never launched another vessel of comparable size, making do with ships awarded as war reparations to replace the vacant slots in the express timetable. Then there was a scandal regarding the finances of Lord Kylsant..."

"Who?" Bruce interjected, his mind clearly spotting an unfamiliar name, despite his growing horror.

"Right, I'm sorry; he hasn't been elevated to the peerage yet," she said, staring off into the distance and muttering to herself for a moment. Then her expression cleared. "Okay, you know him as Owen Philipps, Chairman of RMSPC."

"Ah, the Royal Mail Steam Packet Company," he nodded. "Yes, Mr Philipps is a personage I am acquaintance with."

"Cool, we're on the same page. By the end of the 1920s, Philipps was 1st Baron Kylsant, and through RMSPC he had obtained ownership of something like twenty shipping lines, including White Star, gathering his holdings together as the biggest shipping group in the world. Then a government investigation revealed Kylsant's group was fraudulently paying dividends despite trading at a loss, and had liabilities to the tune of ten million pounds. Kylsant was arrested for falsely reporting accounts and issuing a deceptive stock prospectus, and the banks moved in on his assets. On top of that the global economy crashed; with White Star on the verge of a financial deep-six the government stepped in to save British shipping, but would only offer financial aid if White Star merged with an equally-troubled Cunard."

She clapped her palms together. "And lo, out of this union didst flower Cunard White Star, with old Samuel Cunard's firm as the dominant partner."

Reaching out for her cup, she downed the last of her tea and cleared her throat. "By that point most of White Star Line's remaining ships were either second-hand or nearing the end of their service lives, so Cunard White Star was able to discretely dispose of them. Oh, it probably sounded reasonable enough at the time, especially with men desperate for work at the scrapyards, but the fact that they scrapped *Olympic* when she was still popular, seaworthy and running better than ever was a clear sign that they were trying to erase the memory of their oldest rival. In 1950 the line's name reverted back to just Cunard, in 1961 the last ship inherited from White Star was broken up, and until the line was revived with *Oceanic*, the only WSL vessel left in the world was *Nomadic*."

"*Nomadic*, you mean the little *ferry*, the Cherbourg tender?"

"Yup, all 1200 tons of her," Pip sighed, staring into her tea-leaves. "The last vestige of a maritime empire." She smiled wanly and laughed. "Back home the nostalgia for all things *Titanic* is so great that *Nomadic* is being restored. She's enshrined at her birthplace in Belfast, in the same yard that launched so many great ships, including this young lady. Touch wood, I'll probably get to see her with my own eyes when we go back to our future."

Her knuckles rapped lightly on the table, and before Bruce could so much as bend his mind around her words of prophecy she seemed to crumple. "Of course, if we can't go home, I'll see more than my far share of contemporary shipping; either that or the inside of a jail-cell for being some kind of '*hysteric eastern aberration*'."

Bruce, unsure of what to say and afraid of being misinterpreted, suddenly felt his heart go out to this lost lamb. He was just about to open his mouth in an attempt to offer some comfort when she looked abruptly up at him.

"Tell me this, Bruce. Humour me a trivial question," she said, in the voice of someone clearly trying to distract their mind from an unwelcome issue. "There's something that's been argued over for years back in my time. The third sister of the *Olympic*-class, the one under construction right now back in Belfast; what name do you have planned for her?"

Against his instincts, Bruce felt his moustache twitch into a half-smile, finding it amusing that a matter of some debate back at the White Star offices in Liverpool was still an issue a century hence. And if it helped assuage her of her fear, then he'd gladly exposit on all matters White Star.

"Well," he said. "When we first placed the order with Harland & Wolff for a third ship the intended name was *Gigantic*. It made for a nice symmetry alongside *Olympic* and *Titanic*, with all being named for races from classical myth; the Olympians, the Titans and the Giants."

She nodded, snorting in sardonic amusement. "Kinda appropriate; if I recall the gods of Mount Olympus defeated the Titans of Mount Othrys in the war of the Titanomachy, and the Giants rose up in protest, leading to the Gigantomachy, which also ended with the Olympians giving the Giants the smack-down."

"How is that fitting?"

"Because of your three super-ships, only the 'Old Reliable' *Olympic* would have been left standing by the end, and even then she had her share of accidents as well as glories. In the present day some morons think the entire class was cursed from birth." She paused, and then shrugged. "And then you have the crazies who insist *Titanic* and *Olympic* were switched as part of some massive insurance scam; you might as well say the ship was sunk by Godzilla, or a giant red robot."

"Yes, well… Lloyds of London only carry part of the ships' insurance value, we cover the rest from the line's in-house 'pot'," Bruce shrugged, unable to think of a decent riposte. "Returning to your question, however; there are those in White Star who feel that the name *Gigantic* is too blunt, too direct and crude. In the spirit of national pride, and to better reflect our competition with *Imperator* and the other new ships being built for Germany's HAPAG Line, it is felt that it would be more fitting to name her-"

"-the *Britannic*…" Pip finished for him, waving a fragment of Danish pastry to punctuate her words. "Well, it should tickle you patriotic fancy to know that after the First World War White Star was awarded *Imperator*'s sister *Bismarck* as war reparations. She sailed for fourteen years under the name *Majestic*… of course, that now might not happen."

She popped the last of the pastry in her mouth and chewed morosely, hands clasped to her mouth as if in prayer. Then she looked across the table at him."And Bruce, assuming the war doesn't come, you need to be ready to fight White Star's corner twice as hard to keep the line afloat, otherwise HAPAG are going to dance all over you *and* Cunard with *their* trio of super-ships. The *Olympics* might be good, but *Imperator*, *Vaterland* and *Bismarck* are going to be *stellar*."

Bruce's hand clenched, scrunching up the tablecloth. He had heard multiple critics express the belief that White Star was destined to fail, but this girl almost made it seem as if his father's company was doomed from the outset.

Something must be done, but should it be me who takes action?

There was a soft clatter as a figure dressed in white emerged from the door that connected the Cafe Parisien to the à La Carte Restaurant and the pantry. Charles Joughin, the ship's Chief Baker, was pushing a small tray loaded with slightly stale pastries, and was taking great delight in providing them freely for their enjoyment. After the dispirited mood she had heretofore exhibited, Bruce was relieved to see Pip abruptly sit up and take notice as the robust baker laid out his choice offerings, smiling as sweetly as if she was regarding an eccentric but much-beloved uncle.

"He survived the sinking, but nearly didn't..." she explained to Bruce once Joughin had left. "He got out of a lifeboat before it was lowered, to make room for others, and stayed on the ship right until she went down, holding onto the stern rail. The legend goes that he didn't freeze to death in the water because he was drunk at the time, but I call bullshit on that. His testimony was too coherent for a man allegedly soaked to the gills with whiskey."

Bruce lifted his eyebrows at her language, before sighing and resting both his hands on the table, lacing the fingers together as he might when chairing a meeting.

"What about myself?" he asked, fielding the question that had dwelt heaviest on his mind the past few hours, feeling a sympathetic twinge of pain from his injured leg as he spoke. "From your reaction to me when we first met, and events on *Oceanic*, I take it the world does not have a favourable opinion of me."

"I dunno Bruce, what do you think happened?" she asked, now stirring her tea with a crescent-shaped fragment of pastry, her eyes focused on him, challenging him.

"Well, based on what I know of the temper of popular opinion, either I survived in a manner that was deemed cowardly, or that blame for the disaster is placed on me so disproportionately great as to offset any glory I might have gained by going down with the ship."

"Right on both counts," she said, holding out her scrap of pastry as if awarding a prize. "You got off in one of the last lifeboats to safely leave the ship, and people accused you of pressuring Captain Smith to go full speed into the ice field in an attempt to get into New York a day early, beating the time it took *Olympic* to complete her maiden voyage last June. Again, while the evidence supports claims that *Titanic* was making better time than *Olympic*, I call bullshit on the idea that you personally ordered Smith to damn the torpedoes and go all ahead, but that became the public zeitgeist. 'J. Brute Ismay', villain of the *Titanic*."

He exhaled and looked away from her, gazing out the nearest window into night. *Olympic* was just coming into view astern, and for a meditative moment it seemed as if *Titanic* and her sister were indeed challenging one another in a race.

"Well," he said at last. "I don't deny that we've been making good time, but might I guess that William Randolph Hearst had something to do with stirring up public opinion against me?"

"The newspaper mogul?" she snickered. "Citizen Kane himself, the master of yellow journalism… yeah, I've heard things along those lines."

There was a pause, and Bruce supposed his emotional distress must have made itself known, for when she next spoke her tone was more sympathetic.

"It's well-known that there was some bad blood between you and Hearst, and back up in my day it was a popular theory that Hearst deliberately spun the *Titanic* disaster in an attempt to publicly shame you. He actually put out a cash prize for anyone who might have dirt on your conduct during the voyage, but still… where are you going?"

Bruce had risen and was wiping at the corners of his mouth with a napkin.

"Excuse me," he said. "But I must gather my thoughts."

"Your thoughts on what?"

"On how I wish to comport myself when we arrive in New York. There will be questions, people will expect answers, and I must be ready to give them."

He was turning to go when Pip called him back.

"You're afraid of reporters aren't you, Bruce?" she said, bluntly, but with some sympathy. "Everyone expects you to have your father's flair for self-promotion, but you've always been the man who simply wanted to stay in an office and try to run the Line as best you could, not wade like some David into the lair of the media lions."

Turning back around, Bruce opened his mouth to protest her arrogance and presumption, but found her gazing evenly at him. No, he couldn't argue with the plain honesty in her eyes.

"You're a decent man Bruce Ismay, otherwise you wouldn't have cared so much about my own well-being. I once read that you made a spontaneous £500 donation to a Liverpool orphanage, out of the goodness of your heart. And yet, you were apparently an anti-unionist, which seems at odds with your social conscience. So, as someone who's also terrified by the prospect of speaking publically, let me give you some advice."

She turned around her laptop so that the screen was facing him, reached over and pressed a button.

Bruce blinked as his own image appeared onscreen, as he had been moments ago, calmly explaining the naming of the *Olympic*-class; affable, relaxed and coolly collected. Seeing his surprise, Pip tapped a small device that was clipped to the top of the screen.

"Portable webcam; I was recording the whole of the conversation."

"Why?" he stammered, face blanching. "Do you intend to blackmail me?"

"What? No! Hell no..." she sighed and tapped at the keys. "There, those files are deleted. What I meant was..." she paused and rubbed at her temples. "I felt guilty for not warning you and others about how history miscast you. I know the whole story of how 'after *Titanic* sank Ismay went off and brooded in misery for the rest of his life' is a gross exaggeration, but after Murdoch confronted me on the issue, I decided that I should at least try and make amends for not warning you in advance."

She folded the laptop up with a sharp click.

"You might not like reporters Bruce, but the camera is possibly your best friend. I hate speaking to crowds, but during the centennial expedition my articles and videos were being consumed across the world; the same technology could enable you to get your words across to multitudes of people without having to face an army of overbearing journalists. So if you want to put your case across, go speak to Margaret Brown on *Oceanic*; I'm told she's started a news service, so have her interview you. That's how you fight back against men like Hearst, by fixing the score before they can get started. You beat them at their own game. Get on camera and get your version of events out to the six thousand people on these ships and admit to your mistakes if you think you've got any to confess. The story will spread from there."

He pondered this. Was she right? Was this was the best opportunity he had to ensure that his image, and the image of White Star, remained intact? It seemed uncertain, full of potential pitfalls, but at the same time, alluring…

"Thank you, Miss Paik," he said at length. "And I wish you the best of luck in your own affairs."

"Heh, thanks Bruce," she replied, and with an exchange of nods he left her to the tender mercies of Baker Joughin and his pastries.

But as he weaved through the ship towards his cabin, Bruce's mind was suddenly active. The girl was right; the next few days at sea were his chance, perhaps his only chance, to clear his name in advance. That in itself, however, was a tacit admission that he was trying to hide some wrongdoing, and if that were the case, he did not know if he could go the rest of his life with such feelings burdening him.

Confess to my mistakes? Well, there was that affair with the telegram from the Baltic…

His footsteps increasing in speed and tempo, he headed towards the Marconi Room.

*

Scott was in the open recess atop *Viking*'s sail, peering off to port where the other ships were smoothly gliding over the rising waves; even *Rescue* and *Californian*, smallest in the fleet, were meeting the rising seas with little complaint.

Viking, on the other hand, was struggling. Designed to travel for long distances *under* the ocean, not *over* it, the submarine kept trying to bury her head in the sea every time she took a wave on the nose, turning her progress into a lumbering, pitching ride that was causing Scott's already restless stomach considerable discomfort.

But we can't dive, because of how we mutilated our own ballast system to help bail out Titanic…

Climbing down into the hull he quickly made his way to the washstand in his cabin and splashed water over his face, calming himself before returning to take the Conn.

"...opportunity to make a change for the better in the world..."

Not far away, in the wardroom, he could hear the sound of a television playing.

"...for Alexandra Press, this is Dean Simmons aboard Oceanic."

The Captain and Major Butt had sequestered themselves in the wardroom for some hours now, turning the volume of the television up to mask their conversation. But what worried Scott was not just the fact that they were trying to hide something, but the attitude being reflected in the broadcast itself. The channel chosen was the one that *Oceanic* was now broadcasting, the one calling itself the Alexandra Press.

It was playing in *Viking's* mess as well. An hour ago he had passed through and seen the men watching in rapt attention as a 1912 girl called Viola or Violet or some such, dressed to the nines in a modern stewardess' uniform, gave the camera crew a guided tour of *Oceanic's* below-deck areas, explaining the operation of the ship for the benefit of her fellow 'passengers', the contemporaries.

"Now that's a bit of alright..." one of *Viking's* crew had said, when the girl led the camera team into *Oceanic's* private crew bar. "There any chance of a few drinks on the house, Mr Thresher?"

It was meant as a joke rather than a breach of discipline, and Scott had laughed along with the men. But the fact that people on *Oceanic* were so clearly trying to ease relations between the two groups of people, between natives and the time-displaced, concerned him deeply.

They're making themselves comfortable here, as if they don't really believe we can go home...

It was the same mindset he feared he saw in how Bob Furness and Major Butt had shut themselves away in the wardroom. The Captain was making a plan, that was for sure, but Scott wished he might be a party to it as *Viking's* XO.

What about our responsibilities to the future? Don't they even care?

He knew that he was being cruel, that people on all the ships were just uncertain, but still he clung to the hope of going back. At the same time, however, he feared the ambition many of them might feel to, as Dean Simmons had put it, 'make a change for the better in this word'.

There was opportunity here, the chance to make fortunes by playing soothsayer with future knowledge. Anyone armed with the right know-how and some technical skill could develop a piece of non-existing technology, like a jet engine or penicillin, and claim it as their own. What kind of cog would that throw into the course of history?

Could that be temptation enough to stay? Would *Viking* and her crew get stuck behind with them? Was this guilt he was feeling at wanting to get back to the future ASAP, now that they had made their mark here and done some definitive good?

He thought of people from both eras mingling over on the *Oceanic*, dining together, exchanging ideas, and suddenly felt a wave of thick, hot nausea wash over him, laced with frustration and anger as numerous thoughts boiled in his mind, clashing and rebounding every time he tried to get a solid footing on where he lay.

Jess. Time travel. History. Destiny. Free Will. Future.

And war. War, war, war. Every history book he had read in his life suddenly seemed like they were trying to drag their way up out of his memory, forcing themselves on him until it felt that his mind should burst from the unwanted influx.

Lusitania, sunk 1915 by the U-20, almost 1,200 civilian deaths… Jutland, 1916, 8,500 lives lost… Battle of May Island, 1918, 270 men killed during a training exercise gone wrong…

More numbers, more statistics, culminating in a possible new entry in the annals of maritime disaster back home;

…HMS Viking. Vanished at sea April 14ᵗʰ 2012. 135 men MIA. 135 families left missing sons, husbands, fathers, with no explanation as to where we've gone… thousands others also grieving from the disappearance of the Oceanic, Anatoly Sagalevich, Rescue and Seguin Laroche…

Something was happening, he suddenly realised. There were raised voices coming from the wardroom, where someone was shouting. Crossing over he threw back the curtain and found Butt and the Captain, staring raptly at the television, upon which *Oceanic*'s grand staircase could be seen, gathered crowds staring at a figure ranting from the top of the stairs.

Margaret Brown had seen the crowds converging on the Grand Staircase from across the Palm Court, the sudden commotion drawing the attention of both herself and her cameraman, Daniel Mervin. Weaving past tables and chairs, they quickly drew close enough to make out the words being yelled.

"...have you no consideration? The consequences of your very presence will be dire, and yet you are going to abandon this age to the very chaos you have sparked!"

Even as she came to the railing and peered down into the staircase well, she recognised the voice of the speaker. Jack Thayer's friend, Milton Long.

"Start filming this, Danny, quick," she instructed, and Mervin trained his camera on Long, wirelessly uploading it live to the ship's internal television channel.

Long was standing before the ship's great clock, the timepiece supported by artistic sculptures embodying Honour and Glory. He was dishevelled, swaying on his feet and moving his arms around in such exaggerated motions that he was evidently drunk. Despite his inebriation, or possibly because of it, he was remarkably eloquent, and made for extremely good TV.

"You come with warnings of wars to come, and presenting yourself as evidence of a society so changed as to be unrecognisable to people of this era. But like children caught in some misdemeanour, you now wish to just run away and escape the consequences. Yes, you are privileged with the gift of future knowledge, but what of the responsibility that knowledge entails?"

His volume and aggressive tone had cleared the immediate area around the staircase, leaving Milt a stage from which to pontificate. And almost immediately he had gathered himself a willing audience. The balconies around them were now crowded with spectators, listening with rapt fascination. Maggie gazed around at them. Her contemporaries were whispering amongst themselves, as if discussing the validity of his points, while the time-travellers seemed more hostile. What they had in common, however, was fear and uncertainty.

The sound of gears whirring caught her ear as Milt paused in the middle of his diatribe for breath. Directly beneath her, on a balcony that protruded out into the atrium, William Harbeck was grinding away at a Jury's Kine Popular camera, creating a black-and-white film record.

Milt must have seen them, and realising he suddenly had the audience of posterity, directed himself towards the watching cameras.

"To those watching on this 'Alexandra Press', I offer you my free and honest thoughts. We have been told that in just two years the Archduke of Austria-Hungary will die by an assassin's bullet; that his death will set in motion a war long in the coming, with Germany held in contempt as the alleged engine of aggression. But what are we to do now? Surely the Archduke will avoid Sarajevo like the plague, but are we to assume that powers in Berlin are still set upon a cause of action, to which his death was just an excuse? Are they more likely to attack now before they lose surprise, or will they step down from a theatre on which they stand to gain land and glory? Should we take action and sanction to prevent such a war from coming, whereas before we would have sat back and awaited its nascent birth, like lambs before the inevitable slaughter? You have relieved us of that fatal innocence, and for that I thank you, but you are now ready to leave us fumbling in a blind, trying to seek out a light amidst the flares of burgeoning war and revolution. Shame on you sirs, that you would leave us to this fate!"

The crowd rippled as several of *Oceanic*'s crew pressed to the front. Three of them came to the foot of the stairs and stood facing Milt, as if ready to charge him.

"You are content to lecture us on the mistakes of our futures past, with your films, and your judgements, and in your brutal, unwarranted attacks on men of high calibre, but you are blind to the mistake you are on the verge of committing. Then you are hypocrites, hypocrites I say! This world is now your responsibility, so much more so than the world you have left behind. If you were to abandon this age, with just the few scraps of information you have passed on to enlighten us, you would condemn millions to death in uncertainty. No, I must insist you remain, and pass onto us in full the wisdom of ages to come. Only with a complete account of the road ahead might we safely travel it without falling off into the mire of chaos…"

*

The television mounted against the bulkhead of *Viking*'s officer's mess cast flickering shadows over the dimmed room. Scott Thresher stood in the doorway while Bob Furness and Archibald Butt sat in silence as the unknown man, broadcast live from *Oceanic*, continued to vent up at the camera filming him.

"…before, but a few of you were in positions of power, but each of you now, by the accident of this new history, have been elevated to the position of potentates, whose word is enough to direct the minds and lives of others. That you weep for the friends, children and loved ones you have left forward is not to be denied, nor is the righteousness of your desire to see them again. But your innate nobility obliged you to render assistance to us upon Titanic, and by that same nobility you are now obliged to stay! Yes, it is your good deeds that have trapped you in this quandary, not your sins but your virtues. For that I am sorry, but you cannot shirk responsibility, not as the parents of the new world born when you chose to intervene to save Titanic! God bless you all, and may He console and succour you in your loss, but in His name, I implore that you not abandon us!"

The man had been staring up at the camera, his face dark and his eyes burning intensely. Now, however, he took a step back and breathed deeply, as if he had just ran a marathon.

"Thank you."

The security officers came running up the stairs and Furness tensed for a moment, sensing a burgeoning fight, but the man who seconds ago had been ranting simply regarded them with a puzzled expression, before raising his hands in surrender to *Oceanic*'s security officers, who quickly and firmly handcuffed him and led him away. He offered no protest.

Bob Furness wondered who he was.

Beside him Archibald Butt sighed in relief, and Bob realised that he had not been the only one stressed during the impromptu broadcast.

"That poor man had no idea what to do with his fists," Butt said at last. "The anger was just for show."

Beneath them, *Viking* thrummed softly, pitching noticeably as she pushed forward through the swells. Bob glanced down at his clenched hands, white-knuckled and numb, He forced them to open, and winced at the dull ache as feeling returning to them.

Uncomfortable silence reigned for several minutes. Butt gazed around the small compartment, taking in details of the fittings and furniture, while Bob Furness sat and mused. The young man onscreen had a very valid point, and he felt inspired, trying to dig out the kernel of an idea taking root in his mind. He had first grasped at it during his tirade for the benefit of the 'Council of Captains', and his fingers were just reaching out now to grab at it when someone rapped on the bulkhead outside. Scott Thresher ducked his head out to speak with whoever had knocked; returning seconds later, expression grim.

"Captain, there's a delegation here from the crew. They wish to speak with you."

Bob stared at him for a second, not comprehending, his derailed train of thought struggling through the wilds back to the tracks. Butt however coughed loudly, and remarked aloud;

"A delegation, you say? To my ears, that sounds like a precursor to mutiny."

The last word jolted Bob back to reality, and he rose to receive these guests. His feet felt leaden, but the familiar tug of command was enough to draw him on.

"Show them in, Mr Thresher," he said at last. "Major, would you care to remain with us?"

Butt nodded in silent response, and after several long seconds three petty officers entered, the youngest among them looking somewhat abashed. They exchanged salutes with the captain, who invited them to sit.

"That won't be necessary, Captain," the senior of the three replied politely. His name was Shires, and even after Bob instructed him to relax, he remained at parade rest. Thresher loomed concernedly in the doorway as the Chief Petty Officer began to speak.

"Sir, you are no doubt feeling some confusion as to what to do in this situation. We wish to make clear that the crew overwhelmingly wish to return to 2012. It is felt that our duty as Royal Navy submariners is to resume our essential duties safeguarding Britain and her allies from nuclear aggression."

Bob nodded curtly. Like Shires, who stood three inches taller than him, he remained on his feet, hands clasped behind his back.

"I understand your feelings, Mr Shires. And I also understand that any decision to remain in this time would separate us permanently from our wives and families. Lieutenant Commander Thresher, for example..." he nodded towards Scott. "Is recently married, and I know that you, Mr Shires, have family waiting back on the Gareloch."

"Yes sir," Shires dipped his own head.

"At the same time, however, I must consider the course of action most beneficial to this new age we find ourselves in, so as not to allow the mistakes that left millions of our ancestors dead on the fields of Europe to be repeated."

"I know that is not an easy decision," Shires persisted. "But this goes beyond the risk involved when we volunteered for the submarine service. Our families knew too that someday we might not come back from a patrol, but these are exceptional circumstances. We have a duty, and people dependant on us, back in the future, and to stay here and play with this new history is to abandon that duty, an action both cowardly and treacherous. The speech that man gave on *Oceanic* has given the men in the mess concerns sir. They feel you might consider it... noble, or heroic, to sacrifice *our* present for the wellbeing of *this* century. And although *Viking* is not a democracy, they question whether they can obey any orders you give that will result in us becoming trapped in this era."

And there it was. The threat of mutiny, no different to what Captain Bligh had encountered aboard HMS *Bounty*. Yet, to be honest, Bob's sympathies had always been with Lieutenant Christian, the mutineer-in-chief. How had it come to this?

"That is all, Captain," Shires concluded, saluting smartly. Now the floor reverted to one Robert Furness, who could respond with discipline or discretion, tyranny or tact.

"Very well," Bob dismissed them, for now valuing prudence as the better part of valour. He needed to judge the mood of the crew himself before he made a critical misstep. "I will put your concerns under due consideration, Mr Shires. For now however, I must ask you men to please return to your stations."

Shires and his wingmen saluted again, and wordlessly left the mess. Bob saw Thresher lurking in the door, and nodded for him to step inside. Major Butt sat in the corner in silence, observing the two of them.

"Well, Scott, you're our live-in idealist," Bob said. "What's your impression of the situation?"

"I think both yourself and Mr Shires are right sir. If we were Army or Air Force then I'd say we'd have to return home without question, as their oath of service specifies their loyalty is to Queen Elizabeth the Second, and Her Heirs and Successors. But given that we never had to swear that oath to get into the Navy, but instead pledged our loyalty to the Crown, I don't see any technical reason for us not to transfer that loyalty to her grandfather. Wherever we are, *whenever* we are, we remain part of the Senior Service, and our duty remains the same."

Scott paused and sighed, running a hand through his hair. "That said, I doubt anyone has ever had to prepare for a contingency like this. The Roswell Files don't contain any orders beyond attempting to secure the *Liberty Bell*. We have a responsibility to our own age, providing the Ultimate Defence of the Realm, but we can't just leave this world to a century of war and chaos."

"So are you suggesting," Bob said softly, feeling clammy around his collar, "that we split the difference?"

Thresher's clean-shaven face was blank and unreadable.

"Yes sir, I am."

The atmosphere seemed to become very dense in the small space. *Viking* heaved slightly as she took a wave on the nose, and the low, metallic groans of hull girders flexing and fittings rattling merged together into a single organic sound, as if they were riding within a living entity with a will of its own, a beast of steel.

Butt seemed to sense the tension, and slowly came to his own feet, holding onto the mess table for support.

"Gentlemen," he enunciated carefully. "Do I mean to presume that you are considering launching your missiles?" His diction was precise and his voice did not quaver, but there was an unspoken challenge in his words. "Are you ready to enforce your will on the rest of the world, using these devastating weapons, weapons which you alone possess?"

"Perhaps we are, sir," Scott began to say. "We could create desolation and call it peace, scare the world into disarmament, and then slip away back to the future…" he stopped abruptly as the captain held up a hand, demanding silence.

"We're thinking on the same page, but let's not get ahead of ourselves, Scott," he said, before turning to Butt.

"Archibald, we are the third HMS *Viking*. The first was a light cruiser, launched only in 1909. She will not be broken up for scrap for years to come, but she was fortunate in that regard. Many of her compatriots, the battleships and dreadnoughts that have been built with such abandon these past few years, will soon be consumed in a firestorm the likes of which you cannot imagine. All across Europe, and America too, and far abroad in Asia, arms have been stocked for years, like wood and kindling. Tensions between and within nations are fermenting like spilled oil. All it will take is but a spark, and all of the world will go up in a conflagration that will define history for a century to come. The Great War they called it, the War to End all Wars. That's a joke; World War One will be the War to Start all Wars! So yes, Major; if, with the weapons afforded to my command, I can create a power vacuum so great as to squeeze the air from that fire before it begins, I will make use of *Viking*'s arms."

Butt rose to protest, but Furness quieted him with another motion of his hand.

"Don't panic, Major. I'm not going to run around firing off nukes willy-nilly. Any action we take will require quiet, methodical action. And before we thrash the world's nations with any stick, we should first try plying them with a carrot of some kind. Furthermore, we should be making sure that those among the Time Fleet who wish to go home, can, and help them on their way."

He turned to Scott.

"Mr Thresher, order engines stopped and have the men run out the Zodiac. If the Major is willing to accompany you, I wish for you to go over to *Rescue* to inspect the *Liberty Bell*, and bring Doctor Oshiro back for further discussion. In the meantime, I'll stay aboard *Viking* and address the concerns of the crew."

"Yes, sir…" Scott said slowly, before turning to shout forward into the control room. "Stop engines, secure the boat and ready the Zodiac for launch."

He vanished forward to carry out the orders and Bob rose, straightening his uniform.

"Well, Major? Do you think me a monster?"

"No, captain," Butt admitted. "But I think you're in a difficult patch. Tell me, do you have family?"

"Yes I do," Bob's fingers clutched at the familygram in his pocket, and he clenched his jaw in an attempt to swell the flood of emotion. "My wife, and a fine nephew."

"Indeed. I can't tell rightly Captain, if you command a crew of heroes or inhuman monsters."

"Can any of us? You've led men in battle; you should have seen the same, right?"

"Never such as this."

"No," Bob acquiesced. "Never such as this."

He pulled himself upright and stepped forward. "Come on, I have a crew to calm, and you have a time machine to inspect."

*

There was a light squall falling, and through the dark the lights of the other ships were blurred streaks. As he came through *Viking*'s deck hatch, Archibald Butt had time to think they looked like running watercolours before someone grabbed him and threw him back off his feet. His head slammed against the lip of the conning tower, fiery pain bursting in his mind like a starburst. Fumbling, he caught hold of whoever had assaulted him, and the attacker's face came into focus.

"Mr Shires!" he demanded. *"What is the meaning of this?"*

The bullet-headed chief petty officer's face was devoid of emotion, and as Butt instinctively lunged forward in an attempt to head-butt him, Shires brought his fist up into the soft tenderness beneath his sternum, bludgeoning the fight out of him. Fumbling weakly for his dress-sword, and realising with a curse that he had allowed himself to be disarmed when he came aboard, Butt suddenly found himself seized bodily and thrown across the edge of the deck. Tumbling on and off his feet, struggling for grip on the wet metal, he fell down *Viking*'s curving flank and pitched into the Zodiac boat, which bobbed alongside in the turbulent sea.

Seconds later, Captain Furness was cast down beside him.

Equally stunned, the two men peered up into the bright glare of a torch directed down on them. Scott Thresher was silhouetted behind it by other lights, his face cast into unreadable shadow. The gilt thread on his shoulder boards burned like soft fire.

"What... what is this, Scott?" Butt heard Captain Furness laugh weakly. "What's... what's the game?"

"No game, Bob," Thresher answered, calling out to make himself heard over the waves and hissing rain. "I'm sorry, but if we're going to do anything for this time, it has to be done *now*, and then we have to go home. All of us from 2012 need to go home, with the *Liberty Bell* in *Viking*'s possession. If you try and get the world powers of 1912 around a table, then you'll be forced to play it slow. By the time you've talked them round, the timelines will surely have parted, and we and the civilians in our care will be trapped here, forev-"

His voice was calm, but caught in a cough on the end of the sentence, as if the man was trying to talk himself up. In Thresher's hand, Butt could see a key glinting on a thin length of silver chain.

"You took my firing key, Scott..." the captain replied. "Are you really willing to launch? Do you honestly think you can?"

Thresher did not reply. Shires stood to one side like a sentinel, a rifle cocked in his hands, but they were the only two on deck.

"Look at you, Scott!" Furness again managed a laugh, and this time Butt heard a forced note of condescension in his voice. "Look at us! You've thrown us into an inflatable when you could have killed us. You're no Cold Warrior; you don't have it in you to commit a holocaust!"

He was calling Thresher's bluff, Butt knew so much as that, but it was still an alarming path that the Captain's words were turning down.

"Don't bullshit me, Lieutenant Commander Scott Thresher!" Furness continued. "You'd better kill us now, because if you don't I swear that I will stop you, somehow."

Thresher shook his head. "No you won't, Bob. You know I'm doing the right thing, the same thing you were planning. I'm just accelerating the timetable, while we still have surprise and a chance to resume our duties in the future, to our country and our families. And even if you tried to stop us, you couldn't find us; we're grey ghosts in the Atlantic, invisible. I'll see you in the future."

Butt saw Thresher pocket the key and disappear down the ladder, followed by Shires. As they dogged the hatch behind them, he threw himself forward to climb back aboard *Viking*, only for Furness to grab him by the hem of his mess-jacket and drag him back into the boat.

"Stay back, Archie! He's going to start engines any second, and we've got to get clear!"

Still sore and wet, their fingers rapidly numbing in the April chill, the two of them struggled to start the Zodiac's outboard motor, and by the time it coughed into life *Viking* was getting herself underway, her huge ducted propeller churning up a rising mound of chop and coming straight at them.

"Hold tight!" Furness shouted, gunning the throttle. The Zodiac shot forward into the low gap between the rearward curve of *Viking*'s deck and the thrashing propeller assembly. The inflatable boat grounded momentarily on the slope of the deck, and then shot itself clear, pushing away from the submarine, which was accelerating away into the night, conning-tower raised like the dorsal fin of a black iron shark.

The two panted, still struggling to catch their breath, and then the walkie-talkie clipped to Furness' belt crackled with Thresher's voice.

"Attention all hands, attention all hands. I regret to inform you that I have relieved Captain Furness of duty. He has been set adrift with his guest, Major Archibald Butt..."

"He can't honestly expect them to obey him..." Butt seethed, but silenced himself when Furness held up a hand, indicating that they should listen to Thresher's continuing elegy.

"Captain Furness was a dedicated officer and leader to us all. But he failed us, the Royal Navy, and the millions entrusted to our care when he considered abandoning our mission to follow his own agenda. We

shall not fail in his place, and shall proceed immediately with securing the Liberty Bell time machine, while safeguarding the future of this new timeline's Britain, with an immediate nuclear attack on the aggres-aajdssssss."

The message began to break up as the distance increased between them and the sub, and Furness began to frantically adjust the frequency on the radio to reacquire the signal.

"Shsmasss –we have spent years, lifetimes, wishing that the evil that has festered recently in the world be excised. We've sat and watched orphaned children and grieving parents on the news, crippled and crying, telling us how their families were killed in Baghdad, in Jerusalem, in New York, and in London. We all know of the blood and treasure that was spilled once at Jutland and on the fields of Flanders, and the innocents destroyed without mercy in the chambers of Auschwitz. These crimes may well occur again in this time. May. Wishing got us nowhere. Now we have a chance for action. The minefields, the checkpoints, the hate and atrocity that gave rise to the evil regimes we still live with, are yet to come. The world can do better. Viking will make sure of it. Captain Furness knew this, but feared to wield that force, even when empowered to do so by the Letter of Last Resort. We will show this world's war hawks a reason to be afraid, we will make a peace through their utter destruction, and when warmongers like Kaiser Wilhelm will no longer have a say in affairs we, and the rest of the Time Fleet, shall go home."

Over the radio Thresher swallowed, and then spoke in firm, clipped tones.

"Our priority now is to secure the USNS Rescue and the Liberty Bell. Rescue is currently under tow from the SS Californian and making twelve knots. Under normal conditions we could capture her with ease, but trapped on the surface in worsening seas we will be hard pressed to run her down, let alone board her. As such, I now issue my first order as Viking's commanding officer; prepare the following firing solution…"

The man had a definite flare for the dramatic. Butt almost expected to hear a jingoistic '*huzzah*' resound through the talkie, but instead there was just a sudden silence as the message terminated, as if a tensioned wire had just snapped under load.

"Action stations…" Furness said softly.

CHAPTER TWENTY SEVEN

"Action stations!" a voice cried over *Viking*'s speakers. *"All hands to action stations."*

Men were running, leaping out of bunks and stowing possessions in lockers, jumping into chairs and playing their hands over the control panels. Electrical displays came to life, glowing in arcane patterns. Like a rock in a swollen sea, Scott Thresher suddenly found himself anchored in place, drowning in the onslaught around him.

Captain Furness had apparently been concerned about him about going beyond initiative into impulse. Now look at what he had done.

You can do this, Scott, he thought to himself, turning over the Captain's firing key in his hand alongside his own. *You've trained so many times for this, gone through the drill.*

But it had all been a sham. Despite all the memorised procedures and launch drills, the training and lectures, the better part of him had been convinced that they would never, *could never*, be called on to launch *Viking*'s armaments in anger. Now he had bitten off more than he could chew, yet the mask of calm battle-readiness fell on as easily as ever, convincing everyone but himself of his resolve.

That was why they had to do this; not just to incapacitate *Rescue* and secure the *Liberty Bell*, not just so that they could go home, but so that he could commit himself. Already he'd staged a mutiny, now he was going to attack an unarmed allied vessel, each deed building up his confidence to the point that he could commit a war crime... for a greater good.

"We have a firing solution on the target, Mr Thresher. Torpedo loaded and ready to fire."

In Scott's mind, bells were ringing as he remembered his wedding day, Jess stepping up beside him to take their vows, a

548

symphony in silk and lace. So loyal, so calm, so accepting of the time that they had spent apart during his patrols. The two of them planned to share the rest of their lives together, and he was going to make sure they would have that time.

"Fire tube one!" he ordered.

The sub kicked back subtly as she spat the torpedo out, and Scott's wedding bells were drowned out by the hysterical shriek of its motor, screaming in his mind.

*

Jordan Jones had been sitting in contemplative silence, feeling the soft rise and fall of *Rescue*'s deck as she ploughed the waves, towed along in *Californian*'s wake. The bridge was a quiet oasis of calm, and, once more alone with his thoughts, he was wondering what to do with himself once they reached port, wherever or whenever that port lay.

Could he perhaps stay in 1912, playing the role of a blind prophet? Blindness in old age was something he had feared all throughout his life, being lost to the same dark that had claimed his father. Now he was living the nightmare, but he still had his life, and his pride in the accomplishments of his ship and her crew filled his heart until it overran with feeling.

And I have a surrogate son in Kai... that's something else to consider...

But in the fringes of his thoughts he could feel something building. There had been a tension at the captain's table on *Titanic*, and now he sensed that a confrontation was approaching fast...

"Captain!"

...so when *Rescue*'s sonar officer gave a panicked shout, and alarms began to ring, he rose to meet this new challenge almost as if he had known it was coming, with a calm that was frightening.

"Report!" he barked.

"Sir, one fast contact detected in the water, speed eighty knots, impact in less than a minute."

Torpedo, he realised.

"Let go of *Californian*'s line, evasive manoeuvres!" he shouted. "Full astern! Helm and bow thrusters hard to port! If we sink no-one goes home!"

Rescue responded exactly as he wished, digging into the water and yanking herself hard to one side, but she was still crippled and not as agile as she should be.

"Sir!" someone shouted in alarm. "The fish isn't tracking with us! It's maintaining course onto *Californian* – she's the target, not us!"

Jones spun on his heel, wishing more than ever that he could see what was happening.

"What?"

*

Stanley Lord had long been described as prudent to the point of staidness; a man so methodical and cautious that he seemed to lack any sense of initiative.

"Captain Lord!" cried an electronically-amplified voice from the *Rescue*. *"You have a torpedo inbound at eighty knots, eight points to port!"*

In another time, in another place, in the controversy surrounding *Californian*'s role in the *Titanic* disaster, that caution would be one of the faults of Lord's character laid against him by his opponents, accusations that he would unsuccessfully challenge until his dying day.

Having learned of history's unfavourable opinion of him, Lord himself had spent much of the past hours pondering the fate he had narrowly avoided, and how best to prevent falling into the same trap again.

"Helm, hard to starboard! Port engine, full astern! Starboard, ahead full!"

Right now however, he was too preoccupied to worry about what history would have to say about him.

The deck bounced as the ship worked to turn, a combination of engine, rudder and momentum swinging her away from *Rescue* and pointing her prow at the incoming threat. It was a deft bit of seamanship, in the spirit of the same manoeuvre that had safely brought her to a halt on the edge of the ice field yesterday evening.

It was not enough.

"Attention all hands!" Lord snatched up a megaphone and bellowed into it. "Clear back from the gunwales and brace for impact!"

And at that point a single Spearfish torpedo, its electronic mind working to outfox any evasion, dived deep, slipped under *Californian*'s hull, and detonated directly beneath her keel.

The ship *ju mped*, as if trying to leap clear of the Atlantic and take flight. The violent lurch knocked Lord flat on his back, and he stared up in disbelief as a towering column of smoke and flame erupted from his ship's single smokestack. The Leyland steamer bellowed in pain, arching like a creature in agony. Then, just as quickly she flopped back into the sea, settling rapid amidships and flexing like a banana.

Groggily, Lord pulled himself upright.

Her back's broken... he realised, feeling the deck tilting beneath his feet. Off to starboard, *Rescue*'s searchlights were turning towards them. *Californian,* however, was another story, already heeling hard over to port, and it took only the most cursory glance at the plunging needle of the inclinometer to confirm that the sturdy little freighter was doomed. Grabbing hold of the whistle chain, Lord held down on it, sounding a faltering, watery cry that signalled the end of his command, and perhaps his entire career.

"All hands, abandon ship!"

*

"We have a hit!" Scott, eyes pressed to *Viking*'s periscope, reported as a bright flash of light far across the water. He glanced to the sonar operator, who confirmed the detonation. "Congratulations gentlemen! Without *Californian*'s assistance, *Rescue* can't evade us on a single screw."

No cheers went up in the control room, but in Scott's mind a chorus of applause fit to lift the roof sang out. Lord Nelson had not received such a fanfare returning triumphant from Trafalgar, albeit dead and pickled in vinegar.

"Ahead, half speed," he instructed. "Navigation, manoeuvre us away from the fleet. Once we're a safe distance off, make ready to launch. Then we'll move in on *Rescue*."

He paused and swallowed before completing the order. "Our first target is Berlin."

"You've lost it, Scott!" a new voice rang out like a bell in a storm. Men stopped and turned where they stood. Scott looked too, towards *Viking*'s Weapons Engineering Officer, who had entered without anyone noticing and now stood with his feet planted solidly on the deck, firm as a pillbox.

"We've all got our reservations, Weps," Scott said calmly, focusing his attention on the displays around him, in an attempt to bar any sudden doubt out of his mind. "But you had no objection just now, when we fired on *Californian*."

"That was different; there was a measurable, objective goal, securing the *Liberty Bell* and our path home. It was not like this, sir. Not an indiscriminate strike, launching an armed missile into the heart of a nation which has not declared war on us."

"Weps," Scott bared his teeth, in a grin that was more friend than fiend. "I've got no intention of nuking a non-combatant without warning; this first launch is just a demonstration."

He forced his expression to harden, turning his attention. "Prepare for a surface launch from *tube one*."

"Tube one?" The WEO pulled himself around the periscope, not allowing Scott to break eye-contact. "You mean that…"

"As I said," Scott intoned, cutting him off. "It's a message to the leaders of 1912, a declaration that we can reach out and touch our finger to any point on the world we choose. They'll listen to that; they'll have to."

Scott reached under the chart table and reverentially produced Major Butt's ceremonial sword. Drawing the gleaming blade from its well-oiled scabbard, he looked the other man in the eye, feeling like St. George readying to slay the dragon.

"Your key please, WEO."

*

"Come over, quick! Jump for it!"

Californian was heeling heavily away from *Rescue*, but the other ship was throwing across ropes and gangways in an attempt to bring men to safety. Chest heaving, stumbling on the uneven surface, Charles Groves ran up the length of the deck to one of the torpedoed steamer's lifeboats, now hanging inboard from the davits due to the increasing list, impossible to launch. Grabbing hold of its gunwale, he boosted himself inside and crawled under the weather sheet, feeling around for the duffle bag he had stowed here earlier.

Then his groping hand made contact, and he sighed in relief. It was still there.

Suddenly he felt the lifeboat lurch, the wooden craft swinging violently from the falls as *Californian* rolled. Pulling his penknife from a trouser pocket, Groves stabbed upwards with the blade, cutting through the tarpaulin and creating a space in which he could stand up. The ship was capsizing, falling right over onto her beams, masts shattering as they toppled. Men fell along her decks as she tumbled, some of them striking ventilators and fittings with sickening force. Her funnel tore away as it slammed into the water, steam and fragments of broken machinery vomiting out of the shaft. As her flooding curve inverted the ship finally plunged, Groves' lifeboat splashing into the water as his side of the deck submerged.

Before the ship could drag him down with it, Groves had scrambled across the tarpaulin to both ends of the tiny craft, pounding on the release mechanisms to free it from the falls. No sooner had he done so than *Californian* slid under, the sea bubbling wildly where she had sunk in mere seconds.

Heart racing, Groves let himself fall back in the lifeboat, one hand patting at the duffle bag under the tarpaulin. Satisfied that the laptop and iPad were still safe, he smiled. Then, hearing cries for help coming from all around, he began to haul swimming survivors up into the boat, as *Rescue* slowly manoeuvred closer on her one good engine.

*

Smith had seen an explosive flash of light off to *Titanic*'s starboard side, and through binoculars had witnessed *Californian*'s rapid and unexpected sinking.

"Did her boilers explode?" a sweating Murdoch asked. "Or did something go wrong with that *Liberty Bell* machine aboard *Rescue*?"

Before Smith could answer him, Harold Bride came running from the wireless room, waistcoat unbuttoned and face panicked.

"Captain Smith, Captain Smith! We've just received a message from *Rescue* over the speaking radio!"

"And what did they say? What's happened man!?"

"Sir, the SS *Californian* was torpedoed!"

Smith felt himself grow cold, and he turned to peer out into the dark, out towards where he had last seen *Viking*.

"My God, what are they doing?"

*

"Mr Thresher, we're getting reports that *Rescue* is closing to draw *Californian*'s survivors from the water."

I'd expected Captain Jones to run, Scott mused as he tapped Butt's cutlass thoughtfully against the deck. Then he shook his head, deferring to destiny.

"It makes no difference. *Rescue* will now be preoccupied, and can't outrun us in a straight sprint in these conditions, not without both screws turning. Once we've delivered our message to Berlin, then we'll go after the *Liberty Bell*."

He turned to the firing computer; all of the arming keys were set in place, and now he turned them one-by-one, completing the circuit that brought the fuelled missile, poised in its firing tube, to launch readiness.

"WEO," he spoke softly into a handheld microphone. "Permission to fire."

"Supervisor WEO, initiate fire one."

Scott almost imagined he could hear the gentle click of the firing trigger before all sound was drowned out, overwhelmed by the roar of the rocket motor igniting under the missile somewhere aft. *Viking* bowed beneath his feet as the ICBM eagerly flexed its muscles, and then, with deceptive speed, the roar dwindled to a gentle, distant buzz.

"One away."

Launch. Scott stopped and forced himself to breathe. They had launched. He could feel his heart pounding in his chest and neck, and his uniform suddenly felt ten pounds heavier as he let himself fall backwards into his chair.

"WEO, stand down from firing stations, continue tracking the missile's progress, report when orbital apogee is reached."

Now they played the waiting game.

*

Something burst bright as a flare out beyond *Titanic*'s starboard side, as if something had just shone a torch in Smith's eye. He threw up an arm to protect his night vision, but then a sound like a cannon firing struck him head-on, the shockwave that followed knocking him to the deck like a sack of potatoes. *Titanic* quivered beneath him like a live thing, the whole hull ringing from the same force that had felled him. That blast of sound matured, becoming a booming rush that roared in his ears with deafening force. Hands pressed to the side of his head, chest wheezing, Smith rolled onto his knees and pushed himself upright.

"What happened?!" he shouted, drowning in the surge of raw sound coming from off to the north. Lurid red light was pouring in through the bridge windows, lending a horrific glow to all the fixtures, as though *Titanic* was steaming through St John's Revelation. To Smith's eyes, Murdoch and the other crew were dark blots in greatcoats, stark outlines against the glare.

"*Viking* launched some kind of firework, sir!" the Scotsman yelled, struggling to be heard. Suddenly comprehending, Smith's gaze snapped from the stunned officer's face to the source of his awe.

"No..." he shouted in horror, and heart flailing in his chest, he ran to the rail. "Lord God Almighty, no!"

Running on the surface as she was, *Viking*'s position was clear to see, the vessel lit from above with a ruddy glare, a biblical pillar of smoke connecting the submarine to a jet of brilliant fire that was racing into the sky. Already the device was at least a mile up, highlighting the clouds in hellish hues of red. The roar was subsiding, but all Smith could hear was the roar of blood in his ears. He tipped his head back, eyes following this new star climbing the ladder of heaven.

"Furness!" he growled. "Blast it, he wasn't lying about her abilities!"

555

"Captain, what is it?" Murdoch shouted in concern. "What's happening?"

"It's *Viking!* She's launched one of her damned missiles!"

"Her what!?"

"Rocket-bombs, William! Rocket-bombs!" Smith snapped, one hand pressed tight to his chest. He was struggling to breathe, his lungs burning as they fought for oxygen. Still his eyes remained fixed high upon the dwindling light of the missile, as it slowly began to tip away towards the east.

He's fired it towards Europe... God above, no.

His mouth struggled to form more words, but they wouldn't come. In his mind he imagined his little daughter Mel standing outside their home in Southampton, pointing innocently at the pinprick of light crossing the sky like a shooting star. And then that star fell to Earth, and Mel's wail of fear mingled with the shriek of the missile as it plunged into the heart of the town, and everything turned to fire.

"Captain Smith? Edward, what's wrong!?" he heard Murdoch shouting dimly, far away beyond Mel's dying screams. "EJ, EJ!"

He was screaming with Mel, roaring in pain, his heart bursting like rotten fruit, then he was falling backwards, legs collapsing as he sprawled back on the deck, some unseen hand driving a spike through his chest.

"Oh Lord, it's his heart! Quick, get Doctor O'Loughlin!"

Overhead the twinkling missile continued to ascend on its pillar of smoke. Lying prone, one hand clawing at his breast, Smith could still see it, and through the fiery pain stabbing all through him felt tears on his face.

It looked like a distress flare.

"God save our souls," he said, in shuddering breaths, forcing the prayer out with the last of his strength.

Cold oblivion rushed in on him. Once more he was drowning in darkness.

Then nothing...

*

"Heavens above!" Butt gaped in horror as the rain poured down on them, staring up through sleeting rain at the missile now rocketing upwards. "He did it; the madcap bastard actually did it!"

"That's Scott Thresher for you…" Furness commented darkly from where he was manning the Zodiac's tiller. They were still in the tiny inflatable, and had been granted a first-hand view of the launch. "Impulsive to the end."

"Impulsive?" Butt turned to face *Viking*'s deposed master, face livid. "You make it sound like a boyish prank, but God alone knows how many people that diabolic weapon is going to kill, and all because you could not maintain a firm enough grip on your subordinate!"

Furness gazed back at him with reptilian calm, before speaking slowly. "I wanted Scott to remain my XO on *Viking* for at least another patrol before he was offered his own command. If he hadn't shaped up by the end of that period, I was planning on recommending he be transferred out of the ballistic submarine fleet and redeployed on the attack boats."

He pointed up at the rocket flickering miles overhead. "Now he might be an idiot, but he's not going to jump straight to mass murder. Did you see the checkerboard telemetry markings on the side of the rocket? Those aren't standard; meaning he intentionally launched the D5 Life Extension test package that we were scheduled to fire from off the coast of Florida. It was a dummy, a warning-shot across history's bow."

"You sound as if you approve," Butt glowered. "Armed or not, the use of such a weapon is still monstrous."

"Of course it's monstrous!" Furness snapped back. "That's what I've been trying to beat into you these past few hours, *Archie*. Nuclear arms are a zero-sum arsenal! But launching a blank one enables him to demonstrate what he can do to the world, with minimal casualties. That is genius!"

"So is that it? Do you intend for him to get away with it?"

"Hell no. He's already torpedoed a ship and launched the test missile; he's working his courage up to do something definitive, and I'm either taking my sub back from him before he can, or sending her to the bottom."

With that, Furness put the tiller over with a snap and revved the engine, sending the Zodiac flying across the open sea towards *Rescue*. The waves were rising into white-capped rollers, and a stiff breeze was forming, pushed ahead of the developing weather front.

*

"Give him air, step back!" Murdoch shouted off the gathering crew as he knelt beside Captain Smith and searched for a pulse. Nothing. He quickly laid his ear to the captain's mouth, which hung slackly open.

"He's not breathing," he realised, before repeating another futile cry for Doctor O'Loughlin, gazing along the open deck in the hope that the good Doctor might suddenly come running. But all that met his eyes was the tiny, shrunken figure of Philippa Paik, the girl standing at the open First Class staircase door, staring up in slack-jawed disbelief at the ascending rocket.

"Miss Paik!" he cried out, feeling a desperate surge of hope.

She did not seem to hear him. He shouted again, and she turned, seeing the group of figures clustered together at the entrance to the bridge. Murdoch jumped to his feet and waved her frantically over. "Come quickly! Captain Smith is dying!"

Now she ran. Dropping back to his knees Murdoch smacked the captain about the cheeks, muttering frantically. "Come on EJ, wake up dammit!"

The sound of men being shoved aside heralded Ms Paik's arrival, and she practically threw herself down onto her knees beside the prone Smith. "Oh God! What happened?"

"He fell down clutching at his chest when he saw... that!" Will snapped, gesticulating at the missile's trail, a plume of smoke now fading into the encroaching dark. She nodded, but only stared hopelessly at him for a second. "Well?"

"Well what?" she repeated, uncomprehending.

"Don't you have some fantastic machine or technique for reviving the dead?" Will heard himself demand. "What good is it coming from the future if you've not found some way of staving off heart failure!?"

558

"I'm not a Doctor, Mister Murdoch!" she answered, eyes flashing with anger, before her attention fell back upon Smith. "But I do know CPR."

"What's CPR?"

"Watch…" Grabbing Smith's head with both hands Paik tipped it back and pinched his nose, before opening her own mouth and clamping it over his. Murdoch recoiled for a second, thinking she was molesting the dead Captain's body; then he saw her chest heaving, and realised that she was actually breathing into Smith's mouth, and doing the work of his lungs for him. After several seconds she removed her mouth and, resting her hands over Smith's upper chest, pressed down several times.

"There, you see…" she explained, teeth gritted and arms flexing. "CPR. Cardio, pulmonary, resuscitation. You've got to do the work of his heart and lungs for him, until he either regains consciousness, or a doctor arrives."

At that moment Doctor O'Loughlin did arrive, the Irishman immediately shouldering in beside Murdoch and reaching for Smith's wrist. After several seconds he released it, and spoke quietly.

"It's bad, Mr Murdoch, very bad."

Will slowly removed his cap and pushed the hair back from his face. Looking away, O'Loughlin's curled moustache twitched as he finally noticed Philippa Paik, still alternating between compressing Smith's chest with her hands and breathing into his mouth.

"My dear girl, what are you doing?"

"I'm trying to keep his brain alive!" she replied. "See!"

She paused in her cycle of actions for a second, and both Murdoch and the Doctor saw Smith's body reflexively exhale by itself. Spreading her hands in a show of victory, Pip then folded them back together and began to compress on the Captain's chest once more. Murdoch stared in silent consternation as the Doctor grabbed Smith's wrist and counted to himself, before standing.

"Still no pulse, but I do see!" O'Loughlin said, his eyes lighting up. "You're forcing oxygen into his lungs and keeping it flowing to his brain…" He pushed himself to his feet, and turned towards the door to the officer's quarters. "Where's the speaking wireless? I need to speak to *Oceanic's* doctors immediately!"

"What do we do until then?" Murdoch replied, gesturing for Pitman to show the Doctor the way.

"Assist her!" O'Loughlin pointed down at Smith. "His heart's not beating but the old boy's not dead yet! This young lady's keeping him back from the brink!"

*

Jack Thayer was tired, and somewhat lost, but after emerging from the stifling, choking heat of the boiler rooms an aimless wander through *Titanic's* corridors seemed welcome. The only other activity was that of a handful of stewards checking to ensure that each cabin was locked, in case anyone attempted to loot the possessions of now-absent passengers. Beyond them, and a few other volunteer firemen groggily trying to find their beds after exhausting themselves in the stokeholds, the liner seemed all but deserted.

But despite the weariness, and the pain burning slowly in all his limbs, Jack felt strangely accomplished, and at the same time thoughtful. Even a few hours work in the boiler-rooms had been an eye-opening experience. As he ambled about the ship, walking in laps on C-Deck, he was for the first time aware of how many men laboured thanklessly below decks, feeding the burning heart of the ship. Pausing for a moment, he glanced down, trying to reconcile how the opulent passenger accommodations floated on a metal skein over a fiery slice of Hell.

Is this why she thinks of us as monsters...? he considered. *Because of the contrast between our comfortable lifestyles, and the drudgery that supports us?*

A more cynical part of him began to wonder if Philippa Paik's own world showed a similar disparity between economic classes, or if wealth and affluence was the status quo from New York to New Guinea. It seemed doubtful.

"Hello there, I say, what's happened?"

Jack looked up in surprise. His amblings had brought him to where the corridor opened out onto the Second Class promenade, but to his left was an open door marked *'Ship's Hospital'*. Standing in it was a heavily bandaged-man. He wore a pullover over a hospital gown, and his face was severely reddened, either from exhaustion or injury.

"I… I don't understand…" Jack gaped, and the man grunted.

"I'm officer Lightoller, of the ship's company. A few moments ago something happened outside. Some manner of weapon that my fellow patient identified as a 'missile' was launched. What exactly happened?"

"I'm afraid I'll be of no help to you," Jack explained. "Until but a few moments ago I was assisting in the boiler rooms." He held up his filthy hands as evidence, feeling a sudden new anxiety gnawing away at him.

"Listen!" the man named Lightoller held up a hand, pointing towards the ceiling, and straining his ears Jack clearly heard the sound of multiple men running aft.

"Come on…" the injured officer grunted. "Let's see what's happened."

Jack was about to protest that his new companion was in no shape to be leaving the hospital, but Lightoller seemed to have an indomitable will, limping out aft onto the promenade in spite of his evident discomfort. Uncertain, but following on, Jack kept pace as they came out into the aft well-deck, and heard the sound of men labouring hard up on the ship's sterncastle.

*

"Move, men, move. Clear them all away!"

As members of the deck crew hastened in the hissing rain to take down the removable railings around *Titanic's* poop-deck, Will Murdoch paced on the aft docking bridge and fretted. The open structure, normally used only for co-ordinating the ship's arrival at a harbour, stretched right across the ship's stern, and was fitted with a secondary helm and order telegraphs.

"I've got those tools, Mr Murdoch," one of the men spoke up from below, and Murdoch came to the rail. It was Quartermaster Olliver, and he was carrying a collection of saws and lump hammers.

"Good," Murdoch pointed at the aftermost point of the hull, a stumpy pole from which flags were flown near to shore. "Cut the stern staff down."

"Beggin' your pardon sir, but *what*?"

"Cut it down, knock it down, whatever, but get rid of it!" Murdoch ordered, before turning his attention towards the horizon. Over the sounds of men working, the wash from the propellers and the sizzling rain, something else was making itself heard, a rhythmic pulsing that rose over the chaos into a steady mechanical drone. He peered into the dark, and saw a cluster of lights at the level of his eyes, skimming across the water, drawing nearer with every second.

"Cut it down, Mr Olliver!" he repeated himself, waving an arm to encompass the poop deck. "We need to clear as much space as possible!"

The approaching noise was now hard to ignore, sounding like several unbalanced propellers charging away. Olliver turned towards the lights, and Murdoch saw comprehension dawn upon the man.

"Understood sir," the quartermaster said, and taking the heaviest hammer in both hands he began to lay into the stern staff.

"What's happening, Will?" someone else called. It was Charles Lightoller, who despite being heavily salved and bandaged was surreptitiously climbing the stairs to join him on the docking bridge. *Titanic's* Second Officer had pulled a jersey on over his hospital-issue pyjamas, and was accompanied by a young man who looked to be from the scratch crew of firemen.

"Lights," Will said in disbelief. "You're meant to be in bed!"

"Well, I could not help but notice when Doctor O'Loughlin received an urgent call from the bridge, only to charge off out of the hospital like a man possessed," Lightoller replied. "And it seems to me that right now you need a helping hand." His easy words were laced with a quiet concern. "What's happening, Will?"

"The Captain nearly died, Lights," Will said bluntly. "His heart stopped with shock when *Viking* fired one of her weapons."

Lightoller took a step back and grabbed the rail. "First Mr Wilde, now Captain Smith?"

"Not quite yet," Will pointed towards the lights, reaching out like a man grasping at salvation. "Miss Paik is trying to keep him alive with a kind of heart massage, and *Oceanic* is sending out a Doctor and modern appliances that they claim can help him."

Something crackled, and Murdoch turned to grab a walkie-talkie from where it had been resting on a locker. "This is *Titanic*, please repeat your message."

"Roger Titanic, this is Bell 88 approaching you from the east. How do you want to handle this transfer?"

Murdoch sensed Lightoller step up next to him and turned. The second officer's eyes were wide open with fascination, and Will smirked slightly, unable to resist. "I understand your craft can hover; we're clearing a space now for it to berth upon."

"I can see that Titanic, but it's going to be a tight fit. There's a lot of clutter on your deck."

Lowering the talkie, Murdoch regarded all the capstans littering the deck like manganese-bronze mushrooms. Wooden benches were nuzzled among them for the use of Third Class passengers. "We can't do much about that, I'm afraid. If we stop our engines you might have a better chance of landing, but we will not be able to control the ship's drift. The current might take her out from under you as you try to come down."

"Toss him a line," Lightoller suggested with a shrug. Will briefly turned and regarded him as if he was mad, and then nodded. Seeing the simplicity of Lights' idea, he spoke back into the talkie.

"Actually sir, we might have a solution."

While he explained the plan into the radio, Lights crossed to the auxiliary engine order telegraphs and rang down to the Engine Room for minimum speed, steerage only. The pulsations of the propellers under their feet slowed obligingly, and as Olliver succeeded in felling the stern staff, Murdoch saw the flying machine ease forward into the dim light cast by *Titanic*.

"So that's their 'helicopter', is it," he heard Lightoller say appreciatively. "Strike me if that's not impressive."

Will Murdoch found himself agreeing with a silent nod of the head. Bell 88 looked not so much a machine as a creature born of the air, its blue hull shimmering like the carapace of an insect. The source of the attending noise became clear; the craft hovered effortlessly beneath a wide propeller, one that spun so fast as to lend the whole machine the semblance of a hummingbird. Through a tinted glass canopy at the front he could spy the helmsman, cautiously easing forward towards *Titanic*.

"Come on, come on!" Murdoch waved him closer. Inching forward and hovering just above the level of the poop-deck, the flying machine eased its sleek nose over the edge of *Titanic*'s stern. Keeping their heads ducked low, several of the ship's crew ran forward and threaded a pair of lightweight mooring lines around the two skids that protruded from its underside. Quickly rejoining their mates, they looped the ropes around two of the capstans and, taking up the effort as a team, began to haul the helicopter in as if reeling in a catch. The pilot in turn maintained his mount in a hover, allowing it to be towed aboard the ship, until with a glad thump its twin skids landed on the deck, straddling one of the smaller bollards and the stump of the stern staff. The craft's tail, however, still hung out over the Atlantic, and the spinning propeller that gave it lift was flashing around only scant feet away from the elevated docking bridge, at a perfect height to decapitate anyone standing on it if the helicopter shifted forward.

It was perhaps the most risky, the most *foolhardy* piece of seamanship, or airmanship, ever attempted. In Will Murdoch's mind it was second in folly only to last night's scrape with the iceberg, but as he scrambled down the stairs and ran to the helicopter's doors, he did not give a single care so long as it meant Captain Smith's survival. He had already lost one friend to this madness in the death of Henry Wilde, and did not intend to lose another.

As he approached to the craft, the door to its passenger cabin slammed open, and down stepped a distinguished-looking gentleman carrying two thick holdalls. He introduced himself as Doctor Montgomery, and was accompanied by 'Nurse Patton', a dark-skinned woman who looked decidedly shaken from the flight. Will shouted his thanks, and with the two of them in tow ran forward, leading them towards the starboard side of the boat deck.

"Orbital apogee has been reached, Mr Thresher; the missile should now be commencing re-entry, impact in less than five minutes."

"All right, extend the radio antennas. We want to make sure no-one misses what we have to say next."

*

Captain Smith was still laid out on the deck, just inside the bridge awning. When Murdoch had left to oversee docking the helicopter, Doctor O'Loughlin and Miss Paik had been alternating the duties of compressing the captain's heart and breathing air into his mouth. Since then they had undone his jacket, waistcoat and shirt to expose his chest, and as Murdoch's entourage approached at full speed, he saw O'Loughlin stand with a hopeful look on his face.

"His heart is beating again, but it is extremely out of step."

"What are the specifics?" Montgomery said, wasting no time for introductions.

"Adult male, sixty-two years old," O'Loughlin replied briskly. "Very irregular heartbeat, laboured breathing."

Will glanced down to confirm the Doctor's words, and saw that although Miss Paik was still doing his breathing for him, Smith's hands were weakly flexing on the own.

"Thank you, Lord," he said beneath his breath, and turned back to O'Loughlin, who was still briefing Doctor Montgomery.

"…it's now been sixteen minutes since he collapsed, and three minutes since his heart restarted. We had been ready to give up on him at that point."

"Lazarus syndrome," Montgomery nodded, sighing in relief. "Does he have any relevant medical history?"

"None that I know of."

"And does he smoke or drink alcohol frequently?"

O'Loughlin's expression reflected confusion as to why either would be relevant, but nodded. "Yes, he smokes cigars and enjoys a drink, but never on a voyage. He would not have touched either since… Tuesday evening in Southampton, over six days ago now."

"Very well," Montgomery glanced down as the nurse eased Philippa Paik away from Smith. "Have you been resuscitating him the whole time?"

"Yes, under Miss Paik's instruction," O'Loughlin replied. As a flushed Pip took a moment to catch her own breath, Will shot the girl a look which he hoped reflected his gratitude.

"Excellent," Montgomery turned towards his patient. "Then we can defibrillate immediately, Terri."

The female nurse was down on her knees, applying a sort of jelly to two metal paddles she had removed from a medical case. They were connected by wires to another one of those ubiquitous computer-devices that so annoyed Will, and as she fiddled with the control panel the machine suddenly began to hum in a low tone, suggesting incredible power contained within.

The power of life itself? he wondered. *I'd have thought that blasphemous, but if they save the captain then I'll repent from ever judging these people again.*

But before he could question their methods, Montgomery laid the paddles on Smith's chest.

"Clear!"

Patton pressed her thumb down on a button, and with a sound like the crack of a whip, Smith's body jolted. From somewhere inside the 'life-machine' a series of blips suggested the Captain's heart fluttering like a crippled bird.

"Again! Clear!"

Once more Smith's body lifted off of the deck, back arching. But this time the blips were steady, beating with a natural rhythm. Smith's eyes fluttered open as he breathed weakly, and then suddenly his chest heaved, and he vomited sideways onto the deck.

"That's actually a good sign," said Doctor Montgomery. Will laughed with weak relief, and then Smith turned to look up at him, mouth moving in a near silent whisper. Getting to his knees, Will put his ear close to the other man's mouth; Smith repeated himself hoarsely, and this time the words were legible.

Will Murdoch righted himself in surprise.

"I... I understand, EJ," he nodded as Smith, ashen-faced but composed, was helped onto a stretcher. Will stood as well, ready to escort him to the helicopter, but then turned when he heard someone shouting his name.

"Mr Murdoch! Mr Murdoch!" Harold Bride, face flushed, came running through the crowd. "You're needed sir, in the wireless room!"

Murdoch glanced down at Smith, who was now being injected in the arm by Doctor Montgomery. The professionals had him in their care now.

"Very well," he said, turning his attention upon the wireless operator. "What is it, Sparks?"

"It's *Viking* – she's declared war."

"On who?"

"*On everyone, sir!*"

Launching himself forward into a run, William McMaster Murdoch headed for the Marconi room, Smith's final order echoing in his mind.

"You've got to… stop them… stop Viking, Captain Murdoch."

CHAPTER TWENTY EIGHT

Charles Lightoller had been chatting with the helicopter's 'pilot', a term he found to have been horribly reconceptualised over the course of a century, when the craft's radio had suddenly began to squawk. Hearing it, the young man who had followed him up to *Titanic*'s stern, Mr Thayer, had shouted for quiet and pulled open the door to the flying machine's cabin so that all could hear.

"This is HMS Viking, transmitting on the Standard Intership Frequency. No doubt you have all noticed the missile we launched not long ago. I will now reveal its target to be Berlin, specifically the Wannsee Lakes on the River Havel. Many of you understand the devastating power of an intercontinental ballistic missile, so I must assure you that this first strike made use of a test warhead, and so, coupled with the selection of a water target, will not lead to fatalities. It is merely to send part of a message..."

*

"It has now been twenty minutes since launch, and the missile should very soon be making impact. As such, it is time to send the second part of that message, which I require forwarded on our behalf by Marconi wireless..."

Jack Phillips' hand flew over a sheet of paper as he struggled to keep up with the words issuing out of Cameron's jerry-rigged radio set, transcribing the message the madman had for Berlin.

"To all nations currently involved in war preparations. The recent explosion in Wannsee, Berlin, was the impact of a ballistic weapon launched from the North Atlantic, by the time-displaced submarine Viking, at 0330 local time. Between then and the time of impact it travelled a distance of three-thousand miles in less than thirty minutes..."

There was a bang as the door flew open and someone entered the cabin. In the corner of his eyes Jack saw it was Mr Murdoch, but he did not stop copying down Thresher's words.

"...*this should illustrate that Viking can easily fire upon any point we so choose on the surface of the Earth. The missile we launched tonight was not armed. The ones that follow will be. Each has a destructive power equal to its great speed and range, and is capable of levelling an entire city.*"

Phillips paused for a moment in shock, and he heard Murdoch take a sharp breath. As if seeking confirmation the two of them looked over to Cameron, whose expression was black as death.

"He's not joking; he really could do it," the radioman said softly.

"...*we are not belligerent, and do not wish to see lives lost. However, unless the German, Austro-Hungarian and Russian Empires do not immediately renounce their policies of inciting violence and sedition for political gain within Europe, we will launch a second weapon as a demonstration of our powers, at 0500 hours, local time. It will be armed. Any nation that retaliates upon us, either on behalf of Germany or to further their own goals, will find their capital cities levelled in a similar manner. In order to avoid such an unwinnable conflict, we urge the German Empire to respond to our demands immediately. HMS Viking, in the North Atlantic.*"

The channel cleared as Thresher ended his speech, and Phillips felt Mr Murdoch grab hold of the back of his chair, looking for support.

"They're evil bastards, those who brought the world to this, past, present and future..." *Titanic's* Acting Captain seethed, before snapping out as Phillips' hand reached for the Morse key. "Don't you *dare* relay that message; the panic incited if you do will be beyond comparison!"

Then, turning on his heel, Murdoch strode out of the cabin. Awestruck, Phillips found himself following, leaving Bride and Cameron to maintain contact with the other ships.

"Mr Pitman!" Murdoch called to the Third Officer as they came onto the bridge. "Run aft and tell them to get Captain Smith off the ship and away to safety as quickly as possible, and order Doctor O'Loughlin and Charles Lightoller off with him, get them all to a hospital better than our own."

Not giving Pitman time to object, he came up to the telephones mounted inside the wheelhouse and flipped up the one marked 'Engine Room'.

"Joseph, Mr Andrews, Mr Alinka, or whoever's there! This is William Murdoch speaking," Phillips heard him briskly order. "Bring up the pressure and prepare to go full steam ahead on my command. That is all!"

*

"There's no room for stretchers; he'll have be seated in the passenger cabin!"

Bell 88's engine was spooling back up, the down-blast from its rotor making conversation difficult on the poop deck. Captain Smith, brought aft on a stretcher carried between Doctor Montgomery and Bruce Ismay, was now breathing with the assistance of a hand-operated pump as Nurse Patton assisted him into the craft and strapped him in. Landing and navigation lights blazed all around, lending the entire scene a surreal, alien air.

Shielding his eyes from the glare, Jack Thayer hung to one side, yearning to help, but unable to do anything productive. Turning at the sound of pounding footfalls, he looked forward and saw a ship's officer running up in a fluster.

"Mr Murdoch says you're to take off immediately!" the man shouted over the roar of the helicopter. "I think he means to chase down the *Viking!*"

The words ran through Jack like electric current, raising goose pimples on his arms and legs, spurring his heart into a pounding rhythm.

"What?" protested another crewman. "He can't do that, the ship's not sound up in the bows. Go full speed and all the repairs will work loose!"

"I think as the new Captain he can, and he will."

Jack was inclined to agree. *Titanic* was the one ship present not carrying passengers or precious cargo; by any definition, they were standing aboard the only vessel that could be considered *expendable...*

"Now get this machine off the deck quick-smart!" The officer whipped round, looking for someone. "And where's Lights? Will wants him off the ship and in medical hands as well."

*

"Up you come, quick now!"

"Al'ama!" Nashat Abu Shakra hissed as Charles Lightoller got an arm around him and pulled him out of his hospital berth. "What's going on?"

"There's a 'helicopter' come to evacuate Captain Smith," Charles said. "And you're going with it."

"Just, just let me stay here," the Arab replied, clearly finding breathing still painful, let alone speaking. "I'll be fine."

"Not a chance in Hell, lad. Will Murdoch's captain now and I think he means to take this ship into battle; I'll be damned before I leave you here alone."

Making their way through the hospital was a struggle, both of them being injured to greater and lesser extents. Charles's whole body still burned like it was made of fire, and he could not help but notice at how Abu Shakra continually clutched at his wounds' dressings, but at last they made it to the foot of the stairs that led up to C-Deck.

"Damn and blast. This is going to be tricky."

Before Lights could contemplate the difficulty of getting a person up the short, steep flight, however, someone else ducked in through the door at the top.

"Have I missed all the fun?" Jack Thayer asked.

"I'll give you fun," Charles growled, nonetheless relieved to see an extra pair of hands. "Get down here and help me bear this man's weight up the stairs."

It was indeed easier, and with Abu Shakra carried between them, the two men made it aft to the Poop Deck.

"Hey!" Thayer shouted, waving an arm as the three of them fought their way up the last flight of stairs. "One more for the Skylark?"

The two Doctors and the nurse assisting them quickly had the young Arab seated alongside Captain Smith and shot full of sedatives. Then they themselves scrambled aboard, and as the engine of the helicopter roared to the peak of its power and the pilot prepared to lift off, one last person arrived, ascending the stairs from the aft well-deck with a video-camera in hand.

"Miss Paik!" young Thayer and Charles said in unison, before turning to face one another, confusion written in broad strokes across both their faces.

"You know this young lady?" Charles shouted to be heard, hair flying around his head in the turbulent wind swept up by the helicopter.

"Yes, I'm afraid that I was a bit of a cad to her last night!" Thayer replied.

"And I myself!" Charles turned to face the person in question, expression regretful. "Miss Paik, I must apologise for something that occurred last night, a misunderstanding on your part that I did not correct."

"You mean Fred Barrett, right?" she replied, smiling sadly when he reacted with some surprise. "Yeah, I worked out later that there was something odd going on before Boiler Room 5 flooded."

"You said at the time that Engineer Shepherd should have been moved aft into the next compartment before the bunker door collapsed," Lightoller said mournfully. "It was my actions, not your inaction that brought about that change in circumstances and Barrett's death. I realised it at the time, but had not the courage to admit as such to you."

"You've not spent the whole day stressing over that, have you?" she answered incredulously. "Fuck it, Lights, it took me a while myself but it was *you* who got me round to thinking that everything that happened last night was the fault of *everyone, including ourselves.*"

Charles' confusion must have been apparent, because she immediately looked around, waving an arm to encompass the ship. "That's the whole point of *Titanic;* people always want an easy target to blame, like Bruce Ismay or Captain Smith or even *you*, but it's not one person's fault, and it never was! It's everyone's fault, all society, all the whole world's fault that *Titanic* sank as she did, and the whole of two worlds' fault that this is happening right now!"

She paused and laughed aloud. "So get over your sense of self-importance, Lights!"

He felt a smile come to his face, feeling the unmistakable lightness that came with forgiveness and redemption.

"And Jack…" she turned to the Thayer lad. "The same goes for you, and me. I was an idiot last night just as much as you were! You offered me your support, and I drove you away by not thinking about how my actions might affect you. This is your world and I was an uncouth guest in it."

"Well, I'll forgive your sins against me," Thayer said, rubbing at the back of his head. "If you can forgive mine against you."

"Deal!" she replied brightly, eyes shining as she looked from him to Charles. "You guys, I've looked up to the two of you ever since I first discovered *Titanic* for myself. Last night I found myself doubting everything I had ever invested emotionally in you, but seeing the two of you helping that kid to the helicopter reminded me why you drew my attention as a kid; you're two of the genuine heroes of *Titanic*, then and now."

"I hope you count yourself among those heroes now, Miss Paik," Lightoller replied, deflecting her praise right back at her.

"Oh, trust me," she answered, shifting her gaze to peer past his shoulder. "It's a much larger list than it originally was a hundred years from now."

Charles turned and saw that her focus was on Bruce Ismay, who was shaking his head as the helicopter's pilot tried to coax him aboard.

"Some additions are more unexpected than others!" Paik added, and Charles found himself nodding as they watched the White Star magnate shake Captain Smith's hand in farewell, and then step back to slam the cabin's door shut.

"We've got one free seat left!" the pilot turned and yelled towards them. "If no-one takes it we're going now!"

"We've someone right here!" Lightoller shouted back, indicating his youngest companion. "Miss Paik, your place is on that machine."

"No, yours is, you're hurt!" she said firmly. "I'm a historian of *Titanic*, and I'm staying to see this thing play out to the end. Besides, if something goes wrong, I could still be useful; I probably know my way round the ship better than anyone bar Thomas Andrews!"

"I'm not leaving either!" put in Jack Thayer. "If Mr Murdoch is really going into a chase after *Viking* then I'm putting my hands to the furnaces. Sir Cosmo Duff-Gordon is slaving away beside the other stokers below, giving *Titanic* the steam she needs, and I'm going back down to help them! She's right, Mr Lightoller, you should go!"

Charles looked at them both, uncomfortable. "The both of you are pushing me to save myself, but I refuse to go if one of you might be taken in my place."

"We have to take off now!" shouted the pilot. "Murdoch's getting antsy on the radio!"

"You're injured, Lights," Paik pressed. "And you've got a wife waiting for you back home who I know to be destined to spend a long and happy life with you! Jack and I are both healthy, and single!"

The she pointed out into the black void surrounding the ship. "Besides, Murdoch needs your help in spotting *Viking* from the air!"

Charles' teeth clenched as he wrestled with himself.

Are you a righteous man, Charles Lightoller? Maybe not, but that is up to powers beyond yourself to decide. Right now you have a clear duty, to do as these people tell you!

"Thank you both," he said simply, bobbing his head once before limping over to the helicopter and climbing in beside the pilot, who was shouting into his mouthpiece.

"Alright, we're going up! Bell 88 to Captain Murdoch, good luck and Godspeed!"

Charles held on tight, peering out of the window in stunned disbelief as *Titanic* dropped away beneath him.

*

Engine howling, the helicopter rose rapidly off of *Titanic*'s deck, the draught from the rotors billowing out the jackets and overcoats of everyone gathered around the docking bridge. Jack threw an arm around Pip to steady her, and mentally cheered as she returned the gesture.

"You do what you have to do!" he shouted. "And I'm going below to help raise steam! If you need me, I'll be in Boiler Room 4!"

"Alright!"

*

"Thank you Bell 88, *Titanic* out!" Will Murdoch said crisply into Cameron's microphone, before releasing the 'speak' key and turning his attention to the radio operators.

"Keep in contact with them; let me know the second they spot *Viking*'s wake," he stressed to the radio operators, quickly hurrying forward out of the Marconi Suite onto the ship's bridge.

"Half ahead, make revolutions for eleven knots!" he ordered. Pitman and Moody were manning the engine telegraphs, and leapt to carry out his order. Boxhall was in the wheelhouse, keeping a weather eye on the compass binnacle, while Lowe stood by on the starboard wing, binoculars in hand as he swept the open sea.

"Hard a'starboard! Bring us about by one hundred and eighty degrees!" Will called out, hearing Boxhall repeat the order, followed by the sound of the helmsman throwing the helm over until the wheel hit the rudder stops with a bang.

"Hard over!"

"The helm's hard over, sir!"

Beyond the bridge windows, the stars on the horizon wheeled as the ship turned back towards the rest of the flotilla. Most of the fleet had circled the wagons when *Californian* was struck, turning in lazy circles, while *Titanic* had kept on going to facilitate the landing of the helicopter. Now she was several miles away from the other ships, but steaming back with a running sea behind her.

"Do you mean to really go through with this, sir?" Herbert Pitman said softly, stepping to his side. Will flicked his eyes at the man, remembering that Pitman was the one member of *Titanic*'s officer complement to have not served in the Royal Naval Reserve, unlike himself, who carried the acting naval rank of Lieutenant, or Boxhall, Lowe and Moody, all Sub-Lieutenants.

"It can't be helped, Bert," he said. "We're effectively at war now, and unless we act fast the entire world might be. Only *Titanic* is in a position to go after her without endangering massive numbers of innocent lives."

Pitman clenched his jaw, but nodded softly. "I'll see to it that our remaining lifeboats are run out and ready to launch."

"Good man, Bert," Will affirmed. "And ensure that the portside Engelhardt collapsibles have been brought down from the deckhouse roof."

As Pitman strode off to begin preparations to evacuate the ship's remaining company, *Titanic's* acting Captain turned his gaze back upon the darkened sea.

"Where are you, you pirates?" he seethed, peering ahead with his eyes narrowed. "Show yourselves." High above in the night sky he could hear the thumping, pulsing sound of the helicopter, and could clearly make out its navigation lights as it struck straight and true towards *Oceanic*.

"C'mon, Lights, be my eyes in the sky..." he breathed, hoping that *Viking* was still incapable of submerging, and that travelling on the surface her passage would churn up a wake that would lead straight to them. All he needed now was some clue as to which direction he should head in.

Suddenly the helicopter banked to one side, veering to the north as if catching the scent of prey. Will held his breath, and was rewarded with the sudden sound of footsteps.

"Mr Murdoch!" Jack Phillips came flying down the corridor from the wireless room. "Mr Lightoller has spotted a disturbance on the surface two thousand yards east north east from us. White water and phosphorous bacteria churned up by the passage of a large vessel."

"Mr Boxhall!" Will shouted over his shoulder. "We have a bearing! Starboard helm, turn by five points. We'll dogleg until we find her track and then go after her."

"Sir, Mr Lightoller also says that *Viking* appears to be making for the *Rescue!*"

"Is that so?" Will glanced forward and steeled himself. "Then he means to go after the *Liberty Bell*. Mr Boxhall, belay that last order. Head instead towards the gap between *Oceanic* and *Olympic*, make it seem as if we're simply returning to the rest of the fleet. Maintain half speed until we spot *Viking*..."

He smiled grimly and peered in *Rescue*'s direction. The salvage vessel appeared to be making very slow headway, and somewhere in the darkness around her was *Viking*.

"...make ourselves look harmless, and we might just catch them with their britches down."

*

"Mr Thresher!" a lookout called down into *Viking*'s control room. "*Titanic* is crossing our path astern."

"There's radio chatter going on between them and the helicopter as well," came another report from communications. "They're looking for us."

"So is everyone else in the fleet," Scott replied, scrambling up the ladder to the top of *Viking*'s sail, coming out into the open and turning aft to check on *Titanic* for himself. The venerable liner seemed to be on a course taking her back towards *Oceanic*, which would take her clear of *Viking* by well over a mile. The other vessel was also travelling slowly, at no more than ten knots.

"More news is coming through!" the comms officer continued. "Captain Smith had a heart attack, but they were able to revive him. That helicopter is taking him and several other casualties back to *Oceanic*."

Landing a helicopter on a ship like the *Titanic*? Scott felt his mouth twitch into a grin. It was an accomplishment both mad and impressive. But that was beside the point now.

"Set speed five," he ordered, turning to face forward. Only half a mile ahead of them was *Rescue*, ablaze with lights and attempting to limp even further away from the rest of the fleet.

Captain Jones is endeavouring to keep everyone else at a safe distance, he decided. *It does make him an open target, though. He knows we're coming after the Liberty Bell.*

Or was it that Jones was attempting to get far enough away from the fleet as to warp his ship alone back to 2012, leaving the rest of them all trapped in the past? The thought of being abandoned here was enough to set Scott growling in tune to *Viking*'s own prop.

He checked his watch. It was 4.15am; forty-five minutes until they were due to launch on Berlin.

"WEO," he said softly into the sail's communications microphone. "Prepare the first live missile for launch."

"Ready missile for launch, aye," came the response. The WEO was uncertain with this course of action, Scott knew as much, but that was why the launch of the test missile had been intended to placate the man, and others who also had doubts, as well as allow himself time to build up courage for the game-ending move. He did not expect any reply from Berlin, even assuming that the message had been relayed onward for them by *Titanic*. No, he had done his soul-searching and was now ready to drop the bomb; he did not intend to bluff with Kaiser Bill.

"Security team to the deck!" he ordered, readying to board *Rescue*. Despite no doubt having taken lives by sinking *Californian*, no less than *British* lives, the thought of killing anyone from their own time seemed distasteful to him. Privately he hoped there would be no further fatalities. This was all so that they could go home, all of them, when the time was right.

That was just common sense, wasn't it?

*

"There they are…" Archibald Butt said softly. Standing at *Rescue*'s bridge rail, a modern pistol awkwardly holstered at his side, he lowered his binoculars and pointed to where *Viking* was just appearing out of the dark. "They are evidently here for the time machine, so what can we expect their next gambit to be?"

"Scott will have armed men on deck in the event of resistance," Furness said, arms folded sternly. The two of them had been brought aboard minutes after *Californian* sank, and with the rest of *Rescue*'s crew had done the best they could in preparing to repel boarders. Their own meagre arsenal was a mixture of low-calibre weapons liberated from *Rescue*'s small-arms locker and two assault rifles wielded by the Royal Navy petty officers who had been guarding the *Liberty Bell*, both of whom had immediately declared their support for Captain Furness. It was a clear disparity, but regardless of how unevenly they were matched, any conflict between the two crews would surely result in a bloodbath.

"Is that all you've got planned?" asked Jordan Jones. "To get back onboard *Viking* and overwhelm the crew to our side by the force of your personality?"

"Somehow, yes," Butt heard Furness reply.

"You might have the opportunity you need," called *Californian*'s Captain Lord, who was peering off towards the south. "*Titanic* is adjusting course in this direction!"

"Well I'll be, so he is…" Furness whispered, turning to confirm. "And I doubt he's coming for a social call. We need to keep *Viking* distracted from *Titanic* as long as possible."

"Is that all?" laughed Jones, before blindly swiping Butt's pistol from its holster.

"All hands!" he bellowed. *"Hit the deck!"*

Everyone ducked behind the gunwale as Jones repeatedly fired the gun randomly over the side, out towards open water. Moments later the submarine's boarding party began to wildly return fire.

"There you go," Jones said smugly, to everyone else's disbelief.

"Three captains, an army major and myself," hissed Doctor Oshiro, shielding his head, "and the best idea we could come up with by pooling our minds was setting off a *faux shootout!?*"

"Well, they're definitely now distracted," Jones replied, handing the gun back over for Butt. "Could someone please try and put a few rounds into her conning tower, just to add some extra viscerality to their experience?"

"We're a genuine brains trust, aren't we?" muttered Furness as he let off several rounds straight up in the air.

"Less talky, more shooty!"

*

"Got you," Will Murdoch muttered, seeing through his binoculars where *Rescue*'s lights shone on a dark metal object, riding low in the water alongside her. "Ahead all engines; let her run to her fullest!"

Boxhall and Moody grabbed the handles for the engine room telegraphs and shoved them forward with enough force that he momentarily feared they might have torn the linkages. Half-expecting Thomas Andrews or Chief Engineer Bell to telephone up and object to working the ship up to unsafe speeds, he held back a sigh of relief when the telegraph bells rang to signify 'order acknowledged' and the indicator needles jumped like frightened cats to '*Full Ahead*'. Through the deck the rumble of the engines stepped up in tempo, and he felt *Titanic* surge forward on her carefully conserved power.

"James!" he shouted, calling Moody to his side. "Get on the whistle and sound on it repeatedly. Warn off *Rescue*; we're coming through!"

*

"Shit!" Scott cursed, crouched in the recess in *Viking*'s sail. "What are those idiots doing?"

For at least a minute the exchange of gunfire had continued, shots being fired from both ships. But strangely, Scott only heard the odd round connecting with *Viking*, though plenty could be heard ricocheting off of *Rescue*.

"Mr Thresher!" a voice shouted up the hatch. "Radar shows a large contact coming towards us from astern, less than a mile away!"

"What is it?"

"Skipper... she's the *Titanic*, she's changed course and is putting on speed!"

At that moment a proud triple-chime whistle roared out with shocking volume, its sheer proximity cutting short the gunfire. Scott cautiously peered past the lip that he had ducked behind for protection and stared in stunned silence at the vessel charging directly at him.

"Rudder, port fifteen!" he cried, suddenly finding his tongue. "Main engine, ahead full!"

The turbines engaged, the deck surged beneath their feet, and *Viking* powered away from the *Rescue*, her blunt nose crashing through the chop as she made for the safety of open water.

And chasing her was the Royal Mail Steamship *Titanic*, blasting a further note of challenge on her whistles and belching a warrior's plume of smoke from her funnels. *Rescue*, her single working propeller racing away, all but spun on a point to try and get out of the larger ship's path, and *Titanic* charged past only two hundred yards away, her wake and bow wave swatting the salvage vessel safely aside.

As the tiny ship heeled over before righting herself, the men crouched on her port bridge wing rose cautiously, staring after the liner pursuing *Viking* and hurtling headlong into the night.

"Captains, Major, Doctor?" asked Lord. "What do we do now?"

A burst of sparks from below drew their attention to the rail, where they could see down into the hold in which the *Liberty Bell* was stored. Electricity crackled where water from *Titanic*'s wake had washed in and doused the power conduits.

"Is it usable, Doctor Oshiro?" Furness asked softly.

"Why, this is hardly an opportune moment for us to go home," the Japanese engineer replied curtly.

"No, I agree," the RN skipper's voice quavered, and he took a breath to steel himself. "But I've had a thought. Even if *Titanic* runs *Viking* down, Scott may still be able to launch one of the missiles, and if he's set his mind on it then he certainly will try…"

"So instead you want us to remove *Viking* from the equation?" Lord said thoughtfully.

"Yes… I think this machine is our trump card, gentlemen. We get *Rescue* alongside *Viking*, fire up the *Liberty Bell*, and drag Scott and the sub back into our future, where they can face the good justice of Her Majesty for mutiny, dereliction of duty, and attempting to incite war in another time."

"What about your contemporaries?" pointed out Butt. "If the radius of the Bell's effect is too limited to encapsulate the other ships, then they'll all be trapped here, never able to return home."

Furness smiled grimly in answer. "Harsh as it sounds, their safety is outweighed by the lives that will be lost if we let Scott drop a nuke into the heart of Berlin."

581

They stared from one to the other for a moment, before Lord turned to Oshiro. "Well, Doctor, can it be done?"

"Yes, but the *Liberty Bell* is not even fully charged… as the Major said, we wouldn't be able to move all of the fleet, but if we pumped as much voltage from *Rescue's* engines into it as possible, perhaps would could warp an area about an eighth of a mile in diameter…"

"That's more than we need," said Jones, before turning and barking out orders towards Lieutenant Miller. "Sam, take us after *Titanic*, with as much speed as *Rescue* can give! And sound the emergency muster, all crew to evacuation stations!"

*

"All crew up top!"

"Get to the Boat Deck immediately!"

Pip and Bruce Ismay were working their way through *Titanic's* middle decks, ordering any of the few stewards, caterers and deckhands still aboard to abandon their posts and gather alongside the remaining starboard boats.

The stokehold crews and engineering staff will have to fend for themselves though, Pip realised. *Including Jack.*

"What does Murdoch have in mind?" Ismay shouted as they climbed the stairs to the B-Deck promenade.

"Ship to ship combat perhaps?" Pip suggested as she ran to the rail and peered ahead.

"What?"

"Do you know a man called Bertram Hayes?"

"Yes, he's a captain for the line…"

"In the once-and-future time," Pip said, gripping hold of the rail with both hands, bracing her feet. "He commanded *Olympic*, and won her the distinction of being the only merchant vessel to ram and sink an enemy combatant during the First World War, a German submarine! I think Murdoch's channelling the same spirit."

She saw his face pallor as he joined her in looking forward along the length of *Titanic's* bow, the two of them holding on tight as the liner vaulted from wave to wave, surging forward, her prow aimed towards *Viking* as the submarine tried to make its escape.

Bruce Ismay swallowed, and his expression hardened. "Very good."

*

"Chief Engineer!" Scott shouted down the radio from *Viking*'s sail. "How much longer before you can finish repairs to the ballast system!?"

"A minute, two at most!"

"Mr Thresher! *Titanic*'s gaining on us and she's still accelerating!"

Scott turned and peered into the sleeting water thrown up by *Viking*'s screw. *Titanic*, huge and terrible, was emerging from the rain, and from the bow wave she was pushing she was not hanging about.

"What's he doing? her bow's too compromised to be charging along like that!"

Even as Scott said it, he saw *Titanic* rise over a swell and crash back down into the following trough, shockwaves rippling over her hull plates as if they had turned to liquid. Wincing, he picked up a megaphone and shouted through it.

"RMS *Titanic!* Please maintain your distance!" he shouted, but even when amplified, his voice seemed like the cries of a gnat glancing off the hide of a charging rhino. "If you come nearer we will fire upon you!"

With what, Scott? a voiced laughed in his head. *All you've got are torpedoes, and I don't think you've got it in you to gut the Titanic of all ships. Look at her; she's already dying just trying to get to you – but isn't she glorious!?*

Sure enough, *Titanic* was visibly down by the bow; only a few degrees, but evidence enough that least some of the repairs had failed. But in spite of it all she kept on coming, stalwart and unyielding.

Frowning, Scott spun to address the lookouts and navigator.

"All hands below, make ready to dive, quickly!"

*

Will Murdoch had never run with the hounds or joined a hunt, though he remembered them well enough though from his childhood in Dalbeattie, Scotland. But right now, with *Titanic* chasing after *Viking*, he felt himself to be riding as high as any of the fine Lords to whom he had touched his cap as a boy.

"Water's coming into Cargo Hold 2! It's shooting up through the floor grates!"

"Close watertight doors, maintain full speed!"

Engines thrashing away at their fullest revolutions, *Titanic* cleaved the waves with furious speed, the damaged bow shuddering alarmingly as she took the weather on the chin. Will, a walkie-talkie in his hand screaming dire warnings of damage below, saw the forecastle briefly whip sideways independently of the rest of the ship, before the whole hull took up the springing motion. He saw deck planking shatter, heard the liner's bones groaning, but still shouted down for the engineering staff to keep up the effort.

"Just a little more, just a few revolutions more! We're coming alongside her!"

They were overhauling *Viking*. From how the atomic submarine was wallowing in the rising sea, he could tell she was not built to travel on the surface under such conditions, and even with her atomic engine racing away at full tilt she was struggling to keep headway. Whereas *Titanic*, for all her faults and the injuries she had sustained, was built to take the Atlantic's worst head-on and still maintain a timetable speed of nineteen knots. The ship seemed to be effortlessly loping closer to *Viking*, which he could now see riding over a particularly large pair of rollers like a twig carried in a stream.

As *Titanic*'s bow came abreast of *Viking*'s stern, Murdoch saw a lone figure on her conning tower direct some sort of hand gesture at them, before disappearing down the hatch.

"She's preparing to dive!" he heard himself say calmly, his blood running slow with ice. "Hard a'starboard, and then reverse the helm to port, put us right on her!"

For several long moments *Titanic* continued to plough onwards, almost running past *Viking* before her rudder bit into the sea; then she lurched sideways into a high-speed reverse-turn, deck tilting steeply first in one direction and then the other as she swung herself around towards the submarine.

"Another 'port-around', Will?" asked Moody, seeing the irony between trying to avoid an iceberg and intentionally steering into another vessel.

"Well, they used to accuse Captain Smith of driving us up the Hudson like speedboats," Will smiled, before composing his face and willing *Titanic* to push on harder. "Ram her! Helmsman, maintain the turn, and aim for aft of her tower; that's her magazine!"

"Aye aye Captain!" the quartermaster shouted in response, as Moody ran to ring for even more speed on the engines. Still turning hard, *Titanic* seemed to respond to this last command and thundered towards *Viking* with a final burst of knots.

The submarine, venting air and already sitting lower in the water, was trying to come around as well, to keep inside *Titanic*'s own radius and avoid collision. From what Murdoch could see, she had a nice, tight turning circle.

It was not enough. *Titanic* was now bearing right down on her.

"Rudder amidships! Brace for impact!"

As the White Star liner came on top of the other vessel, the waves tore apart, and with the water pulled out from under her, *Viking* fell off into a trough. Bowsprit rearing out of the sea, *Titanic* hung for a moment on the crest of a wave, poised like a hammer over an anvil, and then came crashing down with vengeful force.

*

"Repairs complete! Boat rigged for dive!"

"Crash dive, now! Flood all tanks, ten degrees down bubble!"

Scott Thresher had just dropped into the control room when *Viking* slid away into a trough, the deck nearly falling out from under him.

"Up scope!"

The periscope smoothly telescoped up out of its floor cavity and Scott clung to it as the sub skidded to the bottom of the slope. Like an express elevator making an emergency stop the momentum forced him into a crouch, hanging between the deck and where his hands were latched onto the periscope's handles.

"Vents and valves open, all tanks flooding freely, sir!"

Scott opened his mouth to reply "very good", but as he got his feet under him and pressed his eyes to the scope, the words turned to ash in his mouth.

Titanic's towering bow reared over them, an iceberg wrought in steel.

"Full astern!" he screamed, hands and eyes locked to the periscope. *"Main engine full astern!"*

Before the order could be repeated, however, the Atlantic waves coiled underneath *Viking*'s hull, and like a cornered animal she made a desperate pounce, springing up at the larger ship as *Titanic*'s bow powered over the last swell and came rushing down on them.

And then forty-five-thousand tons of liner and one-point-five billion pounds sterling-worth of missile submarine came crashing together.

The whole world seemed to end. *Viking* lurched, and the smash rolled the room on its side, flinging Scott from the periscope shaft and hurling him into the sonar operators. Emergency lights spluttered as men's voices screamed in time to the screech of rending metal.

Then *Titanic* smote them again, and *Viking* turned right over.

*

The impact shook *Titanic* from end to end, her hull ringing like a bell. Holding to the bridge rail, Murdoch maintained his balance and ran to the wing cab, trying to see what had happened. The ship's reinforced stem had bitten right into *Viking*, and they were pushing the submarine ahead of them as if sweeping the sea clean with a gigantic brush.

"We're right in her!" he shouted to the bridge, seeing Moody reaching for the telegraph. "Hands away James! Keep going!"

The waves shouldered into the conjoined vessels again, giving *Titanic* the chance to heft herself up on top of the submarine now wrapped around her bow. Pinning *Viking* under the turn of her keel the ship bit down again, forcing the other vessel underwater and drawing her under the liner's hull.

*

Emergency lights burnt red in the spinning mess of the control room, which tumbled up and around as *Titanic* spun them over again and again, trampling the submarine underfoot every time it tried to surface. Even lying dazed among several of the crew, Thresher could hear the grating rush of the ship powering over their heads. For a few moments the sub righted itself, before something embedded into the hull above with an almighty smash, and the whole room lurched sideways, before seemingly tearing free.

And then *Titanic* was gone, the turbulent roar of her screws fading into the distance, and *Viking* painfully came back into an even beam, the pressure hull groaning as she settled deeper.

We were rammed by the Titanic, he had time to think in awestruck disbelief, *like a car getting smashed by a train.* The absurdity of it made him smile before he suddenly felt *Viking* settle back on her haunches, sinking by the stern. Seeing the depth gauge spinning down he snapped back to lucidity, pulling himself forward on his hands and knees.

"Surface the boat! Emergency blow, planes to rise!"

As injured men struggled back to their stations the deck reared back even further. Wrapping his arms around the periscope, Scott Thresher fought his way back onto his feet. *Titanic* had struck somewhere behind the control room; the weight of water now rushing into one of the aft compartments was pulling the sub down like a drowning man whose lungs had filled with water. For a second it seemed that *Viking*'s fall was too fast to arrest, but then the air lines vented with a blessed roar, and he felt the deck surge up beneath his feet. As the men shouted and cheered in relief, Scott held on tight and gritted his teeth, the firing keys clenched between his bleeding fingers.

"WEO! Make missile ready for launch. All non-essential crew, prepare to abandon ship!"

*

"There is she!" Butt shouted, pointing from *Rescue*'s bridge into the distance. Furness pulled himself up beside the captain and breathed an awestruck prayer.

Titanic, now heeling by the bow, had just run over a foaming patch of sea, and no sooner had the great ship's stern counter cleared the spot before *Viking* surfaced with a roar. For a moment Bob feared it was the missile launching, but to his relief saw the submarine shoot two-thirds of her length out of the choppy waves, seemingly trying to make it to the stars. *Viking* hung poised for several seconds, and then, leaning heavily to one side, she fell back into the water like a broaching whale.

He shared a glance with Furness.

"Can she still launch?" the Major asked.

"The Royal Navy builds their submarines to deal out war even when crippled," *Viking*'s true skipper replied, feeling a touch of pride show through, even in the circumstances.

"Then we're going after them!" shouted Captain Jones. "Captain Lord, get ready to take us in!"

"Aye, Captain!" Lord was gripping *Rescue*'s helm, Lieutenant Miller, the crew and the survivors from *Californian* having been ordered to evacuate.

"You need to leave the ship as well, Archie," Bob added, leaving no room for argument. "President Taft will need your account of tonight's events to make an informed response."

"Gentleman, I salute your courage," Butt replied simply. He grabbed Bob's hand, gripped it tightly for a second, and then launched himself down the aft companionway to where motorboats, inflatable dinghies and even the one lifeboat successfully launched from *Californian* were being filled with men and shoved overboard.

"All hands! Abandon ship! Abandon ship!" Jones bellowed from the bridge, before yelling down the shipboard tannoy. "Doctor! What's the situation on the *Liberty Bell!?*"

*

Throwing himself down the main companionway, Oshiro came to *Rescue*'s engine-room, where the diesels were turning over at half-speed.

"Bringing all engines to full power!" he shouted, before heaving the throttles against their stops. The turbocharged Rolls-Royce Bergens jolted in their bedplates and then surged ahead, dumping their full six megawatts into the ship's distributor board. Running between fusing lights and thundering engines, Oshiro grabbed the valve that plumbed the *Liberty Bell* into *Rescue*'s cooling system and forced the tap lever over. Gauges spun as the lines pressurised with a roar, and not pausing to catch his breath he hurtled aft into the hold, up to the time machine, grabbed the mode selector switch on the main panel and shoved it from **CHARGE** to **PRIME**.

The *Liberty Bell*'s control board lit up like a Christmas tree, ammeters soaring and status lights blazing different colours as the machine readied itself for discharge. A klaxon began to howl as the sequencing completed itself, the lights all blinked to green and the words **CRITICAL MASS** flashed up on the display.

Beside them, a message burned in digital letters:

EXECUTE RETURN
04/14/2012
23:40
Y/N

Amid the crashing noises of pounding sea and racing machinery, Oshiro suddenly felt a moment's serene clarity; what would happen if they arrived back home in their own 2012 and the missile still got away?

There would be no time to explain circumstances, no defence that could be mounted. Within thirty minutes of their return, Berlin would be plunged into an atomic holocaust, and seeing a thermonuclear event, panicked hands across Earth might just reach for arming keys and nuclear footballs.

Saving this era could kick their own into Armageddon.

The only way to avoid it is to not go home at all…

Sweating, he reached out and pressed 'N', followed by a string of numbers as he inputted a new destination date. Then, before he could second-guess himself, he turned the selector from **PRIME** to **RUN**, grabbed the main breaker and screamed up through the hatch at the top of his lungs.

"*Liberty Bell* ready to fire!"

"Light it!" Jones' voice blasted through the speaker system. "Light that thing off or countless people will die!"

Oshiro hauled down on the switch, the breakers churned noisily inside the machine's hull, and the *Liberty Bell*'s hull began to shimmer...

"Temporal discharge in five minutes!"

Then he groped beneath his shirt and drew out the disarm key for the self-destruct. Slowly, he looked from it, to the time machine.

CHAPTER TWENTY NINE

Thomas Andrews had been in *Titanic*'s Reciprocating Engine Room when Murdoch rang down for maximum revolutions, and as the crew responded to the order and worked up the speed, he and Kai Alinka began running backward and forward along the full length of the mechanical spaces, from the Electric-Engine Room right through the six Boiler Rooms, searching for any sign of incoming water.

He had not guessed that *Titanic*'s new captain had meant to ram *Viking*, but the sudden turn to port had warned him that something was amiss; then the reverse to starboard threw him into the arms of one of the firemen, and everyone had instinctively braced, knowing that something was coming.

Seconds later, the liner had torn into what he hoped was *Viking*, and danced victoriously over the remains. But in the process she had wounded herself badly, and no sooner had Thomas seen water begin mushrooming up into Boiler Room 5 from under the floor grates than he felt a second, horrendous impact from further astern, heralded by the terrible sound of rending metal and machinery running amok. He ran aft, hoping beyond hope that his ship was still seaworthy.

It was a false hope. He reached the engine room just in time to see the great portside engine churn to a stop, then stared in horror at the broken monolith of steam that was the starboard engine; it had jumped off its bedplates whilst *still turning*, and torn itself to pieces, hurling connecting-rods and cylinders into the side of the hull as it did. Water was pouring in, and the engine's mighty crankshaft had smashed down onto the starting platform. In the dim lights, figures moved and screamed and shouted for help in a hellish fume of smoke, steam and oil.

He found Kai Alinka assisting Joseph Bell. The Chief Engineer was shaken and bloodied, but remained resplendent in full uniform, and most importantly was still alive.

"We started to shut off steam when we felt the impact, in case something fouled the propellers, but then something came up through the bottom of the hull like a knife!" Bell exclaimed in answer to what had happened. "I think it was the submarine's conning-tower!"

"Yeah, it was the sail!" Alinka confirmed. "They're reinforced to punch through ice-sheets when surfacing to launch! It only penetrated a few feet, but it was enough to gut the starboard engine from underneath; then was dragged through the aft bulkhead into the turbine engine room!"

"Show me!"

With Thomas helping to support Bell, the three of them struggled aft. The water was already rising up to the level of the floor plates, the surface black with a scummy cocktail of oil and grease. More worrying to Thomas, though, was the way he could feel the deck working under his feet. The damage was worse than either of them had even contemplated.

"That impact didn't just open up the double-bottom," he shouted to Bell. "It's knackered the keel. Just listen to her twisting!"

They reached the bulkhead door, and peered into the stygian gloom of the Turbine Room. Even half-shrouded in steam, it was not a pleasant sight. Dim lighting barely illuminated the half-drowned remains of the mammoth Parsons turbine.

"If we can keep her afloat now," Bell admitted, "it will be with spit and gauze and a prayer, but we'll do our damnedest to save her."

"No," said Kai Alinka, his face serious and bearing upright. "She can't survive this, not with the keel fractured, even if she wasn't already flooding further forward. Trying to keep her afloat won't save anyone now. *Titanic* is going to go down like a brick."

Thomas stared at the Hawaiian in surprise, and Kai looked back evenly at him. Steam and spray batted around their faces, slicking down their hair.

"It's time to let her go, Tom."

For a moment the three of them stood, listening to the pained screams of men and metal as the ship struggled to maintain buoyancy, fighting for her very life. Hearing her pain, Tom's gut wrenched. After so much blood and treasure, after braving hope and despair, it had come to this?

Then, at last, he nodded.

"Get your men out immediately, Joseph," he said, forcing aside grief in favour of action. "And the firemen too. I'll carry a report to Mister Murdoch immediately."

"Aye," Bell said grimly, before turning and regarding the broken cathedral that was the engine room. His eyes were sad, yet the sorrow was tinged with fury.

"And we came so close too!" he hissed, before straightening up to roar out his final orders as *Titanic*'s Chief Engineer. "Finished with Engines! Everyone out now! Pass the word aft to the generator room as well. We'll take electrical power from the emergency dynamos on D-Deck while we evacuate the ship!"

"Tom!" called Alinka, grabbing Thomas' arm before he could dart off. "I said it was pointless to try and save *Titanic*, but is there one part of her you'd want to preserve for posterity; something small enough to not take up much space in a lifeboat?"

Thomas breathed heavily for a moment, mind reeling through everything carried on the ship. All the components and lovingly crafted fittings...

"Yes," he said with sudden conviction, settling almost immediately on a single item. "*Plymouth Harbour*, the painting that hangs over the fireplace in the First Class Smoke Room."

"I'll get it to a boat, I promise!" Kai replied, before vanishing off, grabbing a set of tools as he went. Leaving him and Bell to do their jobs, Thomas himself ran back up through the length and height of the ship, dragging his oiled boots through the fine carpets and linoleum with little regard for the decor.

Then, momentarily, he caught a glimpse of his own reflection in a window; a man in a futuristically tailored boiler-suit, face smeared with oil and water, an electronic telecommunications device hanging from his belt. Struggling for something familiar at the sight, he tried to remember dressing for dinner on the night they struck the iceberg. It was less than a day and a half ago, but now it seemed far away and distant, a time-before-time when everything had seemed assured and confident. He struggled to even remember what he looked like in a tuxedo.

"This is all beyond bedlam!" he cursed to himself.

Yet why, underneath it all, did he feel a spark of excitement?

He got his answer when he came on deck and caught sight of the broached *Viking* lying prone to *Titanic*'s stern; because everything was so new and unexpected, tinged with a touch of destiny, of discovery. Turning, he saw Philippa Paik and Bruce Ismay at the rail, and without pause for decorum he grabbed each of them by the arm and led them forward.

"Stand by the lifeboats," he instructed. "We're going to have to launch them any second!"

"Wait, no. Tom, wait, what happened?!" Philippa said, forcing him to stop in order to answer. They had come abaft of the forward funnel, on the port side, where boats not launched the night before still hung from Axel Welin's Patent Quadrant Davits, swung out and ready for action. The remaining two Engelhardt liferafts, the emergency boats with collapsible sides, were laid out beside them like canvas body shrouds, open to receive.

"That last blow was fatal to her, wasn't it Thomas?" Ismay said as he pulled his arm free, his soft voice as low as that of a man in the dock.

"I'm afraid so," Tom struggled to express the magnitude of his feeling. "The keel has been compromised; now she's flooding uncontrollably in the turbine and reciprocating engine rooms, as well as forward where the repairs were knocked about. *She's going to sink*, Bruce."

"Is that so…" Ismay's moustache twitched, and his shoulders fell in resignation. "Well, if she must sink, I'm glad White Star's flagship went out in a manner befitting the comport of the men who built and crewed her. Captain Murdoch must be informed at once…"

It was a magnanimous gesture from a man who stood to lose so much from *Titanic*'s sinking, possibly even the prestigious shipping line he had inherited from his father.

"Come on, sir," Thomas said at last. "We'd best tell him together."

With Ismay following him as if to the gallows, Thomas turned and pointed at Philippa Paik, who had moved to join their party. "Stay by this lifeboat, Miss Paik. You may be from the future but I'll be damned if I let you endanger yourself anymore than I already have done."

"But-"

"Stay by these lifeboats!" he repeated, jabbing his finger towards the davits, his eyes fixed on hers. Satisfied, he spun on his heel and ran with Ismay towards the bridge.

As they did, he spared a glance towards *Viking*. In slewing to a halt, *Titanic* had turned beam-on to the crippled submarine, and he could see *Rescue* and *Oceanic* emerging through the rain. But where *Oceanic* was maintaining a cautious distance, as one might an animal that could suddenly lash out, tiny *Rescue* actually seemed to be trying to harry *Viking*.

*

Stanley Lord hauled on *Rescue*'s helm and adjusted the speed of the bow thrusters, marvelling at the ship's responsiveness even as he struggled to bring her smoothly alongside *Viking*, fighting as he was against the action of the sea and the uneven thrust of *Rescue*'s single remaining propeller.

"She's taking water through that breach there!" Bob Furness said, pointing towards *Viking*. "It's exposed the missile compartment, but he can still launch as long as whatever tube he ordered prepped is undamaged."

Lord cursed as another attempt to match *Rescue*'s movement to *Viking*'s failed; the submarine, although almost torn in two by *Titanic*'s attack, hull breached and most of her conning-tower bent over like the cocked brim of a hat, seemed to still have power, judging from the foam churning at her stern. In spite of all her wounds, she was continually managing to foil their attempts to raft alongside.

"You absolutely must get on board?" he yelled across to Captain Furness.

"*Yes!*"

Lord chewed his lip and pushed back his hair, his hat having been lost at some point in the madness. Through the wind-slicked windscreen, *Viking* was a cobalt-grey blur in the dark, the most visible part of her being the black breach halfway along the length of her hull.

They called me a fool who stood by in that other time, stood by while lives were wasted... he thought, feeling a sense of grim destiny at work *Now an entire city is at stake, and I promised myself I would not fail again when fate knocked at my door. Thus there's only one course left open for me to steer...*

"Blast it!" he cursed, and pointed forward. "Very well, Captain Furness; go right into *Rescue*'s bows, and hold tight."

"I have the helm!" called Captain Jones, and grabbing hold of Lord's greatcoat, *Rescue*'s blinded master pulled the other man aside and assumed his place at the controls.

"I can steer her with my eyes shut!" he said jovially. "Just tell me where to point her."

"Very good, Captain," Lord swallowed and strode forward to peer through the windows. "Port helm and full ahead, then straighten up the rudder on my word!"

"Aye-aye!" Jones reached out to push the throttle forward, and with *Rescue*'s single engine churning away, all three diesel generators racing below deck, he spun the wheel over and helmed her as Lord asked...

...aiming right for the rent *Titanic* had ripped in the submarine.

Once more into the breach dear friends, once more! Lord thought to himself, before shouting out his intent.

"We're going to ram ourselves into her, impale *Rescue* into that gouge! Then you can jump down onto *Viking*'s deck, Captain Furness!"

"Bloody hell! I like it!" Furness shook his head in disbelief, before saluting. "As you were, gentlemen!"

Then he ran forward, eliciting a small smile from Lord and a laugh from Jones.

"So, Captain Lord, I see the seamen of the twentieth century can be as stark raving mad as us of the twenty-first."

"Indeed..."

Pip threw herself into the vacant cabin assigned for her temporary use on *Titanic*'s A-Deck, and began stuffing scattered memory-cards back into her carry-case, along with her laptop and camera. She might have been ordered to stand by the lifeboats by no less than Thomas Andrews himself, but she was not going to let the photographic record she had assembled of *Titanic* go to waste. Andrews could thank her for it later.

"Ahem... hello?" a voice said pleadingly from outside the door. Pip spun, and found herself facing a dark-haired and stunningly-attired woman, one she had last seen coming aboard *Titanic* in the company of her husband.

"Lady Duff-Gordon..." she replied cautiously. "Please, come in."

Lucille Duff-Gordon stepped hesitantly into the stateroom, warily eyeing the laptop bag and camera. Pip blinked at the transformation in the haute-couture fashionista. Lucille's face, although as perfectly composed as in any photograph of her Pip had ever seen, was now as rigid as a mask, and she was subtly wringing her hands.

"Is something wrong?"

"Ah, yes..." Lucille swallowed. "The ship has, ah, apparently struck something, and, my husband is working down below. I can't find a steward and... I saw you come down the stairs from the Boat Deck. Can you please, ah, please summon Cosmo, with your speaking device?"

She pointed vaguely towards the cell-phone lying useless on the mantle, and Pip felt a sudden sympathy with someone else completely out of their depth.

"It... it doesn't work..." she replied lamely. "I ran the battery down reading old text messages from my... my sister."

"Oh my dear... you have family in the future?"

"Had..." Pip shrugged as bravely as possible. "Marilyn designs fashion, like yourself..."

Lucille's eyes, very dark and alluring, lit up with interest, only for that light to be consumed in worry when the ship suddenly trembled. Pip forcibly snapped herself back to reality. *Titanic* was sinking, and this time there was no way of arresting that process. History was, in some small way, coming full circle.

"I'm sorry, there's not much time," she said, coming to her feet and crossing to the closet. "The ship is sinking, for real this time."

She searched through the shelves and found a rigid white lifejacket, which she offered to Lucille. "Please, put this on, and go up to the boats."

Quickly she helped Lucille tie the floatation vest in place, and then grabbed the ruined dress Marilyn had made her, brought over from *Rescue* earlier, and pressed it and the laptop bag into the other woman's hands.

"This is almost everything I have left. My memories, my work, everything I have left to remember my family by... please keep them safe."

Lucille was somewhat overwhelmed, but took the carry-case without question and slung it over her shoulder as if it was a handbag.

"But where are you going?"

Pip was reaching for her cap, the one sourced from *Rescue*, repeating a now-familiar mantra to herself: *For I Am Full Of Spirit And Resolve.*

Pulling the cap on she turned, zipping up her jacket as she did.

"I'm going to find your husband, and my... boyfriend."

*

"Active Target Package, Missile Spinning Up!" Scott Thresher confirmed with the Weapons Engineering Officer over the comm. *Viking* was hurting bad, but could still fire, and he would see this through. He would save future history...

"Roger!" came the reply. *"Target set as 52.30'N, 13.24'E, Berlin. I have the system."*

Scott clutched a wadded cloth to his forehead, stemming the bleeding of a gash sustained when he was thrown across the room. Was this guilt, or hesitation? No, it was just so chillingly familiar a procedure, exactly as they had drilled. Right now the WEO would have 'the system' in hand, a firing trigger mounted to a handgun stock.

One click and missile away...

"Sir, awaiting your order to fire."

Scott opened his mouth, and then he was drowned out by the roar of a ship's horn echoing down the open hatch leading up on deck, alarmingly close.

Has Titanic come back? No, it sounds too modern to be a steam whistle...

"WEO stand by! You have the Conn, Mr. Winters," he shouted in turn to the Navigation Officer, before grabbing hold of the ladder and pulling himself up onto the deck.

He came out under *Viking*'s battered sail. The submarine was settling in the centre, bending in a way that she was never meant to, and coming right at them was the now-worryingly familiar sight of a ship's prow.

"*Rescue*," he said, before starting in surprise at the sight of a familiar figure standing in the prow of the salvage tug. *"Bob!?"*

"Hullo Scott!" Robert Furness shouted as *Rescue* reared up to strike. "Permission to come aboard!?"

"Fuck that!" Scott began to say, but then the salvage vessel ploughed with a crash into the gash *Titanic* had made, fitting as snugly as if it been tailored for her. Scott was knocked back into the open gangway hatch as once again *Viking* heeled over, but this time her mass was greater than that of the ship that had struck her, and she held fast, absorbing the blow with a fighting groan. Shaken and hurting, Scott got back to his feet, and saw Furness jump down from *Rescue*'s bow onto the submarine's deck. Glancing once in Scott's direction, the Captain ran to the breach in the hull and scrambled down into Sherwood Forest, the missile compartment.

Seriously, fuck it all!

"Flooding below, WEO requests permission to abandon ship, sir!" Winters shouted as Scott dropped back into the control room, landing hard enough to probably crack one of his ankles. Ignoring the exquisite pain blossoming in his heel, he grabbed the radio mike and opened the channel.

"Bridge to WEO, what is your status?"

"Lieutenant, the bulkhead is compromised and water is flooding into the launch compart-"

"What is your status WEO!" he bellowed.

"Weapons system is in readiness for strategic launch, but-"

"Attention all hands!" Bob Furness' voice suddenly boomed from the speakers, and Scott dropped the mouthpiece in surprise. *"This is Captain Robert Furness speaking on the emergency channel from the missile bay. I hereby resume command and relieve Lieutenant Thresher of duty on grounds of my attempted murder, and I am issuing orders for all hands to abandon ship! Put lifesaving procedures into play and evacuate immediately, with priority in the liferafts to go to any wounded!"*

The men in the control room responded immediately, stepping away from their stations and flowing towards their emergency stations, some in pairs carrying injured between them.

"Bob!" Scott roared aloud, before snatching the microphone off of the floor and holding down on the switch. "Belay that order! I am still in command of this vessel, and we have a duty to save Britain from the wars to come! Do not abandon your post WEO, launch now!"

"No, sir, we are standing down from launch readiness," came the firmly defiant reply. *"I have injured boys here, and orders to get them to safety. And I will not launch a missile with men trying to evacuate from off of Viking's back. Good luck, Scott."*

Scott felt his face flush as the WEO rang off, and gritted his teeth. The roars of adulation in his imagination were now turning to mocking cries.

"Lieutenant-Commander?"

At the sound of the Navigation Officer's voice he looked up from his shaking fists.

"Get out," he said mildly.

"Sir?"

Scott pointed up the escape ladder. "Abandon ship immediately, Justin."

Winters lingered for a second, and then, pausing only to secure his station and grab a life vest, he disappeared up the hatch. Focusing, Scott unclenched his hands, and then reached across the chart table for Butt's ceremonial sword, forgotten amidst the chaos.

Fly me to the moon, and let me play among the stars…

Humming softly, he buckled the scabbard around his waist, and then with slow, heavy footsteps on the increasingly listing deck, he set off towards the Launch Control Station, deep in *Viking*'s belly, trying his best to ignore the sounds of water rushing into the submarine's gutted hull.

Eventually, wading through rising water, he pushed open the final door and stepped into the compartment, which was lit with gloomy red light thrown by the firing console. The 'system', the launch trigger, was teetering on the edge of the station, and he lunged forward to grab it before it fell. Gingerly he adjusted his grip so that his finger rested on the firing switch. Then, still softly humming snippets of Sinatra, he settled down into a half-submerged chair and began flipping switches, repeating the final steps of arming the missile, as he waited for the Captain.

*

Pip hurtled down the stairs to *Titanic*'s E-Deck and once again found herself in the Scotland Road passageway. Engineers and Firemen were fleeing the lower compartments through the escape trunks, and she had to fight against the flow of human traffic as she pushed forward.

Boiler Room 4. Jack said he had been working with Cosmo Duff-Gordon in Boiler Room 4. There might be a chance the two of them were still there.

Coming up to the correct escape trunk, she scrambled through onto the ladder that led down along the boiler uptakes. The lights were still on, but she could hear water rushing in below. Trying to not imagine the plummeting drop beneath her (would the water cushion an impact?), she began to go hand-over-hand down the rungs, pausing halfway.

"Hello!?" she lit a torch tucked into one pocket and directed it below her, illuminating only clouds of drifting smoke from the stifled fires. "Is anyone there!?"

"Philippa!?" she heard Jack's voice cry out in answer. "What are you doing down here!?"

She sighed in relief and adjusted her grip.

"I came looking for you and Cosmo Duff-Gordon. Is he there!?"

"Yes, but he's in a bad way! He got half-buried in coal when the ship went over whatever that was we hit! The other men evacuated before I could draw attention to his plight!"

"It was *Viking* that we struck!" she called back. "What about Gordon? Can I help?"

"No, it's too dangerous. Run and find some of the crew…"

Before she could shout a reply, she heard Jack curse aloud and then retract his statement.

"*Dammit,* there's no time for that; yes, please come down quick! A second pair of hands might be enough to get him free!"

Pip blinked in surprise at his change of heart, then grabbed hold of the ladder's uprights and slid down into the murk, landing up to her knees in the incoming water. The numbing cold in her legs was matched only by the stifling sweat running down her back and sleeves, but torch in hand she followed Jack's voice.

Then she spotted him crouched over Duff-Gordon, who was unconscious and buried almost up to his neck in a small avalanche of coal; it must have poured out of a bunker and overwhelmed him. Wading closer, she found the water shallowed as the deck rose, but it was still almost up to Duff-Gordon. If he wasn't having enough difficulty breathing with all the coal on his chest, he was surely going to drown in just a few minutes.

"Here!" Jack looked up and handed her a shovel. "Dig quickly, and try not to hit his limbs."

The two of them set to work, hurling the black diamonds off of the comatose baronet. As the water rose higher it reached another furnace, the flooded firebox gasping as the water overwhelmed it. With every second the angle of the ship increased and the agonized groans of the over-stressed hull girder grew louder. *Titanic* was succumbing, painfully. Through the effort of shovelling, Pip dimly realised that she was suddenly an eyewitness to the death of the great ship.

She prayed that she would live to see it through to the finish.

*

Scott did not have to wait long. Slow, heavy footsteps heralded the arrival of Furness, who came in through the companionway from the missile room, ducking to fit through the hatch. He was not armed, and the only weapon in the compartment was the sword in Scott's hand.

The two officers regarded each other for a moment. Furness' arms hanging at his side as if exhausted. Scott felt a small flame of triumph rekindling in him, roaring loudly in his moment of victory.

And then Furness cocked his head to the ceiling and smiled.

"Well done, Scott," he said, grinning widely. "I was wondering myself whether or not setting a missile off would demonstrate *Viking*'s power, but you've made the decision for me, and the use of the Trident LE test-package was a stroke of brilliance."

Scott paused, the cheers in his mind once again losing their lustre. This was not what he had expected…

"You can't honestly have come here to try and talk me out of launching?" he said, brandishing Butt's sword. "It took me a while to psych myself up, but I'm resolved in this, Bob. If *Viking*'s going to sink, then I am taking out Imperial Germany while I have the chance!"

"No, Scott, you're not getting that chance," Furness smiled weakly. "And I didn't come over here to talk you down, just to keep you talking long enough to distract you."

"Distract me until what?"

Viking creaked ominously under their feet, and then slowly began to shudder, unseen forces pulling at her steel skeleton. Scott felt the sword in his hand beginning to tremble…

"What the hell?" he said, and looked up from the sword to see Furness grinning coldly. "What now, Bob, *what did you do!?*"

"I distracted you until the *Liberty Bell* could discharge," *Viking*'s captain said.

Butt's sword was suddenly ripped itself out of Scott's grasp and flew across the compartment. Clutching his hand in pain, Scott turned and saw the firing trigger, caught by the same force, leap free of the table, only for the wire connecting it to firing console to halt it in mid-air, like a kite at the end of a string… a string that was beginning to fray.

Scott threw himself across the console, snatched the trigger system out of the air and clenched his fist, squeezing down on the firing switch.

"One away!"

The roar of the engine igniting burst onto the scene as brightly as his triumphant grin.

"I win Bob. I win."

He turned and felt the blood flee from his face.

"Oh shit…" he said, as the strength left him and he fell back in the chair.

Bob Furness was pinned against the pressure hull by Butt's sword, the blade of which had gone right through his upper chest. Expression dumbfounded, Furness' hands came up to grasp at the hilt, trying to pull the cutlass out of himself, but the forces acting on the weapon kept him skewered to the wall like a spitted pig.

"Well… that's, a surprise," he said dumbly, before his knees buckled and he collapsed, the sword's crossguard keeping his body fixed up in a forward-slumped position.

Scott's lungs heaved, and his heart hurled itself around inside his chest cavity like a panicked animal as he stared at the fresh corpse. Furness' face was fixed in a victorious grin, the eyes glazing over but the lips drawn back to expose his teeth in an expression of triumph.

Why, at the end, had he been smiling?

And then Scott turned his head to the ceiling, realising that he could still hear the roar of the missile's rocket engine, not dimmed by distance.

As if something was holding it in place…

*

Jordan Jones heard Lord inhale sharply, seconds before a powerful concussive roar echoed across the open sea. He raised his hand to steady the sunglasses that still masked his blinded eyes and called out.

"Something's happening Captain… I can feel it." He rested a hand on the trembling helm. "*Rescue*'s telling me."

"Yes… the missile launched."

"I assumed as such," Jones replied with not a hint of sarcasm. "But then…"

"Well sir…" Lord replied hesitantly. Jones envisioned the other man hopelessly trying to depict a shape with his hands, and cut him off.

"Just tell me what you're seeing."

"Well…" Lord paused as the wind whipped back their hair. Jones leaned closer, feeling his arms prickle with goosebumps as the former master of the *Californian* began to hesitantly describe what he could see.

"The missile is frozen in the sky, about fifteen hundred feet up. We and *Viking* are underneath, twisted together, and everything around is glowing… burning with white light."

"The *Liberty Bell*?"

"Yes, it must be the cause of this. The force is reeling the missile in, and it's also creating a visible boundary. The sea immediately around us is flying up into a dome overhead, like a bubble of light and spray."

Rescue groaned and twisted beneath their feet, metal flexing and shattering under the action of the temporal event manifesting within her hold. Spray pelted them in the faces and thunder cracked heavily overhead. Jones felt forward and pulled himself to the rail. He could feel tears running out from under his glasses. "Christ alive, I wish I could see it."

"It's beautiful, Captain… shimmering and shot through with rainbows."

*

"Full astern!" Lloyd Waters bellowed, turning from the iridescent light towards *Oceanic*'s gawking bridge crew. "Stand off immediately!"

"But, Captain, that's our path home!" a helmsman protested. "*Our only way home!*"

"*That* is a tug-of-war between a time machine and a nuclear missile! I'm not endangering our passengers by getting involved! *Full astern!*"

605

"Our families sir, our lives, our future, they're all on the other side of that light, *we should be getting in closer!*" the wretched man said, before another hand reached past him and hauled the throttle levers back as far as they would go.

"Full astern, Captain," acknowledged Safety Officer Vickers.

"Thank you, Catherine," Lloyd sighed, struggling to not let his own anguish show. Stepping forward, he lightly patted the helmsman on the shoulder. "I'm sorry, but it looks like this is home now, and we've got to live in it."

"Radar's failing, Captain!" came a call. "Just like last night. But we've still got radio contact with *Rescue*, barely."

Lloyd nodded, mouth pursed in silence.

"Sir," added Vickers. "Should we relay anything to Captain Jones? A message to the future, a confirmation we're alive and trapped in the past, a request for help?"

Lloyd turned and looked off to port, eyes squeezed almost shut against the glare being thrown off as reality fluxed.

"Wish them Godspeed, and then leave the channel open. If they've got something to tell us, we'll need all ears open to hear it…"

*

"*Good luck Rescue,*" the radio crackled. "*We won't forget your sacrifice.*"

"Thank you *Oceanic!*" Stanley Lord heard Captain Jones shout into the helm's radio handset. "And Bon Voyage to you and the *Anatoly Sagalevich!*"

Despite everything, despite the forces being exerted on her, *Rescue*'s remaining propeller was still thundering forward at full power, keeping her prow forced into the crippled *Viking*. Lord was assisting Jones in keeping the ship pinned against the submarine, gripping the helm with one hand whilst the other shielded his eyes from the blinding light that was flowing across every surface, including himself. Bright sparks burst painlessly off of his fingertips, droplets of energy exploding like rockets viewed from a great distance.

Turning, he peered over his shoulder, squinting to see through the storm of spray laced with faceted light. Beyond the wall of fracturing time, he could see *Oceanic* retreating to a safe distance, turning to put her great mass between the vortex and where the men evacuated from *Rescue*, including *Californian*'s surviving crew, would be struggling in the water. Seizing the radio from Jones with a word of apology, he essayed off a quick message of thanks for Captain Waters' seamanship, even if *Oceanic* was still a lumbering giant too big for her own draft, in Lord's humble opinion.

"Captain Jones, Captain Lord! It's working!" someone shouted. "The Schwarzschild horizon is contracting to form the singularity, pulling us in!"

Lord turned to see Doctor Oshiro clawing his way up the companionway to the bridge. Something small and metal dangled from his hand on a length of chain. Lord squinted and saw that it was a key. Then, his expression somewhere between awestruck terror and elation, the Japanese engineer hurled the small scrap of metal overboard, and spun to face the two of them.

"This is it!" he cried out. "I need to make a radio transmission, now!"

"Here!" Lord bellowed, holding up the handset. Seeing it, Oshiro threw himself down the canting deck and, steadying himself against the navigation panel, he took the device and began to shout into it.

Lord himself felt empty, focusing instead on the reality of the wheel in his hands and the defiant surging of *Rescue*'s engines as he stared up into the howling eye of the storm, which was focused around the immobile glare of the missile's engine. Then he felt Jones clap a hand on his shoulder.

"Congratulations, Captain Lord! You're a shining hero!"

Before Lord could reply, *Rescue* heeled under an immense wave, and with a cry of alarm Oshiro was carried away, disappearing in a sudden deluge that swept through the bridge. Lord wrapped his arms around the helm and held tight as *Rescue* tore away from *Viking* and rolled sideways onto the next wave, listing so hard as to dip her gunwales into the water. With a percussive snapping of guy-lines the ship's twin cranes swung out, and seawater poured down the open hatches into the cargo holds.

As her diesel generators finally died, *Rescue* howled piteously, and Lord saw the bow flex upwards.

Another ship that's broken her back, he thought with no small touch of sadness, and looked towards *Viking*. The submarine was sinking at both ends, illuminated brilliantly by the glare of the Trident's engine, wreathed with exhaust gasses and seawater that had been flash-boiled to steam.

*

The launch control room was now draining of water as the sub reared up. It would come rushing back when she sank proper. Scott sighed and looked towards the control panels, now descending into a mess of error prompts.

"It could have been so glorious, Bob," he said, addressing the corpse stuck to the wall. "Germany's power-grab stamped out in an instant."

But what about our power-grabbing, Scott? he imagined Bob replying quietly, sitting calmly opposite him. *The British Empire's seeding the whirlwind right now in its overseas Dominions, and playing the Great Game with Russia for who controls the Middle East. Would you have nuked London as well?*

"If need called, until people got the message."

But where would continuously upping the ante have ended? Everyone would take up arms against you, doing their best to enrich themselves with nuclear tech, and then we've gone right back round to where we came from. The world needs more ploughshares now to fight imperialism, not swords.

"Will that be our legacy?" Scott spoke aloud, his eyes closed. It was as if they were discussing strategy over a board game in the wardroom. Nothing so distinguished as chess though; maybe Risk, or Snakes and Ladders.

No, but it might be the legacy of those we leave behind.

The room convulsed violently, and Scott was thrown from his seat against the launch console. Glancing off it he landed hard against the wall, one of his legs twisted under him at a cockeyed angle.

"Bloody hell, Bob," he said quietly, before glancing towards the skipper's body and laughing like a damned man who finally sees the joke. "How did we come to this?"

Water was poured in through the aft hatch. The emergency lights were flickering in and out. With his injured leg dragging behind him, Scott Thresher limped to the ladder and began to pull himself up out of what had become a sinking metal coffin.

*

"We don't have long!" Pip paused in shovelling and shouted to be heard over *Titanic*'s, the cavernous size of the boiler room only amplifying and exaggerating the ship's death throes. "The hull can't take this kind of punishment much longer."

"I'm quite aware of that, thank you, stewardess..." Cosmo Duff-Gordon replied groggily, still pinned by the coal but having regained consciousness when the icy water reached him.

Jack met Pip's eyes with a look of apology, rolling his eyes, while Duff-Gordon, somewhat dazed, continued to remove individual pieces of coal from his chest, as if selecting ice cubes for a drink. If he was aware of the water now rising up his neck, he was doing a remarkable show of concealing it.

"Right, that's enough!" Jack threw down his shovel and got his hands underneath Duff-Gordon's right arm, while Pip mimicked him on the other side. "Together now! Heave!"

They strained, and the coals clattered, slowly giving up their hold on the semi-conscious man.

"Steady on," Cosmo complained lightly, faint comprehension in his eyes. "What happened, did I fall down an open sewer or some such?"

"No Cosmo, you volunteered for manual labour," replied Jack, teeth gritted as they pulled again.

"Who'd have thunk it?" Pip added. "One more pull, his legs are almost free!"

"One, two, *THREE!*" they bellowed together, and finally they dragged Cosmo clear of the collapsed pile of coal.

"Come on, we've got to get out of here, quickly!" Pip shouted. "If we don't get to the Boat Deck before the last boat launches, we're just going to freeze to death in the Atlantic!"

Urging on Duff-Gordon, who was slowly coming back to full awareness, they climbed the ladder out of the drowned boiler room and reached Scotland Road, the lights around them buzzing and stuttering as the ship's emergency dynamos struggled to keep up with demand.

Pip glanced around, winded and catching her breath after the climb. All three of them were blackened with filthy water and coal-dust, contrasting against the white walls like night with day. Turning to Jack, feeling more the poster-image of a wild-child than ever before, she suddenly found herself embraced in an enthusiastic hug.

"You wonderful girl!" he declared. "You wonderful, courageous, uncultured girl."

Pip, somewhat flustered, felt a second hand clap her on the shoulder, and turned to find Cosmo Duff-Gordon, 5th Baronet of Halkin and co-founder of the London Fencing League, staring with stern eyes at her.

"I misjudged you time-travellers, it seems…" he said at length. "You are, by every measure, persons worthy of praise."

"You're not so bad yourself, Cosmo," she managed a laugh. "Two days ago I'd never have thought of you, the man who got off in a lifeboat with only eleven other people, volunteering to work in a stokehold."

As if noticing himself for the first time, Duff-Gordon glanced down at his begrimed shirt and waistcoat. "So I see."

"I guess we're more than what we seem, not stereotypes or… characters in someone else's story," she said, echoing William Murdoch's words to her and smiling wanly at the irony.

The passageway's lights flickered, momentarily plunging them into total darkness, before fading back in. From fore and aft, the soft rippling of water could be heard.

"Come on…" Jack said, and Pip saw both his and Cosmo's eyes widen at the sudden reminder of their situation. "We can praise and adulate one another later."

"Right. Grand Staircase, this way…" Pip pointed, and in a blind sprint they climbed the five flights. Taking the final set of steps two-at-a-time, Pip hurled himself at the vestibule onto the Boat Deck and held the door open for the others, exiting last and almost running into Jack from behind.

He had stopped dead, and was staring up at the sky in disbelief, as was Duff-Gordon. Following their example, she turned her face to the heavens.

"Oh, my God!"

*

There was a cry, and Jordan Jones fell away from *Rescue*'s helm, disappearing into the water now consuming her decks. Suddenly alone on the bridge, Stanley Lord stared up into the very heart of the event coalescing around him. Bolts of blue light arced between the missile and the ocean surface, between the ship and the submarine, forming an elaborate pattern of energy that shimmered through the spray and fog. He could see shapes within it, shadow plays and bursts of light coming together to form images. Dark ships seemed to float on a burning sea, hands entwining and striking, forming a dark shadow that rose up over all, suddenly broken by a multitude of bright flashes that tore it apart like a veil at first dawn.

He grabbed hold of the wheel as the immense mechanical grinding of the portal's formation seemed to reach its peak. More sparks of light fizzed between his fingers and the metal spokes, and across from him *Viking*'s stern was rearing up out of the water, her propeller scrabbling at the sky.

Lord felt the deck roll beneath him as *Rescue* twisted in two. It was too great a force for him to maintain his grip, and as the bridge inverted he was flung from the helm and into darkness.

*

On the bridge of *Olympic*, Herbert Haddock stared in open-eyed amazement across an open mile of water, towards *Rescue* and *Viking*. The rain had stopped, and the two vessels could just be made out as a pair of shadows enveloped within a shimmering dome of flying water and splintered light.

Suddenly the dome seemed to pulse from within, immediately engulfing itself in a half-sphere of light, hazy and indistinct. Gazing briefly into the void beneath reality, Haddock threw up his hands moments before a shockwave blasted out over the water, crashing against ships and flattening waves, knocking down every soul on *Olympic*'s decks as if they were tenpins. As the liner's hull cavitated from end to end, amplifying the bellowing roar, Haddock clamped his hands over his ears and hoped for it all to end.

"..."

Time seemed to shatter, and reality raced back in to fill the sudden void. Total silence fell, as if the source of the maelstrom had been suddenly drawn up through a hole in the sky, creating a brief and perfect moment entirely absent of sound.

Haddock slowly lowered his hands, then struggled to his feet and approached *Olympic*'s rail.

"My God..."

The blinding speck of light at the core of the vortex had stretched into a biblical shaft of white fire, rising like a tower from the surface of the sea into the sky. Within seconds it extinguished itself, energy cascading throughout the gathered clouds in a rippling surge. Almost immediately the swirling clouds collapsed, revealing an open night sky brilliant with ethereal colours.

Another aurora, he realised. Distant thunder boomed, as if a great door had slammed shut. It spoke of finality, that whatever had transpired was over.

It is finished...

Unable to find absolution in the skies, he turned his head down to where *Rescue* and *Viking* had collided, the epicentre of where reality had broken. The two vessels were gone, though whether into the sea or out of time he could not say. All that remained was a field of bubbles writhing on the surface of the ocean, brilliantly lit by the streams of light now rippling across the sky.

Then the ocean rolled back in, wiping the patch of disturbed water clean, as if nothing had happened. To Haddock's eyes it seemed as if the removal of the *Liberty Bell* had placated the

Atlantic's temper, for the weather seemed calmer than it had been, the waves dwindling back towards whitecaps and small rollers, accompanied by a freshness on the air that hinted of dawn.

"They're gone…" he said quietly, glancing at his fob-watch to confirm the time, then turning to regard the lights of *Oceanic* and the *Anatoly Sagalevich*, hove to off of *Olympic*'s side. "And they are now trapped here…"

He considered the two ships with a moment's sadness, and then frowned. Something was missing, something had eluded him…

…he spun on his heel with sudden realisation.

"Where's *Titanic*?!"

Blank faces turned to him with no answers, and then everyone peered out into the dark, searching for the other liner's lights. Had she gotten pulled up in the vortex?

"Signal lights and flares!" he shouted. "Get every ship in the fleet searching for *Titanic!*"

"I see her!" a female voice called out, high and clear, and running to the bridge wing Haddock saw Connie Ramirez had climbed high into the rigging strung from *Olympic*'s forward mast, higher even than the crow's nest, and was pointing away into the night.

"She's out that way, half a mile west of where that pillar of light originated… *and she's going down!*"

CHAPTER THIRTY

Titanic was dying, and no amount of pumping could rescue her now. But in some way, part of her would survive. The people aboard would see to that.

In the Marconi Room, Jack Phillips and Harold Bride were making their contribution. Even as they rushed to help Cameron dismantle and evacuate the precious speaking radio to a lifeboat, they were shoving reams of documentation into spare mail sacks, ripping the wireless flimsies from their office skewers and saving them up for posterity.

"Is that it?" Bride asked, even as he bundled up the radio's antenna cabling.

"That's it, Harry. Go, quick. I'll be with you in a second."

Giving his junior a quick shove to hasten him on his way, Phillips turned and gave the wireless suite a final once-over. The mess they had made notwithstanding, everything was pristine and new, ready to give years of service, a life that would now be cut short. Brass and wood fittings gleamed, and the Marconi equipment hummed with quiet confidence.

Feeling an unexpected wave of emotion, he stepped through into the silent room, and found his attention drawn towards the rotary spark distributor, the installation that formed the heart of *Titanic*'s transmitting station. Only yesterday he had found it bizarre that the time-travellers had, in the future-that-was, gone to great efforts to salvage such a mundane piece of equipment from the ship's wreck, and yet now, with the weight of history bearing down on him, he felt like he understood, and with that understanding came the desire to preserve *something*…

The distributor was too big to save, he knew that much, but there was… yes, that would do.

Crossing back into the actual receiving room, he pulled out his pen-knife; with a quick moment's work he cut the wiring that connected the transmitting key to the rest of the wireless set. Repeating the process with the headphones, he carefully packaged up the instruments by which *Titanic* had whispered her story, wrapping his watertight greatcoat around them.

Fastidious to the end, he reached across the desk and pulled the knife-switches, shutting down the equipment for the last time. Only then, with his bundle underarm, did Jack Phillips cross to the entrance and gave the room a parting glance, his finger hovering over the light switch.

"MGY, signing off," he whispered aloud, and turned out the lights.

*

Deep in the bowels of the ship, the refrigeration hold repurposed as a morgue was flooding. In the original timeline, these sealed and watertight food stores had maintained their structural integrity well after the ship vanished beneath the surface, uncompromised until the stern sank to such a depth that immense water pressure brought about their implosion, the subsequent eruptions of air tearing the wreck apart from within. Far above, survivors in the lifeboats had heard these deep and distant blasts, and witnessed so much cork insulation float to the surface that it seemed as if the Atlantic had been carpeted in wood.

This time was different. With the keel structurally compromised, the immense frames that cradled the holds had begun to shift, fracturing the bulkheads, creating pathways for the floodwaters. They rose around the occupied body bags, those inhabited by Henry Wilde, Robert Hichens, Frederick Barrett, Adrian Abercrombie, and so many others.

One by one, the lights failed, until at last the morgue and its mortal cargo were plunged into darkness, and committed to the deep.

*

The blast wave thrown off by the collapsing vortex had knocked Pip back across *Titanic*'s Boat Deck, slamming her into something soft, something that grunted in pain, before a wall of sound overtook them like the onrushing roar of a runaway train. Pip had screamed along with it, hands pressed against her ears, whomever she had hit wrapping their arms around her in protection.

Then, in an instant, the tempest passed by, racing away into the distance. Eyes wide, Pip turned and stared up from the deck as the flickering light of the singularity winked out, a few final glistening bolts of plasma bursting in the sky. Overhead, *Titanic*'s wireless aerials and masts were glowing like overheated filaments.

She felt her mouth form the words *"Oh my God"*, but all she could hear was a tinny ringing in her ears. The sound added an eerie cast to events; arcane lightning crackled overhead one last time, before the up-swirling dome of water thrown up by the *Liberty Bell* collapsed, with all the horrific slowness of a demolished building.

Then the spray began to fall like rain, the cool wetness slicking her hair down and clinging tight to her clothes. It was like a baptism, washing away her fear and leaving only awe at the incredible sight.

Slowly she looked around to find who she had been knocked into, and to her relief, but with no surprise, she found a coal-encrusted Jack Thayer, not grinning or blushing but regarding her with head bowed and eyes full of questions. Still the handsome youth she had quietly obsessed over for years.

She took his hand, and smiled wearily.

"Hey, you okay?"

With a sigh of his own Jack returned the gesture by lightly grabbing her free hand, his own expression guarded.

"Pardon me if this borders on cliché, but yes, I feel better for speaking to you again."

The two of them stood like that for some time, the world around them fading away. Pip was dimly aware that someone was shouting something, but their voice sounded a hundred years away. Water atomised by the timestorm was still raining down on the two of them, and all around them men were running and shouting as they piled into the remaining lifeboats.

"*Phillipa! Mr Thayer!*" a voice finally broke through to them, and they looked to their side to see Thomas Andrews, the shipwright now animated by a fierce energy.

"It's time to go," he said, beckoning towards a readied lifeboat, into which Fourth Officer Boxhall was hurling charts, documentation, packets of wireless messages and a thick book that could only be the ship's log.

Nodding, and briefly looking to Jack for confirmation, Pip stepped forward. And then she stopped, staggering as a sudden tremor ran through the deck. Andrews grabbed hold of a guy line to keep his footing, while the two teenagers fell against each other for support.

"What was that?" she heard Jack call aloud. Thomas began to explain, but glancing along the deck Pip could see for herself that amidships, beyond the third funnel, the deck was writhing like some live thing, the teak planking shearing as the whole ship was flexed.

She's breaking up…

"The boat, now!" Andrews shouted, but before any of them could reach their footing *Titanic* heaved beneath their feet, throwing them to the deck. Somebody shouted *"lower away now!"* and the boat slid out of sight below the rail, the men lowering it having jumped aboard, dragging the falls with them.

*

In the forward holds, water was gushing up in geysers through the floor. Carefully stowed among the general plethora were countless wares, crates of cargo, general goods, artworks, mechanical components, and a bejewelled copy of *The Rubaiyat of Omar Khayyam*, auctioned for £400 in London just weeks before. All were already sodden from last night's immersion in the sea, and were now being reclaimed by the ocean.

On a higher level, in the Mail Hold, several sacks lay about, their contents reduced to papier-mâché. The majority had been safely removed the night before, however, and transferred to *Oceanic* by the industrious mail-staff, hand-picked from the best men the Royal Mail and United States Postal Service had to offer.

Deeper within the holds, packed in protective wood casing, was a 25 horsepower Renault automobile, recently purchased by Mr William Carter of Bryn Mawr, Pennsylvania. Transported partially dismantled for ease of shipping, the car's fine coachwork now glistened with droplets of water like beads of sweat, metal fittings tinkling in time to *Titanic*'s death-throes.

The ship's hull flexed, the forward bulkhead collapsed, and the car was lost beneath the deluge of water that followed.

*

"The Engelhardt boats!" Pip pushed herself to her knees, peering forward. "The collapsibles!"

"Less talking, more running!" Andrews shouted, leading the way forward. *Titanic* was bending forward and aft like a ruler, but this section of the Boat Deck was right on the highest part still afloat, buoyed up by the uncompromised compartments underneath. But the combined forces were conspiring to snap the great ship, ripping her apart.

"Mr Murdoch!" Thomas shouted as he, Pip, Jack, Cosmo and the few crew still aboard ran up. *Titanic*'s Acting Captain was struggling with several of the deck crew to carry one of the two Engelhardt liferafts to the lifeboat davits. Chief Engineer Bell was there as well as Bruce Ismay, the two of them winching the falls back up to receive the boat. Running past them, Pip looked forward and saw that although the forecastle still stood above the water, the forward well deck was quickly submerging.

Then she peered aft. *Titanic*'s deck sloped downhill away from her, and then bent back up to form the elevated stern, dimly visible as a black shadow against the sky, set with a handful of dimly-burning lights.

"There's no time to launch it!" Andrews was shouting, even as he and the other men leapt in to manhandle the Engelhardt towards the rails. "Push it overboard!"

Murdoch paused to argue, but then Pip ran up, drawing attention by her sheer energy.

"Listen to him!" she burst in. "When the ship sank the first time round, two of these collapsibles floated right off! One was upside-down but it still floated! Just shove them over the gunwale and jump down to them!"

Far aft something burst with an electric bang, and the lights fused, plunging the deck into darkness mitigated only by the faint gleam of torches. Pip's own handheld LED light cast Murdoch's face into a deathly contrast, his eyes as sunken and black as sockets in a skull.

"This is where it happened, isn't it?" he said levelly.

"No, it was on the other side of the ship, to starboard," she replied, knowing instinctively he was referring to his alleged suicide. "And it's not going to happen this time."

"Right…" Murdoch spun away, raising his voice. "You heard the experts! Push the two liferafts off the deck. After that, it's every man for himself. Godspeed to you all!"

It was confused mayhem, torch beams picking out blurring hands and frightened faces. Crew and passengers who had volunteered for the stokeholds heaved together, and the first Engelhardt boat vanished overboard, followed seconds later by a splash. Pip, the smallest person present, suddenly found herself almost knocked to the deck and trampled as men ran back to grab the second boat. Everything dissolved into a confused mix of shouting voices and *Titanic*'s aching groans as the ship laid herself down to die.

"Twilight is in just ten minutes. Hold off till then and we can work better!"

"No time. Water's already risen to the A-Deck promenade amidships, in ten minutes the deck will be too tilted to work."

"You there sir, jump for it!"

"No chance, old man. I'm a yachtsman and as good a sailor as any here! I'm climbing down the falls!"

Someone slammed into Pip, toppling her off her feet. As she fell to the deck she lost hold of her torch. Scrabbling blindly she suddenly felt the ship lunge downwards; screaming, she slid down the tilting deck towards the black water, its arms open to receive her.

*

Water foamed up through the hole smashed in the bottom of *Titanic*'s swimming-pool; ripping the gap wide open, it surged with immense force up the corridor into the Turkish Baths, scattering furniture and shredding panelled woodwork. Relentless and remorseless, it then cascaded aft, flooding through the holes cut for *Viking*'s suctions into the Third Class Dining Saloon, drowning tables still set for a hearty breakfast of porridge, smoked fish, jacket potatoes, and ham with eggs.

Wooden chairs and china crockery floated for several minutes, before the water rose to the roof, submerging the room…

*

Jack heard a familiar voice shriek with terror, dwindling rapidly as if rushing into the distance.

"*Philippa! Pip!*" he shouted, shoving aside other men in the darkness. Even as the ship dived he managed to keep his footing, grabbing hold of davits and funnel stays to steady himself. "*Philippa! Where are you?!*"

No-one answered. He peered aft, where the cry of alarm had come from. There, in the crook of a deck fitting, was a small patch of bright light. Was it her? Stumbling and sliding, he scrambled down to the glowing speck, and found Pip's brilliant white torch, lying against the entrance to the Grand Staircase.

"*Look out!*" someone shouted, and Jack saw something dark slide past him down the length of the deck. It was the second liferaft. He shone the torch after it, and its light caught not only the boat splashing down into the water, capsized, but a flash of reflective material bobbing beside it. It was Pip's jacket. But if it was her, why didn't she swim for the boat? Had it struck her when it slid off the deck, was she unconscious?

"*Philippa!*" he shouted. "*I'm coming!*"

And then, with a foolhardiness born both of teenage emotion and gentlemanly decorum, he swung himself around the edge of the First Class vestibule, lay flat on his back and slid down the deck after the liferaft.

Working in the boiler-room, and wading through the inflowing water to rescue Gordon, would, Jack thought, have inured him to extremes of temperature.

Splashing into the Atlantic, he released that was a false assumption. Cold pain shot through his veins like white fire, robbing him of even the strength to gasp. He thrashed wildly, instinctively trying to find the deck again, and then, suddenly possessed of a terror of the ship dragging him down, he kicked towards the open ocean. The torch was gone, dropped when he hit the water, now he was drowning in cold oblivion…

…his hand, flailing fitfully, fell upon something warm.

It was Pip.

*

The First Class spaces were quickly succumbing to the water. Amidships, the opulent suite of rooms occupied by John and Madeleine Astor was being smashed to splinters by the hull tearing apart around it.

The Smoking Room on A-Deck was faring no better, carved columns exploding and wall sconces tearing apart as the superstructure buckled. Images of great White Star ships of ages past, depicted on the walls in stained glass, now shattered one-by-one like broken dreams.

The advancing waters hesitated for a moment when they reached the fireplace, over which a bare wall could be seen where minutes before artist Norman Wilkinson's masterpiece *'Plymouth Harbour'* had hung. Churning and thrashing as if cheated of a prize, the Atlantic waters retreated for a moment.

Then, with a single heaving motion, the room imploded.

*

"Captain Waters, Ms Vickers says we've taken on the last of the people evacuated from *Rescue*."

"Excellent, make ready to head towards *Titanic*. Is she still showing on our radar?"

"Yes sir, but her return is shrinking. I think she's settling fast."

Lloyd Waters had once heard the sinking of a ship described as *"the slow and painful destruction of a very large piece of machinery"*, but in truth he had always regarded the concept in somewhat abstract terms. Recent events surrounding the sinking of the *Costa Concordia* had shaken him out of that complacency, but now, peering out over the open water towards where *Titanic* lay bellowing in pain, the full horror of a shipwreck struck him like a blow. The sounds of the liner breaking up reached through the open windows on *Oceanic*'s bridge and touched him like a cold knife.

"Once our lifeboats are back aboard, head towards *Titanic!*" he called out to the helmsman. "But slowly. Lookouts, keep an eye out for boats and survivors. Watch for flares coming from the surface."

How many people had been aboard *Titanic?* He struggled to remember. There was the deck-crew, engineering staff, the scratch crew of firemen, and a handful of others. That there was at least several hundred people. Had there been enough time to abandon ship?

Slowly *Oceanic* pushed forward, gingerly passing right over the spot where *Viking* and *Rescue* had been plucked from the sea. About a mile ahead, *Olympic* was also easing forward.

But the ocean between them was just a featureless black field. With even her emergency lights extinguished, *Titanic* had vanished, and even the dim light of the aurora above was not enough to reveal her position.

"Come on, come on!" Lloyd whispered under his breath. "Where are they?"

Then, suddenly, one of the lookouts shouted, followed by a cacophony of reports.

"Green flare to port captain!"

"Another two points to starboard!"

"Lifeboats sighted. Two lashed together!"

"Survivors in the water, swimming!"

"Launch two of our own boats, send them to pick survivors from the sea, quickly, before they all freeze!"

"Captain!" another voice called out. "The sun is about to rise!"

"So?"

"Just look sir!"

Lloyd crossed to the far side of the bridge, and slowly exhaled. "Is that *Titanic?* God Almighty…"

The Grand Staircase was being put through a wood-chipper, the walls and floor grinding like millstones, erasing *Titanic's* iconic centrepiece from existence. Rapidly-rising seawater seeped into the mechanism of the clock borne between the carved reliefs of Honour and Glory readying to crown it, and the hands stopped at fifteen minutes past six…

*

"Hold on the oars!" shouted Joseph Bell from the tiller of Collapsible D. "*Olympic* has seen us!"

Their breath misting, Bruce Ismay and Thomas Andrews rested their weight on the oars, and shared a glance. Each other's faces were just visible in the cold light of dawn.

"Do you really want to see her sink, Thomas?"

"Not really, sir, but I think we should anyway."

Nodding in accord, the two of them turned on their seats, and Andrews's breath left him.

"Oh, she's going!"

Titanic, black against the morning twilight, was still settling in the middle, her back broken below the fourth funnel, the base of which was already submerged. The stern was rising, tipping up under the weight of the water in the engine rooms, until at last her propellers hefted clear of the water, bronze caps glinting.

"Her head's coming up as well," Ismay pointed, and he was right. Despite the water coming in through the damage inflicted by her two collisions, first with the iceberg, and then with *Viking*, the weight of the sinking stern was levering *Titanic's* bow upwards, so that the ship appeared to be vainly reaching out towards the west, towards Halifax and safe harbour.

Groaning, creaking like some immense mechanism straining under the load, the bow rose higher, exposing her forefoot, bent rudely aside from where she had struck the submarine. Further aft, part of the deformed double-bottom peeked momentarily above the waterline, spotted with grey polyurethane patches.

"It was a miracle she floated as long as she did, as badly damaged as she was…" Thomas said quietly, and for the first time in days he heard Bruce Ismay laugh softly in reply.

"No miracle, Tom, just very good shipbuilding. You built her strongly, and she did as asked…"

"Thank you, Bruce…" Thomas smiled ruefully. "I promise you that we'll do even better next time."

There was a sudden rending series of bangs and screams as the ship finally broke in two, and the bow plunged, burying its nose in the sea. As the funnels and masts toppled, the two halves of the ship momentarily righted themselves, and then began to sink. The stern went first, poop-deck disappearing into a mushrooming column of water. Then, the Atlantic racing up her deck, the bow section sank, the weight of the flooded boiler rooms lifting the forecastle upright into a near vertical position.

At that moment, like a fire bursting into life on the horizon, the sun rose, throwing brilliant light into the ship's final moments. Even as it sank, the bow looked impeccable, anchor chains neatly laid out, decking freshly varnished, the capstans gleaming with polish. Briefly the light caught the ship's name picked out on her prow, the sans-serif letters glittering with golden promise.

From across the water *Olympic* sounded her whistles in remembrance of her sister, and moments later her mournful cries were joined by *Oceanic*'s bellowing claxons. The *Anatoly Sagalevich* roared her appreciation in turn, the impromptu fleet sending off its flagship with the tribute she deserved.

For a moment the bow hesitated in its final plunge, the forecastle pointing straight up in salute to the other ships.

And then, exhaling spray and air as if giving up her spirit, *Titanic* collapsed down into the sea, and vanished beneath the waves.

*

"Let the log show," Herbert Haddock dictated, glancing to *Olympic*'s bridge clock, "that the RMS *Titanic* sank on the morning of April 16th 1912, at 6.20am, at approximately 42.18'N, 52.20'W."

"Over a hundred nautical miles from where she originally sank," Connie Ramirez observed. "Never the same way twice."

"Quite," Haddock nodded, removing his hat to pat down his hair. "And I suppose that this makes your bed for you, Lieutenant." He sighed softly. "My sympathies."

She shrugged in response. "Thank you, Captain, but I've had a day and a bit to think things over, and I'd like to think of this as an opportunity." Then she grinned widely, like a child rewarded for good behaviour. "I mean, I'm going to get to live through the golden age of aviation. If I play my cards right, I might even get to be one of those pioneers, flying the first biplanes, maybe even a jet! I've got a chance to be this timeline's Amelia Earhart!"

Who? Haddock thought to himself, even as he smiled in understanding. "Just promise to leave a few passengers for us poor sea-lubbers, pilot."

"Certainly captain…" she laughed, mockingly raising a hand to her head in salute. Then she turned towards where *Titanic* had sunk, and her expression grew thoughtful. "Though there is one thing I'd like to do…"

She explained what she wanted, and Haddock nodded in approval. It was an eminently suitable gesture.

"Come, we can make arrangements once we've taken tally of the survivors…" he extended a hand out onto the bridge wing, and the two of them stepped out into the growing dawn. Attentive officers stood at *Olympic*'s rails, calling out when they spotted an approaching boat.

"All of *Titanic*'s rigid portside boats are accounted for, Captain," came a speedy report. "Along with one of the Engelhardt collapsible boats. They're rowing towards us now. But the remaining collapsible is still unaccounted for."

"I have her!" another lookout shouted, having climbed onto the roof of the wheelhouse. "She's capsized, but there are people on her back, about two miles off!"

"Excellent," Haddock nodded. "Send word to the wireless room, they are to signal *Oceanic* as best they can and ask that she send one of her superb motorboats to the aid of that particular collapsible. We will continue taking on survivors from the others. And ask Captain Waters to make it sharp; those poor souls must surely be half-frozen to death by now!"

Jack was balanced precariously in a squat on the upturned back of Collapsible B, the lifeboat that had slid down the deck past him when *Titanic* plunged. His breath was misting between chattering teeth, and his exposed arms were pale, but were still wrapped weakly around the figure sitting in his embrace.

"Pip..." he shook her softly, and got no response. "Philippa, can you hear me?"

She said nothing, and when he struggled to feel for a pulse in her jugular, he found that his fingers were too numbed even to detect one.

"I think she's gone, Mr Thayer..." said a man standing upright, his arms outstretched in an attempt to maintain the boat's balance.

"What should I do, Mr Murdoch?" Jack said listlessly. "Just cast her adrift like a piece of flotsam?"

"Don't talk rubbish!" *Titanic*'s final master replied. "The poor thing deserves a full funeral, with every honour available."

Jack's shoulders twitched, though whether from the cold or a fickle laugh he could not say. "Is that the best we can do for these people?"

Murdoch had no answer, and instead straightened up slightly, peering towards the horizon. "There's another craft coming. It's one of *Oceanic*'s lifeboats. It's heading our way."

The few other souls crowded onto the back of the boat, twelve in all counting Murdoch, Jack and Pip, murmured appreciatively.

"I'd call for three cheers..." Cosmo Duff-Gordon said. "But I'd fear that might tip us all over."

Like Murdoch and several of the other men, Cosmo was on his feet, shifting his weight around cautiously in an attempt to keep the boat stable. Jack slowly looked from face to face. Crew and passengers, work-clothes and dinner-shirts equally ruined by coal-dust and water; one of *Titanic*'s wireless operators, still resplendent in the uniform of the Marconi Wireless Company; and Murdoch, greatcoat missing but cap of office clamped firmly onto his head.

He looked down to Pip's own headgear, the baseball cap from *Rescue* that still held a wad of bandages in place around her head.

"Did you hear that, Pip... there's a boat coming."

She did not reply. Cautiously, Jack he pushed two of his fingers up under the brim of her cap and probed beneath the bandages, finding a few stitches holding together what must have surely been a nasty gash. A tiny rivulet of warmth ran down one of his fingers. Slowly, trembling with more than just the cold, he withdrew his hand. His fingertips were red with blood, the fluid vivid against his pale fingers and the slate-grey sea.

Dead bodies do not bleed...

"She's still alive..." he said aloud, and suddenly felt hot tears dribbling down his face as he cradled her head in relief, his hand resting against her hair, matted and crusty with ice.

"Come on Pip... come on, it's Jack here..." reflexively he turned her face to him, her skin as pale as Snow White. He considered kissing her, hoping that it would wake her like in the fairytales, and discarded that option quickly. She might have opened his eyes to many new schools of thought, but to go so far as to force himself on her without invitation, no...

His mind cast itself backwards, trying to find something that might reach her, and then he hit on something.

"Pip, you said you wanted to experience *Titanic*, to know it truly. Well, right now, you're riding on an upturned lifeboat, just like your Mr Lightoller did." Eyes closed his he held her close and whispered fervently. "Come on Pip, this is your life's dream; you missed the ship sinking, don't miss the rest of it..."

"...your breath really stinks, Jack."

His eyes flew open, and he saw her own hazel-green pools squinting in the harsh daylight. After a few seconds she blinked as if trying to orientate herself and looked around, taking in the handful of men clustered onto the tiny wooden island with them.

"Wow..." she said softly. "It wasn't a dream."

For some reason, Jack was glad that she did not define the past few days as a nightmare. As *Oceanic*'s boat came within hailing distance, she felt him squeeze his hand.

"Did I ever mention that I get seasick, Jack?"

He chuckled and patted her hair down. "No, but if it helps, I would not object if you were sick on me right now. It might warm the both of us up."

"...you're disgusting," she said calmly, before joining him in laughter. In the corner of his eye Jack could see Murdoch shaking his head at them, but the officer was smiling all the same, as if indulging the antics of two lunatics.

Well, let anyone think him mad. All Jack felt himself to be now was happy, rejoicing in Pip's laughter and her evident joy.

She was going to be alright. He would see to it that she was.

CHAPTER THIRTY ONE

Tens of nautical miles away, the blast of light from the *Liberty Bell* had spread in a flat disc along the full length of the horizon. Aboard *Carpathia*, the agonising wait for the roar of the singularity to catch up seemed to tarry for eternity.

And then the thunderous crash overtook the Cunarder, and passed swiftly, leaving only the steady, confident and reassuring rhythm of the stalwart vessel's engines. Far astern, a few high-climbing bursts of energy rained in droplets from the sky, burning gobs of plasma that boiled away before they dropped below the horizon. Around it the clouds had been pushed back, leaving a perfect circle of open sky where the pillar of light had spread itself in all directions, like the branches of a tree, pouring light and energy into the newborn aurora.

Gradually, night seeped back in, and after a quiet, contemplative period of time, the sun had risen, golden daylight chasing away the dark. As the golden disc pulled itself free of the eastern horizon, Joanna Laroche felt Jabril Hab Allah shift slightly beside her.

"We are all God's prophets now," he whispered under his breath.

His name, she had learnt, apparently meant *Gabriel, the Gift of God*. Now he slowly rose from where he had been bent reflectively over the rail, drawing himself up straight. Not for the first time, she noticed what a strikingly handsome man he was. Strong cheeks flanked an aquiline nose that in turn was crowned with a pair of extremely piercing eyes. His hair, dark and thick, fell in natural waves over his shoulders.

All of this passed through her mind with a sterile objectivism; she had deigned to work with this man, to share their skills and knowledge for a common end, and she suspected at one point she might share more with him; but she did not love him, could not and would not. He had killed Marc, and his intentions for the use of the *Liberty Bell* had been horrific, or so she supposed.

What was that quote from Shakespeare? she thought. *No beast so fierce but knows some touch of pity, but I no none, and therefore am no beast...*

But the man did have his own nobility, and she had it in her to forgive. But not to forget.

"So", he sighed softly, one hand rubbing at his beard. "Something has gone wrong, and the *Liberty Bell* has been used again..."

"Do you think any of them were able to go back?"

"I'm sure we'll know soon enough through the wireless, but I certainly hope so; for their families to have some closure if nothing..." he paused, glancing at her suddenly darkened face. "Have you not considered that, as far as the world we have left behind is concerned, we and several thousand others are dead, vanished at sea in an instant?"

He snapped his fingers, and she twitched as he continued to speak. "The Titanic Memorial Fleet will be remembered as a disaster beyond measure, one just as tragic, perhaps even more so, than the actual sinking of the *Titanic...*"

"...or perhaps," she countered, resting her own weight on the rail, high above *Carpathia*'s foaming wake. "Perhaps, there is just one world... one timeline, and we are writing a new destiny over the one we knew. The people we loved, our triumphs, our mistakes, perhaps now they've never happened, *never will happen*, and we are just ghosts, fragments of memory dancing in the dreams of a world waiting to awake..."

"Do you honestly believe that?"

"No, but I'm French, we're entitled to spout high philosophy..."

"*Oui*, mademoiselle..." He replied, attention focused on a phial of crystals he was turning over in his hand. Curious, she in turn produced the coin-shaped piece of metal she had recovered from the *Seguin Laroche* before the ship sank.

"What is it the Americans like to say?" she said, holding the disc up for him to see. "My eye for your eye?"

He smiled and laughed. "I think the phrase you're thinking of is, '*I'll show you mine if you show me yours*'."

"Whatever, do you want to hear the story behind this thing or don't you?"

He chuckled. "It is your grandfather's medal, conferred on him by the State of Israel for his noble deeds during Hitler's genocide. It honours him as *'Righteous among the Nations'*."

Jo nodded, her surprise comingled with humour.

"May I?" He extended his hand, palm up, at the same time offering her his phial.

Nodding her assent they exchanged totems. The phial she now held in her hand was made of glass, and the small crystals it carried sparkled softly in the dim light. The stylised image of a bell was etched on the surface, along with a serial number and the words US NAVY.

"This is from Project Lesterpack?" she asked.

"Yes…" Jab was tracing his fingers, which were long and slender, over the medal. Stamped into it was a pair of emaciated, skeletal hands clutching at strands of barbed wire, which in turn twisted together into a cord that strangled the Earth. "Your grandfather, I am supposing he smuggled Jews out of Europe?"

"Yes, that's right. He had hidden compartments built into the fleet's ships, disguised in the double-hull and bottom. Papa took me down into one on the *Louvier Laroche* just before she was scrapped…" Joanna paused and lightly shook the phial beside her ear, listening to the crystals tinkling.

"So these are…"

"…a failed sample of the compound essential to the functions of the *Liberty Bell*; the Nazis dubbed it Xerum 525, the Americans codenamed it Apergy after a substance described in present-day science-fiction, and popular culture refers to it as Red Mercury. There were rumours that the United States had built time-engines, but I had not dared to believe in them until some years ago, when that phial arrived in the post from one of my contacts in America. I thought that God himself had sent me a divine message, and set to work gathering the contacts and resources needed to secure a working model."

He held up the medal to the hole in the sky miles astern, as if to plug it. "Great success!"

"So what was your dream?" she asked softly.

"I wanted…" he paused, for the first time looking abashed. "I wanted to travel back in time, and meet the prophet at the end of his life…"

"The Prophet?" she repeated, incredulous. "You wanted to meet with *Mohammed?*"

"Yes, the guardian of Islam. I thought, that if I could bring him *forward* in time, bring him back with us, he could be the leader that Muslims throughout the world need, the one authority we could all agree upon, above all these mad Ayatollahs and Caliphates. I thought that the Prophet alone, blessed with divine wisdom, could reconcile all Islam with the struggles of western democracy, with capitalism, socialism, women's emancipation, technology, and show us all a better path, a holy path…"

His eyes had remained downcast throughout, his fingers turning the Israeli medal in his hands. Slowly he looked up, and his eyes were wet, and his voice trembling. "A path without bloodshed, and hate. As the Prophet said, *'the ink of scholars'*, which I took to mean great thinkers, scientists and lawmakers, *'is more sacred than the blood of martyrs'*."

She stared at him for one second, chin resting on one fist, her head shaking in awe.

"That's beautiful, Jab. And all this time I thought you wanted to use it as some kind of… time-bomb, but you actually wanted to use it to bring about peace…"

He laughed sadly, and held up the medal in one hand. "The foolish dreams of a boy… but your grandfather, he needed no divine mandate, no holy path, to do something powerful, and good. That is the path of true righteousness…"

"My family have their own share of sins…" Jo said slowly. "My grandfather's just a little boy in this day and age, and grew up to be a saint in a time of sinners, but his ancestors, well…"

She lapsed into silence for a moment, before shrugging. "You remember yesterday, when I mentioned that I might have family travelling aboard *Titanic?* For years I'd wondered if there was a connection between me and them, but yesterday, when I had the chance to discover the truth, I couldn't…"

She saw him nod. At the time Jo had claimed that she was putting the bigger picture first, but the truth was that…

"I was afraid of what I would find. Because if I am related, or connected, to the Laroche family of Haiti, then it means I'm descended from *slave traders*..."

He looked at her slowly, intelligence in his eyes. Then, he slowly nodded, and she knew that he understood.

But then he held up the Israeli medal, and smiled.

"This is an award given to a man who fought heart and soul for humanity... and I see no sign of his granddaughter lacking in equal spirit."

Carefully, he handed the totem back over. "Do not hold yourself to blame for crimes in which you had no part, *capitaine*, or seek to atone for them through good deeds. Strive for right for right's sake alone. Your grandfather did, without any awareness of possible black stains upon his family honour, and I'm sure he'd be proud of what you are doing now."

"What we're both doing, Jab..." she leaned in close, unsure of herself, and took his hand and gave it a comforting squeeze. "As it says, *'righteous among the nations'*. And maybe we'll both find the absolution we're looking for."

He trembled for a second as if she had shouted at him, and then slowly closed his hand around hers, returning the gesture.

"Merci, mon Capitaine."

Joanna could forgive, but she would not forget, that this was a man who was once a boy, and who had dreamed, and though he had taken a life, he had unknowingly given her a purpose beyond clinging to the faded scraps of her family's heritage.

It was not love she was feeling, but she had to give him something back.

Adjusting her position, she looped her arms around his back and hugged him. Right now, between the two of them, cast adrift in time, the best she could offer was a gesture of comfort.

*

Captain Arthur Rostron quietly watched as the two people embraced awkwardly, and lifted his cap slightly. His lips began to move in quiet prayer, an old habit of his, and then he paused, for once at a loss and struggling to find the right words to say.

In his hand he held a long sheet of paper. Cottam, the wireless operator, had at length transcribed it from a lengthy transmission being put out from the distant *Olympic*. Rostron had expected it to be a repeat of the missive Captain Smith had prepared for the world, and to his surprise instead found it to be an account of recent events, attached to a transcription of a sermon prepared by a Father Thomas Byles. In plain English the priest spoke of the act of marriage, the connexion by which two incomplete halves become one. Byles then went on to elegantly present the unique situation in which the world now found itself as just such a marriage, an inseparable union made before the presence of an Almighty power.

"Our times are as two broken souls, stained with tragedy and sin, but not beyond redemption. In this most mysterious and divine of events, we are given a chance by which these two souls might come together as one, and begin to heal, to draw from the wisdom each has to offer, and build in completeness a house of perfect peace, in which we might all raise our children."

Rostron paused in his reading, and looked up, a slight grin tugging at his weathered features. He understood that his peers and crews had nicknamed him *The Electric Spark*, on grounds of the energy he could invest in those serving beneath him, but he felt that Father Byles' excellent words were to be the spark that might set the whole world ablaze with the light of illumination.

And in them he had found the prayer that he sought, watching over the two people still embracing on the deck of his ship.

Let those whom God have brought together, let no man put asunder.

*

"They that go down to the sea in ships, and do their business in great waters; these men see the works of the Lord, and his wonders in the deep..."

Thomas Byles' words softly drifted around *Oceanic*, amplified by the public address system. The ship was quiet, the public rooms becoming bubbles of low activity in which *Titanic*'s passengers were congregating and talking amongst themselves.

Adrienne McKinn found herself making 'the rounds', roving from one part of the ship to another and speaking a few words here and there, and gradually she found herself migrating towards the Promenade Deck.

"Addy..." someone said, and she found herself confronted with a middle-aged couple, recognising them as Colin and Sylvia Daniels, a British couple who had been on the ship celebrating their pearl anniversary. She had dined with them on the first night out of Southampton, and had found them altogether charming. Now, however, they were distraught. Colin was nervously trying to hide a shake in his hand, and Sylvia, eyes wet with tears behind her glasses, was trembling on the brink between despair and anger.

"Is this it?" she whispered hoarsely. "Are we trapped here now?"

Adrienne swallowed, and slowly nodded. "It seems that way, yes... I'm sorry." She looked to Sylvia's husband, struggling to not stare at his repressed tremors. "Colin, I don't know what we're going to do about your medication, but we will find a way to ensure you receive some kind of treatment..."

"I'm not worried about myself," he replied, with enough conviction in his voice that she almost believed him. "What about our two sons back home, and our daughter...? they'll be destroyed by this! What about them?"

She had nothing to say, not even empty platitudes. Instead she murmured another apology and took her leave, just as she had done at every other place she had called at since daybreak.

She felt numb, like when as a teenager she had fallen off a horse and been temporarily paralysed. That time she had made a full recovery. Now, she felt like a deep crack had formed right through her very being.

A change had come over the ship as well. The loss of the *Liberty Bell*, and the second sinking of *Titanic*, seemed to have touched a raw nerve in many of her contemporary passengers, the realisation that they could now never go home. The majority had retreated to their cabins in an attempt to isolate their pain, and the remainder were draining the ship's stocks of alcohol. A few, whose grief must have been too great to endure, had simply disappeared. Lloyd Waters had posted extra lookouts to keep an eye for jumpers, but a few had simply climbed over their balcony railings and let go...

Pausing, she glanced over her shoulder, back towards the Daniels couple, isolated in grief. Sylvia was leaning into Colin's chest, and his arms were wrapped shakily around her, his face pressed into her hair. They were the very image of inconsolable grief; Adrienne understood that Colin suffered from Parkinson's Disease, and in lieu of a cure required regular doses of dopamine agonists to keep his condition manageable. Cut off forever from their families, however, sure in the knowledge that the only quantity left of Colin's medication in the whole world was that which they had brought aboard *Oceanic* with them, would they too simply choose to 'disembark', mid-ocean?

The thought caused her to shiver; but fearful of intruding on their already delicate emotions, she forced herself to walk away, focusing on simply keeping her feet moving. Why was she walking in orbits of the ship? Where was her old spark, the vivacity that had brought Project 401 into being? She wasn't sure, but now there was a deep sense of weight in her stomach, a black mass that she had hoped to mitigate simply by speaking to people.

But no, their fears and tears had only deepened her own sense of guilt...

"It's not your fault..." someone cut in as she stalked through the Palm Court, and she looked down to the next level of the Grand Staircase. It was Lloyd Waters, smiling up at her, sadly but knowingly. "You shouldn't blame yourself for this."

He climbed the stairs to her level, and beckoned for her to walk with him through the Palm Court, weaving among the various eateries. They found a quiet spot around an empty table in the *Tentacolino*, an Italian-themed seafood restaurant, and he held out a seat for her.

"It is my fault," she said softly as she sat herself down. The eyes of a cartoon octopus seemed to stare accusingly from the face of the menu, and she reached out to turn it face-down on the table. "The whole of Project 401 was my idea, my brainchild. If I hadn't tried to make the Centennial of *Titanic*'s sinking into a spectacle, none of this would have happened..."

She paused and laughed bitterly. "Shit, Lloyd, I was part of the Congressional Group that got Britain involved in the damn Trident Life Extension program! If it wasn't for my contributions to that end, the fucking sub wouldn't have been anywhere near the fleet... no *Viking* means no missile launch, and we'd have been able to go home without any complications!"

"Yes, I'll grant you that much," he acquiesced, nodding his head sagely. "But look at it this way. You had nothing to do with events surrounding the *Liberty Bell*... that time machine would most likely have gone off with or without Project 401's involvement, except that it would have probably been on the open ocean, with no other ships nearby. Think what it would mean for *Titanic*'s passengers if we and *Rescue* and yes, even *Viking*, were not there to save them."

She looked slowly towards him, feeling the weight in her stomach momentarily lighten as he continued to expand on his ideas.

"Consider, Adrienne, that without you, they would have died again."

"How do you do that, Lloyd; turn a double-negative into a victory?"

"Perspective, Addy," he laughed, wearily sliding off his peaked cap and resting it on the table. "It's all a matter of perspective."

Returning the laugh softly, Adrienne turned to gaze off through the windows, out onto the open sea.

"What are we doing here, Lloyd?" she mused, one hand supporting her chin. "It's 1912, and right now my grandparents are still living in Poland."

"You're Polish?" he asked in surprise.

"My maiden name is Jablonsky," she replied, voice distant. "My grandparents came from a little town called Brony, about seventy miles west of Warsaw; they immigrated to America in 1921, and my father was born ten years later, their youngest child. He drove trains on the Butte, Anaconda & Pacific Railroad from the day he was old enough to work right until he retired, in the same year I started my law practice and met my husband..."

She turned to face him, a self-deprecating grin on her face.

"Believe it or not, my ancestors came over on 'Old Reliable' *Olympic*, Cherbourg to New York... I discovered that after I founded Project 401. Weird how these things work out, huh?"

"Not at all," he said gently. "Do you want to hear another coincidence? My own father was a train-driver. When I was a boy growing up, I used to go out behind our house in Bronwydd Arms to watch him take the milk train past every week… and right now he's not even a gleam in my granddad's lecherous old eye."

"That's cute…" she smiled, before frowning. "I wonder if either of them will ever be born now, our fathers… is it murder if the changes we cause lead to people not coming into being, people who otherwise might have had full and rich lives?"

"If that's the case then every decision we've ever made was a murder," he replied. "We're always reshaping the future, every second of every day. It's always about perspective." His voice grew solemn. "But right now we've got several thousand other people to worry for as well. The decisions we make in the next few days are going to define our relationship with this era. And that's what I need from you now, to chart the course we must follow after we reach New York."

"So we're heading for NYC?" she said, feeling a curious eyebrow perk.

"Yes," he nodded. "We don't have the supplies to stay at sea much more than a week, not with the number of souls onboard. And since we're no longer bound by the need to shepherd *Titanic* to safety, the other captains and I have decided to make for America. Dealing with one single nation, rather than European politics, seemed the wisest choice."

He reached over to gingerly rest his hand over hers, and she straightened up. "You're the best person to hand for political advice, Addy. What's going to happen to our passengers if we're even allowed past customs and immigration? Ellis Island might object to several thousand persons of unknown background and medical history disembarking onto Manhattan."

She sat in silence for several moments, and then began to tick off points on her fingers, building in speed and conviction as she gathered momentum.

"We'd need assurance of their rights, and a guarantee that they would not receive harassment or persecution for acting contrary to social mores, perhaps securing the ships as a sanctuary for 2012 law. Freedom of travel for those who want to return to their parent nations is essential, as is some form of financial support until they can find their feet. And for those who want to stay in America, some process of naturalisation and/or citizenship."

"Now that's the Adrienne McKinn I know," he laughed, at which point she turned to face him, eyes narrowed and mouth smirking. "You're a leader, Addy, and the passengers of this ship are your people. Be the rock they need right now."

"Don't lay it all on me, Lloyd," she answered teasingly. "You've got a part to play here too; in fact you're going to provide the bartering chip we need to finance all this…"

"Oh really?" he said, rapping his knuckles on the table. "Are we thinking the same thing?"

"I'm pretty sure we are," she grinned, before standing to look around them. "Come on, we're going to need contemporary legal counsel, and words with Bruce Ismay and *Titanic*'s officers. Access to both of the helicopters would be useful too, if they've got enough fuel left for what I have in mind. And I'm going to need an aide…"

"What are you planning, Addy?"

"To put on a show; a demonstration of what we can offer to the twentieth century, in return for protection and respect."

With that in mind, the two of strode out of the Palm Court, Adrienne's lingering guilt balanced with a sudden renewal of purpose.

*

"The last survivors from *Titanic* have been brought aboard…" report a quartermaster to *Olympic*'s bridge, and Herbert Haddock allowed himself a moment's pause for thought.

"Do we have a final head-count?" he asked.

"Yes sir. Before *Titanic* struck *Viking*, we believe there were about three-hundred and seventy souls aboard her. Of those, thirty are unaccounted for."

"And from *Viking*, *Rescue* and *Californian?*"

"*Oceanic* says she's picked up just over a hundred and twenty survivors from the three ships, with about a hundred more dead or… missing."

Haddock's shoulders twitched. The fact that the submarine and the salvage ship had been thrown out of time would make it impossible to establish a final death toll.

"Very well," he nodded, and paced out onto the bridge wing.

Lieutenant Ramirez and her colleagues Jenkins and Orion awaited him, a piece of card and a pen in the female aviator's hand.

"We have an approximate tally..." he said after a heavy pause. "Between all our losses, including those who I understand have taken their own lives on *Oceanic* and the *Anatoly Sagalevich*, an approximate one hundred and ninety people have either perished or been 'lost'."

"Thank you, Captain," she replied, scribbling the figure on the card before securing it to the face of the wreath that she had brought aboard from the wreck of Flight 401. Then she paused and regarded it for a moment, before nodding.

"We're ready."

"Three blasts on the whistle," Haddock called towards the bridge. "Make sure we have the fullest attention of the fleet. Then sound eight bells."

Passengers were already gathering on deck, and as *Olympic* roared out to the other ships an abrupt silence fell. Then her bell rang out in the traditional signal marking the commission to the deep of lives whose watches were at an end.

As the last peal died away, the ship's string company began to softly play a hymn, the slow, melancholy notes crisp and clear in the cold air.

"Eternal Father, strong to save, whose arm hath bound the restless wave..." someone began to sing in time to the music, and other voices took up the hymn.

"It is with great respect and reverence," Ramirez began to read aloud, "that we mark the sinking of the RMS *Titanic* on April 16th 1912, and remember the 190 souls who perished during these fateful few days. Presented in proxy of the International Ice Patrol and the United States Coast Guard by the company of the RMS *Olympic*, Project 401, the Titanic Centennial Expedition, and the Time Fleet."

Haddock looked along *Olympic*'s deck, seeing passengers clustered to the rails on the boat deck and promenades, even clustering in the well deck, all peering towards his small group on the bridge wing, and the majority of them singing.

"Most Holy Spirit! Who didst brood,
Upon the Chaos Dark and Rude,
And bid its angry tumult cease,
And give, for wild confusion, peace;
Oh, hear us when we cry to Thee,
For those in peril on the sea…"

The impromptu choir gradually faded away with polite applause as Ramirez, Jenkins and Orion stepped in solemn march to the rail, and between them raised the wreath before dropping it into the sea and saluting crisply. It was closure for them, he hoped, to have completed the mission they had embarked on at the start of all this.

And now, a whole new book lay ahead of them, pages waiting to be filled with history.

Oh, hear us when we cry to Thee, for those lost in eternity… Haddock thought to himself, wondering what new hymns and prayers would be written in light of the past few days' revelations, before standing tall and taking his place on the bridge.

"Half speed ahead," he called out to the officers on the engine telegraphs. "Lay in course for New York City."

*

Milton Long felt a distant rumble underfoot as *Oceanic*'s engines turned over. Around him, crystal and cut glass began to tinkle in their stands as the ship got underway.

"Here we go again," he muttered aloud. "Heaven knows where…"

"I'll give thee a wind, and I another," replied Lawrence Beesley absently, the bookish science teacher examining a polished smoking pipe, into which was carved the White Star pennant. *"I myself have all the other."*

"More Shakespeare?" Milton asked, and Lawrence nodded in confirmation.

"*Macbeth*, the Weird Sisters."

"No more weird than our current circumstances…"

The two of them were in Woolworths, a small retail arcade that adjoined the Belgrave Square Lobby on Deck 3. A helpful plaque informed them that it was named in honour of the thriving British shopping chain, whose flagship store opened on Liverpool's Church Street in 1909. With nothing much to do, the two of them were ambling in and out of the various boutiques, glancing at all manners of fineries and fripperies; china, cutlery, books, perfume, jewellery and *objets d'art*. Beesley had taken the time to procure himself a packet of tobacco, and was now enquiring about the price of the pipe and whether or not he could purchase it using the cards issued at boarding. He seemed in good cheer, and Milton felt a deep sense of gratitude to the man for having sought out the Master-of-Arms and helped secure his release, after that show on the Grand Staircase.

But for his part, Milt himself was in a quiet funk, nursing both a hangover and a terrible sense of having made a fool of himself last night. By all rights he should have felt relieved, as after all his wish had been granted; the time-travellers were now bound to remain in this time, providing the fullest of their knowledge in service of history. Yet he feared the price paid was terrible, and was possessed of a paranoid concern that his actions last night had contributed in bringing affairs to their bloody head.

Caught up in such mental convolutions, he suddenly paused, sighting a familiar pair of figures. Adjacent to the arcade named Woolworths was a long gallery which had been decked out as a kind of exhibition space. Framed photographs lined the walls, almost all of them sepia-toned. A sign proclaimed them to be *'Faces of Titanic'*.

"Lawrence," he called to his escort. "I'll just be in the next room. Please excuse me for a moment."

The two figures were Janice and Terri Patton, the nurse still in her green 'scrubs' and her wife holding one of the tiny future cameras. She was snapping pictures of a third person standing before the wall, a young woman dressed in what was surely 2012 attire; a scandalously-cut skirt that stopped just above the knee, paired with a tailored blouse and jacket. Somewhat curious, and in search of a diversion that might distract from the gnawing in his gut, Milt approached them in what he hoped was a nonchalant manner. Not nonchalant enough, however, for as he drew near

Terri turned and fixed him with a stare so singular and intense that he suspected it was trademarked in her name.

"Hello again, Mr Long," she said coolly. "What brings you down here?"

"My feet, and nothing else," he answered, managing to effect a degree of glibness. "I heard of your heroic exploits last night. Might I ask of Captain Smith's condition?"

"He's weak, but stable," she acquiesced. "I can't speak for his long-term health, but he should be released from hospital before we make landfall."

"So, do I take it that you know whence we are bound?"

"New York, but there's going to be an announcement soon, so it's hardly a secret."

"Ah… might I ask what is going on?"

"Jan's just sourcing inspiration for her next collection of pictures," the mulatto nurse replied, a smile of affection around her lips. "She's determined to have painted something before we get back to port."

She spoke with an easy tone, and yet Milt could not help but notice a tremor in her shoulders, and a catch in her voice that spoke of deep unease.

"Back to the good ol' US-of-A," she added, with such sudden bitterness that the very air seemed to sour. "Back to where we started."

Milton winced. All at once he felt his turbulent thoughts resurface, as though they were *Viking*'s malignant ghost returning from the depths, and his heart went out to their plight, trapped in an unfamiliar and unwelcoming time, returned to square one of a long struggle to see their love affirmed in law and society.

"Do you have any documentation?" he asked, his hesitation drawing a curious glance. "Something that confirms your state of marriage, bearing the seal of the Commonwealth of Massachusetts?"

"We've got scans of the Marriage License, and the Certificate of Marriage," she replied at last, her tone bordering on hostility. "We made sure we travelled with duplicates of both. What's it to you?"

"You said you were wed in Springfield," Milt swallowed. "You may recall that I described my father, Charles Long, as being a respected man there; he was formerly the city mayor, and is currently the judge of Hampden County's Probate Court..."

"Hampden Probate and Family Court is where we applied for our Marriage License..." she replied guardedly. "Are you offering your father's services to... legitimise our marriage?"

"I would have to speak with him in person, but it is entirely possible that he would be willing to adjudicate on the matter, or at the very least bring your case before the relevant authorities," he said, shrugging. "I studied law at Harvard and Columbia, but in truth was somewhat of a slacker. I did not even complete my course at Columbia... yet I am quite certain that wheels might be set in motion to see your union acknowledged – which of course would set legal precedent for future cases."

"It would be a start," she mused, one finger tracing her lower lip in thought, and at last she offered him a guarded smile. "Perhaps we'll take you up on that offer."

"I'm glad to be of service," he replied, bowing slightly at the waist, and it was at this point that Janice rejoined them, an almost manic energy possessing her as Milt repeated his proposal.

"That's fantastic, amazing!" she cried out, and then suddenly drew forward the young woman she had been photographing. "I completely forgot, introductions; Milton Long, Violet Jessop. Violet Jessop, Milton Long."

"It's, it's a pleasure..." the woman replied. She was perhaps a few years younger than Milt, and in truth, quite winsome when properly seen in her attire. Milton guessed at her being another 'young professional' from somewhere uphill in the time stream.

"The pleasure is all mine Miss Jessop," he replied, tipping his head. "Might I ask what your work involves?"

"Violet's a writer," Terri answered, before the woman in question could open her mouth. "She wrote one of history's most respected accounts of the *Titanic*."

"A historian?" he said, at this point finding little surprise in anything events threw at him. "That is most impressive."

The girl blushed, something that he found quite charming, and finding it strangely hard to keep his eyes upon her he glanced back at the Pattons, whose faces had suddenly acquired the most devious of grins, every inch two cats sharing a particularly plump canary.

Oh no... he realised, seconds before they took their leave.

"Well, we've got things to discuss, really should be going," Janice said briskly. "After all, Terri needs to get back to the hospital and I'm going to try and paint *Olympic* from life. Mr Long, would you be a gentleman and escort Violet back to her cabin?"

"I... of course, but... what exactly is happening here?" Milt stammered, his sense of decorum assaulted by this turn of events. They did not deign him an answer however, disappearing off forward in a cloud of excited whispers.

"That was unexpected, did you see them both blushing?"

"I know! Quick thinking Terri!"

Feeling uncomfortably hot under the collar, Milton turned his attention back to the companion now foisted upon him.

"Ah, well, Miss Jessop, where might we be heading? Up to the cabins I presume?"

"No..." she replied quietly, head bowed. "Ah, I'm berthed below-decks, with the crew..."

"But surely, as a passenger, a respected author..." he paused, realising something was not right here; and looking up he caught sight of Violet's face... among the many *'Faces of Titanic'*.

"Oh..." he said. "Then you are not a... a time traveller."

"No sir, just a stewardess," she tugged at the hem of her skirt. "Or at least I was... according to the chief steward, our employment technically ended the moment *Titanic* sank. I've been assisting *Oceanic*'s crew, but they insisted I take a few hours to enjoy myself, even leant me these clothes. Except now I've found myself at somewhat of a loose end."

"Well, I can sympathise with that," he managed, suddenly feeling rather awkward, his physical attraction to her at immediate odds with their opposing social standing. "And ah, what was that about your being an author?"

"Oh, my memoirs..." she suddenly smiled, producing from her handbag a slim volume. She handed it over to him, and he glanced at the title: '*Titanic Survivor, The Memoirs of Violet Jessop*'. "Apparently I had these written down when I was an old biddy. Lots of people on the ship tell me they've read them, including Lady McKinn."

"The formidable 'First Lady' of *Oceanic*?" Milton said, feeling an eyebrow flex. "I've heard much about her, but as of yet nothing certain..."

"Oh, she's ever so kindly," Violet beamed. "She asked me to briefly sit with herself and several ladies from First Class, and said I was her inspiration."

That of course prompted further questions, and Milt soon found himself drawn into discussion.

*

Lawrence Beesley saw all of it. Having made a remarkable discovery in the ship's bookstore, he had been hotfooting his way towards the gallery, aiming to share his find with Milton, when he suddenly found himself accosted by two young women and dragged into the lee of a doorway.

"Sorry, sorry," they immediately apologised, holding fingers to lips and '*shushing*' him. "But we didn't want *them* to be interrupted."

They pointed, and discretely Lawrence looked around the corner of the door and saw Milt trying to make conversation with a third young woman. There was a definite hint of bashful awkwardness in the air, and having seen similar mannerisms on countless young students he could not help but smile.

Journeys end in lovers meeting, he thought to himself. *Twelfth Night, Act II, Scene III.*

"Terri, Janice, what's going on?" another voice interrupted his musing, and turning, Lawrence and his captors paid witness to an elegant woman approaching them, accompanied by someone who could only be *Oceanic*'s Captain Waters, attired as he was in full uniform. "Have any of you seen Violet Jessop, because I need an assistant and thought she could-"

"Hush!" Lawrence's abductors hissed. "We just managed to set her up on a date!"

"You did what?" the woman grinned widely, ducking in beside Lawrence to get a better view.

"There you go, Addy," chuckled the captain. "You're not the only one meddling in 'inter-temporal relations'…"

"Quiet, Lloyd… and oh wow, nicely done girls. Who's the tall, dark and handsome stranger she's caught the eye of?"

"Milton Long," came a quick reply. "Student of law and gentleman-at-leisure."

"Long? As in Jack Thayer's friend?" pressed the woman named 'Addy', who Lawrence suddenly suspected was the Adrienne McKinn of whom so much had been spoken this past day. "And you say he's a lawyer; is he any good?"

"Claims not to be, but his daddy is a judge."

"Reaaaallly," McKinn drawled, her smile turning predatory. "Oh, this is perfect!" Then, finally noticing Lawrence, she turned and brushed back her hair, offering a hand in greeting. "Sorry for pressing in against you like that, I'm Adrienne McKinn. To whom do I have the pleasure?"

"Lawrence Beesley," he answered, taking her hand and finding himself actually having to incline his head to speak to her, she being rather tall for a woman. He saw her eyes light up in recognition of his name, and pre-empting her he held up the remarkable book he had discovered in one of the shops. "Author of *'The Loss of the S.S. Titanic'*…"

"First Jack Thayer, then Helen Candee and Violet Jessop, now Lawrence Beesley," Captain Waters marvelled. "All you need now is Charles Lightoller and Archibald Gracie, and you'll have completed the set of famous survivors who wrote up their experiences!"

"Mr Beesley," Lady McKinn leaned in closer. "I have urgent need of articulate individuals with experience of present-day affairs. Might I ask of your help?"

"I'd be glad to," he agreed readily, and she brought her hands together in delight, rubbing them as if ready to get down to business.

"Wonderful, and now to recruit our next two colleagues." Striding forward past Lawrence, she proceeded into the gallery, calling out in greeting as she did. "Violet, there you are! I wanted to ask for your help, if you're not too busy that is. And who is this…?"

"She's quite the tempest," Lawrence marvelled aloud, prompting a laugh from Captain Waters.

"You have no idea, and it's about to be turned loose on the establishment of 1912… hopefully we'll all be the better for it."

*

The sun was melting into the horizon as Jack leaned on *Oceanic*'s rail and breathed deeply of the cool air. Despite the circumstances, he felt strangely at peace, shutting out the people around him and focusing on the surface of the sea, shimmering with blue and silver as the sun reached the zenith of its arc.

"Jack?"

He turned and smiled. "Mother."

Marian Thayer approached and adjusted her son's jacket. "Stand up straight, Jack. It doesn't become a hero of the *Titanic* to slouch."

He smiled and shook his head wordlessly, before her expression became inquisitive. "What of young Miss Paik? Where is she?"

"In the ship's hospital…" Jack replied, eyes focusing on some point far beyond his mother's shoulder. "She was in a pretty bad way when we finally got her onto a proper boat."

"I see…"

"So, mother…" he said, his eyes coming down to meet hers. "What was so important that you ventured alone among the barbarians to find me?"

Looking not in the least perturbed, Marian reached into some hidden compartment amongst the folds of her dress and produced a thin book, which she pushed into his hands.

"That I might beg your indulgence Jack, and ask that you consider this intriguing text."

Jack examined the book, in truth little bigger than a large pamphlet, and he recognised it straight away as the book that Pip had tried to present to him in *Oceanic*'s library only yesterday.

"*The Sinking of the SS Titanic,*" he read aloud, "By John B Thayer Jr".

"It was one of the few first-hand accounts these people possessed from the *Titanic*'s sinking. Mrs McKinn informed me of its existence, and I located this copy in the ship's library," she said slowly, as if confessing to some horrible crime. "I smuggled it out in the folds of my dress."

"Have you read it?" he asked, eyes narrowing.

"Not a word. Among our family, it is to your eyes alone that your other self's most intimate thoughts should be first revealed."

Eyeing her warily Jack rested his weight back on the rail and turned to the preface, cleared his throat and began to read.

"*This account of the sinking of the S.S. 'Titanic' has been written primarily as a family record for the information of my...*" his voice caught and he paused for a second before he continued, "*...of my children and perhaps their children in memory of my Father, John Borland Thayer, the third of that name, who lost his life in the disaster...*"

A sharp motion to his left caught his eye, and he turned to see Mother clasping her hands to her mouth in shock. And approaching her from behind was his father. As John Thayer stepped up, Marian took her husband's arm and held it tightly.

Looking back to the book cradled in his hands, Jack's eyes fell to the next paragraph...

Just as no two happenings in the stream of space time are identical...' it read, and he grinned ruefully at the appropriate turn of phrase. As motionless as a pillar of salt he read on, except for where his hand moved to turn the pages, trying to envision the man who had penned these words. Quickly he reached the final line of the preface, and looking up gazed across a sparkling sea to *Olympic*'s familiar silhouette, so similar to her sister *Titanic*. Overhead, one of the two helicopters was hovering in a low orbit over what remained of the fleet, presumably recording the image for posterity.

The breeze began to flick at the pages in his hands, as if the wash from the helicopter was reaching out to turn them.

"*These were ordinary days,*" he continued slowly, reciting his own future words. "*And into them had crept only gradually the telephone, the talking machine, the automobile. The airplane due to have so soon such a stimulating yet devastating effect on civilization, was only a few years old, and the radio as known today, was still in the scientific laboratory..."*

He looked up to see the helicopter playing in the coils of smoke rising from *Olympic*'s funnels, keeping its height above that of the liner's wireless masts. Then, dragging the words up from a great depth within him, he managed to speak;

"This account was written in nineteen-forty, only twenty-eight years hence. But this man, this *me*, he sounds so bitter."

"He grew up in a world of constant upheaval, Jack," a familiar female voice intruded, gently cutting his thoughts short. "He was obviously going to look back on life before *Titanic* with nostalgia..."

Jack turned, almost fearful of what he would find. Philippa Paik, a little pale but otherwise seeming in the fullest flush of health, was standing only a few feet away, dressed in a dry change of clothes but with the ever-present baseball cap from *Rescue* still proudly worn on her head. Jack feebly waved 'hello' with the book, and then his idling thoughts snatched up their last thread.

"How did he... what happened to him, to me..."

Pip's mouth clenched as if she was trying to hold back a wave of nausea, and only after a lengthy pause did she speak.

"He had a son named Edward, who was killed in the Second World War. Your future self, he... he took it badly. His body was found in a car, with his wrists cut, in September of 1945."

"That is my fate?" he spoke in sudden horror. "My father dead, a future son and family lost, my life ultimately amounting to a death by *suicide*, by self-murder?"

"Nonsense!" a new voice interjected, and John Borland Thayer Senior put his best foot forward, his free arm coming to rest on his son's shoulder. "Jack Thayer is a young man of boundless curiosity and optimism, a man whose future is one of infinite potential and possibility, ungoverned by any will but his own."

Obviously so, since he died by his own hand, Jack thought bitterly, shaking himself free from his father's grasp and turning towards Pip.

"Philippa, you tried to show this same book to me in the library last night. Why? What did you hope to accomplish from this, if not to taunt me with a destiny already written?"

"To show you that you have a choice…" she responded. "You are not that man!"

As Jack struggled to control his breathing, blood threatening to pound in his ears, he looked back at the book in his hands. His thumb still marked the prefix page, and his eyes again lighted on the words *just as no two happenings in the stream of space time are identical*.

He flexed the bound pages, considered the name on the cover, and then, with an easy flick of the wrist, tossed the book overboard.

"What!?" Pip flailed over the rail fruitlessly as the account fluttered down and splashed into the choppy sea, a tiny speck in the blue. For a second it bobbed on the surface like a life-raft, and then sank quickly, the cream-white cover briefly visible beneath the surface, before it vanished into *Oceanic*'s wash.

"Why did you do that!?" she exclaimed, gesturing in shock and disbelief. "That might have been the only print copy left in the whole world!"

The sight of her indignation was enough to make Jack laugh, and he felt a great sense of release, the sudden weight on his shoulders falling away.

"Because it's just a work of fiction now!" he said, feeling like he could bound easily up to *Oceanic*'s topmost deck with just a single step. "That man saw the world change around him and could only wish for how things could go back to the way they were…"

He spun on his heel, taking in the ships and people in a giddy whirl. "But all I can see is a future of endless possibility!"

Halting, he pointed towards the helicopter now wheeling overhead. "I could become a pilot, or a motion-picture director, or a sportsman."

Then he turned to his parents, holding each other with faint smiles gracing their faces. "I could run, run for political office, or run naked through the streets praising all Creation."

His gaze whipped back to Pip, and he took in all of her, the petite frame that concealed such strength of character, the soft yet winningly boyish face, and those bright, brilliant, inquisitive eyes.

"Or I could get married, to whomever I choose."

Carried away on the sudden euphoria, he ducked in and planted a quick, flighty kiss on her lips. Then, bouncing away with the springy step of a vaudeville performer, Jack returned to the railing.

"Everything is possible!" he declared, arms spread... at which point he abruptly processed her lingering taste on his lips, and he realised what he had done. *Oh good Lord!*

Suddenly cold, and once again dreading what he would find, he turned back to the three other people, holding onto the railing behind him as if letting go would cause him to fall into the sea, weighed down with mortification. His father's hand was raised to his face with embarrassment, and his mother's eyes were narrowed, though a glint of amusement shone in them. Philippa Paik, on the other hand was blushing, a lone finger tracing over her lips as if trying by touch to determine what had just happened.

"I... oh my goodness," he stammered. "Miss Paik, please accept my fullest apolo-"

Pip sprang forward and grabbed the sides of his face with both hands, pulling him down for a second kiss.

ACT FIVE

FINISHED WITH ENGINES

CHAPTER THIRTY TWO

Washington DC seemed tense, and even a heavy fall of rain the night before had not washed away the feeling of oppressive weight now bearing down over the city.

Theodore Roosevelt, gazing from the grounds of the White House, to which he had been summoned by President Taft, likened the atmosphere to the forced calm just before battle, and instinctively reached for his (absent) sword and revolver; he could feel the barely-contained excitement of a coming fight rising inside him. He heard a horse rear out on Pennsylvania Avenue, whinnying like its rider was driving it towards enemy lines, and Roosevelt allowed that tempered fighting instinct to express itself in a smile; all that was missing was the thundering drumbeats of artillery.

One way or another, I was going into a brawl this year, he thought to himself, peering towards the great spire of the Washington Monument. *Mounting a stand for the sake of this Union, but now I find myself against a wholly different adversary than backsliding Republicans, or even the Democrats...*

For months now, Roosevelt had felt himself increasingly distanced from the politics of the incumbent President Taft, his former friend and associate. Both had campaigned as Republicans, but now Taft appeared to be backsliding on the policies Roosevelt himself had set as precedent during his own administration. Thus, despite having pledged to the party to not run for a third term, 'Teddy' found himself increasingly convinced that something had to be done.

Others might accuse him of petty spite, as he was sure they would, but he felt a moral imperative at work; he *had* to take action, even if it was just a token opposition in the face of Taft's bid for re-election. That obligation had driven him to cautiously feel out for supporting progressive-thinkers, and to start training his body back into some semblance of the fighting fitness he had possessed before sloth and politics had fattened him. Now he felt as strong as a bull moose, and ready to sound the charge.

But then everything had changed, and he suddenly felt himself to be conflicted. After months of preparation, the past week had thrown all plans and expectations to the winds.

Teddy Roosevelt was not given to superstition or fancy, too pragmatic a man was he, but word was spreading of what had transpired out at sea, and it harkened to a doom-prophecy as surely as the call to Caesar to beware the Ides of March. Word had come that his plan of action, to campaign as representative of a new 'Progressive Party', was fated to split the right-wing vote, leading to a Democrat assuming the Presidency. That alone was worrying, but most alarming was the source of this ill news.

Time travel. Incredible ships and technologies, and several thousand people displaced from out of time to this present age.

He would have laughed it off, and then gotten angry if the story persisted, had not hard evidence been presented to him. Six or so days ago, something had fallen with tremendous force from the skies in Berlin, killing a few innocents boating on the Wannsee lakes. At about the same time, an incredible fleet had appeared in the North Atlantic, putting out the most amazing messages, and claiming responsibility for averting a second attack that would have eradicated the Imperial German capital.

All this because the Titanic apparently sank, or would have sunk, with great loss of life... but thank Heavens that Archie Butt is, from what fractured accounts we have, alive and well...

The relief at his friend's survival was not enough to stave off his concerns, however. That mysterious fleet was now hove to several miles off of New York, just outside American territorial waters and sitting in silence. He understood that Taft had sent the USS *Chester* and several other warships to stand by in the event these vessels came any closer to the Eastern Seaboard, but so far the fleet had made no attempt to draw closer or even communicate, flying flags of quarantine and ignoring all attempts at communication via Morse lamp or wireless.

So Washington DC brooded, awaiting the inevitable spark that would set off this powder-keg. Roosevelt himself was but one of many figures summoned at the President's pleasure to offer counsel on the situation, among them another of his friends, the Englishman James Bryce, His Majesty's Ambassador to the United States, as well as Johann Heinrich von Bernstorff, plenipotentiary representative of Kaiser Wilhelm.

American politicians were much in evidence too, particularly Senator Smith of Michigan. Like Teddy himself, Smith was an ardent trust-buster, and had seen in the rumoured sinking of the *Titanic* a chance to put the thumbscrews to the sprawling octopus controlled by arch-monopolist JP Morgan. Smith had found his attempts to force an immediate enquiry foxed, however, both by the mysterious fleet's hesitance to enter US territorial waters, and by Ambassador Bryce, who was advocating a less reactionary course of action, almost surely in support of Britain's interests. For all his sympathy to Smith's cause, Roosevelt did feel Bryce's advice of caution to be sound. After all, events at sea had evidently transcended a mere shipwreck, and taken on the semblance of an international crisis, hence the rogue's gallery of 'advisors' that had been 'invited' to the White House.

Speak of the Devil, here comes one now... he thought as he spotted a tall, upright figure emerging from the Executive Wing of the Presidential Mansion.

Woodrow Wilson, the Democratic governor of New Jersey, resembled in Roosevelt's eyes nothing so much as an autocratic schoolmaster, lacking only the mortarboard necessary to complete the image. Normally carrying himself with an aloof confidence that affronted Roosevelt's gutsier approach to life, the man now seemed shaken, one hand dabbing lightly at his brow with a handkerchief. He appeared to be taking the air to steady himself, and Roosevelt, feeling an unanticipated surge of alarm, found himself briskly approaching what under other circumstances might have been his sworn nemesis.

"Governor, are you quite alright, sah?" he said by way of greeting, keeping his hands firmly clasped behind his back.

Wilson straightened up, as if seeing Roosevelt for the first time, a touch of colour returning to his face as he visibly struggled to maintain composure.

"Theodore… yes sir, fine, perfectly fine."

The two men exchanged a nod of curt understanding, and after a held moment, Wilson seemed to wilt slightly, an impression strengthened by his great height and top hat.

"I presume, then," he said, "that the President has confided in you as well."

"If by which you mean the supposed results of the coming election, then yes sah, he has…" Roosevelt replied, pushing his hands into his jacket pockets, elbows akimbo. "My congratulations, Mr President-Elect… or should I say President-Prophet?"

A look of shock appeared on Wilson's face, and Roosevelt had to resist the urge to laugh while the other man struggled to regain his bearing.

"Please do not joke so; I have won no election, and doubt the American body politic will accept a declaration of how they 'would have' voted… this is something beyond the pale of my expectations."

"Mine too, sah. Question is, what do we do about 'em, these time-travellers?"

"I should think that were obvious. Arrest them all on grounds of sedition, which is mild compared to what others might do. Ambassador von Bernstorff is with the President right now, presenting a direct petition from the Kaiser that all these people be turned over to Berlin for charges of murder and assault."

"Indeed!" Roosevelt laughed again, a single sardonic bark. "Might I imagine that the good Ambassador finds himself at odds with his orders?"

Wilson begrudged him a thin-lipped smile, and Roosevelt held back another chortle. It was no secret that the dapper von Bernstorff, so enamoured of Anglo-German friendship, was often at loggerheads with his feckless monarch. Until recently such strife had been touched with a degree of political comedy… but no longer, not amidst the prophecies being whispered in highest echelons.

A war was foretold, a great and terrible war that would make chuck steak of the very flower of European and American manhood; hence the calls from countless men of state that affairs surrounding the 'convergence' or 'time wreck' be approached with delicacy. The fact that Roosevelt was among these advocates of diplomacy had done much to cool the hotheads; the realisation that not even the brash and adventurous 'TR' was so crazed with excitement as to charge ahead into this ice field had sloshed considerable water upon the fires of the reactionaries.

All of these thoughts flitted briskly through Teddy's mind. Slowly, he turned his attention back to the Washington monument.

"Things are never so simple, Governor Wilson…" he voiced. "And what example of human progress would America be were we to incarcerate or turn away these people, assuming they wish to become citizens, or already possess citizenship from some future time? We have no law or procedure to deal with this situation, and until they deign to communicate with us, no means of asking what they desire of us."

"Not so, Theodore," Wilson smirked, as if possessing a winning hand. "Word has just come in; they are on their way here right now."

"What!? Where, when, how?" Roosevelt's self-composure kept him from snapping his head about like a startled scout, but his words were still laced with interrogative demand.

Wilson laughed politely, like an undertaker confiding some private joke to a corpse. "A cable arrived from New York at the same time as the German Ambassador presented Kaiser Wilhelm's petition. Two flying machines have taken off from the decks of the mysterious ships, and were last seen flying south along the coast of New Jersey. We presume they are travelling to Washington right now."

Roosevelt's mind reeled. Flying machines were one of the rumoured technological miracles suddenly bequeathed into 1912, but he had only faintly grabbed at the potential. What if these travellers had weapons that could be fired from the air onto cities below? In such an event, no gun could be elevated high enough to strike back…

…*no, that is panic speaking, not the man who led the Rough Riders up San Juan Hill. Think Teddy, think…*

"Very well, then!" he straightened up and exhaled. "Let us go, Governor!"

He began to stride forward, as purposeful as he had ever been. Wilson dallied for a moment and then hurried after him.

"Go where?"

"To the future, my dear sah!" Roosevelt barked, before moderating his tone, seeing naught but perplexed confusion decorating Wilson's face. "To the Mall, sah! If they have flying machines then it stands to reason that they will need open space in which to land, and the Mall is the most perfect spot in Washington 'pon which to do so! Onward sah, onward!"

*

It was not so simple as all that, of course. President Taft was the one in charge, and it was at his discretion that Roosevelt and Wilson were allowed to join a train of carriages summoned at all speed to carry the Presidential entourage to the Mall. Within minutes, armed soldiers of the National Guard had also descended upon the city to guard the streets, supported by the police.

As the caravan of carriages exited the gates of the White House, a new sound began to rise over the clatter of wheels and hooves, a rhythmic, mechanical pulsing that emanated from somewhere over their heads and out of sight. Hearing it, Roosevelt felt a gleeful certain touch of frontier spirit and jumped to the reins, pushing the poor coachman aside and whipping the horses up into a dash that snatched at the traces and sent the carriage careening past the Washington Monument and onto the Mall, the rest of the convoy tailing behind. Riding in back, Wilson had fearfully clung to his top hat, until he suddenly bolted to his feet and pointed past Roosevelt into the open sky.

"There! There they are!"

Roosevelt glanced and then hauled on the reins, leading the horses into a screeching curve so that they doubled-back towards a low hill at the far end of the Mall's Reflecting Pool.

"This is the perfect spot!" he bellowed, standing up at the reins so that the other carriage drivers could see him. "Circle the wagons!"

It was like living the Western Frontier all over again as the Presidential convoy came to a halt, forming a protective hoop of wood and horses two hundred feet across, minutemen and police rushing to close the gaps and keep back the curious masses now crowding onto the Mall. Finally, Roosevelt looked towards the far end of the Mall, where the Capitol sat in stately majesty on a low rise. The Stars and Stripes proudly flew from its post atop the central dome, and hovering about it, as if in salute to the great flag, were a pair of gravity-defying machines.

It is a most beautiful sight, Roosevelt thought to himself.

"That's quite the jockey steering those machines!" he said to Wilson, as calmly as if judging participants in a rodeo. "I can't image trying to fly something like that in these winds."

*

"*This is fantastic!*" Bell 88's pilot shouted over the radio. "*Clear skies, no air-traffic, no air-traffic-control, and no FAA to tell us off!*"

"Simmer down, cowboy!" Connie Ramirez replied into her headset. "We just want to give them a good show, not crash right down on top of them."

Connie herself was piloting the *Anatoly Sagalevich*'s Sikorsky Seaking, but she had to admit that Bell 88's pilot was right; it was strangely liberating to be the only thing in the sky, gazing out over the unfolding roofs of Washington, almost perched atop the Capitol. She suddenly felt a great surge of gratitude to the late Gareth King for persuading her to pursue her rotary-wing pilot's license, without which she would not be here, making history.

Yes, it felt amazing.

"How are you doing, Mr Lightoller?" said asked sidelong to the man riding beside her in the co-pilot's seat, several maps spread out over his knees.

"Perfectly fine, *Lefthenant!*" replied her acting navigator, his calm words unable to hide his excitement.

"And is everyone in alright in back?" she called to her passengers on the intercom, receiving a few words of assent.

"A little woozy, but none the worse for wear…" said Archibald Butt, and Connie could not help but giggle mentally, envisioning the Major in his full dress uniform squeezed up against the window-seat.

"Just put us down already!" Kai Alinka said softly. "Any longer and some of those crowds might get a little shooty."

"Not on your life!" cried Dean Simmons, who she guessed had one of the cameras out. "These visuals are great. No-one's had a chance to film DC like this since the No-Fly ordinances went into effect after 9/11!"

"Can you see where best to land?" Adrienne McKinn called, acting as the elected head of this first delegation from the Time Fleet. "Violet is feeling a little travel-sick, and I'd rather we met with President Taft sooner than later."

"We're going to begin our final approach in a second!" Connie called back. "They seem to be gathering at the far end of the reflecting pool, and I think they've cleared us a landing space at the foot of where the Lincoln Memorial's going to be built.

"Fitting, I wonder whose idea that was..." spoke Milton Long. "Well, Mrs McKinn, ready to give your Gettysburg Address?"

"I suspect it might be more akin to the Emancipation Proclamation," laughed Margaret Brown. "What happens here is going to start turning the whole world on its head!"

She and Adrienne shared a moment's laughter before the former Congresswoman's tone turned serious.

"Well, there's no putting this off any further. Set us down in 1912 please, Lieutenant Ramirez."

"Roger ma'am, commencing final approach for touchdown. Landing gear down!"

*

Dean Simmons' and Margaret Brown's recordings of that first meeting beside the Reflecting Pool remain preserved in the Library of Congress.

Just as the first of the two helicopters touches onto the grass, Simmons pushes the door open and jumps down to assist Brown out, before she also starts her camera. The two of them take up flanking positions beside the door, filming the disembarkation of the various passengers and the reactions of the receiving delegation.

First out is the grandly-attired Major Butt, who quickly strides forward and salutes President Taft, a rotund but otherwise unremarkable figure dressed in a style better suiting a banker. Then a stocky man in glasses, Roosevelt, pushes through the small crowd of dignitaries and envelops Butt in a full-armed bear-hug. Taft settles for a handshake, before Butt turns towards the helicopter and introduces the various representatives.

Charles Lightoller, here to support Butt in giving an assessment of the time travellers' character, is bandaged and salved, yet manages to retain a heroic bearing. Looking back in later years, Charles, then Commodore of the White Star Aviation Fleet, remarked that history shall forever remember him for being the man who was grinning like a fool when he met the President.

The next person to disembark from is Lieutenant Miller of the *Rescue*, carrying a laptop computer containing video footage of *Viking*'s missile launch, as well as the second time-displacement that threw her and *Rescue* into the time stream. These are more for the benefit of Ambassador von Bernstorff than anyone else, as assurance that there is no further threat to Germany, as well as serving as bona fides of their story.

Accompanying Miller, blinking in the sunlight and walking somewhat unsteadily, is Kai Alinka, future consultant for the Newport News Shipbuilding Company and co-founder of renowned marine architects Gibbs & Alinka, designers of the American Transport Line's much-beloved flagship, the SS *Columbia*. Called to speak repeatedly regarding the sinking of the *Titanic*, his expert testimony proved instrumental in shaping legislation requiring merchant ships to be fitted with reinforced double hulls and carry sufficient lifeboats for all aboard.

The Governor of New Jersey and later founder of the Stateright Party, Woodrow Wilson, can be seen reacting with some disquiet to Alinka's ethnic heritage. Seconds later, however, his lip visibly curls as Connie Ramirez steps down from the Sikorsky's cockpit, resplendent in her borrowed uniform. She, however, merely salutes politely and presents herself as a representative of the future United States Armed Forces. When writing her own memoirs, 'Amelia's Shadow', Ramirez scathingly contrasted Wilson's instant condescension with the open-mindedness displayed by Herbert Haddock, future Commodore of the White Star Line.

Behind her, Bell 88's pilot grins and smiles for the camera as he shuts down the helicopter's engine. Bell 88 now resides in the Smithsonian; unlike the longer-ranged Sikorsky, it had insufficient fuel reserves to return to the fleet, and was instead dragged by teams of packhorses off the Mall, never to fly again. An open dais engraved with the image of a helicopter rotor marks the exact spot where it landed, however, directly in front of the current Lincoln Memorial, reconstructed after the 1931 shelling of Washington.

Various other delegates emerge from each helicopter; last but by no means least is Adrienne McKinn, attended by her personal staff. The former Congresswoman for Montana, and future Progressive Vice President, causes a noticeable stir in the crowd, given her elegant bearing and commanding height, but merely raises a hand in response, waving politely, before walking forward so that Major Butt might introduce her to his friend the President.

Behind her, attired in the manner of the twentieth-first century, are Milton Long and Violet Jessop, who would work together under Mrs McKinn for many years, marrying in 1915. Ms Jessop, icon of the Suffrage movement, looks visibly nervous, and sways slightly as she attempts to recover her land-legs after nearly two weeks at sea. Long, future Congressional Representative for the state of Massachusetts, seems disquieted to be at the centre of attention. In his hand he carries a briefcase, and at Mrs McKinn's request, opens it so that a single-page document might be presented to the President for his consideration.

An amended version of that document, entered into the record as Executive Order 1521 is, like the visual record, preserved in the Congressional Library beside the Declaration of Independence, Constitution and Bill of Rights.

*

In recognition of the event known variously as the Titanic Incident, the Convergence, the Time Wreck, or the *Liberty Bell* Event, the following ordinances are declared:

663

1: The merchant vessels *Olympic, Oceanic III* and *Anatoly Sagalevich* are permitted to enter into New York Harbor, where they shall be quarantined at berth until such time as the Board of Immigration declare their passengers and crew present no medical threat. In the light of crowded conditions aboard these ships proving deleterious to the health of their occupants, additional accommodation shall be arranged aboard other vessels.

2: That an Inquiry into the events surrounding the Titanic Incident be held aboard the *Oceanic III*, to which persons-of-interest aboard said vessels shall consent to providing expertise and testimony in the aid of, accepting limitations on their rights to travel until such inquiries are concluded.

3: That the United States shall set in motion diplomatic efforts to make said Inquiry an International venture, representing the full spectrum of nations to whom the events of the Titanic Incident bear relevance.

4: That persons native to 1912 who are of no interest to said Inquiry be allowed to depart these ships subject to receiving a clean bill of health from the Board of Immigration, subject to standard Immigration and Customs procedures.

5: That time-displaced persons holding foreign citizenship be allowed to return to their nation of choice, if they so desire, at the close of said enquiry, unless subject to criminal charge.

6: That the life, liberty, property and right to happiness of all time-displaced persons seeking asylum in the United States of America shall be recognised, regardless of nationality, birth, place, time or culture of origin, and that no attempt shall be made to constrain, prosecute or persecute said persons subject to their acting within the spirit and letter of the laws of the United States when ashore.

7: Furthermore, consequent to receiving a clean bill of health by the Board of Immigration, at the close of said Inquiry said persons seeking asylum shall be allowed to travel as appropriate within the United States, and to retain the full protection of the law thereof, until such time that Congress may appoint a proper system by which these persons may apply for naturalisation and citizenship.

8: The masters of the vessels *Oceanic III* and *Anatoly Sagalevich* are, in concordance of the spirit of the *1910 Brussels Convention for the Unification of Certain Rules with Respect to Assistance and Salvage at Sea*, recognised as salvors-in-possession of their respective vessels, with full rights to dispose of the material assets of said ships as they see fit, under the new precept of Temporal Salvage.

9: So that all time-displaced persons may have a place of assembly and association wherein the laws to which they are accustomed apply, the right of the Captains of the *Oceanic III* and *Anatoly Sagalevich* to follow, practice, modify and enforce the civil laws of the United Kingdom of Great Britain and Northern Ireland, and the Russian Federation, aboard their respective vessels, in the form said laws existed on April 14th 2012, shall be respected.

(signed)

Wm. H. Taft.

The White House

April 22nd, 1912.

CHAPTER THIRTY THREE

Courtesy of the United States Post Office and the Marconi Wireless Company

To Lloyd Waters, Captain, Oceanic

He signed! Bring them in!

Love, Adrienne.

PS: I met Teddy Roosevelt! He actually said Bully to me when I explained our plans! Lifelong dream achieved!

*

Georgine O'Brien was too young to understand what had her father so excited, but happily followed him hand-in-hand over the Brooklyn Bridge, two embers in the firestorm crowd converging on Manhattan. Below them, the surface of the East River was barely visible for the flotilla of boats and ferries forging their way downstream towards New York Bay, vessels jostling for space and shouldering one another aside as they competed for pole position, glowing warmly in the evening light.

It was little different up on the bridge, and eventually Georgie's father grabbed his ten-year old daughter underarm and swung her up onto his shoulders, rather than lose her in the surging crowds.

"Look at all the boats, father!" she yelled in delight, looking down over the walkway at the growing armada.

"Georgie, can you see the harbour from up there?" he asked in reply.

She frowned. It was strange for Father to ask questions like that of her, but obligingly she turned her head and tried to stretch her neck out, gazing over the roofs of buildings out towards the south.

"Yes father, I can see."

"Are there any big ships out there?"

Georgie peered, squinting in concentration and all but standing up on his shoulders. It was hard to see the harbour, because a massive glare of light from what looked to be a skyscraper turned on its end was drowning out everything...

"Oh!"

"Georgie?"

"It is a ship father, but bigger, so much *bigger!*" Georgie threw her arms apart to depict the incredibly huge craft. "Bigger than this bridge, bigger than the city!"

"That huge, really?" Mr O'Brien laughed softly, indulging his daughter's flight of fancy, before increasing his pace. "Come on, we'd best try and get to the Hudson waterfront, we might even get as far as the Battery if we can hotfoot it to the subway quick enough."

*

Harbor Pilot George Seeth Sr. stood ramrod-stiff in the centre of *Oceanic*'s bridge, assailed on all sides by an arsenal of beeping, blinking electronics. A Danish-born veteran of the Sandy Hook Pilots Association, with over forty years' experience of New York's waters under his belt, Seeth was clearly working hard to maintain his composure in a radically new environment. Yet he had conducted himself with nary so much as a tremor, the only signs of any anxiety being a subtle loosening of his collar and occasional dab of a handkerchief against his sweating brow.

Lloyd Waters could not help but be impressed by the pilot's professional *mien*, remembering all too well the barely-suppressed panic he himself had felt when *Oceanic* first eased out of the graving dock at Harland & Wolff. In truth he was finding himself as much as odds as Seeth; as *Oceanic* approached the Eastern Seaboard of 1912, assailed on all sides by curious craft equipped with neither radio, radar or positional transponders, he had ordered the liner's uppermost promenade deck closed off to all but a select few passengers, making use of the freed-up space to post extra lookouts, each armed with binoculars and two-way radios.

At last they had closed the gap to the Ambrose Light, an actual lightship in this day and age, picked up Seeth from a tiny launch, and begun to slowly motor up the Ambrose Channel, pooling Seeth's experience with real-time data of the sea bed mapped out by *Oceanic*'s navigation suite. Finally, they had transitioned through the Narrows and entered into New York Harbor itself.

Now they were competing for space with hundreds of ships, from soot-stained tugs and filthy cargo steamers to tiny sail-rigged lighters and rowboats, all stewing together in a turbid and chaotic soup. Stately ocean liners that Lloyd had never expected to see with his own eyes sat like islands amidst the channels and anchorages. But none of them were quite so grand as *Oceanic*, he supposed, and he felt a touch of pride.

"Where now, Mr Seeth?" he asked. "We normally berth at Brooklyn; do we make for the Buttermilk Channel, or maintain course?"

"My orders are to bring you in at the Hudson terminals, Captain Waters," Seeth clarified. "So we'll drop anchor off of Liberty Island for now." He gestured to where no less than a dozen tugboats were escorting *Olympic* up the Anchorage Channel and into the mouth of the Hudson. "We'll hold there until further tugs are available to aid our passage up the river."

"Are you certain *Oceanic* requires assistance, sir?" Lloyd said mildly, turning to share a secret smirk with Captain Edward John Smith, who was up and about on his own two feet again, although requiring the aid of a cane to support his weight.

"Quite certain, yes," nodded Seeth, a touch of testiness revealing itself in the tone of his voice. "The currents in the lower Hudson can make it tricky to manoeuvre larger ships into the piers."

"Is that so…" Lloyd chuckled, before calling over to the navigation station. "Helm, bow-thrusters and Azimuth pods. Turn us about if you please."

There was a grinding murmur from below deck. Then, with the perfect grace of a pirouetting ballerina, *Oceanic* began to slowly spin like a top, presenting herself with a flourish to the city of New York.

"Do not panic, George," said Captain Smith, smiling genially at the stunned pilot. "As when you and I brought *Olympic* in on her maiden voyage, one becomes used to such wonders remarkably quickly."

"We nearly sank a tug docking *Olympic* for the first time, EJ…" Seeth retorted. "The poor *OL Hallenbach* almost had her stern ripped off when she fouled that propeller…"

"I do remember, and I feel it lends further credence to the argument for allowing *Oceanic* to berth herself with minimum assistance. After all, Captain Waters and his crew understand the handling characteristics of their ship, where we do not."

Seeth looked forward, jaw working silently. Feeling his heart go out to the man, Lloyd intervened.

"She'll still need three or four tugs to help swing her into the dock, but *Oceanic* is perfectly capable of proceeding unassisted into the Hudson; it's only when we hove to that she requires a bit of a helping hand."

"Very well, then," said Seeth. Marvelling at how a ship three times the size of the largest he had ever brought into the Port could be made to dance so easily, he swallowed and managed a nervous smile, indicating forward to show where the channel was deepest. "Aim between Liberty and Governors Islands, Captain. Make revolutions for five knots… once you're done showing off."

The Sandy Hook Pilots had once commented that *Olympic* docked so easily that she might have done it herself, unassisted by human hands. Faced with Captain Waters and his mind-boggling command, that glib observation now felt more akin to prophecy, and George Seeth resolved to never again complain about the difficulties of bringing in the *Lusitania* or the *Kaiser Wilhelm der Grosse*.

Sliding easily about on her variable-attitude thrusters, *Oceanic* motored forward past the Statue of Liberty, sounding a salute to the green giantess as she did so.

"That fine lady," EJ Smith reflected aloud, contemplating the statue. "Is surely one thing has not changed between eras."

"No, EJ," replied Lloyd softly. "No she has not."

*

"Give me your tired, your poor. Your huddled masses yearning to breathe free..." Pip whispered to herself, peering up at the familiar profile of Lady Liberty. The words of Emma Lazarus's *'The New Colossus'*, which she had memorised in grade-school, now seemed portentous.

"Her name is Mother of Exiles," another voice spoke, continuing the sonnet. Pip, who had been resting her weight on the rail of *Oceanic*'s Sun Deck, turned to the new speaker.

"Mister Murdoch, hello."

William Murdoch, looking somewhat uncomfortable in a modern White Star uniform borrowed from one of *Oceanic*'s officers, nodded a polite greeting back in her direction, and then directed his attention back up towards the statue, a deep silhouette against the setting sun.

"Send these, the homeless, tempest-tossed to me," he recited, finishing the poem. *"I lift my lamp beside the golden door."*

Pip kept her eyes on the statue until it passed away astern, and then drew herself up, toying with the fabric of her dress. It was the silk affair that Marilyn had put together for her presentation on the night of the Centennial, and although the fabric was badly damaged from contact with seawater, blood and oil, she had felt a need to wear it back into New York.

"So, after captaining *Titanic*, how does this ship suit your tastes, Will?" she asked at last, peering forward towards where Manhattan was beginning to reveal itself.

"*Oceanic* is... extraordinary," Murdoch said, seeming to struggle in quantifying that one word. "The past few days have certainly been a learning curve, but an interesting one. At least I can finally stand on her bridge without panicking."

"So, what is your exact position right now, advisor or an actual ship's officer?"

His mouth twisted. "Officially I am... well, the word they used was a 'consultant'. Now though the matter of *Oceanic*'s ownership has been both clarified and confused – Captain Waters has been declared salvor-in-possession, yet I believe he plans to lease it to White Star..."

"Ha!" she snorted. "For sale, one superliner, 160,000 tons gross displacement, slightly used, one careful previous owner. Asking bid, one billion dollars."

"Yes… I expect that I'll be offered a position aboard this ship, most likely as a liaison between management and her actual crew. I intend to decline, however, and continue along the path I've trod, if the Line will still have me. Bertram Hayes or Charles Bartlett might be better suited to serving as Captain Waters' deputy…"

"What? You'd really throw away a chance to help command a ship three times larger than any other in existence?"

"As you yourself said, I captained the *Titanic*, if only for a short while, and that's a fine enough achievement for any seaman." He managed a small smile. "And I don't doubt many are going to have questions to me as to what transpired on the night we struck the iceberg, and during the days after. Besides, I have other responsibilities to consider."

"Your family?"

"And Henry Wilde's…" he answered, and seeing her curiosity at the mention of *Titanic*'s late Chief Officer, sighed and expanded. "Henry was a good friend, and he had four little children back home. I'd like to suggest to Ida, my wife, that she and I make some approach as to providing for them, at least in part."

"That's a nice gesture, Will," she managed to say, but the words sounded hollow to her ears. Sighing in frustration she rapped her fists on the rail and looked back at the stiff-backed officer. "What sort of man was he like, Henry Tingle Wilde?"

Murdoch looked down at his feet for a second.

"A good friend and a devoted father," he said at last, looking up to regard her. "An excellent officer as well, very much deserving of his own command. If it wasn't for the miners' strike confusing the timetables, I think he would right now be master of the *Cymric*, a fine little ship, or he might have taken over Captain Haddock's old command, *Oceanic*."

She raised an eyebrow and indicated the enormous vessel they were standing upon.

"The old *Oceanic*," he clarified, chuckling for a moment, before his face became sombre. "Or he might have commanded *Titanic* on her next voyage, when EJ took his well-earned retirement, and

671

if I had not been so much of a fool as to steer her right into an iceberg."

Pip nodded in understanding, waiting for him to go on. When Murdoch made no move to proceed, she voiced the question that had been lurking at the corners of her mind for years, growing in volume with recent days.

"What happened on that night, Will? What went wrong?"

Pausing, Murdoch removed his cap and seemed to come unbuttoned. Resting his weight on the rail a few feet along from her, he checked once about to make sure that the immediate area was empty but for themselves. Except for the extra lookouts and a few VIP passengers conversing amongst themselves, the Sun Deck was empty.

"We should never have struck that iceberg…" he said at last. "I knew there was something ahead of us the second Fleet rang the bell in the nest, but I saw it with my own eyes just as Moody received the call; I ordered the rudder hard over before James had time to acknowledge what Fleet had seen. So I turned her nose to port, and then reversed the helm, at just the wrong moment. In trying to swing the stern clear, I steered her right over the shelf that gutted her…"

Aware that just a week ago she would have hanging on his every word like an adoring fan, Pip said nothing, withholding her opinion until he had finished speaking.

"…but it should not even have gone that far; we knew we would encounter ice sometime after eleven, and in the minutes before the collision I suspected we were amongst the bergs. The smell of them was in the air, and whiskers of ice were dancing around the ship's lights. Captain Smith's orders were for him to be summoned if the situation looked in any way doubtful. He wasn't asleep in his cabin, but resting in the chart room so that he would be alert and ready when called, as he expected to be called, during my watch…"

Pausing, Murdoch cupped his hands together. "But I didn't call for him, and didn't take any action of my own until that blasted berg loomed out of the dark, just kept up steam and maintained course…"

He trailed off, letting the moment dangle, and then struck the rail with his fist in a moment of venting frustration. "I was just so *sure*, convinced that we were safe, that I was in charge and in command! I failed to do anything before the collision, and when presented with the iceberg, I failed to make the right choice!"

"You made the right choice against *Viking*…" she answered, and when he snorted and shrugged his shoulders she leaned in closer. "Listen to your captive historian, Mr Murdoch; ramming head-on into that berg wouldn't have done anything, so stop second-guessing your decision to port around, because it kept *Titanic* afloat on an even beam long enough to get the boats away. Striking it head-on at full speed would have crumpled her bow up to the foremast at the very least, and the shock transmitted through the hull could have caused her to spring leaks along the greater part of her length. Felling the mainmast also means the wireless antennas would be compromised, meaning less chance of rescue for any survivors in the boats. Even if she did stay afloat, you'd have the lives of all the firemen and steerage passengers quartered in the bow on your conscience, and everyone would have lambasted you for not trying to dodge the obstruction, insisting the ship would have easily survived a brush down the side, because no-one could have imagined a disaster on a scale like *Titanic* until it *actually happened*."

"What of the engines?" he insisted. "What if I'd not attempted to protect the propeller by ordering 'all stop', but left them at 'full ahead'? The mere act of the screws slowing down must have sapped her of a few precious knots, reduced the rotating effect of the rudder. Might she have missed the berg, or just glanced it, if I hadn't jumped to the engine telegraphs?"

"You can't just let it go, can you?" Pip shook her head. And yet she had asked the same questions of history: had seen the what-ifs and the might-have-beens of *Titanic* debated and dissected on *Encyclopaedia Titanica* and countless other message boards, safe and quarantined from the cold reality of that April night. But to be the person to have made those fateful choices, to have the weight of everything that did happen, *which might have happened*, weighing upon your shoulders… no, she did not envy Murdoch right now.

"Someone must take the blame," he said at last. "It's not Charles Lightoller's fault for failing to supply binoculars to the crow's nest, not that they would have helped, and it's certainly not the lookouts' fault that they failed to spot the berg before we came onto it. It was small as they go, and probably did not rise much above the horizon from their vantage point in the crow's net. It was my watch, my fault, my responsibility…"

After another prolonged silence he laughed bitterly, mouth pursed in shame. "I don't doubt that the other me shot himself during the sinking."

"You can't know that, Will," she replied, sympathy and conviction flooding her voice in equal parts. "It might have been you, or it might have been Wilde, maybe even the Captain. There weren't many survivors who stayed on the ship late enough to witness the final plunge of the Boat Deck, and I think they had more pressing things on their mind than identifying whoever shot himself, even if someone did."

He seemed little convinced, his attention focused on his right hand, which he was flexing pensively. Bracing herself for a backlash, Pip pressed harder. "How could a passenger have identified a casualty among the officers? You guys didn't exactly go ambling around the cabins making yourselves well-known. There have even been theories that James Moody or Purser McElroy could have been the suicide, with pretty well-reasoned arguments behind them too."

"Moody and McElroy were not issued with arms during the sinking," Murdoch snapped, voice as taught as a fraying cable. "I've had plenty of chances to confirm as such these past few days, within *Oceanic*'s archives."

His words trailed off into silence, and Pip turned around so that her back was to the rail. Staring up she regarded the pale sky above them, first with frustration, then with calm. At least, she began to speak.

"After what you said to me back on *Titanic*, after all your heroism in taking her into battle against *Viking*, why are you trying to argue yourself into the spotlight, going along with what the myths of my day say happened that night? Throw yourself on the sword of public opinion and the sharks are going to rip you apart once they smell your blood in the water. Bruce Ismay seems ready to drag himself through the muck for his part in this, and it's almost expected of him due to his position, but why you?"

"Because…" Murdoch said quietly, as if trying to convince himself. "Because Henry Wilde deserves better than being slandered as a man who would have put a bullet in his own head."

"You're doing this to protect his reputation?" she replied, whipping her head around to face him, shock written on her features. "To divert negative attention off of Wilde and onto yourself?"

"As I said, he was a good friend," Murdoch said, smiling with growing confidence. "And as *you* said, I'm apparently the hero of the hour, and that will go some way to easing my burden. So let the shadow of the suicide fall on me, because I can take it. I've faced worse squalls in the past and I'll weather this one, though it might be hard on Ida. But I know she'll understand."

Pip's mouth hung open, unable to frame an answer, and Murdoch never gave her a chance, suddenly straightening up and graciously extending a hand towards *Oceanic*'s wheelhouse.

"It's not normal for guests to be allowed on the bridge," he said, smiling wistfully. "In fact Captain Smith took a considerable lashing for giving the Prince of Wales a tour once, back on *Olympic*. But this is hardly normal circumstances, and the Captains say you're welcome to join us if you so wish."

"Thank you Mr Murdoch… Captain Murdoch," she corrected herself, returning his smile sadly. "But I think I'll take a little stroll around the deck, and have a think."

Nodding Murdoch replaced the cap on his head, every inch the stalwart seaman, and calmly walked away.

Choosing an uncertain fate… Pip thought to herself. *But walking to it with his head held high.*

Ahead, the heart of New York was coming into view, and she turned to meet it.

I've got to be strong.

But it was hard, so very hard. As the sun slowly began to settle towards the New Jersey shore she found herself facing something that was recognisably Manhattan, but which was not *home*. What hurt the most was that she could recognise many of the buildings, like the Metropolitan Life Tower, rising like a spire through the centre of the city, and there was the Woolworth Building, still under construction and draped with scaffolding, but those landmarks only drove home how many others just appeared to have vanished. After 9/11 the Manhattan skyline had seemed broken without the double-barrelled Twin Towers, but now there was no Trump Tower or Citigroup Centre, no Chrysler Building, not even the Empire State.

A dread began to seep through her, one that she had first felt when the ship had entered into the Upper Bay without having to pass under the Verrazano Bridge. Some part of her, more that she might have admitted, had clung to the faint, childish hope that they would arrive off the Eastern Seaboard and find... home. Glass and concrete and waterfronts strung with freeways and hotdog stands, the old jetties either broken and decayed or undergoing renovation.

Instead, she found a brick-and-stone metropolis still coming into shape, girt with busy docks and bustling steamships, horses and carts jostling for space in the crowded thoroughfares. *Olympic*, pushing her way up the Hudson ahead of *Oceanic*, was making for the White Star Terminal at Pier 59, exactly where the *Titanic* Metropolitan Museum was being built when Pip had left port. The *Anatoly Sagalevich*, the ship she had been upon for that departure, now trailed behind *Oceanic*, returning almost to the very berth from where this voyage had begun.

That was just a month ago. And from her perspective, the city had gone through a cataclysmic metamorphosis.

There, between the brownstones and burgeoning skyscrapers, she caught sight of the building in which Marilyn had set up her business, where this very dress had been gifted to her.

Despite all her attempts to hold it all in, Pip began to cry. Marilyn was gone. New York, her New York, was gone. Everything that had made her life hers. Her friends and acquaintances, the places she treasured, the shops where she blew her money. Her favourite message boards and websites, Twitter and Facebook, all obliterated.

She sobbed uncontrollably, clutching at her shoulders and hugging herself. A light wind was whistling through the streets, whipping steam and smoke from a thousand chimneys into the air like flurries of snow.

It was then that *Olympic* bellowed on her whistles, shaking Pip from her anguish. And looking up, she gasped.

Behind her the sun was beginning to melt into the New Jersey Ramparts, casting brilliant firelight over the city. Buildings striving towards an egg-blue sky suddenly lit up with red and gold reflections, creating a mural of light as their windows caught the sunset. Far above, the few clouds in the sky were wreathed in pink and orange hues.

She had seen this before, but where?

And then she remembered. The New York Public Library, on Fifth Avenue. The ceiling murals there depicted sunset as it historically had looked from any New York street, before the skyscrapers rose to such a height that they had stolen away the sky, casting their deep shadows on the city.

It was a touch of the familiar, a reminder of what she had known, and almost as if the city was welcoming back a lost child.

This still was New York, a little younger, perhaps a lot less polished, but still home.

Olympic's chime whistles were still roaring from up ahead, the light pall of smoke cast from her funnels trailing across the sky, drifting with the wind. The liner was singing out in double-bursts, as if she was calling out *"Look here!"* in all directions as the tugboats led her arm-in-arm into the dock. *"Look here, and look who I brought with me!"*

And then ships and tugs all along the Hudson began to call out in response, water spraying in great arcs from their fire-hoses as they welcomed *Oceanic* and the *Anatoly Sagalevich* for the first time, in this time, like a ship arriving on her maiden voyage. Awestruck, Pip's arms came close around her and she hugged herself in tear-struck silence as whistles and foghorns resounded in the bright dawn, *Olympic* leading the song.

This was the welcome intended for Titanic, she realised, a shiver running down her spine as *Oceanic* finally sang out with blasts from her own horns, each warbling note rising above the chorus of ships and automobiles, the lost liner thanking the city for a warm welcome.

And as the whistle-cries and sirens echoed away, many minutes later, she heard music drifting up from somewhere aft, a very familiar tune. Curious, she slowly walked back and peered over the rail, gazing down on *Oceanic*'s terraced stern, where Wallace Hartley, bandmaster of the *Titanic*, was leading his fellows in providing music for the passengers. Pip had first witnessed them perform the evening after *Viking* and *Rescue* were sucked out of time, playing funereal hymns as the bodies of those lost over the course of several tumultuous days were committed to sea. The sight and sound of Hartley and his band striking up *'Autumn'* and *'Nearer My God to Thee'*, as they had allegedly done in the other world, just before *Titanic* plunged, had reduced her to tears.

Now, she was laughing. The contemporary band had begun experimenting over the course of the voyage to New York, seeking out music from modern times and playing variations on those familiar songs. In a moment of supreme irony, they were now performing the love theme from the *'Titanic'* movie, and putting a remarkable amount of feeling into the song.

Seeing that, with the lyrical tones rising up around her, Pip looked towards New York and smiled bravely.

I'm here, I'm not afraid, I'm going to make the most of this, she resolved to herself. *And I know that my heart will go on…*

"Miss Paik?" someone said softly. "Philippa?"

Swallowing, Pip turned and smiled.

"Hello, Jack."

*

On a cleared table in *Oceanic*'s champagne bar, *The Magic Stick*, a general arrangement drawing for the *Olympic*-class of ships was unrolled. Then, multiple hands reached in and began to make annotations;

Oil-fired

Insert double-hull here (subdivide for use as fuel bunkerage?)

Reconstruct stern entirely – consideration to rudder arrangement

Fourth funnel entirely ornamental – remove?

Relocate wireless room adjacent to bridge

New design of exhaust turbine (consult with Oceanic's Chief Engineer)

Modify hull-form for improved hydrodynamics (contact D.W. Taylor and V. Yourkevitch)

Extend key bulkheads up to the Bridge Deck

Elevate bridge for improved visibility

Possible radar installation, and bow thrusters? Can technology be reverse-engineered?

Thomas Andrews felt alive, full of vitality as never before. In the days since *Titanic* had sunk he had been given full access to *Oceanic's* technical mysteries, and had found in the ship a wealth of ideas and developments that could easily be applied to contemporary ship design.

And, to his delight, he had discovered that she had apparently been built at Harland & Wolff, the cost being secured by a government guarantee, the previous absence of which had seen the construction of her older sister, the *Queen Mary 2*, outsourced to Saint-Nazaire in France. Apparently H&W had fallen on hard times, as had British shipbuilding in general, and he was resolved to avoid retreading the same ignominious destiny.

We built this ship once, and we shall build many like her again... he had vowed, thinking of the magnificent model displayed in this ship's Cafe Parisien, of the proposed *Oceanic III* of 1928. He would see to it that no such vessel would ever sit stillborn on the Belfast stocks, and providence had given him the perfect hull on which to test both his resolve and these new ideas: Yard Number 433, the third sister of the *Olympic*-class, on which construction had only just commenced back in Belfast.

That was how he found himself gathered around this table with the Harland & Wolff Guarantee Group, radically revising the plans for *Gigantic*, or *Britannic*, or whatever she was to be named. Thomas found himself possessed by fresh energies of enthusiasm; *Olympic* and *Titanic* were mostly the brainchild of his predecessor, Alexander Carlisle, but this third vessel would now truly be his own creation.

The Guarantee Group, men ranging from fitters and plumbers to a young apprentice, were all together brainstorming what could be done with the new ship, while Roderick Chisholm, Thomas' leading draughtsman, sat to one side, sketching away furiously on a pad of paper, trying to amalgamate all of the ideas into a single unified concept.

"What are we going to do about the lifeboats, Mr Andrews?" asked one man. "I mean, it's true that we need to get more onto the ship, but I don't like the idea of cantilevering them over the promenade like they do here on *Oceanic* – it would turn the boat deck into a gloomy tunnel!"

"In the other world, they furnished the *Britannic* with these huge and rather unsightly gantry davits, but they seem to have performed very well when that ship sank in their First World War. Something similar might work here, but we would need to push the deckhouses up so that the davits and boat-racks don't impinge on the lines of the ship…"

"That would also mean a lot of extra space in First Class, Thomas. You might be able to fit a theatre or a cinema in."

"It's all very well and good to be talking about how we can re-imagine the *Gigantic*, but has anyone considered what to do about Belfast?" someone suddenly asked, and Thomas turned.

"Mr Millar!" he smiled in greeting. "Good to see you again sir."

Tommy Millar, one of *Titanic*'s deckhands, had suddenly appeared in the doorway of *The Magic Stick*, uniform rumpled and expression dour. Thomas himself had known Millar as a qualified apprentice and gifted carpenter, who had left Harland & Wolff after an unfortunate bout of sectarian violence, managing to secure work with White Star.

"What's on your mind, Tommy?" Andrews asked. He gestured for the other man to sit, but Millar remained standing, lingering in the entrance to the bar like some malevolent manifestation.

"Catholics and Protestants are tearing Belfast apart, Mr Andrews. Now I hear tell that this is gonna escalate until all of Ireland is torn in twain. I decided to get out when violence got bad in the shipyard, but you're stuck there, and I think as the new Managing Director at Harland & Wolff you need best consider your own views. Are you still a Unionist, or are you now backing your uncle Lord Pirrie in favour of Home Rule?"

It was a crude question, one that broke Thomas' cheery mindset as surely as a crowbar dropped into a working engine. When construction on *Titanic* had begun, Harland & Wolff had been a model of co-operation, Protestants and Catholics employed side by side. But then, as construction on the ship had proceeded, relations between the two faiths had degraded, spurred on by the rising debate as to whether Ireland should remain a part of the United Kingdom, ruled from Westminster, or gain a degree of self-governance. The resulting violence in the shipyard had taught Thomas that politics and religion were deadly when combined.

"You're right, Mr Millar…" he said at last. "And I think that my first edict when we return to Belfast will be that the rabble-rousers stirring up violence in the yards are to be thrown out on their ear. Ireland can ill-afford to be defined by decades of conflict, bloodshed and resentment, so I intend to make Harland & Wolff a symbol of what we can become, unified despite our differences, attracting the best minds and ideas to the mutual prosperity of all…"

He sighed and rubbed at his eyes. "And as for my politics, well, I'm now wondering if all this tension can be ameliorated by a degree of Irish liberty, separated slightly from the United Kingdom, but still ruled by the House of Saxe-Coburg-Gotha as part of a… British Commonwealth… again, united despite our differences, as we are united with these time-travellers regardless of when we come from."

"Aye, well it's good to know where you stand I suppose, but it's going to take more than just pretty words to make it happen," Millar said, before turning away. "Good luck to you all."

And with that the former carpenter retreated away into the crowd, probably to get his first view of New York, the city in which he had expressed a hope to settle with his two young boys. Thomas pondered the man's unhappy life, knowing only that Mrs Millar was dead, a victim of disease brought on by the substandard living-conditions rife in the working-class communities of Belfast.

"It all has to change…" he said to the rest of the group. "Our conceptions of society, nationality, class, must all change, if we are to learn from the lessons forced on us this past week."

He rested his hand on the annotated blueprints. "This ship must be an instrument of that change. *Olympic* and *Titanic* were beloved in Belfast while being built, a subject of great pride and affection. Let their new sister be a model for the society we want to build. One where all can benefit from the prosperity we hope to bring into the world."

A few uncertain murmurs went around the group, and Thomas pointed to the upper deck. "We just said we are going to be creating extra public space by enlarging the superstructure. Well, why not share that among all three classes by giving Second and Third Classes their own libraries, gymnasiums, swimming-pools and open, broad promenades? Conditions on White Star liners for the lesser-off classes are already superior to those on competitors' ships, but what if we were to elevate the steerage passengers into human beings, not mere statistics to be crammed like sardines into the lower decks? Is that not a worthy example to set for Belfast, and an agenda to be addressed by Ireland, and every nation on Earth?"

Heads were now nodding in agreement, men smiling at the idea being suggested. Most of them were from the same impoverished background as Mr Millar, and their voyage aboard *Titanic*, booked into Second Class, must have been an incredible experience even before an iceberg and a time-machine conspired to throw the whole universe off its axis. The idea of sharing that experience with their peers surely excited them...

"It's an ambitious challenge, Thomas, merging shipbuilding with the shaping of nations," interjected the familiar voice of Bruce Ismay, who now slowly limped into the champagne bar and lowered himself gingerly into a seat alongside them. "But then, these ships have always been a symbol of national pride. We and Cunard have been at war with the Germans' HAPAG and Norddeutscher Lloyd lines for years, seeking to outdo one another. Now it seems to me that you want to turn that to an actual political end."

He paused for a moment, and then looked up. "White Star Line is to purchase *Oceanic* from Captain Waters, in several instalments. I've cleared the necessary share issue with JP Morgan and the Board of Directors by wireless. The good Captain aims to divide the monies equally among all those now lost in time, providing some funds for them to find their feet and establish themselves in this world."

"But... what will you do with her, Bruce?" Thomas replied, aghast. "She's too ahead of our time to run in regular service, unsuitable for use on the Atlantic Ferry as an immigrant ship, and too big for any dry dock in the world to house!"

"Well, there you have it..." Ismay shrugged, smiling slightly. "We may get some years service out of her as a floating emissary, a sort of oceangoing ambassador for peace, but it is my hope that eventually *Oceanic* will return to Belfast, becoming a floating hotel that the great and the good of the world will flock to experience for themselves, at a premium, while Harland & Wolff reverse-engineer her technological marvels. And in the spirit of your bold idea, I suggest the wisdom gained from her be shared freely with the shipbuilders of the world, in a gesture of accord and peace."

Thomas rubbed at his brow, letting the idea turn over slowly. It seemed so farcically simple, but was there a touch of brilliance lurking within? But it could be made to go hand-in-hand with his own idea, by making Belfast a hub of global diplomacy, and *Oceanic* a place for the free exchange of ideas and cultures...

"God above, Bruce, I think you might have a notion there..."

Ismay smiled abashedly, before turning his gaze up to a television mounted on the wall.

"Barkeep," he called. "Could you please turn the volume up?"

The woman behind the bar obliged, and Thomas turned in his own seat to see Ismay's own face on-screen, giving an interview to Margaret Brown's Alexandra Press.

"There are allegations, Mr Ismay, that you interfered in the navigation of Titanic during the voyage," enquired the interviewer, Daniel Mervin. *"How would you respond to such accusations?"*

"I would say... that they are not wholly unjustified..." replied onscreen Ismay, and Thomas turned in disbelief to regard Bruce's own inscrutable face as his doppelganger continued to speak;

"...I did not directly pressure Captain Smith to go faster, nor did I step onto the bridge until after the encounter with the iceberg, but I'm sure my very presence had some effect. And there is also the matter of this telegram, received on Sunday morning from the RMS Baltic..."

Television Ismay produced a slip of paper as if by sleight-of-hand, and began to read.

"Captain Smith, Titanic. Have had moderate, variable winds and clear, fine weather since leaving. Greek steamer Athinai reports passing icebergs and large quantity of field ice today in latitude 41.51'N, longitude 49.52'W. Last night we spoke with German oil tanker Deutschland, Stettin to Philadelphia, not under control, short of coal; latitude 40.42'N, longitude 55.11'W. Wishes to be reported to New York and other steamers. Wish you and Titanic all success."

Thomas could not help but notice the calm and good grace that Ismay seemed to possess when in front of the camera, in sharp contrast to the snub-nosed reluctance he usually displayed when called to speak publicly.

"Captain Smith brought this telegram to me and placed it in my hand, which I now believe to have been his subtly asking me if Titanic should go to the aid of the Deutschland, adrift in the Atlantic without fuel. I held onto the telegram for some time, arguing with myself as to what would be better to the company; for Titanic to arrive in New York on time at the end of a glorious maiden voyage, or to be seen to have gone nobly to the aid of a lesser ship, and a German one at that. In the end I decided in favour of the former, and conveyed as such to Captain Smith when I returned the telegraph to him, which may have encouraged him to maintain our course and to keep on speed..."

"Is that true, Bruce?" Tom said, looking to the ship-owner with eyebrows raised, finding the whole story dubious when matched against his own memories of that fateful Sunday.

"It will be, now," Ismay replied mildly, one hand cupped to his mouth so as to mask his expression. "Miss Paik said I needed to control how my story is told, let this be the first step. My tacit expression of guilt will no-doubt be magnified by the press beyond all scale, but I hope my good and well-evidenced deeds will serve to trip up any fantastical narrative Hearst and his bloodhounds try to construct around me..."

Tom thought back over the past few days, and the impressive archive of photo and video material already being assembled of the events set in motion on the night of the iceberg encounter, collating the work of countless amateur filmmakers and passengers who had piecemeal-documented the entire Time Wreck on cameras and those terrifyingly ingenious 'smart phones'. Bruce was front and centre in much of the newly archived material, along with countless other figures that history and myth had vilified in constructing a 'narrative' of *Titanic*'s sinking, and was shown in the captured footage to be what he truly was: a man who did his best.

"Let William Randolph Hearst or his ilk try and slander me, or any persons aboard these ships for that matter; be they from 1912 or 2012, these are our fellows in an adventure like no other, and if anyone tries to garner newspaper sales or prestige by slandering their characters or actions, then they shall be *buried* under a mountain of evidence to the contrary, a mountain that shall only grow as authorities collect further testimony as to recent events."

Bruce Ismay paused, lowering his hand to reveal a smile both savage and sanguine. "Hearst has no conception of the emotive power captured in moving picture accounts of these past few days, and of its power to fight his sensationalised stories. Should he try and furnish the truth of what we have experienced with lies, then I shall see him eat his own poisoned pen!"

He paused and took a moment to compose himself. "And if he still manages to force me into the role of scapegoat for *Titanic*'s encounter with the iceberg, then so be it. At least then it will be my name that is dragged through the mud, not White Star's."

"It's a dangerous game you're playing, Bruce," Tom slowly shook his head, marvelling at Ismay's willingness to sacrifice himself to save face for his father's company.

"But a very interesting one..." Ismay smiled. "I am told that our 'yellow press' is but a forerunner of radical journalists yet to come, thus I think bringing such a movement low in its infancy might be a very worthwhile use of my time in the service of mankind. Hence, I have put myself forward as a partner and financier to Mrs Brown's worthy endeavour, the Alexandra Press, with the goal of expanding it into a journal of international affairs."

Tom felt a slight smile tug at his mouth, but could not hide a flicker of doubt that must have shown in his eyes, for Ismay then leaned in closer and laughed.

"I can bear this cross, Thomas, and am quite excited at the prospect of embarking in a new professional field, so do not worry for me. I've been seeking to retire from both White Star Line and IMM for some time, to finally part ways with my father's legacy.

Harold Sanderson was scheduled to take over from me next year anyway, and I hope that my small contributions give both him and yourself a solid foundation to build upon."

Swivelling on his seat, Thomas looked around the elegant room, imagining powerful heads of state and captains of industry conversing over drinks, enjoying superb views over Belfast Lough and the Ulster hills beyond, while in the other direction a mighty new vessel grew on Harland & Wolff's slipways.

The new world would be shaped in Belfast, in iron and steel and human spirit.

"I'd certainly say you have, Bruce," he said softly. "We'll do our best to not squander those opportunities."

"Excellent…" Bruce replied, tipping his head in respect. "Well, Mr Chisholm, what do you have to show us?"

Roderick Chisholm had finished with his pencils some time ago, and had waited in silence for the two men to finish speaking before he presented a conceptual drawing for the re-imagined third sister of the *Olympic*-class. Now, with all the men in the room sitting in eager anticipation, he flipped over the sketchbook in his hands, and a cry of appreciation went up from them all.

Thomas felt a slow grin grow on his face. The new ship still bore a close family resemblance to *Olympic* and *Titanic*, but seemed taller, longer, and even more graceful. Her bridge had been raised up by another deck, creating room beneath for a lounge clad in shimmering glass. Her bow reared forward as if eager to leap off the page, overhanging a bulbous forefoot somewhat like *Oceanic*'s. The fourth funnel was gone, and the remaining ones had been rescaled to match the ship's new proportions. The decks now stepped down slowly to the stern, creating vast new areas of open space for Second and Third Class, as well as room for additional public rooms and accommodations.

Below the waterline, a large paddle-like rudder shielded the central propeller, while forward a paired set of bow thrusters were integrated into the hull. Above, nestled below the funnels and on the open rear decks were racks of lifeboats cradled within gantry-davits, positioned so as to seem to support the upper works like flying buttresses, lending a suggestion of great strength to the vessel.

She was sleek and grand, both modern and elegant, a fusion of two eras over a century apart.

"Magnificent..." breathed Ismay. "An entirely new generation in marine architecture. Can you build her, gentlemen?"

"There will be challenges, but what an accomplishment would it be if we succeed," Thomas could only say, feeling ready to begin working up the designs immediately. "But she is guaranteed to be the first post-*Titanic* ship to slip into the water; HAPAG's *Imperator* and *Vaterland* are too advanced in construction for major changes to be incorporated into them, and it's the same with Cunard's new *Aquitania*. We, however, have only just started work on the third *Olympic*-class, and have the freedom to take her right back to the drawing-board. We'll only have this opportunity once, so I say the risk is worth the reward."

"As you say, Thomas," Ismay chuckled lightly. "Well, if authorising the construction of this ship is to be my swansong with White Star, I will be most proud. But she'll need a new name. '*Gigantic*' is replete with ostentation, and '*Britannic*' suggests continued hostilities with Germany on the North Atlantic..."

He nodded to himself, and extended a hand as if struck by sudden inspiration. "You wish this ship to be a vanguard for the new world being forged, so why not let her be named... *Heraldic*."

"*Yes!*" Thomas exclaimed in delight, reaching out to grasp Bruce Ismay's hand. "Oh, very yes indeed!"

And so, sealed with a handshake between gentlemen, the RMS *Heraldic* was born.

*

"Well, Lloyd," EJ Smith said softly as *Oceanic* swung about, three tugs assisting her in guiding her nose into the next pier along from where *Olympic* was being docked. "I suspect this will be the last time I venture onto the bridge of a liner."

"You're going to follow through with your retirement?" *Oceanic's* master questioned.

"Yes..." Smith felt his heart softly thumping away inside his chest. "I've pushed my luck far enough as it is, prolonging my career as long as I have. Now I want to step down and be the husband and father my family nearly lost. I hope it does not seem impecunious of me to leave sorting out this mess to younger souls."

"Not at all, EJ," Waters nodded. "But, as Commodore of the White Star Line, would you do me the honour of giving the order to dock us?"

"Heh-heh," Smith chuckled softly. "Are you certain this behemoth will even fit in the dock?"

"Oh, her stern will stick out into the Hudson a fair bit, but if you'll recall, she actually draws an inch less in draught than *Olympic* and *Titanic* did…" Waters laughed.

"Well, if you're so sure, I would be glad," Smith replied, and confirming the order with Pilot George Seeth, he drew himself up straight and held the grip of the cane tightly between his hands, readying himself to issue his final orders as Captain and Commodore.

"Helm amidships, slow ahead, all engines!" he barked briskly, and *Oceanic's* crew jumped to obey.

*

Georgine and her father had managed to secure themselves a spot in the cheering crowds just in view of the White Star Dock. *Olympic*, an increasingly familiar sight on the metropolis' waterways, was just being made secure to the pier, and minutes later the immense ship that had followed her into the harbour nosed her way into the mouth of the next dock upstream from the smaller ship, making a matching pair. But despite its huge size, the larger ship only had a handful of tugs lashed to its hull, as if for appearances sake alone, and its mates attending to *Olympic's* docking were forced to scuttle quickly out of the way to avoid the proud bow that towered over their stubby funnels.

"Is that the *Titanic?*" Georgine asked aloud. "It's much bigger than the other boat. And where's all the little boats to help it?"

Her father stirred uncomfortably, shifting from foot to foot beneath her.

"I don't know, Georgie. People have been saying that this ship has travelled through time."

"Mother said not to tell lies father, you know it's wrong."

She felt him laugh, but before he could answer their attention was drawn by the excited shouts of a newsboy for the *New York American*, waving his hawked wares overhead like battle-flags.

"Extra, extra! *Titanic* sinks at sea after ramming rogue submarine! Time-travelling supership *Oceanic* arrives in New York in the heroic liner's place! Mr and Mrs Astor to give their first interview by wireless! President Taft meets with Lady Adrienne McKinn of Montana! Read everything here!"

Georgie's father tipped him a cent and unfolded the copy he received in return. Georgie felt her eyes open wide as he showed her the banner headline, and underneath a photograph of a very tall and beautiful woman shaking hands with a man whose face Georgie had seen on the wall of her schoolhouse, before she had left school to help raise her little brothers and sisters.

That wasn't what the paper showed this morning! she thought to herself. *They printed it twice! That's cheating!*

And yet, she suddenly had questions to which she wanted answers. Who was this woman, and where had she come from? Why didn't she have a husband escorting her?

"It's very strange, isn't it Georgie?"

"Yes father..." Georgine O'Brien replied, now peering up at the huge ship now docked beside *Olympic*, its forward-thrust bow pointing out towards them and shutting out the last of the sunset. She suddenly felt very confused, but curious, and wanted answers to her questions.

If I worked hard, and helped mother during the rest of the day, maybe I could go back to school, and then I might understand more...

She suddenly had a whole future's worth of new ideas to explore, and began to bounce on her father's shoulders with excitement, hardly able to wait.

CHAPTER THIRTY FOUR

Lights flashed in the night sky over New York Harbor, accompanied by a roaring sound that the Big Apple had grown increasingly familiar with this past week. Rotor blurring, landing lights strobing brightly, a huge Sikorsky helicopter came in to a gentle landing on *Oceanic*. It was the third 'Washington run' the big chopper had made this week, and already a complement of the ship's crew were ready to receive it.

Countless curious bystanders watched from the waterside as well, streets and shore alive with activity. The City of New York was doing a roaring trade from the innumerable multitudes flooding in to catch a glimpse of the 'Great Wonder' that was *Oceanic*, and so a deal had been struck whereby the city agreed to freely keep both the 'Big O' and the *Anatoly Sagalevich* well-supplied with food, drink and basic necessities, at least until a more permanent solution could be achieved.

Lloyd Waters was in attendance for the Sikorsky's landing as well, Captain's hat clamped under one arm and uniform jacket rustling in the downdraught. As the helicopter's landing gear made contact with the reinforced helipad atop the Sun Deck, an attending crewman motioned for the receiving team to step in and begin the tasks of securing and refuelling the huge flying machine.

Fuel, that's another thing we're going to soon run short of… he brooded to himself. One of his hands was pushed deep into his jacket pocket, fingers turning a small box over-and-over, as if imploring it to lend him strength. *Thank God that Oceanic's main engines burn Heavy Fuel Oil, at least it's not too different from the grades already in production in this day and age: I'm not so sure about the more complex fractions of Kerosene, Avgas and Marine Gas Oil we need for the helicopters and the ship's auxiliary engines though…*

It was just one of countless responsibilities that now fell to him as master and de-facto owner of *Oceanic*. Fortunately, some duties were more pleasant than others…

…such as JJ Astor asking if his little lad could please be baptized in Oceanic's bell, once he's strong enough to leave the hospital. Most certainly! And what a name they've chosen for him!

And, as was traditional of a shipboard baptism, Lloyd had already notified the senior chef aboard, the Executive Chef, of his responsibility to prepare the ship's bell in preparation for its service as a font.

Last I saw of him, he was looking for a can of Brasso and a rag…

Feeling a smile growing, both on his lips and in his heart, Lloyd saw the landing team leader issue him a thumbs-up, indicating that it was safe for him to approach the helicopter. Returning the gesture, he did so, running in a ducked half-crouch up to the cockpit door and swinging it open.

"Honey, I'm home," co-pilot Adrienne McKinn shouted over the roar of the engine, removing her helmet as she assisted Lieutenant Ramirez in shutting down the engines.

"Welcome back, Addy!" he called back, bringing his voice back to a reasonable volume as the thrashing rotor spooled down. "Have got any new guests for our little madhouse?"

"A few more of Senator Smith's aides," she answered, swinging down from the cockpit and indicating a group of pale-faced gentlemen being assisted out of the Sikorsky's cabin. "How is the honourable gentleman from Michigan faring?"

"Still chomping at the bit to get the hearing underway," Lloyd shrugged. "But he still seems content for now to issue subpoenas and dig through the Project 401 archives."

"What about the Brits? We saw a ship negotiating the Narrows as we came in, is it them?"

"Yes indeed," Lloyd grinned, issuing her a thumbs-up. "The RMS *Lusitania* arrived off of Sandy Hook around sunset, and she should be docking in the next hour or so. Captain Charles wired the Port Authorities to confirm she made the crossing at an average of over twenty-six-and-a-half knots, which I think qualifies her to take the Blue Riband back from *Mauretania*."

"That's what happens when your ship is commandeered by His Majesty's Government, I suppose!"

"Come on," he said, reaching out to take her hand and feeling his heart flutter when she accepted it. "Let's get you indoors and out of that flight suit!"

Quickly they negotiated their way off the Sun Deck and into the ship's superstructure, ending their journey at what, until a week ago, had been the Captain's Cabin. Now, with Adrienne's stateroom having effectively become the ship's Foreign Office and Consulate, she had moved in with him. Some of the wags among the crew were already referring to the shared cabin as the Honeymoon Suite.

"Well, let them laugh," Lloyd had said at the time, chuckling himself. "We need something to find funny right now."

It was no secret that he and Adrienne had grown close this past year, especially after she had taken permanent residence aboard the ship. His hand brushed over the box in his pocket once more; it contained a simple ring that had been in the Waters family since the earliest days of steam, having in fact been turned during his great-great-great-grandfather's apprenticeship at the Newcastle workshops of Robert Stephenson & Co. He had been working up his courage to present it to her since before this voyage had even begun.

Now, with the both of them facing immense challenges, he was resolved to ask this question of the woman already spoken of as *Oceanic*'s First Lady.

"So, did *Lusitania* confirm their complement?" Adrienne pressed, stripping down to her underwear the second the cabin door swung shut behind them. "Oh, God, I need a shower."

"To get the sweat off, or wash away the stink of the cesspool on the Potomac?" Lloyd ribbed, and seeing her cut a dark glance in his direction he threw up his hands in supplication. "Mercy, have mercy please!"

A brief chuckle later, he perched himself on the edge of the cabin's newly-installed double-bed, keeping up polite conversation as Adrienne stepped into the en-suite, tossing her lacy unmentionables aside as she did. "Captain Charles reported no casualties during the voyage, so Rufus, Mersey, Buxton and Winnie are all safe and sound…"

"The Attorney General, the Commissioner of Wrecks, the President of the Board of Trade, and First Lord of the Admiralty Winston Churchill," she called back over the sound of running water. "We are favoured greatly."

"Them and almost a thousand of Europe's top brass, packed aboard the same ship," he chuckled. "Dinners must have been an interesting affair."

"We'll know soon enough for ourselves," she replied, and the sentiment cut at Lloyd like a knife. Even after everything that had happened, he could not get his head around the ramifications of what he was now involved in.

Part of the deal surrounding the Fleet being permitted to enter New York had been for the companies of *Oceanic*, *Olympic* and the *Anatoly Sagalevich* to submit to testifying at an official inquiry into the whole mess that had transpired out on the Atlantic. Adrienne had managed to work President Taft around to making it an international affair, and the governments of Europe had reacted with remarkable speed. London had commandeered Cunard's *Lusitania*, temporarily laid up due to the coal strike, and as the stately ship made ready to sail with lightning speed, Whitehall showed equal vigour both in assembling a delegation to the enquiry and extending *Lusitania*'s services to all interested parties; in response, the French, Germans and Russians had immediately boarded their finest statesmen, legal minds, military advisors and historians onto crack expresses and rolled them west to Cherbourg. Now, less than five days after weighing anchor, the speedy Cunarder had whisked this floating Congress of Nations across an entire ocean and brought them safely to the door of the New World.

Within the next few weeks, those same figures would be cross-examining witnesses, including Lloyd himself, bringing the twenty-first century under the full scrutiny of the twentieth. But he was resolved to not allow it to be a one-sided affair, and with all witnesses protected under the laws of 2012 when aboard ship, was sure that an equally critical light would be thrown on the mores and means of 1912.

"If anything, the situation's gotten even more complicated," Addy added, lifting her voice for him to hear her over the spraying showerhead. "Ambassador von Bernstorff confirmed to me that Kaiser Bill has been chomping at the bit to see the wonders of the future with his own eyes. It took something like half of the nobility in Prussia exerting pressure to keep him from jumping aboard the *Lusitania* with the rest of the German delegation, but I'm pretty sure we'll see him treading *Oceanic's* decks within the next month."

The shower cut off, and hearing the bathroom door open he looked up. Adrienne, tall and soft-skinned, looked absolutely radiant even when wrapped in nothing more than a terrycloth bathrobe.

"So, where do we go from here, oh Captain my Captain?" she murmured, lips curving into a smile that promised him the entire world.

Lloyd swallowed and then smiled back, a blush rise to his cheeks. He motioned for her to join him on the edge of the bed, and when she obliged, brow quirked in good-natured confusion, he dropped the bombshell.

"Well, I thought we might go and have a word with Father Byles..."

Slowly, he sank to one knee beside the bed, and produced from his pocket that tiny box. And before he had even time to open the lid or ask the question, Addy was embracing him, arms wrapped tightly around his chest, whispering fervent yeses.

Let 1912 say what it would of *Oceanic's* passengers and crew, but the leaders of both were committed to bringing their lives together in Union, and would prove *formidable*...

*

The small office attached to *Oceanic's* hospital was quiet, except for the scratching of a pen, followed by the frustrated sound of crumpling paper as Doctor George Montgomery, late of the *Viking*, wadded the sheet he had been writing on up into a ball and threw it over arm into a wastepaper basket. Game, set and hole in one.

"This is damned hard…" he muttered to himself, pulling a fresh piece of stationary towards himself and starting again. He was working alone, as Tony Jackson, *Oceanic*'s remaining staff doctor, had taken his leave to get some much-needed sleep.

This was not the first time George had put pen to paper to in the last week. In fact, most days had been spent in the company of various nurses, medics, patients and doctors from among his 2012 contemporaries, passengers and crew alike, distilling everything they knew into countless advisory notes for the health authorities of 1912;

A report on the theory and practice of molecular biology…

A report on 'Human Immunodeficiency Virus' infection and 'Acquired Immune Deficiency Syndrome'…

A report on the Influenza pandemic of 1918, and the likelihood of a reoccurrence…

A report into the medical applications of the genus 'Penicillium'…

There were requisitions as well, not just for medical essentials like bandages, but urgent missives such as Doctor Jackson's request for facilities to immediately vaccinate all of the time-travellers against smallpox, a previously 'extinct' disease against which no-one born post-Thrash Metal possessed a natural immunity to. Desperate pleas were also being composed to the medical establishments and institutions of 1912 in an attempt to bootstrap into being countless 'routine' procedures and medications essential to the quality of life of numerous individuals brought back in time. In addition to Colin Daniels's Parkinson's Disease, *Oceanic* had among her company numerous diabetics, individuals undergoing cancer treatment, six persons likely to require open-heart surgery in the next three to five years and somewhere in the order of a hundred other ailments ranging from minor to potentially life-threatening.

The good news was that the medical knowledge relevant to these cases existed, even if in a fragmented and incomplete form. The bad news was that it would take years to reverse-engineer the decades of technological development that underpinned the practical application of that knowledge. But the first steps had been taken, and he hoped a few initial steps could be taken to ease the burden of many of his patients.

His current task, however, was the hardest thing he had yet to write. It was not a report, nor was it couched in scientific jargon, but was a letter to another human being, and thus proving singularly difficult to crack.

To His Royal Highness Nicholas II, Tsar of All The Russias...

Before George could proceed further, however, someone knocked at the door, and when he shouted "come in" that someone revealed herself to be Terri Patton, greeting him with all the brash decorum he had come to expect in the past week.

"Sorry to bother you, Doc, but the press are here to see the Astors."

Was it time already? George glanced towards the wall-clock. He had come in here and begun scribbling not long after sundown, and now the clock was showing it to be nearly two hours hence. It was easy to lose track of time in a windowless office, he supposed.

"Very well..." he pulled his hands over his cheeks and massaged his eyes. "Did Mrs Astor follow my instructions and take some rest?" How he hoped she had not; it would be a pleasure to send the journalists away for the sake of her well-being. Maybe then he could get some sleep as well.

As if reading his mind, Terri grinned impishly. "No luck, Monty. She's rested and ready to greet them. And JJ's chomping at the bit to present their son to the world."

"Well, I suppose we can't keep fending them off. Show the hounds in, but keep an eye on them. If any start rabble-rousing, do that judo that you do."

"You're not coming?" she enquired, and George gestured towards the scattered papers and medical textbooks on his desk. "Oh come on, Monty..." she persisted. "You're not going to want to miss this."

He waved a hand in deference, shooing her away, and turned his attention back to the paper, only to find that in the margins he had been idly doodling the lyrics to another song by his favourite band.

Should I stay or should I go now?
Should I stay or should I go now?
If I go there will be trouble,
And if I stay it will be double.

As he read the words over he even found himself humming the familiar tune, and with another resigned sigh he consigned the failed missive to a place beside its brothers and sisters in the bin. Terri was right; he needed to stretch his legs, and maybe his mind.

Not wanting to draw attention away from the Astors, he slipped out through the hospital's side door, into one of the ship's back-alley passages. Not far away he could hear the sound of carousing from '*The Broken Sole*', the crew bar and nightclub. He supposed most of the ship's company suddenly felt at a loss as to what came next, and were probably turning to the solace of alcohol. While at sea they had duties to fulfil and passengers to care to, but now, with many of the contemporaries disembarking, the delegates to the inquiry arriving, and *Oceanic*'s very ownership in question, he supposed many of them felt cut adrift.

His own status as one of *Viking*'s former crew was no easier a position to bear. He did not doubt that once he stepped ashore he would probably be subpoenaed to give evidence at an official enquiry into everything that had happened, and how close the world had come to tasting thermonuclear war at the receiving end of *Viking*'s armament.

But at least he had it better than the submarine's other survivors. *He* had the alibi of having been aboard *Oceanic* and *Titanic* providing medical care during the whole debacle; *they* had attempted to commit a war crime. Those of *Viking*'s number who had made it to her liferafts had been interred aboard *Olympic* for the rest of the voyage, confined to a part of Third Class which had been turned into a giant brig. Hardly welcome aboard *Oceanic*, and guaranteed to be cross-examined most fiercely by contemporary representatives of the Royal Navy, United States and Imperial Germany, he did not doubt that some, if not most, would find that impromptu interment extended into actual prison terms.

Men he had served with, men who were his friends and colleagues, men who had been cut adrift in time, and had understandably rallied to the leadership of a charismatic man who, at the very least, had a vision for their future. Hence why George found himself writing these interminable letters and missives; not just in the service of bettering medical practice, but so that his conduct reflected well upon his fellow sailors, in the hope that any judgements made upon them would thus be guided by justice, and not vengeance.

Damn, he needed a cigarette right now. The nicotine craving was something he worked through during tours of duty as a submariner, but it was strong now, and his will was crumbling in the face of everything that was happening.

The ship's cigar lounge. He'd surely be able to find a smoke there.

As he passed the main door back into the hospital, he tried to make himself inconspicuous, but quickly realised there was no need. The handful of contemporary press crowding into the small space, holding the doors open to hear every word the Astors spoke, were far too focused on the wealthy couple of the hour to pay him any heed.

Pausing at the back, he gazed over the crowd's shoulders and made eye-contact with Terri Patton, standing beside the proud parents. She smiled sweetly and tipped her head towards Astor.

Pay attention, the gesture seemed to say.

"And so," JJ was saying, one hand resting on the seated Madeleine's shoulder, "it is only thanks to the heroic and noble efforts of these various ships' medical staff that we are able to present our newborn son to you."

George and the other staff had forbidden the use of flash photography in *Oceanic's* newly-established 'maternity ward', and so the only cameramen present were the Alexandra Press, who slowly panned right to where the premature child was resting in the makeshift incubator, tiny limbs flexing.

"Here he is..." Astor said with pride. "Terrance Jackson Montgomery Astor."

The four words knocked George Montgomery back as if he had been punched.

"...born aboard *Oceanic*, and soon to be baptized in her bell, an event that I hope will be attended upon by all those excellent individuals who made possible his miracle birth."

As the Astors continued to sing their praises of all the time-travellers, Janice Patton looked towards George and smirked. *Told you that you'd not want to miss this.*

Stunned, he backed away from the hospital and slowly began to pace forwards towards the Grand Staircase. For some reason the look of pride in Astor's face stuck in his mind, the way his aloof manner collapsed with the simple joy he took in his child. It touched a raw nerve in Montgomery, reminding him of the day his wife Jess had given birth to their twins...

George stopped, suddenly feeling a great weight on him, a force welling up from within like tears, and then he turned around and with a few brisk strides burst back into his office. Quickly, before the momentary muse left him, he seized the pen and dragged it over the paper in a hurried rush, scribing words into the surface with enough force to almost snap the nib.

To his Royal Highness Nicholas II, Tsar of all the Russias
Sir,

I am Doctor Montgomery of the HMS Viking, one of several vessels recently displaced from the year 2012. Please forgive my intrusion, but I believe I may be of service to your beloved son Prince Alexei. I understand he suffers from a bleeding disorder known as Haemophilia, or the Royal Disease, which you have sought to treat for some time.

I can say with confidence that although a cure for your son's disorder is not currently possible, I can provide advice on how to control it. Prince Alexei's blood lacks a substance that will someday be named Factor VII, which is essential to the forming of blood clots. There were means of producing Factor VII for intravenous administration in my time, but the procedure will be difficult to reproduce quickly.

However, you may be aware of the Austrian Doctor Landsteiner's recent discovery of blood groups, and the new practice of blood transfusion. This is the key to treating your son – his haemophilic blood must be periodically supplemented with blood donated from a healthy individual of the same blood group as his own – this blood, rich in Factor VII, will allow his body to form clots and prevent extensive bleeding.

I must also advise against doctors administering the painkiller Aspirin to your son, as it has the side-effects of acidifying the blood and increasing bleeding. If possible, the Prince must also be kept in an atmosphere of calm and ease, free of panic and hysteria, as these will only serve to increase his blood pressure and so the chance of bleeding. Careful, regular exercise will also build up muscle tissue in his joints, so strengthening their ability to armour his blood vessels in the event of a fall or accident.

In the world I left behind, I had a wife and two beautiful daughters, who I am now parted from, as surely as if they were dead. Please understand that I know your grief as a father faced with the loss of that which he holds most dear, and wish to help.

You will see from the papers that myself and my contemporaries have been fortunate enough to have already saved the life of one child who might otherwise have died, and while I cannot make a full promise, I believe we can be of great assistance in improving the quality and quantity of the future Tsar's life.

Presented to you in faith

Doctor George Lathrop Montgomery, resident of the RMS Oceanic

He paused, and massaged his aching wrist as he checked over what he had written. Simple, sufficiently detailed without being long-winded, and most importantly, appealing to the man Nicholas as a father, not as an autocrat or head of state.

And although he was hesitant, it was not about the rightness of this course of action. He had sworn as a doctor to preserve life. Prince Alexei was one such life, but on his fragile shoulders also rested the Tsar's peace of mind, and through him the fate of the Russian Empire, corrupt and yet not beyond saving. That the deprivations of Lenin's revolution, and all that followed, could be said to revolve around the health of a seven-year old princeling, was like a tragic comedy, but as a grieving father he could well imagine the concerned Russian royals fretting over their ailing son, unaware of the discontent fermenting in Russia, so preoccupied were they with issues of family...

No, don't go there. It hurts too much to think of. Courage man, courage.

Courage, hah. The only reason he hung back in sending off this message now was whether or not he had the strength to commit to it. Actually getting it to the Tsar would be simple; there was surely a Russian embassy or consulate somewhere in New York, and from there things would take their course. No, he just needed the courage to take the first step. His family would want it if nothing else, that he help someone, carry on doing good work, even if separated from them...

A teardrop fell onto the paper, followed by another, and he bit his lip in an attempt to hold back memories of Jane, Claire and

Hannah. They would be waiting for him; would not even know he was missing until *Viking* failed to return from her tour. They would be playing right now, making pictures to show him when he came home, planning for the holiday to Disneyland Paris they had promised the girls in August. *Oh God...*

The tears came hard and fast now. He really needed that cigarette.

'Should I stay or should I go?
Should I stay or should I go?'

Stuffing the sheet into his pocket, he slowly began to climb through the ship, towards the cigar lounge in the upper decks. Ascending into the public spaces he found groups of people milling around the Belgrave Square Lobby, mingling and merging and dividing. All talking, all making plans, or discussing hopes and dreams lost and found. In a cordoned-off space at the top of the Grand Staircase he saw Terri's wife, Janice Patton, proudly giving a lecture to attending press on a painting that had been recovered from the *Titanic* just before she sank. The canvas in question, standing on an easel beside Janice, showed a bright daytime scene of Plymouth Harbour in England, red-sailed yachts vying for space with a stately battle cruiser before the white spire of a lighthouse.

"...Norman Wilkinson's immortal artworks, carried on *Olympic* and *Titanic*, were what inspired my style in creating the interior art for *'Titanic Century'*. You can see the same attempt to balance colour and detail reflected in..."

As Janice spoke on, George's eyes slid to a second artwork standing beside 'Plymouth Harbour', something the young artist had produced during the voyage, and felt a sudden surge of emotion mounting up within him, pushing into his chest like a horror movie monster.

The painting showed *Titanic*, stationary on a brisk sea, battered and scarred from where she had taken a beating from the iceberg, but afloat, just as she had looked to his eyes on the morning of April 15th. On either side of the great ship were *Rescue* and *Viking*, tending to her wounds, while the *Oceanic*, *Anatoly Sagalevich*, *Californian* and *Carpathia* stood careful watch. All of the ships were glowing brightly in the light of an unseen sunrise, careful brushstrokes of colour lending their hulls a lustrous gleam.

It was overly sentimental, not hinting at the cost paid in blood and treasure since then, or of the conflict that was just about to arise among the ships of the Fleet, but it felt right. Optimistic, brave…

"…this is the point about *Titanic*, this is why we continue to be fascinated with her…" Janice Patton was saying, still lecturing whoever happened to pause nearby. "We don't cry for her sister-ship *Britannic*, sunk in World War One with minimal loss of life, and we don't cry for *Olympic*, scrapped after becoming redundant in the 1930s. We cry for the people who died, we weep because their humanity becomes bound up in the story of the ship, making a mass of iron and steel something… more. As much as we love the ships, it's the people, not the ships themselves, which give their stories meaning. That's what Wilkinson showed in his paintings of Plymouth and New York Harbours, not what something looks like, but what it truly means… and that's what I tried to do with *Titanic* in this painting. Yes, she still sunk, but look at what has been accomplished, what's going to be accomplished, all because of this ship, and the fact that people loved her story…"

A flash of hospital green at the corner of his eye drew his attention. Terri Patton had emerged up the stairs, having evidently felt it safe to leave the Astors to the tender mercies of the press. George turned and watched as she crossed the lobby to her wife, who broke away from the artworks on display and embraced her. With her soft blonde hair and bright eyes, Janice looked so much like he imagined his own girls would when they grew up that it pained him to see her so happy.

He watched the two women speaking with one other, Terri no-doubt relating what had happened with the Astors and baby Terrance Montgomery… damn, he felt his shoulders slump, another nerve touched.

"Hey, Doctor!" Janice was waving towards him, and Terri was standing behind her, arms folded cockily, ready to take on the world. "Come, on, *Lusitania*'s docking, and they're going to fire the last of the fireworks to greet her. Don't stay here and brood…"

"No," George said as they drew near, raising his hand and smiling. "You two go be together."

"Ah, Doc…" Terri's grin was now one of victory as she pulled a small packet of Virginia Slims from her pocket and waved it at him. "You look like a man who could use a smoke right now. Come outside, get some air and just be happy to be alive. We can all cry or whatever later, but I know I won't be able to enjoy my evening if I know there's some old coot tearing himself up somewhere because he's forcing himself to be alone."

He could not help but return her grin. These girls were about to go and throw themselves to the lions, ready to try and be the Martin Luther Kings of a new timeline, yet here they were taking the time to worry about him.

They deserve to win…

His hand, pushed deep in his pocket, clenched around the message he had scribbled out. Here, for some reason, was the courage he needed.

"Alright, I'll be there in just a second…"

Terri seemed hesitant to leave him, but then seemed to accept that the lust for nicotine would ensure his eventual co-operation. Giving Janice a peck on the cheek, she led her wife out onto the promenade. Through the open doors he caught a brief glimpse of other couples at the rail, marvelling at the New York of 1912.

Turning away, George spared Janice's new artwork another glance. In trying to express herself the young woman had crafted a masterpiece that seemed to reflect all of the hopes and fears bound up the past few days, and all that was to come.

Underneath the painting was a small handwritten plaque.

Dawn of a New World

George Montgomery smiled and walked towards the promenade, for the first time able to think back to his family without crying.

*

Further forward and several decks down, the Mayflower Theatre was alive with activity, as hotel staff and engineering crew went about the process of converting it into an appropriate venue for the coming International Inquiry. Several rows of seats had been removed from the stalls and replaced with furniture 'borrowed' from *Oceanic*'s conference suites. The stage itself was undergoing equally radical changes; desks and benches being fastened into place, cable ducting laid and projection equipment tested. A quick raid of the ship's flag locker had even turned up several national standards with which to bedeck the stage, with the various New York consulates providing those unrepresented in the twenty-first century, consequently prompting a somewhat scathing argument as to whether or not 'Old Glory' should sport forty-six or fifty stars.

Most impressive, however, were the selection of visual aids awaiting use 'backstage'. As part of her role as the focus of Project 401 and the Titanic Memorial Fleet, *Oceanic* had already carried scale models of herself, *Titanic* (pre and post-sinking), *Carpathia* and *Californian*, which were perfect for the inquiry's needs. Aided by experienced hands from the Harland & Wolff guarantee group, the ship's workshops had laid into the task of 'completing the set' with a will, and working from countless photographs and reference books had spent several days rendering the rest of the Fleet in brass, wood and plastic.

Rescue was here, paint still drying on her miniature hull. The ill-fated Flight 401 and both of the helicopters were represented, as was the *Anatoly Sagalevich*. *Viking*'s duplicate was practically a museum-quality piece, with cutaway sections allowing the interior of the vessel to be exposed, complete with scaled Trident missiles and Spearfish torpedoes.

"So is it accurate?" a voice pressed. "Is that what it looked like? We did our best with the dossier from *Viking*, but you actually got a proper look at the thing."

Nashat Abu Shakra was not here to advise on any of *those* models however, no. Seated in a wheelchair, gut still bandaged, his attention was directed by a Harland & Wolff draughtsman towards the two final creations.

One depicted the *Seguin Laroche*, foredeck stacked with crates. Looking at it the young Arab engineer felt his stomach clench with shame and regret, but that was nothing compared to what he felt when he looked on the final model.

It was the *Liberty Bell*, somewhat crude and lacking in detail, but quite a serviceable representation. Confronted with the device into which so much hope and faith had been placed, over which so many lives had been saved and sacrificed, he felt terribly humbled.

"Yes," he nodded, mouth parched. "That's what it looked like."

"...from what little you saw of it," a third voice interjected. It was Thierry Maillard, formerly the *Seguin Laroche*'s Chief Engineer. "I doubt you got much of a chance to examine it in detail, after you were forced to work on it at gunpoint."

The man from Harland & Wolff blanched in sympathy, and Nash managed to fake a brave smile, playing the role of the put upon victim.

"If I may," Maillard rumbled, taking hold of the handles of Nash's wheelchair, "I think my young friend needs some air..."

Minutes later, they were on deck, anonymous amongst the crowds.

"What are we going to do?" Nash hissed, both out of lingering pain and emotional anxiety. "The lie won't hold once we're in court; they're going to find out the truth!"

Maillard did not answer.

"And what about Jabril and the Capitaine; *we* don't even know where they are right now, only that they slipped away on *Carpathia*, and I don't doubt that Captain Rostron's strength of character will compel him to tell the truth if he's put on the stand!"

"Right now, we're in the clear," Maillard said softly. "There's no evidence to suggest that *ma petite* Jo and Monsieur Hab Allah were not still aboard the *Rescue* when she... vanished. Unless someone testifies otherwise, we're safe."

"*Rescue*'s Lieutenant Miller suspects something, you know. Him and half of our contemporaries are suspicious enough of Muslims to draw a connection between us making up a substantial part of the crew of the ship that *just happened* to be smuggling a time-machine! All it takes is one whispered word and the whole lie comes undone."

"We have to run that risk..." Maillard acknowledged, before something caught his eye. "Look there."

Gently he pushed the wheelchair around, and Nash caught sight of a family standing some distance along the promenade, staring out towards the city. They were an increasingly rare sight on *Oceanic*, passengers brought aboard from *Titanic* on the night of the sinking. Most of their contemporaries in Second and Third Class had been deemed irrelevant to the coming inquiry and so, in dribs and drabs, had been allowed to depart the ship and embark on the adventure that was Customs and Immigration, the poorer among them armed with nothing but the clothes on their backs and a compensation pay-out White Star Line had arranged for property lost when *Titanic* sank.

This family, however, seemed to have either been overlooked or pushed to the back of the queue, and a quick glance suggested an awfully easy explanation as to why; though their mother was white, the two children were of mixed-race, and their father was black.

"They are a mixed French-Haitian family," Maillard said softly. "The *pere* was the only African passenger aboard Titanic. Do you know his name?"

Nash silently shook his head, and he heard the Chief Engineer's grip tighten on the wars of the wheelchair.

"He is Joseph Phillipe Lemercier *Laroche*..."

Those two final syllables hung in the air, and Nash once again felt his skin pallor, a chill rushing along his arms.

"Is he... the *capitaine's* ancestor!?"

"No, but *petit*-Jo long wondered if he was a distant cousin, or something more awful... the Laroches have always been sailors, and at least some of them voyaged to Haiti, during the age of the *slave trade.*"

It was a chilling observation, one that set Nash's mind churning. Was there a blood connection between the missing *capitaine* and the family now standing before him, hinting at a darker relationship, one that eventually culminated in a freed slave taking the name of their former master?

"There's never been a definite connection, but ever since she unearthed her name's connection to the *Titanic*, Jo has searched for answers," Maillard rumbled. "After her grandfather did such good for the Jews of Europe, she was horrified to realise that the family might have committed an awful crime against the peoples of Africa..."

He subtly turned the wheelchair away, leaving the Laroche family to their unknown destiny. "After all that searching, I thought she would jump at the chance to come aboard *Oceanic* and meet Monsieur Laroche, hoping to either embrace her kin or plead forgiveness. But she could not bring herself to take that step; instead she asked me to return the *Seguin Laroche*'s bell to her ancestors in Le Havre, while she herself focused on continuing to make amends for a crime she never committed, conspiring with Hab Allah to continue the work of her grandfather... yet I wonder if she feared Monsieur Laroche's absolution more than she did his condemnation."

Nash took in the words, mouth pursed tight as he stared across at *Olympic*, moored across the dock from *Oceanic*. The steamer was being coaled from countless barges, her white superstructure begrimed with thick black dust that rose in clouds from countless shovels, hoisted bags and bunker ports.

"They made me promise – her and Jab," he said, at last feeling the right words well up in him. "Made me promise that I'd do everything I could to ensure the functions of the *Liberty Bell* remain secret. They said we had a chance to make amends for past sins, and did not need anyone else tampering in the flow of events..."

Maillard hummed in low approval, and Nash lapsed back into silence. The atmosphere on deck was becoming excited, word of the imminent arrival of *Lusitania* having spread. Seeing a quartet of funnels painted in Cunard umber-red approaching from behind the dockside warehouses, he let out a deep breath and managed a wan smile.

"I'm just glad my laptop went down with the *Seguin Laroche*; it contained a complete set of working schematics for the device."

At once he felt the atmosphere chill. Maillard, moving with amazing speed, squatted down beside him, staring him in the face. Steam whistles roared as *Lusitania* hove into view, forcing him to shout to make himself heard.

"You don't have your laptop!?"

"No..." Nash shook his head, confusion tinged with sudden fear. "I've not seen it since the night of the accident. I thought it must have been destroyed in the fire, or gone down with the ship... Thierry, what's wrong?"

"Nashat... those of the crew who still have our computers... we've been using *Oceanic*'s wireless network to re-establish peer-to-peer communications. When we pinged the old CML client's contact list, your account *responded!*"

*

"Ah, ah, don't peek," Jack chided Pip lightly, as she tried to peek between the blinds of the carriage. "It wouldn't be a surprise if you knew where we were going."

"Did I mention that I'm claustrophobic?" she replied, struggling to put on a convincing face, and failing. In her hands she held a subpoena that had been presented to her the second she stepped ashore, the document compelling her to attend the coming inquiry. But until the cited date for her swearing-in, she was free to travel under protection of the law, and was making the most of it.

"I think you're lying," Jack smirked, leaning over to whisper in her ear, lightly flicking her nose with his own writ of summons as he did. "Otherwise why else did you come to the rescue of Cosmo and myself in the boiler room?"

"Shove off..." she lightly pushed him back, dimly aware of John and Marian Thayer, riding on the facing side of the carriage, sharing a long-suffering smile at their antics. "I said I was claustrophobic; that doesn't mean that I can't be a stupid and headstrong claustrophobe."

"Taffeta suits you, my dear," Marian put in, breaking up the mutual put-downs being bounced across the opposite bench. "It complements your Oriental features."

"Thank you..." Pip looked down and self-consciously straightened the fabric of the flowing travelling-dress she was wearing. Despite how she had felt on arrival in New York, she had to admit that the silk ensemble Marilyn had made her had been far too tattered to wear in public; when Jack had proposed he take her ashore with his parents for the evening, they having all been cleared as medically harmless to the populace of 1912, she suddenly found herself at a loss as what to wear, even while arguing with herself that she was better off staying onboard the ship. But she was a New Yorker, and some deep-bred instinct was telling her to go out into the city, even if to see if it was as different as it seemed. Thus she found herself back in her cabin on the *Anatoly Sagalevich* for the first time in a long, long fortnight, searching through her wardrobe and finding only work-clothes and casual wear that to the eyes of 1912 would be more likely to mark her out as someone who did favours for sailors down on the waterfront.

Unexpected salvation had come from Lucille Duff-Gordon, who suddenly appeared in the cabin with her husband, having been reunited with him once she had received permission to disembark from *Olympic*. Only intending to return Pip's laptop, she had immediately fallen head over heels in love with the clothes thrown about the room. Nylon and polyester (and worryingly, latex) were like newfound treasures to her, even if she found Pip's natural style of a T-Shirt thrown over denim jeans to be an abomination to ladies everywhere.

But she absolutely adored the bras, treating the simplicity of their design and underwired heft as a divine revelation in comparison to the battery of crinolines, bustles and whalebone corsets still waging war against the female figure in upmarket boutiques across the world. Less candidly, she eventually confessed to Pip that, while on *Olympic*, she had managed to charge and activate the laptop, subsequently scrolling with child-like delight through the picture archives of Pip modelling various dresses of Marilyn's design, mementos of countless fittings endured prior to the centennial voyage's departure from New York.

"Your sister's style is fresh, bold, very much of the future but still close enough to our own tastes as to be acceptable to contemporary fashion..." she had fawned, eventually wrangling out an agreement whereby Pip would allow her to attempt to recreate some of Marilyn's designs in return for monetary compensation, and a promise that the name 'Marilyn Paik' would be associated with any clothing produced.

In a gesture of goodwill, Lucille even volunteered her services to restore Pip's own damaged dress, and when she learned that she needed something to wear tonight, had immediately taken her measurements and charged off in a horse-drawn trap into the city, returning within the hour with some stunning concoction of blue taffeta and silk. Where she had found a dressmaker open for service after sundown, Pip had no desire to know.

And so now here she was, attired like a lady of the period, travelling out with an eligible bachelor and his parents to a mystery destination. Against her best wishes, Pip found herself sweating buckets, and waved some air onto her face with a Chinese fan that came with the dress. She had spurned the matching hat, however, an abomination of feathers and silk flowers, and Lucille had settled for just styling her hair. The whole affair had consequently taken about two hours longer than it should, but even Cosmo Duff-Gordon, pushed aside and left to wait like an unwanted puppy, conceded that it was worth the effort when Lucille finally presented Pip to Jack Thayer, who was dressed in a simple three-piece suit and waiting at the open door of a carriage on the wharf-side.

Remembering Marilyn and Captain Waters' advice, Pip had descended the *Anatoly Sagalevich*'s gangplank as elegantly as possible, curtsied slightly, and then accepted Jack's helping hand into the carriage, keeping her composure throughout, despite wanting to burst out laughing at how his jaw seemed on the verge of falling through the pavement. She couldn't fault him, because it had only taken a brief glimpse of her own reflection in a mirror to set her blushing. As with the uniform issued her aboard *Rescue*, she felt strangely empowered when wearing the right clothes.

Inevitably, however, once the carriage had been set in motion, she and Jack had started heckling one other. It wasn't the romantic horse-drawn ride through Central Park she had long envisioned as her first date, but she was relaxed enough to enjoy herself and argue good-naturedly, in the company of people she trusted, and dressed so perfectly that the little girl in her who still wanted to be a movie princess was jumping up and down in glee, waving her sceptre about with ecstatic regality.

She felt the carriage brake abruptly and turn off the street. Now they were coming to a halt, bumping and rattling over the last of the cobblestones into what, from the echoes, sounded to Pip to be a gigantic concourse. This time it was Jack who lifted the corner from one of the blinds.

"Ah, we're here."

Smiling, he turned to her with a note of triumph gleaming in his eyes, swung the door open and, with John helping Marian down on the other side, extended his hand to Pip, who was pulling on a pair of ladies' gloves and making a considerable mess of it. Eventually she mastered the lace finger-traps and, parasol and skirts in hand, accepted his help in stepping off the carriage. As she did, she heard the familiar whistle and bang of fireworks from far away – someone on *Oceanic* must have been firing the last of their display from the night of the Centennial. Most likely it was to mark the arrival of *Lusitania*. A week ago Pip would have been climbing over herself to see the ill-fated Cunarder with her own eyes, and yet right now there was nowhere else she would rather be than here, wherever 'here' was.

Startled by the retorts, the horses abruptly reared in their harnesses, and their cries reverberated eerily in the cavernous space in which the carriage had drawn up. Lamp fixtures cast a dim light through the mist that drifted between towering Doric pillars that supported a vaulted roof. Other carriages were drawn up at the kerb, passengers and uniformed porters streaming in and out of high-fronted doors. Taking Jack's arm and mimicking the posture of the other ladies, Pip followed the Thayer parents into the flow of the crowd, trying all the while to work out where they were. This giant marble... well, 'temple' was the only word she could use to describe it, looked like no building in New York that she had ever seen. And she knew this part of Manhattan well, the Midtown district. While bickering with Jack in the cab she had been counting every time they turned a corner, and was sure they were still very close to Pier 59, somewhere on Eighth Avenue near to where Madison Square Gardens would someday be built...

"*No!*" she all but shouted, all trace of decorum forgotten as realisation hit her, and she felt Jack tighten his grip on her arm as if afraid she'd suddenly bolt off and start climbing the walls to get a better view.

"Wait and see, just wait..." he whispered in her ear, giving her hand a reassuring squeeze. Stepping off the concourse, they passed through the doors into a huge atrium of pink marble walls, surmounted by an elaborate roof lovingly crafted from shining glass and iron latticework.

"This is... oh my God, it really is..." she gasped, mouth hanging open as she craned her head back, examining every pane of glass, every rivet, the polished wooden ticket stands against one wall, prospective passengers cueing.

"You're not dreaming, Pip," Jack replied, with the pride of someone presenting a Christmas present long in the procuring. "I saw in *Oceanic*'s library that this building had been demolished long before your time, but here it's but a few years old, and I know you appreciate your history."

He extended a hand all around them as they passed between potted palms and onto a long bridge that arched across multiple railroad tracks and platforms. Electric locomotives sizzled below, hitched to long rakes of parlour cars. Gently pulling free of Jack, Pip slowly turned, taking in the huge, beautiful space, a painfully romantic icon that she knew to have been bulldozed in the 1960s.

"It's Penn Station... the *original* Pennsylvania Station, before they knocked it down to build Madison Square Gardens on top..."

Her breath caught in her throat and her hands flew to her mouth as if to hold back a scream.

"How could they have demolished something like this? It's incredible!"

"Not so incredible as time-travel, or persons such as yourself..." interrupted John Borland Thayer, standing just to one side, Marian's arm entwined with his own. Pip turned her attention towards them, and in response, the vice-president of the Pennsylvania Railroad dipped his head and bowed at the waist, and his wife, so elegant and composed, curtsied.

"Thank you, Philippa, for all our sakes..." Jack's father said, smiling kindly, before turning to regard his son with a gimlet eye. "My boy, our private car is attached to the Philadelphia train. It leaves at the top of the hour. If I see you arrive there without this young lady in your company, I shall want to know why. And if you don't turn up at all, then well-done to you, but I warn you..." he raised an admonishing finger. "Treat her, or yourself, with anything less than the respect you both deserve, then I shall skip beyond questions and proceed straight to the disciplining."

He stepped forward and clasped Jack's hands. "You are a fine man, my son, but you're not too old for a hiding yet."

Yet for all that, his eyes were smiling, and turning to an abashed Pip the smile spread to his face. "Thank you again, Miss Paik. Regardless of whatever happens next, I will hold Jack to his promise to name a city in your honour someday, should the American Arctic Railroad come to fruition."

And with another polite bow, reciprocated by Marian, the Thayer parents took their leave.

"I... I don't understand..." Pip said. "You're staying behind?"

"Staying behind with you – if you'll have me. Or, should you wish, taking you home for a few days; home to Philadelphia."

Again Pip's breathing stalled, and her world momentarily reeled before the weight of what he was saying struck home, sinking with a heavy weight into her stomach and anchoring her to the floor. She wasn't going to faint, at least, not yet, but she feared what he was going to say, was afraid that he was suddenly going to propose to her, and terrified that she might say "yes", without thinking of all that the simple word might mean. Mentally she steeled herself against what flowery platitudes he was going to send her way...

"I love you."

...and those defences crumbled in the two seconds it took him to say those three little words.

"I... I love you too, but..." she said slowly, turning to face towards the floor, before he suddenly cupped her chin gently and lifted her eyes to meet his. His confident, easygoing smile had vanished, replaced with what she could only describe as shame.

"It was, wrong of me, in every way possible, to speak to you as I did, that night in the library..." he spoke slowly, with several pauses, as if struggling to make his feelings clear. "And you were right. It is easy, far too easy, to sit in a lofty position and pass casual judgement on people in a lesser position..."

That prompted a flash of annoyance on her part, causing him to quickly amend his choice of words. "Less well off, I mean to say."

Pip maintained what she hoped was a look of quiet defiance, even as they held hands, and Jack swallowed. "But… but when we were on that collapsible together, and I thought you were dead, I was so… afraid that I might be about to lose you, more frightened than I was for my own life at any time during the sinking. I'd only know you for a few days, but you had worked your way into my mind so deeply that the thought of not seeing you again, not hearing you argue, was hard to bear…"

Pip could feel her own emotions coming to the fore, pushing their way out to express themselves on her face.

"I know how you feel, Jack," she replied, mouth pinched into as brave a smile as she could manage. "Since we docked, I'm not been able to stop thinking about you. I've always had a crush on you, ever since I read those memoirs, but after meeting you I convinced myself it was just that, a crush. Or friendship, if I was lucky. But then we fought, and I decided that what I'd felt wasn't real…" her shoulders heaved. "But after the collision with *Viking*, when I came to find you in the boiler rooms, I realised that what I was feeling was so much… *more*. And it hurts, and it scares me, but… but…"

Suddenly she threw her arms up and looped them behind his head, pulling his lips to hers, a brief encounter still brilliant enough to light up both of their minds like the sun breaking through the clouds.

"…*but it feels right*! To be near you, to be holding you…"

Despite the powerful emotions she was feeling, and the way her chest heaved, Pip felt a bashful smile come to her face at the realisation of what she had just done, and she laughed in self-depreciation. "Look at me… I'm a mess Jack. I'm flighty, and vain, and insecure and…"

"…and kind, and brave, and willing to sacrifice your chance at happiness to help us in the pursuit of our own. Your resolve speaks of exceptional courage, and compassion… and in return… I, I would like to…"

"…don't go down on one knee, Jack," she said quietly, a small, serenely sad smile hiding in her slightly parted lips. She released his hands and hugged herself, as if from the cold. "I don't want you to feel you have to propose to me, or repay me in any way, just because of what we did…"

"No," he said with conviction that surprised her, and himself as well from what Pip could see. "No, that's not what I brought you here to say…"

"Go on…" she replied, head downcast, only for her to snap back and meet his eyes when Jack blurted out his next words.

"I would like to offer you a home!"

"What!?" she exclaimed, but Jack was still speaking, hands open palms-out to her.

"All your life you've feared that you were unwanted, and that… that there was no place for you. Well, my parents and I would, would be honoured, if you chose to come live with us, as a guest, or a friend, or even… even as family. You have done far more for us that we could have asked, and as such, there will always be a place for you in our home… your home, if you so wish."

"I'm… I don't…"

"And it's not just because we feel indebted Philippa, or because… because I love you like a lovesick schoolboy. It's more than that. It's because…" she saw him swallow. "Well, because I would like to know you better, Pip. You're like no other girl, or woman, I have ever met. Somewhat rough around my edges, but… so bright and courageous."

She laughed. "You do have a way with words Jack…"

"And you're pretty…" he blurted out. "I mean, beautiful… I would want nothing more than to be close to you."

He reached out with one hand, as if offering her a lifeline. "Anything you wish; friendship, support, guidance, or even a student or husband. I will be whatever you wish me to be, if it can ease your journey through this world."

Pip had clapped a hand to her mouth, trying to hide both the blush rising to her cheeks, and the unexpected tears pricking at her eyes. She looked closely at him, and then around herself. She was standing in Penn Station, living a historian's dream, and Jack Thayer, a *Titanic* enthusiasts' dream, was offering her his hand in… well not something so far as marriage, but more than friendship.

"You're hurting…" he said, his words earnest and his face hopeful. "And we're… we're not blinded to the world around us, but there's more that we could see, and so much you could show to us and our circles. There's not just a place for you, but a home, and a role – not as a housewife or a caregiver, but as the scholar of history that you are."

Pip's shoulders were shaking uncontrollably, and her breath was coming in shallow sobs. In the back of her mind a vision of Marilyn was smiling, arms wrapped around her little sister's shoulders, holding her tightly.

He came to you, Pip. I said he would, someday.

Slowly, she reached out and tentatively told hold of Jack's hand, and then drew herself up high, the two of them drawing close enough to kiss, long and tenderly. Jack brought his free hand down to her waist and wrapped gently around her, holding them close together in the middle of the swirling bustle of the station.

"Thank you," she said at last. Breaking the contact between them and dipping her head, she rested it against his chest, while her eyes peered up to the clock hanging overhead.

"Five minutes before the train leaves…"

She did not want to break away from him, comfortable in his arms.

"It can wait…" he said softly.

Five minutes could be ten, or twenty, or none at all. For now, there was just the two of them, together under the gleaming, warmly glowing arches of the station. Fired from far away, the last of *Oceanic*'s fireworks burst brightly over the city, brilliant white stars cascading down like the tears of angels.

They were together.

And they were happy.

Time no longer mattered.

*

Time was everything.

Captain Anton Gorbachev was alone in his quarters on the *Anatoly Sagalevich*, repeatedly playing back an audio file on his personal computer. Outside, fireworks could be heard screaming overhead, trading their bangs in a market exchange of whistles and horns as *Oceanic*, *Olympic* and *Lusitania* strived to out-voice the other. Anton closed them all out, however, focusing instead on trying to pierce through the heavy static that made up most of the file.

It was a record of a radio transmission that had been picked up on the *Sagalevich*'s bridge in the chaotic moments just before *Viking* and *Rescue* had been sucked into the time vortex. Interference from the *Liberty Bell* had scrambled most of what was being said, but he could recognise the voice screaming down the line as being that of Akira Oshiro.

He suspected it was important, and so no time could be wasted in trying to make sense of it. Enough had been lost already in the shipboard technicians' heroic efforts in cleaning up the file enough for it to be considered even faintly legible.

What were you trying to say, Gospodin Doctor? he thought to himself, concern eating away at him.

He clicked the 'play' button again, and made out what might be two syllables.

"*Tha-tee...*" he said aloud, writing them down on a pad. "Perhaps, thirty, the number."

Immediately after those two syllables was a static pulse, a spike that masked part of Oshiro's next word, but which seemed to be '*is*'.

Thirty is... Anton thought to himself. *Thirty is what?*

As he sat and replayed the file, concern worried at him. Akira Oshiro was someone he considered a good friend, and moreover, one who well knew the effects nuclear war could have on a nation. It seemed impossible to Anton that Oshiro would, as everyone else in the fleet seemed to have assumed, have warped *Viking* back to their own time, when there was the imminent threat of a missile launch.

If Viking reappeared in 2012, and missile got away, radar defences in Russia and America would see, and not know what to think. Would launch back, fearing preliminary strike, and so all world would burn. Do svidaniya, Doctor Strangelove, everybody dies...

No... he was certain that Akira had weighed himself in the balance and decided that he could not risk setting off World War Three, so he would have adjusted the settings on the *Liberty Bell*, taking *Rescue*, and *Viking*, and the missile... *somewhen* else.

717

He clicked 'play' again, and as the few seconds of audio looped, it suddenly all dropped into place.

Thirty years… Akira was saying thirty years!

Anton Gorbachev felt himself grow cold.

Unable to risk destroying their home, a world he knew to be littered with nuclear weapons, Akira had instead used the *Liberty Bell* to warp everything within its event horizon *forward through this new timeline*, and then tried to warn them over the radio.

Warn them to be ready.

Because in thirty years' time, on the morning of April 16th 1942, *Viking*, *Rescue*, and the missile, would be coming back.

EPILOGUE

SYMPATHY FOR THE DEVIL

Vienna in the spring was chillingly cold, even in the second week of May. The icy air bit at Joanna Laroche's face and made the fillings in her teeth ache. And walking on icy paths in lace-up high-heeled shoes was not the easiest of things.

But at least she was getting used to the dress, even if she refused to wear the corset when her trusty old sports bra would do. She had to admit that she liked the way her reflection carried herself in the shop windows, a proud and confident society woman elegantly attired in the latest fashion. Mentally she thanked Arthur Rostron for rounding up some clothes from among *Carpathia*'s First Class passengers.

"*Aktuelle Nachrichten!*" a newsboy shouted, waving copies of '*Die Presse*'. "*Der Kaiser trifft sich mit Präsident Taft an bord die Oceanic!*"

Curious, she handed over a few krona and accepted one of his folded broadsheets. Her German was fragmented, but the photograph on the front page told the story in of itself. Kaiser Wilhelm, puffed-up with self-grandeur and bejewelled with medals like a popinjay, was shaking hands with President Taft. Standing in between them like a minister about to wed a couple was Lloyd Waters, a somewhat strained but relieved smile on his lips. The headline practically screamed itself in inch-high letters, a touch of tabloid journalism making itself felt already in this new time.

Turning through the pages, Joanna's eyes lit for a moment on a photograph of Adrienne McKinn, posing for the camera and attired in a tailored suit of pants, waistcoat and jacket, blonde hair falling down her back and her subtle bosom pushing up underneath the starched shirt. She tried to imagine the cries of

719

scandal erupting in response the image, and laughed to herself. Underneath Adrienne, the caption *'Das Grosse Staatsmannin'* declared Madame McKinn to be the Great Stateswoman.

Rolling the paper up underarm she resumed her quiet walk through the streets, a small basket of goods carried in front of her where the sheer line of the billowing petticoats did not get in the way. Passing gentlemen tipped their heads to her courteously, while she in turn nodded to them.

Turning down an undistinguished alley, in which some children were playing around a small fire, burning scraps of rubbish, she stopped outside a faded green door. Beside it, a handmade sign advertised postcards and portraits done on commission by the resident artist, whose name was printed underneath. Knocking for entry, after a few moments she was received by a dark-haired youth whose imperious expression softened to a kind of begrudging respect when his gaze alit on her.

"Willkommen back, Frau Laroche."

"Guten Morgen, Herr Shickelgruber," she replied, restraining a shudder at the flash of anger in the youth's bright blue eyes. She understood that he hated that particular surname, and had worked to discard it. The fact that she insisted on addressing him by it seemed to by turns infuriate and fascinate him.

"Please, comenzi in…" The straggly edges of his moustache twitched slightly as he held the door open and beckoned her inside. His English was poor, heavily accented, but he had picked up quite a respectable smattering of it in the past two weeks. "Herr Gabriel ist here already."

"Wunderbar," she replied, stepping through. Moving to close it, the man paused for a second, regarding the urchins squatting on his squalid doorstep. For a second his face clouded with a petulant anger, and then he caught her disapproving expression and swallowed. Hesitantly, like a man compelled against his will, he produced a few coins from a pocket and handed it over to the children, directing them towards the nearest bakery. As they ran off she heard him muttering to himself, and yet a slight smile touched on his lips. It struck her that he enjoyed being in a position where he could afford to hand out a few coins at his choosing.

"Why do you hate them so much?" she asked, trying to enunciate clearly. "Did you not spend time living on the streets?"

"It is different!" he said curtly. "I was there not by choice. The chanz to do vell was denied me by the Jeuden…"

He paused again, seeing the stern expression on her face, and brushed off his previous statement.

"They are just too lazy to find werk."

The hypocrisy struck her hard, but she did not comment as they climbed the stairs to a tiny suite of rooms she and Jab had rented for his use. At the top Shickelgruber took her hat and gloves with affected courtesy and directed her to the studio. Jab was sitting in an upright pose against the wall that received most of the light shining through the sole window, posing for a canvas set up facing him. Nodding a greeting, she took her place beside him while Shickelgruber began to fuss among the clutter on the sideboard.

"What took you so long?" Jab enquired quietly in French, the language they chose to use when they wanted to speak in private.

"Stopped to buy a newspaper," she replied, handing *Die Presse* over, taking some satisfaction at the way his eyebrows rose at the headline.

"Interesting…" he said, glancing over the rest of the article, translating a few key details for her.

"…a tentative agreement to meet with other world powers to discuss a mutual approach to future knowledge."

"When?"

"…July, in Stockholm, to coincide with the end of the Summer Olympics. *Oceanic* will be anchored in the harbour there at the same time. Fascinating how two eras are beginning to juxtapose, isn't it?"

He turned a few more pages, smirking slightly at the Great Stateswoman and describing items of interest.

"The inquiry in New York is moving ahead; they've been using *Oceanic*'s archives of the original inquiries to cross-examine witnesses called to testify on matters relating to *Titanic*'s construction and operation prior to the iceberg collision… and Harriet Quimby, the first woman to fly across the English Channel, has become the first contemporary person to pilot a helicopter…"

Jab's expression darkened as he found another article. "Mr Groves from the *Californian* has been arrested in New York; he managed to smuggle a laptop computer off of the *Oceanic*..."

"Wait, what?"

He read in silence for several seconds and then lowered the paper, gauging her reaction.

"He confessed to removing it from the *Seguin Laroche*... if it is the one that belonged to Nashat, then possibly the American government now possess a complete set of plans and schematics to the *Liberty Bell*..."

She shook her head. "Even if they do, that's out of our hands now..."

He sighed and nodded, before reading onwards. "Many are calling for a list of people of future historical significance to be released, so that their lives might be protected from others who might want to benefit from their deaths."

As if thinking together, the two of them looked towards Shickelgruber, who was now mixing up paint on a palette.

"I thought we came to Vienna to do just that," she said quietly. "And now we've rented him a room, commissioned a portrait from him, even indulged him with information."

"Are you worried we're falling victim to a sinister, and admittedly legendary, cult of personality?" Jab asked thoughtfully, and she nodded.

Shickelgruber, oblivious, was humming along to Joanna's MP3 player as he prepared for the session, the buds pushed deep into his ears. Neither Jab nor Joanna had concealed from him that they were time-travellers, and indeed had used that to keep hold of his attention; several times during the past two weeks he had walked out in a fit of pique, and yet always came back, unrepentant but brimming with more questions, their conversations going on long after he'd laid down his brushes for the night. Drawings and doodles based on their descriptions of future technology and architecture were scattered around the room, along with a number of preliminary drafts and sketches of the painting they had commissioned from him. His first, unsatisfactory efforts at capturing their likenesses were rigid and lifeless, but by sheer dint of effort they had managed to coax something increasingly human out of him… perhaps even of sufficient quality to gain him admission to the city's *Akademie* of Fine Arts.

In every regard possible, they had become his patrons and source of both income and inspiration.

"When we stepped off *Carpathia* I was ready to do just that," Jab admitted, and Joanna nodded. Captain Rostron had set them off at Gibraltar, and Jab had immediately secured a handgun and contrived a way of hiding it in their luggage, along with a few scraps of future technology.

"But…" he trailed off.

But then we found not a maddened dictator but a young, impassioned and self-deluded twenty-something year-old, doing pictures for money on the streets. Jo thought to herself. *We'd planned to simply lure him into a dark alley and… murder him. Instead…*

"…we took pity on him," she spoke aloud. "We've made the mistake of feeling sympathy for the devil."

"The devil, *Shaitan*?" Jab gently corrected, before reverting to German with a cough, drawing Shickelgruber's attention. "Adolph, what do you make of this headline?"

Curiously taking the MP3 buds out of his ears, the man who in one timeline grew up to become Adolph Hitler glanced over the front page, his brows wrinkling first in confusion, and then relaxing with relief.

"This is wonderful news," he said.

"Would you please explain why for Frau Laroche."

"Well, *peace*," Adolph's mouth worked with momentary distaste around the word "…peace between the nations will mean that the wars you warned of will not come to pass, and those 'fascist' traitors and the communists will not get their hands on Deutschland, not tear her apart, and she will not be burdened with the shame of the mass murder of die *Judenvolk*."

His words began to run together as his excitement rose, voice pitching up and down like a furious rollercoaster. "…with the Kaiser strong and resolute as leader, not shamed and disgraced! And the *Vaterland* will grow beside him in strength, building on new ideas and new technologies, becoming the leader of the world not by invasion and conquest, but by example, of the

German peoples united, in a single purpose, the pursuit of a perfect, peaceful Reich!"

His hands twitched as he spoke, the clutched paintbrush flying around like the stick of a crazed conductor. And the voice, delivering a frenzied conflagration of pidgin-English and German, was chillingly familiar, harking back to the history classrooms of Joanna's childhood. But the substance was changed, altered, transformed.

As Adolph continued to fantasise about a Germany that would build the best skyscrapers and aircraft in the world, a Germany other nations would respect and admire and aspire to imitate, not fear and despise and seek to destroy, Jab looked to her with an eyebrow arched in triumph.

"The devil," he said to her in French, "has already made his mistakes, and been damned for it. This man has not."

The touch of smugness in his voice both annoyed and amused her, and then she realised that Adolph had fallen silent.

"This is me..."

They turned, to find him holding the paper open on another page. His face was blank, unreadable, the eyes transfixed on the text as he read aloud.

"...people fated to shape history, many of whom are yet to be born, with others already living, including philanthropists, scientists and heads of state. It is now known, for example, that Winston Churchill, *Engerland's* First Lord of the Admiralty, was fated to lead his nation in a war against a German dictator named Hitler, orchestrator of a mass genocide against the Juden of Europe, many millions strong."

"I should have read the article in full, *merde!*" Jab seethed. Joanna felt him shift in the chair beside her, and wondered where he had concealed the gun purchased in Gibraltar.

Schickelgruber – Hitler – Adolph looked slowly up from the page, knuckles turning white and clenched fingers threatening to tear through the paper. His mouth was pinched into a hard line, the blue eyes burning with a hypnotic passion. For a moment, Vienna was transposed with Nuremberg.

"Those 'fascists' you spoke of, the men who I said should hang for dragging Deutschland into shame and infamy, are to be led by me!?"

Their silence gave him his answer, and when he asked if they had known this when they had commissioned an artwork from him, Joanna merely nodded. Jab was sitting upright in his chair, one hand resting just under his chin, the other drifting close to his jacket, eyes focused piercingly on the man standing beside the easel and canvas, who suddenly seemed like an animal caught in the headlights of history.

"I... I have a choice to make here, ya?"

"Yes, Herr Schickelgruber," Joanna said evenly. "We all have those choices, throughout our lives. But you are an interesting example. How was it that an unknown Austrian boy, spoilt by his mother and abused by his father, self-indulgent and petulant, by turns lazy and energetic, artistically inclined but otherwise unremarkable, should become the man who perhaps had the greatest influence on the twentieth century? A man who hated the Jews for little reason than hate's sake itself, and yet who managed to single-handedly install the state of Israel as recompense for his crimes; a man who devoted himself to building up Germany from the rubble of one ruinous war, but then eagerly plunged it into another that all but reduced it to ash; a man who saw his mission as being to oppose international communism, and yet who in his death dowry left half of Europe to a Soviet dictator second only to his own evil. What choices did you make, Adolph Shickelgruber, to become Adolph Hitler, *the most despised man to have ever lived?*"

Jab had drawn the gun from under his jacket, and laid it across one of his knees. Adolph's own eyes were darkened, and nervously he wetted his lips and turned towards the canvas.

"Then... right now, I choose to finish this painting."

Jabril Hab Allah and Joanna Laroche, self-exiled ghosts in time, both nodded and settled back down in their chairs, Joanna musing on something her companion had told her in Gibraltar, after they had bartered some future trinkets for a fair sum of money.

"I had prayed for a Prophet, a leader to unite Islam and the world. Instead I got four thousand, and more. Everyone who came back in time, everyone who we touch and spread our ideas to, all of us... all of us are God's prophets now..."

Yes, she thought to herself, thinking back on the events that had brought them to this point, while regarding the man who might have been the Fuhrer feverishly painting her likeness.

But where we go from here? The path this world now takes depends entirely on the choices we make right now...

What should they do next?

POSTCRIPT

THE DEEP AND TIMELESS SEA

The ships slept.

Far overhead, as governments and institutions adapted to their new reality, as the course of history changed, the ships slept in eternal rest.

By coincidence, the actions of ocean currents had led to the *Seguin Laroche* sinking within a few miles of Titanic's historic resting place. She had sunk in an unbalanced state, and now lay on her starboard side like a beached whale, otherwise intact. Countless containers littered the darkened plains around her, a cemetery of steel gravestones, each a monument to a cargo that would never be delivered. Had it not been for the events surrounding the *Liberty Bell*, she would have given further steadfast service, until time, tide and the skinflint attitudes of M&B Holdings sank her in a tropical storm two hundred miles east of Australia. Lost with all hands, it was later established that the late Captain Laroche-Pètain had been correctly steering the container vessel's prow into the storm, before a complete failure of her engine plant caused the ship to slew beam-on to the waves, at which point she had been swamped, and capsized.

Back broken before she even slipped below the waves, gallant *Californian* had plunged to her grave with such haste that vast amounts of compressible air were trapped within her holds and sealed compartments. Before her hulk had descended past a thousand feet, water pressure had compressed the hull around these gasses like a crushed soda can. What came to rest over two miles down little resembled a ship, but instead a scattering of steel confetti. Yet this too was a far better fate than might have awaited *Californian*. Originally torpedoed during government service in 1915, little interest had ever been expressed in hunting for the wreck of the ship alleged to have stood by and watched as *Titanic* floundered. Now, however, her name would be whispered with awe; for although *Californian* had been sunk in a callous act of betrayal, her master had been among those who had sacrificed himself to preserve Berlin from a pocket Armageddon, and the nobility of Stanley Lord reflected itself well upon his little ship.

Rescue and *Viking* were gone, yet a marker of their final moments remained. The gash *Titanic* ripped into the submarine's hull had dislodged a considerable part of her missile compartment, and the action of *Rescue* holding herself like a knife in the wound had ripped that chunk of flesh away. Sinking so quickly that it was not pulled within the *Liberty Bell's* event horizon, it had fallen in a single piece, landing in a twisted mess less than five miles from her final victim, *Californian*. Among the buckled girders and twisted beams were two Trident II missiles, and although the Atlantic's overwhelming weight had collapsed their fuel tanks and rocket motors, the warheads remained, though mercifully inert through the action of seawater.

The same could not be said for the wreck but five hundred yards from *Viking's* marker, however, an aberrant ship that none in 1912 or 2012 had ever laid eyes upon. She was a motor-vessel, twin prop-shafts revealed where rending time had bisected her aft third. Her welded hull, pockmarked with shell-impacts, was painted battleship-grey, except for where the characters ID40 had been stencilled in huge white letters near her prow. The name *Paradox V* graced her wheelhouse, as did two plaques, the first commemorating her launch from the Newport News Shipyards in 1939, and the second proclaiming her deployment as an auxiliary vessel in the service of the Arctic Atlantic Treaty Organisation. And unlike the other wrecks, something persisted here. No dead crewed her, no corpses drifted her flooded companionways, yet something brooded within her iron heart. A casual eye would have noticed odd antennae ribbing her upper works, and if one was able to follow those coils and capacitors into the belly of the *Paradox V*, they would eventually discover an armoured compartment in which a ceramic bell brooded, its hull gently shimmering…

The largest wreck on the ocean floor, however, was half a mile away, and it was this sainted vessel that curious eyes would soon dive to, and in the process discover so much more. *Titanic* sat upright, broken in two below her fourth funnel, yet strangely intact. Although *Viking* had smashed the liner's keel under her main engine room, the hull had sheared up the void of the Turbine Engine's casing, leaving the mighty reciprocating engines protruding from the after end of the bow section. As in history, she sat upright, her bow and stern half a mile apart, crumpled and collapsed around the break, yet intact and undefiled by the actions of time, nature and man alike.

Titanic slept in peace, as yet undisturbed. Around her rested her sisters, family in death, consigned to the deep and timeless sea…

…in the depths of Timeline C.

THE END

BIBLIOGRAPHY

Though it would be impossible to list every source that either helped inspired me or served as a source of information for '*Timewreck Titanic*', I would like here to list some of the most notable:

NON-FICTION

101 Things You Thought You Knew About The Titanic... But Didn't, Tim Maltin, 2010

Anatomy of the Titanic, Tom McCluskie, 1998

A Night To Remember, Walter Lord, 1955

Damned by Destiny, David L. Williams and Richard P. De Kerbrech, 1982

Expedition: Bismarck, James Cameron (Discovery Channel, 2002)

Ghosts of the Abyss, James Cameron (Walt Disney Pictures, 2003)

HMHS Britannic, the Last Titan, Simon Mills, 1992

Hostage to Fortune, Simon Mills, 2002

K Boats, Steam-powered Submarines in World War 1, Don Everitt, 1999

Modern Seamanship, Don Dodds, 1995

Racing Through The Night; Olympic's Attempt to Reach Titanic, Wade Sisson, 2011

RMS Olympic: Titanic's Sister, Mark Chirnside, 2004

The History of the White Star Line, Robin Gardiner, 2001

The Loss of the S.S. Titanic, its Story and Lessons, Lawrence Beesley, 1912

The New Cunard Queens, Nils Schwerdtner, 2011

The Sinking of the S.S. Titanic, John B. Thayer Jr, 1940

The Truth About the Titanic, Col. Archibald Gracie, 1913

The Unsinkable "Titanic": The Triumph Behind a Disaster, Allen Gibson, 2012

The U.S. Navy Salvage Engineer's Handbook (Volume One), Department of the Navy, 1997

Titanic and Other Ships, Commander C.H. Lightoller, 2003 online edition

Titanic: Answers from the Abyss, David Elisco (Discovery Channel, 1999)

Titanic: Birth of a Legend, Granada Televison, 2005

Titanic Survivor: the Memoirs of Stewardess Violet Jessop, John Maxtone-Graham, 1998

Today's Royal Navy in Colour, Jeremy Flack, 1995

Shadow of the Titanic, Andrew Wilson, 2011

FICTION

Back to the Future, Robert Zemeckis (Universal Studios, 1985)

Outpost, Steve Barker, (Black Camel Pictures, 2008)

Raise the Titanic, Clive Cussler, 1976

The 1633 (Ring of Fire) Series, Eric Flint, 2000-

The Philadelphia Experiment, (Cinema Group Ventures, 1984)

The Time Travel Journals: Shipbuilder, Marlene Dotterer, 2011

The White Star Voyages Series, Joseph L'Episcopo, 2009-

Titanic, James Cameron (Lightstorm Entertainment, 1997)

Titanic: Adventure Out Of Time, Cyberflix, 1996

Titanic: The Ship That Never Sank, Robin Gardiner, 1998

Zipang, Kaiji Kawaguchi

WEBSITES

Alternatehistory.com – the Alternate History Discussion Board

Encyclopedia Titanica

Marconigraph.com

Markchirnside.co.uk – Mark Chirnside's Reception Room

Msc.navy.mil – the Military Sealift Command

The Nautical Site

The Slacktivist

Titanic1.org – the *Titanic* Historical Society

Titanic-Model.com

Titanicology

Wikipedia, the Online Encyclopedia

ACKNOWLEDGEMENTS

I started writing this novel on October 3rd of 2011. Since then its success has been entirely due to the support, advice and inspiration I have received from a number of people, the most prominent of which I wish to thank here:

My father Cledwyn Davies, and my best friend, Doug Walters, for their services as editors and proof-readers on the First Edition.

My mother, brother, sister and friends, who all provided encouragement through the long months of this project.

Doug's mother, Katie Pace, for medical advice essential to scenes involving the Astors and their baby.

Eric Flint, Harry Turtledove, Marlene Dotterer, Joseph L'Episcopo and Kaiji Kawaguchi, whose own time-travel and alternate-history works inspired me to try my own hand at the genre.

Sam Halpern, Parks Stephenson, David G. Brown and Mark Chirnside, for their expertise on all matters *Titanic*, especially with regard to potential flooding scenarios, possible iceberg damage, engine arrangements, and her Marconi apparatus.

Richard Edwards, for his magnificent models of White Star Line's proposed *Oceanic* III of 1928.

Jayant Roy of 'The Nautical Site'.

The Crew and Officers of the USNS Grapple.

Professor George Green of Furness College, Lancaster University.

LUMAS, the Lancaster University Manga & Anime Society.

Fred Clark, the Slacktivist.

Karl Sedgwick and Matt Long of Trinity Saint David's College, Carmarthen, for organising the contest to design the original cover, and to all who participated, not least of all the three finalists, Gwalchmai Doran, Robert Stephenson and Josh Hutchinson.

Jack Tindale, who built on their sterling work to create the cover Sea Lion Press would place on this book.

Everyone on the Encyclopaedia Titanica Message Boards and Titanic-Model.com, whose tireless research and debate informed my personal vision of the *Titanic* and made this all possible.

Dan Price, who helped me with the title.

The Gwili Steam Railway, of Bronwydd Arms, Carmarthen, who nurtured my love for all things steam-power.

And lastly, James Cameron, for introducing me to 'The Big T' all those years ago.

ABOUT THE AUTHOR

Rhys Byron Davies was born in 1986, and from a young age displayed both a passion for anything old-fashioned, and an alarming talent at telling tall tales. Nurtured on a diet of steam trains and fiction ranging from Enid Blyton to Crichton, Clancy and Cussler, he eventually decided he wanted to become a writer.

What followed were three years at Lancaster University (English Lit with Creative Writing), resulting in *Timewreck Titanic*, which he very much hopes you enjoyed reading.

SEA LION PRESS

Sea Lion Press is the world's first publishing house dedicated to alternate history. For our full catalogue, visit **sealionpress.co.uk**.